A TEXT BOOK OF

ENGINEERING
MATHEMATICS - III

FOR

Semester – III

Second Year Degree Course in Mechanical Engineering / Mechanical & Automation Engineering

Also Use for Civil, Electrical & E & TC Engg. Branches

As Per New Revised Syllabus of Shivaji University, Kolhapur, June 2014

Dr. NAVNEET D. SANGLE
M. Sc, Ph. D (Mathematics)
Professor and Head, Department of Basic Sciences
Annasaheb Dange College of Engineering & Technology,
Ashta, (Tal : Walwa, Dist. Sangli)

Dr. M. Y. GOKHALE
M. Sc. (Pure Maths.), M. Sc. (App. Maths.)
Ph. D. (I. I. T., Mumbai)
Professor and Head, Deptt. of Mathematics,
Maharashtra Institute of Technology,
PUNE.

Dr. N. S. MUJUMDAR
M. Sc., M. Phil., Ph. D. (Maths.)
Professor in Mathematics,
JSPM's Rajarshi Shahu
College of Engineering,
Tathawade, PUNE.

N 2200

ENGINEERING MATHEMATICS – III (S.E. MECH. SEM. III SU)   ISBN 978-93-5164-221-3

First Edition : **September 2014**

© : **Authors**

Published By :
NIRALI PRAKASHAN
Abhyudaya Pragati, 1312, Shivaji Nagar,
Off J.M. Road, PUNE – 411005
Tel - (020) 25512336/37/39, Fax - (020) 25511379
Email : niralipune@pragationline.com

DISTRIBUTION CENTRES

PUNE

Nirali Prakashan
119, Budhwar Peth, Jogeshwari Mandir Lane
Pune 411002, Maharashtra
Tel : (020) 2445 2044, 66022708, Fax : (020) 2445 1538
Email : bookorder@pragationline.com

Nirali Prakashan
S. No. 28/25, Dhyari,
Near Pari Company, Pune 411041
Tel : (022) 24690204 Fax : (020) 24690316
Email : dhyari@pragationline.com
bookorder@pragationline.com

MUMBAI
Nirali Prakashan
385, S.V.P. Road, Rasdhara Co-op. Hsg. Society Ltd.,
Girgaum, Mumbai 400004, Maharashtra
Tel : (022) 2385 6339 / 2386 9976, Fax : (022) 2386 9976
Email : niralimumbai@pragationline.com

DISTRIBUTION BRANCHES

NAGPUR
Pratibha Book Distributors
Above Maratha Mandir, Shop No. 3, First Floor,
Rani Jhanshi Square, Sitabuldi, Nagpur 440012,
Maharashtra, Tel : (0712) 254 7129

BENGALURU
Pragati Book House
House No. 1, Sanjeevappa Lane, Avenue Road Cross,
Opp. Rice Church, Bengaluru – 560002.
Tel : (080) 64513344, 64513355,
Mob : 9880582331, 9845021552
Email:bharatsavla@yahoo.com

JALGAON
Nirali Prakashan
34, V. V. Golani Market, Navi Peth, Jalgaon 425001,
Maharashtra, Tel : (0257) 222 0395
Mob : 94234 91860

KOLHAPUR
Nirali Prakashan
New Mahadvar Road,
Kedar Plaza, 1st Floor Opp. IDBI Bank
Kolhapur 416 012, Maharashtra. Mob : 9855046155

CHENNAI
Pragati Books
9/1, Montieth Road, Behind Taas Mahal, Egmore,
Chennai 600008 Tamil Nadu, Tel : (044) 6518 3535,
Mob : 94440 01782 / 98450 21552 / 98805 82331, Email : bharatsavla@yahoo.com

RETAIL OUTLETS

PUNE

Pragati Book Centre
157, Budhwar Peth, Opp. Ratan Talkies,
Pune 411002, Maharashtra
Tel : (020) 2445 8887 / 6602 2707, Fax : (020) 2445 8887

Pragati Book Centre
Amber Chamber, 28/A, Budhwar Peth,
Appa Balwant Chowk, Pune : 411002, Maharashtra,
Tel : (020) 20240335 / 66281669
Email : pbcpune@pragationline.com

Pragati Book Centre
676/B, Budhwar Peth, Opp. Jogeshwari Mandir,
Pune 411002, Maharashtra
Tel : (020) 6601 7784 / 6602 0855

PBC Book Sellers & Stationers
152, Budhwar Peth, Pune 411002, Maharashtra
Tel : (020) 2445 2254 / 6609 2463

MUMBAI
Pragati Book Corner
Indira Niwas, 111 - A, Bhavani Shankar Road, Dadar (W), Mumbai 400028, Maharashtra
Tel : (022) 2422 3526 / 6662 5254, Email : pbcmumbai@pragationline.com

www.pragationline.com   info@pragationline.com

This Book is Dedicated to…

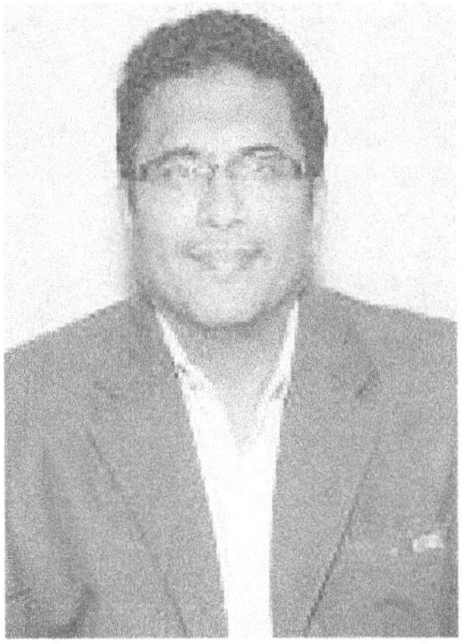

Prof. R. A. KANAI

…Authors

PREFACE

The book is written mainly for the Second Year Students of Mechanical Engineering / Mechanical & Automation Engineering for the Subject **'Engineering Mathematics – III'**. It is strictly written as per the New Revised Syllabus of Shivaji University, Kolhapur 2014.

Keeping in view the limited time at the disposal of Engineering students preparing for University Examinations, the book contains fairly large number of solved problems taken from various recently examination papers of Different Universities and Autonomous colleges so that students may not find any difficulty while answering problems in Final University Examination.

This book is divided in to the six chapters. Sincere efforts have been made to present the subject matter in a lucid and comprehensive manner so that an average student may follow the subject easily. At the end of each sub topics exercise is given so that the students may try for the problem and assess their confidence of answering the problems after studying the sub topics.

We take this opportunity to express our thanks to **Shri. Dineshbhai Furia** and **Shri. Jignesh Furia** and **Shri. M.P. Munde** for publishing this book in time.

We are also take this opportunity to express our thank all the staff members of Nirali Prakashan namely Mrs. Shilpa Kale and Miss. Mandakini for their tremendous dedication and hard work in bringing out this book in an excellent form.

We are also thankful to **Mr. Virdhaval Shinde,** Branch Manager, Kolhapur Office and **Mr. Ashok Nanaware,** Branch Manager, Sangli District for their valuable help and efforts for promotion of my book.

We would also like to thank family members, colleagues and friends for their inspiration and consistent encouragement.

Suggestions, critical evaluations for improvement of this book will be highly appreciated and thankful acknowledged.

September 2014

Pune   **Authors**

SYLLABUS

Unit 1 : Linear Differential Equations [7]

1.1 Linear Differential Equations with constant coefficients Definition, Complementary function and Particular integral (without method of variation of Parameters).

1.2 Homogeneous Linear differential equations.

Unit 2 : Applications of Linear Differential Equations with Constant Coefficients [7]

2.1 The Whirling of Shafts.

2.2 Mass – spring Mechanical system

2.2.1 Free oscillations

2.2.2 Damped Oscillations

2.2.3 Forced oscillations without damping.

Unit 3 : Vector Differential Calculus [6]

3.1 Differentiation of vectors

3.2 Gradient of scalar point function and Directional derivative

3.3 Divergence of vector point function and Solenoidal vector fields.

3.4 Curl of a vector point function and Irrotational.

Unit 4 : Laplace Transform [7]

4.1 Definition, Transforms of elementary functions, Properties of Laplace transform.

4.2 Transforms of derivatives and Integral.

4.3 Inverse Laplace transforms formulae.

4.4 Inverse Laplace transforms by using partial fractions and Convolution theorem.

4.5 Solution of Linear differential equation with constants coefficients by Laplace transforms method.

Unit 5 : Fourier Series [6]

5.1 Definition, Euler"s Formulae, Dirchilt"s Condition.

5.2 Functions having points of discontinuity

5.3 Change of interval

5.4 Expansion of odd and even periodic functions

5.5 Half range series.

Unit 6 : Application of Partial Differential Equations [7]

6.1 The Wave Equation.

6.1.1 The method of separation of variables.

6.1.2 Fourier Series solution of wave equation.

6.2 One dimensional heat flow equation

6.2.1 The method of separation of variables.

6.2.2 Fourier Series solution of heat equation.

6.3 The Laplace equation in two dimensional heat flow (Steady State).

6.3.1 Solutions of Laplace equations by the Gauss – Siedel iterative method.

CONTENTS

Unit 1 : Linear Differential Equations — 1.1-1.54

Unit 2 : Applications of Linear Differential Equations with Constant Coefficients — 2.1-2.26

Unit 3 : Vector Differential Calculus — 3.1-3.52

Unit 4 : Laplace Transform — 4.1-4.114

Unit 5 : Fourier Series — 5.1-5.88

Unit 6 : Application of Partial Differential Equations — 6.1-6.70

◈ ◈ ◈

UNIT - I

LINEAR DIFFERENTIAL EQUATIONS

1.1 INTRODUCTION

Differential equations are widely used in fields of Engineering and Applied Sciences. Mathematical formulations of most of the physical problems are in the forms of differential equations. Use of differential equations is most prominent in subjects like Circuit Analysis, Theory of Structures, Vibrations, Heat Transfer, Fluid Mechanics etc. Differential equations are of two types : Ordinary and Partial Differential Equations. In ordinary equations, there is one dependent variable depending for its value on one independent variable. Partial differential equations will have more than one independent variables.

In what follows, we shall discuss ordinary and partial differential equations, which are of common occurrence in engineering fields. Applications to some areas will also be dealt.

1.2 PRELIMINARIES

I. Second Degree Polynomials and Their Factorization :

(a)

(i) $D^2 - 2D - 3 = (D + 1)(D - 3)$ (ii) $D^2 + 5D + 6 = (D + 2)(D + 3)$

(iii) $D^2 + 2D + 1 = (D + 1)^2$ (iv) $D^2 - 5D + 6 = (D - 2)(D - 3)$

(v) $D^2 + 3D + 2 = (D + 2)(D + 1)$ (vi) $D^2 - D - 2 = (D - 2)(D + 1)$

(vii) $D^2 - 4D + 4 = (D - 2)^2$ (viii) $D^2 - a^2 = (D - a)(D + a)$

(ix) $D^2 + a^2 = (D + ia)(D - ia)$

(b) The roots of $ax^2 + bx + c = 0$ are $x = \dfrac{-b \pm \sqrt{b^2 - 4ac}}{2a}$, these roots are imaginary if $b^2 - 4ac < 0$.

(i) $D^2 + 2D + 2 = 0 \Rightarrow D = \dfrac{-2 \pm \sqrt{4 - 8}}{2} = -1 \pm i$

(ii) $D^2 + D + 1 = 0 \Rightarrow D = \dfrac{-1 \pm \sqrt{1 - 4}}{2} = \dfrac{-1}{2} \pm \dfrac{\sqrt{3}}{2} i$

If $D = \dfrac{-1}{2} \pm i \dfrac{\sqrt{3}}{2} = \alpha \pm i\beta$ then $\alpha = -\dfrac{1}{2}, \beta = \dfrac{\sqrt{3}}{2}$, β is always positive; α may be positive, negative or zero.

(iii) $D^2 + 1 = 0 \Rightarrow D^2 = -1$ i.e. $D = \pm i$ $\therefore$ $\alpha = 0, \beta = 1$.

(iv) $D^2 + 4 = 0 \Rightarrow D^2 = -4$ i.e. $D = \pm 2i$ $\therefore$ $\alpha = 0, \beta = 2$.

(1.1)

II. Third Degree Polynomials and Their Factorization :

(a) (i) $D^3 - a^3 = (D - a)(D^2 + aD + a^2)$ (iii) $D^3 + a^3 = (D + a)(D^2 - aD + a^2)$

(ii) $D^3 + 3D^2 + 3D + 1 = (D + 1)^3$ (iv) $D^3 - 3D^2 + 3D - 1 = (D - 1)^3$

(b) Use of synthetic division :

(i) $f(D) = D^3 - 7D - 6 = 0$; for $D = -1$, $f(-1) = 0$ $\therefore$ $(D + 1)$ is one of the factors.

-1	1	0	-7	-6
		-1	1	6
	1	-1	-6	$\lfloor 0$

$\therefore$ $D^3 - 7D - 6 = 0 \Rightarrow (D + 1)(D^2 - D - 6) = 0$

$(D + 1)(D - 3)(D + 2) = 0 \Rightarrow D = -1, -2, 3.$

(ii) For $D^3 - 2D + 4 = 0$; $D = -2$ $\therefore$ $f(-2) = 0$ $\therefore$ $(D + 2)$ is one of the factors.

-2	1	0	-2	4
		-2	4	-4
	1	-2	2	$\lfloor 0$

$\therefore$ $D^3 - 2D + 4 = 0 \Rightarrow (D + 2)(D^2 - 2D + 2) = 0$

$D = -2$ and $D = 1 \pm i$, $\alpha = 1$, $\beta = 1$.

III. Fourth Degree Polynomials and Their Factorization :

(a) $D^4 - a^4 = (D^2 - a^2)(D^2 + a^2) = (D - a)(D + a)(D + ia)(D - ia)$

(b) Making a perfect square by introducing a middle term :

(i) For $D^4 + a^4 = 0$; consider $(D^2 + a^2)^2 = D^4 + 2a^2 D^2 + a^4$

$$D^4 + a^4 = (D^4 + 2a^2 D^2 + a^4) - (2a^2 D^2) = (D^2 + a^2)^2 - \left(\sqrt{2}\, a D\right)^2$$

$$D^4 + a^4 = \left(D^2 - \sqrt{2}\, a D + a^2\right)\left(D^2 + \sqrt{2}\, a D + a^2\right)$$

(ii) For $D^4 + 1 = D^4 + 2D^2 + 1 - 2D^2 = (D^2 + 1)^2 - \left(\sqrt{2}\, D\right)^2$

$$D^4 + 1 = \left(D^2 - \sqrt{2}\, D + 1\right)\left(D^2 + \sqrt{2}\, D + 1\right)$$

(c) $D^4 + 8D^2 + 16 = (D^2 + 4)^2$, $D^4 + 2D^2 + 1 = (D^2 + 1)^2 = (D + i)^2 (D - i)^2$

$D^4 + 10D^2 + 9 = (D^2 + 9)(D^2 + 1) = (D + 3i)(D - 3i)(D + i)(D - i)$

(d) (i) $f(D) = D^4 - 2D^3 - 3D^2 + 4D + 4 = 0$, for $D = -1, f(-1) = 0$

-1	1	-2	-3	4	4
		-1	3	0	-4
-1	1	-3	0	4	$\lfloor 0$
		-1	4	-4	
2	1	-4	4	$\lfloor 0$	
		2	-4		
	1	-2	$\lfloor 0$		

$\therefore$ Factors are $(D + 1)^2 (D - 2)^2 = 0.$

On a similar line,

(ii) $D^4 - D^3 - 9D^2 - 11D - 4 = (D + 1)^3 (D - 4)$

(e) Perfect square of the type $(a + b + c)^2$

(i) $D^4 + 2D^3 + 3D^2 + 2D + 1 = (D^2)^2 + 2 \cdot D^2 \cdot D + D^2 + 2D^2 + 2D + 1$

$$= (D^2 + D)^2 + 2(D^2 + D) + 1$$

$$= [(D^2 + D) + 1]^2 = (D^2 + D + 1)^2$$

(ii) $D^4 - 4D^3 + 8D^2 - 8D + 4 = (D^2)^2 - 2D^2 \cdot 2D + (2D)^2 + 4D^2 - 8D + 4$

$$= (D^2 - 2D)^2 + 4(D^2 - 2D) + 4$$

$$= [(D^2 - 2D) + 2]^2 = (D^2 - 2D + 2)^2$$

IV. Fifth Degree Polynomials and Their Factorization :

(i) $D^5 - D^4 + 2D^3 - 2D^2 + D - 1 = D^4(D - 1) + 2D^2(D - 1) + 1(D - 1)$

$$= (D^4 + 2D^2 + 1)(D - 1) = (D - 1)(D^2 + 1)^2$$

$$= (D - 1)(D + i)^2 (D - i)^2$$

1.3 THE nth ORDER LINEAR DIFFERENTIAL EQUATION WITH CONSTANT COEFFICIENTS

A differential equation which contains the differential coefficients and the dependent variable in the first degree, does not involve the product of a derivative with another derivative or with dependent variable, and in which the coefficients are constants is called a *linear differential equation with constant coefficients.*

The general form of such a differential equation of order "n" is

$$\boxed{a_0 \frac{d^n y}{dx^n} + a_1 \frac{d^{n-1} y}{dx^{n-1}} + a_2 \frac{d^{n-2} y}{dx^{n-2}} + \ldots + a_{n-1} \frac{dy}{dx} + a_n y = f(x)} \qquad \ldots (1)$$

Here $a_0, a_1, a_2 \ldots$ are constants. Equation (1) is a nth order linear differential equation with constant coefficients.

e.g. Put $n = 3$ in equation (1), we get $a_0 \frac{d^3 y}{dx^3} + a_1 \frac{d^2 y}{dx^2} + a_2 \frac{dy}{dx} + a_3 y = f(x)$ which is a 3rd order linear differential equation with constant coefficients.

Using the differential operator D to stand for $\frac{d}{dx}$ i.e. $Dy = \frac{dy}{dx}$; $D^2 y = \frac{d^2 y}{dx^2}$, $\ldots$

$D^n y = \frac{d^n y}{dx}$, the equation (1) will take the form

$$a_0 D^n y + a_1 D^{n-1} y + a_2 D^{n-2} y + \ldots + a_{n-1} Dy + a_n y = f(x)$$

OR $(a_0 D^n + a_1 D^{n-1} + a_2 D^{n-2} + \ldots + a_{n-1} D + a_n) y = f(x)$ $\qquad \ldots (2)$

in which each term in the parenthesis is operating on y and the results are added.

Let $\phi(D) \equiv a_0 D^n + a_1 D^{n-1} + a_2 D^{n-2} + \ldots + a_{n-1} D + a_n$, $\phi(D)$ is called as n^{th} order polynomial in D.

$\therefore$ Equation (2) can be written as $\boxed{\phi(D) \, y \, = f(x)}$ ... (3)

Note : In equation (1), if a_0, a_1, ... a_n are functions of x then it is called n^{th} order linear differential equation.

1.4 THE NATURE OF DIFFERENTIAL OPERATOR "D"

It is convenient to introduce the symbol D to represent the operation of differentiation with respect to x. i.e. $D \equiv \dfrac{d}{dx}$, so that

$$\frac{dy}{dx} = Dy; \quad \frac{d^2 y}{dx^2} = D^2 y; \quad \frac{d^3 y}{dx^3} = D^3 y; \quad \ldots\ldots; \quad \frac{d^n y}{dx^n} = D^n y \text{ and } \frac{dy}{dx} + ay = (D + a) y$$

The differential operator D or (D^n) obeys the laws of Algebra.

Properties of the operator D :

If y_1 and y_2 are differentiable functions of x and "a" is a constant and m, n are positive integer then

(i) $D^m (D^n) y = D^n (D^m) y = D^{m+n} y$

(ii) $(D - m_1) (D - m_2) y = (D - m_2) (D - m_1) y$

(iii) $(D - m_1) (D - m_2) y = [D^2 - (m_1 + m_2) D + m_1 m_2] y$

(iv) $D (au) = a \cdot D(u);$ $D^n (au) = a \cdot D^n (u)$

(v) $D (y_1 + y_2) = D (y_1) + D(y_2);$ $D^n (y_1 + y_2) = D^n (y_1) + D^n (y_2).$

1.5 LINEAR DIFFERENTIAL EQUATION ϕ (D) y = 0

Consider $\phi(D) y = 0$ ... (4)

where, $\phi(D) = a_0 D^n + a_1 D^{n-1} + a_2 D^{n-2} + a_3 D^{n-3} + \ldots + a_{n-1} D + a_n$ is n^{th} order polynomial in D and D obeys the laws of algebra, we can in general factorise $\phi(D)$ in n linear factors as $\phi(D) = (D - m_1) (D - m_2) (D - m_3) \ldots (D - m_n)$ where $m_1, m_2, m_3, \ldots m_n$ are the roots of the algebraic equation $\phi(D) = 0$

$\therefore$ Equation (4) can be written as

$\phi(D) y = (D - m_1) (D - m_2) (D - m_3) \ldots (D - m_n) y = 0$ ... (5)

Note : These factors can be taken in any sequence.

1.6 AUXILIARY EQUATION (A.E.)

The equation $\phi(D) = 0$ is called as an *auxiliary equation* (A.E.) for equations (3), (4).

e.g. $\dfrac{d^2 y}{dx^2} - 5 \dfrac{dy}{dx} + 6y = 0$

By using operator D for $\dfrac{d}{dx}$, we have $(D^2 - 5D + 6) y = 0$

$\therefore$ $\phi(D) = D^2 - 5D + 6 = 0$ is the A.E.

$\therefore$ $(D^2 - 5D + 6) y = (D - 3) (D - 2) y = (D - 2) (D - 3) y.$

1.7 SOLUTION OF $\phi(D)\, y = 0$

Being n^{th} order DE, equation (4) or (5) will have exactly n arbitrary constants in its general solution.

The equation (5) will be satisfied by the solution of the equation $(D - m_n)\, y = 0$

i.e. $\dfrac{dy}{dx} - m_n\, y = 0$

On solving this 1st order 1st degree DE by separting variables, we get $y = c_n\, e^{m_n x}$, where, c_n is an arbitrary constant.

Similarly, since the factors in equation (5) can be taken in any order, the equation will be satisfied by the solution of each of the equations $(D - m_1)\, y = 0$, $(D - m_2)\, y = 0$ ... etc., that is by $y = c_1\, e^{m_1 x}$, $y = c_2\, e^{m_2 x}$ .... etc.

It can, therefore, easily be proved that the sum of these individual solutions, i.e.

$$y \;=\; c_1\, e^{m_1 x} + c_2\, e^{m_2 x} + \dots + c_n\, e^{m_n x} \qquad \dots (6)$$

also satisfies the equation (5) and as it contains n arbitrary constants, and the equation (4) is of the nth order, (6) constitutes the general solution of the equation (4).

$\therefore$ **The general solution of the equation $\phi(D)\, y = 0$ is**

$$y = c_1\, e^{m_1 x} + c_2\, e^{m_2 x} + \dots + c_n\, e^{m_n x}$$

where $m_1, m_2, \dots m_n$ are the roots of the auxiliary equation $\phi(D) = 0$.

Ex. 1 : Solve $\dfrac{d^3 y}{dx^3} - 6\dfrac{d^2 y}{dx^2} + 11\dfrac{dy}{dx} - 6y = 0.$

Sol. : Let D stand for $\dfrac{d}{dx}$ and the given equation can be written as

$(D^3 - 6D^2 + 11D - 6)\, y = 0.$

Here auxiliary equation is $D^3 - 6D^2 + 11D - 6 = 0$

i.e. $(D - 1)(D - 2)(D - 3) = 0 \Rightarrow m_1 = 1,\ m_2 = 2,\ m_3 = 3$, are roots of AE.

$\therefore$ The general solution is $y = c_1\, e^x + c_2\, e^{2x} + c_3\, e^{3x}$.

2. For $(4D^2 - 8D + 1)\, y = 0$, $D = 1 \pm \dfrac{\sqrt{3}}{2} \Rightarrow y = c_1\, e^{\left(1 + \frac{\sqrt{3}}{2}\right) x} + c_2\, e^{\left(1 - \frac{\sqrt{3}}{2}\right) x}$.

1.8 DIFFERENT CASES DEPENDING UPON THE NATURE OF ROOTS OF THE AUXILIARY EQUATION $\phi(D) = 0$.

A. The Case of Real and Different Roots :

If roots of $\phi(D) = 0$ be $m_1, m_2, m_3 \dots m_n$, all are real and different, then the solution of $\phi(D)\, y = 0$ will be

$$\boxed{y \;=\; c_1\, e^{m_1 x} + c_2\, e^{m_2 x} + c_3\, e^{m_3 x} + \dots + c_n\, e^{m_n x}}$$

B. The Case of Real and Repeated Roots (The Case of Multiple Roots) :

Let $m_1 = m_2, m_3, m_4 \ldots m_n$ be the roots of $\phi(D) = 0$, then the part of solution corresponding to m_1 and m_2 will look like

$$c_1 e^{m_1 x} + c_2 e^{m_1 x} \, (m_1 = m_2) \ = \ (c_1 + c_2) \, e^{m_1 x} \ = c' e^{m_1 x}$$

But this means that number of arbitrary constants now in the solution will be $n - 1$ instead of n. Hence it is no longer the general solution. The anomaly can be rectified as under.

Pertaining to $m_1 = m_2$, the part of the equation will be $(D - m_1)(D - m_1) \, y = 0$

Put $(D - m_1) \, y = z$, temporarily, then we have $(D - m_1) \, z = 0 \quad \therefore \ z = c_1 e^{m_1 x}$

Hence putting value of z in $(D - m_1) \, y = z$, we have

$$(D - m_1) \, y \ = \ c_1 e^{m_1 x} \quad \text{or} \quad \frac{dy}{dx} - m_1 \, y \ = \ c_1 e^{m_1 x}$$

which is a linear differential equation. Its I.F. $= e^{-\int m_1 dx} = e^{-m_1 x}$ and hence solution is

$$y\left(e^{-m_1 x}\right) \ = \ \int c_1 e^{m_1 x} \cdot e^{-m_1 x} \ dx + c_2 = c_1 x + c_2$$

$$\therefore \qquad\qquad y \ = \ (c_1 x + c_2) \, e^{m_1 x}$$

If $m_1 = m_2$ are real, and the remaining roots $m_3, m_4, m_5, \ldots, m_n$ are real and different then solution of $\phi(D) \, y = 0$ is

$$\boxed{y \ = \ (c_1 x + c_2) \, e^{m_1 x} + c_3 e^{m_3 x} + c_4 e^{m_4 x} + \ldots + c_n e^{m_n x}}$$

Similarly, when three roots are repeated. i.e. if $m_1 = m_2 = m_3$ are real, and the remaining roots $m_4, m_5, \ldots m_n$ are real and different then solution of $\phi(D) \, y = 0$ is

$$\boxed{y \ = \ (c_1 x^2 + c_2 x + c_3) \, e^{m_1 x} + c_4 e^{m_4 x} + \ldots + c_n e^{m_n x}}$$

If $m_1 = m_2 = m_3 = \ldots = m_n$ i.e. n roots are real and equal then solution of $\phi(D) \, y = 0$ is

$$\boxed{y \ = \ (c_1 x^{n-1} + c_2 x^{n-2} + \ldots + c_{n-1} x + c_n) \, e^{m_1 x}}$$

Ex. 1. For $(D^2 - 6D + 9) \, y = 0$ A.E. $= (D - 3)^2 = 0$ and solution is $y = (c_1 x + c_2) \, e^{3x}$

  2. For $(D - 1)^3 (D + 1) \, y = 0$, solution is $y = (c_1 x^2 + c_2 x + c_3) \, e^x + c_4 e^{-x}$

  3. For $(D - 1)^2 (D + 1)^2 \, y = 0$, solution is $y = (c_1 x + c_2) \, e^x + (c_3 x + c_4) \, e^{-x}$.

C. The Case of Imaginary (Complex) Roots

For practical problems in engineering, this case has special importance. Since the coefficients of the auxiliary equation are real, the imaginary roots (if exists) will occur in conjugate pairs. Let $\alpha \pm i\beta$ be one such pair. Therefore $m_1 = \alpha + i\beta$, $m_2 = \alpha - i\beta$

The corresponding part of the solution of the equation $\phi(D) \, y = 0$, then takes the form

$$y = A \, e^{(\alpha + i\beta) x} + B \, e^{(\alpha - i\beta) x}$$
$$= e^{\alpha x} \left[A \, e^{i\beta x} + B \, e^{-i\beta x} \right]$$

$$= e^{\alpha x}\,[A\,(\cos \beta x + i \sin \beta x) + B\,(\cos \beta x - i \sin \beta x)]$$
$$= e^{\alpha x}\,[(A+B)\cos \beta x + i\,(A-B)\sin \beta x]$$

$$\boxed{y \;=\; e^{\alpha x}\,[c_1 \cos \beta x + c_2 \sin \beta x]}$$

where, $c_1 = A + B$ and $c_2 = i\,(A - B)$ are arbitrary constants.

Using $c_1 = C \cos \theta$, $c_2 = -\sin \theta$, this can also be put sometimes into the form as given below (recall SHM).

$$\boxed{y \;=\; C\, e^{\alpha x} \cos (\beta x + \theta) \text{ where } C,\ \theta \text{ are arbitrary constants.}}$$

ILLUSTRATIONS

Ex. 1 : *Solve* $(D^2 + 2D + 5)\,y = 0.$

Sol. : The auxiliary equation is $D^2 + 2D + 5 = 0$ whose roots are $D = -1 \pm 2i$ which are both imaginary. Here $\alpha = -1$, $\beta = 2$. Hence the solution is

$$y \;=\; e^{-x}\,[A \cos 2x + B \sin 2x]$$

Ex. 2 : *Solve* $\dfrac{d^4y}{dx^4} - 5\dfrac{d^2y}{dx^2} + 12\dfrac{dy}{dx} + 28y = 0.$

Sol. : The auxiliary equation is $D^4 - 5D^2 + 12D + 28 = 0$ having roots $D = -2, -2,\ 2 \pm \sqrt{3}\ i.$

(Here $\alpha = 2$, $\beta = \sqrt{3}$). Hence the solution is

$$y \;=\; (c_1 x + c_2)\, e^{-2x} + e^{2x}\left[A \cos \sqrt{3}\, x + B \sin \sqrt{3}\, x\right]$$

Ex. 3 : For $(D^2 + 4)y = 0$, $D = 0 \pm 2i$ (Here $\alpha = 0$, $\beta = 2$) $\Rightarrow$ $y = A \cos 2x + B \sin 2x.$

D. The Case of Repeated Imaginary Roots :

If the imaginary roots $m_1 = \alpha + i\beta$ and $m_2 = \alpha - i\beta$ occur twice, then the part of solution of $\phi\,(D)\,y = 0$ will be

$$y \;=\; (A x + B)\, e^{m_1 x} + (C x + D)\, e^{m_2 x} \qquad \text{... (by using case B)}$$
$$= (A x + B)\, e^{(\alpha + i\beta)\,x} + (C x + D)\, e^{(\alpha - i\beta)\,x}$$
$$= e^{\alpha x}\left[(A x + B)\, e^{i\beta x} + (C x + D)\, e^{-i\beta x}\right]$$
$$= e^{\alpha x}\,[(A x + B)\,\{\cos \beta x + i \sin \beta x\} + (C x + D)\,\{\cos \beta x - i \sin \beta x\}]$$
$$= e^{\alpha x}\,[(A x + B + C x + D)\cos \beta x + i\,(A x + B - C x - D)\sin \beta x]$$

$$\boxed{y \;=\; e^{\alpha x}\,[(c_1 x + c_2)\cos \beta x + (c_3 x + c_4)\sin \beta x]}$$

with proper changes in the constants c_1, c_2, c_3 and c_4.

ILLUSTRATIONS

Ex. 1 : *Solve* $\dfrac{d^6y}{dx^6} + 6\dfrac{d^4y}{dx^4} + 9\dfrac{d^2y}{dx^2} = 0.$

Sol. : The auxiliary equation $D^6 + 6D^4 + 9D^2 = 0$ has roots $D = 0, 0, \pm i\sqrt{3}, \pm i\sqrt{3}$ where the imaginary roots $\pm i\sqrt{3}$ are repeated. Hence the solution is

$$y = c_1 x + c_2 + (c_3 x + c_4)\cos\sqrt{3}\, x + (c_5 x + c_6)\sin\sqrt{3}\, x$$

Ex. 2 : $(D^4 + 2D^2 + 1)\, y = 0.$

Sol. : The auxiliary equation $D^4 + 2D^2 + 1 = 0$ has roots $D = \pm i, \pm i$, repeated imaginary roots. Hence the solution is

$$y = (c_1 x + c_2)\cos x + (c_3 x + c_4)\sin x$$

Now we will summarise the four cases for ready reference.

Case 1 : Real and Distinct Roots : A.E. $\Rightarrow (D - m_1)(D - m_2)(D - m_3) \ldots (D - m_n) = 0$

$\therefore$ **Solution is** $y = c_1 e^{m_1 x} + c_2 e^{m_2 x} + c_3 e^{m_3 x} + \ldots + c_n e^{m_n x}$

Case 2 : Repeated Real Roots :

For $m_1 = m_2 \Rightarrow$ A.E. $\Rightarrow (D - m_1)(D - m_1)(D - m_3) \ldots (D - m_n) = 0$

Solution is $y = (c_1 x + c_2) e^{m_1 x} + c_3 e^{m_3 x} + \ldots + c_n e^{m_n x}$

For $m_1 = m_2 = m_3 \Rightarrow$ A.E. $\Rightarrow (D - m_1)(D - m_1)(D - m_1)(D - m_4) \ldots (D - m_n) = 0$

Solution is $y = (c_1 x^2 + c_2 x + c_3) e^{m_1 x} + c_4 e^{m_4 x} + \ldots + c_n e^{m_n x}$

Case 3 : Imaginary Roots : For $D = \alpha \pm i\beta$

Solution is $y = e^{\alpha x}[c_1 \cos \beta x + c_2 \sin \beta x]$

Case 4 : Repeated Imaginary Roots : For $D = \alpha \pm i\beta$ be repeated twice

Solution is $y = e^{\alpha x}[(c_1 x + c_2)\cos \beta x + (c_3 x + c_4)\sin \beta x]$

ILLUSTRATIONS

1. Solve $\dfrac{d^2 x}{dt^2} + 4x = 0.$ Let D stand for $\dfrac{d}{dt}$.

$\therefore$ A.E. : $D^2 + 4 = 0 \Rightarrow D = 0 \pm 2i$

$\therefore$ The solution is $x = c_1 \cos 2t + c_2 \sin 2t.$

2. Solve $\dfrac{d^4 y}{dz^2} - 16y = 0.$ Let D stand for $\dfrac{d}{dz}$.

$\therefore$ A.E. : $D^4 - 16 = 0, \ (D - 2)(D + 2)(D^2 + 4) = 0.$

$\therefore$ The solution is $y = c_1 e^{2z} + c_2 e^{-2z} + c_3 \cos 2z + c_4 \sin 2z.$

Special Case : If the two real roots of $\phi(D)\, y = 0$ be m and $-m$ [e.g. $D^2 - m^2 = 0$], then the corresponding part of the solution is

$$y = A\, e^{mx} + B\, e^{-mx}$$

OR $y = A(\cosh mx + \sinh mx) + B(\cosh mx - \sinh mx)$

OR $y = (A + B)\cosh mx + (A - B)\sinh mx$

i.e. $\boxed{y = c_1 \cosh mx + c_2 \sinh mx}$

We note here that (in some particular cases) solution of $D^2 - m^2 = 0$ can be written as

$$y = c_1 e^{mx} + c_2 e^{-mx} \quad \text{or} \quad y = c_1 \cosh mx + c_2 \sinh mx.$$

e.g. 1. $(D^2 - 1)y = 0 \Rightarrow y = c_1 \cosh x + c_2 \sinh x.$

  2. $(D^2 - 4)y = 0 \Rightarrow y = c_1 \cosh 2x + c_2 \sinh 2x.$

EXERCISE 1.1

Solve the following differential equations :

1. $\dfrac{d^2y}{dx^2} - 5\dfrac{dy}{dx} - 6y = 0.$ **Ans.** $y = c_1 e^{-x} + c_2 e^{6x}$

2. $2\dfrac{d^2y}{dx^2} - \dfrac{dy}{dx} - 10y = 0.$ **Ans.** $y = c_1 e^{-2x} + c_2 e^{(5/2)\,x}$

3. $\dfrac{d^3y}{dx^3} + 2\dfrac{d^2y}{dx^2} + \dfrac{dy}{dx} = 0.$ **Ans.** $y = c_1 + e^{-x}(c_2 x + c_3)$

4. $(D^4 - 2D^3 + D^2)y = 0.$ **Ans.** $y = c_1 x + c_2 + (c_3 x + c_4)e^x$

5. $(D^6 - 6D^5 + 12D^4 - 6D^3 - 9D^2 + 12D - 4)y = 0.$

Ans. $y = (c_1 x^2 + c_2 x + c_3)e^x + (c_4 x + c_5)e^{2x} + c_6 e^{-x}$

6. $(D^3 + 6D^2 + 11D + 6)y = 0.$ **Ans.** $y = c_1 e^{-x} + c_2 e^{-2x} + c_3 e^{-3x}$

7. $4y'' - 8y' + 7y = 0.$ **Ans.** $y = e^x\left[A\cos\left(\dfrac{\sqrt{3}}{2}x\right) + B\sin\left(\dfrac{\sqrt{3}}{2}x\right)\right]$

8. $\dfrac{d^2x}{dt^2} + 2\dfrac{dx}{dt} + 5x = 0,\ x(0) = 2,\ x'(0) = 0.$ **Ans.** $x = e^{-t}(2\cos 2t + \sin 2t)$

9. $\dfrac{d^2s}{dt^2} = -16\dfrac{ds}{dt} - 64\,s,\ s = 0,\ \dfrac{ds}{dt} = -4$ when $t = 0.$ **Ans.** $s = -4e^{8t}\,t$

10. $(D^3 + D^2 - 2D + 12)y = 0.$ **Ans.** $y = c_1 e^{-3x} + e^x\left[A\cos\sqrt{3}\,x + B\sin\sqrt{3}\,x\right]$

11. $(D^2 + 1)^3(D^2 + D + 1)^2 y = 0.$

Ans. $y = (c_1 + c_2 x + c_3 x^2)\cos x + (c_4 + c_5 x + c_6 x^2)\sin x$

$$+ e^{-x/2}\left[(c_7 + c_8 x)\cos\left(\frac{\sqrt{3}}{2}x\right) + (c_9 + c_{10} x)\sin\left(\frac{\sqrt{3}}{2}x\right)\right]$$

12. $\dfrac{d^4y}{dx^4} + m^4 y = 0.$ **Ans.** $y = e^{(mx/\sqrt{2})}\left[A\cos\left(\dfrac{mx}{\sqrt{2}}\right) + B\sin\left(\dfrac{mx}{\sqrt{2}}\right)\right]$

$$+ e^{-(mx/\sqrt{2})}\left[C\cos\left(\frac{mx}{\sqrt{2}}\right) + D\sin\left(\frac{mx}{\sqrt{2}}\right)\right]$$

13. $4\dfrac{d^2s}{dt^2} = -9s.$ **Ans.** $s = c_1 \sin\dfrac{3t}{2} + c_2 \cos\dfrac{3t}{2}$

14. The equation for the bending of a strut is $EI\dfrac{d^2y}{dx^2} + Py = 0$. If $y = 0$ when $x = 0$

and $y = a$ when $x = \dfrac{l}{2}$, find y. **Ans.** $y = \dfrac{a\,\sin\sqrt{\dfrac{P}{EI}}\,x}{\sin\sqrt{\dfrac{P}{EI}}\cdot\dfrac{l}{2}}$

1.9 THE GENERAL SOLUTION OF THE LINEAR DIFFERENTIAL EQUATION $\phi(D)\,y = f(x)$

The general solution of the equation $\phi(D)y = f(x)$ can be written as $\boxed{y = y_c + y_p}$ where,

1. y_c is the solution of the given equation with $f(x) = 0$, that is of equation $\phi(D)\,y = 0$ (which is known as Associated equation or Reduced equation) and is called the *complimentary function* (C.F.). It involves n arbitrary constants and is denoted by C.F. then $\boxed{\phi(D)\,y_c = 0}$.

2. y_p is any function of x, which satisfies the equation $\phi(D)\,y = f(x)$, so that

$$\boxed{\phi(D)\,y_p = f(x)}$$

y_p is called the particular integral and is denoted by P.I. It does not contain any arbitrary constant.

Thus, on substituting $y = y_c + y_p$ in $\phi(D)\,y$,

$$\phi(D)\,[y_c + y_p] = \phi(D)\,y_c + \phi(D)\,y_p = 0 + f(x) = f(x)$$

$\therefore\ y = y_c + y_p$ satisfies the equation $\phi(D)\,y = f(x)$ and as it contains exactly n arbitrary constants, is the general (or complete) solution of the equation.

Note : 1. The complete solution of $\phi(D)\,y = f(x)$ is $y = \text{C.F.} + \text{P.I.} = y_c + y_p$.

2. The general solution of $\phi(D)\,y = f(x)$ has *arbitrary constants equal in number to the order of the differential equation.*

1.10 THE INVERSE OPERATOR $\dfrac{1}{\phi(D)}$ AND THE SYMBOLIC EXPRESSION FOR THE PARTICULAR INTEGRAL

We define $\dfrac{1}{\phi(D)}\,f(x)$ as that function of x which when acted upon by the differential operator $\phi(D)$ gives f(x).

Thus by this definition, $\phi(D)\left\{\dfrac{1}{\phi(D)}\,f(x)\right\} = f(x)$ and so $\left\{\dfrac{1}{\phi(D)}\,f(x)\right\}$ satisfies the equation $\phi(D)\,y = f(x)$ and so is the P.I. of the equation $\phi(D)\,y = f(x)$.

Thus the P.I. of the equation $\phi(D)\, y = f(x)$ is symbolically given by

$$\boxed{\text{P.I.} = y_p = \frac{1}{\phi(D)}\, f(x)}$$

e.g.   1. $(D^2 - 1)\, y = x^2 \quad \therefore \quad y_p = \frac{1}{D^2 - 1}\, x^2$

2. $(D^2 - 3D + 2)\, y = \sin e^x \quad \therefore \quad y_p = \frac{1}{D^2 - 3D + 2}\, \sin e^x.$

1.11 METHODS OF OBTAINING PARTICULAR INTEGRAL

There are three methods to evaluate the particular integral $y_p = \dfrac{1}{\phi(D)}\, f(x)$.

(A) General method

(B) Short-cut methods

Now we will discuss these methods in detail.

(A) General Method :

This method is useful when the short-cut methods given in (B) are not applicable. This method involves integration.

(i) $\dfrac{1}{D-m}\, f(x)$: By definition of the P.I., $\dfrac{1}{D-m}\, f(x)$ will be the P.I. of the equation $(D - m)\, y = f(x)$ i.e. the part in the solution of this equation which does not contain the arbitrary constant. We have, $\dfrac{dy}{dx} - my = f(x)$ (linear)

$$\text{I.F.} = e^{-mx} \text{ and the general solution is}$$

$$y\, e^{-mx} = \int f(x) \cdot e^{-mx}\, dx + c_1$$

$$\therefore \qquad y = (c_1 e^{mx}) + \left(e^{mx} \int e^{-mx} f(x) \cdot dx \right)$$

$$\text{i.e.} \quad y = y_c + y_p$$

Here $c_1 e^{mx}$ is the C.F. and $e^{mx} \displaystyle\int e^{-mx} f(x)\, dx$ must be the P.I.

$$\therefore \qquad \boxed{y_p = \text{P.I.} = \frac{1}{D-m}\, f(x) = e^{mx} \int e^{-mx} f(x)\, dx}$$

Similarly,

$$\boxed{y_p = \text{P.I.} = \frac{1}{D+m}\, f(x) = e^{-mx} \int e^{mx} f(x)\, dx}$$

Put $m = 0$

$$\boxed{y_p = \frac{1}{D}\, f(x) = \int f(x)\, dx}$$

Also,

$$y_p = \frac{1}{D^2}\, f(x) = \frac{1}{D}\left[\frac{1}{D}\, f(x) \right]$$

$$= \frac{1}{D} \left[\int f(x)\, dx \right] = \int \left[\int f(x)\, dx \right] dx$$

$\therefore$

$$\boxed{y_p = \frac{1}{D^2} f(x) = \int \left[\int f(x)\, dx \right] dx}$$

Similarly,

$$\boxed{y_p = \frac{1}{D^3} f(x) = \int \left\{ \int \left[\int f(x)\, dx \right] dx \right\} dx}$$ … and so on.

(ii) $\dfrac{1}{(D - m_1)(D - m_2)}\ f(x)$:

$$y_p = \frac{1}{(D - m_1)(D - m_2)}\ f(x) = \frac{1}{(D - m_1)}\ e^{m_2 x} \int e^{-m_2 x} f(x)\, dx$$

$$y_p = e^{m_1 x} \int e^{-m_1 x} \left[e^{m_2 x} \int e^{-m_2 x} f(x)\, dx \right] dx$$

(iii) Use of Partial Fraction :

$$y_p = \frac{1}{(D - m_1)(D - m_2)}\ f(x)$$

$$= \frac{1}{(m_1 - m_2)} \left[\frac{1}{D - m_1} - \frac{1}{D - m_2} \right] f(x)$$

$$= \frac{1}{m_1 - m_2} \left\{ \frac{1}{D - m_1} f(x) - \frac{1}{D - m_2} f(x) \right\}$$

$$y_p = \frac{1}{m_1 - m_2} \left\{ e^{m_1 x} \int e^{-m_1 x} f(x)\, dx - e^{m_2 x} \int e^{-m_2 x} f(x)\, dx \right\}$$

ILLUSTRATIONS ON GENERAL METHOD

Ex. 1 : *Solve* $\dfrac{d^2 y}{dx^2} + 3\dfrac{dy}{dx} + 2y = e^{e^x}$

Sol. : For C.F.,   A.E. is $D^2 + 3D + 2 = 0 \Rightarrow (D + 2)(D + 1) = 0$

Hence $D = -1, -2$ and C.F. $= c_1 e^{-x} + c_2 e^{-2x}$

Here   P.I. $= y_p = \dfrac{1}{(D + 2)(D + 1)}\ (e^{e^x})$

$$= \frac{1}{D + 2} \left[\frac{1}{D + 1}\ e^{e^x} \right]$$

$$= \frac{1}{D + 2} \left[e^{-x} \int e^x e^{e^x}\, dx \right] \qquad [\text{put } e^x = t \therefore e^x\, dx = dt]$$

$$= \frac{1}{D + 2} \left[e^{-x} \int e^t\, dt \right]$$

$$= \frac{1}{D + 2} \left[e^{-x} e^{e^x} \right]$$

$$= e^{-2x} \int e^{2x} e^{-x} e^{e^x} \, dx$$

$$\text{P.I.} = e^{-2x} \int e^x e^{e^x} \, dx = e^{-2x} e^{e^x}$$

Hence the complete solution will be

$$y = c_1 e^{-x} + c_2 e^{-2x} + e^{-2x} e^{e^x}$$

Ex. 2 : *Solve* $\dfrac{d^2y}{dx^2} + \dfrac{dy}{dx} = \dfrac{1}{1 + e^x}.$

Sol. : We have $(D^2 + D)\, y = \dfrac{1}{1 + e^x}$, here $D \equiv \dfrac{d}{dx}$

$\therefore \quad$ AE $\Rightarrow D\,(D + 1) = 0 \quad \therefore \quad D = 0, -1.$

$\therefore \qquad\qquad$ C.F. $= y_c = c_1 + c_2 e^{-x}$

$$\text{P.I.} = \frac{1}{D\,(D + 1)} \left(\frac{1}{1 + e^x} \right)$$

$$= \left(\frac{1}{D} - \frac{1}{D + 1} \right) \left(\frac{1}{1 + e^x} \right) \qquad \text{by partial fraction}$$

$$= \frac{1}{D} \left(\frac{1}{1 + e^x} \right) - \frac{1}{D + 1} \left(\frac{1}{1 + e^x} \right)$$

$$= \int \frac{1}{1 + e^x} \, dx - e^{-x} \int e^x \frac{dx}{1 + e^x}$$

$$= \int \frac{e^x \, dx}{e^x\,(1 + e^x)} - e^{-x} \int e^x \frac{dx}{1 + e^x} \qquad \begin{bmatrix} \text{put } 1 + e^x = t \\ e^x \, dx = dt \end{bmatrix}$$

$$= \int \frac{dt}{t\,(t - 1)} - e^{-x} \int \frac{dt}{t}$$

$$= \int \left(\frac{1}{t - 1} - \frac{1}{t} \right) dt - e^{-x} \log\,(e^x + 1)$$

$$= \log\,(t - 1) - \log t - e^{-x} \log\,(e^x + 1)$$

$$= \log\,(e^x) - \log\,(1 + e^x) - e^{-x} \log\,(e^x + 1)$$

$$= x - \log\,(1 + e^x) - e^{-x} \log\,(e^x + 1)$$

Hence the complete solution is

$$y = c_1 + c_2 e^{-x} + x - \log\,(1 + e^x) - e^{-x} \log\,(1 + e^x)$$

Ex. 3 : *Solve* $(D^2 + 5D + 6)\, y = e^{-2x} \sec^2 x\,(1 + 2\tan x)$

Sol. : $D^2 + 5D + 6 = 0$ gives $(D + 2)\,(D + 3) = 0 \Rightarrow D = -2, -3$

$\qquad$ C.F. $= c_1 e^{-2x} + c_2 e^{-3x}$

$$\text{P.I.} = \frac{1}{(D + 3)\,(D + 2)} \left[e^{-2x} \sec^2 x\,(1 + 2\tan x) \right]$$

$$= \frac{1}{D + 3} \left[e^{-2x} \int e^{2x} \cdot e^{-2x} \sec^2 x\,(1 + 2\tan x)\, dx \right]$$

$$= \frac{1}{D+3} \left[e^{-2x} \int \sec^2 x \, (1 + 2\tan x) \, dx \right] \quad \text{put } \tan x = t, \ \sec^2 x \, dx = dt$$

$$= \frac{1}{D+3} \left[e^{-2x} \int (1 + 2t) \, dt \right]$$

$$= \frac{1}{D+3} \left[e^{-2x} (t + t^2) \right]$$

$$= \frac{1}{D+3} \left[e^{-2x} (\tan x + \tan^2 x) \right]$$

$$= e^{-3x} \int e^{3x} \cdot e^{-2x} \left[(\tan x - 1) + \sec^2 x \right] dx$$

$$= e^{-3x} \int e^{x} \left[(\tan x - 1) + \sec^2 x \right] dx$$

$$= e^{-3x} \left[e^{x} (\tan x - 1) \right] \qquad\qquad \because \int e^{x} \left[f(x) + f'(x) \right] dx = e^{x} f(x)$$

$$= e^{-2x} (\tan x - 1)$$

Hence the complete solution is

$$y = c_2 e^{-3x} + e^{-2x} \left[c_1 + \tan x - 1 \right]$$

$$= c_2 e^{-3x} + e^{-2x} \left[c_3 + \tan x \right]$$

Ex. 4 : *Solve* $\dfrac{d^2 y}{dx^2} + 9y = \sec 3x$

Sol. : A.E. is $D^2 + 9 = 0$,   or $D = \pm 3i$

$$\text{C.F.} = c_1 \cos 3x + c_2 \sin 3x \text{ and}$$

$$\text{P.I.} = \frac{1}{D^2 + 9} (\sec 3x) = \frac{1}{(D + 3i)(D - 3i)} \sec 3x$$

$$= \frac{1}{6i} \left[\frac{1}{D - 3i} - \frac{1}{D + 3i} \right] \sec 3x$$

$$= \frac{1}{6i} \frac{1}{D - 3i} \sec 3x - \frac{1}{6i} \frac{1}{D + 3i} \sec 3x \qquad\qquad \ldots (1)$$

Now, $\dfrac{1}{D - 3i} \sec 3x = e^{3ix} \int e^{-3ix} \sec 3x \, dx$

$$= e^{3ix} \int \frac{\cos 3x - i \sin 3x}{\cos 3x} \, dx$$

$$= e^{3ix} \int \left[1 - i \tan 3x \right] dx$$

$$= e^{3ix} \left[x + \frac{i}{3} \log (\cos 3x) \right]$$

Changing i to $-i$ in this, we have

$$\frac{1}{D + 3i} (\sec 3x) = e^{-3ix} \left[x - \frac{i}{3} \log (\cos 3x) \right]$$

Putting values in (1), we have

$$\text{P.I.} \;=\; \frac{1}{6i}\left[e^{3ix}\left\{ x + \frac{i}{3}\log(\cos 3x)\right\} - e^{-3ix}\left\{ x - \frac{i}{3}\log(\cos 3x)\right\} \right]$$

$$=\; \frac{x}{6i}\cdot e^{3ix} + \frac{e^{3ix}\log(\cos 3x)}{18} - \frac{x\, e^{-3ix}}{6i} + \frac{e^{-3ix}\log(\cos 3x)}{18}$$

Combining the like terms, we get

$$=\; \frac{x}{3}\left[\frac{e^{3ix} - e^{-3ix}}{2i}\right] + \frac{1}{9}\left[\frac{e^{3ix} + e^{-3ix}}{2}\right]\log(\cos 3x)$$

$$\text{P.I.} \;=\; \frac{x}{3}\sin 3x + \frac{1}{9}\cos 3x \,\log(\cos 3x)$$

Hence the general solution will be

$$y \;=\; c_1\cos 3x + c_2\sin 3x + \frac{x}{3}\sin 3x + \frac{1}{9}\cos 3x \cdot \log(\cos 3x)$$

Ex. 5 : *Solve* $\dfrac{d^2y}{dx^2} - \dfrac{dy}{dx} - 2y = 2\log x + \dfrac{1}{x} + \dfrac{1}{x^2}$

Sol. : $(D^2 - D - 2)\, y = 2\log x + \dfrac{1}{x} + \dfrac{1}{x^2}$

$$\text{A.E.} \;:\; D^2 - D - 2 = 0 \qquad \therefore \quad (D-2)(D+1) = 0$$

$$\therefore \qquad y_c \;=\; c_1 e^{2x} + c_2 e^{-x}$$

$$y_p \;=\; \frac{1}{(D-2)(D+1)}\left(2\log x + \frac{1}{x} + \frac{1}{x^2}\right)$$

$$=\; \frac{1}{D-2}\left[e^{-x}\int e^{x}\left(2\log x + \frac{1}{x} + \frac{1}{x^2}\right) dx \right]$$

$$=\; \frac{1}{D-2}\left[e^{-x}\int e^{x}\left\{2\log x + \frac{2}{x} - \frac{1}{x} + \frac{1}{x^2}\right\} dx \right]$$

$$=\; \frac{1}{D-2}\left\{ e^{-x}\int e^{x}\left[\left(2\log x - \frac{1}{x}\right) + \left(\frac{2}{x} + \frac{1}{x^2}\right)\right] dx \right\}$$

$$=\; \frac{1}{D-2}\, e^{-x}\cdot e^{x}\left(2\log x - \frac{1}{x}\right) \;=\; \frac{1}{D-2}\left(2\log x - \frac{1}{x}\right)$$

$$=\; e^{2x}\int e^{-2x}\left(2\log x - \frac{1}{x}\right) dx$$

$$=\; e^{2x}\left\{\int 2\log x \cdot e^{-2x}\, dx - \int e^{-2x}\frac{1}{x}\, dx\right\}$$

$$= e^{2x} \left\{ 2 \log x \left(\frac{e^{-2x}}{-2} \right) - \int \frac{2}{x} \cdot \left(\frac{e^{-2x}}{-2} \right) dx - \int e^{-2x} \cdot \frac{1}{x} \, dx \right\}$$

$$= e^{2x} \left\{ - \log x \cdot e^{-2x} + \int e^{-2x} \frac{1}{x} \, dx - \int e^{-2x} \frac{1}{x} \, dx \right\}$$

$$= e^{2x} \left\{ - \log x \, e^{-2x} \right\} \ = - \log x$$

$$\therefore \qquad y \ = \ C.F. + P.I. \ = \ y_c + y_p$$

$$y \ = \ c_1 e^{2x} + c_2 e^{-x} - \log x$$

Ex. 6 : *Solve $(D^2 - 1) y = e^{-x} \sin e^{-x} + \cos e^{-x}$.*

Sol. : AE : $D^2 - 1 = 0$ or $(D - 1)(D + 1) = 0 \Rightarrow D = -1, +1 \ \therefore y_c = c_1 e^x + c_2 e^{-x}$

$$y_p \ = \ \frac{1}{(D - 1)(D + 1)} \ (e^{-x} \sin e^{-x} + \cos e^{-x})$$

$$= \ \frac{1}{D - 1} \left\{ e^{-x} \int e^x (\cos e^{-x} + e^{-x} \sin e^{-x}) \, dx \right\} \left\{ \text{Use } \int e^x [f + f'] \, dx = e^x \cdot f \right\}$$

$$= \ \frac{1}{D - 1} \{ e^{-x} \cdot e^x \cos e^{-x} \} = \frac{1}{D - 1} \cdot \cos e^{-x}$$

$$= \ e^x \int e^{-x} \cos e^{-x} \, dx = - e^x \int \cos e^{-x} (- e^{-x} \, dx) \qquad\qquad \{ \text{Use } e^{-x} = t \}$$

$$= \ - e^x \sin e^{-x}$$

$$\therefore \qquad y \ = \ c_1 e^x + c_2 e^{-x} - e^x \sin e^{-x} .$$

Ex. 7 : *Solve $(D^2 - 1) y = (1 + e^{-x})^{-2}$.*

Sol. : 　　　A.E. : 　$D^2 - 1 = 0$

$$C.F. \ = \ c_1 e^x + c_2 e^{-x}$$

$$P.I. \ = \ \frac{1}{(D + 1)(D - 1)} \ (1 + e^{-x})^{-2}$$

$$= \ \frac{1}{D + 1} \ e^x \int e^{-x} (1 + e^{-x})^{-2} \, dx$$

$$= \ \frac{1}{D + 1} \ (- e^x) \int (1 + e^{-x})^{-2} (- e^{-x} \, dx)$$

$$= \ \frac{-1}{D + 1} \ [- e^x (1 + e^{-x})^{-1}]$$

$$= \ e^{-x} \int \frac{e^x \cdot e^x}{1 + e^{-x}} \, dx$$

$$= \ e^{-x} \int \frac{e^{2x} \cdot (e^x \, dx)}{1 + e^x} \ (1 + e^x = t)$$

$$= \ e^{-x} \int \frac{(t - 1)^2}{t} \, dt$$

$$= e^{-x} \left[\frac{t^2}{2} - 2t + \log t \right]$$

$$= e^{-x} \left[\frac{(1 + e^x)^2}{2} - 2(1 + e^x) + \log(1 + e^x) \right]$$

$$\therefore \quad y = c_1 e^x + c_2 e^{-x} + \frac{e^{-x}}{2}(1 + e^x)^2 + e^{-x} \log(1 + e^x) - 2e^{-x} - 2$$

or $\quad y = A e^x + B e^{-x} + e^{-x} \left[\frac{(1 + e^x)^2}{2} + \log(1 + e^x) \right] - 2$

Ex. 8 : *Solve $(D^2 + 3D + 2)y = e^{e^x} + \cos e^x$.*

Sol. :　A.E.　:　$D^2 + 3D + 2 = (D + 2)(D + 1) = 0$

C.F. $= c_1 e^{-2x} + c_2 e^{-x}$

$$\text{P.I.} = \frac{1}{(D + 2)(D + 1)} (e^{e^x} + \cos e^x)$$

$$= \frac{1}{D + 2} e^{-x} \int e^x (e^{e^x} + \cos e^x) \, dx$$

$$= \frac{1}{D + 2} e^{-x} (e^{e^x} + \sin e^x)$$

$$= e^{-2x} \int e^{2x} e^{-x} (e^{e^x} + \sin e^x) \, dx$$

$$= e^{-2x} \int e^x (e^{e^x} + \sin e^x) \, dx$$

$$= e^{-2x} (e^{e^x} - \cos e^x)$$

$$\therefore \quad y = c_1 e^{-2x} + c_2 e^{-x} + e^{-2x} (e^{e^x} - \cos e^x)$$

Ex. 9 : *Solve $(D^2 + 3D + 2)y = \sin e^x$.*

Sol. : A.E. : $D^2 + 3D + 2 = (D + 2)(D + 1) = 0 \Rightarrow D = -2, -1.$

C.F. $= c_1 e^{-2x} + c_2 e^{-x}$

$$\text{P.I.} = \frac{1}{(D + 2)(D + 1)} \sin e^x = \frac{1}{D + 2} e^{-x} \int e^x \sin e^x \, dx$$

$$= \frac{1}{D + 2} e^{-x} (- \cos e^x) = - e^{-2x} \int e^x \cos e^x \, dx$$

$$= - e^{-2x} \sin e^x$$

$$\therefore \quad y = c_1 e^{-2x} + c_2 e^{-x} - e^{-2x} \sin e^x$$

Ex. 10 : *Solve $\dfrac{d^2 y}{dx^2} + y = \csc x$.*

Sol. : A.E. : $D^2 + 1 = (D + i)(D - i) = 0 \Rightarrow D = \pm i.$

C.F. $= c_1 \cos x + c_2 \sin x$

$$\text{P.I.} = \frac{1}{D^2+1}\,\text{cosec}\,x = \frac{1}{2i}\left(\frac{1}{D-i}-\frac{1}{D+i}\right)\text{cosec}\,x$$

$$= \frac{1}{2i}\left[\frac{1}{D-i}\,\text{cosec}\,x - \frac{1}{D+i}\,\text{cosec}\,x\right]$$

$$= \frac{1}{2i}\left[e^{ix}\int e^{-ix}\,\text{cosec}\,x\,dx - e^{-ix}\int e^{ix}\,\text{cosec}\,x\,dx\right]$$

$$= \frac{1}{2i}\left[e^{ix}\int(\cos x - i\sin x)\,\text{cosec}\,x\,dx - e^{-ix}\int(\cos x + i\sin x)\,\text{cosec}\,x\,dx\right]$$

$$= \frac{1}{2i}\left[e^{ix}\int(\cot x - i)\,dx - e^{-ix}\int(\cot x + i)\,dx\right]$$

$$= \frac{1}{2i}\left[e^{ix}(\log\sin x - ix) - e^{-ix}(\log\sin x + ix)\right]$$

$$= \frac{1}{2i}\left[\log\sin x)(e^{ix}-e^{-ix}) - ix(e^{ix}+e^{-ix})\right]$$

$$= \sin x\,\log\sin x - x\cos x$$

$$\therefore\quad y = c_1\cos x + c_2\sin x + \sin x\,\log\sin x - x\cos x$$

(B) Short-cut Methods for Finding P.I. in Certain Standard Cases

Although the general method (A) discussed in the previous article will always work in the theory, it many a times leads to laborious and difficult integration. To avoid this, short methods of finding P.I. without actual integration are developed depending upon the particular form of function f(x).

Case I : P.I. when $f(x) = e^{ax}$, a is any constant.

To obtain $y_p = \dfrac{1}{\phi(D)}\,e^{ax}$, we have $D\,e^{ax} = a\,e^{ax}$, $D^2 e^{ax} = a^2 e^{ax}$ …… $D^n e^{an} = a^n e^{ax}$

$\therefore\quad (a_0 D^n + a_1 D^{n-1} + \ldots\ldots + a_n)\,e^{ax} = (a_0 a^n + a_1 a^{n-1} + \ldots\ldots + a_n)\,e^{ax}$

or $\qquad\qquad \phi(D)\,e^{ax} = \phi(a)\,e^{ax}$

Operating on both sides by $\dfrac{1}{\phi(D)}$, we have

$$\frac{1}{\phi(D)}\,[\phi(D)\,e^{ax}] = \frac{1}{\phi(D)}\,[\phi(a)\,e^{ax}]$$

or $\qquad\qquad e^{ax} = \phi(a)\,\dfrac{1}{\phi(D)}\,(e^{ax}),\qquad\qquad \left(\because \dfrac{1}{\phi(D)}\text{ is a linear operator}\right)$

Dividing by $\phi(a)$, we have the formula

$$\boxed{\frac{1}{\phi(D)}\,e^{ax} = \frac{1}{\phi(a)}\,e^{ax} \text{ provided } \phi(a)\neq 0} \qquad\qquad \ldots\text{(A)}$$

Case of failure : If $\phi(a) = 0$, above rule fails and we proceed as under.

Since $\phi(a) = 0$, $D - a$ must be a factor of $\phi(D)$ (by Factor Theorem).

Let
$$\phi(D) = (D - a)\,\psi(D) \quad \text{where, } \psi(a) \neq 0. \text{ Then}$$

$$\frac{1}{\phi(D)}\,(e^{ax}) = \frac{1}{D-a}\,\frac{1}{\psi(D)}\,e^{ax}$$

$$= \frac{1}{D-a}\,\frac{e^{ax}}{\psi(a)} \qquad \text{... from (A)}$$

$$= \frac{1}{\psi(a)}\,\frac{1}{D-a}\,e^{ax}$$

$$= \frac{1}{\psi(a)}\,e^{ax}\int e^{-ax}\,e^{ax}\,dx \qquad \text{... (refer 1.11-A (i))}$$

$$= \frac{1}{\psi(a)}\,e^{ax}\int dx$$

$$= x \cdot \frac{1}{\psi(a)}\,e^{ax}, \quad \text{where } \psi(a) = \phi'(a) \neq 0.$$

i.e.
$$\boxed{\frac{1}{\phi(D)}\,e^{ax} = x \cdot \frac{1}{\phi'(a)}\,e^{ax} \text{ provided } \phi'(a) \neq 0} \qquad \text{... (B)}$$

If $\phi'(a) = 0$ then we shall apply (B) again to get

$$\boxed{\frac{1}{\phi(D)}\,(e^{ax}) = x^2\,\frac{1}{\phi''(a)}\,e^{ax}, \text{ provided } \phi''(a) \neq 0} \ , \text{ and so on.}$$

Remark 1 : Since
$$\phi(D) = (D - a)\,\psi(D)$$
$$\phi'(D) = (D - a)\,\psi'(D) + \psi(D)$$
$\therefore$
$$\phi'(a) = 0 + \psi(a)$$
or
$$\phi'(a) = \psi(a)$$

Remark 2 : It can also be established that $\dfrac{1}{(D-a)^r\,\psi(D)}\,e^{ax} = \dfrac{1}{\psi(a)}\,\dfrac{x^r}{r!}\,e^{ax},\ \psi(a) \neq 0.$

Remark 3 : Any constant k can be expressed as $k = k \cdot e^{0x}$

$\therefore$
$$y_p = \frac{1}{\phi(D)}\,(k) = \frac{1}{\phi(D)}\,k \cdot e^{0x} = k \cdot \frac{1}{\phi(D)}\,e^{0x}$$

$$= k \cdot \frac{1}{\phi(0)}, \ \phi(0) \neq 0$$

Remark 4 : If $f(x) = a^x$ then we use $a^x = e^{x \log a}$

$\therefore$
$$y_p = \frac{1}{\phi(D)}\,a^x = \frac{1}{\phi(D)}\,e^{x \log a}$$

$$= \frac{1}{\phi\,(\log a)}\,a^x \qquad\qquad \text{Replace D with } \log a.$$

If $f(x) = a^{-x}$ then we use $\quad a^{-x} = e^{x\,\log\,1/a} = e^{x\,(-\log a)}$

$$\therefore \qquad y_p = \frac{1}{\phi(D)}\,a^{-x} = \frac{1}{\phi(D)}\,e^{x\,(-\log a)}$$

$$= \frac{1}{\phi(-\log a)}\,a^{-x}. \qquad\qquad \text{Replace D with } -\log a.$$

Formulae for Ready Reference :

1. $\dfrac{1}{D-a}\,e^{ax} = x \cdot e^{ax}$ 2. $\dfrac{1}{(D-a)^2}\,e^{ax} = \dfrac{x^2}{2!}\,e^{ax}$ 3. $\dfrac{1}{(D-a)^3}\,e^{ax} = \dfrac{x^3}{3!}\,e^{ax}$

4. $\dfrac{1}{(D-a)^r}\,e^{ax} = \dfrac{x^r}{r!}\,e^{ax}$

5. $\dfrac{1}{(D-a)^r\,\psi\,(D)}\,e^{ax} = \dfrac{1}{\psi(a)}\,\dfrac{1}{(D-a)^r}\,e^{ax} = \dfrac{1}{\psi(a)}\,\dfrac{x^r}{r!}\,e^{ax},\ \ \psi(a) \neq 0$

ILLUSTRATIONS

Ex. 1 : *Find the Particular Integral of $(D^2 - 5D + 6)\,y = 3\,e^{5x}$.*

Sol. : $\text{P.I.} = \dfrac{3}{D^2 - 5D + 6}\,(e^{5x}) = \dfrac{3\,e^{5x}}{5^2 - 5.5 + 6} = \dfrac{e^{5x}}{2}$

Ex. 2 : *Find the Particular Integral of $\dfrac{d^2y}{dx^2} + 4\dfrac{dy}{dx} + 3y = e^{-3x}$*

Sol. : Here $\qquad\qquad \text{P.I.} = \dfrac{1}{D^2 + 4D + 3}\,(e^{-3x}),\qquad \phi\,(D) = D^2 + 4D + 3$

But $\qquad\qquad \phi\,(-3) = 9 - 12 + 3 = 0$ hence $\quad \phi\,(-3) = 0$ and case I fails.

$$\therefore \qquad\qquad \text{P.I.} = \frac{x\,e^{-3x}}{\phi'\,(a)} = x \cdot \frac{1}{2D + 4} \cdot e^{-3x},\ D \to a = -3$$

$$= \frac{x\,e^{-3x}}{2\,(-3) + 4} = \frac{x\,e^{-3x}}{-2}$$

Ex. 3 : *Find the Particular Integral of $(D - 1)^3 y = e^x + 2^x - \dfrac{3}{2}$.*

Sol. : $\qquad y_p = \dfrac{1}{(D-1)^3}\,e^x + \dfrac{1}{(D-1)^3}\,2^x - \dfrac{3}{2}\,\dfrac{1}{(D-1)^3}\,e^{0x}$

$$= \frac{x^3}{3!}\,e^x + \frac{1}{(\log 2 - 1)^3}\,2^x - \frac{3}{2}\,\frac{1}{(0-1)^3}$$

$$= \frac{x^3}{6}\,e^x + \frac{1}{(\log 2 - 1)^3}\,2x + \frac{3}{2}$$

Ex. 4 : *Find the Particular Integral of $(D - 2)^2\,(D + 1)\,y = e^{2x} + 2^{-x}$*

Sol. : $\qquad y_p = \dfrac{1}{(D-2)^2\,(D+1)}\,e^{2x} + \dfrac{1}{(D-2)^2\,(D+1)}\,2^{-x}$

$$= \frac{1}{(D-2)^2} \cdot \frac{1}{(2+1)}\,e^{2x} + \frac{2^{-x}}{(-\log 2 - 2)^2\,(-\log 2 + 1)}$$

$$= \frac{1}{3} \cdot \frac{x^2}{2!} \; e^{2x} + \frac{2^{-x}}{(-\log 2 - 2)^2 \, (-\log 2 + 1)}$$

Case II : P.I. when $f(x) = \sin(ax + b)$ or $\cos(ax + b)$.

To obtain $y_p = \dfrac{1}{\phi(D^2)} \sin(ax + b)$ or $\dfrac{1}{\phi(D^2)} \cos(ax + b)$, we have

$$D \sin(ax + b) = a \cos(ax + b)$$
$$D^2 \sin(ax + b) = -a^2 \sin(ax + b)$$
$$D^3 \sin(ax + b) = -a^3 \cos(ax + b)$$
$$D^4 \sin(ax + b) = a^4 \sin(ax + b)$$

or
$$(D^2)^2 \sin(ax + b) = (-a^2)^2 \sin(ax + b)$$

Similarly
$$(D^2)^p \sin(ax + b) = (-a^2)^p \sin(ax + b)$$

and we may generalise that

$$\phi(D^2) \sin(ax + b) = \phi(-a^2) \sin(ax + b)$$

Operating on both sides by $\dfrac{1}{\phi(D^2)}$, we have

$$\frac{1}{\phi(D^2)} \, [\phi(D^2) \sin(ax + b)] = \frac{1}{\phi(D^2)} \, [\phi(-a^2) \sin(ax + b)]$$

$$\sin(ax + b) = \phi(-a^2) \frac{1}{\phi(D^2)} \, \sin(ax + b)$$

Dividing now by $\phi(-a^2)$, we have

$$\boxed{\frac{1}{\phi(D^2)} \sin(ax + b) = \frac{1}{\phi(-a^2)} \sin(ax + b), \text{ provided } \phi(-a^2) \neq 0}$$

Case of failure : But if $\phi(-a^2) = 0$, above rule fails and we proceed as under :

We know by Euler's Theorem that $\cos(ax + b) + i \sin(ax + b) = e^{i(ax + b)}$ hence

$$\frac{1}{\phi(D^2)} \, \sin(ax + b) = \text{Imag. Part of } \frac{1}{\phi(D^2)} \, e^{i(ax + b)}$$

$$= \text{I.P. of } \frac{1}{\phi(D^2)} \, e^{i(ax + b)}$$

$$= \text{I.P. of } x \frac{1}{\phi(D^2)} \, e^{i(ax + b)}, \quad (D^2 = -a^2)$$

Hence
$$\boxed{\frac{1}{\phi(D^2)} \sin(ax + b) = x \frac{1}{\phi'(-a^2)} \sin(ax + b) \text{ provided } \phi'(-a^2) \neq 0}$$

Add if $\phi'(-a^2) \neq 0$, we have

$$\frac{1}{\phi(D^2)} \sin(ax+b) = x^2 \frac{1}{\phi''(-a^2)} \sin(ax+b), \text{ provided } \phi''(-a^2) \neq 0$$

Similarly formulae for cos (ax + b) viz.

$$\frac{1}{\phi(D^2)} \cos(ax+b) = \frac{1}{\phi(-a^2)} \cos(ax+b), \text{ provided } \phi(-a^2) \neq 0$$

But if $\phi(-a^2) = 0$, we have

$$\frac{1}{\phi(D^2)} \cos(ax+b) = x \frac{1}{\phi'(-a^2)} \cos(ax+b), \text{ provided } \phi'(-a^2) \neq 0$$

And if $\phi'(-a^2) = 0$, we have

$$\frac{1}{\phi(D^2)} \cos(ax+b) = x^2 \frac{1}{\phi''(-a^2)} \cos(ax+b), \text{ provided } \phi''(-a^2) \neq 0$$

and so on and so forth.

Additional Results :

$$\frac{1}{\phi(D^2)} \sin ax = \frac{1}{\phi(-a^2)} \sin ax, \quad \phi(-a^2) \neq 0 \quad (\text{Replace } D^2 \text{ with } -a^2)$$

$$\frac{1}{\phi(D^2)} \cos ax = \frac{1}{\phi(-a^2)} \cos ax, \quad \phi(-a^2) \neq 0, \quad (\text{Replace } D^2 \text{ with } -a^2)$$

For the case of failure, it can also be established that

$$\frac{1}{D^2 + a^2} \sin(ax+b) = -\frac{x}{2a} \cos(ax+b)$$

$$\frac{1}{D^2 + a^2} \cos(ax+b) = \frac{x}{2a} \sin(ax+b)$$

$$\frac{1}{(D^2 + a^2)^r} \sin(ax+b) = \left(\frac{-x}{2a}\right)^r \frac{1}{r!} \sin\left(ax+b+\frac{r\pi}{2}\right)$$

$$\frac{1}{(D^2 + a^2)^r} \cos(ax+b) = \left(\frac{-x}{2a}\right)^r \frac{1}{r!} \cos\left(ax+b+\frac{r\pi}{2}\right)$$

Useful Formulae :

$$\sin^2 x = \frac{1 - \cos 2x}{2} = \frac{e^{0x}}{2} - \frac{\cos 2x}{2}$$

$$\cos^2 x = \frac{1 + \cos 2x}{2} = \frac{e^{0x}}{2} + \frac{\cos 2x}{2}$$

$$\sin A \sin B = \frac{1}{2} [\cos (A - B) - \cos (A + B)]$$

$$\sin A \cos B = \frac{1}{2} [\sin (A + B) + \sin (A - B)]$$

$$\cos A \cos B = \frac{1}{2} [\cos (A + B) + \cos (A - B)]$$

$$\sin x = 2 \sin \frac{x}{2} \cos \frac{x}{2}; \sin 2x = 2 \sin x \cos x.$$

Note : Write $D^3 = D^2 \cdot D$; $D^4 = (D^2)^2$; $D^5 = (D^2)^2 \cdot D$. Always replace D^2 by $- a^2$ and *keep D as it is.* To get D^2 in the denominator, rationalise the denominator and then replace D^2 by $- a^2$. Now numerator will contain an operator in D, therefore open the bracket.

ILLUSTRATIONS

Ex. 1 : *Solve $(D^2 + 2D + 1) y = 4 \sin 2x$.*

Sol. : A.E. is $D^2 + 2D + 1 = 0 \implies D = - 1, - 1$.

$$\text{C.F.} = (c_1 x + c_2) e^{-x}$$

$$\text{P.I.} = \frac{1}{D^2 + 2D + 1} (4 \sin 2x)$$

$$= \frac{1}{-4 + 2D + 1} (4 \sin 2x) \qquad \text{(putting } D^2 = - 2^2 = - 4)$$

$$= \frac{4}{2D - 3} (\sin 2x)$$

$$= \frac{4 (2D + 3)}{4 D^2 - 9} (\sin 2x)$$

$$\qquad\qquad [(\text{Multiply numerator and denominator by } (2D + 3)]$$

$$= \frac{4 (2D + 3)}{4 (-4) - 9} (\sin 2x) \qquad \text{(replace } D^2 \text{ with} - 4)$$

$$= - \frac{4}{25} (2D + 3) (\sin 2x)$$

$$= - \frac{4}{25} [4 \cos 2x + 3 \sin 2x]$$

$\therefore$ General solution is $y = (c_1 x + c_2) e^{-x} - \frac{4}{25} [4 \cos 2x + 3 \sin 2x]$

Ex. 2 : *Solve $\frac{d^3y}{dx^3} + 4 \frac{dy}{dx} = \sin 2x$.*

Sol. : A.E. will be $D^3 + 4D = 0 \implies D (D^2 + 4) = 0$

Hence $D = 0$ and $D = \pm 2 i$.

$$\text{C.F.} = \text{Complementary Function} = c_1 + c_2 \cos 2x + c_3 \sin 2x$$

$$\text{P.I.} = \frac{1}{D\,(D^2+4)}\,(\sin 2x) \qquad\qquad [\because D^2+4=0,\ \text{for } D^2=-2^2=-4\,]$$

$$= x\,\frac{1}{3\,D^2+4}\,(\sin 2x),\ \left[\frac{d}{dD}(D^3+4D)=3D^2+4,\ \text{then put } D^2=-4\right]$$

$$= x\cdot\frac{1}{3\,(-4)+4}\,(\sin 2x)$$

$$= -\frac{x}{8}\,\sin 2x.$$

Hence the solution is

$$y = c_1 + c_2\cos 2x + c_3\sin 2x - \frac{x\sin 2x}{8}$$

Ex. 3 : *Solve $(D^2+1)\,y = \sin x \sin 2x$.*

Sol. : A.E. is $D^2+1=0 \Rightarrow D=\pm i$

$\therefore \qquad\qquad$ C.F. $= c_1\cos x + c_2\sin x$

We have $\qquad$ P.I. $= \dfrac{1}{D^2+1}\,(\sin x \sin 2x)$

$$= \frac{1}{D^2+1}\left[\frac{1}{2}\,(\cos x - \cos 3x)\right]$$

$$= \frac{1}{2}\,\frac{1}{D^2+1}\,\cos x - \frac{1}{2}\,\frac{1}{D^2+1}\,\cos 3x$$

$$(D^2 \to -9 \text{ in 2nd term, case fails for 1st term})$$

$$= \frac{1}{2}\,x\cdot\frac{1}{2D}\,\cos x - \frac{1}{2}\,\frac{1}{-9+1}\,\cos 3x$$

$$= x\cdot\frac{1}{4}\,\frac{D}{D^2}\,\cos x + \frac{1}{16}\,\cos 3x,\ (D^2 \to -1)$$

$$= \frac{1}{4}\,x\cdot\frac{D\,(\cos x)}{-1} + \frac{1}{16}\,\cos 3x$$

$$= \frac{1}{4}\,x\sin x + \frac{1}{16}\,\cos 3x$$

Hence the solution is $y = c_1\cos x + c_2\sin x + \dfrac{1}{4}\,x\sin x + \dfrac{1}{16}\,\cos 3x$

Case III : P.I when $f(x) = \cosh(ax+b)$ or $\sinh(ax+b)$.

To find $y_p = \dfrac{1}{\phi(D^2)}\cosh(ax+b)$ or $\dfrac{1}{\phi(D^2)}\sinh(ax+b)$

As earlier on the similar line, we can prove that

$$\frac{1}{\phi(D^2)} \cosh(ax+b) = \frac{1}{\phi(a^2)} \cosh(ax+b), \quad \phi(a^2) \neq 0$$

$$\text{and} \quad \frac{1}{\phi(D^2)} \sinh(ax+b) = \frac{1}{\phi(a^2)} \sinh(ax+b), \quad \phi(a^2) \neq 0$$

ILLUSTRATION

Ex. 1 : *Solve* $\dfrac{d^3y}{dx^3} - 4\dfrac{dy}{dx} = 2\cos h\, 2x$

Sol. : A.E. is $D^3 - 4D = 0 \Rightarrow D(D^2 - 4) = 0, \; D = 0, \; \pm 2$

Hence   C.F. $= c_1 + c_2 e^{2x} + c_3 e^{-2x}$

$$\text{P.I.} = \frac{1}{(D^2-4)}\left[\frac{1}{D}(2\cosh 2x)\right]$$

$$= \frac{1}{D^2-4} \int 2\cosh 2x \, dx$$

$$= \frac{2}{D^2-4}\left(\frac{\sinh 2x}{2}\right)$$

$$= \frac{1}{D^2-4}(\sinh 2x) \qquad [\text{case of failure, hence differentiate } \phi(D)]$$

$$= \frac{x(\sinh 2x)}{2D} = \frac{x\, D(\sinh 2x)}{2D^2}$$

$$= \frac{x}{2}\frac{D(\sinh 2x)}{(4)} = \frac{x}{8}D(\sinh 2x)$$

$$= \frac{x}{4}\cosh 2x$$

$\therefore$ Solution is $y = c_1 + c_2 e^{2x} + c_3 e^{-2x} + \dfrac{x}{4}\cosh 2x$

Case IV : P.I. when f(x) $= x^m$

To find $y_p = \dfrac{1}{f(D)}x^m$, we write $\dfrac{1}{\phi(D)}(x^m) = [\phi(D)]^{-1}x^m$.

We shall now expand $[\phi(D)]^{-1}$ in ascending powers of D as far as the term in D^m and operate on x^m term by term. Since $(m+1)^{th}$ and higher derivatives of x^m will be zero, we need not consider terms beyond D^m.

Important Formulae :

$$\frac{1}{1+x} = (1+x)^{-1} = 1 - x + x^2 - x^3 + \ldots\ldots$$

$$\frac{1}{1-x} = (1-x)^{-1} = 1 + x + x^2 + x^3 + \ldots\ldots$$

$$(1 + x)^n = 1 + nx + \frac{n(n-1)}{2!} x^2 + \ldots\ldots\ldots$$

Also note that $D^n (x^n) = n!$ and $D^{n+1} (x^n) = 0$.

Note : To find $y_p = \dfrac{1}{\phi(D)} x^m$

(i) we always take constant term common from the denominator and use the formulae $(1 + x)^{-1}, (1 - x)^{-1}, (1 + x)^n, (1 - x)^n$.

(ii) if constant term is absent in the denominator then the minimum power of D is taken common from the denominator.

e.g.

$$\frac{1}{D^2 - 3D - 2} x^m = \frac{1}{-2\left[1 - \left(\dfrac{D^2 - 3D}{2}\right)\right]} x^m$$

$$\frac{1}{D^2 - 3D + 3} x^m = \frac{1}{3\left[1 + \left(\dfrac{D^2 - 3D}{3}\right)\right]} x^m$$

$$\frac{1}{D^3 - 3D^2 + 2D} x^m = \frac{1}{2D\left[1 + \left(\dfrac{D^2 - 3D}{2}\right)\right]} x^m$$

ILLUSTRATION

Ex. 1 : *Find the particular solution of $\dfrac{d^2y}{dx^2} - \dfrac{dy}{dx} + y = x^3 - 3x^2 + 1$.*

Sol. : It can be put as $(D^2 - D + 1) y = x^3 - 3x^2 + 1$.

$$\text{P.I.} = \frac{1}{(1 - D + D^2)} (x^3 - 3x^2 + 1)$$

$$= [1 - (D - D^2)]^{-1} (x^3 - 3x^2 + 1)$$

Expanding by Binomial theorem upto D^3 terms

$$= [1 + (D - D^2) + (D - D^2)^2 + (D - D^2)^3 + \ldots] (x^3 - 3x^2 + 1)$$

$$= [1 + D - D^2 + D^2 - 2D^3 + \ldots + D^3 + \ldots] (x^3 - 3x^2 + 1)$$

$$= (1 + D - D^3) (x^3 - 3x^2 + 1)$$

$$= x^3 - 6x - 5$$

Hence   P.I. $= x^3 - 6x - 5$.

Case V : P.I. when $f(x) = e^{ax} V$, where V is any function of x.

To find $y_p = \dfrac{1}{f(D)} e^{ax} V$, we have

$$D (e^{ax} V) = e^{ax} DV + ae^{ax} V = e^{ax} (D + a) V$$

and $$D^2 (e^{ax} V) = e^{ax} D^2 V + 2a\, e^{ax} DV + a^2\, e^{ax} V$$

$$= e^{ax} (D + a)^2 V$$

and proceeding similarly, we may have in general

$$D^n (e^{ax} V) = e^{ax} (D + a)^n V$$

Hence $\quad \phi(D)(e^{ax} V) = e^{ax} \phi(D+a) V \qquad \qquad \dots (I)$

Now, let $\quad \phi(D+a) V = V_1 \Rightarrow V = \dfrac{1}{\phi(D+a)} V_1$

If we put value of V in (I), we have

$$\phi(D)\left[e^{ax} \dfrac{1}{\phi(D+a)} V_1 \right] = e^{ax} V_1$$

Operating on both sides by $\dfrac{1}{\phi(D)}$ now, we get

$$e^{ax} \dfrac{1}{\phi(D+a)} V_1 = \dfrac{1}{\phi(D)}(e^{ax} V_1)$$

Here V_1 is any function of x, and hence, we have the formula

$$\boxed{\dfrac{1}{\phi(D)}(e^{ax} V) = e^{ax} \dfrac{1}{\phi(D+a)}(V)}$$

ILLUSTRATION

Ex. 1 : *Solve $(D^2 - 4D + 3) y = x^3 e^{2x}$.*

Sol. : $\qquad\qquad$ A.E. $= D^2 - 4D + 3 = (D-1)(D-3) \Rightarrow D = 1, 3.$

Hence $\qquad\qquad\qquad$ C.F. $= c_1 e^x + c_2 e^{3x}$

$$\text{P.I.} = \dfrac{1}{D^2 - 4D + 3}(x^3 e^{2x})$$

$$= e^{2x} \dfrac{1}{(D+2)^2 - 4(D+2) + 3}(x^3) \qquad \dots (D \to D+2)$$

$$= e^{2x} \dfrac{1}{D^2 + 4D + 4 - 4D - 8 + 3}(x^3)$$

$$= e^{2x} \dfrac{1}{D^2 - 1}(x^3) = -e^{2x}(1 - D^2)^{-1}(x^3) \qquad \text{(by case IV)}$$

$$= -e^{2x}[1 + D^2 + D^4 + \dots\dots](x^3) = -e^{2x}[x^3 + 6x]$$

Hence solution is $\qquad y = c_1 e^x + c_2 e^{3x} - e^{2x}(x^3 + 6x)$

Case VI : P.I. when $f(x) = x^m \sin ax$, or $x^m \cos ax$.

To find $y_p = \dfrac{1}{f(D)} x^m \sin ax$ or $\dfrac{1}{f(D)} x^m \cos ax$, we have

$$\dfrac{1}{\phi(D)} x^m[\cos ax + i \sin ax] = \dfrac{1}{\phi(D)} x^m e^{iax}$$

$$= e^{iax} \dfrac{1}{\phi(D + ia)} x^m$$

Now $\dfrac{1}{\phi(D + ia)} x^m$, can be evaluated by method of case IV and equating the Real and Imaginary parts, we get the required results.

ILLUSTRATION

Ex. 1 : *Solve $(D^4 + 2D^2 + 1)\, y = x^2 \cos x$.*

Sol. : A.E. is $(D^2 + 1)^2 = 0 \Rightarrow D = \pm i,\ \pm i$.

$\therefore$ C.F. $= (c_1 x + c_2) \cos x + (c_3 x + c_4) \sin x$

For Particular Integral, we have

$$\frac{1}{(D^2 + 1)^2}\,[x^2(\cos x + i\sin x)] = \frac{1}{(D^2 + 1)^2}\ x^2 \cdot e^{ix}$$

$$= e^{ix}\ \frac{1}{[(D + i)^2 + 1]^2}\ (x^2) = e^{ix}\ \frac{1}{(D^2 + 2iD)^2}\ (x^2)$$

$$= e^{ix}\ \frac{1}{-4D^2\left(1 - \dfrac{iD}{2}\right)^2}\ (x^2) \qquad \left(\because \frac{1}{i} = -i\right)$$

$$= -\frac{e^{ix}}{4}\ \frac{1}{D^2}\ \left(1 - \frac{iD}{2}\right)^{-2}\ (x^2)$$

$$= -\frac{e^{ix}}{4}\ \frac{1}{D^2}\ \left(1 + iD - \frac{3}{4}D^2 + \dots\right)(x^2)$$

$$= -\frac{e^{ix}}{4}\ \frac{1}{D^2}\ \left[x^2 + 2ix - \frac{3}{2}\right]$$

$$= -\frac{e^{ix}}{4}\ \left[\frac{x^4}{12} + \frac{ix^3}{3} - \frac{3}{4}x^2\right]\ \text{Integrating twice}$$

$$= -\frac{1}{4}\ [\cos x + i\sin x]\ \left[\frac{x^4}{12} + \frac{ix^3}{3} - \frac{3}{4}x^2\right]$$

Equating the real parts on both sides,

$$\frac{1}{(D^2 + 1)^2}\ (x^2 \cos x) = -\frac{1}{4}\left(\frac{x^4}{12} - \frac{3}{4}x^2\right)\cos x + \frac{1}{12}\ x^3 \sin x$$

Hence the general solution is

$$y = (c_1 x + c_2)\cos x + (c_3 x + c_4)\sin x + \frac{x^3 \sin x}{12} - \frac{(x^4 - 9x^2)}{48}\cos x$$

Case VII : P.I. when $f(x) = x\,V$, V being any function of x.

To find $\dfrac{1}{f(D)}\,xV$ we have by successive differentiations

$$D\,(xV) = x\,DV + V$$
$$D^2\,(xV) = x\,D^2V + 2DV$$
$$D^3\,(xV) = x\,D^3V + 3D^2V$$

and so on, we may have

$$D^n\,(xV) = x\,D^n V + n\,D^{n-1}\,(V)$$

Or $\qquad\qquad D^n\,(xV) = x\,D^n V + \dfrac{d}{dD}\,(D^n)\,V \qquad\qquad \dots (A)$

Since $\phi(D)$ is a polynomial in D, we may write in general from (A) using

$$\phi'(D) = \frac{d}{dD} \phi(D)$$

$$\phi(D)(xV) = x\,\phi(D)\,V + \phi'(D)\,V \qquad \ldots (B)$$

Now, put $\phi(D)\,V = V_1$ so that $V = \dfrac{1}{\phi(D)}\,V_1$ in equation (B), we have

$$\phi(D)\left[x\,\frac{1}{\phi(D)}\,V_1\right] = x\,V_1 + \phi'(D)\,\frac{1}{\phi(D)}\,V_1$$

Operating on both sides by $\dfrac{1}{\phi(D)}$, we get

$$x \cdot \frac{1}{\phi(D)}\,V_1 = \frac{1}{\phi(D)}\,[xV_1] + \frac{1}{\phi(D)}\,\phi'(D)\,\frac{1}{\phi(D)}\,V_1$$

and if we adjust the terms on both sides, we get

$$\frac{1}{\phi(D)}\,[xV_1] = \left[x - \frac{1}{\phi(D)}\,\phi'(D)\right]\frac{1}{\phi(D)}\,V_1$$

But here V_1 is any function of x, hence we have the formula

$$\boxed{\;\frac{1}{\phi(D)}\,[xV] = \left[x - \frac{1}{\phi(D)}\,\phi'(D)\right]\frac{1}{\phi(D)}\,V\;}$$

Remark : 1. The rule xV is applied if

(i) power of x is one

(ii) $\dfrac{1}{\phi(D)}\,V$ is not a case of failure.

2. If power of x is one and $\dfrac{1}{\phi(D)}\,V$ is a case of failure then do not apply xV rule.
In this case, apply rule given by case (VI).

e.g. $\qquad\qquad y_p = \dfrac{1}{D^2 + 1}\,x \sin x$

Here $\dfrac{1}{D^2 + 1}\,\sin x$ is a case of failure. Therefore use case (VI) method.

ILLUSTRATIONS

Ex. 1 : *Solve* $\dfrac{d^2y}{dx^2} + 4y = x\sin x.$

Sol. : $\qquad\qquad$ A.E. : $\; D^2 + 4 = 0 \;\Rightarrow\; D = \pm\, 2i$

$\therefore \qquad\qquad$ C.F. $= c_1 \cos 2x + c_2 \sin 2x,$

and $\qquad\qquad$ P.I. $= \dfrac{1}{D^2 + 4}\,(x \sin x)$

$$= \left[x - \frac{2D}{D^2 + 4}\right]\frac{1}{D^2 + 4}\,(\sin x) \qquad\qquad \text{[by case (VII)]}$$

$$= \left[x - \frac{2D}{D^2+4} \right] \frac{1}{-1+4} \,(\sin x)$$

$$= \frac{1}{3} \left[x - \frac{2D}{D^2+4} \right] \sin x \;=\; \frac{1}{3} \left[x \sin x - \frac{2D}{D^2+4} \sin x \right]$$

$$= \frac{1}{3} \left[x \sin x - \frac{2D\,(\sin x)}{-1+4} \right] = \frac{1}{3} \left[x \sin x - \frac{2}{3}\,(\cos x) \right]$$

$$= \frac{1}{3}\, x \sin x - \frac{2}{9}\, \cos x.$$

Hence the complete solution is

$$y \;=\; c_1 \cos 2x + c_2 \sin 2x + \frac{x \sin x}{3} - \frac{2}{9} \cos x$$

Ex. 2 : *Solve $(D^2 - 2D + 1)\, y = x\, e^x \sin x$*

Sol. :   A.E. : $D^2 - 2D + 1 = 0$

$$\Rightarrow (D - 1)^2 = 0, \; D = 1, 1.$$

Hence   C.F. $= (c_1 x + c_2)\, e^x$

$$\text{P.I.} \;=\; \frac{1}{(D-1)^2}\, [x\, e^x \sin x]$$

$$= e^x \, \frac{1}{(D+1-1)^2}\, (x \sin x) \qquad\qquad \text{(by case V)}$$

$$= e^x \frac{1}{D^2}\, (x \sin x)$$

$$= e^x \left[x - \frac{2D}{D^2} \right] \frac{1}{D^2}\, (\sin x) \qquad\qquad \text{(by case VII)}$$

$$= e^x \left[x - \frac{2}{D} \right] (-\sin x) \;=\; -e^x \left[x \sin x - \frac{2}{D} \sin x \right]$$

$$= -e^x\, [x \sin x + 2 \cos x]$$

Hence the complete solution is

$$y \;=\; (c_1 x + c_2)\, e^x - e^x\, [x \sin x + 2 \cos x]$$

Now, we will summarise the short-cut methods of P.I. and the corresponding formulae :

Case I : $\quad \dfrac{1}{\phi(D)}\, e^{ax} = \dfrac{e^{ax}}{\phi(a)}, \;\; \phi(a) \neq 0$	
Case of failure : If $\phi(a) = 0,\; \dfrac{1}{\phi(D)}\, e^{ax} = x \cdot \dfrac{1}{\phi'(a)}\, e^{ax},\, \phi'(a) \neq 0$	
$\dfrac{1}{(D-a)^r}\, e^{ax} = \dfrac{x^r}{r!}\, e^{ax}; \quad \dfrac{1}{\phi(D)}\,(k) = k \cdot \dfrac{1}{\phi(0)}\, ,\; \phi(0) \neq 0$	
$\dfrac{1}{\phi(D)}\, a^x = \dfrac{a^x}{\phi(\log a)}$	

Case II : $\dfrac{1}{\phi(D^2)}$ $\sin(ax+b)$ $=$ $\dfrac{1}{\phi(-a^2)}$ $\sin(ax+b),$ $\phi(-a^2) \neq 0$

$$\dfrac{1}{\phi(D^2)}\cos(ax+b) = \dfrac{1}{\phi(-a^2)}\cos(ax+b), \ \phi(-a^2) \neq 0$$

Case of failure : If $\phi(a^2)=0,$ $\dfrac{1}{\phi(D^2)}\sin(ax+b) = x \cdot \dfrac{1}{\phi'(-a)^2}\sin(ax+b),$ $\phi'(-a)^2 \neq 0$

If $\phi(a^2)=0,$ $\dfrac{1}{\phi(D^2)}\cos(ax+b) = x \cdot \dfrac{1}{\phi'(-a^2)}\cos(ax+b),$ $\phi'(-a^2) \neq 0$

Case of failure formulae :

$$\dfrac{1}{D^2+a^2}\sin ax = -\dfrac{x}{2a}\cos ax; \quad \dfrac{1}{D^2+a^2}\cos ax = \dfrac{x}{2a}\sin ax$$

$$\dfrac{1}{(D^2+a^2)^r}\sin(ax+b) = \left(-\dfrac{x}{2a}\right)^r \dfrac{1}{r!}\sin\left(ax+b+r\dfrac{\pi}{2}\right) \text{ and}$$

$$\dfrac{1}{(D^2+a^2)^r}\cos(ax+b) = \left(-\dfrac{x}{2a}\right)^r \dfrac{1}{r!}\cos\left(ax+b+r\dfrac{\pi}{2}\right)$$

Case III : $\dfrac{1}{\phi(D^2)}\sinh ax = \dfrac{1}{\phi(a^2)}\sinh ax, \ \phi(a^2) \neq 0$ and

$$\dfrac{1}{\phi(D^2)}\cosh ax = \dfrac{1}{\phi(a^2)}\cosh ax, \ \phi(a^2) \neq 0$$

Case IV : $\dfrac{1}{\phi(D)}x^m = [\phi(D)]^{-1}x^m,$ expand by using Binomial theorem.

Case V : $\dfrac{1}{\phi(D)}e^{ax}V = e^{ax}\boxed{\dfrac{1}{\phi(D+a)}}V$

Case VI : $\dfrac{1}{\phi(D)}x^m \sin ax = $ I.P. of $\dfrac{1}{\phi(D)}x^m e^{iax} = $ I.P. of $e^{iax}\dfrac{1}{\phi(D+ia)}x^m$

$$\dfrac{1}{\phi(D)}x^m \cos ax = \text{R.P. of } \dfrac{1}{\phi(D)}x^m e^{iax} = \text{R.P. of } e^{iax}\dfrac{1}{\phi(D+ia)}x^m$$

Case VII : $\dfrac{1}{\phi(D)}xV = \left[x - \dfrac{\phi'(D)}{\phi(D)}\right]\dfrac{1}{\phi(D)}V$

ILLUSTRATIONS ON SHORT-CUT METHODS

Ex. 1 : *Solve $(D^2 + 2D + 1)\, y = 2\cos x + 3x + 2 + 3e^x$.*

Sol. : Here AE is $(D+1)^2 = 0 \ \Rightarrow \ D = -1, -1$

$\therefore \qquad$ C.F. $= (c_1 x + c_2)\, e^{-x}$

and $\qquad$ P.I. $= 2\dfrac{1}{D^2+2D+1}\cos x + \dfrac{1}{[1+(2D+D^2)]}(3x+2) + 3\dfrac{1}{(D+1)^2}e^x$

$$= \dfrac{1}{-1+2D+1}2\cos x + [1+(2D+D^2)]^{-1}(3x+2) + \dfrac{3e^x}{4}$$

$$= \int \cos x \, dx + [1 - 2D - D^2 + \ldots](3x + 2) + \frac{3}{4} e^x$$

$$= \sin x + 3x + 2 - 6 + \frac{3e^x}{4}$$

$$= \frac{3e^x}{4} + \sin x + 3x - 4$$

Hence the complete solution is

$$y = (c_1 x + c_2) e^{-x} + \frac{3e^x}{4} + \sin x + 3x - 4$$

Ex. 2 : *Solve* $\dfrac{d^2y}{dx^2} + a^2y = \dfrac{a^2R}{p} (l - x)$ *where a, R, p and l are constants, subject to the conditions* $y = 0,\ \dfrac{dy}{dx} = 0$ *at* $x = 0$.

Sol. : Given equation is

$$(D^2 + a^2)\, y = \frac{a^2R}{p} (l - x)$$

$$\text{A.E.} = D^2 + a^2 = 0 \quad \text{or} \quad D = \pm\, ia$$

$$\text{C.F.} = c_1 \cos ax + c_2 \sin ax$$

$$\text{P.I.} = \frac{1}{D^2 + a^2}\, \frac{a^2 R}{p}\, (l - x) = \frac{a^2 R}{p} \cdot \frac{1}{a^2}\, \frac{1}{\left(1 + \dfrac{D^2}{a^2}\right)}\, (l - x)$$

$$= \frac{R}{p} \left(1 + \frac{D^2}{a^2}\right)^{-1} (l - x) = \frac{R}{p} \left[1 - \frac{D^2}{a^2}\right] (l - x) = \frac{R}{p}\, (l - x)$$

Hence the general solution is

$$y = c_1 \cos ax + c_2 \sin ax + \frac{R}{p}\, (l - x) \qquad\qquad \ldots (1)$$

For initial conditions, now put $y = 0$ when $x = 0$ in (1), we get

$$0 = c_1 + \frac{R}{p}\, l \implies c_1 = \frac{-Rl}{p}$$

If we differentiate equation (1),

$$\frac{dy}{dx} = -ac_1 \sin ax + ac_2 \cos ax - \frac{R}{p}$$

Putting $x = 0$ and $\dfrac{dy}{dx} = 0$ in this, we get

$$0 = ac_2 - \frac{R}{p}, \text{ hence } c_2 = \frac{R}{ap}$$

Now put values of c_1 and c_2 in A, then the required particular solution is

$$y = \frac{R}{p}\left[\frac{\sin ax}{a} - l\cos ax + l - x\right]$$

Ex. 3 : *Solve* $(D^3 - 1)\,y = (1 + e^x)^2$.

Sol. : A.E. : $D^3 - 1 = 0$ or $(D - 1)(D^2 + D + 1) = 0$ $\therefore D = 1, -\dfrac{1}{2} \pm i\dfrac{\sqrt{3}}{2}$

$$y_c = c_1 e^x + e^{(-1/2)x}[c_2 \cos(\sqrt{3}/2)\,x + c_3 \sin(\sqrt{3}/2)\,x]$$

$$y_p = \frac{1}{D^3 - 1}(1 + e^x)^2 = \frac{1}{D^3 - 1}(1 + 2e^x + e^{2x})$$

$$= \frac{1}{D^3 - 1}e^{0x} + 2\frac{1}{D^3 - 1}e^x + \frac{1}{D^3 - 1}e^{2x}$$

$$= -1 + \frac{2}{3}xe^x + \frac{1}{7}e^{2x}$$

$\therefore \qquad y = c_1 e^x + e^{(-1/2)x}[c_2 \cos(\sqrt{3}/2)\,x + c_3 \sin(\sqrt{3}/2)\,x] - 1 + \frac{2}{3}xe^x + \frac{1}{7}e^{2x}$

Ex. 4 : *Solve* $(D - 1)^2 (D^2 + 1)^2\, y = \sin^2 \dfrac{x}{2}$.

Sol. : A.E. : $(D - 1)^2 (D^2 + 1)^2 = 0$, $D = 1, 1, \pm i, \pm i$.

$$y_c = (c_1 x + c_2)\,e^x + (c_3 x + c_4)\cos x + (c_5 x + c_6)\sin x.$$

$$y_p = \frac{1}{(D - 1)^2 (D^2 + 1)^2}\sin^2\frac{x}{2} = \frac{1}{(D - 1)^2 (D^2 + 1)^2}\left(\frac{1 - \cos x}{2}\right)$$

$$= \frac{1}{2}\left[\frac{1}{(D - 1)^2 (D^2 + 1)^2}e^{0x} - \frac{1}{(D - 1)^2 (D^2 + 1)^2}\cos x\right]$$

$$= \frac{1}{2}\left[1 - \frac{1}{(D^2 + 1)^2 (-1 - 2D + 1)}\cos x\right]$$

$$= \frac{1}{2}\left[1 + \frac{1}{2}\frac{1}{(D^2 + 1)^2}\sin x\right]$$

$$= \frac{1}{2}\left[1 + \frac{1}{2}x^2\frac{1}{-8}\sin x\right]$$

$$\left\{\frac{d^2}{dD^2}(D^2 + 1)^2 = \frac{d}{dD}2(D^2 + 1)\,2D = 4(3D^2 + 1),\ \text{then put}\ D^2 = -1\right\}$$

$$= \frac{1}{2} - \frac{1}{32}x^2 \sin x$$

$$y = (c_1 x + c_2)\,e^x + (c_3 x + c_4)\cos x + (c_5 x + c_6)\sin x + \frac{1}{2} - \frac{1}{32}x^2 \sin x$$

Ex. 5 : *Solve* $(D^4 - 2D^3 - 3D^2 + 4D + 4)\, y\ = x^2\, e^x.$

Sol. :　　A.E.　:　$(D-2)^2 (D+1)^2 = 0$

$$y_c = (c_1 x + c_2)\, e^{2x} + (c_3 x + c_4)\, e^{-x}$$

$$y_p = \frac{1}{(D^2 - D - 2)^2}\, e^x \cdot x^2 = e^x \frac{1}{[(D+1)^2 - (D+1) - 2]^2}\, x^2$$

$$= e^x \frac{1}{(D^2 + D - 2)^2}\, x^2 = \frac{e^x}{4}\, \frac{1}{\left[1 - \left(\dfrac{D^2 + D}{2} \right) \right]^2}\, x^2$$

$$= \frac{e^x}{4} \left[1 + (D^2 + D) + \frac{3}{4} (D^2 + D)^2 + \dots \right] x^2$$

$$= \frac{e^x}{4} \left[1 + D + \frac{7}{4} D^2 + \dots \right] x^2 = \frac{e^x}{4} \left[x^2 + 2x + \frac{7}{2} \right]$$

$\therefore$　　　　$$y = (c_1 x + c_2)\, e^{2x} + (c_3 x + c_4)\, e^{-x} + \frac{e^x}{4} \left(x^2 + 2x + \frac{7}{2} \right).$$

Ex. 6 : *Solve* $(D^4 - 1)\ y = \cos x \cosh x$

Sol. :　　A.E.　:　$(D-1)(D+1)(D+i)(D-i) = 0$

$$y_c = c_1 e^x + c_2 e^{-x} + c_3 \cos x + c_4 \sin x.$$

$$y_p = \frac{1}{D^4 - 1}\, \cos x \left(\frac{e^x + e^{-x}}{2} \right)$$

$$= \frac{1}{2}\, \frac{1}{D^4 - 1}\, e^x \cos x + \frac{1}{2} \cdot \frac{1}{D^4 - 1}\, e^{-x} \cos x$$

$$= \frac{e^x}{2}\, \frac{1}{(D+1)^4 - 1}\, \cos x + \frac{e^{-x}}{2}\, \frac{1}{(D-1)^4 - 1}\, \cos x$$

$$= \frac{e^x}{2} \cdot \frac{1}{D^4 + 4D^3 + 6D^2 + 4D + 1 - 1}\, \cos x +$$

$$\frac{e^{-x}}{2}\, \frac{1}{D^4 - 4D^3 + 6D^2 - 4D + 1 - 1}\, \cos x$$

$$= \frac{e^x}{2}\, \frac{1}{1 - 4D - 6 + 4D}\, \cos x + \frac{e^{-x}}{2}\, \frac{1}{1 + 4D - 6 - 4D}$$

$$= \frac{e^x}{2} \cdot \frac{\cos x}{-5} + \frac{e^{-x}}{2}\, \frac{\cos x}{-5} = \frac{\cos x}{-5}\, \cosh x$$

$\therefore$　　　　$$y = c_1 e^x + c_2 e^{-x} + c_3 \cos x + c_4 \sin x - \frac{\cos x \cosh x}{5}$$

Ex. 7 : *Solve* $(D^4 + 1)\, y\ = 2 \sinh x \sin x.$

Sol. :　A.E. :　$D^4 + 1 = 0$　　$\therefore$　$D^4 + 2D^2 + 1 - 2D^2 = 0$

or $(D^2 + 1)^2 - (\sqrt{2}\, D)^2 = 0$ or $(D^2 - \sqrt{2}\, D + 1)\,(D^2 + \sqrt{2}\, D + 1) = 0$

$\therefore \qquad D = \dfrac{1}{\sqrt{2}} \pm \dfrac{1}{\sqrt{2}}\, i, \qquad\qquad D = \dfrac{-1}{\sqrt{2}} \pm \dfrac{1}{\sqrt{2}}\, i$

$$y_c = e^{x/\sqrt{2}} \left[c_1 \cos \frac{x}{\sqrt{2}} + c_2 \sin \frac{x}{\sqrt{2}} \right] + e^{-x/\sqrt{2}} \left[c_3 \cos \frac{x}{\sqrt{2}} + c_4 \sin \frac{x}{\sqrt{2}} \right]$$

$$y_p = \frac{1}{D^4 + 1}\ 2 \sinh x \sin x$$

$$= \frac{1}{D^4 + 1}\ (e^x - e^{-x}) \sin x$$

$$= \frac{1}{D^4 + 1}\ e^x \sin x - \frac{1}{D^4 + 1}\ e^{-x} \sin x$$

$$= e^x \frac{1}{(D + 1)^4 + 1}\ \sin x - e^{-x} \frac{1}{(D - 1)^4 + 1}\ \sin x$$

$$= e^x \cdot \frac{1}{D^4 + 4D^3 + 6D^2 + 4D + 2} \sin x - e^{-x} \frac{1}{D^4 - 4D^3 + 6D^2 - 4D + 2} \sin x$$

$$= e^x \frac{1}{(-1)^2 + 4D\,(-1) + 6\,(-1) + 4D + 2} \sin x$$

$$\quad - e^{-x} \frac{1}{(-1)^2 - 4D\,(-1) + 6\,(-1) - 4D + 2} \sin x$$

$$= e^x \left(\frac{\sin x}{-3} \right) - e^{-x} \left(\frac{\sin x}{-3} \right)$$

$$= \frac{-2}{3} \sin x \cdot \left(\frac{e^x - e^{-x}}{2} \right) = -\frac{2}{3} \sin x \sinh x$$

$\therefore \qquad y = \text{C.F.} + \text{P.I.}$

$$y = e^{x/\sqrt{2}} \left[c_1 \cos \frac{x}{\sqrt{2}} + c_2 \sin \frac{x}{\sqrt{2}} \right] + e^{-x/\sqrt{2}} \left[c_3 \cos \frac{x}{\sqrt{2}} + c_4 \sin \frac{x}{\sqrt{2}} \right] - \frac{2}{3} \sin x \sinh x$$

Ex. 8 : *Solve* $\dfrac{d^3y}{dx^3} - 7\dfrac{dy}{dx} - 6y = e^{2x}\,(1 + x).$ **(SUK June 14)**

Sol. : Given D.E. is written as

$$(D^3 - 7D - 6)\, y = e^{2x}\,(1 + x) \ \text{ where } D \equiv \frac{d}{dx}$$

A.E. : $D^3 - 7D - 6 = 0 \quad \therefore \quad (D + 1)\,(D + 2)\,(D - 3) = 0$

$\therefore \qquad\qquad \text{C.F.} = c_1\, e^{-x} + c_2\, e^{-2x} + c_3\, e^{3x}$

$$\text{P.I.} = \frac{1}{D^3 - 7D - 6}\ e^{2x}\,(1 + x)$$

$$= e^{2x} \frac{1}{(D+2)^3 - 7(D+2) - 6}(1+x), \qquad \text{by } D \to D+2$$

$$= e^{2x} \frac{1}{D^3 + 6D^2 + 5D - 12}(1+x)$$

$$= \frac{-e^{2x}}{12}\left[1 - \frac{D^3 + 6D^2 + 5D}{12}\right]^{-1}(1+x)$$

$$= \frac{-e^{2x}}{12}\left[1 + \frac{5D}{12} + \dots\right](1+x)$$

$$= \frac{-e^{2x}}{12}\left(1 + x + \frac{5}{12}\right) = \frac{-e^{2x}}{12}\left(x + \frac{17}{12}\right)$$

$$\therefore \qquad y = \text{C.F.} + \text{P.I.} = c_1 e^{-x} + c_2 e^{-2x} + c_3 e^{3x} - \frac{e^{2x}}{12}\left(x + \frac{17}{12}\right)$$

Ex. 9 : *Solve $(D^2 - 1)\, y = x\sin x + (1 + x^2)\, e^x$.*   **(SUK Dec. 13)**

Sol. :   A.E. : $D^2 - 1 = 0$

$$(D-1)(D+1) = 0 \qquad \therefore \ \text{C.F.} = c_1 e^x + c_2 e^{-x}$$

$$\text{P.I.} = \frac{1}{D^2 - 1}\, x\sin x + \frac{1}{D^2 - 1}\, e^x (1 + x^2)$$

$$= x\frac{1}{D^2 - 1}\sin x - \frac{2D}{(D^2 - 1)^2}\sin x + e^x \frac{1}{(D+1)^2 - 1}(1 + x^2)$$

$$= \frac{x\sin x}{-2} - \frac{2D}{4}\sin x + e^x \frac{1}{D^2 + 2D}(1 + x^2)$$

$$= -\frac{x}{2}\sin x - \frac{\cos x}{2} + e^x \frac{1}{2D}\left(1 - \frac{D}{2} + \frac{D^2}{4} + \dots\right)(1 + x^2)$$

$$= -\frac{x}{2}\sin x - \frac{\cos x}{2} + \frac{e^x}{2}\,\frac{1}{D}\left(1 + x^2 - x + \frac{1}{2}\right)$$

$$= -\frac{x}{2}\sin x - \frac{\cos x}{2} + \frac{e^x}{2}\left(\frac{x^3}{3} - \frac{x^2}{2} + \frac{3x}{2}\right)$$

$$y = c_1 e^x + c_2 e^{-x} - \frac{1}{2}(x\sin x + \cos x) + \frac{e^x}{12}(2x^3 - 3x^2 + 9x)$$

Ex. 10 : $(D^2 - 4D + 4)\, y = e^x \cos^2 x.$ **(SUK Dec. 11)**

Sol. : A.E. is $D^2 - 4D + 4 = 0 \quad \therefore \ D = 2, 2$

$$y_c = (c_1 x + c_2)\, e^{2x}$$

$$y_p = \frac{1}{(D-2)^2}\, e^x \cos^2 x = e^x \frac{1}{(D-1)^2}\cos^2 x$$

$$= e^x \frac{1}{(D-1)^2}\left(\frac{1 + \cos 2x}{2}\right) = 0$$

$$= \frac{e^x}{2}\left[\frac{1}{(D-1)^2}\,e^{0x} + \frac{1}{D^2-2D+1}\,\cos 2x\right]$$

$$= \frac{e^x}{2}\left[1 - \frac{1}{(2D+3)}\cos 2x\right] = \frac{e^x}{2}\left[1 - \frac{(2D-3)}{4D^2-9}\cos 2x\right]$$

$$= \frac{e^x}{2}\left[1 + \frac{1}{25}\,(2D-3)\cos 2x\right] = \frac{e^x}{2}\left[1 - \frac{1}{25}(4\sin 2x + 3\cos 2x)\right]$$

$$y = (c_1 x + c_2)\,e^{2x} + \frac{e^x}{2}\left[1 - \frac{1}{25}(4\sin 2x + 3\cos 2x)\right]$$

Ex. 11 : *Solve $(D^2 + 1)\,y = x^2 \sin 2x$.*

Sol. : A.E. is $D^2 + 1 = 0$ $\therefore$ $D = \pm i$.

$$y_c = c_1 \cos x + c_2 \sin x$$

$$y_p = \frac{1}{D^2+1}\,x^2 \sin 2x = \text{I.P. of } \frac{1}{D^2+1}\,e^{i2x}\,x^2$$

$$= \text{I.P. of } e^{i2x}\frac{1}{(D+2i)^2+1}\,x^2 = \text{I.P. of } e^{i2x}\frac{1}{D^2+4iD-4+1}\,x^2$$

$$= \text{I.P. of } \frac{e^{i2x}}{(-3)}\frac{1}{\left[1-\frac{1}{3}(4iD+D^2)\right]}\,x^2 = \text{I.P. of } \frac{e^{i2x}}{(-3)}\left[1-\frac{1}{3}(4iD+D^2)\right]^{-1}\,x^2$$

$$= \text{I.P. of } \frac{e^{i2x}}{(-3)}\left[1+\frac{1}{3}(4iD+D^2) + \frac{1}{9}(-16D^2+8iD^3+D^4) + \dots\right]x^2$$

$$= \text{I.P. of } \frac{e^{i2x}}{(-3)}\left[1+\frac{4}{3}iD - \frac{13}{9}D^2 + \dots\right]x^2$$

$$= \text{I.P. of } \frac{(\cos 2x + i \sin 2x)}{(-3)}\left[\left(x^2 - \frac{26}{9}\right) + i\,\frac{8}{3}x\right]$$

$$= -\frac{1}{3}\left(x^2 - \frac{26}{9}\right)\sin 2x - \frac{8}{9}x\cos 2x$$

$$\therefore \quad y = c_1 \cos x + c_2 \sin x - \frac{1}{3}\left(x^2 - \frac{26}{9}\right)\sin 2x - \frac{8}{9}x\cos 2x$$

Ex. 12 : $(D^2 + D + 1)\,y = x \sin x.$

Sol. : A.E. is $D^2 + D + 1 = 0$ $\therefore$ $D = -\frac{1}{2} \pm i\frac{\sqrt{3}}{2}$.

$$y_c = e^{(-1/2)x}\left[c_1 \cos (\sqrt{3}/2)\,x + c_2 \sin (\sqrt{3}/2)\,x\right]$$

$$y_p = \frac{1}{D^2+D+1}\,x \sin x = \left[x - \frac{2D+1}{D^2+D+1}\right]\frac{1}{D^2+D+1}\sin x$$

$$= \left[x - \frac{2D+1}{D^2+D+1} \right] \frac{1}{D} \sin x = \left[x - \frac{2D+1}{D^2+D+1} \right] (-\cos x)$$

$$= -x \cos x + (2D+1) \frac{1}{D} \cos x$$

$$= -x \cos x + (2D+1) \sin x$$

$$= -x \cos x + 2 \cos x + \sin x$$

$$\therefore \quad y = e^{(-1/2)x} [c_1 \cos (\sqrt{3}/2) x + c_2 \sin (\sqrt{3}/2) x] - x \cos x + 2 \cos x + \sin x$$

Ex. 13 : $(D^2 + 2D + 1) y = x e^{-x} \cos x.$

Sol. : A.E. is $D^2 + 2D + 1 = 0 \quad \therefore \quad D = -1, 1.$

$$y_c = (c_1 x + c_2) e^{-x}$$

$$y_p = \frac{1}{(D+1)^2} e^{-x} x \cos x = e^{-x} \frac{1}{D^2} x \cos x$$

$$= e^{-x} \left[x - \frac{2D}{D^2} \right] \frac{1}{D^2} \cos x = e^{-x} \left[x - \frac{2}{D} \right] (-\cos x)$$

$$= e^{-x} (-x \cos x + 2 \sin x)$$

$$y = (c_1 x + c_2) e^{-x} + e^{-x} (-x \cos x + 2 \sin x)$$

Ex. 14 : *Solve* $(D^2 + 4) y = x \sin^2 x.$

Sol. : A.E. : $D^2 + 4 = 0 \quad \therefore \quad D = \pm 2i$

$$y_c = c_1 \cos 2x + c_2 \sin 2x$$

$$y_p = \frac{1}{D^2+4} x \cdot \left(\frac{1 - \cos 2x}{2} \right) = \frac{1}{2} \cdot \frac{1}{D^2+4} x - \frac{1}{2} \frac{1}{D^2+4} x \cos 2x.$$

$$= y_{P_1} + y_{P_2}$$

$$y_{P_1} = \frac{1}{2} \cdot \frac{1}{D^2+4} x = \frac{1}{8} \frac{1}{1 + \frac{D^2}{4}} x = \frac{1}{8} \left(1 - \frac{D^2}{4} + \ldots \right) x = \frac{x}{8}$$

$$y_{P_2} = -\frac{1}{2} \cdot \frac{1}{D^2+4} x \cos 2x.$$

Here we can not apply "xV" rule (case VII) because $\dfrac{1}{D^2+4} \cos 2x$ is a case of failure.

$$\therefore \quad \frac{1}{D^2+4} x e^{i2x} = e^{i2x} \frac{1}{(D+2i)^2 + 4} x$$

$$= e^{i2x} \frac{1}{D^2 + 4iD} x = \frac{e^{i2x}}{4iD} \left(\frac{1}{1 - \frac{Di}{4}} \right) x$$

$$= -\frac{e^{i2x} i}{4D} \left(1 + \frac{iD}{4} \right) x = \frac{- e^{i2x} i}{4D} \left(x + \frac{i}{4} \right)$$

$$= -\frac{e^{i2x}\,i}{4}\left(\frac{x^2}{2}+\frac{ix}{4}\right)$$

$$= -\frac{1}{16}\,(\cos 2x + i\sin 2x)\,(-x + i\,2x^2)$$

Taking real parts on both sides,

$$\frac{1}{D^2+4}\;x\cos 2x \;=\; -\frac{1}{16}\,(-x\cos 2x - 2x^2\sin 2x)$$

$$\therefore \qquad y_{p_2} \;=\; -\frac{1}{2}\left[\frac{1}{16}(x\cos 2x + 2x^2\sin 2x)\right]$$

$$y_p \;=\; \frac{x}{8} - \frac{1}{32}\,(x\cos 2x + 2x^2\sin 2x)$$

$$y \;=\; c_1\cos 2x + c_2\sin 2x + \frac{x}{8} - \frac{1}{32}\,(x\cos 2x + 2x^2\sin 2x)$$

EXERCISE 1.2

Solve the following differential equations :

(A) On General Method :

1. $(D^2 + 5D + 6)\,y = e^{e^x}$. **Ans.** $y = c_1 e^{-2x} + c_2 e^{-3x} + (e^{-2x} - 2e^{-3x})\,e^{e^x}$.

2. $\dfrac{d^2y}{dx^2} + a^2 y = \tan ax$ **Ans.** $y = c_1\cos ax + c_2\sin ax - \dfrac{1}{a^2}\cos ax\,\log[\sec ax + \tan ax]$

3. $(D^2 - 3D + 2)\,y = \dfrac{1}{e^{e^{-x}}} + \cos\left(\dfrac{1}{e^x}\right)$ **Ans.** $y = c_1 e^{2x} + c_2 e^x + e^{2x}\left[e^{-e^{-x}} - \cos(e^{-x})\right]$

4. $(D^2 - 9D + 18)\,y = e^{e^{-3x}}$ **Ans.** $y = c_1 e^{6x} + c_2 e^{3x} + \dfrac{e^{6x}}{9}\,e^{e^{-3x}}$

5. $(D^2 - 2D - 3)\,y = 3e^{-3x}\sin(e^{-3x}) + \cos(e^{-3x})$ **Ans.** $y = c_1 e^{3x} + c_2 e^{-x} - \dfrac{e^{3x}}{3}\sin e^{-3x}$

(B) On Short Methods :

1. $\dfrac{d^2y}{dx^2} - 7\dfrac{dy}{dx} + 6y = e^{2x}$ **Ans.** $y = c_1 e^{6x} + c_2 e^x - \dfrac{e^{2x}}{4}$

2. $\dfrac{d^2y}{dx^2} - 4y = (1 + e^x)^2 + 3$ **Ans.** $y = c_1 e^{2x} + c_2 e^{-2x} - 1 - \dfrac{2}{3}e^x + \dfrac{xe^{2x}}{4}$

3. $(D^3 - 5D^2 + 8D - 4)\,y = e^{2x} + 2e^x + 3e^{-x} + 2$

    Ans. $y = c_1 e^x + (c_2 + c_3 x)\,e^{2x} + \dfrac{e^{2x}x^2}{2} + 2xe^x - \dfrac{e^{-x}}{6} - \dfrac{1}{2}$

4. $(D^4 - 4D^3 + 6D^2 - 4D + 1)\,y = e^x + 2^x + \dfrac{1}{3}$.

    Ans. $y = (c_1 x^3 + c_2 x^2 + c_3 x + c_4)\,e^x + \dfrac{x^4}{24}e^x + \dfrac{1}{(\log 2 - 1)^4}2^x + \dfrac{1}{3}$

5. $\dfrac{d^2y}{dx^2} + 4y = \cos x \cdot \cos 2x \cdot \cos 3x$

Ans. $y = A \cos 2x + B \sin 2x + \dfrac{1}{16} + \dfrac{x \sin 2x}{16} - \dfrac{1}{48} \cos 4x - \dfrac{1}{128} \cos 6x$

6. $(D^5 - D^4 + 2D^3 - 2D^2 + D - 1)\, y = \cos x$

Ans. $y = c_1 e^x + (c_2 x + c_3) \cos x + (c_4 x + c_5) \sin x + \dfrac{1}{16}\left[(x^2 + 2x) \cos x - x^2 \sin x\right]$

7. $(D^4 - m^4)\, y = \sin mx$

Ans. $y = c_1 e^{mx} + c_2 e^{-mx} + c_3 \cos mx + c_4 \sin mx + \dfrac{x}{4m^3} \cos mx$

8. $(D^3 + D)\, y = \cos x$ **Ans.** $c_1 + c_2 \cos x + c_3 \sin x - \dfrac{x \cos x}{2}$

9. $\operatorname{cosec} x \dfrac{d^4y}{dx^4} + y \operatorname{cosec} x = \sin 2x$

Ans. $y = e^{\frac{x}{\sqrt{2}}}\left[c_1 \cos \dfrac{x}{\sqrt{2}} + c_2 \sin \dfrac{x}{\sqrt{2}}\right] + e^{-\frac{x}{\sqrt{2}}}\left[c_3 \cos \dfrac{x}{\sqrt{2}} + c_4 \sin \dfrac{x}{\sqrt{2}}\right] + \dfrac{1}{2}\left(\dfrac{\cos x}{2} - \dfrac{\cos 3x}{82}\right)$

10. $\dfrac{d^2x}{dt^2} + 9x = 4 \cos\left(\dfrac{\pi}{3} + t\right)$, given that $x = 0$ at $t = 0$ and $x = 2$ at $t = \dfrac{\pi}{6}$.

Ans. $x = \dfrac{1}{4} \cos 3t + 2 \sin 3t + \dfrac{1}{2} \cos\left(\dfrac{\pi}{3} + t\right)$

11. $\dfrac{d^2y}{dt^2} + 2\dfrac{dy}{dt} + 5y = \sin^2 t$

Ans. $y = e^{-t}\left[A \cos 2t + b \sin 2t\right] + \dfrac{1}{10} - \dfrac{1}{34}\left[4 \sin 2t + \cos 2t\right]$

12. $\dfrac{d^2y}{dx^2} + 2\dfrac{dy}{dx} + 2y = \sin 2x - 2 \cos 2x$, given that $y = 0$ and $\dfrac{dy}{dx} = 0$ when $x = 0$.

Ans. $y = e^{-x} \sin x - \dfrac{1}{2} \sin 2x$

13. $\dfrac{d^2y}{dx^2} + n^2 y = h \sin px$, where h, p and n are constants satisfying the condition $y = 0$, $\dfrac{dy}{dx} = b$ for $x = 0$.   **Ans.** $y = a \cos nx + \left[\dfrac{b}{n} - \dfrac{ph}{n(n^2 - p^2)}\right] \sin nx + \dfrac{h \sin px}{(n^2 - p^2)}$

14. $(D^3 + 1)\, y = \cos(2x - 1) - \cos^2 \dfrac{x}{2}$

Ans. $y = c_1 e^{-x} + e^{x/2}\left[c_2 \cos \dfrac{\sqrt{3}}{2} x + c_3 \sin \dfrac{\sqrt{3}}{2} x\right]$

$+ \dfrac{1}{65}\left[\cos(2x - 1) - 8 \sin(2x - 1)\right] - \dfrac{1}{2} - \dfrac{1}{4}(\cos x - \sin x)$

15. $\dfrac{d^2y}{dx^2} - 2\dfrac{dy}{dx} + 5y = 10 \sin x.$

Ans. $y = e^x (A \cos x + B \sin x) + 2 \sin x + \cos x$

16. $(D^4 + 10D^2 + 9)\, y = 96 \sin 2x \cos x$

Given that at $x = 0$, $y = 0$, $y' = -2$, $y'' = -8$, $y''' = -18$.

Ans. $y = \cos 3x - \cos x + x (\cos 3x - 3 \cos x)$

17. $(D^4 + 6D^2 + 8)\, y = \sin^2 x \cos 2x$

Ans. $y = c_1 \cos 2x + c_2 \sin 2x + c_3 \cos \sqrt{2}\, x + c_4 \sin \sqrt{2}\, x - \dfrac{x \sin 2x}{16} - \dfrac{1}{32} - \dfrac{\cos 4x}{672}$

18. $(D^3 + 3D)\, y = \cosh 2x \sinh 3x.$

Ans. $y = c_1 + \left(c_2 \cos \sqrt{3}\, x + c_3 \sin \sqrt{3}\, x\right) + \dfrac{\cosh 5x}{280} + \dfrac{\cosh x}{8}$

19. $(D^3 - 25D)\, y = \cosh 2x \sinh 3x.$

Ans. $y = c_1 + c_2 e^{5x} + c_3 e^{-5x} + \dfrac{x}{100} \sinh 5x - \dfrac{1}{48} \cosh x$

20. $(D^4 - 1)\, y = \cosh x \sinh x$ **Ans.** $y = c_1 e^x + c_2 e^{-x} + c_3 \cos x + c_4 \sin x + \dfrac{1}{30} \sinh 2x$

21. $(D^2 + 13D + 36)\, y = e^{-4x} + \sinh x.$

Ans. $y = c_1 e^{-9x} + c_2 e^{-4x} + \dfrac{x}{5} e^{-4x} - \dfrac{1}{1200} (13 \cosh x - 37 \sinh x)$

22. $(D^3 + 1)\, y = \sin (2x + 3) + e^{-x} + 2^x.$

Ans. $y = c_1 e^{-x} + e^{(1/2)\, x} [c_2 \cos (\sqrt{3}/2)\, x + c_3 \sin (\sqrt{3}/2)\, x]$

$+ \dfrac{1}{65} [\sin (2x + 3) + 8 \cos (2x + 3)] + \dfrac{x}{3} e^{-x} + \dfrac{2^x}{(\log 2)^3 + 1}$

23. $\dfrac{d^2y}{dx^2} + 6\dfrac{dy}{dx} + 10y = 50 x$ with $y = 0$, $\dfrac{dy}{dx} = 1$ at $x = 0$

Ans. $y = 5x - 3 + e^{-3x} (3 \cos x + 5 \sin x)$

24. $(D^2 - 2D + 5)\, y = 25x^2.$ **Ans.** $y = e^x [c_1 \cos 2x + c_2 \sin 2x] + 5x^2 + 4x - \dfrac{2}{5}$

25. $(D^4 + D^2 + 1)\, y = 53x^2 + 17$

Ans. $y = e^{-x/2}\left[c_1 \cos \dfrac{\sqrt{3}}{2} x + c_2 \sin \dfrac{\sqrt{3}}{2} x \right] + e^{x/2}\left[c_3 \cos \dfrac{\sqrt{3}}{2} x + c_4 \sin \dfrac{\sqrt{3}}{2} x \right] + 53x^2 - 89$

26. $(D^2 + 5D + 4)\, y = x^2 + 7x + 9.$ **Ans.** $y = c_1 e^{-4x} + c_2 e^{-x} + \dfrac{1}{4}\left(x^2 + \dfrac{9x}{2} + \dfrac{23}{8} \right)$

27. $(D^4 + 6D^2 + 25)\, y = x^4 + x^2 + 1.$

Ans. $y = e^x [c_1 \cos 2x + c_2 \sin 2x] + e^{-x} [c_3 \cos 2x + c_4 \sin 2x] + \dfrac{1}{25}\left[x^4 - \dfrac{47}{25} x^2 + \dfrac{589}{625} \right]$

28. $(D^2 - D + 1)\, y = x^3 - 3x^2 + 1$

Ans. $y = e^{x/2}\left[c_1 \cos \dfrac{\sqrt{3}}{2} x + c_2 \sin \dfrac{\sqrt{3}}{2} x \right] + x^3 - 6x - 5$

29. $(D^3 - 3D^2 + 3D - 1) y = 2x^3 - 3x^2 + 1.$

Ans. $y = (c_1 x^2 + c_2 x + c_3) e^x - (2x^3 + 15x^2 + 54x + 85)$

30. $(D^3 - 2D + 4) y = 3x^2 - 5x + 2.$

Ans. $c_1 e^{-2x} + e^x (c_2 \cos x + c_3 \sin x) + \dfrac{1}{4}(3x^2 - 2x + 1)$

31. $\dfrac{d^3 y}{dx^3} + 8y = x^4 + 2x + 1.$

Ans. $y = c_1 e^{-2x} + e^x \left[A \cos \sqrt{3}\, x + B \sin \sqrt{3}\, x\right] + \dfrac{1}{8}(x^4 - x + 1)$

32. $(D^2 - 3D + 2) y = x^2 + \sin x.$

Ans. $y = c_1 e^x + c_2 e^{2x} + \dfrac{1}{2}\left(x^2 + 3x + \dfrac{7}{2}\right) + \dfrac{1}{10}\sin x + \dfrac{3}{10}\cos x$

33. $(D^3 + 3D^2 - 4) y = 6e^{-2x} + 4x^2.$ **Ans.** $y = c_1 e^x + (c_2 x + c_3) e^{-2x} - x^2 e^{-2x} - x^2 - \dfrac{3}{2}$

34. $(D^3 + 6D^2 + 12D + 8) y = e^{-2x} + x^2 + 3^x + \cos 2x.$

Ans. $y = (c_1 x + c_2 x + c_3) e^{-2x} + \dfrac{x^3}{6} e^{-2x} + \dfrac{1}{8}(x^2 - 3x + 3)$

$$+ \dfrac{1}{(\log 3 + 2)^3} 3^x + \dfrac{1}{32}(\sin 2x - \cos 2x)$$

35. $(D^2 - 4D + 4) y = 8(e^{2x} + \sin 2x + x^2).$

Ans. $y = (c_1 x + c_2) e^{2x} + 4x^2 e^{2x} + \cos 2x + 2\left(x^2 + 2x + \dfrac{3}{2}\right)$

36. $(D^5 - D) y = 12 e^x + 8 \sin x - 2x$

Ans. $y = c_1 + c_2 e^{-x} + c_3 e^x + A \cos x + B \sin x + 3x e^x + 2x \sin x + x^2$

37. $(D^2 - 1) y = e^x + x^3.$ **Ans.** $y = c_1 e^x + c_2 e^{-x} + \dfrac{1}{2} x e^x - x^3 - 6x$

38. $(D^2 - 4D + 4) y = e^{2x} + x^3 + \cos 2x$

Ans. $y = (c_1 + c_2 x) e^{2x} + \dfrac{1}{2} x^2 e^{2x} - \dfrac{1}{8}\sin 2x + \dfrac{1}{8}[2x^3 + 6x^2 + 9x + 6]$

39. $(D^5 - D) y = 12e^x + 85mx + 2^x$

Ans. $y = c_1 + c_2 e^x + c_3 e^{-x} + c_4 \cos x + c_5 \sin x + 3x e^x - 35\, m\, \dfrac{x^2}{2} + \dfrac{2^x}{(\log 2)^5 - \log 2}$

40. $(D^2 - 4) y = e^{3x} x^2.$ **Ans.** $y = c_1 e^{2x} + c_2 e^{-2x} + \dfrac{e^{3x}}{125}(125x^2 - 60x + 62)$

41. $\dfrac{d^3 y}{dx^3} - 7\dfrac{dy}{dx} - 6y = e^{2x}(1 + x^2)$ **Ans.** $y = c_1 e^{-x} + c_2 e^{-2x} + c_3 e^{3x} - \dfrac{e^{2x}}{12}\left[\dfrac{169}{72} + x^2 + \dfrac{5x}{6}\right]$

42. $(D^3 - 3D^2 + 3D - 1) y = \sqrt{x}\, e^x.$ **Ans.** $y = (c_1 x^2 + c_2 x + c_3) e^x + \dfrac{8e^x x^{7/2}}{105}$

43. $(D^2 - 4D + 4) y = e^{2x} \sin 3x$ **Ans.** $y = (c_1 + c_2 x) e^{2x} - \dfrac{1}{9} e^{2x} \sin 3x$

44. $(D^3 - D^2 + 3D + 5)\, y = e^x \cos 3x$

$$\text{Ans. } y = c_1 e^{-x} + e^x (c_2 \cos 2x + c_3 \sin 2x) - \frac{e^x}{65} (3 \sin 3x + 2 \cos 3x)$$

45. $(D^2 + 2D + 1)\, y = \dfrac{e^{-x}}{x + 2}$

$$\text{Ans. } y = (c_1 + c_2 x)\, e^{-x} - e^{-x} [x \log (x + 2) + 2 \log (x + 2) - x]$$

46. $(D^2 + 6D + 9)\, y = \dfrac{1}{x^3}\, e^{-3x}$ $\text{Ans. } y = (c_1 x + c_2)\, e^{-3x} + \dfrac{e^{-3x}}{2x}$

47. $(D^4 - 3D^3 - 2D^2 + 4D + 4)\, y = x^2 e^x.$

$$\text{Ans. } y = (c_1 x + c_2)\, e^{-x} + (c_3 x + c_4)\, e^{2x} + \frac{e^x}{4} \left(x^2 + 2x + \frac{7}{2}\right)$$

48. $(D^3 - 3D - 2)\, y = 540\, x^3\, e^{-x}.$

$$\text{Ans. } y = (c_1 x + c_2)\, e^{-x} + c_3\, e^{2x} - 180 e^{-x} \left(\frac{x^5}{20} + \frac{x^4}{12} + \frac{x^3}{9} + \frac{x^2}{9}\right)$$

49. $\dfrac{d^2 y}{dx^2} + 2\dfrac{dy}{dx} + 2y = e^{-x} \sec^3 x$ $\text{Ans. } y = e^{-x} \left[c_1 \cos x + c_2 \sin x + \dfrac{\sin x}{2} \tan x\right]$

50. $(D^2 + 2D + 1)\, y = e^{-x} \log x.$ $\text{Ans. } y = (c_1 x + c_2)\, e^{-x} + \dfrac{e^{-x} x^2}{4} (2 \log x - 3x^2)$

51. $(D^4 + D^2 + 1)\, y = e^{-x/2} \cos \left(\dfrac{\sqrt{3}}{2} x\right)$

$$\text{Ans. } y = e^{x/2} \left[c_1 \cos \frac{\sqrt{3}}{2} x + c_2 \sin \frac{\sqrt{3}}{2} x\right] + e^{-x/2} \left[c_3 \cos \frac{\sqrt{3}}{2} x + c_4 \sin \frac{\sqrt{3}}{2} x\right]$$
$$+ \frac{1}{4\sqrt{3}}\, x\, e^{-x/2} \left[\sin x \frac{\sqrt{3}}{2} + \sqrt{3} \cos x \frac{\sqrt{3}}{2}\right]$$

52. $(D^3 - D^2 - D + 1)\, y = \cosh x \sin x.$

$$\text{Ans. } y = (c_1 x + c_2)\, e^x + c_3\, e^{-x} + \frac{e^x}{10} (\cos x - 2 \sin x) - \frac{e^{-x}}{50} (3 \cos x - 4 \sin x)$$

53. $\dfrac{d^2 y}{dx^2} - y = \cosh x \cos x$ $\text{Ans. } y = c_1 e^x + c_2 e^{-x} + \dfrac{1}{5} (2 \sinh x \sin x - \cosh x \cos x)$

54. $(D^2 + 40D + 8)\, y = 12 e^{-2x} \sin x \sin 3x.$

$$\text{Ans. } y = e^{-2x} (c_1 \cos 2x + c_2 \sin 2x) + \frac{3}{2} x\, e^{-2x} \sin 2x + \frac{1}{2} e^{-2x} \cos 4x$$

55. $(D^3 - 6D^2 + 11D - 6)\, y = e^x x + \sin x + \cos x.$

$$\text{Ans. } y = c_1 e^x + c_2 e^{2x} + c_3 e^{3x} + \frac{e^x}{2} \left(\frac{x^2}{3} + \frac{3}{2} x\right) - \frac{1}{10} \cos x + \frac{1}{10} \sin x$$

56. $\dfrac{d^2 y}{dx^2} + 5\dfrac{dy}{dx} + 6y = e^{-2x} \sin 2x + 4x^2 e^x$

$$\text{Ans. } y = c_1 e^{-2x} + c_2 e^{-3x} - \frac{e^{-2x}}{10} (\cos 2x + 2 \sin 2x) + \frac{e^x}{3} \left(x^2 - \frac{7}{6} x + \frac{37}{72}\right)$$

57. $\dfrac{d^3y}{dx^3} - \dfrac{d^2y}{dx^2} = 3x + x\,e^x.$ **Ans.** $y = c_1 + c_2 x + c_3 e^x - 2x\,e^x + \dfrac{x^2 e^x}{2} - \dfrac{x^3}{2} - \dfrac{3x^2}{2}$

58. $\dfrac{d^2y}{dx^2} - 3\dfrac{dy}{dx} + 2y = x\,e^{3x} + \sin 2x.$

Ans. $y = c_2 e^x + c_1 e^{2x} + e^{3x}\left(\dfrac{x}{2} - \dfrac{3}{4}\right) + \dfrac{1}{20}\,(3\cos 2x - \sin 2x)$

59. $(D^2 - 6D + 13)\,y = 8\,e^{3x}\sin 4x + 2^x$

Ans. $y = e^{3x}(A\cos 2x + B\sin 2x) - \dfrac{2e^{3x}\sin 4x}{3} + \dfrac{2^x}{(\log 2)^2 - 6\log 2 + 13}$

60. $(D^4 + D^2 + 1)\,y = ax^2 + be^{-x}\sin 2x.$

Ans. $y = e^{(-1/2)\,x}\,[c_1\cos(\sqrt{3}/2)\,x + c_2\sin(\sqrt{3}/2)\,x]$

$+ e^{(1/2)\,x}\,[c_3\cos(\sqrt{3}/2)\,x + c_4\sin(\sqrt{3}/2\,x] + a\,(x^2 - 2) - \dfrac{b}{481}\,e^{-x}\,(20\cos 2x + 9\sin 2x)$

61. $(D^2 - 4)\,y = x\sinh x$ **Ans.** $y = c_1 e^{2x} + c_2\,e^{-2x} - \dfrac{1}{3}\,[x\sinh x + \dfrac{2}{3}\cosh x]$

62. $(D^2 - 20D + 1)\,y = x^2\,e^x\sin x.$ **Ans.** $y = (c_1 x + c_2)\,e^x - e^x\,[4x\cos x + (x^2 - 6)\sin x]$

63. $\dfrac{d^2y}{dx^2} - 4\dfrac{dy}{dx} + 4y = 8x^2 \cdot e^{2x}\sin 2x.$

Ans. $y = e^{2x}\,[c_1 + c_2 x + 3\sin 2x - 2x^2\sin 2x - 4x\cos 2x]$

64. $(D^2 + 2D + 1)\,y = x\cos x$ **Ans.** $y = (c_1 x + c_2)\,e^{-x} + \dfrac{1}{2}\,(x\sin x + \cos x - \sin x)$

65. $\dfrac{d^2y}{dx^2} + 3\dfrac{dy}{dx} + 2y = x\sin 2x$

Ans. $y = c_1 e^{-2x} + c_2\,e^{-x} + \left(\dfrac{7 - 30x}{200}\right)\cos 2x + \left(\dfrac{12 - 5x}{100}\right)\sin 2x$

66. $(D^4 + 2D^2 + 1)\,y = x\cos x.$

Ans. $y = (c_1 x + c_2)\cos x + (c_3 x + c_4)\sin x - \dfrac{x^3}{24}\cos x + \dfrac{x^2}{2}\sin x$

67. $(D^2 + 1)^2\,y = 24x\cos x.$

Ans. $y = (c_1 x + c_2)\cos x + (c_3 x + c_4)\sin x - x^3\cos x + 3x^2\sin x$

68. $(D^2 + 2D + 5)^2\,y = x\,e^{-x}\cos 2x.$

Ans. $y = e^{-x}\,[(c_1 x + c_2)\cos 2x + (c_3 x + c_4)\sin 2x] - \dfrac{e^{-x}}{32}\left[(x^3 - x^2)\cos 2x - \dfrac{2}{3}x^3\sin 2x\right]$

69. $(D^2 - 2D + 4)^2\,y = xe^x\cos\left[\sqrt{3}\,x + \alpha\right]$

Ans. $y = e^x\left[(c_1 + c_2 x)\cos\sqrt{3}\,x + (c_3 + c_4 x)\sin\sqrt{3}\,x\right]$

$-\dfrac{e^x}{12}\left[\dfrac{x^3}{6}\cos(\sqrt{3}\,x + \alpha) + \dfrac{x^2}{2\sqrt{3}}\sin(\sqrt{3}\,x + \alpha)\right]$

70. $(D^2 - 4D + 4)\,y = x\,e^{2x}\sin 2x.$ **Ans.** $y = (c_1 x + c_2)\,e^{2x} - \dfrac{e^{2x}}{4}\,[x\sin 2x + \cos 2x]$

1.12 EQUATIONS REDUCIBLE TO LINEAR WITH CONSTANT COEFFICIENTS

We shall now study two types of linear differential equations with *variable coefficients* which can be reduced to the case of linear differential equation with constant coefficients by suitable transformations of variables.

1.13 CAUCHY'S OR EULER'S HOMOGENEOUS LINEAR DIFFERENTIAL EQUATION

An equation of the type

$$(a_0 x^n D^n + a_1 x^{n-1} D^{n-1} + \dots + a_{n-1} x D + a_n) y = F(x)$$

where a_0, a_1, a_2 ...... a_n are constants is called Cauchy's Homogeneous Equation. It is sometimes attributed to Euler also. It may also be written as

$$a_0 x^n \frac{d^n y}{dx^n} + a_1 x^{n-1} \frac{d^{n-1}y}{dx^{n-1}} + \dots + a_{n-1} x \frac{dy}{dx} + a_n y = F(x) \qquad \dots (1)$$

It can be reduced to linear differential equation with constant coefficients by putting

$$x = e^z \text{ or } z = \log x \qquad \dots (2)$$

Now

$$\frac{dy}{dx} = \frac{dy}{dz}\frac{dz}{dx} = \frac{1}{x}\frac{dy}{dz}$$

or

$$x \frac{dy}{dx} = \frac{dy}{dz} = Dy, \text{ here we took } D \equiv \frac{d}{dz}$$

Also,

$$\frac{d^2 y}{dx^2} = \frac{d}{dx}\left(\frac{1}{x}\frac{dy}{dz}\right) = -\frac{1}{x^2}\frac{dy}{dz} + \frac{1}{x}\frac{d}{dz}\left(\frac{dy}{dz}\right)\frac{dz}{dx}$$

$$= -\frac{1}{x^2}\frac{dy}{dz} + \frac{1}{x}\left(\frac{d^2 y}{dz^2}\right)\frac{1}{x}$$

$$= -\frac{1}{x^2}\frac{dy}{dz} + \frac{1}{x^2}\frac{d^2 y}{dz^2}$$

Hence

$$x^2 \frac{d^2 y}{dx^2} = -Dy + D^2 y = D(D-1) y$$

Similarly, we can show that

$$x^3 \frac{d^3 y}{dx^3} = D(D-1)(D-2) y \text{ and so on.}$$

$$\dots\dots\dots\dots\dots\dots\dots\dots\dots\dots\dots$$

$$\dots\dots\dots\dots\dots\dots\dots\dots\dots\dots\dots$$

$$x^r \frac{d^r y}{dx^r} = D(D-1)(D-2)\dots\dots(D-r+1) y \qquad \dots (3)$$

Making these substitutions in (1) it can be reduced to linear differential equation with constant coefficients. The following examples can clarify further.

ILLUSTRATIONS

Ex. 1 : *Solve* $x^2 \dfrac{d^2y}{dx^2} - x \dfrac{dy}{dx} + 4y = \cos (\log x) + x \sin (\log x)$

Sol. : Given equation is Cauchy's homogeneous linear differential equation. We use substitution $z = \log x$ or $x = e^z$ and let $D \equiv \dfrac{d}{dz}$.

Then we note from article (1.18),

$$x^2 \frac{d^2y}{dx^2} = D(D-1)\,y, \quad x\frac{dy}{dx} = Dy, \text{ where } D \equiv \frac{d}{dz}$$

and equation is transformed into

$$D(D-1)\,y - Dy + 4y = \cos(z) + e^z \sin z$$

$$\text{or} \qquad (D^2 - D - D + 4)\,y = \cos(z) + e^z \sin z$$

$$\text{or} \qquad (D^2 - 2D + 4)\,y = \cos(z) + e^z \sin z$$

which is linear with constant coefficients in y and z. Now

A.E. is $D^2 - 2D + 4 = 0 \;\Rightarrow\; D = 1 \pm i\sqrt{3}$

Hence $\qquad$ C.F. $= e^z \left[A \cos \sqrt{3}\,z + B \sin \sqrt{3}\,z \right]$

and $\qquad$ P.I. $= \dfrac{1}{D^2 - 2D + 4} \cos z + \dfrac{1}{D^2 - 2D + 4} e^z \sin z$

$$= \frac{1}{-1 - 2D + 4} \cos z + e^z \frac{1}{(D+1)^2 - 2(D+1) + 4} \sin z$$

$$= \frac{1}{3 - 2D} \cos z + e^z \frac{1}{D^2 + 3} \sin z$$

$$= -\frac{2D + 3}{4D^2 - 9} \cos z + e^z \frac{1}{-1 + 3} (\sin z)$$

$$= -\frac{(2D + 3) \cos z}{-4 - 9} + e^z \frac{1}{2} \sin z$$

$$= \frac{1}{13} [-2 \sin z + 3 \cos z] + \frac{1}{2} e^z \sin z$$

Hence the general solution in terms of y and z is

$$y = e^z \left[A \cos (\sqrt{3}\,z) + B \sin (\sqrt{3}\,z) \right] + \frac{1}{13} [3 \cos z - 2 \sin z] + \frac{1}{2} e^z \sin z$$

Changing to y and x, we have

$$y = x \left[A \cos \sqrt{3}\,(\log x) + B \sin \sqrt{3}\,(\log x) \right]$$

$$+ \frac{1}{13} [3 \cos (\log x) - 2 \sin (\log x)] + \frac{1}{2} x \sin (\log x)$$

Ex. 2 : *Find the equation of the curve, which satisfies the differential equation*

$4x^2 \dfrac{d^2y}{dx^2} - 4x \dfrac{dy}{dx} + y = 0$ *and crosses the x-axis at an angle of* 60° *at* $x = 1$.

Sol. : Given equation is Cauchy's homogeneous linear differential equation. The solution will be the equation of the curve.

Put $x = e^z \Rightarrow z = \log x$, and $\dfrac{d}{dz} \equiv D$, then the given equation is transformed into

$$[4 D (D - 1) - 4 D + 1] \; y = 0$$

A.E. is $4D^2 - 8D + 1 = 0 \therefore D = 1 \pm \dfrac{\sqrt{3}}{2}$

$$\text{C.F.} = c_1 e^{\left(1 + \frac{\sqrt{3}}{2}\right) z} + c_2 e^{\left(1 - \frac{\sqrt{3}}{2}\right) z} \quad \text{and solution is}$$

$$y = c_1 x^{\left(1 + \frac{\sqrt{3}}{2}\right)} + c_2 x^{\left(1 - \frac{\sqrt{3}}{2}\right)} \qquad \ldots (1)$$

But initially when $x = 1$, $y = 0$ and $\dfrac{dy}{dx} = \sqrt{3}$

$$\therefore \quad 0 = c_1 + c_2 \Rightarrow c_1 = - c_2 \qquad \ldots (2)$$

Differentiating (1) w.r.t. x

$$\dfrac{dy}{dx} = \left(1 + \dfrac{\sqrt{3}}{2}\right) c_1 x^{\frac{\sqrt{3}}{2}} + \left(1 - \dfrac{\sqrt{3}}{2}\right) c_2 x^{-\frac{\sqrt{3}}{2}}$$

Put $x = 1$ and $\dfrac{dy}{dx} = \sqrt{3}$ in this

$$\sqrt{3} = \left(1 + \dfrac{\sqrt{3}}{2}\right) c_1 + \left(1 - \dfrac{\sqrt{3}}{2}\right) c_2$$

Solving with (2), we get $c_1 = 1$, $c_2 = - 1$

$\therefore$ Solution or the equation of the curve will be

$$y = x^{\left(1 + \frac{\sqrt{3}}{2}\right)} - x^{\left(1 - \frac{\sqrt{3}}{2}\right)}$$

Ex. 3 : *Solve* $x^3 \cdot \dfrac{d^3y}{dx^3} + 2x^2 \cdot \dfrac{d^2y}{dx^2} + 2y = 10\left(x + \dfrac{1}{x}\right)$

Sol. : The given equation is Cauchy's homogeneous linear differential equation.

Put $x = e^z$, $\Rightarrow z = \log x$ and $\dfrac{d}{dz} \equiv D$ then equation is transformed into

$$[D (D - 1) (D - 2) + 2 D (D - 1) + 2] \; y = 10 (e^z + e^{-z})$$

A.E. is $D^3 - D^2 + 2 = 0$ $\therefore$ $D = - 1, \; 1 \pm i$

$$\text{C.F.} = c_1 e^{-z} + e^z [c_2 \cos z + c_3 \sin z]$$

$$= \dfrac{c_1}{x} + x [c_2 \cos (\log x) + c_3 \sin (\log x)]$$

$$\text{P.I.} = 10 \, \dfrac{1}{D^3 - D^2 + 2} \, (e^z + e^{-z})$$

$$= 10 \left[\frac{1}{D^3 - D^2 + 2} e^z + \frac{1}{D^3 - D^2 + 2} e^{-z} \right]$$

$$= 10 \left[\frac{1}{1 - 1 + 2} e^z + z\, \frac{1}{3D^2 - 2D} e^{-z} \right] = 10 \left[\frac{e^z}{2} + \frac{1}{5} z\, e^{-z} \right]$$

$$= 5\, e^z + 2\, z\, e^{-z} = 5x + \frac{2}{x} \log x$$

Hence the general solution will be

$$y = \frac{c_1}{x} + x\, [c_2 \cos (\log x) + c_3 \sin (\log x)] + 5x + \frac{2}{x} \log x$$

Ex. 4 : *Solve* $x^2 \dfrac{d^2y}{dx^2} - 3x \dfrac{dy}{dx} + 5y = x^2 \sin (\log x).$ **(SUK Dec. 11)**

Sol. : Given equation is Cauchy's homogeneous linear differential equation.

Put $z = \log x$ or $x = e^z$ and $\dfrac{d}{dz} \equiv D$, then equation is transformed into

$$[D\, (D - 1) - 3D + 5]\; y = e^{2z} \sin z$$
$$(D^2 - 4D + 5)\, y = e^{2z} \sin z$$

A.E. is $D^2 - 4D + 5 = 0$ $\therefore$ $D = 2 \pm i.$

$$\text{C.F.} = e^{2z} (c_1 \cos z + c_2 \sin z)$$

$$\text{P.I.} = \frac{1}{D^2 - 4D + 5} e^{2z} \sin z = e^{2z} \frac{1}{(D + 2)^2 - 4\, (D + 2) + 5} \sin z$$

$$= e^{2z} \frac{1}{D^2 + 1} \sin z = -e^{2z} \frac{z}{2} \cos z$$

$$= -\frac{1}{2} e^{2z} z \cos z$$

General solution in terms of y and z is

$$y = e^{2z} (c_1 \cos z + c_2 \sin z) - \frac{1}{2} e^{2z} z \cos z$$

General solution in terms of y and x is

$$y = x^2 [c_1 \cos (\log x) + c_2 \sin (\log x)] - \frac{1}{2} x^2 (\log x) \cos (\log x)$$

Ex. 5 : *Solve* $u = r \dfrac{d}{dr} \left(r \dfrac{du}{dr} \right) + r^3.$

Sol. : Given equation is $u = r \left\{ r \dfrac{d^2u}{dr^2} + \dfrac{du}{dr} \right\} + r^3$ or $r^2 \dfrac{d^2u}{dr^2} + r \dfrac{du}{dr} - u = -r^3$

which is a homogeneous equation.

Put $z = \log r$ or $r = e^z$ and using D for $\dfrac{d}{dz}$, equation is transformed into

$$[D\,(D-1) + D - 1]\,u = -e^{3z} \quad \text{or} \quad (D^2 - 1)\,u = -e^{3z}.$$

A.E. is $D^2 - 1 = 0$ $\therefore$ $D = \pm 1$

$$\text{C.F.} = c_1 e^z + c_2 e^{-z}$$

$$\text{P.I.} = \frac{1}{D^2 - 1}(-e^{3z}) = -\frac{1}{8}\,e^{3z}$$

$\therefore$
$$u = c_1 e^z + c_2 e^{-z} - \frac{1}{8}\,e^{3z}$$

The general solution in u and r is

$$u = c_1 r + \frac{c_2}{r} - \frac{r^3}{8}$$

1.14 LEGENDRE'S LINEAR EQUATION

An equation of the type

$$a_0\,(ax + b)^n \frac{d^n y}{dx^n} + a_1\,(ax + b)^{n-1} \frac{d^{n-1} y}{dx^{n-1}} + \ldots + a_n y = F(x)$$

where, $a_0, a_1, a_2 \ldots \ldots a_n$ are constants is called *Legendre's Linear Equation*.

In case of such equations, we put $ax + b = e^z$ to reduce it to linear with constant coefficients.

If we put $ax + b = e^z \Rightarrow z = \log (ax + b)$

then
$$\frac{dy}{dx} = \frac{dy}{dz} \cdot \frac{dz}{dx} = \left(\frac{a}{ax + b}\right) \frac{dy}{dz}$$

$\Rightarrow$
$$(ax + b)\frac{dy}{dx} = a\,\frac{dy}{dx} = a\,Dy \qquad\qquad \left[\because \frac{d}{dz} = D\right]$$

$$\frac{d^2 y}{dx^2} = \frac{d}{dx}\left(\frac{a}{ax + b} \cdot \frac{dy}{dz}\right)$$

$$= \frac{-a^2}{(ax + b)^2}\frac{dy}{dz} + \frac{a}{ax + b}\frac{d}{dz}\left(\frac{dy}{dz}\right)\frac{dz}{dx}$$

$$= -\frac{a^2}{(ax + b)^2}\frac{dy}{dz} + \frac{a^2}{(ax + b)^2}\frac{d^2 y}{dz^2}$$

$$= \frac{a^2}{(ax + b)^2}\left[\frac{d^2 y}{dz^2} - \frac{dy}{dz}\right]$$

$\Rightarrow$
$$(ax + b)^2 \frac{d^2 y}{dx^2} = a^2\,[D^2 - D]\,y = a^2\,D\,(D - 1)\,y$$

Similarly, we shall get

$$(ax + b)^3 \frac{d^3 y}{dx^3} = a^3\,D\,(D - 1)\,(D - 2)\,y \text{ and so on.}$$

If we make these substitutions in the differential equation (Legendre's), we shall see that it has been transformed into one with constant coefficients.

ILLUSTRATIONS

Ex. 6 : *Solve* $(2x + 1)^2 \dfrac{d^2y}{dx^2} - 2(2x + 1)\dfrac{dy}{dx} - 12y = 6x$

Sol. : Put $2x + 1 = e^z \Rightarrow z = \log(2x + 1)$, $\dfrac{dz}{dx} = \dfrac{2}{2x + 1}$, $\dfrac{d}{dz} \equiv D$.

Then we shall have

$$(2x + 1)^2 \frac{d^2y}{dx^2} = 4 \cdot D(D - 1)\,y, \quad (2x + 1)\frac{dy}{dx} = 2\,Dy$$

and the equation is transformed into

$$4D(D - 1)\,y - 4(Dy) - 12y = 6\left(\frac{e^z - 1}{2}\right)$$

$$\Rightarrow \qquad [4(D^2 - D) - 4D - 12]\,y = 3\,e^z - 3$$

$$\Rightarrow \qquad (4D^2 - 8D - 12)\,y = 3\,e^z - 3$$

$$\Rightarrow \qquad (D^2 - 2D - 3)\,y = \frac{3}{4}(e^z - 1)$$

which is now linear with constant coefficient in y, z.

$$\text{A.E.} \quad : \quad D^2 - 2D - 3 = 0 \Rightarrow D = 3, -1$$

$$\text{C.F.} = c_1 e^{3z} + c_2 e^{-z}$$

$$\text{P.I.} = \frac{1}{D^2 - 2D - 3}\,\frac{3}{4}(e^z - e^{0z})$$

$$\text{P.I.} = \frac{3}{4}\left[\frac{1}{D^2 - 2D - 3}e^z - \frac{1}{D^2 - 2D - 3}e^{0z}\right]$$

$$= \frac{3}{4}\left[\frac{e^z}{1 - 2 - 3} - \frac{e^{0z}}{0 - 0 - 3}\right] = \frac{3}{4}\left[\frac{e^z}{-4} + \frac{1}{3}\right]$$

$$= \frac{3e^z}{-16} + \frac{1}{4}$$

Hence the complete solution in terms of y and z is

$$y = c_1 e^{3z} + c_2 e^{-z} - 3\frac{e^z}{16} + \frac{1}{4}$$

Changing back to y and x, we have

$$y = c_1(2x + 1)^3 + c_2(2x + 1)^{-1} - \frac{3}{16}(2x + 1) + \frac{1}{4}$$

Ex. 7 : *Solve* $(1 + x)^2 \dfrac{d^2y}{dx^2} + (1 + x)\dfrac{dy}{dx} + y = 2\sin[\log(1 + x)]$

Sol. : Put $(1 + x) = e^z \Rightarrow z = \log(1 + x)$, $\dfrac{d}{dz} \equiv D$

Then the equation will become

$$D(D - 1)\,y + Dy + y = 2\sin z$$

$$\Rightarrow \qquad (D^2 + 1)\,y = 2\sin z$$

Here   A.E. : $D^2 + 1 = 0$, $D = \pm i$, hence

C.F. $= A \cos z + B \sin z$

$$P.I. = \frac{2 \sin z}{D^2 + 1} = \frac{2 \sin z}{-1 + 1} \quad \text{(case of failure)}$$

$\therefore$ $P.I. = z \dfrac{1}{2D} 2 \sin z = z \displaystyle\int \sin z \, dz = -z \cos z$

General solution in terms of y and z is

$$y = A \cos z + B \sin z - z \cos z$$

$\therefore$ $y = A \cos [\log (1 + x)] + B \sin [\log (1 + x)] - \log (1 + x) \cos [\log (1 + x)]$

Ex. 8 : *Solve* $(3x + 2)^2 \dfrac{d^2 y}{dx^2} + 3 (3x + 2) \dfrac{dy}{dx} - 36y = 3x^2 + 4x + 1.$

Sol. : Given equation is Legendre's linear differential equation.

Put $z = \log (3x + 2)$ or $(3x + 2) = e^z$ and let $\dfrac{d}{dz} \equiv D$ then the equation is transformed

into $[9D (D - 1) + 3.3D - 36] \, y = \dfrac{1}{3} (e^{2z} - 1)$ or $(D^2 - 4) \, y = \dfrac{1}{27} (e^{2z} - 1)$

A.E. is $D^2 - 4 = 0 \quad \therefore \quad D = \pm 2.$

C.F. $= c_1 e^{2z} + c_2 e^{-2z}$

$$P.I. = \frac{1}{27} \frac{1}{D^2 - 4} (e^{2z} - 1) = \frac{1}{27} \left[\frac{1}{D^2 - 4} e^{2z} - \frac{1}{D^2 - 4} e^{oz} \right]$$

$$= \frac{1}{27} \left[\frac{z \, e^{2z}}{4} + \frac{1}{4} \right] = \frac{1}{108} [z e^{2z} + 1]$$

The general solution in y and z is

$$y = c_1 e^{2z} + c_2 e^{-2z} + \frac{1}{108} [z e^{2z} + 1]$$

The general solution in y and x is

$$y = c_1 (3x + 2)^2 + c_2 (3x + 2)^{-2} + \frac{1}{108} [(3x + 2)^2 \log (3x + 2) + 1]$$

EXERCISE 1.4

Solve following differential equations with variable coefficients.

1. $x^2 \dfrac{d^2 y}{dx^2} - 4x \dfrac{dy}{dx} + 6y = x^5$ **Ans.** $y = c_1 x^2 + c_2 x^3 + \dfrac{x^5}{6}$

2. $x^2 \dfrac{d^2 y}{dx^2} - 2x \dfrac{dy}{dx} - 4y = x^2 + 2 \log x$ **Ans.** $y = c_1 x^4 + \dfrac{c_2}{x} - \dfrac{x^2}{6} - \dfrac{1}{2} \log x + \dfrac{3}{8}$

3. $x^2 \dfrac{d^3y}{dx^3} + 3x \dfrac{d^2y}{dx^2} + \dfrac{dy}{dx} + \dfrac{y}{x} = \log x$

> **Ans.** $y = \dfrac{c_1}{x} + \sqrt{x}\left[c_2 \cos (\sqrt{3}/2)\log x + c_3 \sin (\sqrt{3}/2)\log x\right] + \dfrac{x}{2}\left(\log x - \dfrac{3}{2}\right)$

4. $x^3 \dfrac{d^3y}{dx^3} + x^2 \dfrac{d^2y}{dx^2} - 2y = x^2 + x^{-3}.$

> **Ans.** $y = c_1 x^2 + c_2 \cos (\log x) + c_3 \sin (\log x) + \dfrac{x^2}{5}\log x - \dfrac{1}{50} x^{-3}$

5. $(x^3 D^3 + x^2 D^2 - 2)\, y = x + x^{-3}$

> **Ans.** $y = c_1 x^2 + c_2 \cos (\log x) + c_3 \sin (\log x) - \dfrac{x}{2} - \dfrac{1}{50} x^{-3}$

6. $\dfrac{d^2y}{dx^2} + \dfrac{1}{x} \dfrac{dy}{dx} = A + B \log x$ **Ans.** $y = (c_1 + c_2 \log x) + \dfrac{A}{4} x^2 + \dfrac{B}{4} x^2 (\log x - 1)$

7. $\left(\dfrac{d^2}{dx^2} - \dfrac{2}{x^2}\right)^2 y = 0$ **Ans.** $y = c_1 x^4 + c_2 x^2 + c_3 x + \dfrac{c_4}{x}$

8. $\left(\dfrac{d^2}{dx^2} - \dfrac{2}{x^2}\right)^2 y = x^2$ **Ans.** $y = c_3 x^2 + \dfrac{c_4}{x} + c_5 x^4 + c_6 x + \dfrac{x^6}{280}$

9. $(x^2 D^2 - xD + 1)\, y = x \log x$ **Ans.** $y = x\,[A \log x + B] + \dfrac{x}{6} (\log x)^3$

10. $x^2 \dfrac{d^2y}{dx^2} - 3x \dfrac{dy}{dx} + 5y = x^2 \log x.$

> **Ans.** $y = x^2\,[c_1 \cos (\log x) + c_2 \sin (\log x)] + x^2 \log x$

11. $x^3 \dfrac{d^2y}{dx^2} + 3x^2 \dfrac{dy}{dx} + xy = \sin (\log x)$ **Ans.** $y = \dfrac{1}{x}\{c_1 + c_2 \log x - \sin (\log x)\}$

12. The radial displacement 'u' in a rotating disc at a distance 'r' from axis is given by

$\dfrac{d^2u}{dr^2} + \dfrac{1}{r} \dfrac{du}{dr} - \dfrac{u}{r^2} + kr = 0.$ Find the displacement if $u = 0$ for $r = 0, r = a$

> **Ans.** $u = \dfrac{kr}{8} (a^2 - r^2)$

13. $x^2 \dfrac{d^2y}{dx^2} + x \dfrac{dy}{dx} - y = \dfrac{x^3}{1 + x^2}$

> **Ans.** $y = Ax + \dfrac{B}{x} + \dfrac{x}{4} \log (1 + x^2) - \dfrac{x}{4} + \dfrac{1}{4x} \log (x^2 + 1)$

14. $u = r \dfrac{d}{dr}\left[r \dfrac{du}{dr}\right] + ar^3$ **Ans.** $u = Ar + \dfrac{B}{r} - \dfrac{a}{8} r^3$

15. $x \dfrac{d^2y}{dx^2} + \dfrac{dy}{dx} + x = 0$ [**Hint :** Multiply by x]   **Ans.** $y = A + B \log x - \dfrac{x^2}{4}$

16. $(x^3 D^3 + 2 x^2 D^2 + 3 x D - 3) y = x^2 + x$

Ans. $y = c_1 x + c_2 \cos (\log x) + c_3 \sin (\log x) + \dfrac{x}{7} + \dfrac{x}{4} \log x$

17. $x^2 \dfrac{d^2y}{dx^2} + 3x \dfrac{dy}{dx} + y = \dfrac{1}{(1-x)^2}$ **Ans.** $y = \dfrac{1}{x} \left[c_1 \log x + c_2 + \log \left(\dfrac{x}{x-1} \right) \right]$

18. $x^2 \dfrac{d^2y}{dx^2} + x \dfrac{dy}{dx} + y = \sin (\log x^2)$

Ans. $y = c_1 \cos (\log x) + c_2 \sin (\log x) - \dfrac{1}{3} \sin (\log x^2)$

19. $x^3 \dfrac{d^3y}{dx^3} + 3x^2 \dfrac{d^2y}{dx^2} + x \dfrac{dy}{dx} + 8y = 65 \cos (\log x).$ ***SUK: Dec-13***

Ans. $y = c_1 x^{-2} + x (c_2 \cos \sqrt{(3)} \log x + c_3 \sin (\sqrt{3}) \log x)$
$- \sin (\log x) + 8 \cos (\log x)$

20. $(x^2 D^2 + 5xD + 3) y = \left(1 + \dfrac{1}{x} \right)^2 \log x$

21. $(x^2 D^2 - 3xD + 1) y = \log x \left[\dfrac{\sin (\log x) + 1}{x} \right]$

22. $\left(D^3 - \dfrac{4}{x} D^2 + \dfrac{5}{x^2} D - \dfrac{2}{x^3} \right) y = 1$ **Ans.** $y = c_1 x^2 + c_2 \, x^{\left(\frac{5 - \sqrt{21}}{2} \right)} + c_3 \, x^{\left(\frac{5 - \sqrt{21}}{2} \right)} - \dfrac{x^3}{5}$

23. $(x^2 D^2 - 4xD + 6) y = - x^4 \sin x$ **Ans.** $y = c_1 x^2 + c_2 x^3 + x^2 \sin x$

24. $(2x + 3)^2 \dfrac{d^2y}{dx^2} - 2 (2x + 3) \dfrac{dy}{dx} - 12y = 6x$

Ans. $y = c_1 (2x + 3)^3 + c_2 (2x + 3)^{-1} - \dfrac{3}{16} (2x + 3) + \dfrac{3}{4}$

25. $(x + a)^2 \dfrac{d^2y}{dx^2} - 4 (x + a) \dfrac{dy}{dx} + 6y = x$ **Ans.** $y = A (x + a)^3 + B (x + a)^2 + \dfrac{3x + 2a}{6}$

26. $7 (2 + x)^2 \dfrac{d^2y}{dx^2} + 8 (2 + x) \dfrac{dy}{dx} + y = 4 \cos [\log (2 + x)]$

27. $(1 + x)^2 \dfrac{d^2y}{dx^2} + (1 + x) \dfrac{dy}{dx} + y = 4 \cos [\log (1 + x)]$

Ans. $y = c_1 \cos [\log (x + 1)] + c_2 \sin [\log (1 + x)]$

28. $(x + 2)^2 \dfrac{d^2y}{dx^2} - (x + 2) \dfrac{dy}{dx} + y = 3x + 4$

Ans. $y = (x + 2) [c_1 + c_2 \log (x + 2)] + \dfrac{3}{2} (x + 2) [\log (x + 2)]^2 - 2$

29. $(x + 2)^2 \dfrac{d^2y}{dx^2} + 3(x + 2)\dfrac{dy}{dx} + y = 4 \sin[\log(x + 2)]$

Ans. $y = [\{c_1 + c_2 \log(x + 2)\}(x + 2)^{-1} - 2\cos[\log(x + 2)]$

30. $(2x + 1)^2 \dfrac{d^2y}{dx^2} - 6(2x + 1)\dfrac{dy}{dx} + 16y = 8(2x + 1)^2.$

Ans. $y = [c_1 + c_2 \log(2x + 1)](2x + 1)^2 + (2x + 1)^2 [\log(2x + 1)]^2$

31. $(x + 1)^2 \dfrac{d^2y}{dx^2} + (x + 1)\dfrac{dy}{dx} = (2x + 3)(2x + 4).$

Ans. $y = c_1 + c_2 \log(x + 1) + (x + 1)^2 + 6(x + 1) + [\log(x + 1)]^2$

32. $(4x + 1)^2 \dfrac{d^2y}{dx^2} + 2(4x + 1)\dfrac{dy}{dx} + y = 2x + 1.$

Ans. $y = [c_1 + c_2 \log(4x + 1)](4x + 1)^{1/4} + \dfrac{1}{18}(4x + 1) + \dfrac{1}{2}$

33. $(x + 1)^2 \dfrac{d^2y}{dx^2} + (x + 1)\dfrac{dy}{dx} - y = 2\log(x + 1) + x - 1.$

Ans. $y = c_1(x + 1) + c_2(x + 1)^{-1} - 2\log(x + 1) + \dfrac{1}{2}(x + 1)\log(x + 1) + 2$

34. $(x - 1)^3 \dfrac{d^3y}{dx^3} + 2(x - 1)^2 \dfrac{d^2y}{dx^2} - 4(x - 1)\dfrac{dy}{dx} + 4y = 4\log(x - 1)$

Ans. $y = c_1 + c_2(x - 1)^2 + c_3(x - 1)^{-2} - \dfrac{4}{3}(x - 1)\log(x - 1)$

UNIT - II

APPLICATIONS OF LINEAR DIFFERENTIAL EQUATIONS WITH CONSTANT COEFFICIENTS

2.1 MASS-SPRING SYSTEM (VIBRATION OF SPRINGS)

LDE with constant coefficients play very important role in representing vibrating mechanical systems. In this section we discuss the motions of a basic mechanical system, a mass attached to elastic spring (Fig. 2.1). Modelling of Mass-Spring System includes setting up its mathematical equation, solving it and discussing the nature of motion.

2.2 MODEL OF MASS-SPRING SYSTEM (FREE OSCILLATIONS)

Let an ordinary spring (which resists compression as well as extension) be suspended vertically from a fixed support. At the lower end of the spring we attach a body of mass 'm'. When the body is in rest, we describe this position as the equilibrium position. If we pull the body down a certain distance and then release it, it undergoes a motion. We shall determine the motion of mechanical system.

(a) Assumptions : (i) We assume that the body moves strictly vertically.

(ii) We choose the downward direction as the positive direction, thus we consider downward forces as positive and upward forces as negative.

(b) The mass 'm' is subjected to the following forces :

(i) A gravitational force : $W = mg$ of the body acting downward (we note here that $g = 980$ cm/sec^2 = 9.80 m/sec^2).

(ii) Spring restoring force : It has tendency to restore the system to its equilibrium position. It is governed by Hooke's law which states that "the force exerted by a spring, to restore the weight W to its equilibrium position, is proportional to the distance of W from the equilibrium position (briefly restoring force is proportional to stretch). Thus if F is restoring force and x denote the position of W measured from the equilibrium position then

$$F \propto x \quad \text{or} \quad F = -kx$$

Here $k\ (> 0)$ is the constant of proportionality, depends upon the stiffness of spring and is called spring constant and minus sign appears because force F points upward. We note here that a stiff spring has a large k; small stretch s_0.

Model Equation : Consider Fig. 2.1, initially, the spring is unstretched (Fig. 2.1 (a)). When we attach the body of mass 'm' it stretches the spring by amount s_0. This causes an upward force F_0 in the spring. By Hooke's law this force F_0 is proportional to the stretch s_0, thus

$$F_0 = -k\,s_0 \qquad\qquad \dots (1)$$

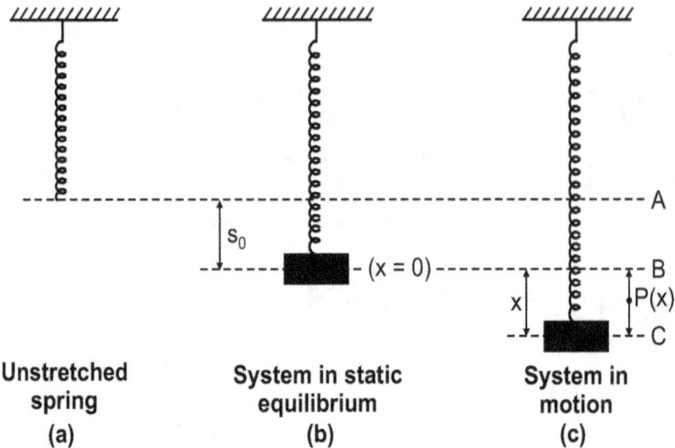

Fig. 2.1 : Mass-Spring System

The extension s_0 is such that F_0 balances the weight W of the body. Consequently,

$$F_0 + W = -k\,s_0 + mg = 0 \qquad \ldots (2)$$

These forces will not affect the motion and the spring and the body again at rest. This is called the *static equilibrium of the system* (Refer Fig. 2.1 (b)). We take this position of the body as origin (i.e. x = 0) and is used to measure the displacement x(t) of the body. From this position x = 0, we pull the body downwards which further stretches the spring by some amount x > 0 (the distance we pull down) (Fig. 2.1 (c)). This causes an additional upward restoring force F_1 in the spring. By Hooke's law this force F_1 is proportional to stretch x. Thus,

$$F_1 = -kx \qquad \ldots (3)$$

Hence, F_1 is the only force causing motion for our mechanical system. This motion is governed by Newton's second law of motion, if x(t) is the displacement of the body and t is the time, then

$$m \times \frac{d^2x}{dt^2} = \text{Resultant force.} \qquad \ldots (4)$$

Remark 1 : From (2), we note that in static equilibrium $mg = ks_0$ (i.e. $F_0 = -W$).

Remark 2 : Resultant force in positive direction can also be calculated as given below.

(i) When the body of mass 'm' is attached to the spring, it stretches a distance s_0 downward, then the tension (force) $T_0 = ks_0 = W$.

(ii) When the body is pulled further by distance x > 0 downwards and released, then the tension (force) $T_1 = k\,(s_0 + x)$.

From (i) and (ii), net force is given by

$$T_0 - T_1 = ks_0 - k\,(s_0 + x) = -kx.$$

It follows that resultant force in the positive direction turns out to be same as given in (3).

2.3 UNDAMPED SYSTEM (FREE, UNDAMPED OSCILLATION)

Every system has damping otherwise it would keep moving forever. But here we consider those mechanical system with very ideal spring where effect of damping may often be negligible (e.g. the external forces such as air resistance and other forces) and oscillation did not decrease. For instance, the motion of an iron ball on a spring during few minutes. Then F_1 is the only force acting in (4), causing motion. Hence from (3) and (4),

$$m \frac{d^2x}{dt^2} + kx = 0 \quad \text{or} \quad \frac{d^2x}{dt^2} + \frac{k}{m} x = 0 \qquad \ldots (5)$$

Putting $\omega^2 = \dfrac{k}{m}$, the equation (5) takes the form

$$\frac{d^2x}{dt^2} + \omega^2 x = 0$$

whose general solution is sinusoidal given by

$$x(t) = c_1 \cos \omega t + c_2 \sin \omega t \qquad \ldots (6)$$

Introducing $c_1 = A \cos \phi$ and $c_2 = -A \sin \phi$, solution (6) can be rewritten as

$$x(t) = A \cos \phi \cos \omega t - A \sin \phi \sin \omega t$$

or
$$x(t) = A \cos (\omega t + \phi) \qquad \ldots (7)$$

where, $A = \sqrt{c_1^2 + c_2^2}$, $\tan \phi = -\dfrac{c_2}{c_1}$. The constant A is called the *amplitude* of the motion and gives the maximum (positive) displacement of the mass from its equilibrium position. Thus the free, undamped motion of the mass is a *simple harmonic motion*, which is periodic. The period of the motion is the time interval between two successive maxima and is given by

$$T = \frac{2\pi}{\omega} = 2\pi \sqrt{\frac{m}{k}} \qquad \ldots (8)$$

The *natural frequency* (or simply frequency) of the motion (or harmonic oscillation) is the reciprocal of the period, which gives the number of oscillations/second. Thus natural frequency is the undamped frequency i.e. frequency of the system without damping.

ILLUSTRATIONS

Ex. 1 : *It is found experimentally that a weight W = 3 N stretches a spring to 15 cm. If the weight is pulled down 10 cm below the equilibrium position and then released*

(i)   find the amplitude, period and frequency of motion,

(ii) determine the position, velocity and acceleration of the weight 1/2 second after it has been released

Sol. : Since a weight W = 3 N stretches a spring 15 cm $\left(=\dfrac{15}{100}\,\text{m} = 0.15\,\text{m}\right)$ downward, by Hooke's law, we have

$$F_0 = ks_0 \Rightarrow 3 = k \times 0.15 \;\; \therefore \;\; k = \frac{3}{0.15} = 20 \text{ N/m (or kg/s}^2)$$

By Newton's second law, the equation of motion of the body is

$$m\frac{d^2x}{dt^2} = -kx \quad \text{or} \quad \frac{W}{g}\frac{d^2x}{dt^2} = -kx$$

$$\therefore \qquad \frac{3}{9.8}\frac{d^2x}{dt^2} = -20\,x \quad \text{or} \quad \frac{d^2x}{dt^2} + \frac{196}{3}x = 0 \qquad\qquad (\because m = \frac{W}{g})$$

which is a linear differential equation with constant coefficients.

$$\text{A.E. is } D^2 + \frac{196}{3} = 0 \;\; \therefore \;\; D = \pm\frac{14}{\sqrt{3}}i$$

$$\text{G.S. is } x = c_1 \cos\frac{14}{\sqrt{3}}t + c_2 \sin\frac{14}{\sqrt{3}}t \qquad\qquad \dots (1)$$

Differentiating (1), with respect to t, we get

$$\frac{dx}{dt} = -c_1\frac{14}{\sqrt{3}}\sin\frac{14}{\sqrt{3}}t + c_2\frac{14}{\sqrt{3}}\cos\frac{14}{\sqrt{3}}t \qquad\qquad \dots (2)$$

The initial conditions are t = 0, x = 10 cm = 0.1 m and since the weight is released, $t = 0, \dfrac{dx}{dt} = 0$. Using these conditions, we obtain

$$0.1 = c_1\,(1) + c_2\,(0) \;\Rightarrow\; c_1 = 0.1$$

$$0 = 0 + c_2\frac{14}{\sqrt{3}}\,(1) \;\Rightarrow\; c_2 = 0$$

Thus, we note that :

(1) $x(t) = (0.1)\cos\dfrac{14}{\sqrt{3}}t$
(2) $v = \dfrac{dx}{dt} = -(0.1)\dfrac{14}{\sqrt{3}}\sin\dfrac{14}{\sqrt{3}}t$

(3) $a = \dfrac{d^2x}{dt^2} = -(0.1)\dfrac{196}{3}\cos\dfrac{14}{\sqrt{3}}t$
(4) Amp. = 0.1 m

(5) Periodic time $T = \dfrac{2\pi}{\omega} = \dfrac{\sqrt{3}\,\pi}{7}$ sec.

(6) Frequency $= f = \dfrac{1}{T} = \dfrac{\omega}{2\pi} = \dfrac{7}{\sqrt{3}\,\pi}$ cycles/sec.

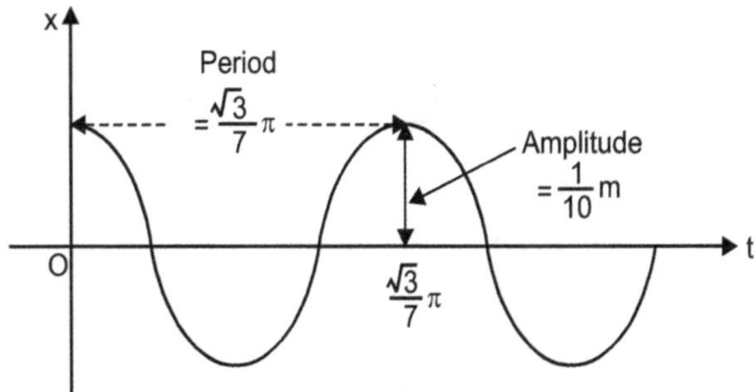

Fig. 2.2

Also, the position, velocity and acceleration of the weight 1/2 second after it has been released is obtained by putting t = 1/2 and using the fact that

$$\frac{7}{\sqrt{3}}\,\text{radian} = \frac{7}{\sqrt{3}}\,\frac{180}{\pi} = 231.56° \text{ approximately.}$$

(1) $x(t)|_{t=1/2} = (0.1)\cos\dfrac{14}{\sqrt{3}}t = -0.0622$

(2) $v|_{t=1/2} = \dfrac{dx}{dt}\bigg|_{t=1/2} = -(0.1)\dfrac{14}{\sqrt{3}}\sin\dfrac{14}{\sqrt{3}}t = 0.633$ m/sec

(3) $a|_{t=1/2} = \dfrac{d^2x}{dt^2}\bigg|_{t=1/2} = -(0.1)\dfrac{196}{3}\cos\dfrac{14}{\sqrt{3}}t = 4.064$ m/sec^2.

Remark : We note here that 1/2 seconds after the weight has been released, it is 0.0622 m above equilibrium position, is travelling downward with velocity 0.633 m/sec and has acceleration downward of 4.064 m/sec^2.

Ex. 2 : *In example 1 suppose the weight is pulled 10 cm below equilibrium position and is then given a downward velocity 60 cm/sec instead of being released from rest. Find the amplitude, period and frequency of motion.*

OR

A body of weight W = 3 N stretches a spring to 15 cm. If the weight is pulled down 10 cm below the equilibrium position and then given a downward velocity 60 cm/sec, determine the amplitude, period and frequency of motion.

Sol. : Differential equation is same as in the example 1.

$$\frac{d^2x}{dt^2} + \frac{196}{3}x = 0$$

A.E. is $D^2 + \dfrac{196}{3} = 0$ $\therefore$ $D = \pm\dfrac{14}{\sqrt{3}}i$

$$\text{G.S. is } x = c_1\cos\frac{14}{\sqrt{3}}t + c_2\sin\frac{14}{\sqrt{3}}t \qquad\qquad …(1)$$

Differentiating (1) with respect to t, we get

$$\frac{dx}{dt} = -c_1 \frac{14}{\sqrt{3}} \sin \frac{14}{\sqrt{3}} t + c_2 \frac{14}{\sqrt{3}} \cos \frac{14}{\sqrt{3}} t \qquad \ldots(2)$$

The initial conditions are $t = 0$, $x = 10$ cm $= 0.1$ m and the since the weight is given downward velocity 60 cm/sec $= 0.6$ m/sec, $t = 0$, $\frac{dx}{dt} = 0$. Using these conditions, we obtain

$$0.1 = c_1 \,(1) + c_2 \,(0) \Rightarrow c_1 = 0.1$$

$$0.6 = 0 + c_2 \frac{14}{\sqrt{3}} \,(1) \Rightarrow c_2 = \frac{3\sqrt{3}}{70}$$

Hence, $$x = 0.1 \cos \frac{14}{\sqrt{3}} t + \frac{3\sqrt{3}}{70} \sin \frac{14}{\sqrt{3}} t$$

or $$x = 0.125 \sin \left(\frac{14}{\sqrt{3}} t + \phi \right), \qquad \phi = 53°\,24' = 0.9337$$

(1) Amplitude $= 0.125$ m.

(2) Periodic time, $T = \dfrac{2\pi}{\omega} = \dfrac{\sqrt{3}\,\pi}{7}$ sec.

(3) Frequency $= f = \dfrac{1}{T} = \dfrac{\omega}{2\pi} = \dfrac{7}{\sqrt{3}\,\pi}$ cycles/sec.

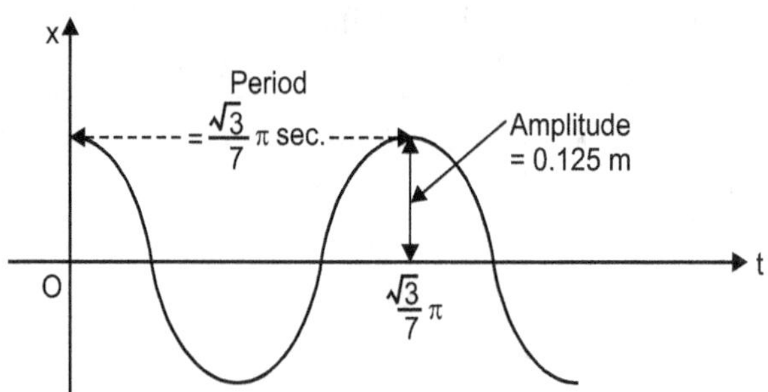

Fig. 2.3

Ex. 3 : *A body of weight W = 1 N is suspended from a spring stretches it 4 cm. If the weight is pulled down 8 cm below the equilibrium position and then released,*

(i)   Set-up a differential equation.

(ii) Find the position and velocity as function of time.

(iii) Find the amplitude, period and frequency of motion.

Sol. : Since a weight $W = 1$ N stretches a spring 4 cm $= 0.04$ m, by Hooke's law,

$$F_0 = k \, s_0 \Rightarrow 1 = k \times 0.04 \quad \therefore \ k = 25 \text{ N/m (or kg/s}^2)$$

By Newton's second law, the equation of motion of the body is

$$m \frac{d^2x}{dt^2} = -kx \quad \text{or} \quad \frac{W}{g} \frac{d^2x}{dt^2} = -kx$$

$$\therefore \quad \frac{1}{9.8} \frac{d^2x}{dt^2} = -25x \quad \text{or} \quad \frac{d^2x}{dt^2} + 245x = 0$$

which is a linear differential equation with constant coefficients.

$$\text{A.E. is } D^2 + 245 = 0 \quad \therefore \quad D = \pm i \sqrt{245}$$

$$\text{G.S. is } x = c_1 \cos \sqrt{245}\, t + c_2 \sin \sqrt{245}\, t \qquad \qquad \dots (1)$$

Differentiating (1) with respect to t, we get

$$\frac{dx}{dt} = -c_1 \sqrt{245} \sin \sqrt{245}\, t + c_2 \sqrt{245} \cos \sqrt{245}\, t \qquad \qquad \dots (2)$$

Using $x = 0.08$ at $t = 0$: $\qquad 0.08 = c_1(0) + c_2(0) \Rightarrow c_1 = 0.08$

Using $\dfrac{dx}{dt} = 0$ at $t = 0$: $\qquad 0 = 0 + c_2 \sqrt{245} \qquad \Rightarrow c_2 = 0$

Thus, we note that :

(1) $x(t) = (0.08) \cos \sqrt{245}\, t$ $\qquad \qquad$ (2) $v = \dfrac{dx}{dt} = -(0.08) \sqrt{245} \sin \sqrt{245}\, t$

(3) Amplitude $= 0.08$ m $\qquad \qquad$ (4) Periodic time $T = \dfrac{2\pi}{\omega} = \dfrac{2\pi}{\sqrt{245}}$ sec

(5) Frequency $= f = \dfrac{1}{T} = \dfrac{\omega}{2\pi} = \dfrac{\sqrt{245}}{2\pi}$ cycles/sec.

Note : For $(D^2 + \omega^2)\, x = 0$, roots are : $D = \pm i\omega$ and G.S. $= x = c_1 \cos \omega t + c_2 \sin \omega t$.

Ex. 4 : *A body weighing W = 20 N is hung from a spring. A pull of 40 N will stretch the spring to 10 cm. The body is pulled down to 20 cm below the static equilibrium position and then released. Find the displacement of the body from its equilibrium position in time t seconds, the maximum velocity and period of oscillation.*

Sol. : Since a pull of $W = 40$ N weight stretches a spring 10 cm $= 0.1$ m, by Hooke's law,

$$F_0 = k\, s_0 \Rightarrow 40 = k \times 0.1 \quad \therefore \quad k = 400 \text{ N/m}$$

By Newton's second law, the equation of motion of the body is

$$m \frac{d^2x}{dt^2} = -kx \quad \text{or} \quad \frac{W}{g} \frac{d^2x}{dt^2} = -kx$$

$$\therefore \quad \frac{20}{9.8} \frac{d^2x}{dt^2} = -400x \quad \text{or} \quad \frac{d^2x}{dt^2} + 196x = 0 \qquad \qquad \left(\because\ m = \frac{W}{g} \right)$$

which is a linear differential equation with constant coefficients.

$$\text{A.E. is } D^2 + 196 = 0 \quad \therefore \quad D = \pm 14i$$

$$\text{G.S. is } x = c_1 \cos 14t + c_2 \sin 14t \qquad \qquad \dots (1)$$

Differentiating (1) with respect to t, we get

$$\frac{dx}{dt} = -c_1\,14\sin\sqrt{245}\,t + c_2\,14\cos\sqrt{245}\,t \qquad \ldots (2)$$

The initial conditions are t = 0, x = 20 cm = 0.2 m and since the weight is released

$t = 0, \dfrac{dx}{dt} = 0.$ Using these conditions, we obtain

$$0.2 = c_1(1) + c_2(0) \ \Rightarrow \ c_1 = 0.2$$
$$0 = 0 + c_2\,14 \qquad \Rightarrow \ c_2 = 0$$

Thus, we note that :

(1) $x(t) = (0.2)\cos 14t$

(2) $v = \dfrac{dx}{dt} = -(0.2)\,14\sin 14t$

(3) Amplitude $= 0.2$ m

(4) Periodic time $T = \dfrac{2\pi}{\omega} = \dfrac{2\pi}{14} = \dfrac{\pi}{7}$ sec.

(5) Frequency $= f = \dfrac{1}{T} = \dfrac{\omega}{2\pi} = \dfrac{7}{\pi}$ cycles/sec.

Ex. 5 : *A body weighing 4.9 N is hung from a spring. A pull of 10 N will stretch the spring to 5 cm. The body is pulled down 6 cm below the static equilibrium position and then released. Find the displacement of the body from its equilibrium position in time t seconds, the maximum velocity and period of oscillation.*

Sol. : Since a pull of W = 10 N weight stretches a spring 5 cm = 0.05 m, by Hooke's law

$$F_0 = k\,s_0 \ \Rightarrow \ 10 = k \times 0.05 \quad \therefore \ k = 200\ \text{N/m}$$

By Newton's second law, the equation of motion of the body is

$$m\frac{d^2x}{dt^2} = -kx \quad \text{or} \quad \frac{W}{g}\frac{d^2x}{dt^2} = -kx \qquad (\because W = mg)$$

$$\therefore \qquad \frac{4.9}{9.8}\frac{d^2x}{dt^2} = -200x \quad \text{or} \quad \frac{d^2x}{dt^2} + 400x = 0$$

which is a linear differential equation with constant coefficients.

$$\text{A.E. is } D^2 + 200 = 0 \quad \therefore D = \pm 20i$$
$$\text{G.S. is } x = c_1\cos 20t + c_2\sin 20t \qquad \ldots (1)$$

Differentiating (1) with respect to t, we get

$$\frac{dx}{dt} = -c_1\,20\sin 20t + c_2\,20\cos 20t \qquad \ldots (2)$$

The initial conditions are t = 0, x = 6 cm = 0.06 m and since the weight is released

$t = 0, \dfrac{dx}{dt} = 0.$ Using these conditions, we obtain

$$0.06 = c_1(1) + c_2(0) \Rightarrow c_1 = 0.06$$
$$0 = 0 + c_2\,20(1) \Rightarrow c_2 = 0$$

Thus, we note that :

(1) $x(t) = (0.06) \cos 20t$

(2) $v = \dfrac{dx}{dt} = -(0.06)\, 20 \sin 20t$ m/sec

(3) Amplitude $= 0.06$ m

(4) Periodic time, $T = \dfrac{2\pi}{\omega} = \dfrac{2\pi}{20} = \dfrac{\pi}{10}$ sec.

(5) Frequency $= f = \dfrac{1}{T} = \dfrac{\omega}{2\pi} = \dfrac{10}{\pi}$ cycles/sec.

2.4 DAMPED SYSTEM (FREE, DAMPED OSCILLATION)

If the motion of the mass m be subjected to an additional force of resistance (damping or frictional forces of medium), the oscillations are said to be damped.

If we connect the dashpot (See Fig. 2.4), we have to take corresponding viscous damping into account. The corresponding damping force has direction opposite to the instantaneous motion. We assume that it is proportional to the velocity $\dfrac{dx}{dt}$ of the body. (For small velocities this is a good approximation.) Thus the damping is of the form

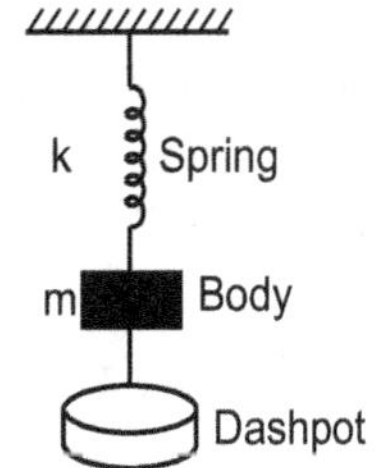

Fig. 2.4 : Damped System

$$F_2 = -c\,\frac{dx}{dt}$$

$c\,(>0)$, constant of proportionality, is called the damping constant.

The resultant force acting on the body is now

$$F_1 + F_2 = -kx - c\,\frac{dx}{dt}$$

Hence, by Newton's second law, motion of the mass with damping force is

$$m\frac{d^2x}{dt^2} + c\frac{dx}{dt} + kx = 0 \quad \text{or} \quad \frac{d^2x}{dt^2} + \frac{c}{m}\frac{dx}{dt} + \frac{k}{m}x = 0$$

Remark : Using short notations $2b = c/m$ and $\omega^2 = k/m$ above equation can be written as

$$\frac{d^2x}{dt^2} + 2b\frac{dx}{dt} + \omega^2 x = 0 \qquad \qquad \dots (9)$$

This shows that the motion of the damped mechanical system is governed by the linear differential equation with constant coefficients. The auxiliary equation of (9) is

$$\lambda^2 + 2b\lambda + \omega^2 = 0$$

The roots are $\lambda_{1,2} = -b \pm \sqrt{b^2 - \omega^2}$ $\qquad \qquad \dots (10)$

The motion of the mass depends on the damping through the nature of discriminant $b^2 - \omega^2$. We note the following three cases :

Case I : $b^2 - \omega^2 > 0$ i.e. $c^2 > 4mk$ Distinct real roots   (Overdamping)

Case II : $b^2 - \omega^2 = 0$ i.e. $c^2 > 4mk$ Repeated real roots   (Critical damping)

Case III : $b^2 - \omega^2 < 0$ i.e. $c^2 > 4mk$ Complex conjugate roots   (Underdamping)

ILLUSTRATION

Ex. 6 : *If a damping force given in N by c = 1.5 kg/s times the velocity in meter per second acts on the weight in the solved example 1 of Article 2.3.*

(i)   Set-up the differential equation and the associated conditions.

(ii) Find the position x of the weight as a function of time.

Sol. : Considering the damping force $- 1.5 \dfrac{dx}{dt}$ in example 1, we write the equation

of motion : $\dfrac{3}{9.8} \dfrac{d^2x}{dt^2} = - 20x - 1.5 \dfrac{dx}{dt}$

$$\Rightarrow \qquad \frac{d^2x}{dt^2} + 4.9 \frac{dx}{dt} + \frac{196}{3} = 0 \qquad \qquad \text{... (1)}$$

The initial conditions are same as in Ex. 1.

i.e. at   t = 0, $x = \dfrac{1}{10}$ m and $\dfrac{dx}{dt} = 0$ $\qquad\qquad$ ... (2)

$$\text{A.E. is } D^2 + 4.9\,D + \frac{196}{3} = 0 \quad \Rightarrow \quad D = -2.45 \pm i\,7.7$$

Hence the general solution of equation (1) will be,

$$x = e^{-(2.45)\,t} [A \cos (7.7)\,t + B \sin (7.7)\,t] \qquad\qquad \text{... (3)}$$

If we apply conditions (2) to this solution, then we have

$$x = e^{-(2.45)\,t} [(0.1) \cos (7.7)\,t + (0.032) \sin (7.7)\,t] \qquad\qquad \text{... (4)}$$

as the complete solution. Which can be written in the form :

$$x = (0.105)\,e^{-(2.45)\,t} \sin [(7.7)\,t + 1.261] \qquad\qquad \text{... (5)}$$

The graph of equation (5) shown in Fig. 3.5 lies between the graphs of

$$x = + 0.105\,e^{-(2.45)\,t} \quad \text{and} \quad x = -0.105\,e^{-(2.45)\,t}$$

[Shown dashed in Fig. 3.5] since sine function varies between −1 and +1.

The constant difference in times between successive maxima (or minima) i.e. $\dfrac{2\pi}{7.7}$ is

called the *Quasi period* (i.e. between the points 0 and T on the t axis).

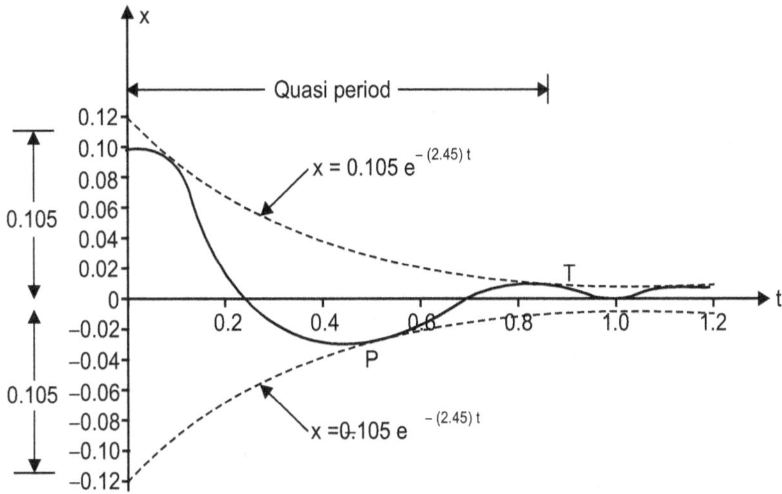

Fig. 2.5

Summary : The motion described in this example is called *Damped oscillatory* or *Damped vibratory* motion. Here equation (5) has the form

$$x = A(t) \sin(\omega t + \phi) \qquad \ldots (6)$$

where $\qquad A(t) = 0.105\, e^{-(2.45)t}$, $\omega = 7.7$ and $\phi = 1.261$

The *quasi period* is given by

$$\frac{2\pi}{\omega} = \frac{2\pi}{7.7}$$

By analogy with the undamped case, A (t) is called *Amplitude* or more exactly *Time-varying amplitude.* It is seen that the amplitude decreases with time, thus agreeing with our experience. Also frequency with damping is less than that without damping. This is possible because one would expect opposition to motion to increase the time for a complete cycle. The undamped frequency i.e. with $\beta = 0$ is often called the *Natural frequency.* It is of great importance in connection with the phenomenon of *Resonance* to be discussed later.

Note : Sometimes the damping force may be too great compared to the restoring force to permit oscillatory motion. This type of motion is called as *Overdamped motion.*

When damping is such that any decrease in it produces oscillations, the motion is called *Critically damped.*

2.5 MASS-SPRING SYSTEM (FORCED OSCILLATIONS)

Earlier we have discussed the problems of spring where only restoring and damping forces were working inspite of the weight W. We now consider cases where other external forces which depend on time may also act. Such forces may occur, for example, when the support holding the spring is moved-up and down in a prescribed manner such as in periodic motion or when the weight is given a little push everytime it reaches the lowest position. If we denote the external force by F(t), the differential equation of motion is,

$$\frac{W}{g}\frac{d^2x}{dt^2} = -kx - c\frac{dx}{dt} + F(t)$$

or $\qquad \dfrac{W}{g}\dfrac{d^2x}{dt^2} + c\dfrac{dx}{dt} + kx = F(t) \qquad\qquad\qquad (W = mg)$

This equation is called the *equation of forced vibrations*. In what follows, we shall now discuss the behaviour of mechanical system for two cases :

(i) damped forced oscillations (c > 0) and (ii) undamped forced oscillations (resonance, c = 0).

Remark : Using short notations, above equation can be written as

$$\frac{d^2x}{dt^2} + 2b\frac{dx}{dt} + \omega^2 x = F_1(t)$$

$$2b = \frac{cg}{W} = \frac{c}{m}, \quad \omega^2 = \frac{kg}{W} = \frac{k}{m} \quad \text{and} \quad F_1(t) = \frac{g}{W}F(t)$$

ILLUSTRATION

Ex. 7 : *In the previous solved example 6, assume that a periodic external force given by* $F(t) = 24\cos\dfrac{14}{\sqrt{3}}t$ *is acting. Find x in terms of t, using conditions given there.*

Sol. : The differential equation will be

$$\frac{3}{9.8}\frac{d^2x}{dt^2} = -20x - 1.5\frac{dx}{dt} + 24\cos\frac{14}{\sqrt{3}}t$$

or $\qquad \dfrac{d^2x}{dt^2} + 4.9\dfrac{dx}{dt} + \dfrac{196}{3}x = 78.4\cos\dfrac{14}{\sqrt{3}}t \qquad\qquad \dots (1)$

with the initial conditions $\quad x = \dfrac{1}{10}, \quad \dfrac{dx}{dt} = 0 \quad$ at $\quad t = 0 \qquad\qquad \dots (2)$

If we solve equation (1), the complementary function is given by,

$$\text{C.F.} = x_c = e^{-(2.45)t}[A\cos(7.7)t + B\sin(7.7)t]$$

and particular integral is

$$\text{P.I.} = x_p = \frac{1}{D^2 + 4.9D + \dfrac{196}{3}}\,78.4\cos\frac{14}{\sqrt{3}}t = 1.979\sin\frac{14}{\sqrt{3}}t$$

Hence the general solution of equation (1) is

$$x = x_c + x_p = e^{-(2.45)t}[A\cos(7.7)t + B\sin(7.7)t] + 1.979\sin\frac{14}{\sqrt{3}}t \ \dots (3)$$

and using the initial conditions (2), we have

$$A = \frac{1}{10}, \quad B = -2.046$$

and hence $\quad x = e^{-(2.45)t}[1\cos(7.7)t - (2.046)\sin(7.7)t] + 1.979\sin\dfrac{14}{\sqrt{3}}t \ \dots (4)$

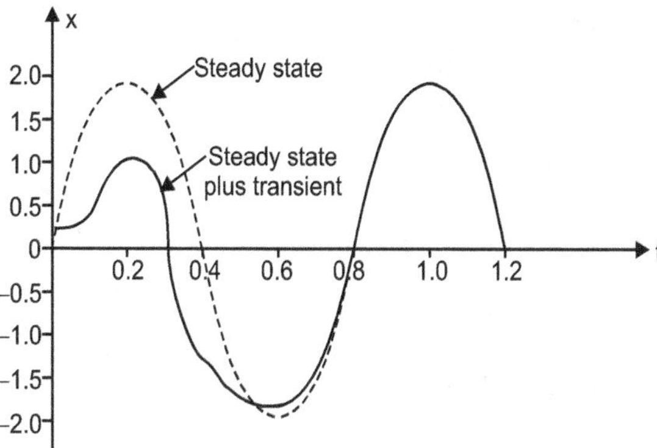

Fig. 2.6

The graph of equation (3) is given in Fig. 2.6. It will be seen that the terms in equation (4) involving $e^{-(2.45)\,t}$, become negligible (die down) when t is large. These terms are called *Transient terms* and are of value only when t is near zero, and these terms in the solution, when they are significant are called *Transient solution.* But when the transient terms are negligible, the term $1.979\ \sin \dfrac{14}{\sqrt{3}}$ t remains. This is called the *Steady state solution* since it indicates the behaviour of the system when things have become steady. It is seen that steady state solution (shown dashed curve in Fig. 2.6) is periodic, having same period as that of applied external force.

2.6 MECHANICAL FORCE

When the frequency of a periodic external force, applied to a mechanical system is *related to the natural frequency* of the system, *Mechanical resonance* may occur, which builds-up the oscillations to such tremendous magnitudes that the system itself may fall apart. A company of soldiers marching in step across a bridge may in this manner cause the bridge to collapse even though it would have been strong enough to carry many more soldiers had they marched out of step. Similarly, it may be possible for a musical note of proper characteristic frequency to shatter a glass. Hence mechanical resonance in general should be avoided by engineers designing structure of vibrating mechanism. The example below will indicate what may be the consequence of resonance.

ILLUSTRATIONS

Ex. 8 : *Suppose an external force given by* $6 \cos \dfrac{14}{\sqrt{3}}$ t *is applied to the spring of the solved example 1 of Art. 2.3. Describe the motion which ensures if it is assumed that initially the weight is at the equilibrium position (x = 0) and that its initial velocity is zero.*

Sol. : The differential equation will be

$$\frac{3}{9.8} \frac{d^2x}{dt^2} = -20\,x + 6 \cos \frac{14}{\sqrt{3}}\ t$$

or
$$\frac{d^2x}{dt^2} + \frac{196}{3}\,x = 19.6 \cos \frac{14}{\sqrt{3}}\ t \qquad \qquad \dots (1)$$

and the initial conditions are

$$x = 0, \qquad \frac{dx}{dt} = 0 \ \text{ at } \ t = 0 \qquad\qquad \text{... (2)}$$

The solution will be (general solution),

$$x = A \cos \frac{14}{\sqrt{3}}\, t + B \sin \frac{14}{\sqrt{3}}\, t + 1.212\, t \sin \frac{14}{\sqrt{3}}\, t \qquad \text{... (3)}$$

and using initial condition, it will be (A = 0 = B)

$$x = 1.212\, t \sin \frac{14}{\sqrt{3}}\, t \qquad\qquad \text{... (4)}$$

Graph of equation (4) will lie between the graphs of x = 1.212 t and x = – 1.212 t as shown in Fig. 2.7.

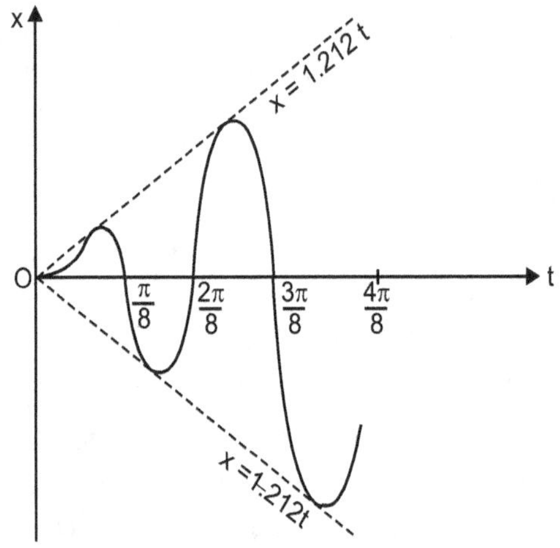

Fig. 2.7

It is seen from the graph that oscillations build-up without limit. Naturally the spring is bound to break within a short time.

It should be noted here that damping was neglected and *Resonance* occurred because the *frequency of the applied external force was equal to the Natural frequency of the undamped system.* This is a general principle. In the case where damping occurs, the oscillations do not build-up without limit but may sometimes become large.

Ex. 9 : *A spring stretches 1 cm under the tension of 2 N and has a negligible weight. It is fixed at one end and is attached to a weight W Newton at the other. It is found that resonance occurs when an axial periodic force 2 cos 2t N acts on the weight. Show that when the free vibrations have died out, the forced vibrations are given by x = ct sin 2t and find the values of W and c.*

Sol. : A weight of 2 N stretches the spring by $\frac{1}{100}$ m

$$\therefore \quad 2 = T = k \cdot \frac{1}{100} \Rightarrow k = 200 \text{ N/m}$$

Let B be the equilibrium position of the weight W attached to A, then

$$W = T_B = k \cdot AB = 200\, AB$$

$$\Rightarrow \qquad AB = \frac{W}{200}\ m$$

At any time t, let the weight be at P where BP = x. Then the tension T at P

$$= k \cdot AP = 200\left(\frac{W}{200} + x\right) = W + 200\,x$$

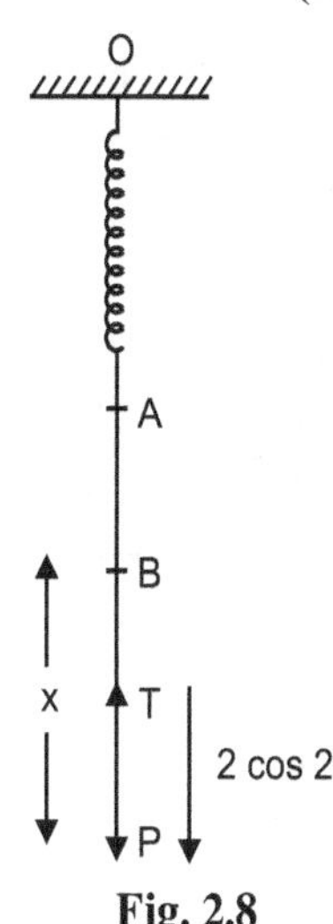

Fig. 2.8

∴   Equation of motion is,

$$\frac{W}{g}\frac{d^2x}{dt^2} = -T + W + 2\cos 2t$$

$$\Rightarrow \qquad \frac{W}{g}\frac{d^2x}{dt^2} = -W - 200\,x + W + 2\cos 2t$$

Or $\qquad \dfrac{d^2x}{dt^2} + 200\,\dfrac{gx}{W} = \dfrac{2g}{W}\cos 2t \qquad\qquad\qquad \ldots (1)$

The phenomenon of resonance will occur when the frequency of free oscillations is equal to the frequency of forced oscillations or (the period of free oscillations is equal to the period of forced oscillations).

If we write equation (1) as $\dfrac{d^2x}{dt^2} + \omega^2 x = \dfrac{2g}{W}\cos 2t$ where, $\omega^2 = \dfrac{200\,g}{W}$, the period of free oscillations is found to be $\dfrac{2\pi}{\omega}$ and the period of the forced oscillations is $2\pi/2 = \pi$.

Hence $\qquad \dfrac{2\pi}{\omega} = \pi \Rightarrow \omega = 2 \quad$ or $\quad \dfrac{200\,g}{W} = \omega^2 = 4$

hence $\qquad W = 50\,g$

Taking this value of W in equation (1), we have

$$\frac{d^2x}{dt^2} + 4x = \frac{1}{25} \cos 2t \qquad \ldots (2)$$

Now free oscillations are given by C.F. and forced oscillations by the P.I. Hence when the free oscillations have died out, the forced oscillations are given by the P.I. of (2).

$$\text{Now P.I. of equation (2)} = \frac{1}{25} \frac{1}{D^2 + 4} \cos 2t = \frac{1}{25} t \frac{1}{2D} \cdot \cos 2t$$

$$= \frac{1}{100} t \sin 2t = ct \sin 2t$$

$$\text{Hence } c = \frac{1}{100}$$

Ex. 10 : *A body of weight 9.8 N is suspended from a spring having constant 4 N/m. Prove that the motion is one of resonance if a force 16 sin 2t is applied and damping force is negligible. Assume that initially the weight is at rest in the equilibrium position.*

Sol. : The differential equation describing phenomenon is

$$m \frac{d^2x}{dt^2} + kx = F(t)$$

$$\frac{9.8}{9.8} \frac{d^2x}{dt^2} + 4x = 16 \sin 2t$$

or

$$\frac{d^2x}{dt^2} + 4x = 16 \sin 2t$$

A.E. is $D^2 + 4 = 0$, Roots are $D = \pm 2i$

C.F. $= c_1 \cos 2t + c_2 \sin 2t$

$$\text{P.I.} = 16 \frac{1}{D^2 + 4} \sin 2t = -4t \cos 2t$$

G.S. $= x(t) = c_1 \cos 2t + c_2 \sin 2t - 4t \cos 2t$

Using $x = 0$ at $t = 0$,

$$0 = c_1 (1) + c_2 (0) - 0 \quad \therefore \ c_1 = 0$$

$\therefore \qquad x(t) = c_2 \sin 2t - 4t \cos 2t.$

Differentiating $x(t)$ with respect to t,

$$\frac{dx}{dt} = 2c_2 \cos 2t - 4 \cos 2t + 8t \sin 2t$$

Using $\dfrac{dx}{dt} = 0$ at $t = 0$,

$$0 = 2c_2 (1) - 4(1) + 8(0) \quad \therefore \ c_2 = 2$$

The position of weight at any time is

$$x(t) = 2 \sin 2t - 4t \cos 2t$$

and its velocity is

$$\frac{dx}{dt} = 4 \cos 2t - 4 \cos 2t + 8t \sin 2t$$

We note that frequency external force is $\dfrac{2}{2\pi} = \dfrac{1}{\pi}$ cycles/sec. Natural frequency of the free undamped system is $\dfrac{\omega}{2\pi} = \dfrac{2}{2\pi} = \dfrac{1}{\pi}$ cycles/sec. Therefore, resonance occurs in the system because the frequency of the external force equals to natural frequency of the system.

Ex. 11 : *A spring which stretches by an amount e under a force mk^2e is suspended from a support P and has a mass 'm' at its lower end. At time $t = 0$, the mass is at rest in its equilibrium position at a point A below P. A vertical oscillation is now given to the support P such that at any time its displacement below its initial position is 'a sin nt'. Show that the displacement x of the mass below A is*

$$\frac{d^2x}{dt^2} + k^2x = k^2 a \sin nt$$

Hence show that if $n \neq k$, the displacement is given by

$$x = \frac{ka}{k^2 - n^2}(k \sin nt - n \sin kt)$$

Sol. : A spring under the action of force mk^2e stretches by an amount e. By Hooke's law,

$$mk^2e = \lambda e \Rightarrow \lambda = mk^2$$

Also, given external periodic force (vertical oscillation) is λ (a sin nt). Therefore, by Newton's second law, the equation of motion is

$$m\frac{d^2x}{dt^2} + \lambda x = \lambda \,(a \sin nt)$$

or $\qquad m\dfrac{d^2x}{dt} + mk^2x = mk^2 \,(a \sin nt)$

or $\qquad \dfrac{d^2x}{dt^2} + k^2x = k^2a \, \sin nt$

$$\text{C.F.} = c_1 \cos kt + c_2 \sin kt$$

$$\text{P.I.} = k^2a \frac{1}{D^2 + k^2} \sin nt = k^2a \frac{1}{(k^2 - n^2)} \sin nt, \ k \neq n$$

$$x = c_1 \cos kt + c_2 \sin kt + ka^2 \frac{1}{(k^2 - n^2)} \sin nt$$

Differentiating with respect to t,

$$\frac{dx}{dt} = -kc_1 \sin kt + kc_2 \cos kt + ka^2n \frac{1}{(k^2-n^2)} \cos nt$$

Using $x = 0$ at $t = 0$,

$$0 = c_1(1) + c_2(0) + 0 \quad \therefore \quad c_1 = 0$$

Using $\dfrac{dx}{dt} = 0$ at $t = 0$,

$$0 = k\,c_1(0) + k\,c_2(1) + k^2an \frac{1}{(k^2-n^2)}(1) \quad \therefore \quad c_2 = -\frac{kan}{k^2-n^2}$$

Hence, if $n \neq k$, the displacement is given by

$$x = -\frac{kan}{k^2-n^2} \sin kt + \frac{k^2a}{k^2-n^2} \sin nt$$

or

$$x = \frac{ka}{k^2-n^2}(k \sin nt - n \sin kt) \text{ when } k \neq n.$$

2.7 COUPLED MASSES

In coupled masses, we get a good application of simultaneous equations, an example will explain better.

ILLUSTRATION

Ex. 12 : *Two particles, each of mass m gram are suspended from two springs of same stiffness k as shown in Fig. 3.9. After the system comes to rest, the lower mass is pulled l cm, downward and released. Discuss their motion.*

Sol. : Let x and y be the displacements of the upper and lower masses, at time t from their respective positions of equilibrium.

Then the stretch of the upper spring is x and that of the lower spring is $y - x$.

$\therefore$ Restoring force acting on the upper mass $= -kx + k(y-x) = k(y-2x)$
and that on the lower mass $= -k(y-x)$

Hence their equations of motion are :

$$m\frac{d^2x}{dt^2} = k(y-2x) \text{ and}$$

$$m\frac{d^2y}{dt^2} = -k(y-x)$$

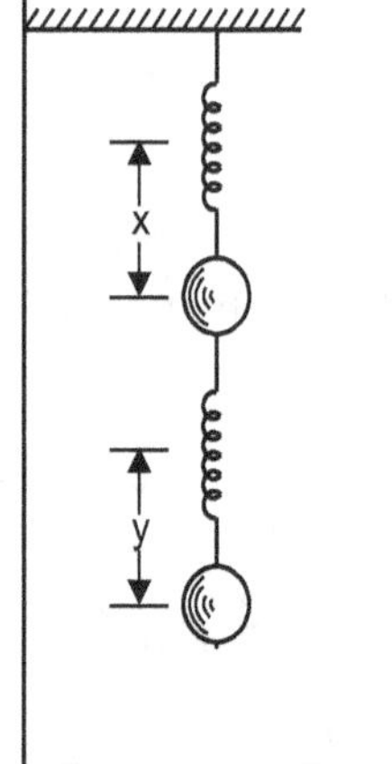

Fig. 2.9

or $\qquad (mD^2 + 2k)x - ky = 0$ $\qquad\qquad$ ... (1)

and $\qquad (mD^2 + k)y - kx = 0$ $\qquad\qquad$ ... (2)

which are the linear simultaneous equations. Operating (1) by $(mD^2 + k)$ and adding to k times (2), we get

$$[(mD^2 + k)(mD^2 + 2k) - k^2]x = 0$$

or $\qquad (D^4 + 3\lambda D^2 + \lambda^2)\, x = 0, \quad$ where $\lambda = \dfrac{k}{m}$.

Its auxiliary equation is $\ D^4 + 3\lambda D^2 + \lambda^2 = 0$

which gives $\qquad D^2 = \dfrac{-3\lambda \pm \sqrt{9\lambda^2 - 4\lambda^2}}{2} = -2.62\,\lambda \ \text{ or } \ -0.38\,\lambda$

$$= -\alpha^2, \ -\beta^2 \ \text{(say)}$$

So that $\qquad D = \pm i\alpha, \ \pm i\beta.$

Hence $\qquad x = C_1 \cos \alpha t + C_2 \sin \alpha t + C_3 \cos \beta t + C_4 \sin \beta t \qquad \ldots (3)$

Also from equation (1), $\ y = \left(\dfrac{D^2}{\lambda} + 2\right) x$

$\therefore \ \ y = \left(2 - \dfrac{\alpha^2}{\lambda}\right)(C_1 \cos \alpha t + C_2 \sin \alpha t) + \left(2 - \dfrac{\beta^2}{\lambda}\right)(C_3 \cos \beta t + C_4 \sin \beta t) \ \ \ldots (4)$

But initially when $t = 0$, $\ x = y = l$, $\ \dfrac{dx}{dt} = 0 = \dfrac{dy}{dt}$

Hence from (3), $\ C_1 + C_3 = l \ \ $ and $C_2\,\alpha + C_4\,\beta = 0$

and from (4), $\qquad l = \left(2 - \dfrac{\alpha^2}{\lambda}\right) C_1 + \left(2 - \dfrac{\beta^2}{\lambda}\right) C_3$

$$0 = \left(2 - \dfrac{\alpha^2}{\lambda}\right) \alpha\, C_2 + \left(2 - \dfrac{\beta^2}{\lambda}\right) \beta C_4$$

when $\qquad C_1 = \dfrac{l\,(\lambda - \beta^2)}{\alpha^2 - \beta^2}, \quad C_3 = \dfrac{l\,(\lambda - \alpha^2)}{\beta^2 - \alpha^2}, \ \ C_2 = C_4 = 0$

Substituting these values of the constants in (3) and (4), we get x and y which show that the motion of the string is a combination of two simple harmonic motions of periods $\dfrac{2\pi}{\alpha}$ and $\dfrac{2\pi}{\beta}$.

2.8 WHIRLING OF SHAFTS

A shaft is a bar or a rod joining parts of a machine, which transmits power to the machine.

2.9 CRITICAL OR WHIRLING SPEEDS

Ordinary a shaft does not rotate about its geometrical axis because there is always some non-symmetrical crookedness in the shaft., but the dead weight of the shaft causes deflection which tends to become large at certain speeds. The speed at which the deflection of the shaft reaches a stage where it may develop fracture unless the speed is lowered is called critical or whirling speed of the shaft.

2.10 DIFFERNTIAL EQUATION OF A ROTATING SHAFT

Consider a shaft of weight W per unit length which is rotating with angular velocity ω. Take its original along horizontal position and the vertical downwards through the end O as the axes of x and y.

We assume that the intensity of the restoring force of the shaft at a point x from some fixed origin is $EI\dfrac{d^4y}{dx^4}$. Where y coordinate is the deflection of the point, E is modular of elasticity, I is moment of inertia of the cross-section. For an element of length δx the restoring force is $EI\dfrac{d^4y}{dx^4}\delta x$ as W is the weight per unit length , therefore $\dfrac{W}{g}\delta x$ is the mass of the element δx, the acceleration of the element along the normal to its length is $y\omega^2$. Therefore centrifugal force is equal to $\dfrac{W}{g}\delta x\, y\omega^2$.

Thus,
$$EI\frac{d^4y}{dx^4}\delta x = \frac{W}{g}\delta x\, y\omega^2$$

$$\Rightarrow \qquad \frac{d^4y}{dx^4} = \frac{W}{g}\frac{\omega^2}{EI}y \ \text{ i.e. } \ \frac{d^4y}{dx^4} - \frac{W}{g}\frac{\omega^2}{EI}y = 0$$

$$\frac{d^4y}{dx^4} - a^4 y = 0$$

Let
$$a^4 = \frac{W}{g}\frac{\omega^2}{EI}$$

Which is the required differential equation of rotating shaft.

Auxiliary equation is
$$D^4 - a^4 = 0 \Rightarrow D = \pm a, \pm ai$$

Hence solution is $\qquad y = C_1 e^{ax} + C_2 e^{-ax} + C_3 \cos ax + C_4 \sin ax$

Which may be put in a better form as
$$y = A \cosh ax + B \sinh ax + C \cos ax + D \sin ax$$

ILLUSTRATION

Ex. 1 : *The differential equation of a whirling shaft is given by* $EI\dfrac{d^4y}{dx^4} - W\dfrac{\omega^2}{g}y = W$ where W is the weight of the shaft and ω is the whirling speed. Taking length of the shaft as 2*l* and origin at the centre and $y = 0$; $\dfrac{d^2y}{dx^2} = 0$ for $x = \pm\, l$.

Prove that $\qquad y = \dfrac{g}{2\omega^2}\left[\dfrac{\cos ax}{\cos al} + \dfrac{\cosh ax}{\cosh al} - 2\right]$

$$W\frac{\omega^2}{EIg} = a^4$$

Sol. : Given

$$EI\frac{d^4y}{dx^4} - W\frac{\omega^2}{g}y = W \text{ dividing by } EI\frac{d^4y}{dx^4} - W\frac{\omega^2}{g}y = W$$

$$\frac{d^4y}{dx^4} - \frac{W\omega^2}{EIg}y = \frac{W}{EI}$$

i.e.
$$\frac{d^4y}{dx^4} - a^4y = \frac{W}{EI}$$

$$\therefore \qquad a^4 = \frac{W\omega^2}{EIg}$$

Auxiliary equation is $D^4 - a^4 = 0 \Rightarrow D \pm a, \pm ai$

Hence Complementary function C.F.is

$$y = A\cosh ax + B\sinh ax + C\cos ax + D\sin ax$$

Now for Particular Integral,

$$P.I = \frac{1}{D^4 - a^4}\frac{W}{EI} = \frac{-1}{a^4\left[1 - \frac{D^4}{a^4}\right]}\frac{W}{EI}$$

$$P.I = \frac{-1}{a^4}\left[1 - \frac{D^4}{a^4}\right]^{-1}\frac{W}{EI}$$

$$P.I = \frac{-1}{a^4}\left[1 + \frac{D^4}{a^4} + \dots\right]\frac{W}{EI} = \frac{-1}{a^4}\frac{W}{EI}$$

$$\Rightarrow \qquad P.I = \frac{-g}{\omega^2} \qquad \because a^4 = \frac{W\omega^2}{EIg}$$

Thus complete solution of the given equation is

$$y = A\cosh ax + B\sinh ax + C\cos ax + D\sin ax - \frac{g}{\omega^2} \qquad \dots(A)$$

Differentiating w. r. t x, we get

$$\frac{1}{a}\frac{dy}{dx} = A\sinh ax + B\cosh ax - C\sin ax + D\cos ax \qquad \dots(B)$$

$$\frac{1}{a}\frac{d^2y}{dx^2} = A\cosh ax + B\sinh ax - C\cos ax - D\sin ax \qquad \dots(C)$$

As $x = \pm l$, $y = 0$, $\dfrac{d^4y}{dx^4} = 0$ sub in equation (A) and (C) we get

$$0 = A\cosh al + B\sinh al + C\cos al + D\sin al - \frac{g}{\omega^2}$$

$$0 = A\cosh al - B\sinh al + C\cos al - D\sin al - \frac{g}{\omega^2} \qquad \dots(D)$$

$$\left. \begin{aligned} 0 &= A \cosh al + B \sinh al - C \cos al - D \sin al \\ 0 &= A \cosh al - B \sinh al - C \cos al + D \sin al \end{aligned} \right\} \qquad \ldots(E)$$

From equation (D)

$$2A \cosh al + 2C \cos al = \frac{2g}{\omega^2} \Rightarrow A \cosh al + \cos al = \frac{g}{\omega^2} \qquad \ldots(F)$$

From equation (E)

$$2A \cosh al - 2C \cos al = 0 \Rightarrow A \cosh al - C \cos al = 0 \qquad \ldots(G)$$

Adding equation (F) and (G), we get

$$2A \cosh al = \frac{g}{\omega^2} \Rightarrow A = \frac{g}{2\omega^2 \cosh al}$$

Again subtracting equation (F) and (G), we get

$$2C \cos al = \frac{g}{\omega^2} \Rightarrow C = \frac{g}{2\omega^2 \cosh al}$$

Further from equation (D) and (E), we get

$$B \sin al + D \sin al = 0 \text{ and } B \sinh al - D \sinh al = 0$$

$$\Rightarrow \qquad B \sinh al = 0 \text{ by adding above equations } \Rightarrow B = 0 \;\because\; al \neq 0$$

$$\text{and} \qquad D \sin al = 0 \text{ by subtracting above equations} \Rightarrow D = 0 \;\because\; al \neq 0$$

Substituting the values of A,B,C and D in equation (A) we get

$$y = \frac{g}{2\omega^2 \cosh al} \cosh ax + \frac{g}{2\omega^2 \cosh al} \sin ax - \frac{g}{\omega^2}$$

i.e.

$$y = \frac{g}{2\omega^2}\left[\frac{\cos x}{\cos al} - 2\right], \; w\frac{\omega^2}{EIg} = a^4$$

Ex. 2 : *The whirling speed of a shaft of length l is given by* $\dfrac{d^4 y}{dx^4} - a^4 y = 0$ *where*

$a^4 = W\dfrac{\omega^2}{gEI}.$ y is the displacement at a distance x from one end of the shaft. If the ends of the shaft are constrained in long bearing, so that the slopes at both ends are zero. Prove that the shaft will whirl when cosh al cos $al = 1$.

Sol. : Given $\quad (D^4 - a^4)\, y = 0$

Auxiliary equation is $D^4 - a^4 = 0 \Rightarrow D = \pm a, \pm ai$

Hence Complementary function C.F. is

$$y = A \cosh ax + B \sinh ax + C \cos ax + D \sin ax \qquad \ldots(A)$$

Differentiating w. r. t x we get

$$\frac{1}{a}\frac{dy}{dx} = A \sinh ax + B \cosh ax - C \sin ax + D \cos ax \qquad \ldots(B)$$

As slope at both ends are zero, wet have $\dfrac{dy}{dx} = 0$ when $x = 0$, $y = 0$

and $\dfrac{dy}{dx} = 0$ when $x = l$, $y = 0$.

Substituting $\dfrac{dy}{dx} = 0$ when $x = 0$, $y = 0$ in equation (A) and (B) we get

$$0 = A + C \Rightarrow A = -C$$

$$0 = B + D \Rightarrow B = -D$$

Again Substituting $\dfrac{dy}{dx} = 0$ when $x = l$, $y = 0$ in equation (A) and (B) we get

$$0 = A \cosh al + B \sinh al + C \cos al + D \sin al \qquad \text{...(C)}$$

and $\qquad 0 = B \sinh al + B \cosh al - C \sin al + D \cos al \qquad \text{...(D)}$

Putting $\qquad A = -C,\ B = -D$

$$0 = A\,[\cosh - \cos al] + B\,[\sinh al - \sin al] \qquad \text{...(E)}$$

and $\qquad 0 = A\,[\sinh a + \sin al] + B\,[\cosh al - \cos al] \qquad \text{...(F)}$

From equation (E) and (F), we get

$$\frac{A}{B} = -\frac{\sinh al - \cos al}{\cosh al - \cos al} \quad \text{and} \quad \frac{A}{B} = -\frac{\cosh al - \cos al}{\sinh al + \sin al}$$

$$\therefore \qquad \frac{\sinh al - \sin al}{\cosh al - \cos al} = \frac{\cosh al - \cos al}{\sinh al + \sin al}$$

$$(\sin al - \sin al)\,(\sinh al + \sin al) = (\cosh al - \cos al)\,(\cosh al - \cos al)$$

$$\sinh^2 al \sin^2 al = \cosh^2 al - 2\cosh al \cos al \cos^2 al$$

$$2\cosh al \cos al = \cosh^2 al - \sinh^2 al + \cos^2 al + \sin^2 al$$

$$\Rightarrow \qquad 2\cosh al \cos al = 1 + 1$$

$$\therefore \qquad 2\cosh al \cos al = 2 \Rightarrow \cosh al \cos al = 1$$

EXERCISE 2.1

1. A 1 N weight suspended from a spring stretches it 4 cm. If the weight is pulled 8 cm below the equilibrium position and released,

    (a) Set-up a differential equation and conditions describing the motion.

    (b) Find the velocity and the position of the weight as a function of time.

    (c) Find the amplitude, period and frequency of the motion.

    (d) Determine the position, velocity and acceleration $\dfrac{\pi}{64}$ sec. after the weight is released.

$$\textbf{Ans.}\ \text{(b)}\ \ x = \frac{2}{25} \cos\,(15.65)\,t,\ \ v = -1.252 \sin\,(15.65)\,t$$

$$\text{(c)}\ \ \text{Amplitude} = \frac{2}{25}\ \text{m},\ \ \text{Period} = T = \frac{\pi}{7.825}\ \text{sec.}$$

$$\text{Frequency} = f = \frac{7.825}{\pi}\ \text{cycles/sec.}$$

2. A 1.5 N weight on a spring stretches it 15 cm. When equilibrium is reached the weight is struck so as to give it a downward velocity of 60 cm/sec. Find :

(a) The velocity and position of the weight at time t sec. after the impact.

(b) The amplitude, period and frequency of the motion.

(c) The velocity and acceleration when the weight is 2.5 cm from the equilibrium position and moving upward.

Ans. (a) $x = (0.074) \sin (8.08) t$, $v = (0.598) \cos (8.08) t$ (ft/sec.)

(b) Amplitude $= 0.074$ m,, $T = 0.4$ sec., $f = \dfrac{4.04}{\pi}$ cycles/sec.

(c) 0.562 met/sec., 1.632 met/sec^2.

3. A weight W Newton is suspended from a vertical spring and produces a stretch of magnitude and when the weight is in equilibrium it is acted upon by a force which imparts to it a velocity V_0 downward. Show that the weight travels a distance

$V_0 \sqrt{\dfrac{a}{g}}$ for a time $\left(\dfrac{\pi}{2}\right) \sqrt{\dfrac{a}{g}}$ before it starts to return.

4. A 2 N weight suspended from a spring stretches it 8 cm. The weight is pulled 15 cm below the equilibrium position and released. Assume that the weight is acted upon by a damping force which in N is numerically equal to 1 V, where V is the instantaneous velocity in m/sec.

(a) Set-up a differential equation and conditions describing the motion.

(b) Determine the position of the spring at any time after the weight is released.

(c) Write the result of (b) in the form A (t) sin (ωt + φ) .

Thus determine the time-varying amplitude and quasi period.

Ans. Note : $c = 1$ kg/s (b) $e^{-(2.45)t} [(0.15) \cos (10.79) t + (0.034) \sin (10.79) t]$

(c) $x = (0.15) e^{-(2.45)t} [\sin (10.79) t + 1.3478]$

$\omega = 10.79$, $\phi = 1.3478$, quasi period $= \dfrac{2\pi}{10.79} = \dfrac{\pi}{5.39}$ sec.

5. A 1 N weight suspended from a spring stretches it 15 cm. A velocity of 150 cm/sec. upward is imparted to the weight at its equilibrium position. Assume a damping force in N is numerically equal to 0.3 V, where V is the instantaneous velocity in m/sec. (a) Find the position and velocity of the spring at any time.

(b) Write a result of (a) in the form A (t) sin (ωt + φ).

Ans. (a) $x = -(0.188) e^{-(1.48)t} \sin (7.95) t$

$V = e^{-(1.48)t} [0.278 \sin (7.95) t - (1.49) \cos (7.95) t]$

(b) $x = (0.188) e^{-(1.48)t} \sin (7.95 t + \pi)$

6. A 3 N weight stretches a certain spring 15 cm. The weight is pulled 10 cm below the equilibrium position and released. A damping force in N equals to 5.75 V, where V being instantaneous velocity in m/sec. is working on the spring. Find x as a function of time t. By drawing the graph of the solution, show that it is a case of overdamped motion.

$$\textbf{Ans.} \quad x = (0.148)\, e^{-(4.615)\, t} - (0.048)\, e^{-(14.65)\, t}.$$

7. A vertical spring having constant 2 N/m has a 8 N weight suspended from it. An external force given by $F(t) = 8 \sin 10t$ is applied. A damping force given numerically in N by 4V, where V is velocity (m/sec.), is assumed to act. Initially the weight is at rest at its equilibrium position.

(a) Determine the position of the weight at any time.

(b) Indicate the transient and steady-state solutions.

(c)   Find the amplitude, period and frequency of the steady-state solution.

$$\textbf{Ans.} \quad (a) \quad x = (0.193)\, e^{-(0.57)\, t} - (0.138)\, e^{-(8.66)\, t}$$
$$- (0.055) \cos 10\, t - (0.109) \sin 10\, t$$

$$(b) \;\; \text{Steady-state part} - 0.55 \cos 10\, t - 0.109 \sin 10\, t = -0.12 \sin (10\, t + \phi)$$
$$- 0.397 \; \sin (10\, t + 3.87)$$

$$(c) \;\; \text{Steady-state amplitude} = 0.12 \text{ m, period} = \frac{\pi}{5} \text{ sec.}$$

$$\text{Frequency} = \frac{5}{\pi} \text{ cycles/sec.}$$

8. A vertical spring having constant 4 kg/m has a 32 N weight suspended from it. A force given by $F(t) = 16 \cos 4t$ is applied. Assuming that the weight initially at the equilibrium position is given an upward velocity 3 m/sec. and that the damping force is negligible, determine the position and the velocity of the weight at any time.

$$\textbf{Ans.} \qquad x = 0.928 \cos (1.106)\, t - 2.712 \sin (1.106)\, t - 0.928 \cos 4t$$
$$V = -1.026 \sin (1.106)\, t - 2.999 \cos (1.106)\, t + 3.928 \sin 4t.$$

9. A vertical spring having constant 2 kg/ft. has a 16 N weight attached to it. A force given by $F(t) = 4 \sin \dfrac{7}{\sqrt{40}}\, t$ is applied. Assuming that at $t = 0$, the weight is at rest at the equilibrium position and the damping force is negligible,

(a) Set-up a differential equation and conditions describing the motion.

(b) Determine the position and velocity of the weight at any time.

(c) Show that the motion is one of Resonance.

$$\textbf{Ans. (b)} \;\; x = 2 \sin \frac{7}{\sqrt{40}}\, t - \frac{7}{\sqrt{10}}\, t \cos \frac{7}{\sqrt{40}}\, t, \quad V = \frac{49}{20}\, t \sin \frac{7}{\sqrt{40}}\, t$$

10. In example 9 above, suppose that at $t = 0$, the weight is 15 cm below the equilibrium position and is struck so as to give a velocity of 1 m/sec. upward. Determine the position and the velocity of the weight at any time.

$$\textbf{Ans. } x = (0.15)\cos\frac{7}{\sqrt{40}}\,t + (1.01)\sin\frac{7}{\sqrt{40}}\,t - \frac{7}{\sqrt{10}}\,t\cos\frac{7}{\sqrt{40}}\,t$$

$$V = (0.16)\sin\frac{7}{\sqrt{40}}\,t + (1.11)\cos\frac{7}{\sqrt{40}}\,t - \frac{7}{\sqrt{10}}\cos\frac{7}{\sqrt{40}}\,t + \frac{49}{20}\,t\sin\frac{7}{\sqrt{40}}\,t$$

11. The equation of forced vibrations of a mass on a vertical spring is

$$m\frac{d^2x}{dt^2} + \beta\frac{dx}{dt} + kx = A\cos\omega t, \quad t > 0,$$

where x is the displacement of a mass from its position of equilibrium and m, β, k, A and ω are positive constants.

(a) Show that a steady-state oscillation is given by

$$x = \frac{A}{\sqrt{(m\omega^2 - k)^2 + \beta^2\omega^2}}\cos(\omega t + \phi)$$

(b) Show that maximum oscillations (Resonance) will occur if ω is so chosen that :

$$\omega = \sqrt{\frac{k}{m} - \frac{\beta^2}{2m^2}} \quad \text{provided } \beta^2 < 2\,km$$

(c) Show that at resonance, the amplitude of oscillation varies inversely as the damping constant β.

12. A mass m suspended from the end of helical spring is subjected to a periodic force $f = F\sin pt$ in the direction of its length. The force f is measured positive vertically downward and initially the mass is at rest in its equilibrium position. If the spring stiffness is k and damping force is negligible, show that the displacement of m at time t from the commencement of the motion is given by

$$x = \frac{F}{m\,(\omega^2 - p^2)}\left[\sin pt - \frac{p}{\omega}\sin \omega t\right], \text{ ωηερε } \omega^2 = \frac{k}{m}.$$

◈ ◈ ◈

VECTOR DIFFERENTIAL CALCULUS

3.1 DEFINITION AND ELEMENTARY RULES

In ordinary differentiation (not involving vectors), the derivative $\dfrac{dy}{dx}$ [where y = f (x)] is defined as

$$\frac{dy}{dx} = \lim_{h \to 0} \left[\frac{f(x+h) - f(x)}{h} \right]$$

Consider vector $\bar{r}$, which may depend for its value on scalar variable t, the functional relationship being $\qquad \bar{r} = \bar{F}(t)$

Here we have vector function $\bar{r} = \bar{F}(t)$ depending upon scalar variable t. Corresponding to a change δt in t, let there be a change $\delta\bar{r}$ in $\bar{r}$ i.e.

$$\delta\bar{r} = \bar{F}(t + \delta t) - \bar{F}(t)$$

The vector derivative can now be defined as

$$\frac{d\bar{r}}{dt} = \lim_{\delta t \to 0} \left[\frac{\bar{F}(t + \delta t) - \bar{F}(t)}{\delta t} \right]$$

This limit when exists is denoted by $\bar{F}'(t)$ or $\dfrac{d\bar{r}}{dt}$ and is called *rate of change of $\bar{r}$ with respect to t*. Thus, the vector derivative is defined in the same way as the scalar derivative and all the laws of scalar differentiation can be suitably extended to cover vector differentiation.

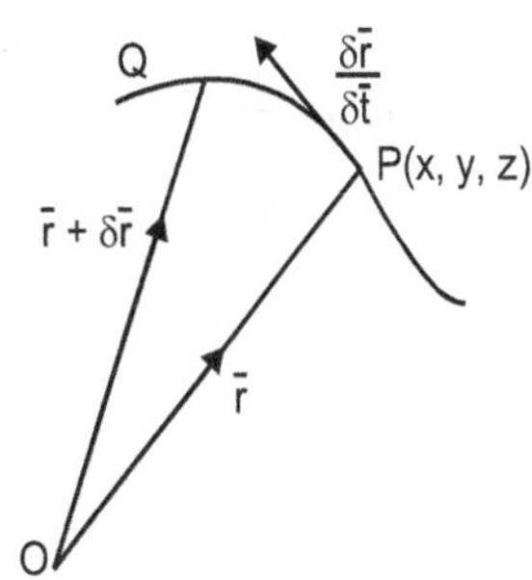

Fig. 3.1

To interpret physically, consider a point P on the curve whose position vector is $\bar{r}(t)$. Corresponding to different values of t, we get different points on the curve. Let t change by an amount δt and the point P move to Q. Let $\bar{r} + \delta\bar{r}$ be the position vector of Q.

$$\vec{PQ} = \vec{OQ} - \vec{OP} = \bar{r} + \delta\bar{r} - \bar{r} = \delta\bar{r}$$

Consider the vector $\dfrac{\vec{PQ}}{\delta t} = \dfrac{\delta\bar{r}}{\delta t}$

Now taking the limit as $\delta t \to 0$, i.e. $Q \to P$, $\displaystyle \lim_{\delta t \to 0} \frac{\overrightarrow{PQ}}{\delta t} = \lim_{\delta t \to 0} \frac{\delta \overline{r}}{\delta t} = \frac{d\overline{r}}{dt}$

In the limiting case when $Q \to P$, the vector $\overrightarrow{PQ}$ assumes the position of tangent vector at P. Thus $\dfrac{d\overline{r}}{dt}$ represents the tangent vector $\overline{T}$ at P (See Fig. 3.1).

In particular, if t is the time variable, $\overrightarrow{PQ}$ represents displacement vector then $\dfrac{d\overline{r}}{dt}$ represents the velocity vector $\overline{V}$.

Thus, in general, $\dfrac{d\overline{r}}{dt}$ will represent tangent vector denoted by $\overline{T}$ and in particular when t is the time variable, $\dfrac{d\overline{r}}{dt}$ represents velocity vector denoted by $\overline{V}$. The second and higher order derivatives can be defined in the same way as first order derivative. $\dfrac{d\overline{V}}{dt} = \dfrac{d^2\overline{r}}{dt^2}$ represents acceleration vector denoted by $\overline{a}$.

In another particular case, if the arc $PQ = \delta s$ and P, Q are very close to each other, chord PQ is approximately equal to arc PQ i.e. δs and from the distance formula,

$$\delta s^2 = \delta x^2 + \delta y^2 + \delta z^2 \text{ (See Fig. 3.1)}$$

Dividing by δs^2 and taking the limit as $Q \to P$ or $\delta s \to 0$

$$1 = \left(\frac{dx}{ds}\right)^2 + \left(\frac{dy}{ds}\right)^2 + \left(\frac{dz}{ds}\right)^2$$

just as $\lim \dfrac{\overrightarrow{PQ}}{\delta t}$ represents tangent vector.

$$\lim \frac{\overrightarrow{PQ}}{\delta s} = \lim \frac{\delta \overline{r}}{\delta s} = \frac{d\overline{r}}{ds} \text{ also represents a tangent vector}$$

Now,
$$\overline{r} = x\overline{i} + y\overline{j} + z\overline{k}$$

$$d\overline{r} = \overline{i}\, dx + \overline{j}\, dy + \overline{k}\, dz$$

$$\therefore \qquad \frac{d\overline{r}}{ds} = \overline{i}\,\frac{dx}{ds} + \overline{j}\,\frac{dy}{ds} + \overline{k}\,\frac{dz}{ds}$$

$$\left|\frac{d\overline{r}}{ds}\right| = \sqrt{\left(\frac{dx}{ds}\right)^2 + \left(\frac{dy}{ds}\right)^2 + \left(\frac{dz}{ds}\right)^2} = 1$$

Thus, $\dfrac{d\overline{r}}{ds}$ represents a tangent vector at P with unit magnitude denoted by $\hat{T}$.

From the definition of vector derivative, following results can be easily established.

For vectors $\overline{u}\,(t),\ \overline{v}(t), \overline{w}\,(t)$

(i) $\dfrac{d}{dt}(\overline{u} + \overline{v}) = \dfrac{d\overline{u}}{dt} + \dfrac{d\overline{v}}{dt}$ $\qquad$ (ii) $\dfrac{d}{dt}(\overline{u} - \overline{v}) = \dfrac{d\overline{u}}{dt} - \dfrac{d\overline{v}}{dt}$

(iii) $\dfrac{d}{dt}(\overline{u} \cdot \overline{v}) = \overline{v} \cdot \dfrac{d\overline{u}}{dt} + \overline{u} \cdot \dfrac{d\overline{v}}{dt}$ (iv) $\dfrac{d}{dt}(\overline{u} \times \overline{v}) = \dfrac{d\overline{u}}{dt} \times \overline{v} + \overline{u} \times \dfrac{d\overline{v}}{dt}$

$$[\text{The order in which } \overline{u},\, \overline{v} \text{ occur is maintained}]$$

(v) $\dfrac{d}{dt}[\overline{u} \times \overline{v} \cdot \overline{w}] = \dfrac{d\overline{u}}{dt} \times \overline{v} \cdot \overline{w} + \overline{u} \times \dfrac{d\overline{v}}{dt} \cdot \overline{w} + \overline{u} \times \overline{v} \cdot \dfrac{d\overline{w}}{dt}$

(vi) $\dfrac{d}{dt}[\overline{u} \times (\overline{v} \times \overline{w})] = \dfrac{d\overline{u}}{dt} \times (\overline{v} \times \overline{w}) + \overline{u} \times \left(\dfrac{d\overline{v}}{dt} \times \overline{w}\right) + \overline{u} \times \left(\overline{v} \times \dfrac{d\overline{w}}{dt}\right)$

$$[\text{In (iv), (v) and (vi) order in which } \overline{u},\, \overline{v},\, \overline{w} \text{ occur is maintained}]$$

(vii) If s is any scalar depending upon t,

$$\frac{d}{dt}(s\,\overline{u}) = \frac{ds}{dt}\,\overline{u} + s\,\frac{d\overline{u}}{dt}$$

(viii) $\dfrac{d}{dt}\left(\dfrac{\overline{u}}{s}\right) = \dfrac{s\,\dfrac{d\overline{u}}{dt} - \overline{u}\,\dfrac{ds}{dt}}{s^2}$

(ix) If s is constant, $\dfrac{d}{dt}(s\,\overline{u}) = s\,\dfrac{d\overline{u}}{dt}$

Since $\dfrac{\overline{u}}{\overline{v}}$ is not defined, hence $\dfrac{d}{dt}\left(\dfrac{\overline{u}}{\overline{v}}\right)$ is also not defined or has no meaning.

If $\bar{u}(x, y)$, $\bar{v}(x, y)$ are vector functions of scalars x, y; the partial derivatives $\dfrac{\partial \bar{u}}{\partial x}, \dfrac{\partial \bar{u}}{\partial y}$ are defined as

$$\frac{\partial \bar{u}}{\partial x} = \lim_{\delta x \to 0}\left[\frac{\bar{u}(x + \delta x, y) - \bar{u}(x, y)}{\delta x}\right], \quad \frac{\partial \bar{u}}{\partial y} = \lim_{\delta y \to 0}\left[\frac{\bar{u}(x, y + \delta y) - \bar{u}(x, y)}{\delta y}\right]$$

if the limits exist.

The mixed derivatives $\dfrac{\partial^2 \bar{u}}{\partial x\, \partial y}$ and higher order partial derivatives $\dfrac{\partial^2 \bar{u}}{\partial x^2}, \dfrac{\partial^2 \bar{u}}{\partial y^2}, \dfrac{\partial^2 \bar{v}}{\partial x^2},$ $\dfrac{\partial^3 \bar{u}}{\partial x^3}$ can be similarly defined and can be computed.

Rules for partial differentiation of vectors are similar to those used in calculus for scalar functions. Following results can be easily established :

$$\frac{\partial}{\partial x}(\bar{u} \pm \bar{v}) = \frac{\partial \bar{u}}{\partial x} \pm \frac{\partial \bar{v}}{\partial x}$$

$$\frac{\partial}{\partial x}(\bar{u} \cdot \bar{v}) = \frac{\partial \bar{u}}{\partial x} \cdot \bar{v} + \bar{u} \cdot \frac{\partial \bar{v}}{\partial x}$$

$$\frac{\partial}{\partial x}(\bar{u} \times \bar{v}) = \frac{\partial \bar{u}}{\partial x} \times \bar{v} + \bar{u} \times \frac{\partial \bar{v}}{\partial x}$$

3.2 APPLICATIONS OF MECHANICS

This includes a study of the motion of particles along curves. Newton's second law of motion states that $\bar{F} = \dfrac{d}{dt}(m\bar{V})$, where $m\bar{V}$ is the momentum of the object. If m is constant, then this becomes $\bar{F} = m\,\dfrac{d\bar{V}}{dt} = m\,\bar{a}$, where $\bar{a}$ is the acceleration of the object. This law is quite useful in the study of dynamics.

(A) **Plane motion of a particle along a circle :** Consider a particle P moving along a circle of radius r with constant angular speed ω.

$$\omega = \frac{d\theta}{dt}$$

$$\bar{r} = \overline{OP} = x\bar{i} + y\bar{j} = r\cos\theta\,\bar{i} + r\sin\theta\,\bar{j}$$

Differentiating w.r.t. t

$$\overline{V} = \frac{d\overline{r}}{dt} = -r\sin\theta\,\overline{i}\,\frac{d\theta}{dt} + r\cos\theta\,\overline{j}\,\frac{d\theta}{dt} = (-r\sin\theta\,\overline{i} + r\cos\theta\,\overline{j}\,)\,\omega$$

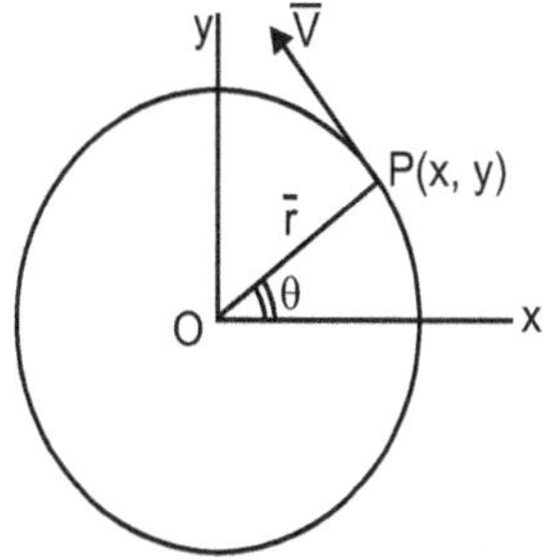

Fig. 3.2

Differentiating again w.r.t. t,

$$\frac{d\overline{V}}{dt} = \overline{a} = \left(-r\cos\theta\,\frac{d\theta}{dt}\,\overline{i} - r\sin\theta\,\frac{d\theta}{dt}\,\overline{j}\right)\omega = (-r\cos\theta\,\overline{i} - r\sin\theta\,\overline{j})\,\omega^2 = -\overline{r}\,\omega^2$$

Hence the acceleration is directed towards the centre.

(B) Radial and Transverse Components of Velocity and Acceleration : Consider a particle moving along a curve C (See Fig. 3.3).

Let $\overrightarrow{OP} = \overline{r}$ be the position vector of point P, $\hat{r}$ and $\hat{s}$ be unit vectors along the radius vector $\overline{r}$ (radial direction) and perpendicular to $\overline{r}$ (transverse direction).

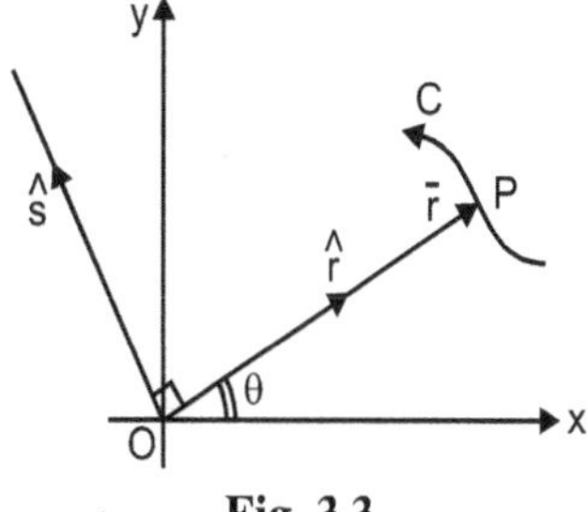

Fig. 3.3

$$\hat{r} = \cos\theta\,\overline{i} + \sin\theta\,\overline{j}$$

$$\hat{s} = \cos\left(\frac{\pi}{2}+\theta\right)\overline{i} + \sin\left(\frac{\pi}{2}+\theta\right)\overline{j}$$

$$= -\sin\theta\,\overline{i} + \cos\theta\,\overline{j}$$

Differentiating both w.r.t. t, we get

$$\frac{d\hat{r}}{dt} = -\sin\theta\,\frac{d\theta}{dt}\,\overline{i} + \cos\theta\,\frac{d\theta}{dt}\,\overline{j} = (-\sin\theta\,\overline{i} + \cos\theta\,\overline{j})\frac{d\theta}{dt} = \hat{s}\,\frac{d\theta}{dt}$$

Similarly, $$\frac{d\hat{s}}{dt} = -\hat{r}\,\frac{d\theta}{dt}$$

Now $$\overline{r} = r\,\hat{r}$$

and $\overline{V}$ the velocity of the point P is

$$\bar{V} = \frac{d\bar{r}}{dt} = \frac{d}{dt}(r\,\hat{r}) = \frac{dr}{dt}\,\hat{r} + r\,\frac{d\hat{r}}{dt}$$

$$\boxed{\bar{V} = \frac{dr}{dt}\,\hat{r} + \left(r\,\frac{d\theta}{dt}\right)\hat{s}} \qquad \ldots (1)$$

Thus the radial and transverse components of velocity are $\dfrac{dr}{dt}$ (or $\dot{r}$) and $r\dfrac{d\theta}{dt}$ (or $r\,\dot{\theta}$) respectively.

To obtain radial and transverse components of acceleration,

$$\bar{a} = \frac{d\bar{v}}{dt} = \frac{d}{dt}\left[\frac{dr}{dt}\,\hat{r} + \left(r\,\frac{d\theta}{dt}\right)\hat{s}\right] = \frac{d^2r}{dt^2}\,\hat{r} + \frac{dr}{dt}\,\frac{d\hat{r}}{dt} + \left(\frac{dr}{dt}\frac{d\theta}{dt} + r\,\frac{d^2\theta}{dt^2}\right)\hat{s} + \left(r\,\frac{d\theta}{dt}\right)\frac{d\hat{s}}{dt}$$

but $$\frac{d\hat{r}}{dt} = \hat{s}\,\frac{d\theta}{dt} \quad \text{and} \quad \frac{d\hat{s}}{dt} = -\hat{r}\,\frac{d\theta}{dt}$$

$\therefore \qquad \bar{a} = \dfrac{d\bar{v}}{dt} = \dfrac{d^2r}{dt^2}\,\hat{r} + \dfrac{dr}{dt}\left(\hat{s}\,\dfrac{d\theta}{dt}\right) + \dfrac{dr}{dt}\dfrac{d\theta}{dt}\,\hat{s} + r\,\dfrac{d^2\theta}{dt^2}\,\hat{s} + r\,\dfrac{d\theta}{dt}\left(-\hat{r}\,\dfrac{d\theta}{dt}\right)$

$$= \left[\frac{d^2r}{dt^2} - r\left(\frac{d\theta}{dt}\right)^2\right]\hat{r} + \left[2\,\frac{dr}{dt}\,\frac{d\theta}{dt} + r\,\frac{d^2\theta}{dt^2}\right]\hat{s}$$

$\therefore \qquad \boxed{\bar{a} = [\ddot{r} - r\,(\dot{\theta})^2]\,\hat{r} + [2\,\dot{r}\,\dot{\theta} + r\,\ddot{\theta}]\,\hat{s}} \qquad \ldots (2)$

Thus $\ddot{r} - r\,\dot{\theta}^2$ is radial and $2\,\dot{r}\,\dot{\theta} + r\,\ddot{\theta}$ is transverse component of acceleration.

(C) Tangential and Normal Components of Acceleration :

$$\bar{V} = \frac{d\bar{r}}{dt} = \frac{d\bar{r}}{ds}\,\frac{ds}{dt}$$

but $$\frac{d\bar{r}}{ds} = \hat{T} \text{ [unit tangent vector] and } \frac{ds}{dt} = v = |\bar{V}| \text{ [speed]}$$

$\therefore \qquad \bar{V} = \dfrac{ds}{dt}\,\hat{T} = v\,\hat{T}$

and $$\bar{a} = \frac{d\bar{V}}{dt} = \frac{dv}{dt}\,\hat{T} + v\,\frac{d\hat{T}}{dt}$$

$$= \frac{d^2s}{dt^2}\,\hat{T} + \frac{ds}{dt}\left(\frac{d\hat{T}}{ds}\,\frac{ds}{dt}\right) = \frac{d^2s}{dt^2}\,\hat{T} + \left(\frac{ds}{dt}\right)^2\frac{d\hat{T}}{ds}$$

From Serret-Frenet formulae,

$$\frac{d\hat{T}}{ds} = k\,\hat{N}, \qquad\qquad [\hat{N} \text{ is unit principal normal vector}]$$

$$\bar{a} = \frac{d^2s}{dt^2}\,\hat{T} + \left(\frac{ds}{dt}\right)^2 k\,\hat{N}, \qquad\qquad [k \text{ is curvature}]$$

$$= \frac{d^2s}{dt^2}\,\hat{T} + \frac{1}{\rho}\left(\frac{ds}{dt}\right)^2 \hat{N}, \quad \left[k = \frac{1}{\rho}, \text{ where } \rho \text{ is radius of curvature}\right]$$

$$\boxed{\bar{a} = \frac{dv}{dt}\,\hat{T} + \frac{v^2}{\rho}\,\hat{N} = a_T\,\hat{T} + a_N\,\hat{N}}$$

$$\text{where} \qquad a_T = \frac{dv}{dt} = \frac{d^2s}{dt^2} = \frac{\bar{r}\cdot\bar{r}}{|\bar{r}|}, \qquad \text{is tangential component of } \bar{a},$$

$$\text{and} \qquad a_N = \frac{v^2}{\rho} = \frac{1}{\rho}\left(\frac{ds}{dt}\right)^2 = \frac{|\bar{r}\times\bar{r}|}{|\bar{r}|}, \qquad \text{is normal component of } \bar{a}.$$

(D) Law of Central Orbits (Orbital Motion) :
Consider a particle P, describing the curve C under the
action of a force F always directed towards the centre
'O'. From equation (2) of (b),

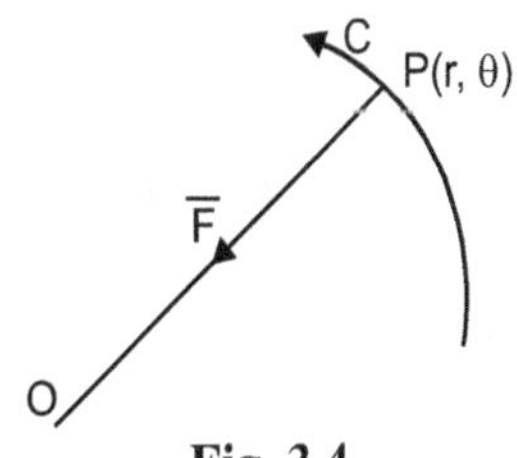

Fig. 3.4

$$F = -\left[\frac{d^2r}{dt^2} - r\left(\frac{d\theta}{dt}\right)^2\right] \qquad\qquad \dots (1)$$

As the force or acceleration is directed towards the centre and since there is no
transverse component of acceleration,

$$2\dot{r}\dot{\theta} + r\ddot{\theta} = 0 \qquad \therefore \qquad \frac{1}{r}\left(2r\dot{r}\dot{\theta} + r^2\ddot{\theta}\right) = 0$$

$$\text{i.e.} \quad \frac{1}{r}\frac{d}{dt}\left[r^2\frac{d\theta}{dt}\right] = 0$$

which implies $r^2\dfrac{d\theta}{dt} = h$ (constant), taking $u = \dfrac{1}{r}$, we get

$$\therefore \qquad \frac{d\theta}{dt} = \frac{h}{r^2} = hu^2 \qquad \Rightarrow \qquad \frac{dr}{dt} = \frac{dr}{d\theta}\frac{d\theta}{dt} = hu^2\frac{dr}{d\theta}$$

$$\text{but} \qquad r = \frac{1}{u} \qquad \Rightarrow \qquad \frac{dr}{d\theta} = -\frac{1}{u^2}\frac{du}{d\theta}$$

$$\therefore \qquad \frac{dr}{dt} = hu^2\left(-\frac{1}{u^2}\frac{du}{d\theta}\right) = -h\frac{du}{d\theta}$$

$$\frac{d^2r}{dt^2} = -h\,\frac{d^2u}{d\theta^2}\,\frac{d\theta}{dt} = -h\,\frac{d^2u}{d\theta^2}\,hu^2 = -h^2u^2\,\frac{d^2u}{d\theta^2}$$

Putting in (1) for $\dfrac{d\theta}{dt},\ \dfrac{d^2r}{dt^2}$

$$F = -\left[-h^2u^2\,\frac{d^2u}{d\theta^2} - \frac{1}{u}\,(h^2u^4)\right] = h^2u^2\left(\frac{d^2u}{d\theta^2} + u\right)$$

$$\therefore \qquad \boxed{F = h^2u^2\left(\frac{d^2u}{d\theta^2} + u\right)}$$

Which gives the law of force or acceleration which is always directed towards the centre (pole) when the particle describes the given orbit. In above discussion, $r^2\,\dfrac{d\theta}{dt}$ = constant, represents moment of velocity of the particle about the centre, which remains constant throughout the motion of the particle.

ILLUSTRATIONS

Ex. 1 : *A curve is given by the equations* $x = t^2 + 1,\ y = 4t - 3,\ z = 2t^2 - 6t.$
Find the angle between tangents at $t = 1$ and at $t = 2$.

Sol. : $\qquad \overline{r} = x\,\overline{i} + y\,\overline{j} + z\,\overline{k}$, where $x = t^2 + 1,\ y = 4t - 3,\ z = 2t^2 - 6t$

$$\therefore \qquad \overline{T} = \frac{d\overline{r}}{dt} = \overline{i}\,\frac{dx}{dt} + \overline{j}\,\frac{dy}{dt} + \overline{k}\,\frac{dz}{dt} = 2t\,\overline{i} + 4\,\overline{j} + (4t - 6)\,\overline{k}$$

$$\therefore \qquad \overline{T}_1 = \{\overline{T}\}_{t=1} = 2\overline{i} + 4\overline{j} - 2\overline{k} \text{ and } \overline{T}_2 = \{\overline{T}\}_{t=2} = 4\overline{i} + 4\overline{j} + 2\overline{k}$$

$$\therefore \qquad \hat{T}_1 = \frac{2\,\overline{i} + 4\,\overline{j} - 2\,\overline{k}}{\sqrt{4 + 16 + 4}} = \frac{2\overline{i} + 4\,\overline{j} - 2\,\overline{k}}{2\sqrt{6}} = \frac{\overline{i} + 2\overline{j} - \overline{k}}{\sqrt{6}}$$

$$\text{and} \qquad \hat{T}_2 = \frac{4\,\overline{i} + 4\,\overline{j} + 2\,\overline{k}}{\sqrt{16 + 16 + 4}} = \frac{4\,\overline{i} + 4\overline{j} + 2\,\overline{k}}{6} = \frac{2\,\overline{i} + 2\,\overline{j} + \overline{k}}{3}$$

Now, $\hat{T}_1 \cdot \hat{T}_2 = |\hat{T}_1|\,|\hat{T}_2|\cos\theta$ $\qquad\qquad$ [θ is the angle between the tangents]

$$\cos\theta = \hat{T}_1 \cdot \hat{T}_2 = \frac{2 + 4 - 1}{3\sqrt{6}} = \frac{5}{3\sqrt{6}}$$

$$\therefore \qquad \theta = \cos^{-1}\left\{\frac{5}{3\sqrt{6}}\right\}$$

Ex. 2 : *For the curve* $x = e^t \cos t$, $y = e^t \sin t$, $z = e^t$ *find the velocity and acceleration of the particle moving on the curve at* $t = 0$.

Sol. :
$$\bar{V} = \bar{i}\,\frac{dx}{dt} + \bar{j}\,\frac{dy}{dt} + \bar{k}\,\frac{dz}{dt}$$

$$= \bar{i}\,\{e^t \cos t - e^t \sin t\} + \bar{j}\,\{e^t \sin t + e^t \cos t\} + \bar{k}\,\{e^t\}$$

$$\bar{a} = \frac{d\bar{V}}{dt} = \bar{i}\,\{e^t \cos t - e^t \sin t - e^t \sin t - e^t \cos t\}$$

$$+ \bar{j}\,\{e^t \sin t + e^t \cos t + e^t \cos t - e^t \sin t\} + \bar{k}\,\{e^t\}$$

$$= \bar{i}\,\{-2\,e^t \sin t\} + \bar{j}\,\{2e^t \cos t\} + \bar{k}\,\{e^t\}$$

$$\bar{V}|_{t=0} = \bar{i} + \bar{j} + \bar{k}$$

$$\bar{a}|_{t=0} = 2\,\bar{j} + \bar{k}$$

Ex. 3 : *If* $\bar{r}$ *is the position vector of a particle of mass m w.r.t. 'O' as origin and* $\bar{F}$ *is the external force on the particle, then show that the moment of* $\bar{F}$ *about O is given by* $\bar{M} = \frac{d\bar{H}}{dt}$, *where* $\bar{H} = \bar{r} \times m\bar{V}$ *and* $\bar{V}$ *is the velocity of the particle.*

Sol. :
$$\bar{M} = \bar{r} \times \bar{F} = \bar{r} \times \frac{d}{dt}(m\bar{V})$$

$$\frac{d\bar{H}}{dt} = \frac{d}{dt}(\bar{r} \times m\bar{V}) = \frac{d\bar{r}}{dt} \times m\bar{V} + \bar{r} \times \frac{d}{dt}(m\bar{V})$$

$$= \bar{V} \times m\bar{V} + \bar{r} \times \frac{d}{dt}(m\bar{V}) = 0 + \bar{r} \times \frac{d}{dt}(m\bar{V})$$

Thus,
$$\bar{M} = \bar{r} \times \frac{d}{dt}(m\bar{V}) = \frac{d\bar{H}}{dt}$$

Ex. 4 : *For the curve* $x = t^3 + 1$, $y = t^2$, $z = t$, *find the magnitude of tangential and normal components of acceleration for a particle moving on the curve at* $t = 1$.

Sol. : Let
$$\bar{a} = a_T\,\hat{T} + a_N\,\hat{N} \qquad\qquad \dots \text{(i)}$$
where a_T, a_N are tangential and normal components of acceleration, respectively.

$$\bar{V} = \frac{d\bar{r}}{dt} = \bar{i}\,\frac{dx}{dt} + \bar{j}\,\frac{dy}{dt} + \bar{k}\,\frac{dz}{dt}$$

$$= \bar{i}(3t^2) + 2t\,\bar{j} + \bar{k} = 3\,\bar{i} + 2\,\bar{j} + \bar{k} \text{ at } t = 1$$

$$\bar{a} = \frac{d^2\bar{r}}{dt^2} = 6t\,\bar{i} + 2\,\bar{j} = 6\,\bar{i} + 2\,\bar{j} \text{ at } t = 1$$

From (i), $\bar{a} \cdot \hat{T} = a_T \hat{T} \cdot \hat{T} + a_N \hat{N} \cdot \hat{T} = a_T$ as $\hat{N} \cdot \hat{T} = 0$

$$\hat{T} = \frac{d\bar{r}/dt}{\left|\dfrac{d\bar{r}}{dt}\right|} = \frac{3\bar{i} + 2\bar{j} + \bar{k}}{\sqrt{9+4+1}} = \frac{1}{\sqrt{14}} (3\bar{i} + 2\bar{j} + \bar{k})$$

$$\bar{a} \cdot \hat{T} = (6\bar{i} + 2\bar{j}) \cdot \frac{1}{\sqrt{14}} (3\bar{i} + 2\bar{j} + \bar{k}) = \frac{1}{\sqrt{14}} (18 + 4) = \frac{22}{\sqrt{14}}$$

Thus $a_T = \dfrac{22}{\sqrt{14}}$ (Magnitude of tangential component of acceleration).

To obtain normal component, consider

$$a_N \hat{N} = \bar{a} - a_T \hat{T}$$

Taking the dot product with itself

$$a_N \hat{N} \cdot a_N \hat{N} = (\bar{a} - a_T \hat{T}) \cdot (\bar{a} - a_T \hat{T})$$

$$a_N^2 = \left((6\bar{i} + 2\bar{j}) - \frac{22}{\sqrt{14}} \frac{(3\bar{i} + 2\bar{j} + \bar{k})}{\sqrt{14}} \right) \cdot \left((6\bar{i} + 2\bar{j}) - \frac{22}{\sqrt{14}} \frac{(3\bar{i} + 2\bar{j} + \bar{k})}{\sqrt{14}} \right)$$

$$\therefore \quad a_N^2 = \left[\left(\frac{84\bar{i} - 66\bar{i} + 28\bar{j} - 44\bar{j} - 22\bar{k}}{14} \right) \cdot \left(\frac{84\bar{i} - 66\bar{i} + 28\bar{j} - 44\bar{j} - 22\bar{k}}{14} \right) \right]$$

$$= \left[\left(\frac{18\bar{i} - 16\bar{j} - 22\bar{k}}{14} \right) \cdot \left(\frac{18\bar{i} - 16\bar{j} - 22\bar{k}}{14} \right) \right]$$

$$= \left(\frac{9\bar{i} - 8\bar{j} - 11\bar{k}}{7} \right) \cdot \left(\frac{9\bar{i} - 8\bar{j} - 11\bar{k}}{7} \right)$$

$$= \frac{1}{49} [81 + 64 + 121] = \frac{266}{49} = \frac{38}{7}$$

$$\therefore \quad a_N = \sqrt{\frac{38}{7}} \qquad \text{[Magnitude of normal component of acceleration]}$$

Ex. 5 : *For the curve $x = \cos t + t \sin t$, $y = \sin t - t \cos t$, find the tangential and normal components of acceleration at any time t.*

Sol. : $\dfrac{dx}{dt} = -\sin t + \sin t + t \cos t = t \cos t$

$\dfrac{d^2x}{dt^2} = \cos t - t \sin t$

$\dfrac{dy}{dt} = \cos t - \cos t + t \sin t = t \sin t$

$\dfrac{d^2y}{dt^2} = \sin t + t \cos t$

$$\bar{r} = x\,\bar{i} + y\,\bar{j}$$

$$\bar{T} = \bar{i}\,\frac{dx}{dt} + \bar{j}\,\frac{dy}{dt} = \bar{i}\,(t\cos t) + \bar{j}\,(t\sin t)$$

$$\bar{a} = \bar{i}\,\frac{d^2x}{dt^2} + \bar{j}\,\frac{d^2y}{dt^2} = \bar{i}\,(\cos t - t\sin t) + \bar{j}\,(\sin t + t\cos t)$$

Let $$\bar{a} = a_T\,\hat{T} + a_N\,\hat{N}$$

$$\bar{a}\cdot\hat{T} = a_T$$

$$\hat{T} = \frac{\bar{i}\,(t\cos t) + \bar{j}\,(t\sin t)}{\sqrt{t^2\cos^2 t + t^2\sin^2 t}} = \bar{i}\,(\cos t) + \bar{j}\,(\sin t)$$

$$\bar{a}\cdot\hat{T} = [\,\bar{i}\,(\cos t - t\sin t) + \bar{j}\,(\sin t + t\cos t)\,]\cdot[\,\bar{i}\,(\cos t) + \bar{j}\,(\sin t)\,]$$

$$= \cos^2 t - t\sin t\cos t + \sin^2 t + t\cos t\sin t = 1$$

Thus $$a_T = \bar{a}\cdot\hat{T} = 1 \qquad\text{(tangential component)}$$

$$a_N\,\hat{N} = \bar{a} - a_T\,\hat{T}$$

$$\therefore\ (a_N\,\hat{N})\cdot(a_N\,\hat{N}) = (\bar{a} - a_T\,\hat{T})\cdot(\bar{a} - a_T\,\hat{T})$$

$$a_N^2 = (\bar{a} - a_T\,\hat{T})\cdot(\bar{a} - a_T\,\hat{T})$$

$$\bar{a} - a_T\,\hat{T} = \bar{i}\,(\cos t - t\sin t) + \bar{j}\,(\sin t + t\cos t) - \bar{i}\,(\cos t) - \bar{j}\,(\sin t)$$

$$= (-t\sin t)\,\bar{i} + (t\cos t)\,\bar{j}$$

$$a_N^2 = [(-t\sin t)\,\bar{i} + (t\cos t)\,\bar{j}\,]\cdot[(-t\sin t)\,\bar{i} + (t\cos t)\,\bar{j}\,]$$

$$= t^2\sin^2 t + t^2\cos^2 t = t^2$$

$$a_N = t \qquad\text{(Normal component of acceleration)}$$

Ex. 6 : *A particle describes the cardioide $r = a\,(1 + \cos\theta)$ under the attraction of a force directed towards the pole. Find the law of force.*

Sol. : From article 3.2 (d), law of force is given by

$$F = h^2 u^2\left(\frac{d^2u}{d\theta^2} + u\right)$$

where $$u = \frac{1}{r} \qquad\qquad u = \frac{1}{a}\,\frac{1}{(1 + \cos\theta)}$$

$$\frac{du}{d\theta} = \frac{1}{a}\left[\frac{1\,(\sin\theta)}{(1+\cos\theta)^2}\right] = \frac{\sin\theta}{a\,(1+\cos\theta)^2}$$

$$\frac{d^2u}{d\theta^2} = \frac{1}{a}\left[\frac{\cos\theta\,(1+\cos\theta)^2 + 2\,(1+\cos\theta)\sin^2\theta}{(1+\cos\theta)^4}\right]$$

$$= \frac{1}{a}\left[\frac{\cos\theta\,(1+\cos\theta) + 2\sin^2\theta}{(1+\cos\theta)^3}\right] = \frac{1}{a}\left[\frac{\cos\theta + 1 + \sin^2\theta}{(1+\cos\theta)^3}\right]$$

$$\frac{d^2u}{d\theta^2} + u = \frac{1}{a}\left[\frac{\cos\theta + 1 + \sin^2\theta}{(1+\cos\theta)^3} + \frac{1}{(1+\cos\theta)}\right]$$

$$= \frac{1}{a}\left[\frac{\cos\theta + 1 + \sin^2\theta + 1 + 2\cos\theta + \cos^2\theta}{(1+\cos\theta)^3}\right]$$

$$= \frac{1}{a}\left[\frac{3\,(1+\cos\theta)}{(1+\cos\theta)^3}\right] = \frac{1}{a}\frac{3}{(1+\cos\theta)^2}$$

$$F = h^2u^2\left(\frac{d^2u}{d\theta^2} + u\right) = h^2\,\frac{1}{a^2\,(1+\cos\theta)^2}\cdot\frac{3}{a}\cdot\frac{1}{(1+\cos\theta)^2}$$

$$= \frac{3h^2\,a}{a^4\,(1+\cos\theta)^4} = \frac{3h^2\,a}{r^4}$$

Or force is proportional to r^{-4}.

Ex. 7 : *A particle describes the curve r = 2a cos θ with constant angular speed ω. Find the radial and transverse components of velocity and acceleration.*

Sol. : From article 3.2 (b),

$$\bar{V} = \frac{dr}{dt}\,\hat{r} + \left(r\frac{d\theta}{dt}\right)\hat{s}$$

$$\bar{a} = \left[\frac{d^2r}{dt^2} - r\left(\frac{d\theta}{dt}\right)^2\right]\hat{r} + \left[2\frac{dr}{dt}\frac{d\theta}{dt} + r\frac{d^2\theta}{dt^2}\right]\hat{s}$$

Consider

$$r = 2a\cos\theta$$

$$\frac{dr}{dt} = -2a\sin\theta\,\frac{d\theta}{dt} = -2a\,\omega\sin\theta \qquad r\frac{d\theta}{dt} = 2a\cos\theta\,\omega$$

Thus, the radial and transverse components of velocity are $-2a\,\omega\sin\theta$ and $2a\,\omega\cos\theta$ respectively.

$$\frac{d^2r}{dt^2} = -2a\,\omega\cos\theta\,\frac{d\theta}{dt} = -2a\,\omega^2\cos\theta$$

Radial component of acceleration is

$$\frac{d^2r}{dt^2} - r\left(\frac{d\theta}{dt}\right)^2 = -2a\,\omega^2\cos\theta - 2a\cos\theta\,\omega^2 = -4a\,\omega^2\cos\theta$$

Transverse component of acceleration is

$$2\frac{dr}{dt}\frac{d\theta}{dt} + r\frac{d^2\theta}{dt^2} = 2\frac{dr}{dt}\,\omega\left[as\ \frac{d^2\theta}{dt^2} = 0\right]$$

i.e. $2(-2a\,\omega\sin\theta)\,\omega = -4a\,\omega^2\sin\theta$

Ex. 8 : *A particle P moves in a plane with constant angular velocity ω about O. If the rate of increase of acceleration is parallel to PO, prove that*

$$\frac{d^2r}{dt^2} = \frac{1}{3}\,r\omega^2$$

Sol. : From result (2) of article 10.2 (b),

$$\bar{a} = \left[\frac{d^2r}{dt^2} - r\left(\frac{d\theta}{dt}\right)^2\right]\hat{r} + \left[2\frac{dr}{dt}\frac{d\theta}{dt} + r\frac{d^2\theta}{dt}\right]\hat{s}$$

In proving this result, we had also seen that

$$\frac{d\hat{r}}{dt} = \hat{s}\,\frac{d\theta}{dt} \qquad\qquad \frac{d\hat{s}}{dt} = -\hat{r}\,\frac{d\theta}{dt}$$

$$\because \qquad \frac{d\theta}{dt} = \omega = \text{constant}$$

$$\bar{a} = \left[\frac{d^2r}{dt^2} - r\omega^2\right]\hat{r} + \left[2\omega\,\frac{dr}{dt}\right]\hat{s} \qquad\qquad \left[as\ \frac{d^2\theta}{dt^2} = 0\right]$$

Differentiating w.r.t. t

$$\frac{d\bar{a}}{dt} = \left[\frac{d^3r}{dt^3} - \frac{dr}{dt}\omega^2\right]\hat{r} + \left[\frac{d^2r}{dt^2} - r\omega^2\right]\frac{d\hat{r}}{dt} + 2\omega\frac{d^2r}{dt^2}\,\hat{s} + 2\omega\frac{dr}{dt}\frac{d\hat{s}}{dt}$$

Putting $\dfrac{d\hat{r}}{dt} = \hat{s}\,\dfrac{d\theta}{dt},\ \ \dfrac{d\hat{s}}{dt} = -\hat{r}\,\dfrac{d\theta}{dt}$

$$\frac{d\bar{a}}{dt} = \left[\frac{d^3r}{dt^3} - \frac{dr}{dt}\omega^2\right]\hat{r} + \left[\frac{d^2r}{dt^2} - r\omega^2\right]\hat{s}\frac{d\theta}{dt} + 2\omega\frac{d^2r}{dt^2}\,\hat{s} + 2\omega\frac{dr}{dt}\left(-\hat{r}\,\frac{d\theta}{dt}\right)$$

Putting ω for $\dfrac{d\theta}{dt}$ and rearranging,

$$\frac{d\bar{a}}{dt} = \left[\frac{d^3r}{dt^3} - \frac{dr}{dt}\omega^2 - 2\omega^2\frac{dr}{dt}\right]\hat{r} + \left[\omega\frac{d^2r}{dt^2} - r\omega^3 + 2\omega\frac{d^2r}{dt^2}\right]\hat{s}$$

Since $\dfrac{d\bar{a}}{dt}$ is parallel to PO i.e. along $\hat{r}$, coefficient of $\hat{s}$ must be zero.

i.e. $3\omega\dfrac{d^2r}{dt^2} - r\omega^3 = 0$ \qquad\qquad Or \qquad\qquad $\dfrac{d^2r}{dt^2} = \dfrac{1}{3}\,r\omega^2$

Ex. 9 : *If* $\bar{r} \times \dfrac{d\bar{r}}{dt} = 0$, *show that* $\bar{r}$ *has a constant direction.*

Sol. : Let $\bar{r} = r\,\hat{r}$, where $\hat{r}$ is a unit vector in the direction of $\bar{r}$ and $r = |\bar{r}|$.

$$\frac{d\bar{r}}{dt} = r\,\frac{d\hat{r}}{dt} + \hat{r}\,\frac{dr}{dt}$$

$$\bar{r} \times \frac{d\bar{r}}{dt} = r\hat{r} \times \left(r\frac{d\hat{r}}{dt} + \hat{r}\frac{dr}{dt}\right) = r^2\hat{r} \times \frac{d\hat{r}}{dt} + r\frac{dr}{dt}\,(\hat{r} \times \hat{r})$$

$$= r^2\,\hat{r} \times \frac{d\hat{r}}{dt}\ [\hat{r} \times \hat{r} = 0]$$

Now, $\qquad \bar{r} \times \dfrac{d\bar{r}}{dt} = 0$ (given) $\qquad \therefore \qquad r^2\hat{r} \times \dfrac{d\hat{r}}{dt} = 0$

i.e. $\qquad \hat{r} \times \dfrac{d\hat{r}}{dt} = 0\ $ [as $r \neq 0$] $\qquad\qquad\qquad\qquad$ ...(i)

Again $\qquad \hat{r} \cdot \hat{r} = 1 \qquad\qquad \therefore \qquad \hat{r} \cdot \dfrac{d\hat{r}}{dt} = 0 \qquad$ ... (ii)

(i) implies $\dfrac{d\hat{r}}{dt}$ is parallel to $\hat{r}$ $\qquad$ (ii) implies $\dfrac{d\hat{r}}{dt}$ is perpendicular to $\hat{r}$

both cannot be true simultaneously $\qquad \therefore \qquad \dfrac{d\hat{r}}{dt} = 0$

which means $\hat{r}$ has constant direction.

Ex. 10 : *Show that tangential and normal components of acceleration are given by*

$$\frac{\bar{V} \cdot \bar{a}}{V} \quad and \quad \frac{|\bar{V} \times \bar{a}|}{|\bar{V}|}$$

Also show that $\qquad \rho = \dfrac{V^3}{|\bar{V} \times \bar{a}|}$

Sol. : Let $\qquad \bar{a} = a_T\,\hat{T} + a_N\,\hat{N}, \quad \bar{V} = V\,\hat{T}$

$\therefore \qquad \bar{V} \cdot \bar{a} = V\hat{T} \cdot (a_T\,\hat{T} + a_N\,\hat{N}) = V\,a_T\,\hat{T} \cdot \hat{T} + V\,a_N\,\hat{T} \cdot \hat{N}$

but $\qquad \hat{T} \cdot \hat{T} = 1, \quad \hat{T} \cdot \hat{N} = 0$

$\therefore \qquad a_T = \dfrac{\bar{V} \cdot \bar{a}}{V} \qquad\qquad\qquad\qquad\qquad\qquad$ ... (1)

$$\overline{V} \times \overline{a} = V\,\hat{T} \times (a_T\,\hat{T} + a_N\,\hat{N}) = V\,a_t\,\hat{T} \times \hat{T} + V\,a_N\,\hat{T} \times \hat{N}$$

but
$$\hat{T} \times \hat{T} = 0$$

$\therefore$
$$|\overline{V} \times \overline{a}| = V\,a_N|\hat{T} \times \hat{N}| = V\,a_N \ \text{ as } |\hat{T} \times \hat{N}| = 1$$

$\therefore$
$$a_N = \frac{|\overline{V} \times \overline{a}|}{V} \quad \text{or} \quad \frac{|\overline{V} \times \overline{a}|}{|\overline{V}|} \qquad \ldots (2)$$

From article 3.2 (c), we know that

$$\overline{a} = \frac{dV}{dt}\hat{T} + \frac{V^2}{\rho}\hat{N}$$

$$\overline{V} \times \overline{a} = V\,\hat{T} \times \left(\frac{dV}{dt}\hat{T} + \frac{V^2}{\rho}\hat{N}\right) = \frac{V^3}{\rho}\,\hat{T} \times \hat{N} \qquad [\because \hat{T} \times \hat{T} = 0]$$

$\therefore$
$$|\overline{V} \times \overline{a}| = \frac{V^3}{\rho}|\hat{T} \times \hat{N}| = \frac{V^3}{\rho}$$

$\therefore$
$$\rho = \frac{V^3}{|\overline{V} \times \overline{a}|} \qquad \ldots (3)$$

(1), (2), (3) are the required results.

Ex. 11 : *If a particle moves along the cardioide $r = a\,(1 + \cos\,\theta)$ with constant velocity, show that $\dfrac{d\theta}{dt}$ is proportional to $\dfrac{1}{\sqrt{r}}$.*

Sol. : From article 3.2 (b), we know that

$$\overline{V} = \frac{d\overline{r}}{dt} = \frac{dr}{dt}\hat{r} + \left(r\frac{d\theta}{dt}\right)\hat{s} = \frac{dr}{d\theta}\frac{d\theta}{dt}\hat{r} + \left(r\frac{d\theta}{dt}\right)\hat{s} = \frac{d\theta}{dt}\left(\frac{dr}{d\theta}\hat{r} + r\,\hat{s}\right)$$

$\therefore$
$$|\overline{V}| = \frac{d\theta}{dt}\left|\frac{dr}{d\theta}\hat{r} + r\,\hat{s}\right| = \frac{d\theta}{dt}\sqrt{\left(\frac{dr}{d\theta}\right)^2 + r^2}$$

$$= \frac{d\theta}{dt}\sqrt{a^2\sin^2\theta + a^2(1 + \cos\,\theta)^2}$$

$$= a\frac{d\theta}{dt}\sqrt{\sin^2\theta + 1 + 2\cos\theta + \cos^2\theta} = \frac{d\theta}{dt}\sqrt{2}\,a\sqrt{1 + \cos\theta}$$

but
$$|\overline{V}| = \text{constant (given)} \quad \text{and} \quad \sqrt{1 + \cos\theta} = \frac{\sqrt{r}}{\sqrt{a}}$$

$\therefore$
$$\frac{d\theta}{dt} = \frac{c\sqrt{a}}{\sqrt{2}\,a\sqrt{r}} = \frac{c}{\sqrt{2}\,a}\frac{1}{\sqrt{r}}$$

$\therefore$ $\dfrac{d\theta}{dt}$ is proportional to $\dfrac{1}{\sqrt{r}}$.

Ex. 12 : *A particle moves along the curve s = a log (sec ψ + tan ψ), where ψ is the angle made by the tangent with x-axis. If the motion is such that the tangent to the curve rotates uniformly, then show that the resultant acceleration of the particle varies as the square of radius of curvature.*

Sol. : Since the tangent rotates uniformly, $\dfrac{d\psi}{dt} = \omega = $ constant.

$$\rho = \frac{ds}{d\psi} = a \cdot \frac{(\sec \psi \tan \psi + \sec^2 \psi)}{\sec \psi + \tan \psi} = a \cdot \frac{\sec \psi (\tan \psi + \sec \psi)}{(\sec \psi + \tan \psi)}$$

$$\rho = a \sec \psi$$

$$\frac{ds}{dt} = \frac{ds}{d\psi} \frac{d\psi}{dt} = a \, \omega \sec \psi$$

From article 10.2 (c),

$$\bar{a} = \frac{d^2 s}{dt^2} \hat{T} + \frac{1}{\rho} \left(\frac{ds}{dt}\right)^2 \hat{N} = a_T \, \hat{T} + a_N \, \hat{N}$$

$$|\bar{a}| = \sqrt{a_T^2 + a_N^2}$$

$$a_T = \frac{d^2 s}{dt^2} = a \, \omega \sec \psi \tan \psi \frac{d\psi}{dt} = a \, \omega^2 \sec \psi \, \tan \psi$$

$$a_N = \frac{1}{\rho} \left(\frac{ds}{dt}\right)^2 = \frac{1}{a \sec \psi} a^2 \, \omega^2 \sec^2 \psi = a \, \omega^2 \sec \psi$$

$$|\bar{a}|^2 = a^2 \, \omega^4 \sec^2 \psi \, \tan^2 \psi + a^2 \, \omega^4 \sec^2 \psi$$

$$= a^2 \, \omega^4 \sec^2 \psi \, (\tan^2 \psi + 1) = a^2 \, \omega^4 \sec^4 \psi$$

$$\therefore \qquad |\bar{a}| = a \, \omega^2 \sec^2 \psi$$

but $\qquad \rho = a \sec \psi \qquad \therefore \; \sec \psi = \dfrac{\rho}{a}$

$$\therefore \qquad |\bar{a}| = a \, \omega^2 \cdot \frac{\rho^2}{a^2} = \frac{\omega^2}{a} \cdot \rho^2 \qquad \therefore \quad |\bar{a}| = k \, \rho^2$$

as ω, a are constants.

$\therefore$ Acceleration varies as the square of radius of curvature.

Ex. 13 : *A particle moves along a curve x = 2t², y = t² – 4t, z = 2t – 5. Find components of velocity and acceleration at t = 1 in the direction $\bar{i} - 3\bar{j} + 2\bar{k}$.*

Sol. :
$$\bar{r} = x\bar{i} + y\bar{j} + z\bar{k}$$

$$= 2t^2 \, \bar{i} + (t^2 - 4t) \, \bar{j} + (2t - 5) \, \bar{k}$$

$$\bar{v} = \frac{d\bar{r}}{dt} = 4t \, \bar{i} + (2t - 4) \, \bar{j} + 2\bar{k}$$

$$\bar{v}|_{t=1} = 4\bar{i} - 2\bar{j} + 2\bar{k}$$

$$\bar{a} = \frac{d^2\bar{r}}{dt^2} = 4\bar{i} + 2\bar{j}, \quad \bar{a}]_{t=1} = 4\bar{i} + 2\bar{j}$$

$$\bar{b} = \bar{i} - 3\bar{j} + 2\bar{k}$$

$$\hat{b} = \frac{\bar{i} - 3\bar{j} + 2\bar{k}}{\sqrt{1+9+4}} = \frac{1}{\sqrt{14}}(\bar{i} - 3\bar{j} + 2\bar{k})$$

Velocity component along

$$\hat{b} = \bar{v} \cdot \hat{b} = (4\bar{i} - 2\bar{j} + 2\bar{k}) \cdot \frac{1}{\sqrt{14}}(\bar{i} - 3\bar{j} + 2\bar{k})$$

$$= \frac{1}{\sqrt{14}}(4+6+4) = \frac{14}{\sqrt{14}} = \sqrt{14}$$

Acceleration component along

$$\hat{b} = \bar{a} \cdot \hat{b} = (4\bar{i} + 2\bar{j}) \cdot \frac{1}{\sqrt{14}}(\bar{i} - 3\bar{j} + 2\bar{k})$$

$$= \frac{1}{\sqrt{14}}(4-6) = -\frac{2}{\sqrt{14}}$$

EXERCISE 3.1

1. Find the angle between tangents to the curve :

   $\bar{r} = (t^3 + 2)\,\bar{i} + (4t - 5)\,\bar{j} + (2t^2 - 6t)\,\bar{k}$ at $t = 0$ and $t = 2$. $\left(\textbf{Ans.}\dfrac{1}{\sqrt{13}\,\sqrt{14}}\right)$

2. For the curve $\bar{r} = e^{-t}\,\bar{i} + \log(t^2 + 1)\,\bar{j} - \tan t\,\bar{k}$, find velocity and acceleration at $t = 0$. $(\textbf{Ans.} -\bar{i} - \bar{k},\ \bar{i} + 2\bar{j})$

3. If $\bar{r} = \bar{a}\,e^{2t} + \bar{b}\,e^{3t}$, where $\bar{a}, \bar{b}$ are constant vectors, then show that

   $$\frac{d^2\bar{r}}{dt^2} - 5\frac{d\bar{r}}{dt} + 6\bar{r} = 0.$$

4. If $\bar{r} = \bar{a}\cos nt + \bar{b}\sin nt$, where $\bar{a} = 2\bar{i} + 2\bar{j} - \bar{k}, \bar{b} = 3\bar{i} - 2\bar{j} + 2\bar{k}$ then

   show that (i) $\dfrac{d^2\bar{r}}{dt^2} + n^2\bar{r} = 0;$ (ii) Find $\bar{r} \cdot \bar{v}$; (iii) $\bar{r} \times \bar{v}$.

   $(\textbf{Ans.}$ (ii) $4\,n\sin 2\,nt$, (iii) $n(2\bar{i} + 7\bar{j} - 10\bar{k}))$

5. A particle describes the straight line $r = a\sec\theta$ with constant angular velocity ω. Find the radial and transverse components of velocity and acceleration.

   $(\textbf{Ans.}$ (i) $a\omega\sec\theta\tan\theta,\ a\omega\sec\theta$, (ii) $2\,a\omega^2\sec\theta\tan^2\theta,\ 2\,a\omega^2\sec\theta\tan\theta)$

6. A particle describes the following curves : (i) $\dfrac{l}{r} = 1 + e \cos \theta$, (ii) $r^2 = a^2 \cos 2\theta$

under the action of a force directed towards the pole. Find the law of force in each case. **(Ans. (i) $F \propto r^{-2}$, (ii) $F \propto r^{-7}$)**

7. Find the tangential and normal components of acceleration at any time t for the curve

$\bar{r} = at \cos t \; \bar{i} + at \sin t \; \bar{j}$.   **(Ans.** $\dfrac{at}{\sqrt{1+t^2}}, \; \dfrac{a(t^2+2)}{\sqrt{1+t^2}}$ **)**

8. The vector $\bar{r}$ satisfies the equation

$$m\frac{d^2\bar{r}}{dt^2} = e\bar{E} + \frac{e}{c}\frac{d\bar{r}}{dt} \times \bar{H}, \text{ where } \bar{E} = E\bar{j}, \bar{H} = H\bar{k}. \text{ Find the solution satisfying the}$$

conditions $\bar{r} = \dfrac{d\bar{r}}{dt} = 0$ at $t = 0$, where e, m, c, E and H are constants.

9. If $\bar{r} \cdot \dfrac{d\bar{r}}{dt} = 0$, then show that $\bar{r}$ has constant magnitude.

10. A particle moves along the curve $x = a \cos t$, $y = a \sin t$, $z = bt$ with constant angular velocity ω. Find the radial and transverse components of its linear velocity and acceleration at any time t.

(Ans. $\dfrac{b^2 t}{\sqrt{a^2 + b^2 \, t^2}}, \; \omega\sqrt{a^2 + b^2 t^2} \; ; \; \dfrac{a^2 b^2}{(a^2 + b^2 t^2)^{3/2}} - \omega^2\sqrt{a^2 + b^2 t^2}, \; \dfrac{2b^2 t \, \omega}{\sqrt{a^2 + b^2 t^2}}$ **)**

11. An electron moves such that its velocity is always perpendicular to its radius vector. Show that its path is a circle.

12. A particle describes an ellipse $\dfrac{l}{r} = 1 + e \cos \theta$ with uniform angular velocity ω. Show that when the particle is at one end of latus rectum through the pole, the component of acceleration towards the pole is $(1 - 2e^2) \, \omega^2 l$.

13. Prove that $\dfrac{d}{dt}\left(\bar{v} \cdot \dfrac{d\bar{v}}{dt} \times \dfrac{d^2\bar{v}}{dt^2}\right) = \bar{v} \cdot \dfrac{d\bar{v}}{dt} \times \dfrac{d^3\bar{v}}{dt^3}$.

14. If $\bar{r} = \bar{a} \, e^{mt} + \bar{b} \, e^{nt}$, where $\bar{a}, \bar{b}$ are constant vectors, show that $\bar{r}$ satisfies the

differential equation $\dfrac{d^2\bar{r}}{dt^2} - (m+n)\dfrac{d\bar{r}}{dt} + mn \, \bar{r} = 0$.

15. Show that tangent at any point on the curve $x = e^t \cos t$, $y = e^t \sin t$, $z = e^t$ makes constant angle with z-axis. $\left(\textbf{Ans. } \phi = \cos^{-1}\dfrac{1}{\sqrt{3}}\right)$

16. If $\bar{r}(t) = t^2\,\bar{i} + t\,\bar{j} - 2t^3\,\bar{k}$, then evaluate $\displaystyle\int_1^2 \bar{r} \times \dfrac{d^2\bar{r}}{dt^2}\, dt$. $\left(\textbf{Ans. } -28\,\bar{i} + 30\,\bar{j} - 3\,\bar{k}\right)$

17. If $\bar{r} = \bar{a}\,\sinh t + \bar{b}\,\cosh t$, then prove that

(i) $\dfrac{d^2\bar{r}}{dt^2} = \bar{r}$ (ii) $\dfrac{d\bar{r}}{dt} \times \dfrac{d^2\bar{r}}{dt^2} = \text{constant}$ (iii) $\bar{r} \cdot \dfrac{d\bar{r}}{dt} \times \dfrac{d^2\bar{r}}{dt^2} = 0$

18. The position vector of a particle at time t is

$$\bar{r} = \cos(t-1)\,\bar{i} + \sinh(t-1)\,\bar{j} + mt^3\,\bar{k}$$

Find the condition imposed on m by requiring that at time $t = 1$, the acceleration is normal to the position vector. $\left(\textbf{Ans. } m = \dfrac{1}{\sqrt{6}}\right)$

19. Prove that if a particle moves always on the surface of the sphere

(i) $\bar{r} \cdot \bar{a} + \bar{V} \cdot \bar{V} = 0$ (ii) $\bar{r} \cdot \bar{a} \leq 0$

20. If a particle P moves along the curve $r = ae^{\theta}$ with constant angular velocity ω, then show that the radial and transverse components of its velocity are equal and its acceleration is always perpendicular to radius vector and is equal to $2\,r\,\omega^2$.

3.3 GRADIENT, DIVERGENCE AND CURL

Before we define these quantities which are so often encountered in vector analysis, we shall introduce certain terms.

(i) Scalar point function : If a scalar quantity ϕ depends for its value on its position say (x, y, z) in space, then $\phi(x, y, z)$ is called scalar point function. Pressure in a fluid usually varies according to its depth, hence $p(x, y, z)$ is a scalar point function. Temperature, density, potential etc. are other examples of a scalar point functions, as these quantities usually take different values at different points.

(ii) Vector point function : If a vector quantity $\bar{F}$ depends for its value on its position (x, y, z) in space, then $\bar{F}(x, y, z)$ is called vector point function. Velocity, Force, Electric Intensity etc. are examples of vector point functions.

In dealing with scalar point function $\phi(x, y, z)$ and vector point function $\bar{F}(x, y, z)$, following operations of differential calculus are found quite useful.

$$d\phi = \frac{\partial\phi}{\partial x}\,dx + \frac{\partial\phi}{\partial y}\,dy + \frac{\partial\phi}{\partial z}\,dz \qquad \frac{\partial\phi}{\partial s} = \frac{\partial\phi}{\partial x}\frac{\partial x}{\partial s} + \frac{\partial\phi}{\partial y}\frac{\partial y}{\partial s} + \frac{\partial\phi}{\partial z}\frac{\partial z}{\partial s}$$

$$d\overline{F} = \frac{\partial\overline{F}}{\partial x}\,dx + \frac{\partial\overline{F}}{\partial y}\,dy + \frac{\partial\overline{F}}{\partial z}\,dz \qquad \frac{\partial\overline{F}}{\partial s} = \frac{\partial\overline{F}}{\partial x}\frac{\partial x}{\partial s} + \frac{\partial\overline{F}}{\partial y}\frac{\partial y}{\partial s} + \frac{\partial\overline{F}}{\partial z}\frac{\partial z}{\partial s}$$

If required these results can be converted into spherical polar or cylindrical co-ordinate system.

(iii) Level surface : Let scalar point function $\phi\,(x,\,y,\,z)$ be continuous and is defined in a certain region of space. *The surface drawn in space containing all those points where $\phi\,(x,\,y,\,z)$ has same value is called a level surface.* Equipotential or isothermal surfaces are examples of level surface.

(iv) Operator 'Del' or 'Nabla' (∇) : The vector differential operator $\overline{i}\dfrac{\partial}{\partial x} + \overline{j}\dfrac{\partial}{\partial y} + \overline{k}\dfrac{\partial}{\partial z}$ is denoted by the symbol ∇ called **Del** or **Nabla**. When it operates on a scalar point function $\phi\,(x,\,y,\,z)$, we get a vector quantity $\nabla\phi = \overline{i}\dfrac{\partial\phi}{\partial x} + \overline{j}\dfrac{\partial\phi}{\partial y} + \overline{k}\dfrac{\partial\phi}{\partial z}$, called Gradient of the scalar point function $\phi\,(x,\,y,\,z)$. This is also written as Gradient ϕ or simply Grad ϕ.

$$\therefore \qquad \text{Grad } \phi = \nabla\phi = \overline{i}\frac{\partial\phi}{\partial x} + \overline{j}\frac{\partial\phi}{\partial y} + \overline{k}\frac{\partial\phi}{\partial z}$$

Consider
$$\overline{r} = x\,\overline{i} + y\,\overline{j} + z\,\overline{k}$$

$$\therefore \qquad d\overline{r} \equiv \overline{i}\,dx + \overline{j}\,dy + \overline{k}\,dz$$

$$\nabla\phi \cdot d\overline{r} \equiv \left(\overline{i}\frac{\partial\phi}{\partial x} + \overline{j}\frac{\partial\phi}{\partial y} + \overline{k}\frac{\partial\phi}{\partial z}\right) \cdot (\overline{i}\,dx + \overline{j}\,dy + \overline{k}\,dz)$$

$$\equiv \frac{\partial\phi}{\partial x}\,dx + \frac{\partial\phi}{\partial y}\,dy + \frac{\partial\phi}{\partial z}\,dz \equiv d\phi$$

This result has many useful applications. To interpret Gradient or $\nabla\phi$ physically, consider the level surfaces through $P(\overline{r})$ and $Q\,(\overline{r} + \delta\overline{r})$ where scalar function has values ϕ and $\phi + \delta\phi$ respectively (See Fig. 3.5).

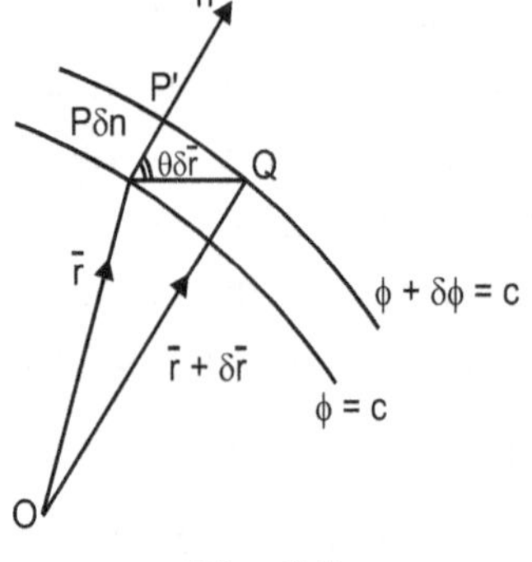

$$\overrightarrow{PQ} = \overline{r} + \delta\overline{r} - \overline{r} = \delta\overline{r}$$

$$\left|\overrightarrow{PQ}\right| = \delta r.$$

Fig. 3.5

Let $\overline{n}$ be a vector normal to the level surface $\phi = c$ at P, $\hat{n}$ be a unit vector in the same direction.

Let θ be the angle between vectors $\overline{\delta r}$ and $\hat{n}$ and let $PP' = \delta n$, then $\dfrac{\partial \phi}{\partial r}$ represents the rate of change of ϕ along the direction $\overrightarrow{PQ}$ and $\dfrac{\partial \phi}{\partial n}$ the rate of change of ϕ along the direction of normal $\hat{n}$.

We can easily see that rate of change of ϕ is maximum along the normal direction.

For
$$\frac{\delta\phi}{\delta r} = \frac{\delta\phi}{\delta n} \cdot \frac{\delta n}{\delta r} = \frac{\delta\phi}{\delta n} \cos\theta$$

$$\lim \frac{\delta\phi}{\delta r} = \frac{\partial\phi}{\partial r} \text{ and } \lim \frac{\delta\phi}{\delta n} = \frac{\partial\phi}{\partial n}$$

Above relation clearly shows that

$$\frac{\partial\phi}{\partial r} \leq \frac{\partial\phi}{\partial n}, \text{ as } \cos\theta \leq 1$$

Since $PP' = \delta n$ = projection of PQ along the normal

We have
$$dn \equiv \hat{n} \cdot \overline{dr}$$

Writing
$$d\phi \equiv \frac{\partial\phi}{\partial n} \, dn \equiv \frac{\partial\phi}{\partial n} \, (\hat{n} \cdot \overline{dr})$$

But
$$d\phi \equiv \nabla\phi \cdot \overline{dr}$$

$\therefore$
$$\nabla\phi \cdot \overline{dr} \equiv \frac{\partial\phi}{\partial n} \, \hat{n} \cdot \overline{dr}$$

Thus
$$\nabla\phi = \frac{\partial\phi}{\partial n} \, \hat{n}$$

Which shows that $\nabla\phi$ (grad ϕ) represents maximum rate of change of ϕ, which is along the outward drawn normal to the level surface, ϕ = constant.

$\dfrac{\partial\phi}{\partial r}$ represents rate of change of ϕ in any other direction and is termed as **directional derivative**. Among all the directional derivatives, $|\nabla\phi| = \dfrac{\partial\phi}{\partial n}$ has the maximum value.

It is also clear that the directional derivative of ϕ along $\overrightarrow{PQ}$ is the scalar resolute of $\nabla\phi$ in that direction. The directional derivative of ϕ along certain direction $\overline{a}$ is given by $\boldsymbol{\nabla\phi \cdot \hat{a}}$
.

By virtue of its definition, the vector differential operator ∇ behaves like ordinary differential operator $D = \dfrac{d}{dx}$.

Following deductions follow from the definition :

For any scalars u and v

(i) $\nabla (u + v) = \nabla u + \nabla v$ (ii) $\nabla (u - v) = \nabla u - \nabla v$

(iii) $\nabla (uv) = u\nabla v + v\nabla u$ (iv) $\nabla \left(\dfrac{u}{v}\right) = \dfrac{v\nabla u - u\nabla v}{v^2}$

(v) $\nabla [f(u)] = f'(u)\,\nabla u$ (vi) $\nabla (au) = a\nabla u.$

ILLUSTRATIONS

Ex. 1 : *Find $\nabla\phi$ for (i) $\phi = x^2 + y^2 + z^2$ at (1, 1, 1).*

(ii) $\phi = r^m$, where $\bar{r} = x\,\bar{i} + y\,\bar{j} + z\,\bar{k}$

(iii) $\phi = e^{-r}\,r^3$, (iv) $\nabla f(r) = \dfrac{f'(r)}{r}\,\bar{r}$, where $\bar{r} = x\,\bar{i} + y\,\bar{j} + z\,\bar{k}$.

Sol. : (i) $\phi = x^2 + y^2 + z^2$

$$\frac{\partial \phi}{\partial x} = 2x,\ \frac{\partial \phi}{\partial y} = 2y,\ \frac{\partial \phi}{\partial z} = 2z.$$

$$\nabla \phi = \bar{i}\,\frac{\partial \phi}{\partial x} + \bar{j}\,\frac{\partial \phi}{\partial y} + \bar{k}\,\frac{\partial \phi}{\partial z} = (2x\,\bar{i} + 2y\,\bar{j} + 2z\,\bar{k})$$

$\therefore$ $\{\nabla \phi\}_{(1,\,1,\,1)} = 2\,\bar{i} + 2\,\bar{j} + 2\,\bar{k},$ [putting $x = y = z = 1$]

(ii) $\phi = r^m$, $\bar{r} = x\,\bar{i} + y\,\bar{j} + z\,\bar{k}$,

$$r = \sqrt{x^2 + y^2 + z^2} \qquad\qquad \frac{\partial \phi}{\partial x} = mr^{m-1}\frac{\partial r}{\partial x}$$

$$\frac{\partial r}{\partial x} = \frac{1.2x}{2\sqrt{x^2 + y^2 + z^2}} = \frac{x}{r} \qquad \therefore\ \frac{\partial \phi}{\partial x} = mr^{m-1}\cdot\frac{x}{r} = mr^{m-2}\cdot x$$

Similarly, $\dfrac{\partial \phi}{\partial y} = mr^{m-2}\,y,\ \dfrac{\partial \phi}{\partial z} = mr^{m-2}\,z$

$$\nabla \phi = \bar{i}\,\frac{\partial \phi}{\partial x} + \bar{j}\,\frac{\partial \phi}{\partial y} + \bar{k}\,\frac{\partial \phi}{\partial z}$$

$$= \bar{i}\ mr^{m-2}\,x + \bar{j}\ mr^{m-2}\,y + \bar{k}\ mr^{m-2}\,z$$

$$= mr^{m-2}\,(x\,\bar{i} + y\,\bar{j} + z\,\bar{k})$$

$$\nabla \phi = mr^{m-2}\,\bar{r}$$

This is taken as a standard result.

(iii) $\phi = e^{-r} r^3$

$$\nabla\phi = \nabla(e^{-r} r^3)$$

$$= r^3 \nabla(e^{-r}) + e^{-r} \nabla(r^3) = r^3(-e^{-r}) \nabla(r) + e^{-r} 3r\,\bar{r}$$

$$= -r^3 e^{-r} \frac{1}{r}\,\bar{r} + 3r\,e^{-r}\,\bar{r} = e^{-r}\,\bar{r}\,(-r^2 + 3r)$$

(iv)

$$\nabla f(r) = f'(r)\,\nabla r \qquad\qquad \left(\because \nabla f(u) = f'(u)\,\nabla u\right)$$

$$= f'(r)\left(\bar{i}\,\frac{\partial r}{\partial x} + \bar{j}\,\frac{\partial r}{\partial y} + \bar{k}\,\frac{\partial r}{\partial z}\right)$$

$$= f'(r)\left(\bar{i}\,\frac{x}{r} + \bar{j}\,\frac{y}{r} + \bar{k}\,\frac{z}{r}\right)$$

$$\boxed{\nabla f(r) = \frac{f'(r)}{r}\,\bar{r}}\ .\ \text{This is also taken as a standard result.}$$

Ex. 2 : *Find the directional derivative of $\phi = xy^2 + yz^3$ at $(1, -1, 1)$,*

(i)   along the vector $\bar{i} + 2\bar{j} + 2\bar{k}$

(ii)   towards the point $(2, 1, -1)$

(iii) along the direction normal to the surface $x^2 + y^2 + z^2 = 9$ at $(1, 2, 2)$.

Sol. : (i) $\dfrac{\partial\phi}{\partial x} = y^2,\ \dfrac{\partial\phi}{\partial y} = 2xy + z^3,\ \dfrac{\partial\phi}{\partial z} = 3yz^2$

$$\nabla\phi = y^2\,\bar{i} + (2xy + z^3)\,\bar{j} + 3yz^2\,\bar{k}$$

$$[\nabla\phi]_{(1,-1,1)} = \bar{i} - \bar{j} - 3\bar{k}$$

$$\bar{a} = \bar{i} + 2\bar{j} + 2\bar{k},\ \hat{a} = \frac{\bar{i} + 2\bar{j} + 2\bar{k}}{\sqrt{1+4+4}} = \frac{1}{3}(\bar{i} + 2\bar{j} + 2\bar{k})$$

$\therefore$ Directional derivative $= \nabla\phi \cdot \hat{a} = (\bar{i} - \bar{j} - 3\bar{k}) \cdot \dfrac{1}{3}(\bar{i} + 2\bar{j} + 2\bar{k})$

$$= \frac{1}{3}[1 - 2 - 6] = \frac{-7}{3}$$

(ii) $\bar{a}$ is along the line joining $(1, -1, 1)$ and $(2, 1, -1)$.

$\therefore$

$$\bar{a} = (2-1)\,\bar{i} + (1+1)\,\bar{j} + (-1-1)\,\bar{k} = \bar{i} + 2\bar{j} - 2\bar{k}$$

$$\hat{a} = \frac{\bar{i} + 2\bar{j} - 2\bar{k}}{\sqrt{1+4+4}} = \frac{1}{3}(\bar{i} + 2\bar{j} - 2\bar{k})$$

$\therefore$ Directional derivative $= \nabla\phi \cdot \hat{a} = (\bar{i} - \bar{j} - 3\bar{k}) \cdot \dfrac{1}{3}(\bar{i} + 2\bar{j} - 2\bar{k})$

$$= \frac{1}{3}(1 - 2 + 6) = \frac{5}{3}$$

(iii) $\phi_1 = x^2 + y^2 + z^2 - 9$ $\nabla\phi_1 = 2x\,\bar{i} + 2y\,\bar{j} + 2z\,\bar{k}$

$\therefore$ $[\nabla\phi_1]_{(1,2,2)} = 2\bar{i} + 4\bar{j} + 4\bar{k}$ $\bar{a} = 2\bar{i} + 4\bar{j} + 4\bar{k}$

$$\hat{a} = \frac{2\bar{i} + 4\bar{j} + 4\bar{k}}{\sqrt{4 + 16 + 16}} = \frac{2\bar{i} + 4\bar{j} + 4\bar{k}}{6}$$

$\therefore$ Directional derivative $= \nabla\phi \cdot \hat{a} = (\bar{i} - \bar{j} - 3\bar{k}) \cdot \left(\dfrac{2\bar{i} + 4\bar{j} + 4\bar{k}}{6}\right)$

$$= \frac{1}{6}(2 - 4 - 12) = \frac{-14}{6} = \frac{-7}{3}$$

Ex. 3 : *If the directional derivative of $\phi = axy + byz + czx$ at (1, 1, 1) has maximum magnitude 4 in a direction parallel to x-axis, find the values of a, b, c.*

Sol. : $\dfrac{\partial\phi}{\partial x} = ay + cz, \quad \dfrac{\partial\phi}{\partial y} = ax + bz, \quad \dfrac{\partial\phi}{\partial z} = by + cz$

$\therefore$ $\nabla\phi = \bar{i}\,(ay + cz) + \bar{j}\,(ax + bz) + \bar{k}\,(by + cx)$

and $[\nabla\phi]_{(1,1,1)} = (a + c)\,\bar{i} + (a + b)\,\bar{j} + (b + c)\,\bar{k}$

Now $(a + c)\,\bar{i} + (a + b)\,\bar{j} + (b + c)\,\bar{k} = 4\,\bar{i}$ (given)

$\therefore$ $a + c = 4, \quad a + b = 0, \quad b + c = 0$

which gives on solving $a = 2, \ b = -2, \ c = 2$.

Ex. 4 : *The directional derivative of $\phi\,(x, y)$ at the point A (3, 2) towards the point B (2, 3) is $3\sqrt{2}$ and towards the point C (1, 0) is $\sqrt{8}$. Find the directional derivative at the point A towards the point D (2, 4).*

Sol. : For function $\phi\,(x, y)$, $\nabla\phi = \bar{i}\,\dfrac{\partial\phi}{\partial x} + \bar{j}\,\dfrac{\partial\phi}{\partial y}$

$$\overrightarrow{AB} = (2 - 3)\,\bar{i} + (3 - 2)\,\bar{j} = -\bar{i} + \bar{j}$$

Directional derivative of $\phi\,(x, y)$ towards $\overrightarrow{AB}$ is

$$\nabla\phi \cdot \widehat{AB} = \left(\bar{i}\,\frac{\partial\phi}{\partial x} + \bar{j}\,\frac{\partial\phi}{\partial y}\right) \cdot \left(\frac{-\bar{i} + \bar{j}}{\sqrt{2}}\right) = 3\sqrt{2}$$

$$\therefore \qquad -\frac{\partial\phi}{\partial x} + \frac{\partial\phi}{\partial y} = 6 \qquad\qquad \dots (1)$$

Directional derivative at A $(3, 2)$ towards C $(1, 0)$ is

$$\nabla\phi \cdot \hat{AC} = \left(\bar{i}\frac{\partial\phi}{\partial x} + \bar{j}\frac{\partial\phi}{\partial y} \right) \cdot \frac{(-2\,\bar{i} - 2\,\bar{j})}{\sqrt{8}} = \sqrt{8}$$

$$\therefore \qquad -2\frac{\partial\phi}{\partial x} - 2\frac{\partial\phi}{\partial y} = 8 \ \text{ or } \ \frac{\partial\phi}{\partial x} + \frac{\partial\phi}{\partial y} = -4 \qquad\qquad \dots (2)$$

From (1) and (2), $\quad \dfrac{\partial\phi}{\partial y} = 1, \ \dfrac{\partial\phi}{\partial x} = -5$

$$\therefore \qquad \nabla\phi = -5\,\bar{i} + \bar{j}$$

Hence, directional derivative at A $(3, 2)$ towards D $(2, 4)$ is

$$\nabla\phi \cdot \hat{AD} = (-5\,\bar{i} + \bar{j}) \cdot \left(\frac{-\bar{i} + 2\,\bar{j}}{\sqrt{5}} \right) = \frac{7}{\sqrt{5}}$$

Ex. 5 : *For the function* $f = x^2y + 2y^2x$, *find the following at the point P $(1, 3)$:*

(i)   the direction of the greatest increase in f.

(ii)   the direction of the greatest decrease in f.

(iii)   the directional derivative of f in the direction of the greatest increase in f.

(iv)   the directions in which the directional derivative is zero.

Sol. : (i) Direction of greatest increase in f is along ∇f

and $\qquad\qquad \nabla f = \bar{i}\dfrac{\partial f}{\partial x} + \bar{j}\dfrac{\partial f}{\partial y} = \bar{i}\,(2xy + 2y^2) + \bar{j}\,(x^2 + 4yx)$

i.e. $\qquad\qquad [\nabla f]_{(1,\,3)} = 24\,\bar{i} + 13\,\bar{j}$

(ii)   Direction of greatest decrease in f is along

$$[-\nabla f]_{(1,\,3)} = -24\,\bar{i} - 13\,\bar{j}$$

(iii)   Directional derivative of f along the direction of greatest increase in f

$$= [\nabla f]_{(1,\,3)} \cdot \frac{(24\,\bar{i} + 13\,\bar{j})}{\sqrt{(24)^2 + (13)^2}} = (24\,\bar{i} + 13\,\bar{j}) \cdot \frac{(24\,\bar{i} + 13\,\bar{j})}{\sqrt{(24)^2 + (13)^2}}$$

$$= \sqrt{(24)^2 + (13)^2} = 27.294$$

(iv) If directional derivative is zero along $a_1 \bar{i} + a_2 \bar{j}$

then $\qquad [\nabla f]_{(1,3)} \cdot (a_1 \bar{i} + a_2 \bar{j}) = 0$

$$(24\,\bar{i} + 13\,\bar{j}) \cdot (a_1 \bar{i} + a_2 \bar{j}) = 0$$

$$24\,a_1 + 13\,a_2 = 0 \qquad \therefore \ \frac{a_1}{13} = \frac{-a_2}{24}$$

$\therefore \quad$ Directions are $\bar{u}_1 = 13\,\bar{i} - 24\,\bar{j}, \ \bar{u}_2 = -13\,\bar{i} + 24\,\bar{j}$.

Ex. 6 : *In what direction from the point (2, 1, –1) is the directional derivative of* $\phi = x^2 yz^3$ *a maximum ? What is the magnitude of this maximum ?*

Sol. : $\qquad\qquad\qquad \phi = x^2 y\, z^3$

$$\nabla\phi = (2xyz^3)\,\bar{i} + (x^2 z^3)\,\bar{j} + (3x^2 yz^2)\,\bar{k}$$

$$(\nabla\phi)_{(2,1,-1)} = -4\,\bar{i} - 4\,\bar{j} + 12\,\bar{k}$$

$\therefore \quad$ Directional derivative of ϕ is maximum in the direction of $\nabla\phi$ i.e. in the direction of $-4\,\bar{i} - 4\,\bar{j} + 12\,\bar{k}$.

The maximum magnitude $= |\nabla\phi| = \sqrt{16 + 16 + 144} = 4\sqrt{11}$.

Ex. 7 : *Find the directional derivative of* $\phi = e^{2x} \cdot \cos yz$ *at (0, 0, 0) in the direction of tangent to the curve* $x = a \sin t; \ y = a \cos t; \ z = at,$ *at* $t = \dfrac{\pi}{4}$. **(SUK Dec. 11)**

Sol. : $\qquad\qquad\qquad \phi = e^{2x} \cos yz$

$$\nabla\phi = (2e^{2x} \cos yz)\,\bar{i} - (e^{2x} z \cdot \sin yz)\,\bar{j} - (e^{2x} y \sin yz)\,\bar{k}$$

$\therefore \qquad (\nabla\phi)_{(0,0,0)} = 2\,\bar{i}$

Also, for $\qquad \bar{r} = x\,\bar{i} + y\,\bar{j} + z\,\bar{k} = (a \sin t)\,\bar{i} + (a \cos t)\,\bar{j} + (at)\,\bar{k}$

tangent to the curve $= \dfrac{d\bar{r}}{dt} = (a \cos t)\,\bar{i} - a \sin t\,\bar{j} + a\,\bar{k}$

$\therefore$ At $t = \dfrac{\pi}{4}, \qquad \dfrac{d\bar{r}}{dt} = \dfrac{a}{\sqrt{2}}\,\bar{i} - \dfrac{a}{\sqrt{2}}\,\bar{j} + a\,\bar{k} = \bar{u}$ (say)

$\therefore$ Directional derivative $= \nabla\phi \cdot \hat{u}$

$$= (2\bar{i}) \cdot \left(\frac{\dfrac{a}{\sqrt{2}}\,\bar{i} - \dfrac{a}{\sqrt{2}}\,\bar{j} + a\,\bar{k}}{\sqrt{\dfrac{a^2}{2} + \dfrac{a^2}{2} + a^2}} \right) = \frac{\sqrt{2}\,a}{\sqrt{2}\,a} = 1$$

Ex. 8 : *If directional derivative of $\phi = ax^2 y + by^2 z + cz^2 x$ at $(1, 1, 1)$ has maximum magnitude 15 in the direction parallel to $\dfrac{x-1}{2} = \dfrac{y-3}{-2} = \dfrac{z}{1}$, hence find the values of a, b, c.*

Sol. :
$$\phi = ax^2 y + by^2 z + cz^2 x$$

$$\nabla\phi = (2axy + cz^2)\,\bar{i} + (ax^2 + 2byz)\,\bar{j} + (by^2 + 2czx)\,\bar{k}$$

$$(\nabla\phi)_{(1,1,1)} = (2a + c)\,\bar{i} + (a + 2b)\,\bar{j} + (b + 2c)\,\bar{k}$$

Given direction is $2\bar{i} - 2\bar{j} + \bar{k}$.

$$\therefore \qquad \frac{2a+c}{2} = \frac{a+2b}{2} = \frac{b+2c}{1}$$

Solving first two $\qquad 3a + 2b + c = 0$

Solving last two $\qquad a + 4b + 4c = 0$

$$\therefore \qquad \frac{a}{4} = \frac{b}{-11} = \frac{c}{10} = \lambda \text{ (say)}$$

$a = 4\lambda, \ b = -11\lambda, \ c = 10\lambda$

$$\therefore \qquad 15 = |\nabla\phi| = \sqrt{(2a+c)^2 + (a+2b)^2 + (b+2c)^2}$$

$$= \sqrt{(18\lambda)^2 + (-18\lambda)^2 + (9\lambda)^2}$$

$$15 = \pm 27\lambda \qquad\qquad \therefore \lambda = \pm\frac{5}{9}$$

$$a = \pm\frac{20}{9}, \quad b = \pm\frac{55}{9}, \quad c = \pm\frac{50}{9}$$

Ex. 9 : *If T be the temperature at a point (x, y, z) then find the directional derivative of T at $(1, 1, 1)$ in the direction of the vector $\bar{i} - \bar{j} + 2\bar{k}$ assuming that ∇T at $(1, 1, 1)$ is $2\bar{i} + 3\bar{j} + 4\bar{k}$ and further estimate the change in the temperature as we move from the point to a distance 0.2 units in the direction of the vector $\bar{i} - \bar{j} + 2\bar{k}$. Also find two unit vectors such that the directional derivative of T is zero at $(1, 1, 1)$.*

Sol. :
$$(\nabla T)_{(1,1,1)} = 2\bar{i} + 3\bar{j} + 4\bar{k}$$

$$\bar{a} = \bar{i} - \bar{j} + 2\bar{k} \qquad \therefore \ \hat{a} = \frac{\bar{i} - \bar{j} + 2\bar{k}}{\sqrt{6}}$$

$$\therefore \ \text{Directional derivative} = (\nabla T) \cdot \hat{a}$$

$$= (2\bar{i} + 3\bar{j} + 4\bar{k}) \cdot \frac{\bar{i} - \bar{j} + 2\bar{k}}{\sqrt{6}} = \frac{7}{\sqrt{6}}$$

The change in T that results from moving away $\Delta s = 0.2$ units from $(1, 1, 1)$ in the direction of $\hat{a}$ is $(\nabla T \cdot \hat{a}) \Delta s = \frac{7}{\sqrt{6}} (0.2) = \frac{7}{5\sqrt{6}}$

Let $\hat{a} = \dfrac{a_1 \bar{i} + a_2 \bar{j} + a_3 \bar{k}}{\sqrt{a_1^2 + a_2^2 + a_3^2}}$ be the unit vector such that directional derivative of T is zero at $(1, 1, 1)$.

$$\therefore \qquad (\nabla T) \cdot \hat{a} = 0 \Rightarrow (2\bar{i} + 3\bar{j} + 4\bar{k}) \cdot (a_1 \bar{i} + a_2 \bar{j} + a_3 \bar{k}) = 0$$

$$2a_1 + 3a_2 + 4a_3 = 0$$

Let $a_3 = 0$

$$\therefore \qquad 2a_1 + 3a_2 = 0$$

$$\frac{a_1}{3} = -\frac{a_2}{2} \qquad \therefore \ \hat{a} = \frac{3\bar{i} - 2\bar{j}}{\sqrt{13}}$$

Similarly, $\qquad \hat{b} = \dfrac{-3\bar{i} + 2\bar{j}}{\sqrt{13}}$

Ex. 10 : *If* $\nabla\phi = (y^2 + 2y + z)\,\bar{i} + (2xy + 2x)\,\bar{j} + x\bar{k}$, *find* ϕ *if* $\phi(1, 1, 0) = 5$.

Sol. :
$$\frac{\partial\phi}{\partial x} = y^2 + 2y + z \qquad\qquad\qquad \text{... (1)}$$

$$\frac{\partial\phi}{\partial y} = 2xy + 2x \qquad\qquad\qquad \text{...(2)}$$

$$\frac{\partial\phi}{\partial z} = x \qquad\qquad\qquad \text{... (3)}$$

Integrating (1) partially w.r.t. x,

$$\phi(x, y, z) = xy^2 + 2xy + zx + c_1 (y, z)$$

$$\frac{\partial\phi}{\partial y} = 2xy + 2x + \frac{\partial c_1}{\partial y} = 2xy + 2x$$

$$\therefore \qquad\qquad \frac{\partial c_1}{\partial y} = 0$$

Integrating, $\qquad c_1 = c_2 (z)$

$$\phi = xy^2 + 2xy + zx + c_2 (z)$$

$$\frac{\partial \phi}{\partial z} = x + 2\frac{dc_2}{dz} = x$$

$$\therefore \qquad \frac{dc_2}{dz} = 0 \quad \text{or} \quad c_2 = c$$

$$\therefore \qquad \phi(x, y, z) = xy^2 + 2xy + zx + c$$

$$\phi(1, 1, 0) = 1 + 2 + c = 5$$

$$\therefore \qquad c = 2$$

$$\therefore \qquad \phi(x, y, z) = xy^2 + 2xy + zx + 2$$

V. DIVERGENCE OF A VECTOR

When a vector differential operator ∇ operates scalarly on vector point function $\overline{F}$, it gives a scalar quantity $\nabla \cdot \overline{F}$, called **Divergence of $\overline{F}$** or **Div $\overline{F}$**.

As an illustration, consider $\overline{r} = x\,\overline{i} + y\,\overline{j} + z\,\overline{k}$

$$\therefore \qquad \nabla \cdot \overline{r} = \left(\overline{i}\frac{\partial}{\partial x} + \overline{j}\frac{\partial}{\partial y} + \overline{k}\frac{\partial}{\partial z}\right) \cdot (x\,\overline{i} + y\,\overline{j} + z\,\overline{k})$$

$$= \frac{\partial}{\partial x}(x) + \frac{\partial}{\partial y}(y) + \frac{\partial}{\partial z}(z) = 1 + 1 + 1 = 3$$

This is taken as a standard result.

In general, if

$$\overline{F} = F_1\,\overline{i} + F_2\,\overline{j} + F_3\,\overline{k}$$

$$\nabla \cdot \overline{F} = \frac{\partial F_1}{\partial x} + \frac{\partial F_2}{\partial y} + \frac{\partial F_3}{\partial z}$$

it is also written as div $\overline{F}$.

In particular, if $\nabla \cdot \overline{F} = 0$, **the vector field $\overline{F}$ is called solenoidal.**

It may also be noted here that, while $\nabla \cdot \overline{F}$ gives divergence of a vector field

$$\overline{F} \cdot \nabla = (F_1\,\overline{i} + F_2\,\overline{j} + F_3\,\overline{k}) \cdot \left(\overline{i}\frac{\partial}{\partial x} + \overline{j}\frac{\partial}{\partial y} + \overline{k}\frac{\partial}{\partial z}\right)$$

$$= F_1\frac{\partial}{\partial x} + F_2\frac{\partial}{\partial y} + F_3\frac{\partial}{\partial z}$$

gives a scalar differential operator.

Note : $\qquad \nabla \cdot \overline{F} \ne \overline{F} \cdot \nabla$

If $\overline{a} = a_1\,\overline{i} + a_2\,\overline{j} + a_3\overline{k}$ is a constant vector and $\overline{r} = x\,\overline{i} + y\,\overline{j} + z\,\overline{k}$

$$(\bar{a} \cdot \nabla)\, \bar{r} \;=\; \left(a_1 \frac{\partial}{\partial x} + a_2 \frac{\partial}{\partial y} + a_3 \frac{\partial}{\partial z}\right)\bar{r} \;=\; a_1 \frac{\partial \bar{r}}{\partial x} + a_2 \frac{\partial \bar{r}}{\partial y} + a_3 \frac{\partial \bar{r}}{\partial z}$$

$$= a_1\,\bar{i} + a_2\,\bar{j} + a_3\,\bar{k} \left[\because \; \frac{\partial \bar{r}}{\partial x} = \bar{i} \text{ etc.}\right]$$

$$\therefore \qquad\qquad (\bar{a} \cdot \nabla)\, \bar{r} \;=\; \bar{a}$$

This is also taken as a standard result.

To interpret divergence of a vector field physically, consider the motion of fluid with velocity $\bar{v} = V_1\,\bar{i} + V_2\,\bar{j} + V_3\,\bar{k}$ at a point A (x, y, z). Consider a small parallelopiped with edges δx, δy, δz parallel to the axes in the mass of fluid with one of its corners at the point A. (See Fig. 3.6).

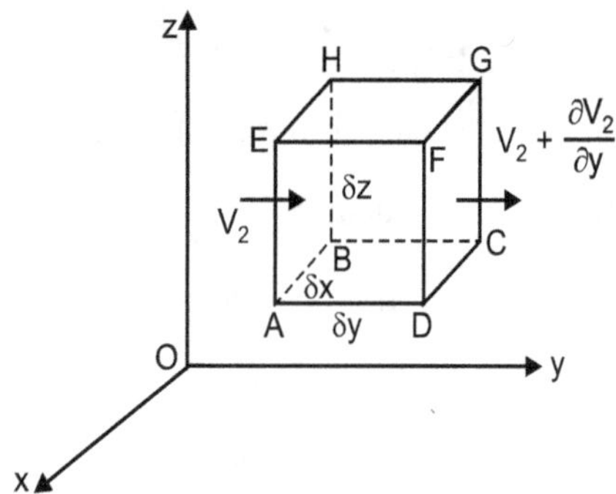

Fig. 3.6

Consider the flow parallel to y-axis that is across the faces ABEH and DCFG. Flow per unit time across the face ABEH $= V_2 \cdot \delta x\, \delta z$

where, V_2 is y component of velocity at the face ABEH.

Now, the y component of velocity at the face DCFG is $V_2 + \dfrac{\partial V_2}{\partial y}\, \delta y$

$\therefore$ Flow per unit time across the face DCFG is $\left(V_2 + \dfrac{\partial V_2}{\partial y}\, \delta y\right) \delta x\, \delta z$.

Thus the rate at which fluid flows out from the elementary volume along the y direction is $\left(V_2 + \dfrac{\partial V_2}{\partial y}\, \delta y\right) \delta x\, \delta z - V_2\, \delta x\, \delta z = \dfrac{\partial V_2}{\partial y}\, \delta x\, \delta y\, \delta z$.

Similarly, the rate of outward flow along x and z directions will be given by $\dfrac{\partial V_1}{\partial x}\, \delta x\, \delta y\, \delta z$, $\dfrac{\partial V_3}{\partial z}\, \delta x\, \delta y\, \delta z$ respectively.

Thus the rate at which fluid flows out of the volume

$$= \left(\frac{\partial V_1}{\partial x} + \frac{\partial V_2}{\partial y} + \frac{\partial V_3}{\partial z}\right) \delta x\, \delta y\, \delta z$$

The rate of outward flow per unit volume

$$= \frac{\partial V_1}{\partial x} + \frac{\partial V_2}{\partial y} + \frac{\partial V_3}{\partial z} = \nabla \cdot \bar{v}$$

Thus the divergence of $\bar{v}$ represents the rate of outward flow through unit volume. Similarly, if $\bar{V}$ represents an electric flux, div $\bar{V}$ is the amount of flux which diverges per unit volume. Various other examples can be quoted to interpret the divergence of $\bar{F}$ in a similar manner.

VI. CURL OF A VECTOR

When a vector differential operator ∇ operates vertorially on vector point function $\bar{F}$, it gives a vector quantity $\nabla \times \bar{F}$, called **curl of $\bar{F}$** or simply **curl $\bar{F}$**.

If
$$\bar{F} = F_1\,\bar{i} + F_2\,\bar{j} + F_3\,\bar{k}$$

$$\text{curl }\bar{F} = \nabla \times \bar{F} = \left(\bar{i}\,\frac{\partial}{\partial x} + \bar{j}\,\frac{\partial}{\partial y} + \bar{k}\,\frac{\partial}{\partial z}\right) \times (F_1\,\bar{i} + F_2\,\bar{j} + F_3\,\bar{k})$$

$$= \bar{k}\,\frac{\partial F_2}{\partial x} - \bar{j}\,\frac{\partial F_3}{\partial x} - \bar{k}\,\frac{\partial F_1}{\partial y} + \bar{i}\,\frac{\partial F_3}{\partial y} + \bar{j}\,\frac{\partial F_1}{\partial z} - \bar{i}\,\frac{\partial F_2}{\partial z}$$

$$= \bar{i}\left(\frac{\partial F_3}{\partial y} - \frac{\partial F_2}{\partial z}\right) + \bar{j}\left(\frac{\partial F_1}{\partial z} - \frac{\partial F_3}{\partial x}\right) + \bar{k}\left(\frac{\partial F_2}{\partial x} - \frac{\partial F_1}{\partial y}\right)$$

Conveniently, this can also be expressed in the determinant form as

$$\text{curl }\bar{F} = \nabla \times \bar{F} = \begin{vmatrix} \bar{i} & \bar{j} & \bar{k} \\ \dfrac{\partial}{\partial x} & \dfrac{\partial}{\partial y} & \dfrac{\partial}{\partial z} \\ F_1 & F_2 & F_3 \end{vmatrix}$$

For
$$\bar{r} = x\,\bar{i} + y\,\bar{j} + z\,\bar{k}$$

$$\nabla \times \bar{r} = \begin{vmatrix} \bar{i} & \bar{j} & \bar{k} \\ \dfrac{\partial}{\partial x} & \dfrac{\partial}{\partial y} & \dfrac{\partial}{\partial z} \\ x & y & z \end{vmatrix} = \bar{i}\left(\frac{\partial z}{\partial y} - \frac{\partial y}{\partial z}\right) + \bar{j}\left(\frac{\partial x}{\partial z} - \frac{\partial z}{\partial x}\right) + \bar{k}\left(\frac{\partial y}{\partial x} - \frac{\partial x}{\partial y}\right)$$

$$\therefore \qquad \nabla \times \bar{r} = 0$$

This result is taken as a standard result and can be used in the solution of problems.

Vector field $\bar{F}$ is called irrotational if $\nabla \times \bar{F} = 0$

To interprete curl of a vector field physically, consider the motion of a rigid body about a fixed axis passing through O [Refer article 3.2 (b) (ii)]. If $\bar{\omega}$ is the angular velocity of the rigid body, $\bar{v}$ the linear velocity of a point P $(\bar{r})$, then

$$\overline{v} = \overline{\omega} \times \overline{r}$$

$$\text{Curl } \overline{v} = \nabla \times (\overline{\omega} \times \overline{r})$$

Let

$$\overline{\omega} = \omega_1 \overline{i} + \omega_2 \overline{j} + \omega_3 \overline{k}$$

$$\therefore \quad \overline{\omega} \times \overline{r} = \begin{vmatrix} \overline{i} & \overline{j} & \overline{k} \\ \omega_1 & \omega_2 & \omega_3 \\ x & y & z \end{vmatrix}$$

$$= \overline{i}\,(\omega_2 z - \omega_3 y) + \overline{j}\,(\omega_3 x - \omega_1 z) + \overline{k}\,(\omega_1 y - \omega_2 x)$$

$$\therefore \quad \nabla \times (\overline{\omega} \times \overline{r}) = \begin{vmatrix} \overline{i} & \overline{j} & \overline{k} \\ \dfrac{\partial}{\partial x} & \dfrac{\partial}{\partial y} & \dfrac{\partial}{\partial z} \\ \omega_2 z - \omega_3 y & \omega_3 x - \omega_1 z & \omega_1 y - \omega_2 x \end{vmatrix}$$

$$= \overline{i}\left\{\frac{\partial}{\partial y}(\omega_1 y - \omega_2 x) - \frac{\partial}{\partial z}(\omega_3 x - \omega_1 z)\right\} + \overline{j}\left\{\frac{\partial}{\partial z}(\omega_2 z - \omega_3 y) - \frac{\partial}{\partial x}(\omega_1 y - \omega_2 x)\right\}$$

$$+ \overline{k}\left\{\frac{\partial}{\partial x}(\omega_3 x - \omega_1 z) - \frac{\partial}{\partial y}(\omega_2 z - \omega_3 y)\right\}$$

$$= \overline{i}\,(\omega_1 + \omega_1) + \overline{j}\,(\omega_2 + \omega_2) + \overline{k}\,(\omega_3 + \omega_3) = 2\,(\omega_1 \overline{i} + \omega_2 \overline{j} + \omega_3 \overline{k})$$

$$\text{curl } \overline{v} = 2\,\overline{\omega}$$

or

$$\overline{\omega} = \frac{1}{2}\,\text{curl } \overline{v}$$

Thus the angular velocity of rotation at any point is equal to half the curl of the velocity vector. **The curl of vector thus signifies rotation.**

3.4 VECTOR IDENTITIES

Given scalar function ϕ and vector functions $\overline{u}$, $\overline{v}$. Following results involving operation of ∇ are quite useful.

(1) $\qquad \nabla \cdot (\phi \overline{u}) = \nabla\phi \cdot \overline{u} + \phi\,(\nabla \cdot \overline{u})$

or $\qquad \text{Div }(\phi \overline{u}) = \overline{u} \cdot \text{Grad }\phi + \phi\,\text{Div }\overline{u}$

Let $\qquad \overline{u} = u_1 \overline{i} + u_2 \overline{j} + u_3 \overline{k}$

$$\therefore \qquad \phi\,\overline{u} = \phi\,u_1\,\overline{i} + \phi\,u_2\,\overline{j} + \phi\,u_3\,\overline{k}$$

$$\text{L.H.S.} = \nabla \cdot (\phi\,\overline{u}) = \frac{\partial}{\partial x}(\phi\,u_1) + \frac{\partial}{\partial y}(\phi\,u_2) + \frac{\partial}{\partial z}(\phi\,u_3)$$

$$= \phi\frac{\partial u_1}{\partial x} + u_1\frac{\partial \phi}{\partial x} + \phi\frac{\partial u_2}{\partial y} + u_2\frac{\partial \phi}{\partial y} + \phi\frac{\partial u_3}{\partial z} + u_3\frac{\partial \phi}{\partial z}$$

$$= \phi\left(\frac{\partial u_1}{\partial x} + \frac{\partial u_2}{\partial y} + \frac{\partial u_3}{\partial z}\right) + u_1\frac{\partial \phi}{\partial x} + u_2\frac{\partial \phi}{\partial y} + u_3\frac{\partial \phi}{\partial z}$$

$$= \phi\,(\nabla \cdot \overline{u}) + (u_1\,\overline{i} + u_2\,\overline{j} + u_3\,\overline{k}) \cdot \left(\overline{i}\frac{\partial \phi}{\partial x} + \overline{j}\frac{\partial \phi}{\partial y} + \overline{k}\frac{\partial \phi}{\partial z}\right)$$

$$= \phi\,(\nabla \cdot \overline{u}) + \overline{u} \cdot \nabla\phi = \text{R.H.S.}$$

Alternatively, the result can be proved by symbolic procedure.

∇ being vector differential operator, it behaves like an operator $D = \dfrac{d}{dx}$ just as

$$D\,(uv) = uDv + vDu = D_u\,(uv) + D_v\,(uv)$$

We can write $\quad \nabla \cdot (\phi\,\overline{u}) = \nabla_\phi \cdot (\phi\,\overline{u}) + \nabla\overline{u} \cdot (\phi\overline{u})$

(the suffix of ∇ is to be treated as constant in each expression.)

$$= \phi\,(\nabla_\phi \cdot \overline{u}) + \overline{u} \cdot \nabla_{\overline{u}}\,\phi$$

Omitting the suffix now $= \phi\,(\nabla \cdot \overline{u}) + \overline{u} \cdot \nabla_\phi$

Symbolic procedure is not rigorous way of presenting the proof of vector identities, but is quite useful in solution of problems.

(2) $\nabla \times (\phi\,\overline{u}) = \nabla\phi \times \overline{u} + \phi\,(\nabla \times \overline{u})$

or $\qquad\qquad \text{curl}\,(\phi\,\overline{u}) = \text{Grad}\,\phi \times \overline{u} + \phi\,\text{curl}\,\overline{u}$

As before, let $\qquad\qquad \overline{u} = u_1\,\overline{i} + u_2\,\overline{j} + u_3\,\overline{k}$

$$\text{L.H.S.} = \nabla \times (\phi\,\overline{u})$$

$$= \begin{vmatrix} \overline{i} & \overline{j} & \overline{k} \\ \dfrac{\partial}{\partial x} & \dfrac{\partial}{\partial y} & \dfrac{\partial}{\partial z} \\ \phi\,u_1 & \phi\,u_2 & \phi\,u_3 \end{vmatrix}$$

$$= \overline{i}\left\{\frac{\partial}{\partial y}(\phi u_3) - \frac{\partial}{\partial z}(\phi u_2)\right\} + \overline{j}\left\{\frac{\partial}{\partial z}(\phi u_1) - \frac{\partial}{\partial x}(\phi u_3)\right\} + \overline{k}\left\{\frac{\partial}{\partial x}(\phi u_2) - \frac{\partial}{\partial y}(\phi u_1)\right\}$$

$$= \bar{i}\left\{\phi\frac{\partial u_3}{\partial y} + u_3\frac{\partial \phi}{\partial y} - \phi\frac{\partial u_2}{\partial z} - u_2\frac{\partial \phi}{\partial z}\right\} + \bar{j}\left\{\phi\frac{\partial u_1}{\partial z} + u_1\frac{\partial \phi}{\partial z} - \phi\frac{\partial u_3}{\partial x} - u_3\frac{\partial \phi}{\partial x}\right\}$$

$$+ \bar{k}\left\{u_2\frac{\partial \phi}{\partial x} + \phi\frac{\partial u_2}{\partial x} - \phi\frac{\partial u_1}{\partial y} - u_1\frac{\partial \phi}{\partial y}\right\}$$

$$= \phi\left[\bar{i}\left(\frac{\partial u_3}{\partial y} - \frac{\partial u_2}{\partial z}\right) + \bar{j}\left(\frac{\partial u_1}{\partial z} - \frac{\partial u_3}{\partial x}\right) + \bar{k}\left(\frac{\partial u_2}{\partial x} - \frac{\partial u_1}{\partial y}\right)\right]$$

$$+ \bar{i}\left(u_3\frac{\partial \phi}{\partial y} - u_2\frac{\partial \phi}{\partial z}\right) + \bar{j}\left(u_1\frac{\partial \phi}{\partial z} - u_3\frac{\partial \phi}{\partial x}\right) + \bar{k}\left(u_2\frac{\partial \phi}{\partial x} - u_1\frac{\partial \phi}{\partial y}\right)$$

$$= \phi\left(\nabla \times \bar{u}\right) + \nabla\phi \times \bar{u}$$

For $\quad \nabla\phi \times \bar{u} \;=\; \begin{vmatrix} \bar{i} & \bar{j} & \bar{k} \\ \dfrac{\partial \phi}{\partial x} & \dfrac{\partial \phi}{\partial y} & \dfrac{\partial \phi}{\partial z} \\ u_1 & u_2 & u_3 \end{vmatrix}$

$$= \bar{i}\left(u_3\frac{\partial \phi}{\partial y} - u_2\frac{\partial \phi}{\partial z}\right) + \bar{j}\left(u_1\frac{\partial \phi}{\partial z} - u_3\frac{\partial \phi}{\partial x}\right) + \bar{k}\left(u_2\frac{\partial \phi}{\partial x} - u_1\frac{\partial \phi}{\partial y}\right)$$

which proves the result.

Alternatively, $\nabla \times (\phi\,\bar{u}) \;=\; \nabla_\phi \times (\phi\,\bar{u}) + \nabla\,\bar{u} \times (\phi\,\bar{u})$

$$= \phi\left(\nabla_\phi \times \bar{u}\right) + \nabla_{\bar{u}} \times (\phi\,\bar{u})$$

$$= \phi\left(\nabla \times \bar{u}\right) + \nabla\phi \times \bar{u} \qquad\qquad \text{(Dropping the suffixes)}$$

(3) $\nabla \cdot (\bar{u} \times \bar{v}) = \bar{v} \cdot (\nabla \times \bar{u}) - \bar{u} \cdot (\nabla \times \bar{v})$

or $\qquad\qquad \mathrm{Div}\,(\bar{u} \times \bar{v}) \;=\; \bar{v} \cdot \mathrm{curl}\,\bar{u} - \bar{u} \cdot \mathrm{curl}\,\bar{v}$

Using symbolic procedure,

$$\nabla \cdot (\bar{u} \times \bar{v}) \;=\; \nabla_{\bar{u}} \cdot (\bar{u} \times \bar{v}) + \nabla_{\bar{v}} \cdot (\bar{u} \times \bar{v})$$

Using the property of scalar triple product and remembering that $\nabla_{\bar{u}}$ must immediately precede $\bar{v}$ as $\bar{u}$ is to be treated as constant and $\nabla_{\bar{v}}$ must precede $\bar{u}$ as $\bar{v}$ is to be treated as constant, we write

$$\nabla \cdot (\bar{u} \times \bar{v}) \;=\; -\bar{u} \cdot (\nabla_{\bar{u}} \times \bar{v}) + \bar{v} \cdot (\nabla_{\bar{v}} \times \bar{u})$$

$$[\bar{a} \cdot \bar{b} \times \bar{c}] \;=\; -\bar{b} \cdot (\bar{a} \times \bar{c}) = \bar{c} \cdot (\bar{a} \times \bar{b})$$

Dropping the suffixes $\;=\; -\bar{u} \cdot (\nabla \times \bar{v}) + \bar{v} \cdot (\nabla \times \bar{u})$

which establishes the result.

Students are advised to establish the result by components method i.e. taking

$$\bar{u} = u_1\bar{i} + u_2\bar{j} + u_3\bar{k} \text{ etc. and proving}$$

$$\text{L.H.S.} = \text{R.H.S. by actually obtaining dot and cross products.}$$

(4) $\nabla \times (\bar{u} \times \bar{v}) = \bar{u}(\nabla \cdot \bar{v}) - (\bar{u} \cdot \nabla)\bar{v} + (\bar{v} \cdot \nabla)\bar{u} - \bar{v}(\nabla \cdot \bar{u})$

$$\nabla \times (\bar{u} \times \bar{v}) = \nabla_{\bar{u}} \times (\bar{u} \times \bar{v}) + \nabla_{\bar{v}} \times (\bar{u} \times \bar{v}) \qquad \ldots (1)$$

Using $\bar{a} \times (\bar{b} \times \bar{c}) = (\bar{a} \cdot \bar{c})\bar{b} - (\bar{a} \cdot \bar{b})\bar{c}$ and remembering that when $\bar{u}$ is to be

treated as constant $\bar{u} \cdot \nabla$ is meaningful rather than $\nabla \cdot \bar{u}$ and $\nabla_{\bar{u}}$ must precede $\bar{v}$ etc.

$$\nabla_{\bar{u}} \times (\bar{u} \times \bar{v}) = (\nabla_{\bar{u}} \cdot \bar{v})\bar{u} - (\bar{u} \cdot \nabla_{\bar{u}})\bar{v},$$

$$\nabla_{\bar{v}} \times (\bar{u} \times \bar{v}) = (\bar{v} \cdot \nabla_{\bar{v}})\bar{u} - (\nabla_{\bar{v}} \cdot \bar{u})\bar{v}$$

Dropping the suffixes and putting the values of $\nabla_{\bar{u}}(\bar{u} \times \bar{v})$ and $\nabla_{\bar{v}} \times (\bar{u} \times \bar{v})$ in (1),

we get $\qquad \nabla \times (\bar{u} \times \bar{v}) = (\nabla \cdot \bar{v})\bar{u} - (\bar{u} \cdot \nabla)\bar{v} + (\bar{v} \cdot \nabla)\bar{u} - (\nabla \cdot \bar{u})\bar{v}$

which establishes the result.

(5) $\nabla(\bar{u} \cdot \bar{v}) = \bar{u} \times (\nabla \times \bar{v}) + (\bar{u} \cdot \nabla)\bar{v} + \bar{v} \times (\nabla \times \bar{u}) + (\bar{v} \cdot \nabla)\bar{u}$

$$\nabla(\bar{u} \cdot \bar{v}) = \nabla_{\bar{u}}(\bar{u} \cdot \bar{v}) + \nabla_{\bar{v}}(\bar{u} \cdot \bar{v}) \qquad \ldots (1)$$

Consider $\bar{u} \times (\nabla_{\bar{u}} \times \bar{v}) = \nabla_{\bar{u}}(\bar{u} \cdot \bar{v}) - (\bar{u} \cdot \nabla_{\bar{u}})\bar{v}$

$\therefore \qquad \nabla_{\bar{u}}(\bar{u} \cdot \bar{v}) = \bar{u} \times (\nabla_{\bar{u}} \times \bar{v}) + (\bar{u} \cdot \nabla_{\bar{u}})\bar{v}$

$$= \bar{u} \times (\nabla \times \bar{v}) + (\bar{u} \cdot \nabla)\bar{v} \qquad \text{(Dropping the suffixes)}$$

Similarly, $\bar{v} \times (\nabla_{\bar{v}} \times \bar{u}) = \nabla_{\bar{v}}(\bar{u} \cdot \bar{v}) - (\bar{v} \cdot \nabla_{\bar{v}})\bar{u}$

$\therefore \qquad \nabla_{\bar{v}}(\bar{u} \cdot \bar{v}) = \bar{v} \times (\nabla_{\bar{v}} \times \bar{u}) + (\bar{v} \cdot \nabla_{\bar{v}})\bar{u}$

$$= \bar{v} \times (\nabla \times \bar{u}) + (\bar{v} \cdot \nabla)\bar{u} \qquad \text{(Dropping the suffixes)}$$

Putting the values of $\nabla_{\bar{u}}(\bar{u} \cdot \bar{v})$ and $\nabla_{\bar{v}}(\bar{u} \cdot \bar{v})$ in (1), the required result is established.

Results (iv) and (v) can also be established by component method.

Using component method, the expressions involving second order differential operators can also be obtained.

Let us find equivalent expressions for

(1) $\nabla \cdot \nabla\phi$ or divergence Grade ϕ

$$\nabla \cdot \nabla\phi \; = \; \nabla \cdot \left\{ \bar{i}\,\frac{\partial\phi}{\partial x} + \bar{j}\,\frac{\partial\phi}{\partial y} + \bar{k}\,\frac{\partial\phi}{\partial z} \right\}$$

$$= \; \frac{\partial}{\partial x}\left(\frac{\partial\phi}{\partial x}\right) + \frac{\partial}{\partial y}\left(\frac{\partial\phi}{\partial y}\right) + \frac{\partial}{\partial z}\left(\frac{\partial\phi}{\partial z}\right)$$

$$= \; \frac{\partial^2\phi}{\partial x^2} + \frac{\partial^2\phi}{\partial y^2} + \frac{\partial^2\phi}{\partial z^2}$$

We can write $\quad \nabla \cdot \nabla\phi \; = \; (\nabla \cdot \nabla)\,\phi \; = \; \nabla^2\phi$

Thus $\qquad\qquad \nabla^2\phi \; = \; \dfrac{\partial^2\phi}{\partial x^2} + \dfrac{\partial^2\phi}{\partial y^2} + \dfrac{\partial^2\phi}{\partial z^2}$

Operator $\qquad\qquad \nabla^2 \; \equiv \; \dfrac{\partial^2}{\partial x^2} + \dfrac{\partial^2}{\partial y^2} + \dfrac{\partial^2}{\partial z^2}$

which is a second order differential operator and is known as Laplacian operator and the equation $\nabla^2\phi = 0$ is called Laplace equation, frequently encountered in engineering problems.

(2) $\nabla \times (\nabla\phi)$ or curl Grad ϕ

$$\nabla \times (\nabla\phi) \; = \; \nabla \times \left\{ \bar{i}\,\frac{\partial\phi}{\partial x} + \bar{j}\,\frac{\partial\phi}{\partial y} + \bar{k}\,\frac{\partial\phi}{\partial z} \right\}$$

$$= \; \begin{vmatrix} \bar{i} & \bar{j} & \bar{k} \\[6pt] \dfrac{\partial}{\partial x} & \dfrac{\partial}{\partial y} & \dfrac{\partial}{\partial z} \\[10pt] \dfrac{\partial\phi}{\partial x} & \dfrac{\partial\phi}{\partial y} & \dfrac{\partial\phi}{\partial z} \end{vmatrix}$$

$$= \; \bar{i}\left\{\frac{\partial^2\phi}{\partial y\partial z} - \frac{\partial^2\phi}{\partial y\partial z}\right\} + \bar{j}\left\{\frac{\partial^2\phi}{\partial x\partial z} - \frac{\partial^2\phi}{\partial x\partial z}\right\} + \bar{k}\left\{\frac{\partial^2\phi}{\partial x\partial y} - \frac{\partial^2\phi}{\partial x\partial y}\right\}$$

$$= \; 0$$

We can write $\quad \nabla \times (\nabla\phi) = (\nabla \times \nabla)\,\phi \; = \; 0$

Thus curl Grad $\phi = 0$

(3) $\nabla (\nabla \cdot \bar{u}) =$ Grad Div $\bar{u}$

Let $\qquad\qquad \bar{u} \; = \; u_1\,\bar{i} + u_2\,\bar{j} + u_3\,\bar{k}$

$$\nabla \cdot \bar{u} \; = \; \frac{\partial u_1}{\partial x} + \frac{\partial u_2}{\partial y} + \frac{\partial u_3}{\partial z}$$

$$\nabla \left(\nabla \cdot \overline{u}\right) = \overline{i}\,\frac{\partial}{\partial x}\left\{\frac{\partial u_1}{\partial x} + \frac{\partial u_2}{\partial y} + \frac{\partial u_3}{\partial z}\right\} + \overline{j}\,\frac{\partial}{\partial y}\left\{\frac{\partial u_1}{\partial x} + \frac{\partial u_2}{\partial y} + \frac{\partial u_3}{\partial z}\right\}$$

$$+ \overline{k}\,\frac{\partial}{\partial z}\left\{\frac{\partial u_1}{\partial x} + \frac{\partial u_2}{\partial y} + \frac{\partial u_3}{\partial z}\right\}$$

$$= \overline{i}\left[\frac{\partial^2 u_1}{\partial x^2} + \frac{\partial^2 u_2}{\partial x\,\partial y} + \frac{\partial^2 u_3}{\partial x\,\partial z}\right] + \overline{j}\left[\frac{\partial^2 u_1}{\partial x\,\partial y} + \frac{\partial^2 u_2}{\partial y^2} + \frac{\partial^2 u_3}{\partial y\,\partial z}\right]$$

$$+ \overline{k}\left[\frac{\partial^2 u_1}{\partial x\,\partial z} + \frac{\partial^2 u_2}{\partial y\,\partial z} + \frac{\partial^2 u_3}{\partial z^2}\right]$$

(4) $\nabla \cdot (\nabla \times \overline{u})$ or Div curl $\overline{u}$

$$\nabla \times \overline{u} = \begin{vmatrix} \overline{i} & \overline{j} & \overline{k} \\ \dfrac{\partial}{\partial x} & \dfrac{\partial}{\partial y} & \dfrac{\partial}{\partial z} \\ u_1 & u_2 & u_3 \end{vmatrix} = \overline{i}\left(\frac{\partial u_3}{\partial y} - \frac{\partial u_2}{\partial z}\right) + \overline{j}\left(\frac{\partial u_1}{\partial z} - \frac{\partial u_3}{\partial x}\right) + \overline{k}\left(\frac{\partial u_2}{\partial x} - \frac{\partial u_1}{\partial y}\right)$$

$$\nabla \cdot (\nabla \times \overline{u}) = \frac{\partial}{\partial x}\left\{\frac{\partial u_3}{\partial y} - \frac{\partial u_2}{\partial z}\right\} + \frac{\partial}{\partial y}\left\{\frac{\partial u_1}{\partial z} - \frac{\partial u_3}{\partial x}\right\} + \frac{\partial}{\partial z}\left\{\frac{\partial u_2}{\partial x} - \frac{\partial u_1}{\partial y}\right\}$$

$$= \frac{\partial^2 u_3}{\partial x\,\partial y} - \frac{\partial^2 u_2}{\partial x\,\partial z} + \frac{\partial^2 u_1}{\partial y\,\partial z} - \frac{\partial^2 u_3}{\partial x\,\partial y} + \frac{\partial^2 u_2}{\partial x\,\partial z} - \frac{\partial^2 u_1}{\partial y\,\partial z} = 0$$

Thus Divergence curl $\overline{u}$ = 0. (Note that scalar triple product with two identical vectors is zero.)

(5) $\nabla \times (\nabla \times \overline{u})$ or curl curl $\overline{u}$

Instead of taking $\overline{u} = u_1\,\overline{i} + u_2\,\overline{j} + u_3\,\overline{k}$, etc., we find the equivalent expression by using the property $\overline{a} \times (\overline{b} \times \overline{c}) = (\overline{a} \cdot \overline{c})\,\overline{b} - (\overline{a} \cdot \overline{b})\,\overline{c}$.

$$\nabla \times (\nabla \times \overline{u}) = \nabla(\nabla \cdot \overline{u}) - (\nabla \cdot \nabla)\,\overline{u} = \nabla(\nabla \cdot \overline{u}) - \nabla^2\overline{u}$$

LIST OF FORMULAE

• $\nabla = \overline{i}\dfrac{\partial}{\partial x} + \overline{j}\dfrac{\partial}{\partial y} + \overline{k}\dfrac{\partial}{\partial z}$	• $\nabla\phi = \overline{i}\dfrac{\partial\phi}{\partial x} + \overline{j}\dfrac{\partial\phi}{\partial y} + \overline{k}\dfrac{\partial\phi}{\partial z}$
• $\nabla(u \pm v) = \nabla u \pm \nabla v$	• $\nabla(uv) = u\nabla v + v\nabla u$
• $\nabla\left(\dfrac{u}{v}\right) = \dfrac{v\nabla u - u\nabla v}{v^2}$	• $\nabla(au) = a\nabla u$
• $\nabla(f(u)) = f'(u)\,(\nabla u)$	• $\nabla f(r) = \left(\dfrac{f'(r)}{r}\right)\overline{r}$
• $d\phi \equiv \nabla\phi \cdot d\overline{r}$	• D.D. of $\phi = \nabla\phi \cdot \hat{a}$

• $\operatorname{div} \bar{F} = \nabla \cdot \bar{F} = \dfrac{\partial F_1}{\partial x} + \dfrac{\partial F_2}{\partial y} + \dfrac{\partial F_3}{\partial z}$	• $\nabla \cdot \bar{F} = 0 \Rightarrow \bar{F}$ is solenoidal
• $\operatorname{rot} \bar{F} = \operatorname{curl} \bar{F} = \nabla \times \bar{F} = \begin{vmatrix} \bar{i} & \bar{j} & \bar{k} \\ \dfrac{\partial}{\partial x} & \dfrac{\partial}{\partial y} & \dfrac{\partial}{\partial z} \\ F_1 & F_2 & F_3 \end{vmatrix}$	• $\nabla \times \bar{F} = 0 \Rightarrow \bar{F}$ is irrotational.
• $\nabla (\bar{a} \cdot \bar{r}) = \bar{a}$	• $\nabla (\bar{a} \cdot \bar{b}) = 0$
• $\nabla \cdot \bar{a} = 0, \ \nabla \times \bar{a} = 0$	• $\nabla \cdot \bar{r} = 3, \nabla \times \bar{r} = 0$
• $\nabla \cdot (\phi \bar{u}) = \phi (\nabla \cdot \bar{u}) + \nabla \phi \cdot \bar{u}$	• $\nabla \times (\phi \bar{u}) = \phi (\nabla \times \bar{u}) + \nabla \phi \times \bar{u}$
• $\nabla \cdot (\bar{u} \times \bar{v}) = \bar{v} \cdot (\nabla \times \bar{u}) - \bar{u} \cdot (\nabla \times \bar{v})$	• $\nabla \times (\bar{u} \times \bar{v}) = \bar{u} (\nabla \cdot \bar{v}) - (\bar{u} \cdot \nabla) \bar{v}$ $\qquad\qquad + (\bar{v} \cdot \nabla) \bar{u} - \bar{v} (\nabla \cdot \bar{u})$
• $\nabla (\bar{u} \cdot \bar{v}) = \bar{u} \times (\nabla \times \bar{v}) + (\bar{u} \cdot \nabla) \bar{v} + \bar{v} \times (\nabla \times \bar{u}) + (\bar{v} \cdot \nabla) \bar{u}$	
• $\nabla \cdot (r^n \bar{r}) = (n + 3) \, r^n$	• $\nabla \times (r^n \bar{r}) = 0$
• $\nabla \cdot (\nabla \phi) = (\nabla \cdot \nabla) \phi$ $\qquad \nabla^2 \phi = \dfrac{\partial^2 \phi}{\partial x^2} + \dfrac{\partial^2 \phi}{\partial y^2} + \dfrac{\partial^2 \phi}{\partial z^2}$	• $\nabla^2 \equiv \dfrac{\partial^2}{\partial x^2} + \dfrac{\partial^2}{\partial y^2} + \dfrac{\partial^2}{\partial z^2}$; $\nabla^2 \phi = 0$ is Laplace equation
• $\nabla \times (\nabla \phi) = 0; \ \nabla \cdot (\nabla \times \bar{u}) = 0$	• Curl curl $\bar{u} = \nabla \times (\nabla \times \bar{u}) = \nabla (\nabla \cdot \bar{u}) - \nabla^2 \bar{u}$
• $\nabla (\nabla \cdot \bar{u}) = \nabla \times (\nabla \times \bar{u}) + \nabla^2 \bar{u}$	• Group operator $\qquad \equiv \bar{a} \cdot \nabla \equiv a_1 \dfrac{\partial}{\partial x} + a_2 \dfrac{\partial}{\partial y} + a_3 \dfrac{\partial}{\partial z}$ $\qquad (\bar{a} \cdot \nabla) \bar{r} = \bar{a}$

ILLUSTRATIONS

Ex. 1 : *Given*

$$\bar{u} = xyz \, \bar{i} + (2x^2 z - y^2 x) \, \bar{j} + xz^3 \bar{k}$$

$$\bar{v} = x^2 \bar{i} + 2yz \, \bar{j} + (1 + 2z) \, \bar{k}$$

$$\phi = xy + yz + z^2$$

Find (i) $\nabla \cdot \bar{u}$ *(ii)* $\nabla \times \bar{v}$ *(iii)* $\nabla \cdot (\phi \bar{u})$ *(iv)* $\nabla \times (\phi \bar{v})$ *at (1, 0, –1).*

Sol. :

(i) $\nabla \cdot \bar{u} = \dfrac{\partial}{\partial x} (xyz) + \dfrac{\partial}{\partial y} (2x^2 z - y^2 x) + \dfrac{\partial}{\partial z} (xz^3) = yz - 2xy + 3xz^2$

$\therefore \qquad [\nabla \cdot \bar{u}]_{(1, 0, -1)} = 3$

(ii)
$$[\nabla \times \bar{v}] = \begin{vmatrix} \bar{i} & \bar{j} & \bar{k} \\ \dfrac{\partial}{\partial x} & \dfrac{\partial}{\partial y} & \dfrac{\partial}{\partial z} \\ x^2 & 2yz & (1+2z) \end{vmatrix}$$

$$= \bar{i}\,(0 - 2y) + \bar{j}\,(0 - 0) + \bar{k}\,(0 - 0) = -2y\,\bar{i}$$

$$\therefore \qquad [\nabla \times \bar{v}]_{(1,0,-1)} = 0$$

(iii)
$$\nabla \cdot (\phi\bar{u}) = \nabla\phi \cdot \bar{u} + \phi\nabla \cdot \bar{u}$$

$$\nabla\phi = \bar{i}\,\frac{\partial\phi}{\partial x} + \bar{j}\,\frac{\partial\phi}{\partial y} + \bar{k}\,\frac{\partial\phi}{\partial z} = y\,\bar{i} + (x+z)\,\bar{j} + (y+2z)\,\bar{k}$$

$$\nabla\phi\,\big|_{(1,0,-1)} = 0 + 0 - 2\,\bar{k} = -2\,\bar{k}$$

$$\phi\,\big|_{(1,0,-1)} = 1, \quad \nabla \cdot \bar{u} = 3$$

$$\therefore \qquad \nabla \cdot (\phi\bar{u}) = -2\,\bar{k} \cdot (-2\,\bar{j} - \bar{k}) + 1\,(3) = 2 + 3 = 5$$

(iv)
$$\nabla \times (\phi\,\bar{v}) = \nabla\phi \times \bar{v} + \phi\nabla \times \bar{v}$$

$$= \nabla\phi \times \bar{v} \text{ as } \nabla \times \bar{v} = 0$$

$$\bar{v}\,\big|_{(1,0,-1)} = \bar{i} - \bar{k}, \quad \nabla\phi = -2\,\bar{k}$$

$$\therefore \qquad \nabla \times (\phi\,\bar{v}) = \nabla\phi \times \bar{v} = -2\,\bar{k} \times (\bar{i} - \bar{k}) = -2\,\bar{j}$$

Ex. 2 : *For scalar functions ϕ and ψ, show that*

(i) $\nabla \cdot (\phi\nabla\psi - \psi\nabla\phi) = \phi\nabla^2\psi - \psi\nabla^2\phi.$

(ii) $\nabla^2(\phi\psi) = \phi\nabla^2\psi + 2\,\nabla\phi \cdot \nabla\psi + \psi\nabla^2\phi$

Sol. : (i)
$$\nabla \cdot (\phi\nabla\psi) = \nabla\phi \cdot \nabla\psi + \phi\,(\nabla \cdot (\nabla\psi)) = \nabla\phi \cdot \nabla\psi + \phi\nabla^2\psi$$

$$\nabla \cdot (\psi\nabla\phi) = \nabla\psi \cdot \nabla\phi + \psi\nabla^2\phi$$

$$\therefore \quad \nabla \cdot (\phi\nabla\psi - \psi\nabla\phi) = \nabla \cdot (\phi\nabla\psi) - \nabla \cdot (\psi\nabla\phi)$$

$$= \nabla\phi \cdot \nabla\psi + \phi\nabla^2\psi - \nabla\psi \cdot \nabla\phi - \psi\nabla^2\phi$$

$$= \phi\nabla^2\psi - \psi\nabla^2\phi$$

(ii)
$$\nabla^2(\phi\psi) = \nabla \cdot \nabla(\phi\psi) = \nabla \cdot (\phi\nabla\psi + \psi\nabla\phi)$$

$$= \nabla \cdot (\phi\nabla\psi) + \nabla \cdot (\psi\nabla\phi)$$

$$= \nabla\phi \cdot \nabla\psi + \phi\nabla^2\psi + \nabla\psi \cdot \nabla\phi + \psi\nabla^2\phi$$

$$= \phi\nabla^2\psi + 2\,\nabla\phi \cdot \nabla\psi + \psi\nabla^2\phi$$

Ex. 3 : *For constant vector $\bar{a}$, show that,*

(i) $\nabla(\bar{a} \cdot \bar{r}) = \bar{a}$ *(ii)* $\nabla \times (\bar{a} \times \bar{r}) = 2\bar{a}$

(iii) $\nabla\left(\dfrac{\bar{a} \cdot \bar{r}}{r^n}\right) = \dfrac{\bar{a}}{r^n} - \dfrac{n(\bar{a} \cdot \bar{r})}{r^{n+2}}\,\bar{r}$

where, $\qquad \bar{r} = x\,\bar{i} + y\,\bar{j} + z\,\bar{k}, \qquad\qquad r = \sqrt{x^2 + y^2 + z^2}$

Sol. : (i) Let $\qquad \bar{a} = a_1\,\bar{i} + a_2\,\bar{j} + a_3\,\bar{k}$

$\therefore \qquad\qquad \bar{a} \cdot \bar{r} = a_1 x + a_2 y + a_3 z$

$$\nabla(\bar{a} \cdot \bar{r}) = \bar{i}\frac{\partial}{\partial x}(a_1 x + a_2 y + a_3 z) + \bar{j}\frac{\partial}{\partial y}(a_1 x + a_2 y + a_3 z)$$

$$+ \bar{k}\frac{\partial}{\partial z}(a_1 x + a_2 y + a_3 z)$$

$$= \bar{i}\,a_1 + \bar{j}\,a_2 + \bar{k}\,a_3$$

$\therefore \qquad\qquad \nabla(\bar{a} \cdot \bar{r}) = \bar{a}$

(ii) $\qquad \nabla \times (\bar{a} \times \bar{r}) = (\nabla \cdot \bar{r})\,\bar{a} - (\bar{a} \cdot \nabla)\,\bar{r}$

$$= 3\bar{a} - \bar{a} \qquad\qquad [(\bar{a} \cdot \nabla)\,\bar{r} = \bar{a}]$$

$$= 2\bar{a}$$

(iii) $\qquad \nabla\left(\dfrac{\bar{a} \cdot \bar{r}}{r^n}\right) = \dfrac{1}{r^n}\nabla(\bar{a} \cdot \bar{r}) + (\bar{a} \cdot \bar{r})\nabla\left(\dfrac{1}{r^n}\right)$

$$= \dfrac{\bar{a}}{r^n} + (\bar{a} \cdot \bar{r})(-n)\,r^{-n-2}\,\bar{r}$$

$$= \dfrac{\bar{a}}{r^n} - \dfrac{n(\bar{a} \cdot \bar{r})}{r^{n+2}}\,\bar{r}$$

Ex. 4 : *With usual notations, show that*

(i) $\qquad \nabla \times [\bar{a} \times (\bar{b} \times \bar{r})] = \bar{a} \times \bar{b}$ $\qquad\qquad$ **(SUK May 12)**

(ii) $\nabla[(\bar{r} \times \bar{a}) \cdot (\bar{r} \times \bar{b})] = \bar{b} \times (\bar{r} \times \bar{a}) + \bar{a} \times (\bar{r} \times \bar{b})$

Sol. : (i) $\qquad \bar{a} \times (\bar{b} \times \bar{r}) = (\bar{a} \cdot \bar{r})\,\bar{b} - (\bar{a} \cdot \bar{b})\,\bar{r}$

$\qquad \nabla \times [\bar{a} \times (\bar{b} \times \bar{r})] = \nabla \times [(\bar{a} \cdot \bar{r})\,\bar{b} - (\bar{a} \cdot \bar{b})\,\bar{r}]$

$$= \nabla \times [(\bar{a} \cdot \bar{r})\,\bar{b}] - \nabla \times [(\bar{a} \cdot \bar{b})\,\bar{r}]$$

$$= \nabla\,(\bar{a}\cdot\bar{r})\times\bar{b} + (\bar{a}\cdot\bar{r})\,\nabla\times\bar{b}$$

$$- \nabla\,(\bar{a}\cdot\bar{b})\times\bar{r} - (\bar{a}\cdot\bar{b})\,(\nabla\times\bar{r})$$

$$= \bar{a}\times\bar{b} \ [\bar{a},\bar{b} \text{ being constant vectors}]$$

$$\nabla\times\bar{b} = 0,\ \ \nabla\,(\bar{a}\cdot\bar{b}) = 0 \text{ and } \nabla\times\bar{r} = 0$$

(ii)   L.H.S. $= \nabla\,[(\bar{r}\times\bar{a})\cdot(\bar{r}\times\bar{b})]$

Let $\bar{p} = \bar{r}\times\bar{a}$

$\therefore$ $(\bar{r}\times\bar{a})\cdot(\bar{r}\times\bar{b}) = p\cdot(\bar{r}\times\bar{b}) = (\bar{p}\times\bar{r})\cdot\bar{b}$ [by interchanging dot and cross]

$$= \{(\bar{r}\times\bar{a})\times\bar{r}\}\cdot\bar{b} = -\{\bar{r}\times(\bar{r}\times\bar{a})\}\cdot\bar{b}$$

$$= -\{(\bar{r}\cdot\bar{a})\,\bar{r} - (\bar{r}\cdot\bar{r})\,\bar{a}\}\cdot\bar{b}$$

$$= -(\bar{r}\cdot\bar{a})\,(\bar{r}\cdot\bar{b}) + (\bar{r}\cdot\bar{r})\,(\bar{a}\cdot\bar{b})$$

$\therefore$ L.H.S. $= \nabla\,[(\bar{r}\cdot\bar{r})\,(\bar{a}\cdot\bar{b}) - (\bar{r}\cdot\bar{a})\,(\bar{r}\cdot\bar{b})]$

$$= \nabla\,\{(\bar{r}\cdot\bar{r})\,(\bar{a}\cdot\bar{b})\} - \nabla\,\{(\bar{r}\cdot\bar{a})\,(\bar{r}\cdot\bar{b})\}$$

$$= (\bar{a}\cdot\bar{b})\,\nabla\,(r^2) - (\bar{r}\cdot\bar{r})\,\nabla\,(\bar{a}\cdot\bar{b}) - (\bar{r}\cdot\bar{b})\,\nabla\,(\bar{r}\cdot\bar{a})$$

$$- (\bar{r}\cdot\bar{a})\,\nabla\,(\bar{r}\cdot\bar{b})$$

Now, $\nabla\,(r^2) = 2\bar{r},\ \ \nabla\,(\bar{a}\cdot\bar{b}) = 0,\ \ \nabla\,(\bar{r}\cdot\bar{a}) = \bar{a},\ \ \nabla\,(\bar{r}\cdot\bar{b}) = \bar{b}$

L.H.S. $= 2\,(\bar{a}\cdot\bar{b})\,\bar{r} - (\bar{r}\cdot\bar{b})\,\bar{a} - (\bar{r}\cdot\bar{a})\,\bar{b}$ $[\nabla\,(\bar{a}\cdot\bar{b}) = 0]$

R.H.S. $= \bar{b}\times(\bar{r}\times\bar{a}) + \bar{a}\times(\bar{r}\times\bar{b})$

$$= (\bar{b}\cdot\bar{a})\,\bar{r} - (\bar{b}\cdot\bar{r})\,\bar{a} + (\bar{a}\cdot\bar{b})\,\bar{r} - (\bar{a}\cdot\bar{r})\,\bar{b}$$

$$= 2\,(\bar{a}\cdot\bar{b})\,\bar{r} - (\bar{r}\cdot\bar{b})\,\bar{a} - (\bar{r}\cdot\bar{a})\,\bar{b}$$

L.H.S. $=$ R.H.S. which proves the result.

Ex. 5 : *Show that*

(i) $\nabla^2\,[\nabla\cdot(\bar{r}/r^2)] = \dfrac{2}{r^4}$

(ii) $\nabla\times\left(\dfrac{\bar{a}\times\bar{r}}{r^3}\right) = -\dfrac{\bar{a}}{r^3} + \dfrac{3\,(\bar{a}\cdot\bar{r})}{r^5}\,\bar{r}$

Sol. : (i) $\nabla\cdot(\bar{r}/r^2) = \nabla\cdot(\bar{r}\,r^{-2}) = \nabla\,(r^{-2})\cdot\bar{r} + r^{-2}\,\nabla\cdot\bar{r}$

$$= -2r^{-4}\,\bar{r}\cdot\bar{r} + 3r^{-2} \qquad\qquad [\because \nabla\cdot\bar{r} = 3]$$

$$= -\frac{2}{r^2} + \frac{3}{r^2} = \frac{1}{r^2}$$

$$\nabla^2 [\nabla \cdot (\bar{r}/r^2)] = \nabla^2 \left(\frac{1}{r^2}\right) = \nabla \cdot \nabla \left(\frac{1}{r^2}\right)$$

$$= \nabla \cdot \{-2r^{-4}\bar{r}\} = -2\,[\nabla\,(r^{-4}) \cdot \bar{r} + r^{-4}(\nabla \cdot \bar{r})]$$

$$= -2\,[-4r^{-6}\bar{r} \cdot \bar{r} + 3r^{-4}] = -2\,[-4r^{-6}r^2 + 3r^{-4}] = \frac{2}{r^4}$$

(ii)

$$\nabla \times \left(\frac{\bar{a} \times \bar{r}}{r^3}\right) = \nabla \times (\bar{a} \times \bar{r}\; r^{-3})$$

$$= \{\nabla \cdot (\bar{r}\; r^{-3})\}\, \bar{a} - (\bar{a} \cdot \nabla)\, \bar{r}\; r^{-3}$$

$$\nabla \cdot (\bar{r}\; r^{-3}) = \nabla\,(r^{-3}) \cdot \bar{r} + r^{-3}\nabla \cdot \bar{r}$$

$$= -3r^{-5}\bar{r} \cdot \bar{r} + 3r^{-3} = -3r^{-3} + 3r^{-3} = 0$$

Treating operator $\bar{a} \cdot \nabla$ like operator D,

$$(\bar{a} \cdot \nabla)\, \bar{r}\; r^{-3} = r^{-3}(\bar{a} \cdot \nabla)\, \bar{r} + \bar{r}\,(\bar{a} \cdot \nabla)\; r^{-3}$$

But

$$(\bar{a} \cdot \nabla)\, \bar{r} = \bar{a}$$

and

$$(\bar{a} \cdot \nabla)\, r^{-3} = \bar{a} \cdot \nabla r^{-3} = \bar{a} \cdot (-3)\, r^{-5}\,\bar{r} = \frac{-3\,(\bar{a} \cdot \bar{r})}{r^5}$$

$\therefore$

$$(\bar{a} \cdot \nabla)\, \bar{r}\; r^{-3} = \frac{\bar{a}}{r^3} - \frac{3\,(\bar{a} \cdot \bar{r})}{r^5}\,\bar{r}$$

$\therefore$

$$\nabla \times \left(\frac{\bar{a} \times \bar{r}}{r^3}\right) = \frac{-\bar{a}}{r^3} + \frac{3\,(\bar{a} \cdot \bar{r})}{r^5}\,\bar{r}$$

Ex. 6 : *Show that*

(i) $\;\nabla^2 f(r) = \dfrac{d^2f}{dr^2} + \dfrac{2}{r}\dfrac{df}{dr}$

(ii) $\;\nabla^4 e^r = e^r + \dfrac{4}{r}\, e^r$

Sol. : (i)
$$\nabla^2 f(r) = \nabla \cdot (\nabla f(r)) = \nabla \cdot \left\{\frac{f'(r)}{r}\,\bar{r}\right\} = \frac{f'(r)}{r}\,(\nabla \cdot \bar{r}) + \nabla\left(\frac{f'(r)}{r}\right) \cdot \bar{r}$$

$$= \frac{f'(r)}{r}\,(3) + \left(\frac{rf''(r) - f'(r)}{r^2}\right)\frac{\bar{r}}{r} \cdot \bar{r}$$

$$= \frac{3\,f'(r)}{r} + \left(\frac{r\,f''(r) - f'(r)}{r^3}\right)(\bar{r} \cdot \bar{r})$$

$$= \frac{3\,f'(r)}{r} + \left(\frac{r\,f''(r) - f'(r)}{r}\right) = \frac{3\,f'(r)}{r} + f''(r) - \frac{f'(r)}{r}$$

$$\therefore \qquad \nabla^2 f(r) = f''(r) + \frac{2}{r}\, f'(r) \qquad \qquad \dots (i)$$

(ii) $\qquad \nabla^4 e^r = \nabla^2 \nabla^2 (e^r)$

Let $f(r) = e^r \Rightarrow f'(r) = e^r, \quad f''(r) = e^r$

$$\therefore \qquad \nabla^2 (e^r) = \frac{2}{r}\, e^r + e^r = \left(\frac{2}{r} + 1\right) e^r \qquad \dots \text{ by result (i)}$$

Let $\qquad F(r) = e^r \left(\frac{2}{r} + 1\right) \Rightarrow F'(r) = e^r \left(\frac{2}{r} + 1\right) + e^r \left(-\frac{2}{r^2}\right)$

$$\therefore \qquad F''(r) = e^r \left(\frac{2}{r} + 1\right) + e^r \left(-\frac{2}{r^2}\right) + \frac{4}{r^3}\, e^r - \frac{2}{r^2}\, e^r$$

$$= e^r \left(\frac{2}{r} + 1 - \frac{4}{r^2} + \frac{4}{r^3}\right)$$

$$\therefore \qquad \frac{2}{r}\, F'(r) = \frac{4}{r^2}\, e^r + \frac{2}{r}\, e^r - \frac{4}{r^3}\, e^r$$

and $\qquad \nabla^4 e^r = \nabla^2 (\nabla^2 e^r) = \nabla^2 \left\{ e^r \left(\frac{2}{r} + 1\right) \right\}$

$$= e^r \left\{ \frac{2}{r} + 1 - \frac{4}{r^2} + \frac{4}{r^3} + \frac{4}{r^2} + \frac{2}{r} - \frac{4}{r^3} \right\} \qquad \dots \text{ by result (i)}$$

$$= \frac{4}{r}\, e^r + e^r.$$

Ex. 7 : *If $\rho \bar{E} = \nabla\phi$, prove that $\bar{E} \cdot \text{curl } \bar{E} = 0$.*

Sol. : $\qquad\qquad \bar{E} = \frac{1}{\rho} \nabla\phi$

$$\therefore \qquad \text{curl } \bar{E} = \nabla \times \left(\frac{1}{\rho} \nabla\phi\right) = \nabla \left(\frac{1}{\rho}\right) \times \nabla\phi + \frac{1}{\rho}\, \nabla \times (\nabla\phi)$$

$$= \nabla \left(\frac{1}{\rho}\right) \times \nabla\phi \qquad\qquad [\text{as } \nabla \times \nabla\phi = 0]$$

$$\bar{E} \cdot \text{curl } \bar{E} = \bar{E} \cdot \left[\nabla \left(\frac{1}{\rho}\right) \times \nabla\phi \right]$$

$$= \nabla \left(\frac{1}{\rho}\right) \cdot [\nabla\phi \times \bar{E}] \qquad [\text{By } \bar{a} \cdot (\bar{b} \times \bar{c}) = \bar{b} \cdot (\bar{c} \times \bar{a})]$$

$$= \nabla \left(\frac{1}{\rho}\right) \cdot [\rho\bar{E} \times \bar{E}] = 0 \qquad [\text{as } \bar{E} \times \bar{E} = 0]$$

Ex. 8 : *For a solenoidal vector field $\bar{E}$, show that curl curl curl curl $\bar{E} = \nabla^4 \bar{E}$.*

Sol. : $\bar{E}$ being solenoidal,

$$\nabla \cdot \bar{E} = 0$$

$$\text{curl curl } \bar{E} = \nabla \times (\nabla \times \bar{E})$$

$$= \nabla (\nabla \cdot \bar{E}) - (\nabla \cdot \nabla) \bar{E}$$

$$= -\nabla^2 \bar{E} \qquad [\text{as } \nabla \cdot \bar{E} = 0]$$

Let
$$\bar{F} = -\nabla^2 \bar{F}$$

$\therefore \qquad \text{curl curl curl curl } \bar{E} = \text{curl curl } \bar{F}$

$$= \nabla \times (\nabla \times \bar{F}) = \nabla (\nabla \cdot \bar{F}) - (\nabla \cdot \nabla) \bar{F}$$

$$= \nabla [\nabla \cdot (-\nabla^2 \bar{E})] - \nabla^2 \bar{F}$$

$$= \nabla [-\nabla^2 (\nabla \cdot \bar{E})] - \nabla^2 (-\nabla^2 \bar{E})$$

$$[\text{By commutative property of partial derivatives}]$$

$$= \nabla^4 \bar{E} \qquad [\text{as } \nabla \cdot \bar{E} = 0]$$

Ex. 9 : *Show that $\bar{F} = (6xy + z^3)\,\bar{i} + (3x^2 - z)\,\bar{j} + (3xz^2 - y)\,\bar{k}$ is irrotational. Find scalar ϕ such that $\bar{F} = \nabla\phi$.*

Sol. :
$$\nabla \times \bar{F} = \begin{vmatrix} \bar{i} & \bar{j} & \bar{k} \\ \dfrac{\partial}{\partial x} & \dfrac{\partial}{\partial y} & \dfrac{\partial}{\partial z} \\ 6xy + z^3 & 3x^2 - z & 3xz^2 - y \end{vmatrix}$$

$$= \bar{i}\left\{\frac{\partial}{\partial y}(3xz^2 - y) - \frac{\partial}{\partial z}(3x^2 - z)\right\} + \bar{j}\left\{\frac{\partial}{\partial z}(6xy + z^3) - \frac{\partial}{\partial x}(3xz^2 - y)\right\}$$

$$+ \bar{k}\left\{\frac{\partial}{\partial x}(3x^2 - z) - \frac{\partial}{\partial y}(6xy + z^3)\right\}$$

$$= \bar{i}\,\{-1 + 1\} + \bar{j}\,\{3z^2 - 3z^2\} + \bar{k}\,\{6x - 6x\} = 0$$

which shows that $\bar{F}$ is irrotational. To find corresponding scalar ϕ, consider the relation

$$d\phi \equiv \nabla\phi \cdot d\bar{r}$$

but
$$\bar{F} \equiv \nabla\phi$$

$\therefore \qquad d\phi \equiv \bar{F} \cdot d\bar{r}$

$$\equiv [(6xy + z^3)\,\bar{i} + (3x^2 - z)\,\bar{j} + (3xz^2 - y)\,\bar{k}] \cdot [\bar{i}\,dx + \bar{j}\,dy + \bar{k}\,dz]$$

$$\equiv (6xy + z^3)\, dx + (3x^2 - z)\, dy + (3xz^2 - y)\, dz$$

$$\equiv (6xy\, dx + 3x^2\, dy) + (z^3\, dx + 3xz^2\, dz) - (z\, dy + y\, dz)$$

$$\equiv d\,(3x^2 y) + d\,(z^3 x) - d\,(yz)$$

Integrating, we get

$$\phi \;=\; 3x^2\, y + z^3\, x \;-\; yz + c$$

Ex. 10 : *Show that the vector field $f(r)\,\bar{r}$ is always irrotational and determine $f(r)$ such that the field is solenoidal also. Also find $f(r)$ such that $\nabla^2 f(r) = 0$.*

Sol. : Consider $\nabla \times f(r)\,\bar{r} \;=\; [\nabla\, f(r)] \times \bar{r} + f(r)\,[\nabla \times \bar{r}]$

$$= \frac{f'(r)}{r}\,\bar{r} \times r + \bar{0} \qquad\qquad (\because \nabla \times \bar{r} = 0)$$

$$= \bar{0} \qquad\qquad (\because \bar{r} \times \bar{r} = \bar{0})$$

Hence the vector field $f(r)\,\bar{r}$ is irrotational. Now, for vector field $f(r)\,\bar{r}$ to be solenoidal, we must have

$$\nabla \cdot [f(r)\,\bar{r}] \;=\; 0$$

$$\nabla \cdot [f(r)\,\bar{r}] \;=\; \nabla\, f(r) \cdot \bar{r} + f(r)\,[\nabla \cdot \bar{r}\,]$$

$$= \frac{f'(r)}{r}\,\bar{r} \cdot \bar{r} + 3\,f(r) = f'(r)\,r + 3\,f(r)$$

$\therefore \qquad f'(r)\,r + 3\,f(r) \;=\; 0 \qquad\qquad \text{or} \qquad\qquad \dfrac{f'(r)}{f(r)} + \dfrac{3}{r} \;=\; 0$

On integrating,

$$\log f(r) + 3 \log r \;=\; \log C \qquad\qquad \text{or} \qquad\qquad \log f(r)\, r^3 \;=\; \log C$$

$\text{or} \qquad\qquad f(r)\, r^3 \;=\; C \qquad\qquad \text{or} \qquad\qquad f(r) \;=\; \dfrac{C}{r^3}$

Now, to find $f(r)$ such that $\nabla^2 f(r) = 0$, we have

$$\nabla^2 f(r) \;=\; f''(r) + \frac{2}{r}\, f'(r)$$

$$\therefore \qquad f''(r) + \frac{2}{r}\, f'(r) \;=\; 0$$

$$\frac{f''(r)}{f'(r)} + \frac{2}{r} \;=\; 0$$

On integrating,

$$\log f'(r) + 2 \log r \;=\; \log C_1$$

$\text{or} \qquad\qquad \log f'(r)\, r^2 \;=\; \log C_1$

or $\qquad f'(r) = \dfrac{C_1}{r^2}$

Again integrating, we have

$$f(r) = \int \dfrac{C_1}{r^2}\, dr + C_2$$

$$f(r) = -\dfrac{C_1}{r} + C_2$$

Ex. 11 : *Prove that* $\nabla \times \left(\bar{a} \times \nabla\dfrac{1}{r}\right) + \nabla\left(\bar{a} \cdot \nabla\dfrac{1}{r}\right) = 0$

Sol. : $\qquad \nabla \times \left(\bar{a} \times \nabla\dfrac{1}{r}\right) = \nabla \times \left(\bar{a} \times -\dfrac{1}{r^3}\bar{r}\right)$

$$= -\nabla \times (\bar{a} \times \bar{r}\ r^{-3})$$

$$= -\left\{[\nabla \cdot (r^{-3}\bar{r})]\,\bar{a} - (\bar{a} \cdot \nabla)\,(\bar{r}\ r^{-3})\right\}$$

$$= -\{0 - [(\bar{a} \cdot \nabla)\,\bar{r}\,]\,r^{-3} - \bar{r}\,[(\bar{a} \cdot \nabla)\,r^{-3}]\}$$

$$= (\bar{a})\,r^{-3} + \bar{r}\,[\bar{a} \cdot \nabla\,(r^{-3})]$$

$$= \dfrac{\bar{a}}{r^3} + \bar{r}\left[\bar{a} \cdot \left(\dfrac{-3}{r^5}\right)\bar{r}\right]$$

$$\nabla \times \left(\bar{a} \times \nabla\dfrac{1}{r}\right) = \dfrac{\bar{a}}{r^3} - \dfrac{3\,(\bar{a} \cdot \bar{r})\,\bar{r}}{r^5} \qquad\qquad \ldots (1)$$

$$\nabla\left(\bar{a} \cdot \nabla\dfrac{1}{r}\right) = \nabla\left[\bar{a} \cdot -\dfrac{1}{r^3}\bar{r}\right]$$

$$= -(\bar{a} \cdot \bar{r})\,\nabla\,(r^{-3}) - r^{-3}\nabla\,(\bar{a} \cdot \bar{r})$$

$$= -(\bar{a} \cdot \bar{r})\left(-\dfrac{3}{r^5}\right)\bar{r} - r^{-3}\bar{a}$$

$$\nabla\left(\bar{a} \cdot \nabla\dfrac{1}{r}\right) = \dfrac{3\,(\bar{a} \cdot \bar{r})\,\bar{r}}{r^5} - \dfrac{\bar{a}}{r^3} \qquad\qquad \ldots (2)$$

By adding (1) and (2), $\nabla \times \left(\bar{a} \times \nabla\dfrac{1}{r}\right) + \nabla\left(\bar{a} \cdot \nabla\dfrac{1}{r}\right) = 0$

Ex. 12 : *Prove that*

(i) $\nabla(\bar{r} \cdot \bar{u}) = \bar{r} \times (\nabla \times \bar{u}) + (\bar{r} \cdot \nabla)\bar{u} + \bar{u}$

(ii) $\nabla \times (\bar{r} \times \bar{u}) = \bar{r}\,(\nabla \cdot \bar{u}) - (\bar{r} \cdot \nabla)\bar{u} - 2\,\bar{u}$

Sol. : (i) We have,

$$\nabla\,(\bar{u} \cdot \bar{v}) = \bar{u} \times (\nabla \times \bar{v}) + (\bar{u} \cdot \nabla)\bar{v} + \bar{v} \times (\nabla \times \bar{u}) + (\bar{v} \cdot \nabla)\,\bar{u}$$

$$\therefore \qquad \nabla\,(\bar r \cdot \bar u\,) \;=\; \bar r \times (\nabla \times \bar u) + (\bar r \cdot \nabla)\,\bar u \;+\bar u \times (\nabla \times \bar r) + (\bar u \cdot \nabla)\,\bar r$$

$$\nabla\,(\bar r \cdot \bar u\,) \;=\; \bar r \times (\nabla \times \bar u) + (\bar r \cdot \nabla)\,\bar u + \bar u$$

$$(\because \nabla \times \bar r = 0, (\bar u \cdot \nabla)\,\bar r = \bar u)$$

(ii) We have, $\nabla \times (\bar u \times \bar v) = \bar u\,(\nabla \cdot \bar v) - (\bar u \cdot \nabla)\,\bar v + (\bar v \cdot \nabla)\,\bar u - \bar v\,(\nabla \cdot \bar u)$

$$\therefore \qquad \nabla \times (\bar r \times \bar u) \;=\; \bar r\,(\nabla \cdot \bar u) - (\bar r \cdot \nabla)\,\bar u + (\bar u \cdot \nabla)\,\bar r - \bar u\,(\nabla \cdot \bar r)$$

$$=\; \bar r\,(\nabla \cdot \bar u) - (\bar r \cdot \nabla)\,\bar u + \bar u - 3\,\bar u$$

$$(\because\ \nabla \cdot \bar r = 3, (\bar u \cdot \nabla)\,\bar r = \bar u\,)$$

$$=\; \bar r\,(\nabla \cdot \bar u) - (\bar r \cdot \nabla)\,\bar u - 2\,\bar u$$

Ex. 13 : *Show that* $\bar F = \dfrac{1}{r}\,[r^2\,\bar a + (\bar a \cdot \bar r\,)\,\bar r]$ *is irrotational. Hence find scalar potential* ϕ.

Sol. :
$$\bar F \;=\; r\,\bar a + (\bar a \cdot \bar r\,)\,\frac{\bar r}{r}$$

$$\nabla \times \bar F \;=\; \nabla \times (r\,\bar a) + \nabla \times \left[(\bar a \cdot \bar r)\,\frac{\bar r}{r}\right]$$

$$=\; r\,(\nabla \times \bar a) + \nabla r \times \bar a + (\bar a \cdot \bar r)\left(\nabla \times \frac{\bar r}{r}\right) + \nabla\,(\bar a \cdot \bar r) \times \frac{\bar r}{r}$$

$$=\; \frac{\bar r}{r} \times \bar a + \bar a \times \frac{\bar r}{r} \;=\; 0$$

$$\therefore\quad \nabla \times \bar F = 0 \;\Rightarrow\; \bar F \text{ is irrotational.}$$

We have $\qquad d\phi \;\equiv\; \nabla\phi \cdot d\bar r$

Since $\bar F$ is irrotational, therefore $\bar F = \nabla\phi$

$$\therefore \qquad d\phi \;\equiv\; \bar F \cdot d\bar r \;\equiv\; \left[r\,\bar a + (\bar a \cdot \bar r)\,\frac{\bar r}{r}\right] \cdot d\bar r$$

$$\equiv\; r\,(\bar a \cdot d\bar r) + (\bar a \cdot \bar r)\,\frac{\bar r \cdot d\bar r}{r}$$

$$\equiv\; r\,d\,(\bar a \cdot \bar r) + (\bar a \cdot \bar r)\left(\frac{r\,dr}{r}\right) \qquad\qquad (\because \bar r \cdot d\bar r = r\,dr)$$

$$\therefore \qquad \equiv r\, d\,(\bar{a} \cdot \bar{r}) + (\bar{a} \cdot \bar{r})\, dr$$

$$\equiv d\,[r\,(\bar{a} \cdot \bar{r})]$$

$$\therefore \qquad \phi = r\,(\bar{a} \cdot \bar{r}) + c$$

Ex. 14 : *Find curl curl $\bar{F}$ at the point (0, 1, 2) where*

$$\bar{F} = x^2 y\,\bar{i} + xyz\,\bar{j} + z^2 y\,\bar{k}$$

Sol.

$$(\nabla \times \bar{F}) = \begin{vmatrix} \bar{i} & \bar{j} & \bar{k} \\[4pt] \dfrac{\partial}{\partial x} & \dfrac{\partial}{\partial y} & \dfrac{\partial}{\partial z} \\[6pt] x^2 y & xyz & z^2 y \end{vmatrix}$$

$$= \bar{i}\,(z^2 - xy) + \bar{j}\,(0 - 0) + \bar{k}\,(yz - x^2)$$

$$\nabla \times (\nabla \times \bar{F}) = \begin{vmatrix} \bar{i} & \bar{j} & \bar{k} \\[4pt] \dfrac{\partial}{\partial x} & \dfrac{\partial}{\partial y} & \dfrac{\partial}{\partial z} \\[6pt] z^2 - xy & 0 & yz - x^2 \end{vmatrix}$$

$$= \bar{i}\,(z) + \bar{j}\,(2z + 2x) + \bar{k}\,(x)$$

$$\therefore \quad \text{curl curl } \bar{F} \text{ at } (0, 1, 2) = 2\bar{i} + 4\bar{j}$$

Ex. 15 : *Show that $\bar{F} = r^2\,\bar{r}$ is conservative and obtain the scalar potential associated with it.*

Sol. :

$$\nabla \times \bar{F} = \nabla \times (r^2\,\bar{r}) = \nabla r^2 \times \bar{r} + r^2\,\nabla \times \bar{r}$$

$$= 2r^{2-2}\,\bar{r} \times \bar{r} + r^2\,\nabla \times \bar{r}$$

$$= 0 + 0$$

$$\therefore \quad \bar{F} \text{ is conservative.}$$

$$d\phi = \bar{F} \cdot d\bar{r}$$

$$= r^2\,\bar{r} \cdot d\bar{r} = \frac{1}{2}\,r^2\,d\,(\bar{r} \cdot \bar{r}) = \frac{1}{2}\,r^2\,d\,(r^2)$$

$$= \frac{1}{2}\,r^2 \cdot 2r\, dr = r^3\, dr$$

$$\phi = \frac{r^4}{4} + c$$

Ex. 16 : *Show that* $\bar{F} = (ye^{xy} \cos z)\,\bar{i} + (xe^{xy} \cos z)\,\bar{j} - e^{xy} \sin z\,\bar{k}$ *is irrotational. Find corresponding scalar* ϕ, *such that* $\bar{F} = \nabla\phi$.

Sol. :

$$\nabla \times \bar{F} = \begin{vmatrix} \bar{i} & \bar{j} & \bar{k} \\ \dfrac{\partial}{\partial x} & \dfrac{\partial}{\partial y} & \dfrac{\partial}{\partial z} \\ ye^{xy}\cos z & x\,e^{xy}\cos z & -e^{xy}\sin z \end{vmatrix}$$

$$= \bar{i}\,(-x\,e^{xy}\sin z + x\,e^{xy}\sin z) + \bar{j}\,(-y\,e^{xy}\sin z + y\,e^{xy}\sin z)$$

$$+ \bar{k}\,(e^{xy}\cos z + xy\,e^{xy}\cos z - e^{xy}\cos z - xy\,e^{xy}\cos z)$$

$$= 0$$

$$d\phi = \nabla\phi \cdot d\bar{r} = \bar{F} \cdot d\bar{r}$$

$$= F_1\,dx + F_2\,dy + F_3\,dz$$

$$= y\,e^{xy}\cos z\,dx + x\,e^{xy}\cos z\,dy - e^{xy}\sin z\,\,dz$$

$$= \cos z\,(y\,e^{xy}\,dx + x\,e^{xy}\,dy) - e^{xy}\sin z\,dz$$

$$= \cos z\,d\,(e^{xy}) + e^{xy}\,d\,(\cos z)$$

$$= d\,(e^{xy}\cos z)$$

$$\therefore \qquad \phi = e^{xy}\cos z + c$$

Ex. 17 : *Evaluate* $\displaystyle\int_C \frac{x\,dx + y\,dy}{(x^2 + y^2)^{3/2}}$ *along the curve* $\bar{r}(t) = e^t \cos t\,\bar{i} + e^t \sin t\,\bar{j}$ *from* (1, 0) to (2π, 0).

Sol. :

$$x = e^t \cos t, \quad y = e^t \sin t$$

$$dx = (e^t \cos t - e^t \sin t)\,dt, \quad dy = (e^t \sin t + e^t \cos t)\,dt$$

$$x^2 + y^2 = e^{2t}(\cos^2 t + \sin^2 t) = e^{2t}$$

$$I = \int \frac{e^{2t}(\cos^2 t - \sin t \cos t + \sin^2 t + \sin t \cos t)\,dt}{e^{2t}}$$

$x = 1, y = 0$ correspond to $t = 0$.

$x = 2\pi, y = 0$ correspond to $t = \log 2\pi$.

$$\therefore \qquad I = \int_0^{\log 2\pi} dt = [t]_0^{\log 2\pi} = \log 2\pi$$

EXERCISE 3.2

1. Find $\nabla\phi$ for

   (i) $\phi = \log(x^2 + y^2 + z^2)$ (ii) $\phi = 2x\,z^4 - x^2 y$; at $(2, -2, 1)$

$$\textbf{(Ans. (i)}\ \frac{2}{(x^2 + y^2 + z^2)}\ (x\,\bar{i} + y\,\bar{j} + z\,\bar{k}),\ \text{(ii)}\ 10\,\bar{i} - 4\,\bar{j} + 6\,\bar{k}\,)$$

2. For $\bar{u} = 3xyz^2\,\bar{i} + 2xy^3\,\bar{j} - x^2yz\,\bar{k}$, $\bar{v} = x^3yz\,\bar{i} + 2xy\,\bar{j} + z^2\bar{k}$, $\phi = 3x^2 - yz$

  find (i) $\nabla \cdot \bar{u}$, (ii) $\bar{u} \cdot \nabla\phi$, (iii) $\nabla \cdot (\phi\,\bar{u})$, (iv) $\nabla \times \bar{v}$, (v) $\nabla \times (\phi\,\bar{u})$,

  (vi) $\bar{u} \times \nabla\phi$ at $(1, 2, -1)$.

$$\textbf{(Ans. (i)}\ 28,\ \text{(ii)}\ 48,\ \text{(iii)}\ 188,\ \text{(iv)}\ 2\bar{i} + 3\,\bar{k},\ \text{(v)}\ \bar{i} - 72\,\bar{j} + 129\,\bar{k},\ \text{(vi)}\ 6)$$

3. If $\bar{v}_1$, $\bar{v}_2$ are the vectors which join the fixed points $P\,(x_1, y_1, z_1)$, $Q\,(x_2, y_2, z_2)$ to the variable point $R\,(x, y, z)$ then, show that

  (i) $\nabla\,(\bar{v}_1 \cdot \bar{v}_2) = \bar{v}_2 + \bar{v}_1$, (ii) $\nabla \times (\bar{v}_1 \times \bar{v}_2) = 2\,(\bar{v}_1 - \bar{v}_2)$, (iii) $\nabla \cdot (\bar{v}_1 \times \bar{v}_2) = 0$.

$$\textbf{(Ans. (i)}\ \text{Irrotational, } xy \sin z + \cos x + y^2 z,\ \text{(ii) Irrotational } \log r,$$
$$\text{(iii)}\ \text{Irrotational, } \frac{1}{2}\,(a \cdot r)^2)$$

4. Show that $\nabla \int f(u)\,du = f(u)\,\nabla u$.

5. If $\bar{F} = (x^2 - y^2 + 2xz)\,\bar{i} + (xz - xy + yz)\,\bar{j} + (z^2 + x^2)\,\bar{k}$

  then show that curl $\bar{F}$ at $(1, 2, -3)$ and $(2, 3, 12)$ are orthogonal.

6. If $u = x + y$, $v = x - y + z$, $w = (2x + z)^2 + (2y - z)^2$ then show that $\nabla u, \nabla v, \nabla w$ are coplanar vectors.

7. If $\bar{F} = 2x^3\,\bar{i} - 3yz\,\bar{j} + xz\,\bar{k}$ and $\phi = 2x - z^3 y$, find

  (i) $\bar{F} \cdot \nabla\phi$, (ii) $\bar{F} \times \nabla\phi$ at the point $(1, 2, 1)$. **(Ans.** (i) 4, (ii) $37\,\bar{i} + 14\,\bar{j} + 10\,\bar{k}$)

8. Find the directional derivative of $\phi = 4xz^3 - 3x^2 y^2 z$ at $(2, -1, 2)$

  (i)   In the direction $2\,\bar{i} - 3\,\bar{j} + 6\,\bar{k}$. (ii) Towards the point $\bar{i} + \bar{j} - \bar{k}$.

  (iii) Along a line equally inclined with co-ordinate axes,

  (iv) Along tangent to the curve $x = e^t \cos t$, $y = e^t \sin t$, $z = e^t$ at $t = 0$.

$$\textbf{(Ans. (i)}\ \frac{664}{7},\ \text{(ii)}\ \frac{64}{\sqrt{14}},\ \text{(iii)}\ \frac{140}{\sqrt{3}},\ \text{(iv)}\ \frac{140}{\sqrt{3}})$$

9. Find directional derivative of $xy^2 + yz^3$ at $(2, -1, 1)$ along the line $2\,(x - 2) = (y + 1) = (z - 1)$.

10. Find the directional derivative of the function $\phi = e^{2x - y - z}$ at $(1, 1, 1)$ in the direction of the tangent to the curve $x = e^{-t}$, $y = 2\sin t + 1$, $z = t - \cos t$ at $t = 0$.

$$\textbf{(Ans.}\ -5/\sqrt{6})$$

11. Find the directional derivative of f at $(1, 2, -1)$ where $f(x, y, z) = x^2y + xyz + z^3$ along normal to the surface $x^2y^3 = 4xy + y^2z$ at the point $(1, 2, 0)$. 　　　　$\left(\textbf{Ans. } -\dfrac{1}{3}\right)$

12. If the directional derivative of $\phi = a(x + y) + b(y + z) + c(x + z)$ has maximum value 12 in the direction parallel to the line $\dfrac{x-1}{1} = \dfrac{y-2}{2} = \dfrac{z-1}{3}$, find the values of a, b, c.

13. Find the values of the constants a, b, c so that the directional derivative of $\phi = axy^2 + byz + cz^2x^2$ at $(2, 1, 1)$ has a maximum magnitude 12 in a direction parallel to x-axis. 　　　　$(\textbf{Ans. } a = 4, \ b = -16, \ c = 2)$

14. The directional derivative of a given function $f(x, y)$ at a point $P(2, 3)$ in a direction towards $Q(1, -1)$ is $\sqrt{17}$ and in a direction towards $R(-2, 1)$ is $\sqrt{20}$. Find the directional derivative of $f(x, y)$ at $P(2, 3)$ towards the point $S(6, 2)$. 　　$\left(\textbf{Ans. } \dfrac{-68}{7\sqrt{17}}\right)$

15. Find the constants a and b, so that the surface $ax^2 - byz = (a + 2)x$ will be orthogonal to the surface $4x^2y + z^3 = 4$ at the point $(1, -1, 2)$.

$$\left(\textbf{Ans. } a = \frac{5}{2}, \ b = 1\right)$$

16. Evaluate (i) $\nabla \cdot (r^3\, \bar r)$, 　　 (ii) $\nabla \cdot [r\nabla (1/r^3)]$ 　$\left(\textbf{Ans. (i) } 3r^3 + 3r, \ \text{(ii) } \dfrac{3}{r^4}\right)$

17. Show that

(i) 　$\nabla \cdot \left(\dfrac{\bar a \times \bar r}{r}\right) = 0$　　　(ii) $\nabla \times \left(\dfrac{\bar a \times \bar r}{r^n}\right) = \dfrac{(2-n)}{r^n}\, \bar a + \dfrac{n}{r^{n+2}}\, (\bar a \cdot \bar r)\, \bar r$.

18. $\bar a \cdot \nabla \left[\bar b \cdot \nabla \left(\dfrac{1}{r}\right)\right] = \dfrac{3\,(\bar a \cdot \bar r)\,(\bar b \cdot \bar r)}{r^5} - \dfrac{\bar a \cdot \bar b}{r^3}$

19. Prove that $\bar b \times \nabla\, [\bar a \cdot \nabla \log r] = \dfrac{\bar b \times \bar a}{r^2} - \dfrac{2\,(\bar a \cdot \bar r)}{r^4}\,(\bar b \times \bar r)$

20. Show that

(i) 　$\nabla^4 (r^2 \log r) = \dfrac{6}{r^2}$　　　(ii) $\nabla \cdot \left[r\, \nabla \left(\dfrac{1}{r^n}\right)\right] = \dfrac{n\,(n-2)}{r^{n+1}}$

(iii) 　$\nabla^2 \left(\dfrac{\bar a \cdot \bar b}{r}\right) = 0$.

21. If $\bar r$ be a position vector such that $r = |\bar r|$ and $\bar u$ be a differentiable vector function, then using vector identities, prove that,

(i) 　$\nabla \int r^n\, dr = r^{n-1}\, \bar r$

(ii) 　$\nabla^2 (r^n \log r) = [n\,(n+1) \log r + 2n + 1]\, r^{n-2}$

22. For scalars ϕ and ψ, show that $\nabla \times (\phi \nabla \psi) = \nabla \phi \times \nabla \psi = -\nabla \times (\psi \nabla \phi)$.

23. If $\bar{F} = (y + z)\,\bar{i} + (z + x)\,\bar{j} + (x + y)\,\bar{k}$ then show that

$$\text{curl curl curl curl } \bar{F} = \nabla^4\,[(y + z)\,\bar{i} + (z + x)\,\bar{j} + (x + y)\,\bar{k}\,]$$

24. If $\bar{w}$ is constant vector and $\bar{v} = \bar{w} \times \bar{r}$, prove that div $\bar{v} = 0$.

25. (i) Prove that $\bar{F} = \dfrac{1}{(x^2 + y^2)}\,(x\,\bar{i} + y\,\bar{j})$ is solenoidal.

(ii) Find the function $f(r)$ so that $f(r)\,\bar{r}$ is solenoidal.

26. If $\bar{u}$ and $\bar{v}$ are irrotational vectors then prove that $\bar{u} \times \bar{v}$ is solenoidal vector.

27. If ϕ, ψ satisfy Laplace equation, then prove that the vector $(\phi\nabla\psi - \psi\nabla\phi)$ is solenoidal.

28. Show that $\bar{F} = \dfrac{\bar{a} \times \bar{r}}{r^n}$ is solenoidal field.

29. If $\bar{F}_1 = yz\,\bar{i} + zx\,\bar{j} + xy\,\bar{k}$, $\bar{F}_2 = (\bar{a} \cdot \bar{r})\,\bar{a}$ then show that $\bar{F}_1 \times \bar{F}_2$ is solenoidal.

30. Verify whether following fields are irrotational and if so, find corresponding potential ϕ.

(i) $(y \sin z - \sin x)\,\bar{i} + (x \sin z + 2\,yz)\,\bar{j} + (xy \cos z + y^2)\,\bar{k}$.

(ii) $\dfrac{\bar{r}}{r^2}$ (iii) $(\bar{a} \cdot \bar{r})\,\bar{a}$.

31. Show that the vector field given by $\bar{F} = (y^2 \cos x + z^2)\,\bar{i} + (2y \sin x)\,\bar{j} + 2xz\,\bar{k}$ is conservative and find scalar field such that $\bar{F} = \nabla\phi$.

32. If the vector field $\bar{F} = (x + 2y + az)\,\bar{i} + (bx - 3y - z)\,\bar{j} + (4x + cy + 2z)\,\bar{k}$ is irrotational, find a, b, c and determine ϕ such that $\bar{F} = \nabla\phi$.

33. Show that $\bar{F} = r^2\bar{r}$ is conservative and obtain the scalar potential associated with it.

34. Show that $\bar{F} = (2xz^3 + 6y)\,\bar{i} + (6x - 2yz)\,\bar{j} + (3x^2z^2 - y^2)\,\bar{k}$ is irrotational. Find scalar potential ϕ such that $\bar{F} = \nabla\phi$.   **(Ans.** $\phi = 6xy + x^2z^3 - y^2z$**)**

35. Show that vector field $\bar{F} = (x^2 - yz)\,\bar{i} + (y^2 - zx)\,\bar{j} + (z^2 - xy)\,\bar{k}$ is irrotational. Find scalar potential ϕ such that $\bar{F} = \nabla\phi$.   **(Ans.** $\phi = x^3/3 + y^3/3 + z^3/3 - xyz + c$**)**

◈ ◈ ◈

UNIT - IV

LAPLACE TRANSFORM

4.1 INTRODUCTION

The theory of Laplace transforms is a very versatile tool, which has proved to be an essential part of mathematical techniques required for engineers, physicists, mathematicians and scientists. Its importance lies in the fact that its application is considerably easier than other available techniques.

Laplace transform method is widely used for solving differential equations and general system analysis. It reduces the problem of solving a differential equation to an algebraic problem. It is also useful in problems where the (mechanical or electrical) driving forces has discontinuities, forces acting for a short time only or are periodic and not merely sine or cosine functions.

In this chapter, we start with definition of the transform and state some sufficient conditions for its existence. We then derive its general properties (and theorems) and develop a table of transforms of some functions which are usually encountered in solutions of linear differential equations.

4.2 DEFINITION

Let $f(t)$ be a function of t defined for all $t > 0$. Then the *Laplace transform* of $f(t)$, denoted by $L[f(t)]$, is defined by

$$L[f(t)] = \int_0^\infty e^{-st} f(t)\, dt = F(s) \qquad \ldots (1)$$

where, s is a parameter which may be real or complex.

The Laplace transform of $f(t)$ exists if the integral in (1) exists i.e. the integral in (1) converges for some value of s.

Note :

(i)   Symbol L is called the Laplace transform operator.

(ii) Generally, the transform will exist for more than one value of the parameter s, and hence $L[f(t)]$ defines a function of s, when it exists, and is denoted by F(s).

(iii) There is one to one correspondence between $f(t)$ and $F(s)$, and the relation transforms $f(t)$, a function of t, into $F(s)$, a function of another variable s.

(iv) The operation just described, which yields $F(s)$ from a given function $f(t)$ is called *Laplace transformation.*

Notation :

(i) Original functions are denoted by lower case letters such as f(t), g(t), y(t) etc. and their transforms by the same letters in capital i.e. F(s), G(s), Y(s) etc.

(ii) A Bar (¯) can also be used to denote the Laplace transform. For example, the Laplace transforms of f(t), ϕ(t), x(t) etc. are $\bar{f}$(s) , $\bar{\phi}$(s) , $\bar{x}$(s) etc.

We shall be using notation **L [f(t)] = F(s)** throughout our discussion.

4.3 THEORETICAL PRELIMINARIES

1. Piecewise Continuous Function

A function f(t) is said to be *piecewise continuous* in an interval a $\le$ t $\le$ b, if f(t) is defined on that interval and is such that the interval can be subdivided into a finite number of subintervals, in each of which f(t) is continuous and has finite limits as t approaches either end point of the interval of subdivision from the interior.

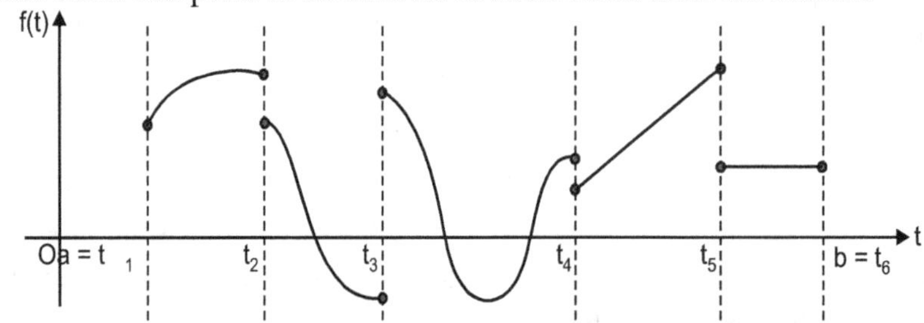

Fig. 4.1 : Example of Piecewise Continuous Function f(t)

2. Functions of Exponential Order

If there is a constant α with the property that $e^{-\alpha t}\left|f(t)\right|$ remains bounded as t $\to$ ∞, then f(t) is said to be a *function of exponential order α as t $\to$ ∞* or, briefly *of exponential order.* In other words, there are constants α, M, and N such that

$$e^{-\alpha t}\left|f(t)\right| < M \qquad \text{for all t} > N.$$

Remark : If a function is of exponential order α, its absolute value must not increase more rapidly than $Me^{\alpha t}$ as t increases.

Example 1 : f (t) = t^2 is of exponential order 3, since $\left|t^2\right| = t^2 < e^{3t}$ for all t.

Example 2 : f(t) = e^{t^2} is not of exponential order, because no matter how large we choose M and α, $e^{t^2} > Me^{\alpha t}$ for all t > N. In other words, $e^{t^2-\alpha t}$ can be made larger than any given constant by increasing t.

Example 3 : Any function which is bounded in absolute value for t $\ge$ 0 such as sin ax, cos ax are of exponential order.

4.4 SUFFICIENT CONDITIONS FOR EXISTENCE OF LAPLACE TRANSFORMS

Theorem : If f(t) is piecewise continuous in every finite interval in the range t $\ge$ 0 and is of exponential order α, then its Laplace transform F(s) exists for all s > α.

Proof : Since f(t) is piecewise continuous, e^{-st} f(t) is integrable over any finite interval for t $\ge$ 0.

$$\therefore \qquad \left| \int_0^b e^{-st} f(t)\, dt \right| \leq \int_0^b \left| e^{-st} f(t) \right| dt = \int_0^b e^{-st} \left| f(t) \right| dt$$

$$< \int_0^b e^{-st} M e^{\alpha t}\, dt = M \int_0^b e^{-(s-\alpha)t}\, dt$$

$$[\because\ f(t) \text{ is of exponential order } \alpha]$$

$$= M \left[\frac{e^{-(s-\alpha)t}}{-(s-\alpha)} \right]_0^b = \frac{M}{(s-\alpha)} [1 - e^{-(s-\alpha)b}]$$

Now if $s > \alpha$ and as $b \to \infty$, then expression on R.H.S. approaches to finite quantity $\dfrac{M}{s-\alpha}$.

$$\therefore \qquad \left| L\,[f(t)] \right| = \left| \int_0^\infty e^{-st} f(t)\, dt \right| < \frac{M}{s-\alpha}, \quad s > \alpha$$

Remark : It should be noted that conditions of this theorem are sufficient to guarantee the existence of the Laplace transform. But these are not necessary conditions, which mean that even if these conditions are not satisfied, Laplace transform of functions exist.

For example, $f(t) = t^{-1/2}$ is infinite at $t = 0$ but its Laplace transform exists.

We shall consider function $f(t)$ as piecewise continuous and of exponential order throughout our discussion.

4.5 LINEARITY PROPERTY

Theorem : If c_1 and c_2 are any constants and $f_1(t)$ and $f_2(t)$ are functions whose Laplace transforms exist, then

$$L\,[c_1\, f_1(t) + c_2\, f_2(t)] = c_1\, L\,[f_1(t)] + c_2\, L\,[f_2(t)]$$

Proof : To prove this, we have by definition

$$L\,[c_1 f_1(t) + c_2 f_2(t)] = \int_0^\infty e^{-st} [c_1 f_1(t) + c_2 f_2(t)]\, dt$$

$$= c_1 \int_0^\infty e^{-st} f_1(t)\, dt + c_2 \int_0^\infty e^{-st} f_2(t)\, dt = c_1\, L\,[f_1(t)] + c_2\, L\,[f_2(t)]$$

The result is easily extended to more than two functions.

Note : The property of Laplace transformation expressed in this theorem is, of course, the property of linearity. In other words, the Laplace transform is a *linear transform.*

4.6 LAPLACE TRANSFORMS OF SOME ELEMENTARY FUNCTIONS

Using the fundamental definition of Laplace transform, we can obtain a table of Laplace transform of some elementary functions.

1. $f(t) = 1$

By the definition of Laplace transform, we obtain

$$L[1] = \int_0^\infty e^{-st} \cdot 1\, dt = \left[\frac{e^{-st}}{-s}\right]_0^\infty$$

$$= \frac{1}{s} \text{ if } s > 0$$

Hence $$\boxed{L[1] = \frac{1}{s} \text{ if } s > 0}$$ ... (2)

2. $f(t) = e^{at}$

By the definition of Laplace transform, we obtain

$$L[e^{at}] = \int_0^\infty e^{-st} e^{at}\, dt = \int_0^\infty e^{-(s-a)t}\, dt = \left[\frac{e^{-(s-a)t}}{-(s-a)}\right]_0^\infty$$

$$= \left\{\lim_{t\to\infty} \frac{e^{-(s-a)t}}{-(s-a)}\right\} + \frac{1}{(s-a)}$$

[The limit depends on sign of $(s-a)$. Under the restriction $s - a > 0$ i.e. $s > a$, limit will be zero.]

$$= 0 + \frac{1}{(s-a)} \text{ if } s > a = \frac{1}{(s-a)} \text{ if } s > a$$

Hence $$\boxed{L[e^{at}] = \frac{1}{s-a} \text{ if } s > a}$$ ... (3)

Note :

(i) If in the result (3) we take $a = 0$, then we get

$$L[e^{0t}] = L[1] = \frac{1}{s} \text{ if } s > 0$$

(ii) If in the result (3) we take $-a$ in place of a, then we get

$$L[e^{-at}] = \frac{1}{s+a} \text{ if } s > -a$$

(iii) If $f(t) = c^{at}$, then we obtain

$$L[c^{at}] = L[e^{at\log c}] = \frac{1}{s - a\log c} \text{ if } s > a\log c,\ c > 0.$$

3. $f(t) = \sin at$

By the definition of Laplace transform, we obtain

$$L[\sin at] = \int_0^\infty e^{-st} \sin at\, dt$$

$$= \left[\frac{e^{-st}}{s^2 + a^2} (- s \sin at - a \cos at) \right]_0^\infty$$

$$= \left\{ \lim_{t \to \infty} \frac{- e^{-st}}{s^2 + a^2} (s \sin at + a \cos at) \right\} + \frac{a}{s^2 + a^2}$$

[The limit depends on sign of s. Under the restriction $s > 0$, $e^{-st} \to 0$ as $t \to \infty$ while $\sin at$ and $\cos at$ remain finite (though not known) as $t \to \infty$.]

$$= 0 + \frac{a}{s^2 + a^2} \text{ if } s > 0 \quad = \frac{a}{s^2 + a^2} \text{ if } s > 0$$

Hence, $\boxed{L \, [\sin at] = \dfrac{a}{s^2 + a^2} \text{ if } s > 0}$ ... (4)

4. $f(t) = \cos at$

By the definition of Laplace transform, we obtain

$$L \, [\cos at] = \int_0^\infty e^{-st} \cos at \, dt$$

$$= \left[\frac{e^{-st}}{s^2 + a^2} (- s \cos at + a \sin at) \right]_0^\infty$$

$$= \left\{ \lim_{t \to \infty} \frac{e^{-st}}{s^2 + a^2} (- s \cos at + a \sin at) \right\} + \frac{s}{s^2 + a^2}$$

$$= 0 + \frac{s}{s^2 + a^2} \text{ if } s > 0 \quad = \frac{s}{s^2 + a^2} \text{ if } s > 0$$

Hence $\boxed{L \, [\cos at] = \dfrac{s}{s^2 + a^2} \text{ if } s > 0}$ ... (5)

Another Method : Assuming that the result (3) holds for complex numbers, then we have

$$L \, [e^{iat}] = \frac{1}{s - ia} = \frac{s + ia}{(s - ia)(s + ia)} = \frac{s + ia}{s^2 + a^2} = \frac{s}{s^2 + a^2} + i \, \frac{a}{s^2 + a^2} \quad ... \text{(i)}$$

But $e^{iat} = \cos at + i \sin at$, hence

$$L \, [e^{iat}] = L \, [\cos at + i \sin at] = L \, [\cos at] + iL \, [\sin at] \qquad ... \text{(ii)}$$

From (i) and (ii), we have on equating real and imaginary parts

$$L \, [\cos at] = \frac{s}{s^2 + a^2} \; ; \quad L \, [\sin at] = \frac{a}{s^2 + a^2} \, .$$

5. $f(t) = \sinh at$

By the definition of Laplace transform, we obtain

$$L \, [\sinh at] = \int_0^\infty e^{-st} \sinh at \, dt = \int_0^\infty e^{-st} \left(\frac{e^{at} - e^{-at}}{2} \right)$$

$$= \frac{1}{2} \left\{ \int_0^\infty e^{-st} e^{at} \, dt - \int_0^\infty e^{-st} e^{-at} \, dt \right\}$$

$$= \frac{1}{2} \left\{ L\,[e^{at}] - L\,[e^{-at}] \right\}$$

$$= \frac{1}{2} \left\{ \frac{1}{(s-a)} - \frac{1}{(s+a)} \right\} \text{ if } s > a \text{ and } s > -a \qquad \text{[By result (3)]}$$

$$= \frac{a}{s^2 - a^2} \text{ if } s > |a|$$

Hence $\boxed{L\,[\sinh at] \;=\; \dfrac{a}{s^2 - a^2} \text{ if } s > |a|}$ ... (6)

6. $f(t) = \cosh at$

By the definition of Laplace transform, we obtain

$$L\,[\cosh at] \;=\; \int_0^\infty e^{-st} \cosh at \, dt \;=\; \int_0^\infty e^{-st} \left(\frac{e^{at} + e^{-at}}{2} \right) dt$$

$$= \frac{1}{2} \left\{ \int_0^\infty e^{-st} e^{at} \, dt + \int_0^\infty e^{-st} e^{-at} \, dt \right\} = \frac{1}{2} \left\{ L\,[e^{at}] + L\,[e^{-at}] \right\}$$

$$= \frac{1}{2} \left\{ \frac{1}{s-a} - \frac{1}{s+a} \right\} \text{ if } s > a \text{ and } s > -a \qquad \text{[By result (3)]}$$

$$= \frac{s}{s^2 - a^2} \text{ if } s > |a|$$

Hence $\boxed{L\,[\cosh at] \;=\; \dfrac{s}{s^2 - a^2} \text{ if } s > |a|}$ ... (7)

Another Method : Using the linearity property of Laplace transformation, we have at once

$$L\,[\sinh at] \;=\; L\left[\frac{e^{at} - e^{-at}}{2} \right] = \frac{1}{2} \left\{ L\,[e^{at}] - L\,[e^{-at}] \right\}$$

$$= \frac{1}{2} \left\{ \frac{1}{(s-a)} - \frac{1}{(s+a)} \right\} = \frac{a}{s^2 - a^2}$$

$$L\,[\cosh at] \;=\; L\left[\frac{e^{at} + e^{-at}}{2} \right] = \frac{1}{2} \left\{ L\,[e^{at}] + L\,[e^{-at}] \right\}$$

$$= \frac{1}{2} \left\{ \frac{1}{(s-a)} + \frac{1}{(s+a)} \right\} = \frac{s}{s^2 - a^2}$$

7. $f(t) = t^n$

By the definition of Laplace transform, we obtain

$$L\,[t^n] \;=\; \int_0^\infty e^{-st} t^n \, dt \text{ put } st = y \;\therefore\; s \, dt = dy \quad \begin{array}{|c|c|c|} \hline t & 0 & \infty \\ \hline y & 0 & \infty \\ \hline \end{array} \text{ and if } s > 0,$$

$$= \int_0^\infty e^{-y} \left(\frac{y}{s}\right)^n \frac{dy}{s}$$

$$= \frac{1}{s^{n+1}} \int_0^\infty e^{-y} \, y^n \, dy \qquad \left\{ \because \int_0^\infty e^{-y} \, y^{n-1} \, dy = \overline{|n} \ \text{ if } n > 0 \right.$$

$$= \frac{\overline{|n+1}}{s^{n+1}} \ \text{ if } s > 0, \ \ n > -1$$

If n is a positive integer, $\overline{|n+1} = n!$,

then $\qquad L[t^n] = \dfrac{n!}{s^{n+1}} \ \text{ if } \ s > 0$

$$\boxed{\ \ \mathbf{L\,[t^n] = } \begin{cases} \dfrac{\overline{|n+1}}{s^{n+1}} \ ; & \text{if } n > -1 \\[2ex] \dfrac{n!}{s^{n+1}} \ \ ; & \text{if n is a positive integer} \end{cases}} \qquad \text{... (8)}$$

Hence

Note :

(i)   If in the result (8) we take n = 0, then we get

$$L[t^0] \ = \ L[1] = \frac{\overline{|1}}{s} = \frac{1}{s}$$

(ii)   If in the result (8) we take $n = \dfrac{-1}{2}$, then we get

$$L[t^{-1/2}] \ = \ \frac{\overline{|-1/2+1}}{s^{-1/2+1}} \ = \ \frac{\overline{|1/2}}{s^{1/2}} \ = \ \sqrt{\frac{\pi}{s}}$$

Remark : Once we know the transforms of these functions given in Table 4.1, nearly all the transforms we shall need, can be obtained with the use of some additional theorems which we consider in the subsequent sections.

The following table gives the Laplace transforms of the above elementary functions for ready reference :

Table 4.1

Table of Elementary Laplace Transforms

Sr. No.	f(t)	F(s) = L [f(t)]
1	1	$\dfrac{1}{s} \ ; \ \ s > 0$
2	e^{at}	$\dfrac{1}{s-a} \ ; \ \ s > a$

3	sin at	$\dfrac{a}{s^2 + a^2}$; $s > 0$
4	cos at	$\dfrac{s}{s^2 + a^2}$; $s > 0$
5	sinh at	$\dfrac{a}{s^2 - a^2}$; $s > |a|$
6	cosh at	$\dfrac{s}{s^2 - a^2}$; $s > |a|$
7	t^n if $n > -1$	$\dfrac{\overline{|n + 1}}{s^{n+1}}$; $s > 0$
8	t^n if n a positive integer	$\dfrac{n!}{s^{n+1}}$; $s > 0$

ILLUSTRATIONS ON LAPLACE TRANSFORM OF ELEMENTARYFUNCTIONS

Ex. 1 : *Find the Laplace transforms of the following functions :*
(i) $4e^{2t} + 5e^{-3t}$ (ii) $(e^{-2t} + e^{3t})^2$ (iii) $e^{at + b}$ (iv) 4^t

Sol. : (i) $L\,[4e^{2t} + 5e^{-3t}]$ $= 4\,L\,[e^{2t}] + 5\,L\,[e^{-3t}]$ (Using the linearity property)

$$= 4\,\frac{1}{s - 2} + 5\,\frac{1}{s + 3}$$

$$= \frac{4}{s - 2} + \frac{5}{s + 3} \text{ where } s > 2$$

(ii) $L\,[(e^{-2t} + e^{3t})^2]$ $= L\,[e^{-4t} + 2e^{t} + e^{6t}]$ (Using the linearity property)

$$= L\,[e^{-4t}] + 2L\,[e^{t}] + L\,[e^{6t}]$$

$$= \frac{1}{s + 4} + 2\,\frac{1}{s - 1} + \frac{1}{s - 6}$$

$$= \frac{1}{s + 4} + \frac{2}{s - 1} + \frac{1}{s - 6} \qquad \text{where } s > 6$$

(iii) $L\,[e^{at + b}]$ $= L\,[e^{at}\,e^{b}] = e^{b}\,L\,[e^{at}]$

$$= e^{b}\,\frac{1}{s - a} = \frac{e^{b}}{s - a} \qquad \text{where } s > a$$

(iv) $L\,[4^t]$ $= L\,[e^{t \log 4}] = L\,[e^{(\log 4)\, t}]$

$$= \frac{1}{s - \log 4} \qquad \text{where } s > \log 4$$

Ex. 2 : *Obtain the Laplace transform of each of the following functions :*
(i) $at + bt^2 + ct^3$ (ii) $4t^3 + t^7 + t^{4/3}$ (iii) $(2t + 3)^3$ (iv) $5t - 7e^{-6t} + t^{5/2}$.

Sol. : (i) $L\,[at + bt^2 + ct^3]$ $= a\,L\,[t] + b\,L\,[t^2] + c\,L\,[t^3]$ (Using the linearity property)

$$= a\,\frac{1}{s^2} + b\,\frac{2\,!}{s^3} + c\,\frac{3!}{s^4}$$

$$= \frac{a}{s^2} + \frac{2\,b}{s^3} + \frac{6\,c}{s^4} \qquad \text{where } s > 0$$

(ii) $\quad$ L $[4t^3 + t^7 + t^{4/3}]$ = 4 L $[t^3]$ + L $[t^7]$ + L $[t^{4/3}]$

$$= 4\,\frac{3!}{s^4} + \frac{7!}{s^8} + \frac{\overline{4/3+1}}{s^{4/3+1}}$$

$$= \frac{24}{s^4} + \frac{5040}{s^8} + \frac{4/3 \cdot 1/3 \,\overline{|1/3}}{s^{7/3}}$$

(iii) $\quad$ L $[(2t+3)^3]$ = L $[(2t)^3 + 3\,(2t)^2\,(3) + 3\,(2t)\,(3)^2 + (3)^3]$

$$= 8 \text{ L } [t^3] + 36 \text{ L } [t^2] + 54 \text{ L } [t] + 27 \text{ L } [1]$$

$$= 8\,\frac{3!}{s^4} + 36\,\frac{2\,!}{s^3} + 54\,\frac{1!}{s^2} + 27\,\frac{1}{s}$$

$$= \frac{48}{s^4} + \frac{72}{s^3} + \frac{54}{s^2} + \frac{27}{s} \qquad \text{where } s > 0$$

(iv) $\quad$ L $[5t - 7e^{-6t} + t^{5/2}]$ = 5 L $[t]$ – 7 L $[e^{-6t}]$ + L $[t^{5/2}]$

$$= 5 \cdot \frac{1!}{s^2} - 7\,\frac{1}{s+6} + \frac{\overline{5/2+1}}{s^{5/2+1}}$$

$$= \frac{5}{s^2} - \frac{7}{s+6} + \frac{\frac{5}{2} \cdot \frac{3}{2} \cdot \frac{1}{2}\,\overline{|\frac{1}{2}}}{s^{7/2}}$$

$$= \frac{5}{s^2} - \frac{7}{s+6} + \frac{15}{8}\,\sqrt{\frac{\pi}{s^7}} \qquad \text{where } s > 0$$

Ex. 3 : *Find the Laplace transform of each of the following functions :*

(i) 2 sin 4t + 5 cos 2t   (ii) sin 2t cos 3t   (iii) cos t cos 2t   (iv) cosh at – cos bt

Sol. : (i) $\quad$ L $[2 \sin 4t + 5 \cos 2t]$ = 2 L $[\sin 4t]$ + 5 L $[\cos 2t]$

$$= 2\,\frac{4}{s^2 + 4^2} + 5\,\frac{s}{s^2 + 2^2}$$

$$= \frac{8}{s^2 + 16} + \frac{5s}{s^2 + 4} \qquad \text{where } s > 0$$

(ii) $\quad$ L $[\sin 2t \cos 3t]$ = L $\left[\frac{1}{2}\,(2 \cos 3t \sin 2t)\right]$ = L $\left[\frac{1}{2}\,(\sin 5t - \sin t)\right]$

$$= \frac{1}{2}\,\{\text{L } [\sin 5t] - \text{L } [\sin t]\} = \frac{1}{2}\,\left\{\frac{5}{s^2 + 5^2} - \frac{1}{s^2 + 1^2}\right\}$$

$$= \frac{2\,(s^2 - 5)}{(s^2 + 25)\,(s^2 + 1)} \qquad \text{where } s > 0$$

(iii) $\qquad$ L [cos t cos 2t] $= L\left[\dfrac{1}{2}\,(2\cos 2t\cos t)\right] = L\left[\dfrac{1}{2}\,(\cos 3t + \cos t)\right]$

$$= \frac{1}{2}\,\{L\,[\cos 3t] + L\,[\cos t]\} = \frac{1}{2}\left\{\frac{s}{s^2 + 3^2} + \frac{s}{s^2 + 1^2}\right\}$$

$$= \frac{s\,(s^2 + 5)}{(s^2 + 9)\,(s^2 + 1)} \qquad \text{where } s > 0$$

(iv) $\qquad$ L [cosh at – cos bt] $=$ L [cosh at] – L [cos bt]

$$= \frac{s}{s^2 - a^2} - \frac{s}{s^2 + b^2} \qquad \text{where } s > |a|$$

Ex. 4 : *Find the Laplace transforms of the following functions :*

(i) 3 cos (4t + 7) (ii) 5 sin (2t + 3) (iii) sin² 4t (iv) cos³ 2t (v) cosh³ 2t

Sol. : (i) $\quad$ L [3 cos (4t + 7)] $=$ 3 L [cos (4t + 7)]

Note : (i) Here we first express cos (4t + 7) as the difference of two terms.

∴ $\qquad$ 3 L [cos (4t + 7)] $=$ 3 L [cos 4t cos 7 – sin 4t sin 7]

$$= 3\ \{\cos 7\,L\,[\cos 4t] - \sin 7\,L\,[\sin 4t]\}$$

$$= 3\left\{\cos 7\,\frac{s}{s^2 + 4^2} - \sin 7\,\frac{4}{s^2 + 4^2}\right\}$$

$$= \frac{3}{s^2 + 16}\,\{s\cos 7 - 4\sin 7\} \qquad \text{where } s > 0$$

(ii) $\qquad$ L [5 sin (2t + 3)] $=$ 5 L [sin (2t + 3)]

$$= 5\,L\,[\sin 2t\cos 3 + \cos 2t\sin 3]$$

$$= 5\,\{\cos 3\,L\,[\sin 2\,t] + \sin 3\,L\,[\cos 2\,t]\}$$

$$= 5\left\{\cos 3\,\frac{2}{s^2 + 2^2} + \sin 3\,\frac{s}{s^2 + 2^2}\right\}$$

$$= \frac{5}{s^2 + 4}\,\{2\cos 3 + s\sin 3\} \qquad \text{where } s > 0$$

(iii) $\qquad$ L [sin² 4 t] $= L\left[\dfrac{1 - \cos 8t}{2}\right] = \dfrac{1}{2}\,\{L\,[1] - L\,[\cos 8t]\}$

$$= \frac{1}{2}\left\{\frac{1}{s} - \frac{s}{s^2 + 8^2}\right\} = \frac{32}{s\,(s^2 + 64)} \qquad \text{where } s > 0$$

(iv) $\qquad$ L [cos³ 2 t] $= L\left[\dfrac{\cos 6t + 3\cos 2t}{4}\right]\ \left\{\because\ \cos 3\theta = 4\cos^3\theta - 3\cos\theta\right\}$

$$= \frac{1}{4} \{L [\cos 6t] + 3 L [\cos 2t]\}$$

$$= \frac{1}{4} \left\{ \frac{s}{s^2 + 6^2} + 3 \frac{s}{s^2 + 2^2} \right\}$$

$$= \frac{s (s^2 + 28)}{(s^2 + 4) (s^2 + 36)} \quad \text{where } s > 0$$

(v) $L [\cosh^3 2t] = L \left[\dfrac{\cosh 6t + 3 \cosh 2t}{4} \right] \quad \left\{ \because \cosh 3\theta = 4 \cosh^3 \theta - 3 \cosh \theta \right\}$

$$= \frac{1}{4} \{L [\cosh 6t] + 3 L [\cosh 2t]\}$$

$$= \frac{1}{4} \left\{ \frac{s}{s^2 - 6^2} + 3 \frac{s}{s^2 - 2^2} \right\}$$

$$= \frac{s (s^2 - 28)}{(s^2 - 4) (s^2 - 36)}$$

Ex. 5 : *Obtain Laplace transforms of*

(i) $3e^{4t} + 6t^2 - 4 \sin 3t + \cos 2t$ (ii) $5e^{-t/2} + t^{-1/2} + 7 \sin \dfrac{t}{2}$.

Sol. : (i) $L [3e^{4t} + 6t^2 - 4 \sin 3t + \cos 2t]$

$$= 3 L [e^{4t}] + 6 L [t^2] - 4 L [\sin 3t] + L [\cos 2t]$$

$$= 3 \frac{1}{s - 4} + 6 \frac{2 !}{s^3} - 4 \frac{3}{s^2 + 3^2} + \frac{s}{s^2 + 2^2}$$

$$= \frac{3}{s - 4} + \frac{12}{s^3} - \frac{12}{s^2 + 9} + \frac{s}{s^2 + 4} \qquad \text{where } s > 4$$

(ii) $L \left[5e^{-t/2} + t^{-1/2} + 7 \sin \dfrac{t}{2} \right] = 5 L [e^{-(1/2) t}] + L [t^{-1/2}] + 7 L \left[\sin \left(\dfrac{1}{2} \right) t \right]$

$$= 5 \frac{1}{s + \dfrac{1}{2}} + \sqrt{\frac{\pi}{s}} + 7 \frac{1/2}{s^2 + \left(\dfrac{1}{2} \right)^2}$$

$$= \frac{5}{s + \dfrac{1}{2}} + \sqrt{\frac{\pi}{s}} + \frac{\dfrac{7}{2}}{s^2 + \dfrac{1}{4}} \quad \text{where } s > 0$$

Ex. 6 : *Obtain Laplace transform of each of the following functions :*

(i) $f(t) = \begin{cases} t, & 0 < t < 4 \\ 5, & t > 4 \end{cases}$ (ii) $f(t) = \begin{cases} \sin 2t, & 0 < t < \pi \\ 0, & t > \pi \end{cases}$

(iii) $f(t) = \begin{cases} t/T, & 0 \le t < T \\ 1, & t > T \end{cases}$

Sol. : (i) $f(t) = \begin{cases} t, & 0 < t < 4 \\ 5, & t > 4 \end{cases}$

Note : Given function is discontinuous and we cannot get Laplace transform by using table of elementary Laplace transforms. Here we use fundamental definition (1) of Laplace transform.

Thus
$$L[f(t)] = \int_0^\infty e^{-st} f(t)\, dt = \int_0^4 e^{-st} t\, dt + \int_4^\infty e^{-st} 5\, dt$$

$$= \left[t\left(\frac{e^{-st}}{-s}\right) - (1)\left(\frac{e^{-st}}{s^2}\right) \right]_0^4 + 5\left[\frac{e^{-st}}{-s}\right]_4^\infty$$

(Using the generalised rule of integration by parts)

$$= \left[\left(-\frac{4e^{-4s}}{s} - \frac{e^{-4s}}{s^2} \right) - \left(0 - \frac{1}{s^2} \right) \right] + 5\left[0 + \frac{e^{-4s}}{s} \right]$$

$$= \frac{1}{s^2} + e^{-4s}\left(\frac{1}{s} - \frac{1}{s^2} \right) \qquad \text{where } s > 0$$

(ii)
$$f(t) = \begin{cases} \sin 2t, & 0 < t < \pi \\ 0, & t > \pi \end{cases}$$

$$L[f(t)] = \int_0^\infty e^{-st} f(t)\, dt = \int_0^\pi e^{-st} \sin 2t\, dt + \int_\pi^\infty e^{-st}\,(0)\, dt$$

$$= \left[\frac{e^{st}}{s^2 + 4} (-s \sin 2t - 2 \cos 2t) \right]_0^\pi$$

$$= \frac{1}{s^2 + 4}\left[e^{-s\pi}(-2) - (-2) \right]$$

$$= \frac{2}{s^2 + 4}(1 - e^{-s\pi}) \qquad \text{where } s > 0$$

(iii)
$$f(t) = \begin{cases} t/T, & 0 \le t < T \\ 1, & t > T \end{cases}$$

$$L[f(t)] = \int_0^\infty e^{-st} f(t)\, dt = \int_0^T e^{-st}\left(\frac{t}{T}\right) dt + \int_T^\infty e^{-st}\, 1\, dt$$

$$= \frac{1}{T}\left[t\left(\frac{e^{-st}}{-s}\right) - (1)\left(\frac{e^{-st}}{s^2}\right) \right]_0^T + \left[\frac{e^{-st}}{-s}\right]_T^\infty$$

$$= \frac{1}{T}\left[T\left(\frac{e^{-sT}}{-s}\right) - \left(\frac{e^{-sT}}{s^2}\right) + \frac{1}{s^2} \right] + \left[0 + \frac{e^{-sT}}{s} \right]$$

$$= -\frac{e^{-sT}}{s} - \frac{(e^{-sT} - 1)}{Ts^2} + \frac{e^{-sT}}{s}$$

$$= \frac{1 - e^{-sT}}{Ts^2} \qquad \text{where } s > 2$$

EXERCISE 4.1

1. Find the Laplace transform of each of the following functions :

   (i) $2e^{3t} + 3e^{-2t}$ (ii) $(e^{-at} - e^{-bt})^2$ (iii) $(2e^{3t} + 5)^2$ (iv) c^{at+b}

Ans. (i) $\dfrac{2}{s-3} + \dfrac{3}{s+2}$ (ii) $\dfrac{1}{s+2a} + \dfrac{2}{s+(a+b)} + \dfrac{1}{s+2b}$

(iii) $\dfrac{4}{s-6} + \dfrac{20}{s-3} + \dfrac{25}{s}$ (iv) $\dfrac{c^b}{s - a \log c}$

2. Obtain the Laplace transform of each of the following functions :

   (i) $t^2 - 3t + 5$ (ii) $t^4 + 5t^3 + t^{1/2}$ (iii) $a + \dfrac{b}{\sqrt{t}}$ (iv) $(t+2)^3 + (e^{2t} + 3)^2$

Ans. (i) $\dfrac{5s^2 - 3s + 2}{s^3}$ (ii) $\dfrac{24}{s^5} + \dfrac{30}{s^4} + \dfrac{\sqrt{\pi}}{2s^{3/2}}$ (iii) $\dfrac{a}{s} + b\sqrt{\dfrac{\pi}{s}}$

(iv) $\dfrac{6}{s^4} + \dfrac{12}{s^3} + \dfrac{12}{s^2} + \dfrac{17}{s} + \dfrac{1}{s-4} + \dfrac{6}{s-2}$

3. Find the Laplace transform of each of the following functions :

   (i) $3 \cos 2t - \sin 2t$ (ii) $\cosh 5t + \cos 5t$ (iii) $\cos 3t \cos 2t$ (iv) $\sin 2t \cos 5t$

Ans. (i) $\dfrac{3s}{s^2+4} - \dfrac{2}{s^2+4}$ (ii) $\dfrac{s}{s^2-25} + \dfrac{s}{s^2+25}$ (iii) $\dfrac{s(s^2+13)}{(s^2+1)(s^2+25)}$ (iv) $\dfrac{2(s^2-21)}{(s^2+9)(s^2+49)}$

4. Find the Laplace transforms of the following functions :

(i) $\cos(\omega t + \alpha)$ (ii) $\sin(\omega t + \alpha)$ (iii) $\cos^2 bt$ (iv) $\sin^3 2t$ (v) $\sinh^3 2t$ (vi) $(\sin t - \cos t)^2$

Ans. (i) $\dfrac{s \cos \alpha - \omega \sin \alpha}{s^2 + \omega^2}$ (ii) $\dfrac{\omega \cos \alpha + s \sin \alpha}{s^2 + \omega^2}$ (iii) $\dfrac{s^2 + 2b^2}{s(s^2 + 4b^2)}$

(iv) $\dfrac{48}{(s^2+4)(s^2+36)}$ (v) $\dfrac{48}{(s^2-4)(s^2-36)}$ (vi) $\dfrac{s^2 - 2s + 4}{s(s^2+4)}$

5. Obtain Laplace transforms of

   (i) $e^{2t} + 4t^3 - 2 \sin 3t + 3 \cos 3t$ (ii) $4 \cos 2t - 5t^2 + 2e^{3t}$

   (iii) $3t^4 - 2t^3 + 4e^{-3t} - 2 \sin 5t + 3 \cos 2t$

Ans. (i) $\dfrac{1}{s-2} + \dfrac{24}{s^4} - \dfrac{6}{s^2+9} + \dfrac{3s}{s^2+9}$ (ii) $\dfrac{4s}{s^2+4} - \dfrac{10}{s^3} + \dfrac{2}{s-3}$

(iii) $\dfrac{72}{s^5} - \dfrac{12}{s^4} + \dfrac{4}{s+3} - \dfrac{10}{s^2+25} + \dfrac{3s}{s^2+4}$

6. Obtain Laplace transform of each of the following functions :

(i) $f(t) = \begin{cases} a, & 0 < t < b \\ 0, & t > b \end{cases}$ (ii) $f(t) = \begin{cases} \cos t, & 0 < t < 2\pi \\ 0, & t > 2\pi \end{cases}$

(iii) $f(t) = \begin{cases} \cos t, & 0 < t < \pi \\ \sin t, & t > \pi \end{cases}$ (iv) $f(t) = \begin{cases} 0, & 0 \leq t < 1 \\ t^2 - 2t + 2, & t \geq 1 \end{cases}$

(v) $f(t) = \begin{cases} 0, & 0 \leq t < 1 \\ t, & 1 < t < 2 \\ 0, & t > 2 \end{cases}$

Ans. (i) $\dfrac{a}{s}\,(1 - e^{-sb})$ (ii) $\dfrac{s\,(1 - e^{-2\pi s})}{s^2 + 1}$ (iii) $\dfrac{s + (s - 1)\,e^{-\pi s}}{s^2 + 1}$

(iv) $e^{-s}\left(\dfrac{1}{s} + \dfrac{2}{s^3}\right)$ (v) $\left(\dfrac{1}{s^2} + \dfrac{1}{s}\right)e^{-s} - \left(\dfrac{1}{s^2} + \dfrac{2}{s}\right)e^{-2s}$

4.7 GENERAL THEOREMS OF LAPLACE'S TRANSFORMS

We shall now derive a number of theorems that will be of considerable use in finding the Laplace transforms of some additional functions (not included in the Table 4.1).

(A) First Shifting Theorem

Theorem : If $L\,[f(t)] = F(s)$, then

$$L\,[e^{-at} f(t)] = F(s + a) = \{L\,[f(t)]\}_{s \to s + a}$$

Proof : By definition,

$$L\,[e^{-at} f(t)] = \int_0^\infty e^{-st}\,[e^{-at} f(t)]\,dt = \int_0^\infty e^{-(s + a)\,t} f(t)\,dt$$

$$= \int_0^\infty e^{-pt} f(t)\,dt \quad \text{where } p = s + a$$

$$= F(p) \qquad\qquad \text{... by def. (1), } s \to p$$

$$= F(s + a)$$

Hence $\boxed{L\,[e^{-at} f(t)] = F(s + a) = \{L\,[f(t)]\}_{s \to s + a}}$ ... (9)

Remark 1 : In words, this theorem states that the Laplace transform of e^{-at} times a function of t is equal to the Laplace transform of the function f(t), with s replaced by s + a.

Remark 2 : The first shifting theorem concerns shifting on the s-axis : the replacement of s in F(s) by s + a corresponds to shifting the graph of F(s) to the left through distance a unit.

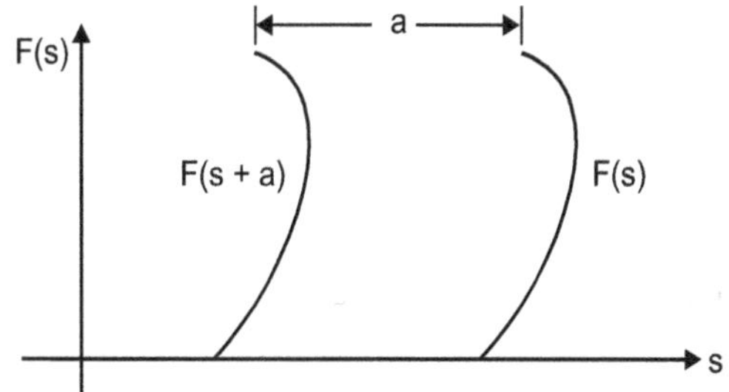

Fig. 4.2 : First Shifting Theorem, Shifting on The s-Axis

Remark 3 : In practice to obtain Laplace transform of $e^{-at} f(t)$, we first obtain Laplace transform of $f(t)$ (i.e. factor e^{-at} is dropped initially) and then replace s by s + a in L [f(t)] to account for the multiplying factor e^{-at}.

ILLUSTRATIONS

Ex. 1 : *Find the Laplace transform of each of the following functions :*

(i) $e^{-at} \sin bt$ (ii) $e^{-at} \cos bt$ (iii) $e^{-at} \sinh bt$ (iv) $e^{-at} \cosh bt$ (v) $e^{-at} t^n$

Sol. : (i) We have

$$L [\sin bt] = \frac{b}{s^2 + b^2} \qquad \text{(From Table 4.1 in sec. 4.6)}$$

$$\therefore \quad L [e^{-at} \sin bt] = \frac{b}{(s + a)^2 + b^2} \qquad \text{(By the First Shifting Theorem)}$$

(ii) We have

$$L [\cos bt] = \frac{s}{s^2 + b^2} \qquad \text{(From Table 4.1)}$$

$$\therefore \quad L [e^{-at} \cos bt] = \frac{s + a}{(s + a)^2 + b^2} \qquad \text{(By the First Shifting Theorem)}$$

(iii) We have

$$L [\sinh bt] = \frac{b}{s^2 - b^2} \qquad \text{(From Table 4.1)}$$

$$\therefore \quad L [e^{-at} \sinh bt] = \frac{b}{(s + a)^2 - b^2} \qquad \text{(By the First Shifting Theorem)}$$

(iv) We have

$$L [\cosh bt] = \frac{s}{s^2 - a^2} \qquad \text{(From Table 4.1)}$$

$$\therefore \quad L [e^{-at} \cosh bt] = \frac{s + a}{(s + a)^2 - a^2} \qquad \text{(By the First Shifting Theorem)}$$

(v) We have

$$L[t^n] = \frac{\overline{|n+1}}{s^{n+1}} \qquad \text{(From Table 4.1)}$$

$$\therefore \qquad L[e^{-at} t^n] = \frac{\overline{|n+1}}{(s+a)^{n+1}} \qquad \text{(By the First Shifting Theorem)}$$

Ex. 2 : *Obtain the Laplace transform of each of the following functions :*

(i) $e^{4t} \cosh 5t$ (ii) $(t+2)^2 e^{4t}$ (iii) $e^{-2t}(3\cos 6t - 5\sin 6t)$ (iv) $e^{-3t}\sin^2 t$ (v) $\cosh at \sin at$

Sol. : (i) We have

$$L[\cosh 5t] = \frac{s}{s^2 - 25}$$

$$\therefore \qquad L[e^{4t}\cosh 5t] = \left\{\frac{s}{s^2-25}\right\}_{s \to s-4} \qquad \text{(By the First Shifting Theorem)}$$

$$= \frac{s-4}{(s-4)^2 - 25} = \frac{s-4}{s^2 - 8s - 9}$$

Another Method :

$$L[e^{4t}\cosh 5t] = L\left[e^{4t}\left(\frac{e^{5t} + e^{-5t}}{2}\right)\right] = \frac{1}{2}L[e^{9t} + e^{-t}]$$

$$= \frac{1}{2}\left\{\frac{1}{s-9} + \frac{1}{s+1}\right\} = \frac{s-4}{s^2 - 8s - 9} \qquad \text{(From Table 4.1)}$$

(ii) We have

$$L[(t+2)^2] = L[t^2 + 4t + 4]$$

$$= \frac{2}{s^3} + \frac{4}{s^2} + \frac{4}{s} = \frac{4s^2 + 4s + 2}{s^3}$$

$$\therefore \qquad L[e^{4t}(t+2)^2] = \left\{\frac{4s^2 + 4s + 2}{s^3}\right\}_{s \to s-4}$$

$$= \frac{4(s-4)^2 + 4(s-4) + 2}{(s-4)^3} = \frac{4s^2 - 28s + 50}{(s-4)^3}$$

(iii) We have

$$L[3\cos 6t - 5\sin 6t] = 3L[\cos 6t] - 5L[\sin 6t]$$

$$= 3\frac{s}{s^2 + 36} - 5\frac{6}{s^2 + 36} = \frac{3s - 30}{s^2 + 40}$$

$$\therefore \ L[e^{-2t}(3\cos 6t - 5\sin 6t)] = \left\{\frac{3s + 30}{s^2 + 36}\right\}_{s \to s+2}$$

$$= \frac{3\,(s+2)-30}{(s+2)^2+36} = \frac{3s-24}{s^2+4s+40}$$

(iv) We have $L\,[\sin^2 t] = L\left[\dfrac{1-\cos 2t}{2}\right] = \dfrac{1}{2}\,\{L\,[1] - L\,[\cos 2t]\}$

$$= \frac{1}{2}\left\{\frac{1}{s} - \frac{s}{s^2+4}\right\} = \frac{2}{s\,(s^2+4)}$$

$\therefore$ $L\,[e^{-3t}\,\sin^2 t] = \left\{\dfrac{2}{s\,(s^2+4)}\right\}_{s\,\to\,s+3}$

$$= \frac{2}{(s+3)\,\{(s+3)^2+4\}} = \frac{2}{(s+3)\,(s^2+6s+13)}$$

(v) $L\,[\cosh at \sin at] = L\left[\left(\dfrac{e^{at}+e^{-at}}{2}\right)\sin at\right]$

$$= \frac{1}{2}\,\{L\,[e^{at}\sin at] + L\,[e^{-at}\sin at]\}$$

$$= \frac{1}{2}\left\{\frac{a}{(s-a)^2+a^2} + \frac{a}{(s+a)^2+a^2}\right\} \quad \left\{\because\ L\,[\sin at] = \frac{a}{s^2+a^2}\right.$$

$$= \frac{1}{2}\left\{\frac{a}{s^2-2as+2a^2} + \frac{a}{s^2+2as+2a^2}\right\} = \frac{a\,(s^2+2a^2)}{s^4+4a^4}$$

(B) SECOND SHIFTING THEOREM

Theorem: If $L\,[f(t)] = F(s)$ and $F(t) = \begin{cases} f(t-a), & t>a \\ 0, & t<a \end{cases}$, then $L\,[F(t)] = e^{-as}\,F(s)$

Proof : By definition,

$$L\,[F(t)] = \int_0^\infty e^{-st}\,F(t)\,dt = \int_0^a e^{-st}\,F(t)\,dt + \int_a^\infty e^{-st}\,F(t)\,dt$$

$$= \int_0^a e^{-st}\,(0)\,dt + \int_a^\infty e^{-st}\,f(t-a)\,dt$$

$$= \int_a^\infty e^{-st}\,f(t-a)\,dt,\ \text{Put}\ t-a = u \therefore dt = du\ \text{and}\ \begin{array}{|c|c|c|}\hline t & a & \infty \\\hline u & 0 & \infty \\\hline\end{array}$$

$$= \int_0^\infty e^{-s\,(a+u)}\,f(u)\,du = e^{-as}\int_0^\infty e^{-su}\,f(u)\,du$$

$$= e^{-as}\,L\,[f(t)] = e^{-as}\,F(s)$$

Hence

$$L\,[F(t)] \;=\; e^{-as}\,F(s), \text{ where } F(t) = \begin{cases} f(t-a) & t > a \\ 0 & t < a \end{cases}$$

... (10)

Remark 1 : The second shifting theorem concerns shifting on t-axis : the replacement of t in f(t) by $(t-a)$ (i.e. shifting graph of f(t) to the right through distance a, corresponds to multiplication of the transform F(s) by e^{-as}.

Remark 2 : In practice to obtain Laplace transform of F(t), we first obtain f(t) from $f(t-a)$ and its Laplace transform F(s) and then required transform is written as $e^{-as}\,F(s)$.

ILLUSTRATIONS

Ex. 1 : *Find the Laplace transforms of the following functions :*

(i) $F(t) = \begin{cases} \cos(t - 2\pi/3), & t > \dfrac{2\pi}{3} \\[2mm] 0, & t < \dfrac{2\pi}{3} \end{cases}$
(ii) $F(t) = \begin{cases} (t-1)^3, & t > 1 \\ 0, & t < 1 \end{cases}$

Sol. : (i) Here $f(t-a) = \cos\left(t - \dfrac{2\pi}{3}\right)$, where $a = \dfrac{2\pi}{3}$.

$\therefore$ $f(t) = \cos t$ and $F(s) = \dfrac{s}{s^2 + 1}$

Hence by the second shifting theorem, with $a = \dfrac{2\pi}{3}$, we have

$$L\,[F(t)] \;=\; e^{-as}\,F(s) \;=\; e^{-2\pi s/3}\left(\dfrac{s}{s^2 + 1}\right)$$

(ii) Here $f(t-a) = (t-1)^3$, where $a = 1$.

$\therefore$ $f(t) = t^3$ and $F(s) = \dfrac{3!}{s^4} = \dfrac{6}{s^4}$

Hence by the second shifting theorem, with $a = 1$, we have

$$L\,[F(t)] \;=\; e^{-as}\,F(s) \;=\; e^{-s}\left(\dfrac{6}{s^4}\right)$$

Ex. 2 : *Obtain the Laplace transforms of the following functions :*

(i) $F(t) = \begin{cases} e^{-4(t-3)} \sin 3\,(t-3), & t > 3 \\ 0, & t < 3 \end{cases}$
(ii) $F(t) = \begin{cases} \sin 2\,(t-\pi), & t > \pi \\ 0, & t < \pi \end{cases}$

Sol. : (i) Here $f(t-a) = e^{-4(t-3)} \sin 3\,(t-3)$ where $a = 3$.

$\therefore$ $f(t) = e^{-4t} \sin 3t$

$\therefore$ $F(s) = \left\{\dfrac{3}{s^2 + 9}\right\}_{s \to s + 4}$ (By the First Shifting Theorem)

$$= \frac{3}{(s+4)^2 + 9} = \frac{3}{s^2 + 8s + 25}$$

Hence by the second shifting theorem, with $a = 3$, we have

$$L[F(t)] = e^{-as} F(s) = e^{-3s} \left(\frac{3}{s^2 + 8s + 25} \right)$$

(ii) Here $\qquad f(t - a) = \sin 2(t - \pi)$ where $a = \pi$

$\therefore \qquad\qquad f(t) = \sin 2t$

$\therefore \qquad\qquad F(s) = \dfrac{2}{s^2 + 4}$

Hence by the second shifting theorem, with $a = \pi$, we have

$$L[F(t)] = e^{-as} F(s) = e^{-\pi s} \left(\frac{2}{s^2 + 4} \right)$$

(C) CHANGE OF SCALE THEOREM

Theorem : If $L[f(t)] = F(s)$, then $L[f(at)] = \dfrac{1}{a} F\left(\dfrac{s}{a}\right)$

Proof : By definition,

$$L[f(at)] = \int_0^\infty e^{-st} f(at)\, dt \quad \text{Put } at = u \therefore a\, dt = du \quad \text{and} \quad \begin{array}{|c|c|c|} \hline t & 0 & \infty \\ \hline u & 0 & \infty \\ \hline \end{array}$$

$$= \int_0^\infty e^{-s(u/a)} f(u)\, \frac{du}{a} = \frac{1}{a} \int_0^\infty e^{-(s/a)u} f(u)\, du$$

$$= \frac{1}{a} F\left(\frac{s}{a}\right) \qquad\qquad \left(\text{by } s \to \frac{s}{a} \text{ in def. (1)} \right)$$

Hence $\qquad\boxed{L[f(at)] = \dfrac{1}{a} F\left(\dfrac{s}{a}\right)} \qquad\qquad\qquad \dots (11)$

ILLUSTRATIONS

Ex. 1 : *If $L[\sin t] = \dfrac{1}{s^2 + 1}$, find $L[\sin at]$.*

Sol. : We have given that

$$L[\sin t] = \frac{1}{s^2 + 1}$$

By the Change of Scale Theorem,

$$L[\sin at] = \frac{1}{a}\, \frac{1}{(s/a)^2 + 1} = \frac{a}{s^2 + a^2}$$

Ex. 2 : If $\quad L\left[\dfrac{\sin t}{t}\right] = \tan^{-1}\left(\dfrac{1}{s}\right)$, find $L\left[\dfrac{\sin at}{t}\right]$.

Sol. : We have given that

$$L\left[\frac{\sin t}{t}\right] = \tan^{-1}\left(\frac{1}{s}\right)$$

By the Change of Scale Theorem,

$$L\left[\frac{\sin at}{at}\right] = \frac{1}{a} L\left[\frac{\sin at}{t}\right] = \frac{1}{a} \tan^{-1}\left\{\frac{1}{(s/a)}\right\} = \frac{1}{a} \tan^{-1}\left(\frac{a}{s}\right)$$

$$\therefore \qquad L\left[\frac{\sin at}{t}\right] = \tan^{-1}\left(\frac{a}{s}\right)$$

Ex. 3 : *If* $L\,[f(t)] = \dfrac{8 + 12s - 2s^2}{(s^2 + 4)^2}$, *find* $L\,[f(2t)]$.

Sol. : We have given that

$$L\,[f(t)] = \frac{8 + 12s - 2s^2}{(s^2 + 4)^2}$$

By the Change of Scale Theorem,

$$L\,[f(2t)] = \frac{1}{2}\left[\frac{8 + 12\,(s/2) - 2\,(s/2)^2}{\{(s/2)^2 + 4\}^2}\right] = \frac{4\,(16 + 12s - s^2)}{(s^2 + 16)^2}$$

(D) LAPLACE TRANSFORMS OF DERIVATIVES

To solve differential equations by Laplace transform method, we require the transforms of the derivatives. We derive below some expressions for the Laplace transforms of $f'(t)$, $f''(t)$ … etc. in terms of the transform of the function itself and in terms of the lower order derivatives of the function at $t = 0$ (i.e. values of the lower order derivatives as $t \to 0$ from positive values).

Theorem : If $L\,[f(t)] = F(s)$, then

$$L\,[f'(t)] = s\,L\,[f(t)] - f(0) = s\,F(s) - f(0) \quad \text{if } f(t) \text{ is continuous}$$

function for $t \geq 0$ and is of exponential order α $\left[\text{i.e. } \lim_{b\to\infty} e^{-sb}\,f(b) = 0 \text{ for } s > \alpha\right]$.

Proof : Using integration by parts (considering e^{-st} as first function), we have

$$L\,[f'(t)] = \int_0^\infty e^{-st}\,f'(t)\,dt = \lim_{b\to\infty} \int_0^b e^{-st}\,f'(t)\,dt$$

$$= \lim_{b\to\infty}\left\{\left[e^{-st}\,f(t)\right]_0^b + s\int_0^b e^{-st}\,f(t)\,dt\right\}$$

$$= \lim_{b\to\infty}\left\{\left[e^{-sb}\,f(b) - f(0)\right] + s\int_0^b e^{-st}\,f(t)\,dt\right\}$$

$$= s\int_0^\infty e^{-st}\,f(t)\,dt - f(0) \quad \{\because\ f(t) \text{ is of exponential order}\}$$

$$= s\,L\,[f(t)] - f(0)$$

$$= s\,F(s) - f(0)$$

Hence $\boxed{L\,[f\,'(t)] \;=\; s\,L\,[f(t)] - f(0) = s\,F(s) - f(0)}$ ... (12)

By applying result (12) to second order derivative f''(t), we obtain

$$L\,[f\,''(t)] \;=\; L\,[\{f\,'(t)\}']$$

$$= s\,L\,[f\,'(t)] - f\,'(0)$$

$$= s\,\{s\,F(s) - f(0)\} - f\,'(0)$$

$$= s^2\,F(s) - s\,f(0) - f\,'(0)$$

Thus $\boxed{L\,[f\,''(t)] \;=\; s^2\,F(s) - s\,f(0) - f\,'(0)}$ ... (13)

Similarly, it can be proved that

$$\boxed{L\,[f\,'''(t)] \;=\; s^3\,F(s) - s^2\,f(0) - s\,f\,'(0) - f\,''(0)}$$ ... (14)

etc. By using mathematical induction, we can obtain the following generalised result :

$$\boxed{L\,[f^n(t)] = s^n\,F(s) - s^{n-1}\,f(0) - s^{n-2}\,f\,'(0) - s^{n-3}\,f\,''(0) - \ldots s^2\,f^{n-3}(0) - s\,f^{n-2}(0) - f^{n-1}(0)}$$

$$... (15)$$

Note 1 : Following observations are quite useful in remembering the result (15) :

(a) Except first all other terms are negative.

(b) Power of s in the first term is n (i.e. the order of the derivative whose Laplace transform is required) and goes on decreasing by one in subsequent term upto zero.

(c) Multiplier of s^n is $F(s) = L\,[f(t)]$ and that of subsequent terms f(0), f'(0), f''(0), ... etc.

(d) Sum of powers of s and order of the derivative of f(0) in every term (except first) is $n - 1$.

Note 2 : Laplace transform of derivative of a function f(t), roughly corresponds to multiplication of transform F(s) by s. This permits replacing operations of calculus by simple algebraic operations on transforms.

ILLUSTRATIONS

Ex. 1 : *Obtain the Laplace transforms of (i) $\dfrac{d^5x}{dt^5}$, (ii) $\dfrac{d^2y}{dt^2} - 3\dfrac{dy}{dt} + 5y$, given that y (0) = 2 and y'(0) = – 4.*

Sol. : (i) We have, from result (15)

$$L\left[\frac{d^5x}{dt^5}\right] \;=\; s^5 \times (s) - s^4\,x\,(0) - s^3\,x'(0) - s^2\,x''(0) - s\,x'''(0) - x^{iv}(0)$$

(ii) $\quad L\left[\dfrac{d^2y}{dt^2} - 3\dfrac{dy}{dt} + 5y\,(t)\right]$

$$= L\left[\dfrac{d^2y}{dt^2}\right] - 3\,L\left[\dfrac{dy}{dt}\right] + 5\,L\,[y(t)]$$

$$= \{s^2\,Y(s) - y(0) - y'(0)\} - 3\,\{s\,Y(s) - y(0)\} + 5\,Y(s)$$

[By results (12) and (13)]

$$= \{s^2\,Y(s) - s(2) - (-4)\} - 3\,\{s\,Y(s) - (2)\} + 5\,Y(s)$$

$$= (s^2 - 3s + 5)\,Y(s) - 2s + 10$$

Ex. 2 : *Obtain the Laplace transform of y(t), if* $\dfrac{d^3y}{dt^3} - \dfrac{d^2y}{dt^2} + 4\dfrac{dy}{dt} - 4y = t$, *given that*

$y(0) = y'(0) = y''(0) = 1.$

Sol. : Taking Laplace transforms of both sides, we get

$$L\left[\dfrac{d^3y}{dt^3}\right] - L\left[\dfrac{d^2y}{dt^2}\right] + 4\,L\left[\dfrac{dy}{dt}\right] - 4\,L\,[y(t)] = L\,[t]$$

$\therefore \quad \{s^3\,Y(s) - s^2\,y(0) - s\,y'(0) - y''(0)\} - \{s^2\,Y(s) - s\,y(0) - y'(0)\}$

$$+ 4\,\{s\,Y(s) - y(0)\} - 4\,Y(s) = \dfrac{1}{s^2}$$

$\therefore \quad (s^3 - s^2 + 4s - 4)\,Y(s) + (-s^2 - s - 1) - (-s - 1) - 4 = \dfrac{1}{s^2}$

$\left\{\because\ y(0) = y'(0) = y''(0) = 1\right\}$

$\therefore \qquad (s^2 + 4)\,(s - 1)\,Y(s) = s^2 + 4 + \dfrac{1}{s^2}$

$\therefore \qquad\qquad Y(s) = \dfrac{1}{(s - 1)} + \dfrac{1}{s^2\,(s - 1)\,(s^2 + 4)}$

(E) LAPLACE TRANSFORM OF INTEGRALS

Theorem : If $L\,[f(t)] = F(s)$, then

$$L\left[\int_0^t f(u)\,du\right] = \dfrac{1}{s}\,F(s)$$

Proof : Let $\qquad\qquad g(t) = \int_0^t f(u)\,du$, then $g'(t) = f(t)$ and $g(0) = 0$

$$\left[\text{Since,}\ \dfrac{d}{dt}\,g(t) = \dfrac{d}{dt}\int_0^t f(u)\,du = f(t)\ \text{and}\ g(0) = \int_0^0 f(u)\,du = 0\right]$$

Taking the Laplace transform of both sides, we have

$$L\,[g'(t)] = L\,[f(t)]$$

$\therefore \qquad\qquad s\,L\,[g(t)] - g(0) = F(s) \qquad\qquad$ [By the result (12)]

$\therefore \qquad\qquad s\, L\,[g(t)] \;=\; F(s) \qquad\qquad\qquad [\because g(0) = 0]$

$\therefore \qquad\qquad L\,[g(t)] \;=\; \dfrac{1}{s}\, F(s)$

or $\qquad\qquad L\left[\displaystyle\int_{0}^{t} f(u)\,du\right] \;=\; \dfrac{1}{s}\, F(s)$

Hence $\qquad \boxed{L\left[\displaystyle\int_{0}^{t} f(u)\,du\right] \;=\; L\left[\displaystyle\int_{0}^{t} f(t)\,dt\right] = \dfrac{1}{s}\, L\,[f(t)] = \dfrac{1}{s}\, F(s)} \qquad$ ... (16)

By using result (16), we can obtain

$$L\left[\int_{0}^{t}\int_{0}^{t} f(t)\,dt\,dt\right] \;=\; L\left[\int_{0}^{t} \phi(t)\,dt\right], \qquad\qquad \text{where } \phi(t) = \int_{0}^{t} f(t)\,dt$$

$$=\; \frac{1}{s}\, L\,[\phi(t)] \;=\; \frac{1}{s}\, L\left[\int_{0}^{t} f(u)\,du\right]$$

$$=\; \frac{1}{s}\left\{\frac{1}{s} F(s)\right\} \;=\; \frac{1}{s^2}\, F(s)$$

Thus $\qquad \boxed{L\left[\displaystyle\int_{0}^{t}\int_{0}^{t} f(t)\,dt\,dt\right] \;=\; \dfrac{1}{s^2}\, F(s)} \qquad$ ... (17)

Remark 1 : Laplace transform of integral of f(t) over (0, t) corresponds to division of transform F(s) by s.

Remark 2 : In general, $\quad L\left[\displaystyle\int_{0}^{t}\int_{0}^{t}\ldots\int_{0}^{t} f(t)\,dt^n\right] = \dfrac{1}{s^n}\, F(s)$

ILLUSTRATIONS

Ex. 1 : *Obtain Laplace transform of* $\dfrac{d^2y}{dt^2} + 3\dfrac{dy}{dt} + 4y + 2\displaystyle\int_{0}^{t} y(t)\,dt.$

Sol. : $L\left[\dfrac{d^2y}{dt^2} + 3\dfrac{dy}{dt} + 4y + 2\displaystyle\int_{0}^{t} y(t)\,dt\right]$

$\qquad\qquad =\; L\left[\dfrac{d^2y}{dt^2}\right] + 3\,L\left[\dfrac{dy}{dt}\right] + 4\,L\,[y(t)] + 2\,L\left[\displaystyle\int_{0}^{t} y(t)\,dt\right]$

$$= \{s^2\, Y(s) - s\, y(0) - y'(0)\} + 3\, \{s\, Y(s) - y(0)\} + 4\, Y(s) + 2\,\frac{1}{s}\, Y(s)$$

$$= \left(s^2 + 3s + 4 + \frac{2}{s}\right)\, Y(s) - (s + 3)\, y(0) - y'(0)$$

Ex. 2 : Verify $\displaystyle L\left[\int_0^t u^2\, e^{-u}\, du\right] = \frac{1}{s}\, L\, [t^2\, e^{-t}]$

Sol. : L.H.S. $= \displaystyle L\left[\int_0^t u^2\, e^{-u}\, du\right] = L\left[\left\{u^2(-e^{-u}) - (2u)(e^{-u}) + (2)(-e^{-u})\right\}_0^t\right]$

$$= L\left[\left\{-(u^2 + 2u + 2)\, e^{-u}\right\}_0^t\right] = L\,[2 - (t^2 + 2t + 2)\, e^{-u}]$$

$$= 2\, L\,[1] - L\,[(t^2 + 2t + 2)\, e^{-u}] = \frac{2}{s} - \left\{\frac{2}{s^3} + \frac{2}{s^2} + \frac{2}{s}\right\}_{s \to s+1}$$

[By the First Shifting Theorem]

$$= \frac{2}{s} - 2\left\{\frac{1}{(s+1)^3} + \frac{1}{(s+1)^2} + \frac{1}{s+1}\right\} = \frac{2}{s\,(s+1)^3} \qquad \ldots \text{(i)}$$

$$\text{R.H.S.} = \frac{1}{s}\, L\,[t^2\, e^{-t}] = \frac{1}{s}\, L\,[e^{-t}\,(t^2)] = \frac{1}{s}\left\{\frac{2}{s^3}\right\}_{s \to s+1} = \frac{2}{s\,(s+1)^3} \quad \ldots \text{(ii)}$$

From (i) and (ii), L.H.S. = R.H.S. and hence the result is verified.

(F) MULTIPLICATION BY POWERS OF t

Theorem : If $L\,[f(t)] = F(s)$, then

$$L\,[t^n\, f(t)] = (-1)^n\, \frac{d^n}{ds^n}\, F(s)$$

Proof : By definition, we have

$$F(s) = \int_0^\infty e^{-st}\, f(t)\, dt$$

Differentiating both sides w.r.t. s, we get

$$\frac{d}{ds}\, F(s) = \frac{d}{ds}\, \int_0^\infty e^{-st}\, f(t)\, dt = \int_0^\infty \frac{\partial}{\partial s}\, e^{-st}\, f(t)\, dt \qquad \ldots \text{(by DUIS rule)}$$

$$= \int_0^\infty -t\, e^{-st}\, f(t)\, dt = -\int_0^\infty e^{-st}\, \{t\, f(t)\}\, dt$$

$$= -L\,[t\, f(t)] \qquad\qquad \text{(By definition)}$$

Hence

$$\boxed{L\,[t\,f(t)] \;=\; -\frac{d}{ds}\,F(s)} \qquad \ldots (18)$$

By using result (18), we can obtain

$$L\,[t^2\,f(t)] \;=\; L\,[t\cdot t\,f(t)] \;=\; -\frac{d}{ds}\,L\,[t\,f(t)]$$

$$=\; -\frac{d}{ds}\left\{-\frac{d}{ds}\,F(s)\right\} \;=\; (-1)^2\,\frac{d^2}{ds^2}\,F(s)$$

Thus

$$\boxed{L\,[t^2\,f(t)] \;=\; (-1)^2\,\frac{d^2}{ds^2}\,F(s)} \qquad \ldots (19)$$

etc. By using mathematical induction, we can obtain the following generalised result :

$$\boxed{L\,[t^n\,f(t)] \;=\; (-1)^n\,\frac{d^n}{ds^n}\,F(s)} \qquad \ldots (20)$$

Note : The result (18) can be interpreted as the differentiation of the transform of a function $f(t)$ corresponds to the multiplication of the function $f(t)$ by $-t$.

ILLUSTRATIONS

Ex. 1 : *Obtain the Laplace transform of each of the following functions :*

(i) $\dfrac{t\,\sin at}{2a}$ *(ii)* $\dfrac{1}{2a^3}\,(\sin at - at\,\cos at)$ *(iii)* $\dfrac{1}{2a}\,(\sin at + at\,\cos at)$

Sol. : (i) We have

$$L\left[\frac{\sin at}{2a}\right] \;=\; \frac{1}{2a}\,L\,[\sin at] \;=\; \frac{1}{2}\,\frac{1}{s^2 + a^2}$$

$$\therefore \qquad L\left[t\,\frac{\sin at}{2a}\right] \;=\; (-1)\,\frac{d}{ds}\left\{\frac{1}{2}\left(\frac{1}{s^2 + a^2}\right)\right\} \qquad \text{[By result (18)]}$$

$$=\; (-1)\,\frac{1}{2}\,\frac{-2s}{(s^2 + a^2)^2} \;=\; \frac{s}{(s^2 + a^2)^2}$$

Another Method : We have

$$L\,[\cos at] \;=\; \int_0^\infty e^{-st}\,(\cos at)\,dt \;=\; \frac{s}{s^2 + a^2}$$

Differentiating with respect to the parameter a [using DUIS rule], we get

$$\frac{d}{da}\int_0^\infty e^{-st}\cos at\,dt \;=\; \int_0^\infty \frac{\partial}{\partial a}\,e^{-st}\cos at\,dt \;=\; \frac{d}{da}\,\frac{s}{s^2 + a^2}$$

$$\therefore \qquad \int_0^\infty e^{-st}\,(-t\,\sin at)\,dt \;=\; -\frac{2as}{(s^2 + a^2)^2}$$

$$\therefore \qquad - L\,[t\,\sin at] \;=\; -\,\frac{2as}{(s^2 + a^2)^2} \qquad\qquad \ldots \text{(by def.)}$$

Hence, $\qquad L\left[\dfrac{t\,\sin at}{2a}\right] \;=\; \dfrac{s}{(s^2 + a^2)^2}$

(ii) $\;L\left[\dfrac{1}{2a^3}\,(\sin at - at\,\cos at)\right]$

$$= \frac{1}{2a^3}\,\{L\,[\sin at] - a\,L\,[t\,\cos at]\}$$

$$= \frac{1}{2a^3}\left[\frac{a}{(s^2 + a^2)} - a\,(-1)\,\frac{d}{ds}\,\frac{s}{s^2 + a^2}\right] \qquad \text{[By result (18)]}$$

$$= \frac{1}{2a^3}\left[\frac{a}{s^2 + a^2} + a\left\{\frac{(s^2 + a^2)\,(1) - s\,(2s)}{(s^2 + a^2)^2}\right\}\right]$$

$$= \frac{1}{2a^3}\left[\frac{a}{s^2 + a^2} + a\left\{\frac{a^2 - s^2}{(s^2 + a^2)^2}\right\}\right]$$

$$= \frac{1}{2a^3}\left[\frac{a\,(s^2 + a^2) + a\,(a^2 - s^2)}{(s^2 + a^2)^2}\right] = \frac{1}{(s^2 + a^2)^2}$$

(iii) $\;L\left[\dfrac{1}{2a}\,(\sin at + at\,\cos at)\right]$

$$= \frac{1}{2a}\,\{L\,[\sin at] + a\,L\,[t\,\cos at]\}$$

$$= \frac{1}{2a}\left[\frac{a}{s^2 + a^2} + a\,(-1)\,\frac{d}{ds}\,\frac{s}{s^2 + a^2}\right] \qquad \text{[By result (18)]}$$

$$= \frac{1}{2a}\left[\frac{a}{s^2 + a^2} - a\left\{\frac{a^2 - s^2}{(s^2 + a^2)^2}\right\}\right]$$

$$= \frac{1}{2a}\left[\frac{a\,(s^2 + a^2) - a\,(a^2 - s^2)}{(s^2 + a^2)^2}\right] = \frac{s^2}{(s^2 + a^2)^2}$$

Ex. 2 : *Find the Laplace transform of each of the following functions :*

(i) $t^2 \sin 4t$, (ii) $t^2 \cos at$, (iii) $t^3 e^{2t}$.

Sol. : (i) We have

$$L\,[\sin 4t] \;=\; \frac{4}{s^2 + 16}$$

$$\therefore \qquad L\,[t^2 \sin 4t] \;=\; (-1)^2\,\frac{d^2}{ds^2}\left(\frac{4}{s^2 + 16}\right) \qquad \text{[By result (19)]}$$

$$= 4\,\frac{d}{ds}\left[-\,\frac{2s}{(s^2 + 16)^2}\right] = -\,8\,\frac{d}{ds}\left[\frac{s}{(s^2 + 16)^2}\right]$$

$$= -8\left[\frac{(s^2+16)^2\,(1) - 2\,(s^2+16)\,(2s)\cdot s}{(s^2+16)^4}\right] = -8\left[\frac{s^2+16-4s^2}{(s^2+16)^3}\right]$$

$$= \frac{24s^2-128}{(s^2+16)^3}$$

(ii) We have $\quad L\,[\cos at] \;=\; \dfrac{s}{s^2+a^2}$

$\therefore\qquad\qquad L\,[t^2\cos at] \;=\; (-1)^2\,\dfrac{d^2}{ds^2}\left(\dfrac{s}{s^2+a^2}\right)$ $\qquad\qquad\qquad$ [By result (19)]

$$= \frac{d}{ds}\left[\frac{(s^2+a^2)\,(1) - s\,(2s)}{(s^2+a^2)^2}\right] = \frac{d}{ds}\left[\frac{a^2-s^2}{(s^2+a^2)^2}\right]$$

$$= \left[\frac{(s^2+a^2)^2\,(-2s) - (a^2-s^2)\cdot 2\,(s^2+a^2)\,(2s)}{(s^2+a^2)^4}\right]$$

$$= \left[\frac{-2s^3-2a^2s-4a^2\,s+4s^3}{(s^2+a^2)^3}\right] = \frac{2s\,(s^2-3a^2)}{(s^2+a^2)^3}$$

(iii) $\qquad\qquad L\,[e^{2t}] \;=\; \dfrac{1}{s-2}$

$\therefore\qquad\quad L\,[t^3\,e^{2t}] \;=\; (-1)^3\,\dfrac{d^3}{ds^3}\left(\dfrac{1}{s-2}\right) = -\,\dfrac{d^2}{ds^2}\left[-\dfrac{1}{(s-2)^2}\right]$ [By result (20)]

$$= \frac{d}{ds}\left[-\frac{2}{(s-2)^3}\right] = \frac{6}{(s-2)^4}$$

(G) DIVISION BY t :

Theorem : If $\quad L\,[f(t)] \;=\; F(s)$, then

$$L\left[\frac{f(t)}{t}\right] \;=\; \int_s^\infty F(s)\,ds, \;\text{ provided } \lim_{t\to 0+}\frac{f(t)}{t} \text{ exists.}$$

Proof : By definition,

$$F(s) \;=\; \int_0^\infty e^{-st}\,f(t)\,dt$$

Integrating both sides w.r.t. s from s to ∞, we get

$$\int_s^\infty F(s)\,ds \;=\; \int_s^\infty\left[\int_0^\infty e^{-st}\,f(t)\,dt\right]ds$$

$$= \int_0^\infty f(t)\left[\int_s^\infty e^{-st}\,ds\right]dt, \;\;\text{(changing the order of integration)}$$

$$= \int_0^\infty f(t) \left[\frac{e^{-st}}{-t}\right]_s^\infty dt = \int_0^\infty f(t) \left[0 + \frac{e^{-st}}{t}\right] dt$$

$$= \int_0^\infty e^{-st} \frac{f(t)}{t} dt = L\left[\frac{f(t)}{t}\right]$$

Hence
$$\boxed{L\left[\frac{f(t)}{t}\right] = \int_s^\infty F(s)\, ds} \qquad\qquad \text{... (21)}$$

By using result (21), we can obtain

$$L\left[\frac{f(t)}{t^2}\right] = L\left[\frac{1}{t}\cdot\frac{f(t)}{t}\right] = \int_s^\infty L\left[\frac{f(t)}{t}\right] ds = \int_s^\infty \int_s^\infty F(s)\, ds\, ds$$

Thus
$$\boxed{L\left[\frac{f(t)}{t^2}\right] = \int_s^\infty \int_s^\infty F(s)\, ds\, ds} \qquad\qquad \text{... (22)}$$

Repeating the above procedure, we can obtain the following generalised result :

$$\boxed{L\left[\frac{f(t)}{t^n}\right] = \underbrace{\int_s^\infty \int_s^\infty \cdots\cdots\cdots \int_s^\infty}_{\leftarrow\ n\ \textbf{integrals}\ \rightarrow} F(s)\, ds\cdot ds\ \underbrace{\cdots\cdots ds}_{\leftarrow\ n\ \textbf{times}\ \rightarrow}} \qquad \text{... (23)}$$

Note : The result (21) can be interpreted as the integration of the transform of a function f(t) corresponds to the division of the function f(t) by t.

ILLUSTRATIONS

Ex. 1 : *Find the Laplace transform of* $\dfrac{\sin at}{t}$ *and hence show that* $\displaystyle\int_0^\infty \dfrac{\sin t}{t}\, dt = \dfrac{\pi}{2}$.

Sol. : We have $\quad L[\sin at] = \dfrac{a}{s^2 + a^2}$

$$\therefore \qquad L\left[\frac{\sin at}{t}\right] = \int_s^\infty \frac{a}{s^2 + a^2}\, ds = \left[\tan^{-1}\frac{s}{a}\right]_s^\infty \qquad\qquad \text{[By result (21)]}$$

$$= \frac{\pi}{2} - \tan^{-1}\frac{s}{a} = \cot^{-1}\frac{s}{a}$$

When a = 1, we have

$$L\left[\frac{\sin t}{t}\right] = \cot^{-1} s$$

or $\qquad \displaystyle\int_0^\infty e^{-st}\,\frac{\sin t}{t}\,dt \;=\; \cot^{-1} s$ $\qquad\qquad\qquad\qquad$ (By definition)

On putting $s = 0$, we obtain

$$\int_0^\infty \frac{\sin t}{t}\,dt \;=\; \cot^{-1}(0) \;=\; \frac{\pi}{2}\,.$$

Ex. 2 : *Obtain the Laplace transforms of the following functions :*

(i) $\dfrac{e^{-at} - e^{-bt}}{t}$, (ii) $\dfrac{\cos at - \cos bt}{t}$.

Sol. : (i) We have

$$L\,[e^{-at} - e^{-bt}] \;=\; \frac{1}{s+a} - \frac{1}{s+b}$$

$\therefore\quad L\!\left[\dfrac{e^{-at} - e^{-bt}}{t}\right] \;=\; \displaystyle\int_s^\infty \left(\frac{1}{s+a} - \frac{1}{s+b}\right)\,ds$ $\qquad\qquad$ [By result (21)]

$$= \big[\log(s+a) - \log(s+b)\big]_s^\infty = \left[\log\frac{s+a}{s+b}\right]_s^\infty = \left[\log \frac{1+\dfrac{a}{s}}{1+\dfrac{b}{s}}\right]_s^\infty$$

$$= \log 1 - \log \frac{1+\dfrac{a}{s}}{1+\dfrac{b}{s}} = 0 - \log \frac{s+a}{s+b} = \log \frac{s+b}{s+a}$$

$$\left[\text{Notice that } L\!\left[\frac{e^{-at}}{t}\right] \text{ or } L\!\left[\frac{e^{-bt}}{t}\right] \text{ does not exist since } \int_s^\infty \frac{1}{s+a}\,ds \text{ or } \int_s^\infty \frac{1}{s+b}\,ds \text{ does not exist.}\right]$$

(ii) We have

$$L\,[\cos at - \cos bt] \;=\; \frac{s}{s^2+a^2} - \frac{s}{s^2+b^2}$$

$\therefore\quad L\!\left[\dfrac{\cos at - \cos bt}{t}\right] \;=\; \displaystyle\int_s^\infty \left(\frac{s}{s^2+a^2} - \frac{s}{s^2+b^2}\right)\,ds$

$$= \left[\frac{1}{2}\log(s^2+a^2) - \frac{1}{2}\log(s^2+b^2)\right]_s^\infty$$

$$= \frac{1}{2} \left[\log \frac{s^2 + a^2}{s^2 + b^2} \right]_s^{\infty} = \frac{1}{2} \left[\log \frac{1 + \dfrac{a^2}{s^2}}{1 + \dfrac{b^2}{s^2}} \right]_s^{\infty}$$

$$= \frac{1}{2} \left[\log 1 - \log \frac{s^2 + a^2}{s^2 + b^2} \right] = \frac{1}{2} \log \frac{s^2 + b^2}{s^2 + a^2}$$

(H) THE CONVOLUTION THEOREM

Definition : The convolution of functions f(t) and g(t) is denoted by f(t) $*$ g(t) and

defined by $\qquad$ $f(t) * g(t) = \int_0^t f(u)\, g(t-u)\, du$ $\qquad\qquad$ ... (24)

Note : $\qquad$ $f(t) * g(t) = \int_0^t f(u)\, g(t-u)\, du$ $\qquad$ Put $t - u = v$ $\quad$ or $\quad$ $u = t - v$

$$\therefore \quad du = -dv \quad \text{and} \quad \begin{array}{|c|c|c|} \hline u & 0 & t \\ \hline v & t & 0 \\ \hline \end{array}$$

$$= \int_0^t f(t-v)\, g(v)\, dv = \int_0^t g(v)\, f(t-v)\, dv$$

$$= g(t) * f(t)$$

This shows that the convolution of f(t) and g(t) obeys the commutative law of algebra. Similarly, the following properties of the convolution can be proved easily :

(i) $\qquad$ $f(t) * [g(t) + h(t)] = f(t) * g(t) + f(t) * h(t)$ $\qquad\qquad$ (Distributive Law)

(ii) $\qquad$ $[f(t) * g(t)] * h(t) = f(t) * [g(t) * h(t)]$ $\qquad\qquad$ (Associative Law)

Theorem : If $L\,[f(t)] = F(s)$ and $L\,[g(t)] = G(s)$, then

$$L\,[f(t) * g(t)] = L \left[\int_0^t f(u)\, g(t-u)\, du \right] = F(s)\, G(s)$$

Proof : $\qquad$ $L\,[f(t) * g(t)] = L \left[\int_0^t f(u)\, g(t-u)\, du \right]$

$$= \int_{t=0}^{t=\infty} e^{-st} \left[\int_{u=0}^{u=t} f(u)\, g(t-u)\, du \right] dt$$

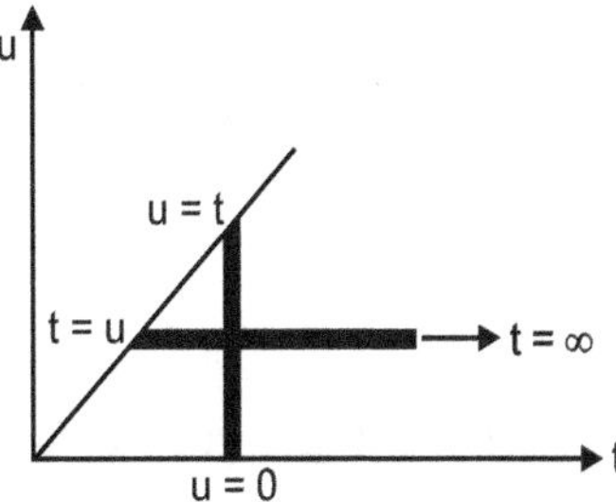

Fig. 4.3 : Region of Integration In The tu-Plane

Changing the order of integration, we get

$$= \int_{u=0}^{u=\infty} \left[\int_{t=u}^{t=\infty} e^{-st} f(u)\, g(t-u)\, dt \right] du = \int_{u=0}^{u=\infty} f(u) \left[\int_{t=u}^{t=\infty} e^{-st} g(t-u)\, dt \right] du$$

$$= \int_{u=0}^{u=\infty} f(u) \left[\int_{v=0}^{v=\infty} e^{-s(u+v)} g(v)\, dv \right] du \qquad \begin{cases} \text{On putting} \\ t-u=v \;\; \therefore\; dt = dv \\ \text{and } \begin{array}{|c|c|c|} \hline t & u & \infty \\ \hline v & 0 & \infty \\ \hline \end{array} \end{cases}$$

$$= \int_{0}^{\infty} e^{-su} f(u)\, du \int_{0}^{\infty} e^{-sv} g(v)\, dv$$

$$= \int_{0}^{\infty} e^{-st} f(t)\, dt \int_{0}^{\infty} e^{-st} g(t)\, dt = F(s)\, G(s)$$

Hence

$$\boxed{\; L\,[f(t) * g(t)] = L\left[\int_{0}^{t} f(u)\, g(t-u)\, du \right] = F(s)\, G(s) \;} \qquad \dots (25\ a)$$

Note 1 : In words, this theorem states that Laplace transform of convolution of two functions is equal to product of their Laplace transforms.

Note 2 : Since convolution of f(t) and g(t) is commutative, we have from result (25 a)

$$\boxed{\; L\left[\int_{0}^{t} f(t-u)\, g(u)\, du \right] = F(s)\, G(s) \;} \qquad \dots (25\ b)$$

Note 3 : The convolution theorem is useful to find inverse transformation.

ILLUSTRATIONS

Ex. 1 : *Verify the convolution theorem for the pair of functions f(t) = t, g(t) = e^{at}.*

Sol. : Here $\qquad\qquad$ f(t) = t $\qquad\qquad \therefore \quad F(s) = \dfrac{1}{s^2}$ $\qquad\qquad$ **(SUK Dec. 13)**

$$\text{and} \qquad g(t) = e^{at} \qquad \therefore \quad G(s) = \frac{1}{s-a}$$

$$\therefore \qquad F(s)\,G(s) = \frac{1}{s^2(s-a)} \qquad \qquad \ldots (i)$$

$$\text{Now} \qquad L[f(t)*g(t)] = L\left[\int_0^t f(u)\,g(t-u)\,du\right] = L\left[\int_0^t u\,e^{a(t-u)}\,du\right]$$

$$= L\left[e^{at}\int_0^t ue^{-au}\,du\right] = L\left[e^{at}\left\{u\left(\frac{e^{-au}}{-a}\right) - (1)\left(\frac{e^{-au}}{a^2}\right)\right\}_0^t\right]$$

$$= L\left[e^{at}\left\{\left(-\frac{te^{-at}}{a} - \frac{e^{-at}}{a^2}\right) - \left(0 - \frac{1}{a^2}\right)\right\}\right] = \frac{1}{a^2}\,L\,[e^{at} - at - 1]$$

$$= \frac{1}{a^2}\left[\frac{1}{s-a} - \frac{a}{s^2} - \frac{1}{s}\right] = \frac{1}{a^2}\left[\frac{s^2 - a(s-a) - s(s-a)}{s^2(s-a)}\right]$$

$$= \frac{1}{s^2(s-a)} \qquad \qquad \ldots (ii)$$

Since results (i) and (ii) are the same, convolution theorem is verified.

Ex. 2 : *Show that 1 * 1 = t, hence prove that*

$$1 * 1 * 1 \ldots\ldots * 1 = \frac{t^{n-1}}{(n-1)!}$$

$$\leftarrow n\text{-}ones \rightarrow$$

Sol. :

$$1 * 1 = \int_0^t 1 \cdot 1\, dt = t$$

$$(1 * 1) * 1 = t * 1$$

$$= \int_0^t u \cdot 1\, dt = \frac{t^2}{2}$$

$$(1 * 1 * 1) * 1 = \frac{t^2}{2} * 1$$

$$= \int_0^t \frac{u^2}{2} \cdot 1\, dt = \frac{t^3}{3!}$$

$$\therefore \qquad 1 * 1 * 1 \ldots\ldots * 1 = \frac{t^{n-1}}{(n-1)!}$$

Table 4.2 : Table of Laplace Transform Theorems

	If $L[f(t)] = F(s)$, then
(A)	$L[e^{-at} f(t)] = F(s + a)$
(B)	$L\left[F(t) = \begin{cases} f(t-a) & t > a \\ 0 & t < a \end{cases}\right] = e^{-as} F(s)$
(C)	$L[f(at)] = \dfrac{1}{a} F\left(\dfrac{s}{a}\right)$
(D)	$L[f'(t)] = s\,F(s) - f(0)$
(E)	$L\left[\displaystyle\int_0^t f(u)\,du\right] = \dfrac{1}{s}\,F(s)$
(F)	$L[t\,f(t)] = (-1)\,\dfrac{d}{ds}\,F(s)$
(G)	$L\left[\dfrac{f(t)}{t}\right] = \displaystyle\int_s^\infty F(s)\,ds$
(H)	$L\left[\displaystyle\int_0^t f(u)\,g(t-u)\,du\right] = F(s)\,G(s)$
(I)	$\displaystyle\lim_{t \to 0} f(t) = \lim_{s \to \infty} s\,F(s)$
(J)	$\displaystyle\lim_{t \to \infty} f(t) = \lim_{s \to 0} s\,F(s)$

ILLUSTRATIONS ON LAPLACE TRANSFORM THEOREMS

Ex. 1 : *Find the Laplace transform of each of the following functions :*

(i)　$e^{-3t}\, t^{-1/2}$　(ii)　$e^{-2t}\,(4\cos 3t - 2\sinh t)$　(iii)　$e^{-at}\,\dfrac{t^{n-1}}{(n-1)\,!}$

Sol. : (i) We have 　　$L[t^{-1/2}] = \dfrac{\overline{|1/2}}{s^{1/2}} = \sqrt{\dfrac{\pi}{s}}$ 　　　　(From Table 4.1)

$\therefore$ 　　　　$L[e^{-3t}\, t^{-1/2}] = \left\{\sqrt{\dfrac{\pi}{s}}\right\}_{s \to s+3} \sqrt{\dfrac{\pi}{s+3}}$

(By the First Shifting Theorem)

(ii)　We have

$L[4\cos 3t - 2\sinh t] = 4L[\cos 3t] - 2L[\sinh t]$

$$= \dfrac{4s}{s^2 - 3^2} - \dfrac{2}{s^2 - 1}$$ 　　　　(From Table 4.1)

$$\therefore\ L\left[e^{-2t}\left(4\cosh 3t - 2\sinh t\right)\right] = \left\{\frac{4s}{s^2-3^2} - \frac{2}{s^2-1}\right\}_{s\to s+2}$$

(By the First Shifting Theorem)

$$= \frac{4(s+2)}{(s+2)^2-9} - \frac{2}{(s+2)^2-1}$$

$$= \frac{4(s+2)}{s^2+4s-5} - \frac{2}{s^2+4s+3}$$

(iii) We have
$$L\left[\frac{t^{n-1}}{(n-1)!}\right] = \frac{1}{(n-1)!}\,L\left[t^{n-1}\right] = \frac{1}{(n-1)!}\,\frac{\lfloor n}{s^n}\quad\text{(From Table 4.1)}$$

$$= \frac{1}{(n-1)!}\,\frac{(n-1)!}{s^n} = \frac{1}{s^n}$$

$$\therefore\qquad L\left[e^{-at}\,\frac{t^{n-1}}{(n-1)!}\right] = \left\{\frac{1}{s^n}\right\}_{s\to s+a} = \frac{1}{(s+a)^n}$$

(By the First Shifting Theorem)

Ex. 2 : *Find L [F(t)] if F(t)* $= \begin{cases}(t-1)^2\ , & t>1\\[4pt] 0\ , & 0<t<1\end{cases}$.

Sol. : Here $\qquad\qquad f(t-a) = (t-1)^2 \qquad\qquad\qquad\qquad$ where $a = 1$

$\therefore\qquad\qquad\qquad\qquad f(t) = t^2\quad$ and $\quad F(s) = \dfrac{2}{s^3}$

Hence by the second shifting theorem [result (10)], with $a = 1$, we have

$$L[F(t)] = e^{-as}\,F(s) = e^{-s}\left(\frac{2}{s^3}\right)$$

Ex. 3 : *If L [f(t)]* $= \dfrac{1}{s}\,e^{-1/s}$, *find L [e^{-t} f(3t)].*

Sol. : We have given that

$$L[f(t)] = \frac{1}{s}\,e^{-1/s}$$

By change of scale theorem [result (11)], with $a = 3$, we have

$$L[f(3t)] = \frac{1}{3}\left(\frac{1}{s/3}\,e^{-3/s}\right) = \frac{1}{s}\,e^{-3/s}$$

Hence, by the first shifting theorem, we get

$$L[e^{-t}f(3t)] = \left\{\frac{1}{s}\,e^{-3/s}\right\}_{s\to s+1} = \frac{e^{-3/(s+1)}}{(s+1)}$$

Ex. 4 : Given $\quad L\left[2\sqrt{\dfrac{t}{\pi}}\right] = \dfrac{1}{s^{3/2}}$, show that $\quad L\left[\dfrac{1}{\sqrt{\pi t}}\right] = \dfrac{1}{\sqrt{s}}$

Sol. : Let $\qquad\qquad\qquad f(t) = 2\sqrt{\dfrac{t}{\pi}}\ \Rightarrow\ f(0) = 0$

$$\therefore \qquad f'(t) = \frac{2}{\sqrt{\pi}} \cdot \frac{1}{2}\, t^{-1/2} = \frac{1}{\sqrt{\pi t}}$$

$$\therefore \qquad L[f'(t)] = L\left[\frac{1}{\sqrt{\pi t}}\right] = s\,F(s) - f(0) \qquad \text{[By result (12)]}$$

$$= s\,\frac{1}{s^{3/2}} - 0 \qquad \left\{ \begin{array}{l} \because\ \text{Given } F(s) = \dfrac{1}{s^{3/2}} \\[2mm] \text{and } f(0) = 0 \end{array} \right.$$

$$= \frac{1}{\sqrt{s}}$$

Ex. 5 : *Given that* $4\,f''(t) + f(t) = 0$, $f(0) = 0$ *and* $f'(0) = 2$, *show that*
$L\,[f(t)] = \dfrac{8}{4s^2 + 1}$.

Sol. : Taking Laplace transforms of both sides, we get

$$4\,L[f''(t)] + L[f(t)] = L[0]$$

$$\therefore \quad 4\,\{s^2\,F(s) - s\,f(0) - f'(0)\} + F(s) = 0 \qquad \text{[By results (12) and (13)]}$$

$$\therefore \quad 4\,\{s^2\,F(s) - s(0) - (2)\} + F(s) = 0 \qquad \text{[as } f(0) = 0 \text{ and } f'(0) = 2]$$

$$\therefore \quad (4s^2 + 1)\,F(s) - 8 = 0$$

$$\therefore \qquad F(s) = L[f(t)] = \frac{8}{4s^2 + 1}$$

Ex. 6 : *Use theorem on Derivative, to derive the following Laplace transforms :*

$$(i)\ L[e^{at}] = \frac{1}{s-a} \quad (ii)\ L[\sin at] = \frac{a}{(s^2 + a^2)}$$

Sol. : (i) Let $f(t) = e^{at}$. Then $f'(t) = a\,e^{at}$, $f(0) = 1$

Now $\qquad\qquad L[f'(t)] = s\,L[e^{at}] - f(0) \qquad\qquad$ [By result (12)]

$\therefore \qquad\qquad L[ae^{at}] = s\,L[e^{at}] - 1$

or $\qquad\qquad a\,L[e^{at}] = s\,L[e^{at}] - 1$

or $\qquad\qquad L[e^{at}] = \dfrac{1}{s-a}$

(ii) Let $f(t) = \sin at$. Then $f'(t) = a \cos at$, $f''(t) = -a^2 \sin at$, $f(0) = 0$, $f'(0) = a$.

Now $\qquad\qquad L[f''(t)] = s^2\,L[f(t)] - s\,f(0) - f'(0) \qquad\qquad$ [By result (13)]

$\therefore \qquad\qquad L[-a^2 \sin at] = s^2\,L[\sin at] - s(0) - a$

or $\qquad\qquad -a^2\,L[\sin at] = s^2\,L[\sin at] - a$

or $\qquad\qquad L[\sin at] = \dfrac{a}{s^2 + a^2}$

Ex. 7 : Find $\quad L\left[\displaystyle\int_0^t \sin 2u\ du\right]$.

Sol. : We have $\quad L\,[\sin 2t]\ =\ \dfrac{2}{s^2+4}$

$$\therefore \qquad \int_0^t \sin 2u\ du\ =\ \frac{1}{s}\left(\frac{2}{s^2+4}\right) \qquad\qquad\qquad \text{[By result (16)]}$$

Ex. 8 : *Find the Laplace transforms of the following functions :*

(i) $t \cos at$ $\quad$ *(ii)* $\dfrac{t \sinh at}{2a}$ $\quad$ *(iii)* $t \sin^3 t$

Sol. : (i) We have

$$L\,[\cos at]\ =\ \frac{s}{s^2+a^2}$$

$$\therefore \qquad L\,[t \cos at]\ =\ (-1)\frac{d}{ds}\left(\frac{s}{s^2+a^2}\right)\ =\ -\left\{\frac{(s^2+a^2)\,(1)-s\,(2s)}{(s^2+a^2)^2}\right\}\quad \text{[By result (18)]}$$

$$=\ \frac{s^2-a^2}{(s^2+a^2)^2}$$

(ii) We have

$$L\left[\frac{\sinh at}{2a}\right]\ =\ \frac{1}{2a}\,L\,[\sinh at]\ =\ \frac{1}{2}\,\frac{1}{s^2-a^2}$$

$$\therefore \qquad L\left[\frac{t \sinh at}{2a}\right]\ =\ (-1)\frac{d}{ds}\left\{\frac{1}{2}\,\frac{1}{(s^2-a^2)}\right\}\ =\ (-1)\frac{1}{2}\,\frac{-2s}{(s^2-a^2)^2}\quad \text{[By result (18)]}$$

$$=\ \frac{s}{(s^2-a^2)^2}$$

(iii) We have $\ L\,[\sin^3 t]\ =\ L\left[\dfrac{3}{4}\sin t-\dfrac{1}{4}\sin 3t\right]\qquad \{\because\ \sin 3t=3\sin t-4\sin^3 t\}$

$$=\ \frac{3}{4}\,L\,[\sin t]-\frac{1}{4}\,L\,[\sin 3t]\ =\ \frac{3}{4}\left(\frac{1}{s^2+1}-\frac{1}{s^2+9}\right)$$

$$\therefore \qquad L\,[t \sin^3 t]\ =\ (-1)\frac{d}{ds}\left[\frac{3}{4}\left(\frac{1}{s^2+1}-\frac{1}{s^2+9}\right)\right]\ =\ -\frac{3}{4}\left[\frac{(-2s)}{(s^2+1)^2}-\frac{(-2s)}{(s^2+9)^2}\right]$$

$$\text{[By result (18)]}$$

$$=\ \frac{3s}{2}\left[\frac{1}{(s^2+1)^2}-\frac{1}{(s^2+9)^2}\right]$$

Ex. 9 : *Find the Laplace transforms of the following functions :*

(i) $\dfrac{1-\cos t}{t}$ $\quad$ *(ii)* $\dfrac{1-\cos t}{t^2}$ $\quad$ *(iii)* $\dfrac{\sin^2 t}{t^2}$

Sol. : (i) We have

$$L\,[1 - \cos t] \;=\; \frac{1}{s} - \frac{s}{s^2 + 1}$$

$$\therefore \qquad L\left[\frac{1 - \cos t}{t}\right] \;=\; \int_{s}^{\infty} \left(\frac{1}{s} - \frac{s}{s^2 + 1}\right) ds \qquad\qquad \text{[By result (21)]}$$

$$= \left[\log s - \frac{1}{2}\log (s^2 + 1)\right]_{s}^{\infty} \;=\; \frac{1}{2}\left[\log s^2 - \log (s^2 + 1)\right]_{s}^{\infty}$$

$$= \frac{1}{2}\left[\log \frac{s^2}{s^2 + 1}\right]_{s}^{\infty} \;=\; \frac{1}{2}\left[\log \frac{1}{1 + 1/s^2}\right]_{s}^{\infty}$$

$$= \frac{1}{2}\left[0 - \log \frac{s^2}{s^2 + 1}\right] \qquad\qquad (\because \;\; \log 1 = 0)$$

$$= \frac{1}{2}\log \frac{s^2 + 1}{s^2} \quad \text{or} \quad \log \frac{\sqrt{s^2 + 1}}{s}$$

$$\left[\text{Notice that } L\left[\frac{\cos t}{t}\right] \text{ does not exist since } \int_{s}^{\infty} \frac{s}{s^2 + a^2}\, ds \text{ does not exist.}\right]$$

(ii) $\quad L\left[\dfrac{1 - \cos t}{t^2}\right] \;=\; L\left[\dfrac{1}{t}\left(\dfrac{1 - \cos t}{t}\right)\right] \qquad\qquad$ [use result of (i) above]

$$= \int_{s}^{\infty} \frac{1}{2}\log \frac{s^2 + 1}{s^2}\, ds \;=\; \frac{1}{2}\int_{s}^{\infty}\left(\log \frac{s^2 + 1}{s^2}\right)\cdot 1\, ds$$

Integrating by parts, we have

$$= \frac{1}{2}\left[\left(\log \frac{s^2 + 1}{s^2}\right)\cdot s - \int \left\{\frac{s^2}{s^2 + 1}\,\frac{s^2\,(2s) - (s^2 + 1)\,(2s)}{s^4}\right\}\cdot s\, ds\right]_{0}^{\infty}$$

$$= \frac{1}{2}\left[s \log \frac{s^2 + 1}{s^2} - \int \left\{\frac{s^2}{s^2 + 1}\left(\frac{-2}{s^3}\right)\right\} s\, ds\right]_{s}^{\infty}$$

$$= \frac{1}{2}\left[s \log \frac{s^2 + 1}{s^2} + 2 \int \frac{1}{s^2 + 1}\, ds\right]_{s}^{\infty}$$

$$= \frac{1}{2}\left[s \log \frac{s^2 + 1}{s^2} + 2 \tan^{-1} s\right]_{s}^{\infty}$$

$$= \frac{1}{2}\left[\left\{0 + 2\left(\frac{\pi}{2}\right)\right\} - \left\{s \log \frac{s^2 + 1}{s^2} + 2 \tan^{-1} s\right\}\right]$$

$$\left\{ \because \lim_{s \to \infty} s \log \left(1 + \frac{1}{s^2}\right) = \lim_{s \to \infty} s \left(\frac{1}{s^2} - \frac{1}{2s^4} + \frac{1}{3s^6} \cdots \right) = 0 \right\}$$

$$= \frac{1}{2} \left[\pi - s \log \frac{s^2 + 1}{s^2} - 2 \tan^{-1} s \right]$$

$$= \frac{1}{2} s \log \frac{s^2}{s^2 + 1} + \cot^{-1} s \qquad \left(\because \frac{\pi}{2} - \tan^{-1} s = \cot^{-1} s \right)$$

(iii) We have $L\left[\sin^2 t\right] = L\left[\dfrac{1 - \cos 2t}{2}\right] = \dfrac{1}{2}\left(\dfrac{1}{s} - \dfrac{s}{s^2 + 4}\right)$

$$\therefore \qquad L\left[\frac{\sin^2 t}{t}\right] = \frac{1}{2} \int_s^\infty \left(\frac{1}{s} - \frac{s}{s^2 + 4}\right) ds = \frac{1}{4} \log \frac{s^2 + 4}{s^2}$$

$$\therefore \qquad L\left[\frac{\sin^2 t}{t^2}\right] = L\left[\frac{1}{t}\left(\frac{\sin^2 t}{t}\right)\right] = \frac{1}{4} \int_s^\infty \left(\log \frac{s^2 + 4}{s^2}\right) \cdot (1)\, ds$$

$$= \frac{1}{4} \left[\left(\log \frac{s^2 + 4}{s^2}\right)(s) - \int \left(\frac{s^2}{s^2 + 4}\right)\left(-\frac{8}{s^3}\right)(s)\, ds \right]_s^\infty$$

$$= \frac{1}{4} \left[s \log \left(1 + \frac{4}{s^2}\right) + 8 \int \frac{1}{s^2 + 4}\, ds \right]_s^\infty$$

$$= \frac{1}{4} \left[s \log \left(1 + \frac{4}{s^2}\right) + \frac{8}{2} \tan^{-1} \frac{s}{2} \right]_s^\infty$$

$$= \frac{1}{4} \left[\left(0 + 4\left(\frac{\pi}{2}\right)\right) - \left\{s \log \left(\frac{s^2 + 4}{s^2}\right) + 4 \tan^{-1} \frac{s}{2}\right\} \right]$$

$$= \frac{1}{4} \left[4\left(\frac{\pi}{2} - \tan^{-1}\frac{s}{2}\right) - s \log \left(\frac{s^2 + 4}{s^2}\right) \right]$$

$$= \frac{1}{4} s \log \frac{s^2}{s^2 + 4} + \cot^{-1} \frac{s}{2}$$

Ex. 10 : *Obtain the Laplace transform of each of the following functions :*

(i) $t\, e^{3t} \sin 2t$

(ii) $t\, e^{-2t} (2 \cosh 3t - 4 \sinh 2t)$ *(iii)* $\dfrac{d}{dt}\left(\dfrac{\sin t}{t}\right)$

(iv) $\displaystyle\int_0^t \frac{\sin t}{t}\, dt$ *(v)* $\displaystyle\int_0^t \frac{1 - e^{-x}}{x}\, dx$

$(vi)\ \displaystyle\int_0^t u\cosh u\ du$

Sol. : (i) We have

$$L\,[\sin 2t]\ =\ \frac{2}{s^2+4} \qquad\qquad \text{[From Table 4.1]}$$

$$\therefore\qquad L\,[t\sin 2t]\ =\ (-1)\,\frac{d}{ds}\left(\frac{2}{s^2+4}\right)=\frac{4s}{(s^2+4)^2} \qquad\qquad \text{[By result (18)]}$$

$$\therefore\qquad L\,[e^{3t}\,t\sin 2t]\ =\ \left\{\frac{4s}{(s^2+1)^2}\right\}_{s\,\to\,s-3} \qquad \text{[By First Shifting Theorem, result (9)]}$$

$$=\ \frac{4\,(s-3)}{[(s-3)^2+1]^2}\ =\ \frac{4\,(s-3)}{(s^2-6s+10)^2}$$

(ii) We have

$$L\,[2\cosh 3t-4\sinh 2t]\ =\ \frac{2s}{s^2-9}-\frac{8}{s^2-4}$$

$$\therefore\quad L\,[t\,(2\cosh 3t-4\sinh 2t)]\ =\ (-1)\,\frac{d}{ds}\left(\frac{2s}{s^2-9}-\frac{8}{s^2-4}\right) \qquad\qquad \text{[By result (18)]}$$

$$=\ -\left\{\frac{(s^2-9)\,(2)-(2s)\,(2s)}{(s^2-9)^2}+\frac{16s}{(s^2-4)^2}\right\}$$

$$=\ \left\{\frac{2\,(s^2+9)}{(s^2-9)^2}-\frac{16s}{(s^2-4)^2}\right\}$$

$$\therefore\quad L\,[e^{-2t}\,t\,(2\cosh 3t-4\sinh 2t)]\ =\ \left\{\frac{2\,(s^2+9)}{(s^2-9)^2}-\frac{16s}{(s^2-4)^2}\right\}_{s\,\to\,s+2}$$

$$=\ \left\{\frac{2\,(s+2)^2+18}{[(s+2)^2-9]^2}-\frac{16\,(s+2)}{[(s+2)^2-4]^2}\right\}$$

$$=\ \frac{2s^2+8s+26}{(s^2+4s-5)^2}-\frac{16\,(s+2)}{(s^2+4s)^2}$$

(iii) We have $\qquad L\,[\sin t]\ =\ \dfrac{1}{s^2+1}$

$$\therefore\qquad L\left[\frac{\sin t}{t}\right]\ =\ \int_s^{\infty}\frac{1}{s^2+1}\ ds\ =\ \left[\tan^{-1}s\right]_s^{\infty} \qquad\qquad \text{[By result (21)]}$$

$$=\ \frac{\pi}{2}-\tan^{-1}s\ =\ \cot^{-1}s$$

$$\therefore\qquad L\left[\frac{d}{dt}\left(\frac{\sin t}{t}\right)\right]\ =\ s\,L\left[\frac{\sin t}{t}\right]-\lim_{t\to 0}\frac{\sin t}{t} \qquad\qquad \text{[By result (12)]}$$

$$=\ s\cot^{-1}s-1$$

(iv) We have from result (iii) above

$$L\left[\frac{\sin t}{t}\right] = \cot^{-1} s$$

$$\therefore \quad L\left[\int_0^t \frac{\sin t}{t}\, dt\right] = \frac{1}{s}\cot^{-1} s \qquad \text{[By result (16)]}$$

(v) We have $L\,[1 - e^{-t}] = \dfrac{1}{s} - \dfrac{1}{s+1}$

$$\therefore \quad L\left[\frac{1 - e^{-t}}{t}\right] = \int_s^\infty \left(\frac{1}{s} - \frac{1}{s+1}\right) ds \qquad \text{[By result (21)]}$$

$$= \left[\log s - \log(s+1)\right]_s^\infty = \left[\log \frac{s}{s+1}\right]_s^\infty$$

$$= \left[\log \frac{1}{1 + 1/s} - \log \frac{s}{s+1}\right]_s^\infty = -\log \frac{s}{s+1} = \log \frac{s+1}{s}$$

$$\therefore \quad L\left[\int_0^t \frac{1 - e^{-x}}{x}\, dx\right] = L\left[\int_0^t \frac{1 - e^{t}}{t}\, dt\right] = \frac{1}{s}\log \frac{s+1}{s} \qquad \text{[By result (16)]}$$

(vi) We have $L\,[\cosh t] = \dfrac{s}{s^2 - 1}$

$$\therefore \quad L\,[t \cosh t] = (-1)\frac{d}{ds}\left(\frac{s}{s^2 - 1}\right) \qquad \text{[By result (18)]}$$

$$= (-1)\left\{\frac{(s^2 - 1)(1) - s(2s)}{(s^2 - 1)^2}\right\} = \frac{s^2 + 1}{(s^2 - 1)^2}$$

$$\therefore \quad L\left[\int_0^t u \cosh u\, du\right] = L\left[\int_0^t t \cosh t\, dt\right] = \frac{1}{s}\left\{\frac{s^2 + 1}{(s^2 - 1)^2}\right\} \qquad \text{[By result (16)]}$$

Ex. 11 : *Obtain Laplace transforms of*

$$(i)\ t\int_0^t e^{-4t}\sin 3t\, dt \quad (ii)\ e^{-4t}\int_0^t t\sin 3t\, dt \quad (iii)\int_0^t t\, e^{-4t}\sin 3t\, dt$$

$$(iv)\ \cosh t \int_0^t e^{t}\cosh t\, dt$$

Sol. : (i) We have $L [\sin 3t] = \dfrac{3}{s^2 + 9}$ [From Table (4.1)]

$\therefore \quad L [e^{-4t} \sin 3t] = \left\{ \dfrac{3}{s^2 + 9} \right\}_{s \to s + 4}$ [By result (9)]

$$= \dfrac{3}{(s + 4)^2 + 9} = \dfrac{3}{s^2 + 8s + 25}$$

$\therefore \quad L \left[\displaystyle\int_0^t e^{-4t} \sin 3t \right] = \dfrac{1}{s} \left(\dfrac{3}{s^2 + 8s + 25} \right)$ [By result (16)]

$\therefore \quad L \left[t \displaystyle\int_0^t e^{-4t} \sin 3t \right] = (-1) \dfrac{d}{ds} \left\{ \left(\dfrac{1}{s} \right) \left(\dfrac{3}{s^2 + 8s + 25} \right) \right\}$ [By result (18)]

$$= \dfrac{1}{s^2} \dfrac{3}{(s^2 + 8s + 25)} + \dfrac{1}{s} \dfrac{3 (2s + 8)}{(s^2 + 8s + 25)^2}$$

$$= \dfrac{3 (s^2 + 8s + 25) + 3s (2s + 8)}{s^2 (s^2 + 8s + 25)^2}$$

$$= \dfrac{3 (3s^2 + 16s + 25)}{s^2 (s^2 + 8s + 25)^2}$$

$$\left\{ \textbf{Note :} L \left[t \int_0^t e^{-4t} \sin 3t \, dt \right] = (-1) \dfrac{d}{ds} \left(\dfrac{1}{s} \{ L [\sin 3t] \}_{s \to s + 4} \right) \right\}$$

(ii) We have $\quad L [\sin 3t] = \dfrac{3}{s^2 + 9}$

$\therefore \quad L [t \sin 3t] = (-1) \dfrac{d}{ds} \left(\dfrac{3}{s^2 + 9} \right) = \dfrac{6s}{(s^2 + 9)^2}$ [Multiplication by t]

$\therefore \quad L \left[\displaystyle\int_0^t t \sin 3t \, dt \right] = \dfrac{1}{s} \dfrac{6s}{(s^2 + 9)^2} = \dfrac{6}{(s^2 + 9)^2}$ $\left[L \displaystyle\int_0^t f(t) \, dt \right]$

$\therefore \quad L \left[e^{-4t} \displaystyle\int_0^t t \sin 3t \, dt \right] = \left\{ \dfrac{6}{(s^2 + 9)^2} \right\}_{s \to s + 4}$ [First Shifting Theorem]

$$= \dfrac{6}{[(s + 4)^2 + 9]^2} = \dfrac{6}{(s^2 + 8s + 25)^2}$$

(iii) We have $\quad L [\sin 3t] = \dfrac{3}{s^2 + 9}$

$\therefore \quad L [t \sin 3t] = (-1) \dfrac{d}{ds} \left(\dfrac{3}{s^2 + 9} \right) = \dfrac{6s}{(s^2 + 9)^2}$ [Multiplication by t]

$$\therefore \qquad L\left[e^{-4t}\, t \sin 3t\right] = \left\{\frac{6s}{(s^2+9)^2}\right\}_{s \to s+4} \qquad \text{[First Shifting Theorem]}$$

$$= \frac{6\,(s+4)}{[(s+4)^2+9]^2} = \frac{6\,(s+4)}{(s^2+8s+25)^2}$$

$$\therefore \qquad L\left[\int_0^t e^{-4t}\, t \sin 3t\right] = \frac{1}{s}\,\frac{6\,(s+4)}{(s^2+8s+25)^2} \qquad\qquad \left[L\int_0^t f(t)\,dt\right]$$

(iv) Let

$$f(t) = \int_0^t e^t \cosh t\, dt$$

$$\therefore \qquad F(s) = L\left[\int_0^t e^t \cosh t\, dt\right] = \frac{1}{s}\, L\left[e^t \cosh t\right]$$

$$= \frac{1}{s}\,\{L\,[\cosh t]\}_{s \to s-1} = \frac{1}{s}\,\left\{\frac{s}{s^2-1}\right\}_{s \to s-1}$$

$$= \frac{1}{s}\,\frac{s-1}{[(s-1)^2-1]} = \frac{s-1}{s\,(s^2-2s)}$$

$$= \frac{s-1}{s^2\,(s-2)}$$

$$\text{Now } L\left[\cosh t \int_0^t e^t \cosh t\right] = L\left[\frac{e^t+e^{-t}}{2}\, f(t)\right] \qquad \left\{\because \ \cosh t = \frac{e^t+e^{-t}}{2}\right.$$

$$= \frac{1}{2}\,\{L\,[e^t f(t)] + L\,[e^{-t} f(t)]\}$$

$$= \frac{1}{2}\,[\{F(s)\}_{s \to s-1} + \{F(s)\}_{s \to s+1}]$$

$$= \frac{1}{2}\,\left\{\frac{(s-1)-1}{(s-1)^2\,[(s-1)-2]} + \frac{(s+1)-1}{(s+1)^2\,[(s+1)-2]}\right\}$$

$$= \frac{1}{2}\,\left\{\frac{s-2}{(s-1)^2\,(s-3)} + \frac{s}{(s+1)^2\,(s-1)}\right\}$$

Ex. 12 : *Obtain Laplace transforms of*

$$(i)\ \frac{e^{-4t}\sin 3t}{t} \quad (ii)\ \int_0^t \frac{e^{-4t}\sin 3t}{t}\,dt \quad (iii)\ e^{-4t}\int_0^t \frac{\sin 3t}{t}\,dt$$

Sol. : (i) We have $L\,[\sin 3t] = \dfrac{3}{s^2+9}$

$$\therefore \quad L\left[\frac{\sin 3t}{t}\right] = \int_s^\infty \frac{3}{s^2+9}\, ds = \left[\tan^{-1}\frac{s}{3}\right]_s^\infty \qquad \text{[By result (21)]}$$

$$= \frac{\pi}{2} - \tan^{-1}\frac{s}{3} = \cot^{-1}\frac{s}{3}$$

$$\therefore \quad L\left[e^{-4t}\frac{\sin 3t}{t}\right] = \left\{\cot^{-1}\frac{s}{3}\right\}_{s\to s+4} \qquad \text{[By result (9)]}$$

$$= \cot^{-1}\frac{s+4}{3}$$

(ii) We have from result (i) above,

$$L\left[e^{-4t}\frac{\sin 3t}{t}\right] = \cot^{-1}\frac{s+4}{3}$$

$$\therefore \quad L\left[\int_0^t e^{-4t}\frac{\sin 3t}{t}\, dt\right] = \frac{1}{s}\cot^{-1}\frac{s+4}{3} \qquad \text{[By result (16)]}$$

(iii) We have from result (i) above,

$$L\left[\frac{\sin 3t}{t}\right] = \cot^{-1}\frac{s}{3}$$

$$\therefore \quad L\left[\int_0^t \frac{\sin 3t}{t}\, dt\right] = \frac{1}{s}\cot^{-1}\frac{s}{3} \qquad \text{[By result (16)]}$$

$$\therefore \quad L\left[e^{-4t}\int_0^t \frac{\sin 3t}{t}\, dt\right] = \left\{\frac{1}{s}\cot^{-1}\frac{s}{3}\right\}_{s\to s+4} \qquad \text{[By result (9)]}$$

$$= \frac{1}{s+4}\cot^{-1}\frac{s+4}{3}$$

Ex. 13 : *Given $L\,[J_0(t)] = \dfrac{1}{\sqrt{s^2+1}}$, show that*

(i) $L\,[J_0(at)] = \dfrac{1}{\sqrt{s^2+a^2}}$ (ii) $L\,[e^{-at}J_0(at)] = \dfrac{1}{\sqrt{s^2+2as+2a^2}}$

(iii) $L\,[t\,J_0(at)] = \dfrac{s}{(s^2+a^2)^{3/2}}$

Sol. : (i) Given that

$$L\,[J_0(t)] = \frac{1}{\sqrt{s^2+1}}$$

$$\therefore \qquad L\,[J_0\,(at)] = \frac{1}{a}\,\frac{1}{\sqrt{(s/a)^2+1}} = \frac{1}{\sqrt{(s^2+a^2)}}$$

[By result (11) of Change of Scale Theorem]

(ii) From result (i) above, we have

$$L\,[J_0\,(at)] = \frac{1}{\sqrt{s^2+a^2}}$$

$$\therefore \qquad L\,[e^{-at}\,J_0\,(at)] = \left\{\frac{1}{\sqrt{s^2+a^2}}\right\}_{s\,\to\,s+a} \qquad \text{[By result (9) of First Shifting Theorem]}$$

$$= \frac{1}{\sqrt{(s+a)^2+a^2}} = \frac{1}{\sqrt{s^2+2as+2a^2}}$$

(iii) From result (i) above, we have

$$L\,[J_0\,(at)] = \frac{1}{\sqrt{s^2+a^2}}$$

$$\therefore \qquad L\,[t\,J_0\,(at)] = (-1)\,\frac{d}{ds}\,\frac{1}{\sqrt{s^2+a^2}} \qquad\qquad \text{[By result (18)]}$$

$$= (-1)\,\left(\frac{-1}{2}\right)\,(s^2+a^2)^{-3/2}\,(2s)$$

$$= \frac{s}{(s^2+a^2)^{3/2}}$$

MISCELLANEOUS EXAMPLES

EVALUATION OF INTEGRALS

Laplace transformation is often useful in evaluating various integrals. This is illustrated in the following examples :

Ex. 14 : *Evaluate each of the following integrals :*

(i) $\displaystyle\int_0^\infty t\,e^{-3t}\,\sin t\;dt$ 　　(ii) $\displaystyle\int_0^\infty t^2\,e^{-t}\,\sin t\;dt$ 　(iii) $\displaystyle\int_0^\infty t^3\,e^{-t}\,\sin t\;dt$

(iv) $\displaystyle\int_0^\infty \frac{e^{-at}-e^{-bt}}{t}\,dt$ 　　(v) $\displaystyle\int_0^\infty \frac{\cos 6t-\cos 4t}{t}\,dt$ 　(vi) $\displaystyle\int_0^\infty e^{-2t}\,\frac{\sinh t}{t}\,dt$

(vii) $\displaystyle\int_0^\infty e^{-t}\,\frac{\sin t}{t}\,dt$ 　(viii) $\displaystyle\int_0^\infty e^{-2t}\,\sin^3 t\;dt$

Sol. : (i) We first obtain Laplace transform of t sin t using properties or theorems already proved.

$$L\,[t\,\sin t] \;=\; (-1)\frac{d}{ds}\,L\,[\sin t] \qquad\qquad \text{[By result (18)]}$$

$$=\; (-1)\frac{d}{ds}\,\frac{1}{s^2+1} \;=\; (-1)\frac{(-1)}{(s^2+1)^2}\,(2s)$$

$$=\; \frac{2s}{(s^2+1)^2}$$

∴　By definition of Laplace transform, we have

$$\int_{0}^{\infty} e^{-st}\,t\,\sin t\,dt \;=\; \frac{2s}{(s^2+1)^2}$$

Putting s = 3, we get

$$\int_{0}^{\infty} e^{-3t}\,t\,\sin t\,dt \;=\; \frac{2\,(3)}{(9+1)^2} \;=\; \frac{6}{100} \;=\; \frac{3}{50}$$

(ii)　We have

$$L\,[t^2\,\sin t] \;=\; L\,[t\,(t\,\sin t)]$$

$$=\; (-1)\frac{d}{ds}\,\frac{2s}{(s^2+1)^2} \;=\; (-1)\left[\frac{(s^2+1)^2\,(2) - (2s)\,2\,(s^2+1)\,(2s)}{(s^2+1)^4}\right]$$

$$=\; -\left[\frac{2-6s^2}{(s^2+1)^3}\right]$$

∴　By definition of Laplace transform, we have

$$\int_{0}^{\infty} e^{-st}\,t^2\,\sin t\,dt \;=\; -\left[\frac{2-6s^2}{(s^2+1)^3}\right]$$

Putting s = 1, we get

$$\int_{0}^{\infty} e^{-t}\,t^2\,\sin t\,dt \;=\; -\left[\frac{2-6\,(1)}{(1+1)^3}\right] \;=\; \frac{1}{2}$$

(iii)　We have　$L\,[t^3\,\sin t] \;=\; L\,[t\,(t^2\,\sin t)]$

$$=\; (-1)\frac{d}{ds}\left[-\left\{\frac{2-6s^2}{(s^2+1)^3}\right\}\right] \qquad\qquad \text{[By result (ii) above]}$$

$$=\; \left[\frac{(s^2+1)^3\,(-12s) - (2-6s^2)\,3\,(s^2+1)^2\,(2s)}{(s^2+1)^6}\right]$$

$$=\; \left[\frac{-12s\,(s^2+1) - 12s\,(1-3s^2)}{(s^2+1)^4}\right] \;=\; \frac{24s\,(s^2-1)}{(s^2+1)^4}$$

$\therefore$ By definition of Laplace transform, we have

$$\int_0^\infty e^{-st}\, t^3 \sin t\ dt = \frac{24s\,(s^2 - 1)}{(s^2 + 1)^4}$$

Putting $s = 1$, we get

$$\int_0^\infty e^{-t}\, t^3 \sin t\ dt = \frac{24\,(1)\,(1 - 1)}{(1 + 1)^4} = 0$$

(iv) We have $\quad L\left[\dfrac{e^{-at} - e^{-bt}}{t}\right] = \int_s^\infty L\,[e^{-at} - e^{-bt}]\ ds \qquad\qquad$ [By result (21)]

$$= \int_s^\infty \left(\frac{1}{s+a} - \frac{1}{s+b}\right) ds = \left[\log \frac{s+a}{s+b}\right]_s^\infty$$

$$= 0 - \log \frac{s+a}{s+b} = \log \frac{s+b}{s+a}$$

$\therefore$ By definition of Laplace transform, we have

$$\int_0^\infty e^{-st}\left(\frac{e^{-at} - e^{-bt}}{t}\right) dt = \log \frac{s+b}{s+a}$$

Putting $s = 0$, we get

$$\int_0^\infty \frac{e^{-at} - e^{-bt}}{t}\ dt = \log \frac{0+b}{0+a} = \log \frac{b}{a}$$

(v) We have

$$L\left[\frac{\cos 6t - \cos 4t}{t}\right] = \int_s^\infty L\,[\cos 6t - \cos 4t]\ ds \qquad\qquad \text{[By result (21)]}$$

$$= \int_s^\infty \left(\frac{s}{s^2 + 36} - \frac{s}{s^2 + 16}\right) ds = \left[\frac{1}{2}\log\,(s^2 + 36) - \frac{1}{2}\log\,(s^2 + 16)\right]_s^\infty$$

$$= \left[\frac{1}{2}\log \frac{s^2 + 36}{s^2 + 16}\right]_s^\infty = \frac{1}{2}\log \frac{s^2 + 16}{s^2 + 36}$$

$\therefore$ By definition of Laplace transform, we have

$$\int_0^\infty e^{-st}\left(\frac{\cos 6t - \cos 4t}{t}\right) dt = \frac{1}{2}\log \frac{s^2 + 16}{s^2 + 36}$$

Putting s = 0, we get

$$\int_0^\infty \frac{\cos 6t - \cos 4t}{t}\, dt = \frac{1}{2}\log\frac{16}{36} = \log\frac{2}{3}$$

(vi) We have $\mathrm{L}\left[\dfrac{\sinh t}{t}\right] = \displaystyle\int_s^\infty \mathrm{L}\,[\sinh t]\, ds$ [By result (21)]

$$= \int_s^\infty \frac{1}{(s^2-1)}\, ds = \frac{1}{2}\int_s^\infty \left(\frac{1}{s-1}-\frac{1}{s+1}\right)ds$$

$$= \frac{1}{2}\left[\log\frac{s-1}{s+1}\right]_s^\infty = \frac{1}{2}\log\frac{s+1}{s-1}$$

∴ By definition of Laplace transform, we have

$$\int_0^\infty e^{-st}\frac{\sinh t}{t}\, dt = \frac{1}{2}\log\frac{s+1}{s-1}$$

Putting s = 2, we get

$$\int_0^\infty e^{-2t}\frac{\sinh t}{t}\, dt = \frac{1}{2}\log\frac{2+1}{2-1} = \frac{1}{2}\log 3$$

(vii) We have $\mathrm{L}\left[\dfrac{\sin t}{t}\right] = \displaystyle\int_s^\infty \mathrm{L}\,[\sin t]\, ds$ [By result (21)]

$$= \int_s^\infty \frac{1}{s^2+1}\, ds = \left[\tan^{-1} s\right]_s^\infty = \frac{\pi}{2} - \tan^{-1} s$$

∴ By definition of Laplace transform, we have

$$\int_0^\infty e^{-st}\frac{\sin t}{t}\, dt = \frac{\pi}{2} - \tan^{-1} s$$

Putting s = 1, we get

$$\int_0^\infty e^{-t}\frac{\sin t}{t} = \frac{\pi}{2} - \tan^{-1} 1 = \frac{\pi}{2} - \frac{\pi}{4} = \frac{\pi}{4}$$

(viii) We have $\mathrm{L}\,[\sin^3 t] = \dfrac{1}{4}\mathrm{L}\,[3\sin t - \sin 3t]$ $\{\because \sin 3t = 3\sin t - 4\sin^3 t\}$

$$= \frac{1}{4}\left(\frac{3}{s^2+1} - \frac{3}{s^2+9}\right) = \frac{6}{(s^2+1)(s^2+9)}$$

∴   By definition of Laplace transform, on LHS, we get

$$\int_0^\infty e^{-st} \sin^3 t \, dt = \frac{6}{(s^2+1)(s^2+9)}, \quad \text{and put } s = 2$$

$$\therefore \quad \int_0^\infty e^{-2t} \sin^3 t \, dt = \frac{6}{(4+1)(4+9)} = \frac{6}{65}$$

EXERCISE 4.2

1. Find the Laplace transform of each of the following functions :

   (i) $t^3 e^{-3t}$ (ii) $e^{at}(2\cos bt - 3\sin bt)$ (iii) $(1 + t\,e^{-t})^3$ (iv) $e^{-t}\{4t^3 + \cos(4t+7)\}$

   (v) $2e^t \sin 4t \cos 2t$ (vi) $\sinh \dfrac{t}{2} \sin \dfrac{\sqrt{3}}{2} t$ (vii) $\cos at \sinh at$ (viii) $e^{4t} t^{3/2}$

   (ix) $\dfrac{\cosh at}{\sqrt{t}}$ (x) $e^{-t} \sin^3 t$

   Ans. (i) $\dfrac{6}{(s+3)^4}$ (ii) $\dfrac{2s-2a-2b}{(s-a)^2+b^2}$ (iii) $\dfrac{1}{s} + \dfrac{3}{(s+1)^2} + \dfrac{6}{(s+2)^3} + \dfrac{6}{(s+3)^4}$

   (iv) $\dfrac{24}{(s+1)^4} + \dfrac{(s+1)\cos 7 - 4\sin 7}{s^2+2s+17}$ (v) $\dfrac{6}{s^2-2s+37} + \dfrac{2}{s^2-2s+5}$

   (vi) $\dfrac{\sqrt{3}}{2} \dfrac{s}{s^4+s^2+1}$ (vii) $\dfrac{a(s^2-2a^2)}{s^4+4a^2}$ (viii) $\dfrac{3}{4} \dfrac{\sqrt{\pi}}{(s-4)^{5/2}}$

   (ix) $\dfrac{1}{2}\left[\sqrt{\dfrac{\pi}{s-a}} + \sqrt{\dfrac{\pi}{s+a}}\right]$ (x) $\left[\dfrac{6}{(s^2+2s+2)(s^2+2s+10)}\right]$

2. Find $L[F(t)]$ if (i) $F(t) = \begin{cases} \cos(t-\alpha) & t > \alpha \\ 0 & t < \alpha \end{cases}$

   (ii) $F(t) = \begin{cases} 5\sin 3(t - \pi/4) & t > \pi/4 \\ 0 & t < \pi/4 \end{cases}$

   Ans. (i) $e^{-\alpha s} \dfrac{s}{s^2+1}$ (ii) $e^{-\pi s/4} \dfrac{15}{s^2+9}$

3. Verify change of scale theorem for $L[e^{2t}\cos 2t]$.   [**Hint :** Consider $f(t) = e^t \cos t$]

4. If $L[f(t)] = \dfrac{s^2-s+1}{(2s+1)^2(s-1)}$, find $L[f(2t)]$.   **Ans.** $\dfrac{s^2-2s+4}{4(s+1)^2(s-2)}$.

5. Given that $y'' + 2y' - 8y = 0$, $y(0) = 1$, $y'(0) = 8$, show that $L[y(t)] = \dfrac{2}{s-2} - \dfrac{1}{s+4}$.

6. Find $L[f'(t)]$ if (i) $f(t) = e^{-5t}\sin t$, (ii) $f(t) = \sin^2 t$.

   Ans. (i) $\dfrac{s}{s^2+10s+26}$ (ii) $\dfrac{2}{(s^2+4)}$ $\left[\textbf{Hint :} f'(t) = \sin 2t, \text{ and } L[\sin 2t] = \dfrac{2}{s^2+4}\right]$

7. If $L[f''(t)] = \tan^{-1}\left(\dfrac{1}{s}\right)$, $f(0) = 2$ and $f'(0) = -1$, find $L[f(t)]$.

Ans. $\quad \dfrac{2s - 1 + \tan^{-1}(1/s)}{s^2}$

8. Verify directly that $L\left[\displaystyle\int_0^t (u^2 - u + e^{-u})\, du\right] = \dfrac{1}{s} L[t^2 - t + e^{-t}]$

9. Find the Laplace transform of each of the following functions :

(i) $t(3 \sin 2t - 2 \cos 2t)$ (ii) $t \cos(4t + 3)$ (iii) $t^2 \sin 2t$

(iv) $t^2 \sinh t$ (v) $(t^2 - 3t + 2) \sin 3t$ (vi) $t^3 \cos t$.

Ans. (i) $\dfrac{8 + 12s - 2s^2}{(s^2 + 4)^2}$ (ii) $\dfrac{s^2 \cos 3 - 8s \sin 3 - 16 \cos 3}{(s^2 + 16)^2}$ (iii) $\dfrac{4(3s^2 - 4)}{(s^2 + 4)^3}$

(iv) $\dfrac{6s^2 + 2}{(s^2 - 1)^3}$ (v) $\dfrac{6s^4 - 18s^3 + 126s^2 - 162s + 432}{(s^2 + 9)^3}$ (vi) $\dfrac{6s^4 - 36s^2 + 6}{(s^2 + 1)^4}$

10. If $L\left[\dfrac{1 - \cos at}{a^2}\right] = \dfrac{1}{s(s^2 + a^2)}$, show that $L\left[\dfrac{t(1 - \cos at)}{a^2}\right] = \dfrac{3s^2 + a^2}{s^2(s^2 + a^2)^2}$.

11. Find the Laplace transform of each of the following functions :

(i) $\dfrac{\sinh t}{t}$ (ii) $\dfrac{e^{2t} - 1}{t}$ (iii) $\dfrac{1 - e^{-t}}{t}$ (iv) $\dfrac{1 - \cos 3t}{t}$ (v) $\dfrac{\cos 2t - \cos 3t}{t}$

Ans. (i) $\dfrac{1}{2} \log \dfrac{s + 1}{s - 1}$ (ii) $\log \dfrac{s}{s - 2}$ (iii) $\log \dfrac{s + 1}{s}$ (iv) $\log \dfrac{\sqrt{s^2 + 9}}{s}$ (v) $\dfrac{1}{2} \log \dfrac{s^2 + 9}{s^2 + 4}$

12. Obtain the Laplace transform of each of the following functions :

(i) $t e^{3t} \cos 2t$ (ii) $\displaystyle\int_0^t e^u u^3\, du$ (iii) $\displaystyle\int_0^t e^x \cos x\, dx$ (iv) $\displaystyle\int_0^t \dfrac{e^t - \cos 2t}{t}\, dt$

Ans. (i) $\dfrac{s^2 - 6s + 5}{(s^2 - 6s + 13)^2}$ (ii) $\dfrac{6}{s(s - 1)^4}$ (iii) $\dfrac{s - 1}{s(s^2 - 2s + 2)}$ (iv) $\dfrac{1}{s} \log \dfrac{\sqrt{s^2 + 4}}{(s - 1)}$

13. Obtain the Laplace transforms of

(i) $t \displaystyle\int_0^t e^{-3t} \sin 2t\, dt$ (ii) $e^{-3t} \displaystyle\int_0^t t \sin 2t\, dt$ (iii) $\displaystyle\int_0^t t e^{-3t} \sin 2t\, dt$

(iv) $\cosh t \displaystyle\int_0^t t \cosh t\, dt$

Ans. (i) $\dfrac{6s^2 + 24s + 26}{s^2(s^2 + 6s + 13)^2}$ (ii) $\dfrac{4}{(s^2 + 6s + 13)^2}$ (iii) $\dfrac{1}{s} \dfrac{2(2s + 6)}{(s^2 + 6s + 13)^2}$

(iv) $\dfrac{1}{2}\left[\dfrac{s^2 - 2s + 2}{(s - 1)(s^2 - 2s)^2} + \dfrac{s^2 + 2s + 2}{(s + 1)(s^2 + 2s)^2}\right]$

14. Obtain the Laplace transforms of

(i) $\dfrac{e^{-3t}\sin 2t}{t}$ (ii) $\displaystyle\int_0^t \dfrac{e^{-3t}\sin 2t}{t}\,dt$ (iii) $e^{-3t}\displaystyle\int_0^t \dfrac{\sin 2t}{t}\,dt$

Ans. (i) $\cot^{-1}\dfrac{s+3}{2}$ (ii) $\dfrac{1}{s}\cot^{-1}\dfrac{s+3}{2}$ (iii) $\dfrac{1}{s+3}\cot^{-1}\dfrac{s+3}{2}$

15. Find the following convolutions :

(i) $1*1$ (ii) $1*e^t$ (iii) $1*\cos t$ (iv) $(e^{-t}-e^{-2t})*e^{-t}$

(v) $t*e^{at}$ (vi) $\cos t*\cos t$ (vii) $\sin t*\sin t$ (viii) $\sin t*\cos t$

Ans. (i) t (ii) e^t (iii) $\sin t$ (iv) $e^{-2t}+(t-1)e^{-t}$ (v) $(e^{at}-1)/a^2-t/a$

(vi) $\dfrac{1}{2}(t\cos t+\sin t)$ (vii) $\dfrac{1}{2}(\sin t-t\cos t)$ (viii) $\dfrac{1}{2}t\sin t$.

Hint : Find $f(t)*g(t)=\displaystyle\int_0^t f(u)\,g(t-u)\,du$ or $f(t)*g(t)\displaystyle\int_0^t f(t-u)\,g(u)\,du.$

16. Verify the convolution theorem for the pair of following functions :

(i) $f(t)=t^2,\ g(t)=e^{-at}$ (ii) $f(t)=t,\ g(t)=\cos t.$

Hint : Show that $L[f(t)*g(t)]=F(s)\,G(s).$

17. Verify the initial value theorem for the functions :

(i) $3e^{-2t}$ (ii) $5+2\cos 3t$ (iii) $(2t-3)^2.$

Hint : Show that (i) $\displaystyle\lim_{t\to 0}f(t)=3=\lim_{s\to\infty}s\,F(s)$ (ii) $\displaystyle\lim_{t\to 0}f(t)=7=\lim_{s\to\infty}s\,F(s)$

(iii) $\displaystyle\lim_{t\to 0}f(t)=9=\lim_{s\to\infty}s\,F(s).$

18. Verify the final value theorem for the functions :

(i) $3e^{-2t}$ (ii) $2+3e^{-2t}\sin 4t$ (iii) $t^3 e^{-4t}$

Hint : Show that (i) $\displaystyle\lim_{t\to\infty}f(t)=0=\lim_{s\to 0}s\,F(s)$

(ii) $\displaystyle\lim_{t\to\infty}f(t)=2=\lim_{s\to 0}s\,F(s)$ (iii) $\displaystyle\lim_{t\to\infty}f(t)=0=\lim_{s\to 0}s\,F(s).$

19. Using Laplace transform, evaluate each of the following integrals :

(i) $\displaystyle\int_0^\infty t\,e^{-2t}\cos t\,dt$ (ii) $\displaystyle\int_0^\infty t^2\,e^{-3t}\sinh 2t\,dt$ (iii) $\displaystyle\int_0^\infty \frac{e^{-t}-e^{-3t}}{t}\,dt$

(iv) $\displaystyle\int_0^\infty \frac{e^{-3t}-e^{-6t}}{t}\,dt$ (v) $\displaystyle\int_0^\infty \frac{\cos 3t-\cos 2t}{t}\,dt$ (vi) $\displaystyle\int_0^\infty e^{3t}\,\frac{\sinh t}{t}\,dt$

(vii) $\displaystyle\int_0^\infty \frac{1-\cos t}{t^2}\,dt$ (viii) $\displaystyle\int_0^t \frac{\sin^2 t}{t^2}\,dt$ (ix) $\displaystyle\int_0^\infty e^{-2t}\,\frac{\sinh t\,\sin t}{t}\,dt$

(x) $\displaystyle\int_0^\infty e^{3t}\,\cos^3 t\,dt$ (xi) $\displaystyle\int_0^\infty \frac{\sin^3 t}{t}\,dt$ (xii) $\displaystyle\int_0^\infty e^{-t}\,\frac{1-\cos t}{t}\,dt$

Ans. (i) $\dfrac{3}{25}$ (ii) $\dfrac{124}{125}$ (iii) $\log 3$ (iv) $\log 2$

(v) $\log \dfrac{2}{3}$ (vi) $-\log\sqrt{2}$

(vii) $\dfrac{\pi}{2}$ (viii) $\dfrac{\pi}{2}$ (ix) $\dfrac{1}{2}\tan^{-1}\left(\dfrac{1}{2}\right)$ (x) $\dfrac{4}{15}$ (xi) $\dfrac{\pi}{4}$ (xii) $\dfrac{1}{2}\log 2$

20. Given $L\,[J_0(t)] = \dfrac{1}{\sqrt{s^2+1}}$, show that

(i) $\displaystyle\int_0^\infty J_0(t)\,dt = 1$, (ii) $\displaystyle\int_0^\infty e^{-t}\,J_0(t)\,dt = \dfrac{\sqrt{2}}{2}$,

(iii) $\displaystyle\int_0^\infty t\,e^{-3t}\,J_0\,(4t)\,dt = \dfrac{3}{125}$

21. Find $L\,[J_0(t)]$, where $J_0(t)$ is the Bessel function of order zero defined by

$$J_0(t) = 1 - \frac{t^2}{2^2} + \frac{t^4}{2^2\,4^2} - \frac{t^6}{2^2\,4^2\,6^2}\,.$$

Ans. $\dfrac{1}{\sqrt{s^2+1}}$

22. Use infinite series to obtain Laplace transform of (i) $\cos \sqrt{t}$ (ii) $\int_0^t \dfrac{\sin u}{u} \, du$.

Ans. (i) $\dfrac{1}{s}\left[1 - \left(\dfrac{1}{2s}\right) + \dfrac{(1/2s)^2}{3} - \dfrac{(1/2s)^3}{3.5} + \dfrac{(1/2s)^4}{3.5.7} - \dfrac{(1/2s)^5}{3.5.7.9} + \cdots\right]$

(ii) (ii) $\dfrac{1}{s} \tan^{-1} \dfrac{1}{s}$.

Hint : $\int_0^t \dfrac{\sin u}{u} \, du = t - \dfrac{t^3}{3 \cdot 3!} + \dfrac{t^5}{5.5!} - \dfrac{t^7}{7 \cdot 7!} + \cdots$

4.8 INVERSE LAPLACE TRANSFORM

We have so far discussed how to find Laplace transform of given function f(t). However, from the application point of view this will not be very useful unless we obtain inverse transform f(t) in time domain, of a given function F(s) in frequency domain.

we shall consider the inverse problem of finding f(t) for a given F(s) i.e. given a function F(s), to find a function f(t) of which F(s) is the Laplace transform. Applications of the Laplace transform to differential equations are also discussed.

4.9 DEFINITION

If the Laplace transform of f(t) is F(s), i.e. L [f(t)] = F(s), then f(t) is called the inverse Laplace transform of F(s) and we write symbolically

$$\boxed{L^{-1} [F(s)] = f(t)}$$ ... (26)

where, L^{-1} is called inverse Laplace Transform Operator.

4.10 LINEARITY PROPERTY

Theorem : If c_1 and c_2 are any constants and $F_1(s)$ and $F_2(s)$ are the Laplace transforms of $f_1(t)$ and $f_2(t)$, respectively, then

$$L^{-1} [c_1 F_1(s) + c_2 F_2(s)] = c_1 L^{-1} [F_1(s)] + c_2 L^{-1} [F_2(s)]$$
$$= c_1 f_1(t) + c_2 f_2(t)$$

Proof : To prove this, we have given

$$F_1(s) = L [f_1(t)] \quad \text{and} \quad F_2(s) = L [f_2(t)]$$

We know by the Linearity property of Laplace transform (see Art. 4.5)

$$L [c_1 f_1(t) + c_2 f_2(t)] = c_1 L [f_1(t)] + c_2 L [f_2(t)]$$
$$= c_1 F_1(s) + c_2 F_2(s)$$

Therefore by definition (1) above, we have

$$L^{-1} [c_1 F_1(s) + c_2 F_2(s)] = c_1 f_1(t) + c_2 f_2(t)$$
$$= c_1 L^{-1} [F_1(s)] + c_2 L^{-1} [F_2(s)].$$

The result is easily extended to the addition of more than two functions.

Note : The property of Laplace transformation expressed in this theorem is, of course, the property of Linearity. In other words, the inverse Laplace transform is a Linear transform.

4.11 METHODS OF FINDING INVERSE TRANSFORMS

Following methods are used to find inverse Laplace transforms :

(I)   Use of Table of inverse Laplace transforms.

(II)   Use of Theorems of inverse Laplace transform.

(III)   Use of Partial fractions.

In what follows we shall illustrate these methods.

4.12 METHOD (I) : USE OF TABLE OF INVERSE LAPLACE TRANSFORMS

From the Table 4.1 of Laplace transforms of elementary functions and by using definition and linearity property, we can obtain corresponding Table of inverse Laplace transform.

1. $\qquad L[1] = \dfrac{1}{s}$ $\qquad \therefore \qquad L^{-1}\left[\dfrac{1}{s}\right] = 1$

2. $\qquad L[e^{at}] = \dfrac{1}{s-a}$ $\qquad \therefore \qquad L^{-1}\left[\dfrac{1}{s-a}\right] = e^{at}$

$\qquad L[e^{-at}] = \dfrac{1}{s+a}$ $\qquad \therefore \qquad L^{-1}\left[\dfrac{1}{s+a}\right] = e^{-at}$

3. $\qquad L[\sin at] = \dfrac{a}{s^2+a^2}$ $\qquad \therefore \qquad L^{-1}\left[\dfrac{1}{s^2+a^2}\right] = \dfrac{1}{a}\sin at$

4. $\qquad L[\cos at] = \dfrac{s}{s^2+a^2}$ $\qquad \therefore \qquad L^{-1}\left[\dfrac{s}{s^2+a^2}\right] = \cos at$

5. $\qquad L[\sinh at] = \dfrac{a}{s^2-a^2}$ $\qquad \therefore \qquad L^{-1}\left[\dfrac{1}{s^2-a^2}\right] = \dfrac{1}{a}\sinh at$

6. $\qquad L[\cosh at] = \dfrac{s}{s^2-a^2}$ $\qquad \therefore \qquad L^{-1}\left[\dfrac{s}{s^2-a^2}\right] = \cosh at$

7. $\qquad L[t^n] = \dfrac{\overline{|n+1}}{s^{n+1}}$ $\qquad \therefore \qquad L^{-1}\left[\dfrac{1}{s^{n+1}}\right] = \dfrac{t^n}{\overline{|n+1}}$

$\qquad L[t^{n-1}] = \dfrac{\overline{|n}}{s^n}$ $\qquad \therefore \qquad L^{-1}\left[\dfrac{1}{s^n}\right] = \dfrac{t^{n-1}}{\overline{|n}}$

If n is a positive integer, $\overline{|n+1} = n!$ and $\overline{|n} = (n-1)!$, then we have

8. $\qquad L[t^n] = \dfrac{n!}{s^{n+1}}$ $\qquad \therefore \qquad L^{-1}\left[\dfrac{1}{s^{n+1}}\right] = \dfrac{t^n}{n!}$

$$L\,[t^{n-1}] \;=\; \frac{(n-1)\,!}{s^n} \qquad \therefore \qquad L^{-1}\left[\frac{1}{s^n}\right] \;=\; \frac{t^{n-1}}{(n-1)\,!}$$

Note : For the units step functions $u(t) = \begin{cases} 0 \,,\, t<0 \\ 1 \,,\, t\geq 0 \end{cases}$ and displaced unit steps function

$u(t-a) = \begin{cases} 0 \,,\, t<a \\ 1 \,,\, t\geq a \end{cases}$ we can also add the following results :

9. $\quad L\,[U(t-a)] \;=\; \dfrac{e^{-as}}{s} \qquad \therefore \qquad L^{-1}\left[\dfrac{e^{-as}}{s}\right] \;=\; U(t-a)$

$\qquad\quad L\,[U(t)] \;=\; \dfrac{1}{s} \qquad\quad \therefore \qquad L^{-1}\left[\dfrac{1}{s}\right] \;=\; U(t)$

Similarly, for Dirac delta or unit impulse function $\delta(t-a) = \displaystyle\lim_{\varepsilon \to 0} F(t)$

where $F(t) = \begin{cases} 0 \,, & t<a \\ 1/\varepsilon \,, & a\leq t\leq a+\varepsilon \\ 0 \,, & t>a+\varepsilon \end{cases}$ we note that

10. $\quad L\,[\delta(t-a)] \;=\; e^{-as} \qquad \therefore \qquad L^{-1}\,[e^{-as}] \;=\; \delta(t-a)$

$\qquad\quad L\,[\delta(t)] \;=\; 1 \qquad\qquad \therefore \qquad L^{-1}\,[1] \;=\; \delta(t)$

The following table gives the inverse Laplace transforms of some elementary functions for ready reference.

Table 4.2 : Inverse Laplace Transforms

Sr. No.	$F(s)$	$f(t) = L^{-1}\,[F(s)]$
1	$\dfrac{1}{s}$	1
2	$\dfrac{1}{s-a}$	e^{at}
3	$\dfrac{1}{s^2+a^2}$	$\dfrac{\sin at}{a}$
4	$\dfrac{s}{s^2+a^2}$	$\cos at$
5	$\dfrac{1}{s^2-a^2}$	$\dfrac{\sinh at}{a}$
6	$\dfrac{s}{s^2-a^2}$	$\cosh at$
7	$\dfrac{1}{s^{n+1}}$	$\dfrac{t^n}{\overline{\lvert n+1}}$
8	$\dfrac{1}{s^{n+1}}$ if n a positive integer	$\dfrac{t^n}{n!}$

ILLUSTRATIONS ON TABLE OF INVERSE LAPLACE TRANSFORMS

Ex. 1 : *Find the inverse Laplace transforms of the following functions :*

(i) $\dfrac{5}{s+3}$ (ii) $\dfrac{1}{2s-3}$ (iii) $\dfrac{4}{3s-1}$ (iv) $\dfrac{2s+1}{s(s+1)}$

Sol. : (i) $\quad L^{-1}\left[\dfrac{5}{s+3}\right] = 5\,L^{-1}\left[\dfrac{1}{s+3}\right] = 5e^{-3t}$

$$\begin{cases}\text{From Table of I.L.T.}\\[4pt] L^{-1}\left[\dfrac{1}{s+a}\right] = e^{-at}\end{cases}$$

(ii) $\quad L^{-1}\left[\dfrac{1}{2s-3}\right] = \dfrac{1}{2}\,L^{-1}\left[\dfrac{1}{s-3/2}\right] = \dfrac{1}{2}\,e^{(3/2)t}$

$$\begin{cases}\text{From Table of I.L.T.}\\[4pt] L^{-1}\left[\dfrac{1}{s-a}\right] = e^{at}\end{cases}$$

(iii) $\quad L^{-1}\left[\dfrac{4}{3s-1}\right] = \dfrac{4}{3}\,L^{-1}\left[\dfrac{1}{s-1/3}\right] = \dfrac{4}{3}\,e^{(1/3)t}$

(iv) $\quad L^{-1}\left[\dfrac{2s+1}{s(s+1)}\right] = L^{-1}\left[\dfrac{s+1+s}{s(s+1)}\right] = L^{-1}\left[\dfrac{1}{s}+\dfrac{1}{s+1}\right]$

$$= L^{-1}\left[\dfrac{1}{s}\right] + L^{-1}\left[\dfrac{1}{s+1}\right] = 1 + e^{-t} \quad \text{[By Linearity property]}$$

Ex. 2 : *Obtain the inverse Laplace transform of each of the following functions :*

(i) $\dfrac{2}{s^2+16}$ (ii) $\dfrac{4s}{s^2-16}$ (iii) $\dfrac{2s-5}{4s^2+25}$ (iv) $\dfrac{3s-12}{s^2+8}$ (v) $\dfrac{s-4}{s^2-4}$ (vi) $\dfrac{s\cos\alpha + \omega\sin\alpha}{s^2+\omega^2}$

Sol. : (i) $\quad L^{-1}\left[\dfrac{2}{s^2+16}\right] = 2\,L^{-1}\left[\dfrac{1}{s^2+16}\right] = 2\,L^{-1}\left[\dfrac{1}{s^2+4^2}\right]$

$$= 2\left(\dfrac{\sin 4t}{4}\right) = \dfrac{\sin 4t}{2}$$

$$\begin{cases}\text{From Table of I.L.T.}\\[4pt] L^{-1}\left[\dfrac{1}{s^2+a^2}\right] = \dfrac{\sin at}{a}\end{cases}$$

(ii) $\quad L^{-1}\left[\dfrac{4s}{s^2-16}\right] = 4\,L^{-1}\left[\dfrac{s}{s^2-16}\right] = 4\,L^{-1}\left[\dfrac{s}{s^2-4^2}\right]$

$$= 4\cosh 4t.$$

$$\begin{cases}\text{From Table of I.L.T.}\\[4pt] L^{-1}\left[\dfrac{s}{s^2-a^2}\right] = \cosh at\end{cases}$$

(iii) $\quad L^{-1}\left[\dfrac{2s-5}{4s^2+25}\right] = \dfrac{1}{4}\,L^{-1}\left[\dfrac{2s-5}{s^2+25/4}\right] = \dfrac{1}{4}\,L^{-1}\left[\dfrac{2s-5}{s^2+(5/2)^2}\right]$

$$= \dfrac{1}{2}\,L^{-1}\left[\dfrac{s}{s^2+(5/2)^2}\right] - \dfrac{5}{4}\,L^{-1}\left[\dfrac{1}{s^2+(5/2)^2}\right]$$

$$\text{[By Linearity Property]}$$

$$= \dfrac{1}{2}\cos\dfrac{5}{2}t - \dfrac{5}{4}\cdot\dfrac{2}{5}\sin\dfrac{5}{2}t = \dfrac{1}{2}\left(\cos\dfrac{5t}{2} - \sin\dfrac{5t}{2}\right).$$

(iv) $\quad L^{-1}\left[\dfrac{3s-12}{s^2+8}\right] = 3\,L^{-1}\left[\dfrac{s}{s^2+8}\right] - 12\,L^{-1}\left[\dfrac{1}{s^2+8}\right] \quad \text{[By Linearity Property]}$

$$= 3\,L^{-1}\left[\dfrac{s}{s^2+\left(2\sqrt{2}\right)^2}\right] - 12\,L^{-1}\left[\dfrac{1}{s^2+\left(2\sqrt{2}\right)^2}\right]$$

$$= 3 \cos \left(2\sqrt{2}\right) t - 12 \frac{1}{2\sqrt{2}} \sin \left(2\sqrt{2}\right) t$$

$$= 3 \cos \left(2\sqrt{2}\right) t - 3\sqrt{2} \sin \left(2\sqrt{2}\right) t.$$

(v) $\quad L^{-1}\left[\dfrac{s-4}{s^2-4}\right] = L^{-1}\left[\dfrac{s}{s^2-4}\right] - 4\,L^{-1}\left[\dfrac{1}{s^2-4}\right]$ [By Linearity property]

$$= \cosh 2t - 4\left(\frac{\sinh 2t}{2}\right)$$

$$= \cosh 2t - 2 \sinh 2t$$

(vi) $L^{-1}\left[\dfrac{s \cos \alpha + \omega \sin \alpha}{s^2 + \omega^2}\right] = \cos \alpha\, L^{-1}\left[\dfrac{s}{s^2 + \omega^2}\right] + \sin \alpha\, L^{-1}\left[\dfrac{\omega}{s^2 + \omega^2}\right]$

$$= \cos \alpha \cos \omega t + \sin \alpha \sin \omega t$$

$$= \cos (\omega t - \alpha)$$

Ex. 3 : *Find each of the following inverse Laplace transforms :*

(i) $L^{-1}\left[\dfrac{a_1}{s} + \dfrac{a_2}{s^2} + \dfrac{a_3}{s^3}\right]$ (ii) $L^{-1}\left[\dfrac{1}{s^4}\right]$ (iii) $L^{-1}\left[\dfrac{s+1}{s^{4/3}}\right]$ (iv) $L^{-1}\left[\dfrac{3\,(s^2-1)^2}{2s^5}\right]$

Sol. : (i) $\quad L^{-1}\left[\dfrac{a_1}{s} + \dfrac{a_2}{s^2} + \dfrac{a_3}{s^3}\right] = a_1 L^{-1}\left[\dfrac{1}{s}\right] + a_2 L^{-1}\left[\dfrac{1}{s^2}\right] + a_3 L^{-1}\left[\dfrac{1}{s^3}\right]$

[By Linearity property]

$$= a_1 + a_2 t + a_3 \frac{t^2}{2!} = a_1 + a_2 t + \frac{a_3 t^2}{2}.$$

$$\left[\begin{array}{l}\text{From Table of I.L.T.}\\[4pt] L^{-1}\left[\dfrac{1}{s^{n+1}}\right] = \dfrac{t^n}{n!}\end{array}\right.$$

(ii) $\quad L^{-1}\left[\dfrac{1}{s^4}\right] = \dfrac{t^3}{3!} = \dfrac{t^3}{6}$

(iii) $\quad L^{-1}\left[\dfrac{s+1}{s^{4/3}}\right] = L^{-1}\left[\dfrac{s}{s^{4/3}}\right] + L^{-1}\left[\dfrac{1}{s^{4/3}}\right] = L^{-1}\left[\dfrac{1}{s^{1/3}}\right] + L^{-1}\left[\dfrac{1}{s^{4/3}}\right]$

$$= \frac{t^{-2/3}}{\overline{\lfloor 1/3}} + \frac{t^{1/3}}{\overline{\lfloor 4/3}} = \frac{1}{\overline{\lfloor 1/3}}\left(t^{-2/3} + 3t^{1/3}\right), \quad \left\{L^{-1}\left[\dfrac{1}{s^n}\right] = \dfrac{t^{n-1}}{\overline{\lfloor n}}\right\}$$

(iv) $\quad L^{-1}\left[\dfrac{3\,(s^2-1)^2}{2s^5}\right] = \dfrac{3}{2}\,L^{-1}\left[\dfrac{s^4 - 2s^2 + 1}{s^5}\right] = \dfrac{3}{2}\,L^{-1}\left[\dfrac{1}{s} - \dfrac{2}{s^3} + \dfrac{1}{s^5}\right]$

$$= \frac{3}{2}\left\{L^{-1}\left[\frac{1}{s}\right] - 2\,L^{-1}\left[\frac{1}{s^3}\right] + L^{-1}\left[\frac{1}{s^5}\right]\right\}$$

$$= \frac{3}{2}\left(1 - 2\frac{t^2}{2!} + \frac{t^4}{4!}\right) = \frac{3}{2}\left(1 - t^2 + \frac{t^4}{24}\right)$$

Ex. 4 : *Determine each of the following :*

(i) $L^{-1}\left[\dfrac{3}{s+2} - \dfrac{2s}{s^2+25} + \dfrac{3}{s^2+9}\right]$ (ii) $L^{-1}\left[\dfrac{5s+4}{s^3} - \dfrac{2s-18}{s^2+9} + \dfrac{24-30\sqrt{s}}{s^4}\right]$

(iii) $L^{-1}\left[\dfrac{6}{2s-3} - \dfrac{3+4s}{9s^2-16} + \dfrac{8-6s}{16s^2+9}\right]$

Sol. : (i) $L^{-1}\left[\dfrac{3}{s+2} - \dfrac{2s}{s^2+25} + \dfrac{3}{s^2+9}\right]$

$$= 3\,L^{-1}\left[\frac{1}{s+2}\right] - 2\,L^{-1}\left[\frac{s}{s^2+5^2}\right] + 3\,L^{-1}\left[\frac{1}{s^2+3^2}\right]$$

$$= 3\,e^{-2t} - 2\cos 5t + 3\left(\frac{\sin 3t}{3}\right) = 3\,e^{-2t} - 2\cos 5t + \sin 3t$$

(ii) $L^{-1}\left[\dfrac{5s+4}{s^3} - \dfrac{2s-18}{s^2+9} + \dfrac{24-30\sqrt{s}}{s^4}\right]$

$$= L^{-1}\left[\frac{5}{s^2} + \frac{4}{s^3} - \frac{2s}{s^2+9} + \frac{18}{s^2+9} + \frac{24}{s^4} - \frac{30}{s^{7/2}}\right]$$

$$= 5t + 4\left(\frac{t^2}{2!}\right) - 2\cos t + 18\left(\frac{\sin 3t}{3}\right) + 24\left(\frac{t^3}{3!}\right) - 30\left(\frac{t^{5/2}}{\overline{\lfloor 7/2}}\right)$$

$$= 5t + 2t^2 - 2\cos t + 6\sin 3t + 4t^3 - \frac{16t^{5/2}}{\sqrt{\pi}}$$

$$\left\{\because\ \overline{\lfloor 7/2} = \frac{5}{2}\cdot\frac{3}{2}\cdot\frac{1}{2}\,\overline{\lfloor 1/2} = \frac{15}{8}\sqrt{\pi}\right\}$$

(iii) $L^{-1}\left[\dfrac{6}{2s-3} - \dfrac{3+4s}{9s^2-16} + \dfrac{8-6s}{16s^2+9}\right]$

$$= L^{-1}\left[\frac{3}{s-3/2} - \frac{1}{3}\left(\frac{1}{s^2-16/9}\right) - \frac{4}{9}\left(\frac{s}{s^2-16/9}\right) + \frac{1}{2}\left(\frac{1}{s^2+9/16}\right) - \frac{3}{8}\left(\frac{s}{s^2+9/16}\right)\right]$$

$$= 3\,e^{3t/2} - \frac{1}{4}\sinh\frac{4t}{3} - \frac{4}{9}\cosh\frac{4t}{3} + \frac{2}{3}\sin\frac{3t}{4} - \frac{3}{8}\cos\frac{3t}{4}.$$

EXERCISE 4.3

1. Find the inverse Laplace transforms of the following functions :

(i) $\dfrac{3}{s+4}$ (ii) $\dfrac{1}{2s-5}$ (iii) $\dfrac{12}{4-3s}$ (iv) $\dfrac{2\pi}{s+\pi}$

Ans. (i) $3e^{-4t}$ (ii) $\dfrac{1}{2}e^{5t/2}$ (iii) $-4e^{4t/3}$ (iv) $2\pi\,e^{-\pi s}$

2. Obtain the inverse Laplace transform of each of the following functions :

(i) $\dfrac{7s}{s^2+4}$ (ii) $\dfrac{3}{s^2-7}$ (iii) $\dfrac{4s+15}{16s^2-25}$ (iv) $\dfrac{3s+5\sqrt{2}}{s^2+8}$ (v) $\dfrac{2s+6}{s^2+4}$ (vi) $\dfrac{5s-10}{9s^2-16}$

Ans. (i) $7\cos 2t$ (ii) $\dfrac{3}{\sqrt{7}}\sinh\sqrt{7}\,t$ (iii) $\dfrac{1}{4}\left(\cosh\dfrac{5t}{4}+4\sinh\dfrac{5t}{4}\right)$

(iv) $3\cos 2\sqrt{2}\,t+\dfrac{5}{2}\sin 2\sqrt{2}\,t$ (v) $2\cos 2t+3\sin 2t$

(vi) $\dfrac{5}{9}\cosh\dfrac{4}{3}\,t-\dfrac{5}{6}\sinh\dfrac{4t}{3}$.

3. Find each of the following inverse Laplace transforms :

(i) $L^{-1}\left[\dfrac{s^2+s+1}{s^{9/2}}\right]$ (ii) $L^{-1}\left[\dfrac{1}{s^5}\right]$ (iii) $L^{-1}\left[\left(\dfrac{1-\sqrt{s}}{s^2}\right)^2\right]$ (iv) $L^{-1}\left[\dfrac{7\,(s^2+1)^2}{5s^5}\right]$

Ans. (i) $\dfrac{t^{3/2}}{\sqrt{9/2}}\left(\dfrac{35}{4}+\dfrac{7}{2}t+t^2\right)$ (ii) $\dfrac{t^4}{24}$ (iii) $\dfrac{t^3}{6}+\dfrac{t^2}{2}-\dfrac{16}{15\sqrt{\pi}}\,t^{5/2}$

(iv) $\dfrac{7}{5}\left(1+t^2+\dfrac{t^4}{24}\right)$

4. Determine each of the following :

(i) $L^{-1}\left[\dfrac{3s-2}{s^{5/2}}-\dfrac{7}{3s+2}+\dfrac{5s}{s^2-1}\right]$ (ii) $L^{-1}\left[\dfrac{3s-8}{s^2+4}-\dfrac{4s-24}{s^2-16}\right]$

(iii) $L^{-1}\left[\dfrac{3\,(s^2-1)^2}{s^5}+\dfrac{4s-18}{9-s^2}+\dfrac{(s+1)\,(2-s^{3/2})}{s^{7/2}}\right]$

Ans. (i) $\sqrt{\dfrac{t}{\pi}}\left(6-\dfrac{8}{3}\,t\right)-\dfrac{7}{3}e^{-2t/3}+5\cosh t$

(ii) $3\cos 2t-4\sin 2t-4\cosh 4t+6\sinh 4t$

(iii) $2-t-3t^2+\dfrac{t^4}{8}+\dfrac{t^{3/2}}{\sqrt{7/2}}\,(5+2t)-4\cosh 3t+6\sinh 3t$.

4.13 METHOD II : USE OF THEOREMS OF INVERSE LAPLACE TRANSFORM

Analogous to the theorems proved in Sec. 4.7, we have the following theorems of Inverse Laplace transform.

(A) FIRST SHIFTING THEOREM

Theorem : If $\qquad L^{-1}[F(s)] = f(t)$, then

$$L^{-1}[f(s+a)] = e^{-at}f(t)$$

Proof : We have proved in the first shifting theorem of Laplace transform that

$$L[e^{-at}f(t)] = F(s+a)$$

$\therefore \qquad L^{-1}\,[F(s + a)] = e^{-at}\,f(t)$

Hence $\qquad \boxed{L^{-1}\,[F(s + a)] = e^{-at}\,f(t)} \qquad\qquad \dots (27)$

Remark 1 : In words, this theorem states that the replacement of s by s + a in F(s) corresponds to multiplication of original function f(t) by e^{-at}.

Remark 2 : In practice, to obtain inverse Laplace transform of F(s + a), obtain that of F(s) first (i.e. first obtain $L^{-1}\,[F(s)]$) and then multiply it by e^{-at}.

ILLUSTRATION

Ex. 1 : *Obtain the inverse Laplace transforms of the following functions :*

$(i)\ \dfrac{1}{(s + 4)^6}\ (ii)\ \dfrac{s}{(s - 3)^5}\ (iii)\ \dfrac{3s + 1}{(s + 1)^4}\ (iv)\ \dfrac{s}{s^2 + 6s + 25}$

Sol. : (i) $\quad L^{-1}\left[\dfrac{1}{(s + 4)^6}\right] = e^{-4t}\,L^{-1}\left[\dfrac{1}{s^6}\right] \qquad$ [By the First Shifting Theorem]

$$= e^{-4t}\,\frac{t^5}{5!} = e^{-4t}\,\frac{t^5}{120} \qquad \left\{\text{By } L^{-1}\left[\frac{1}{s^{n+1}}\right] = \frac{t^n}{n!}\right\}$$

(ii) $\quad L^{-1}\left[\dfrac{s}{(s - 3)^5}\right] = L^{-1}\left[\dfrac{(s - 3) + 3}{(s - 3)^5}\right] = L^{-1}\left[\dfrac{1}{(s - 3)^4}\right] + 3\,L^{-1}\left[\dfrac{1}{(s - 3)^5}\right]$

$$= e^{3t}\,L^{-1}\left[\frac{1}{s^4}\right] + 3e^{3t}\,L^{-1}\left[\frac{1}{s^5}\right] = e^{3t}\,\frac{t^3}{3!} + 3e^{3t}\,\frac{t^4}{4!}$$

[By result (27)]

$$= e^{3t}\,t^3\left(\frac{1}{6} + \frac{t}{8}\right)$$

(iii) $\quad L^{-1}\left[\dfrac{3s + 1}{(s + 1)^4}\right] = L^{-1}\left[\dfrac{3\,(s + 1) - 2}{(s + 1)^4}\right] = 3\,L^{-1}\left[\dfrac{1}{(s + 1)^3}\right] - 2\,L^{-1}\left[\dfrac{1}{(s + 1)^4}\right]$

$$= 3e^{-t}\,L^{-1}\left[\frac{1}{s^3}\right] - 2e^{-t}\,L^{-1}\left[\frac{1}{s^4}\right] = 3\,e^{-t}\frac{t^2}{2!} - 2e^{-t}\frac{t^3}{3!}$$

[By result (27)]

$$= e^{-t}\,t^2\left(\frac{3}{2} - \frac{t}{3}\right)$$

(iv) $\quad L^{-1}\left[\dfrac{s}{s^2 + 6s + 25}\right] = L^{-1}\left[\dfrac{s + 3 - 3}{s^2 + 6s + 9 + 16}\right] = L^{-1}\left[\dfrac{(s + 3) - 3}{(s + 3)^2 + 4^2}\right]$

$$= L^{-1}\left[\frac{s + 3}{(s + 3)^2 + 4^2}\right] - 3\,L^{-1}\left[\frac{1}{(s + 3)^2 + 4^2}\right]$$

$$= e^{-3t} L^{-1}\left[\frac{s}{s^2 + 4^2}\right] - 3e^{-3t} L^{-1}\left[\frac{1}{s^2 + 4^2}\right]$$

$$= e^{-3t}(\cos 4t) - 3e^{-3t}\left(\frac{\sin 4t}{4}\right)$$

$$= e^{-3t}\left(\cos 4t - \frac{3}{4}\sin 4t\right)$$

(B) SECOND SHIFTING THEOREM

Theorem : If $L^{-1}[F(s)] = f(t)$, then

$$L^{-1}[e^{-as} F(s)] = \begin{cases} f(t-a), & t > a \\ 0, & t < a \end{cases}$$

Proof : We have proved in second shifting theorem of Laplace transform that

$$L[F(t)] = e^{-as} F(s), \text{ where } F(t) = \begin{cases} f(t-a), & t > a \\ 0, & t < a \end{cases}$$

$$\therefore \qquad L^{-1}[e^{-as} F(s)] = F(t) = \begin{cases} f(t-a), & t > a \\ 0, & t < a \end{cases}$$

Hence
$$\boxed{L^{-1}[e^{-as} F(s)] = \begin{cases} f(t-a), & t > a \\ 0, & t < a \end{cases}} \qquad \dots (28\ a)$$

Note : Since we can write F(t) in terms of Heaviside unit step functions as $f(t-a)\, U(t-a)$, we have the following equivalent result for the second shifting theorem.

$$\boxed{L^{-1}[e^{-as} F(s)] = f(t-a)\, U(t-a)} \qquad \dots (28\ b)$$

Remark 1 : In words, this theorem states that suppressing the factor e^{-as} in a transform requires that the inverse of what remains be shifted a units to the right and cut-off to the left of the point t = a.

Remark 2 : In practice, to obtain inverse Laplace transform of $e^{-as} F(s)$, we first obtain inverse transform of F(s), say f(t) (i.e. factor e^{-as} is dropped initially), then to account for the factor e^{-as}, replace t by t – a throughout in f(t) and multiply this result by $U(t-a)$.

ILLUSTRATIONS

Ex. : *Obtain the inverse Laplace transforms of the following functions :*

(i) $\dfrac{e^{-\pi s}}{s+a}$ *(ii)* $\dfrac{s\, e^{-4\pi s/5}}{s^2 + 25}$ *(iii)* $\dfrac{e^{-3s}}{(s-2)^4}$ *(iv)* $\dfrac{e^{-\pi s/2} + e^{-3\pi s/2}}{s^2 + 1}$.

Sol. : (i) We have $L^{-1}\left[\dfrac{1}{s+a}\right] = e^{-at}$ (Dropping $e^{-\pi s}$)

Hence by the second shifting theorem, with $a = \pi$, we get

$$L^{-1}\left[\frac{e^{-\pi s}}{s+a}\right] = \begin{cases} f(t-a), & t>a \\ 0, & t<a \end{cases} = \begin{cases} e^{-a(t-\pi)}, & t>\pi \\ 0, & t<\pi \end{cases}$$

or $$L^{-1}\left[\frac{e^{-\pi s}}{s+a}\right] = f(t-a)\,U(t-a) = e^{-a(t-\pi)}\,U(t-\pi)$$

(ii) We have $L^{-1}\left[\dfrac{s}{s^2+25}\right] = \cos 5t$

Hence by the second shifting theorem, with $a = 4\pi/5$, we get

$$L^{-1}\left[\frac{e^{-4\pi s/5}\,s}{s^2+25}\right] = \begin{cases} \cos 5\,(t-4\pi/5), & t>4\pi/5 \\ 0, & t<4\pi/5 \end{cases}$$

or $$L^{-1}\left[\frac{e^{-4\pi/5}\,s}{s^2+25}\right] = \cos 5\,(t-4\pi/5)\,U(t-4\pi/5)$$

(iii) We have $L^{-1}\left[\dfrac{1}{(s-2)^4}\right] = e^{2t}\,L^{-1}\left[\dfrac{1}{s^4}\right] = \dfrac{t^3}{3!}$ (By the First Shifting Theorem)

Hence by the second shifting theorem, with $a = 3$, we get

$$L^{-1}\left[\frac{e^{-3s}}{(s-2)^4}\right] = \begin{cases} e^{2(t-3)}\left[\dfrac{(t-3)^3}{6}\right], & t>3 \\ 0, & t<3 \end{cases}$$

or $$L^{-1}\left[\frac{e^{-3s}}{(s-2)^4}\right] = e^{2(t-3)}\left[\frac{(t-3)^3}{6}\right]U(t-3)$$

(iv) We have $L^{-1}\left[\dfrac{1}{s^2+1}\right] = \sin t$

$\therefore$ $$L^{-1}\left[\frac{e^{-\pi s/2}+e^{-3\pi s/2}}{s^2+1}\right] = L^{-1}\left[\frac{e^{-\pi s/2}}{s^2+1}\right] + L^{-1}\left[\frac{e^{-3\pi s/2}}{s^2+1}\right]$$

Hence by the second shifting theorem, we get

$$L^{-1}\left[\frac{e^{-\pi s/2}+e^{-3\pi s/2}}{s^2+1}\right] = \sin(t-\pi/2)\,U(t-\pi/2) + \sin(t-3\pi/2)\,U(t-3\pi/2)$$

$$= -\cos t\,U(t-\pi/2) + \cos t\,U(t-3\pi/2)$$

$$= \cos t\,[U(t-3\pi/2) - U(t-\pi/2)]$$

(C) CHANGE OF SCALE THEOREM

Theorem : If $L^{-1}[F(s)] = f(t)$, then

$$L^{-1}[F(ks)] = \frac{1}{k}\,f\!\left(\frac{t}{k}\right)$$

Proof : We have proved in change of scale theorem of Laplace transform that

$$L\,[f(at)] \;=\; \frac{1}{a}\,F\left(\frac{s}{a}\right)$$

$$\therefore \qquad L^{-1}\left[\frac{1}{a}\,F\left(\frac{s}{a}\right)\right] \;=\; f(at)$$

Putting $\dfrac{1}{a} = k,$ we get

$$L^{-1}\,[kF(ks)] \;=\; f\left(\frac{t}{k}\right)$$

Hence
$$\boxed{L^{-1}\,[F(ks)] \;=\; \frac{1}{k}\,f\left(\frac{t}{k}\right)} \qquad\qquad \dots (29)$$

ILLUSTRATIONS

Ex. 1 : Prove that $L^{-1}\left[\dfrac{s}{a^2\,s^2 + b^2}\right] = \dfrac{1}{a^2}\,\cos\left(\dfrac{b\,t}{a}\right)$

Sol. : We have $\quad L^{-1}\left[\dfrac{s}{s^2 + b^2}\right] \;=\; \cos bt$

$$\therefore \qquad L^{-1}\left[\frac{as}{(as)^2 + b^2}\right] \;=\; \frac{1}{a}\,\cos b\left(\frac{t}{a}\right) \qquad \text{[By Change of Scale Theorem]}$$

$$\therefore \qquad L^{-1}\left[\frac{s}{a^2 s^2 + b^2}\right] \;=\; \frac{1}{a^2}\,\cos\left(\frac{b\,t}{a}\right)$$

Ex. 2 : If $L^{-1}\left[\dfrac{1}{\sqrt{s^2 + 1}}\right] = J_0\,(t),$ then prove that $L^{-1}\left[\dfrac{1}{\sqrt{s^2 + a^2}}\right] = J_0\,(at)$

Sol. : Since $\qquad L^{-1}\left[\dfrac{1}{\sqrt{s^2 + 1}}\right] \;=\; J_0\,(t)$

$$\therefore \qquad L^{-1}\left[\frac{1}{\sqrt{(s/a)^2 + 1}}\right] \;=\; \frac{1}{1/a}\,J_0\left(\frac{t}{1/a}\right) \qquad \text{[By Change of Scale Theorem]}$$

$$\therefore \qquad L^{-1}\left[\frac{a}{\sqrt{s^2 + a^2}}\right] \;=\; a\,J_0\,(at)$$

$$\therefore \qquad L^{-1}\left[\frac{1}{\sqrt{s^2 + a^2}}\right] \;=\; J_0\,(at)$$

[Note : $J_0\,(t)$ is a Bessel's function**]**

(D) INVERSE LAPLACE TRANSFORMS OF DERIVATIVES

Statement : If $\quad L^{-1}\,[F(s)] \;=\; f(t),$ then

$$L^{-1}\left[\frac{d}{ds}\,F(s)\right] \;=\; -\,t\,f(t)$$

Proof : Since $\quad L[t\,f(t)] = -\dfrac{d}{ds}\,F(s)$

$\therefore \qquad L^{-1}\left[-\dfrac{d}{ds}\,F(s)\right] = t\,f(t) \quad \text{or} \quad L^{-1}\left[\dfrac{d}{ds}\,F(s)\right] = -t\,f(t)$

Hence,
$$\boxed{L^{-1}\left[\dfrac{d}{ds}\,F(s)\right] = -\,t\,f(t)} \qquad \dots (30a)$$

The generalization to higher order derivatives is

$$\boxed{L^{-1}\left[\dfrac{d^n}{ds^n}\,F(s)\right] = (-1)^n\,t^n\,f(t)} \qquad \dots (30b)$$

Remark 1 : The result (30 a) can be interpreted as the differentiation of the transform corresponds to multiplication of the function by $-t$.

Remark 2 : This theorem is often useful when the inverse of the transform cannot conveniently be found but the inverse of the derivative of the transform is known. In particular, when $F(s)$ involves logarithmic or inverse circular functions.

ILLUSTRATION

Ex. 1 : *Find the inverse Laplace transform of each of the following functions :*

$(i)\ cot^{-1}s \quad (ii)\ log\left(\dfrac{s+b}{s+a}\right) \quad (iii)\ \dfrac{s}{(s^2+a^2)^2}$

Sol. : (i) Let $\qquad L^{-1}\left[\cot^{-1}s\right] = f(t)$

$\therefore \qquad L^{-1}\left[\dfrac{d}{ds}\cot^{-1}s\right] = -t\,f(t) \qquad$ [By result (30a)]

$\therefore \qquad L^{-1}\left[-\dfrac{1}{s^2+1}\right] = -t\,f(t)$

$\therefore \qquad \sin t = t\,f(t)$

$\therefore \qquad \dfrac{\sin t}{t} = f(t)$

Hence $\qquad L^{-1}\left[\cot^{-1}s\right] = f(t) = \dfrac{\sin t}{t}$

(ii) Let $\qquad L^{-1}\left[\log\left(\dfrac{s+b}{s+a}\right)\right] = f(t)$

$\therefore \qquad L^{-1}\left[\log(s+b) - \log(s+a)\right] = f(t)$

$\therefore\ L^{-1}\left[\dfrac{d}{ds}\{\log(s+b) - \log(s+a)\}\right] = -t\,f(t) \qquad$ [By result (30a)]

$$\therefore \qquad L^{-1}\left[\frac{1}{s+b}-\frac{1}{s+a}\right] = -t\,f(t)$$

$$\therefore \qquad e^{-bt}-e^{-at} = -t\,f(t)$$

$$\text{or} \qquad \frac{e^{-at}-e^{-bt}}{t} = f(t)$$

$$\text{Hence} \qquad L^{-1}\left[\log\frac{s+b}{s+a}\right] = f(t) = \frac{e^{-at}-e^{-bt}}{t}$$

(iii) [**Note** : Since $\dfrac{d}{ds}\left(\dfrac{1}{s^2+a^2}\right) = \dfrac{-2s}{(s^2+a^2)^2}$ or $-\dfrac{1}{2}\dfrac{d}{ds}\left(\dfrac{1}{s^2+a^2}\right) = \dfrac{s}{(s^2+a^2)^2}$, we use

result (30a), to obtain required transform.]

$$\text{We know that,} \qquad L^{-1}\left[\frac{1}{s^2+a^2}\right] = \frac{\sin at}{a}$$

$$\therefore \qquad L^{-1}\left[\frac{d}{ds}\frac{1}{s^2+a^2}\right] = \frac{-t\sin at}{a}$$

$$\therefore \qquad L^{-1}\left[-\frac{2s}{(s^2+a^2)^2}\right] = \frac{-t\sin at}{a}$$

$$\text{or} \qquad L^{-1}\left[\frac{s}{(s^2+a^2)^2}\right] = \frac{t\sin at}{2a}$$

Another Method : Differentiating w.r.t. parameter a, we find

$$\frac{d}{da}\frac{s}{s^2+a^2} = \frac{-2as}{(s^2+a^2)^2}$$

$$\text{Hence} \qquad L^{-1}\left[\frac{d}{da}\left(\frac{s}{s^2+a^2}\right)\right] = L^{-1}\left[\frac{-2as}{(s^2+a^2)^2}\right]$$

$$\text{or} \qquad \frac{d}{da}L^{-1}\left[\frac{s}{s^2+a^2}\right] = -2a\,L^{-1}\left[\frac{s}{(s^2+a^2)^2}\right]$$

$$\text{or} \qquad \frac{d}{da}(\cos at) = -2a\,L^{-1}\left[\frac{s}{(s^2+a^2)^2}\right]$$

$$\text{or} \qquad -t\sin at = -2a\,L^{-1}\left[\frac{s}{(s^2+a^2)^2}\right]$$

$$\text{i.e.} \qquad L^{-1}\left[\frac{s}{(s^2+a^2)^2}\right] = \frac{t\sin at}{2a}$$

(E) INVERSE LAPLACE TRANSFORM OF INTEGRALS :

Theorem : If $\qquad L^{-1}[F(s)] = f(t)$, then

$$L^{-1}\left[\int_{s}^{\infty} F(s)\, ds\right] = \frac{f(t)}{t}$$

Proof : Since $\qquad L\left[\dfrac{f(t)}{t}\right] = \int_{s}^{\infty} F(s)\, ds$

Hence,

$$\boxed{L^{-1}\left[\int_{s}^{\infty} F(s)\, ds\right] = \frac{f(t)}{t}} \qquad \ldots (31a)$$

We can generalise the above result as

$$\boxed{L^{-1}\left[\int_{s}^{\infty}\int_{s}^{\infty} \ldots\ldots \int_{s}^{\infty} F(s)\, ds \cdot ds \ldots\ldots\ldots ds\right] = \frac{f(t)}{t^n}} \qquad \ldots (31b)$$

Remark 1 : The result (31a) can be interpreted as the integration of the transform of a function corresponds to division of the function by t.

Remark 2 : This theorem is often useful when the integral of a transform is simpler to work.

ILLUSTRATION

Ex. 1 : *Find the inverse Laplace transform of*

(i) $\dfrac{2s}{(s^2-4)^2}$ *(ii)* $\dfrac{2s+1}{(s^2+s+1)^2}$ *(iii)* $\dfrac{s}{(s^2+a^2)^2}$

Sol. : (i) Let $\qquad L^{-1}\left[\dfrac{2s}{(s^2-4)^2}\right] = f(t)$

$\therefore \qquad L^{-1}\left[\displaystyle\int_{s}^{\infty} \dfrac{2s}{(s^2-4)^2}\, ds\right] = \dfrac{f(t)}{t}$ $\qquad$ [By result (31a)]

$\therefore \qquad L^{-1}\left[\left\{-\dfrac{1}{(s^2-4)}\right\}_{s}^{\infty}\right] = \dfrac{f(t)}{t}$

$\therefore \qquad L^{-1}\left[\dfrac{1}{s^2-4}\right] = \dfrac{f(t)}{t}$

$\therefore \qquad \dfrac{\sinh 2t}{2} = \dfrac{f(t)}{t}$

Hence $\qquad L^{-1}\left[\dfrac{2s}{(s^2-4)^2}\right] = f(t) = \dfrac{t\,\sinh 2t}{2}$

(ii) Let

$$L^{-1}\left[\frac{2s+1}{(s^2+s+1)^2}\right] = f(t)$$

$$\therefore \quad L^{-1}\left[\int_s^\infty \frac{2s+1}{(s^2+s+1)^2}\,ds\right] = \frac{f(t)}{t} \qquad \text{[By result (31a)]}$$

$$\therefore \quad L^{-1}\left[\left\{-\frac{1}{(s^2+s+1)}\right\}_s^\infty\right] = \frac{f(t)}{t}$$

$$\therefore \quad L^{-1}\left[\frac{1}{s^2+s+1}\right] = \frac{f(t)}{t}$$

$$\text{or} \quad L^{-1}\left[\frac{1}{(s+1/2)^2+(\sqrt{3}/2)^2}\right] = \frac{f(t)}{t} \qquad \text{[Note this step]}$$

$$\therefore \quad e^{-t/2}\,L^{-1}\left[\frac{1}{s^2+\left(\sqrt{3}/2\right)^2}\right] = \frac{f(t)}{t} \qquad \text{[By the First Shifting Theorem]}$$

$$\therefore \quad e^{-t/2}\,\frac{2}{\sqrt{3}}\,\sin\frac{\sqrt{3}}{2}\,t = \frac{f(t)}{t}$$

$$\text{or} \quad \frac{2t}{\sqrt{3}}\,e^{-t/2}\,\sin\frac{\sqrt{3}}{2}\,t = f(t)$$

$$\text{Hence} \quad L^{-1}\left[\frac{2s+1}{(s^2+s+1)^2}\right] = f(t) = \frac{2t}{\sqrt{3}}\,e^{-t/2}\sin\frac{\sqrt{3}}{2}\,t$$

(iii) Let

$$L^{-1}\left[\frac{s}{(s^2+a^2)^2}\right] = f(t)$$

$$\therefore \quad L^{-1}\left[\int_s^\infty \frac{s}{(s^2+a^2)^2}\,ds\right] = \frac{f(t)}{t} \qquad \text{[By result (31 a)]}$$

$$\therefore \quad \frac{1}{2}\,L^{-1}\left[\left\{-\frac{1}{s^2+a^2}\right\}_s^\infty\right] = \frac{f(t)}{t}$$

$$\therefore \quad \frac{1}{2}\,L^{-1}\left[\frac{1}{s^2+a^2}\right] = \frac{f(t)}{t}$$

$$\therefore \quad \frac{1}{2}\left(\frac{\sin at}{a}\right) = \frac{f(t)}{t}$$

$$\text{Hence} \quad L^{-1}\left[\frac{s}{(s^2+a^2)^2}\right] = f(t) = \frac{t\sin at}{2a}$$

(F) MULTIPLICATION BY POWERS OF s :

Theorem : If $\qquad L^{-1}[F(s)] = f(t)$ and $f(0) = 0$, then

$$L^{-1}[s\,F(s)] = f'(t)$$

Proof : Since $\qquad L[f'(t)] = s\,F(s) - f(0)$

$$= s\,F(s) \qquad \left\{ \because\; f(0) = \lim_{t \to 0} f(t) = 0 \right.$$

$\therefore \qquad L^{-1}[s\,F(s)] = f'(t)$

Hence $\qquad \boxed{L^{-1}[s\,F(s)] = f'(t)\,,\; \text{if } f(0) = 0} \qquad\qquad \dots (32)$

Generalisations to $L^{-1}[s^n\,F(s)]$, $n = 2, 3, \dots\dots$, are possible.

Remark 1 : The result (32) can be interpreted as multiplication of the transform by s corresponds to differentiation of a function of t w.r. to t.

Remark 2 : If the Laplace transform of unknown function f(t) contains the factor s, the inverse of that transform can be found by dropping (suppressing) the factor s, determining the inverse of the remaining portion of the transform and finally differentiating that inverse with respect to t.

ILLUSTRATION

Ex. 1 : *Use result (32), to find*

(i) $L^{-1}\left[\dfrac{s}{s^2+4}\right]$, given that $L^{-1}\left[\dfrac{1}{s^2+4}\right] = \dfrac{\sin 2t}{2}$

(ii) $L^{-1}\left[\dfrac{s}{s^2-4}\right]$, given that $L^{-1}\left[\dfrac{1}{s^2-4}\right] = \dfrac{\sinh 2t}{2}$

Sol. : (i) Given that $\quad L^{-1}\left[\dfrac{1}{s^2+4}\right] = \dfrac{\sin 2t}{2}$

$\therefore \qquad L^{-1}\left[s \cdot \dfrac{1}{s^2+4}\right] = \dfrac{d}{dt}\left(\dfrac{\sin 2t}{2}\right) = \dfrac{2\cos 2t}{2} \qquad [\because\; \sin(0) = 0]$

Hence, $\qquad L^{-1}\left[\dfrac{s}{s^2+4}\right] = \cos 2t \qquad\qquad\qquad\quad [\text{By result (32)}]$

(ii) Given that $\qquad L^{-1}\left[\dfrac{1}{s^2-4}\right] = \dfrac{\sinh 2t}{2}$

$\therefore \qquad L^{-1}\left[s \cdot \dfrac{1}{s^2-4}\right] = \dfrac{d}{dt}\left(\dfrac{\sinh 2t}{2}\right) = \dfrac{2\cosh 2t}{2} \qquad [\because\; \sinh(0) = 0]$

Hence, $\qquad L^{-1}\left[\dfrac{s}{s^2-4}\right] = \cosh 2t \qquad\qquad\qquad\quad [\text{By result (32)}]$

(G) DIVISION BY s :

Theorem : If $\quad L^{-1}[F(s)] = f(t)$, then

$$L^{-1}\left[\frac{F(s)}{s}\right] = \int_0^t f(t)\, dt$$

Proof : Since $\quad L\left[\int_0^t f(t)\, dt\right] = \frac{F(s)}{s}$

Hence,

$$\boxed{L^{-1}\left[\frac{F(s)}{s}\right] = \int_0^t f(t)\, dt} \qquad \ldots (33)$$

Generalisations to $L^{-1}\left[\dfrac{F(s)}{s^n}\right]$, $n = 2, 3, \ldots$, are possible.

Remark 1 : The result (33) can be interpreted as the division of the transform by s corresponds to integration of function of t.

Remark 2 : If the Laplace transform contains the factor $\dfrac{1}{s}$, the inverse of that transform can be found by dropping (suppressing) the factor 1/s, determining the inverse of the remaining portion of the transform, and finally integrating that inverse with respect to t from 0 to t.

ILLUSTRATIONS

Ex. 1 : *Obtain the inverse Laplace transform of the following functions :*

(i) $\dfrac{1}{s\,(s + 2)}$ *(ii)* $\dfrac{1}{s\,(s^2 + 4)}$ *(iii)* $\dfrac{1}{s^3\,(s^2 + 1)}$

Sol. : (i) We have $\quad L^{-1}\left[\dfrac{1}{s+2}\right] = e^{-2t}$ $\qquad$ [Dropping the factor 1/s]

$$\therefore \quad L^{-1}\left[\frac{1}{s}\cdot\frac{1}{s+2}\right] = \int_0^t e^{-2t}\, dt = \left[\frac{e^{-2t}}{-2}\right]_0^t \qquad \text{[By result (33)]}$$

$$= \frac{1 - e^{-2t}}{2}.$$

(ii) We have $\quad L^{-1}\left[\dfrac{1}{s^2+4}\right] = \dfrac{\sin 2t}{2}$

$$\therefore \quad L^{-1}\left[\frac{1}{s}\cdot\frac{1}{s^2+4}\right] = \int_0^t \frac{\sin 2t}{2}\, dt = \frac{1}{2}\left[\frac{-\cos 2t}{2}\right]_0^t \qquad \text{[By result (33)]}$$

$$= \frac{1 - \cos 2t}{4} = \frac{1}{2}\sin^2 t$$

(iii) We have $\qquad L^{-1}\left[\dfrac{1}{s^2+1}\right] = \sin t$

$$\therefore \quad L^{-1}\left[\dfrac{1}{s}\cdot\dfrac{1}{s^2+1}\right] = \int_0^t \sin t\, dt = [-\cos t]_0^t = 1-\cos t \qquad \text{[By result (33)]}$$

$$= f(t)\ (\text{say}), \qquad \text{where } F(s) = \dfrac{1}{s\,(s^2+1)}$$

$$\therefore \quad L^{-1}\left[\dfrac{1}{s}\cdot F(s)\right] = \int_0^t f(t)\, dt = \int_0^t (1-\cos t)\ dt \qquad \text{[By result (33)]}$$

$$= [t-\sin t]_0^t = t-\sin t = \phi(t)\ (\text{say}),$$

$$\text{where } \Phi(s) = \dfrac{1}{s^2\,(s+1)}$$

$$\therefore \quad L^{-1}\left[\dfrac{1}{s}\cdot \Phi(s)\right] = \int_0^t \phi(t)\, dt = \int_0^t (t-\sin t)\, dt \qquad \text{[By result (33)]}$$

$$\text{Hence,}\ L^{-1}\left[\dfrac{1}{s^3\,(s^2+1)}\right] = \left[\dfrac{t^2}{2}+\cos t\right]_0^t = \dfrac{t^2}{2}+\cos t - 1$$

(H) USE OF CONVOLUTION THEOREM

If the function $H(s)$ can be expressed as product of two functions $F(s)$ and $G(s)$ whose inverses $f(t)$ and $g(t)$ respectively are known, then the inverse of the product $H(s) = F(s)\,G(s)$ can be obtained by using convolution theorem.

Theorem : If $\qquad L^{-1}\,[F(s)] = f(t),\ L^{-1}\,[G(s)] = g(t)$ and $H(s) = F(s)\,G(s)$, then

$$L^{-1}\,[H(s)] = L^{-1}\,[F(s)\,G(s)] = \int_0^t f(u)\,g(t-u)\,du = f(t) * g(t)$$

Proof : Since $\qquad L\,[f(t) * g(t)] = L\left[\int_0^t f(u)\,g(t-u)\,du\right]$

$$= F(s)\,G(s) = H(s)$$

Hence, $\qquad \boxed{L^{-1}\,[H(s)] = L^{-1}\,[F(s)\,G(s)] = \int_0^t f(u)\,g(t-u)\,du = f(t) * g(t)} \quad \text{... (9 a)}$

Note 1 : Since convolution of f(t) and g(t) is commutative, f(t) and g(t) are interchangeable in the above result.

$$\text{Hence} \quad \boxed{L^{-1}\,[H(s)] = L^{-1}\,[F(s)\,G(s)] = \int_0^t f(t-u)\,g(u)\,du = f(t) * g(t)} \quad \dots (34\,b)$$

Note 2 : If $L^{-1}\,[F(s)] = f(t)$ and $L^{-1}\,[G(s)] = L^{-1}\left[\dfrac{1}{s}\right] = 1$, then by result (34 a),

$$\text{we get} \qquad L^{-1}\left[\frac{F(s)}{s}\right] = \int_0^t f(u) \cdot 1\,du, \quad \text{(same as result (33))}$$

ILLUSTRATION

Ex. 1 : *Use the convolution theorem to find inverse Laplace transform of the following functions :*

$$(i)\ \frac{1}{s\,(s^2 + a^2)} \quad (ii)\ \frac{s^2}{(s^2 + a^2)\,(s^2 + b^2)},\ a \neq b \quad (iii)\ \frac{1}{(s+1)\,(s^2+1)} \quad (iv)\ \frac{1}{s\sqrt{s+4}}$$

Sol. : (i) We can write $\dfrac{1}{s\,(s^2+a^2)} = \dfrac{1}{s} \cdot \dfrac{1}{s^2+a^2}$.

$$\text{Let} \qquad F(s) = \frac{1}{s} \qquad \text{and} \qquad G(s) = \frac{1}{s^2+a^2},$$

$$\text{so that} \qquad f(t) = L^{-1}\left[\frac{1}{s}\right] = 1 \quad \text{and} \qquad g(t) = L^{-1}\left[\frac{1}{s^2+a^2}\right] = \frac{\sin at}{a}$$

Hence by convolution theorem, we have

$$L^{-1}\left[\frac{1}{s\,(s^2+a^2)}\right] = 1 * \frac{\sin at}{a} = \int_0^t 1 \cdot \frac{\sin au}{a}\,du \quad [\text{Using result (34b)}]$$

$$= \left[\frac{-\cos au}{a^2}\right]_0^t = \frac{1 - \cos at}{a^2}$$

(ii) We can write $\dfrac{s^2}{(s^2+a^2)\,(s^2+b^2)} = \dfrac{s}{s^2+a^2} \cdot \dfrac{s}{s^2+b^2}$

$$\text{Let} \qquad F(s) = \frac{s}{s^2+a^2} \qquad \text{and} \qquad G(s) = \frac{s}{s^2+b^2},$$

$$\text{so that} \qquad f(t) = L^{-1}\left[\frac{s}{s^2+a^2}\right] = \cos at \quad \text{and} \qquad g(t) = L^{-1}\left[\frac{s}{s^2+b^2}\right] = \cos bt$$

Hence by convolution theorem, we have

$$L^{-1}\left[\frac{s^2}{(s^2+a^2)\,(s^2+b^2)}\right] = \cos at * \cos bt = \int_0^t \cos au \cos b\,(t-u)\,du$$

$$= \frac{1}{2} \int_0^t [\cos(au + bt - bu) + \cos(au - bt + bu)]\, du$$

$$[\because\ 2\cos A \cos B = \cos(A + B) + \cos(A - B)]$$

$$= \frac{1}{2} \int_0^t [\cos\{(a - b)u + bt\} + \cos\{(a + b)u - bt\}]\, du$$

$$= \frac{1}{2} \left[\frac{\sin\{(a - b)u + bt\}}{a - b} + \frac{\sin\{(a + b)u - bt\}}{a + b} \right]_0^t$$

$$= \frac{1}{2} \left[\frac{\sin at - \sin bt}{a - b} + \frac{\sin at + \sin bt}{a + b} \right]$$

$$= \frac{a \sin at - b \sin bt}{a^2 - b^2}$$

(iii) We can write $\dfrac{1}{(s + 1)(s^2 + 1)} = \dfrac{1}{(s + 1)} \cdot \dfrac{1}{(s^2 + 1)}$.

Let $\qquad F(s) = \dfrac{1}{s + 1}$ $\qquad$ and $\quad G(s) = \dfrac{1}{s^2 + 1}$

so that $\quad f(t) = L^{-1}\left[\dfrac{1}{s + 1}\right] = e^{-t}$ $\qquad$ and $\quad g(t) = L^{-1}\left[\dfrac{1}{s^2 + 1}\right] = \sin t.$

Hence by convolution theorem, we have

$$L^{-1}\left[\frac{1}{(s + 1)(s^2 + 1)}\right] = e^{-t} * \sin t = \int_0^t e^{-u} \sin(t - u)\, du$$

$$\int_0^t e^{-u} \sin(t - u)\, du = \left[\frac{e^{-u}}{(-1)^2 + (-1)^2} (-\sin(t - u) + \cos(t - u)) \right]_{u=0}^{t}$$

$$= \frac{e^{-t}}{2}(0 + 1) - \frac{1}{2}(-\sin t + \cos t)$$

$$= \frac{1}{2}[\sin t - \cos t + e^{-t}]$$

(iv) We can write $\dfrac{1}{s\sqrt{s + 4}} = \dfrac{1}{s} \cdot \dfrac{1}{\sqrt{s + 4}}$.

Let
$$F(s) = \frac{1}{s} \quad \text{and} \quad G(s) = \frac{1}{\sqrt{s+4}}$$

so that
$$f(t) = 1 \quad \text{and} \quad g(t) = L^{-1}\left[\frac{1}{\sqrt{s+4}}\right] = \frac{e^{-4t}}{\sqrt{\pi\, t}}$$

Hence by convolution theorem, we have

$$L^{-1}\left[\frac{1}{s\sqrt{s+4}}\right] = 1 * \frac{e^{-4t}}{\sqrt{\pi\, t}} = \int_0^t \frac{e^{-4u}}{\sqrt{\pi u}}\, du$$

$$= \frac{1}{\sqrt{\pi}} \int_0^{2\sqrt{t}} e^{-y^2}\, dy$$

$$= \frac{1}{2}\, \mathrm{erf}\left(2\sqrt{t}\right)$$

Put
$$4u = y^2 \quad \therefore\ du = \frac{1}{2}\, y\, dy$$

u	0	t
y	0	$2\sqrt{t}$

In the following table 4.3, we have listed useful inverse Laplace transform theorems for ready reference.

Table 4.3 : of Theorems of Inverse Laplace Transform

	If $L^{-1}\,[F(s)] = f(t)$, then
A	$L^{-1}\,[F(s+a)] = e^{-at} f(t)$
B	$L^{-1}\,[e^{-as} F(s)] = f(t-a)\, U(t-a) = \begin{cases} f(t-a) & t > a \\ 0 & t < a \end{cases}$
C	$L^{-1}\,[F(ks)] = \dfrac{1}{k}\, f\!\left(\dfrac{t}{k}\right)$
D	$L^{-1}\left[\dfrac{d}{ds}\, F(s)\right] = -t\, f(t)$
E	$L^{-1}\left[\displaystyle\int_s^{\infty} F(s)\, ds\right] = \dfrac{f(t)}{t}$
F	$L^{-1}\,[s\, F(s)] = f\,'(t),\ \text{if}\ f(0) = 0$
G	$L^{-1}\left[\dfrac{F(s)}{s}\right] = \displaystyle\int_0^t f(u)\, du$
H	$L^{-1}\,[F(s)\, G(s)] = \displaystyle\int_0^t f(u)\, g(t-u)\, du = f(t) * g(t)$

4.14 METHOD III : USE OF PARTIAL FRACTIONS

In case where F(s) is a rational algebraic fraction, it is often convenient to find inverse Laplace transform by expressing F(s) in terms of partial fractions.

Consider a rational function $F(s) = \dfrac{N(s)}{D(s)}$, where N(s) and D(s) are polynomials with the degree of N(s) less than that of D(s) (i.e. proper fraction). Then $F(s) = \dfrac{N(s)}{D(s)}$ can be resolved into the sum of rational functions (called *partial fractions*) having the form $\dfrac{A}{(as+b)^r}$, $\dfrac{As+B}{(as^2+bs+c)^r}$, where r = 1, 2, 3 ……. By finding the inverse Laplace transform of each of the partial fractions, we can find $L^{-1}[F(s)]$.

Example 1 : When the denominator has non-repeated linear factors, we write

$$L^{-1}\,\frac{11s^2-2s+5}{(s-2)(2s-1)(s+1)} = \frac{A}{s-2} + \frac{B}{2s-1} + \frac{C}{s+1}$$

Example 2 : When the denominator has repeated linear factors, we write

$$\frac{2s-5}{(3s-4)(2s+1)^3} = \frac{A}{3s-2} + \frac{B}{(2s+1)} + \frac{C}{(2s+1)^2} + \frac{D}{(2s+1)^3}$$

Example 3 : When the denominator has non-repeated quadratic factors, we write

$$\frac{s^2+2s-4}{(s^2+2s+5)(s^2+2s+2)} = \frac{As+B}{(s^2+2s+5)} + \frac{Cs+D}{(s^2+2s+2)}$$

Example 4 : When the denominator has repeated quadratic factors, we write

$$\frac{3s^2-4s+2}{(s^2+2s+4)^2(s-5)} = \frac{As+B}{(s^2+2s+4)} + \frac{Cs+D}{(s^2+2s+4)^2} + \frac{E}{s-5}$$

The constants A, B, C etc., can be obtained by clearing of fractions (i.e. by multiplying both sides by the denominator of the given fraction) and equating coefficients of like powers of s on both sides or by using special methods [see solved examples].

For non-repeated linear factors, we have more simple method for finding the constants [see solved examples].

Note : Quadratic factor can also be written as product of linear factors with complex conjugate roots and apply above method.

ILLUSTRATION

Ex. 1 : *Using partial fractions, find the inverse Laplace transforms of :*

(i) $\dfrac{3s+7}{s^2-2s-3}$　(ii) $\dfrac{11s^2-2s+5}{(s-2)(2s-1)(s+1)}$

(iii) $\dfrac{21s-9}{(s+1)(s-2)^3}$　(iv) $\dfrac{3s+1}{(s-1)(s^2+1)}$　(v) $\dfrac{2s^2-1}{(s^2+1)(s^2+4)}$　(vi) $\dfrac{s}{s^4+4a^4}$

Sol. : (i) We have $\dfrac{3s+7}{s^2-2s-3} = \dfrac{3s+7}{(s-3)(s+1)}$.

Here denominator has non-repeated linear factors.

Let $\qquad \dfrac{3s+7}{(s-3)(s+1)} = \dfrac{A}{(s-3)} + \dfrac{B}{(s+1)}$ $\qquad\qquad$ ... (i)

Multiplying both sides of (i) by $(s-3)(s+1)$, we obtain

$$3s+7 = A(s+1) + B(s-3) = (A+B)s + A - 3B$$

Equating coefficients of like powers of s, we have

$$A+B = 3 \quad \text{and} \quad A-3B = 7$$

$\therefore \qquad\qquad A = 4 \quad \text{and} \quad B = -1$

Hence $\qquad \dfrac{3s+7}{(s-3)(s+1)} = \dfrac{4}{s-3} - \dfrac{1}{s+1}$

and $\qquad L^{-1}\left[\dfrac{3s+7}{(s-3)(s+1)}\right] = 4\,L^{-1}\left[\dfrac{1}{s-3}\right] - L^{-1}\left[\dfrac{1}{s+1}\right] = 4\,e^{3t} - e^{-t}$

Another Method : Multiplying both sides of (i) by $(s-3)(s+1)$, we have

$$3s+7 = A(s+1) + B(s-3)$$

Putting $s = 3$, we get $16 = A(4)$ $\qquad \therefore \quad A = 4$

Putting $s = -1$, we get $4 = B(-4)$ $\qquad \therefore \quad B = -1$ etc.

Note : It should be noted that the second method is less tedious. It can be used whenever the denominator has non-repeated linear factors.

(ii) We have $\dfrac{11s^2 - 2s + 5}{(s-2)(2s-1)(s+1)}$

Here the denominator has non-repeated linear factors.

Let $\qquad \dfrac{11s^2 - 2s + 5}{(s-2)(2s-1)(s+1)} = \dfrac{A}{s-2} + \dfrac{B}{(2s-1)} + \dfrac{C}{s+1}$ $\qquad$ ... (i)

Multiplying both sides of (i) by $(s-2)(2s-1)(s+1)$, we obtain

$$11s^2 - 2s + 5 = A(2s-1)(s+1) + B(s-2)(s+1) + C(s-2)(2s-1)$$

Putting $s = 2$, we get $\quad 11(4) - 2(2) + 5 = A(4-1)(2+1)$ $\qquad \therefore \qquad A = 5$

Putting $s = 1/2$, we get $\quad 11(1/4) - 2(1/2) + 5 = B(1/2-2)(1/2+1)$ $\quad \therefore \quad B = -3$

Putting $s = -1$, we get $\quad 11(-1) - 2(-1) + 5 = C(-3)(-3)$ $\qquad \therefore \qquad C = 2$

Hence $L^{-1}\left[\dfrac{11s^2 - 2s + 5}{(s-2)(2s-1)(s+1)}\right] = L^{-1}\left[\dfrac{5}{s-2} + \dfrac{-3}{2s-1} + \dfrac{2}{s+1}\right]$

$$= 5 L^{-1} \left[\frac{1}{s-2}\right] - \frac{3}{2} L^{-1} \left[\frac{1}{s-1/2}\right]$$

$$+ 2 L^{-1} \left[\frac{1}{s+1}\right]$$

$$= 5 e^{2t} - \frac{3}{2} e^{t/2} + 2e^{-t}$$

(iii) We have $\dfrac{21s - 9}{(s+1)(s-2)^3}$

Here the denominator has repeated linear factors.

Given : $F(s) = \dfrac{21s-9}{(s+1)(s-2)^3} = \dfrac{A}{s+1} + \dfrac{B}{s-2} + \dfrac{C}{(s-2)^2} + \dfrac{D}{(s-2)^3}$, (say)   ... (i)

$\therefore 21s - 9 = A(s-2)^3 + B(s+1)(s-2)^2 + C(s+1)(s-2) + D(s+1)$

$\qquad\qquad = A(s^3 - 2s^2 + 4s - 8) + B(s+1)(s^2 - 4s + 4) + C(s^2 - s - 2) + D(s+1)$

$\qquad\qquad = s^3[A+B] + s^2[-2A - 3B + C] + s[4A - C + D]$

$$+ [-8A + 4B - 2C + D]$$

Equating coefficients of identical powered terms of s from both sides

$\therefore$

$\qquad\qquad 0 = A + B$

$\qquad\qquad 0 = -2A - 3B + C$

$\qquad\qquad 21 = 4A - C + D$

and $\qquad -9 = -8A + 4B - 2C + D$

On solving simultaneously we get

$-A = B = C = -2$ and $D = 11$

$\therefore$ Equation (i) $\Rightarrow F(s) = \dfrac{2}{s+1} - \dfrac{2}{s-2} - \dfrac{2}{(s-2)^2} + \dfrac{11}{(s-2)^3}$ ... (ii)

Taking inverse Laplace transform using

$$L^{-1}[G(s+a)] = e^{-at} g(t) \quad \text{and} \quad L^{-1}\left[\frac{1}{s^n}\right] = \frac{t^{n-1}}{(n-1)!}$$

$\therefore$ Equation (ii) $\Rightarrow f(t) = L^{-1}\left[\dfrac{2}{s+1}\right] + L^{-1}\left\{\dfrac{-2}{s} - \dfrac{2}{s^2} + \dfrac{11}{s^3}\right\}_{s \to s-2}$

$$= 2e^{-t} + e^{2t}\left\{-2 - 2t + 11\frac{t^2}{2}\right\}$$

(iv) Here denominator has one linear factor and one quadratic factor.

Let $\qquad \dfrac{3s+1}{(s-1)(s^2+1)} = \dfrac{A}{s-1} + \dfrac{Bs+C}{s^2+1}$ ... (i)

Multiplying both sides of (i) by $(s-1)(s^2+1)$, we obtain

$$3s + 1 = A(s^2 + 1) + (Bs + C)(s - 1) \qquad \text{... (ii)}$$

Putting $s = 1$, we get $4 = A(2)$ $\therefore$ $A = 2$

To determine B and C, equate coefficients of like powers of s^2 and constant terms in (ii), then

$$0 = A + B \quad \text{and} \quad 1 = A - C$$

$$\therefore \quad B = -A = -2 \quad \text{and} \quad C = A - 1 = 1$$

Thus
$$L^{-1}\left[\frac{3s + 1}{(s - 1)(s^2 + 1)}\right] = L^{-1}\left[\frac{2}{s - 1} + \frac{-2s + 1}{s^2 + 1}\right]$$

$$= 2\,L^{-1}\left[\frac{1}{s - 1}\right] - 2\,L^{-1}\left[\frac{s}{s^2 + 1}\right] + L^{-1}\left[\frac{1}{s^2 + 1}\right]$$

$$= 2e^t - 2\cos t + \sin t$$

Another method : Since A = 2, we have from (i)

$$\frac{3s + 1}{(s - 1)(s^2 + 1)} = \frac{2}{s - 1} + \frac{Bs + C}{s^2 + 1} \qquad \qquad \text{... (iii)}$$

To determine B and C we can substitute two values for s, say s = 0 and s = 2 (for example) in (iii); then

$$-1 = -2 + C \qquad \text{and} \qquad \frac{7}{5} = 2 + \frac{2B + C}{5}$$

$$\therefore \qquad C = 1 \qquad \text{and} \qquad B = -2 \,...\, \text{etc.}$$

(v) We have $\dfrac{s}{s^4 + 4a^4}$. Here denominator has non-repeated quadratic factors.

Let
$$\frac{2s^2 - 1}{(s^2 + 1)(s^2 + 4)} = \frac{As + B}{(s^2 + 1)} + \frac{Cs + D}{(s^2 + 4)} \qquad \qquad \text{... (i)}$$

Multiplying both sides of (i) by $(s^2 + 1)(s^2 + 4)$, we have

$$2s^2 - 1 = (As + B)(s^2 + 4) + (Cs + D)(s^2 + 1)$$

$$= (A + C)s^3 + (B + D)s^2 + (4A + C)s + 4B + D \qquad \text{... (ii)}$$

To determine A, B, C and D, equate like powers of s^3, s^2, s and constant terms in (ii), then $A + C = 0$, $B + D = 2$, $4A + C = 0$, $4B + D = -1$

$\therefore$ A = 0 , B = –1, C = 0, D = 3.

Thus
$$L^{-1}\left[\frac{2s^2 - 1}{(s^2 + 1)(s^2 + 4)}\right] = L^{-1}\left[\frac{-1}{s^2 + 1} + \frac{3}{s^2 + 4}\right]$$

$$= -L^{-1}\left[\frac{1}{s^2 + 1}\right] + 3\,L^{-1}\left[\frac{1}{s^2 + 4}\right] = -\sin t + 3\,\frac{\sin 2t}{2}$$

Another method : Since fraction involves only even powers of s, we put $s^2 = p$ so that the given fraction becomes $\dfrac{2p - 1}{(p + 1)(p + 4)}$ which has only non-repeated linear factors in the denominator.

Let
$$\frac{2p - 1}{(p + 1)(p + 4)} = \frac{A}{p + 1} + \frac{B}{p + 4} \qquad \qquad \text{... (iii)}$$

Multiplying both sides of (iii) by $(p + 1)(p + 4)$, we get

$$2p - 1 = A(p + 4) + B(p + 1)$$

Putting $p = -1$, we get $-3 = A(3)$ $\therefore$ $A = -1$

Putting $p = -4$, we get $-9 = B(-3)$ $\therefore$ $B = 3$ ... etc.

(vi) Since $s^4 + 4a^4 = (s^2 + 2a^2)^2 - (2as)^2$

$$= (s^2 + 2as + 2a^2)(s^2 - 2as + 2a^2)$$

Let $\dfrac{s}{s^4 + 4a^4} = \dfrac{As + B}{(s^2 + 2as + 2a^2)} + \dfrac{Cs + D}{(s^2 - 2as + 2a^2)}$ ... (i)

Multiplying both sides by $s^4 + a^4$, we get

$$s = (As + B)(s^2 - 2as + 2a^2) + (Cs + D)(s^2 + 2as + 2a^2)$$

$$= (A + C)s^3 + (-2aA + B + 2aC + D)s^2$$

$$+ (2a^2 A - 2aB + 2a^2 C + 2aD)s + 2a^2 B + 2a^2 D \quad \text{... (ii)}$$

Equating coefficients of s^3, s^2, s and constant terms in (ii), we have

$A + C = 0$, $-2aA + B + 2aC + D = 0$, $2a^2 A - 2aB + 2a^2 C + 2aD = 1$,

$2a^2 B + 2a^2 D = 0$.

$\therefore$ $A = 0$, $B = \dfrac{-1}{4a}$, $C = 0$, $D = \dfrac{1}{4a}$

$\therefore$ $L^{-1}\left[\dfrac{s}{s^4 + 4a^4}\right] = \dfrac{1}{4a} L^{-1}\left[-\dfrac{1}{s^2 + 2as + 2a^2} + \dfrac{1}{s^2 - 2as + 2a^2}\right]$

$$= \dfrac{1}{4a}\left\{-L^{-1}\left[\dfrac{1}{(s + a)^2 + a^2}\right] + L^{-1}\left[\dfrac{1}{(s - a)^2 + a^2}\right]\right\}$$

$$= \dfrac{1}{4a}\left\{-e^{-at} L^{-1}\left[\dfrac{1}{s^2 + a^2}\right] + e^{at} L^{-1}\left[\dfrac{1}{s^2 + a^2}\right]\right\}$$

[By the First Shifting Theorem]

$$= \dfrac{1}{4a}\left\{-e^{-at}\left(\dfrac{\sin at}{a}\right) + e^{at}\left(\dfrac{\sin at}{a}\right)\right\}$$

$$= \dfrac{1}{2a^2} \sin at \left(\dfrac{e^{at} - e^{-at}}{2}\right) = \dfrac{1}{2a^2} \sin at \sinh at$$

Note : In certain cases, with a little insight, the partial fractions can be written directly.

Thus $\dfrac{s}{(s^2 + 2as + 2a^2)(s^2 - 2as + 2a^2)} = \dfrac{1}{4a}\left[\dfrac{-1}{s^2 + 2as + 2a^2} + \dfrac{1}{s^2 - 2as + 2a^2}\right]$

ILLUSTRATIONS ON THEOREMS OF INVERSE LAPLACE TRANSFORM AND PARTIAL FRACTIONS METHOD

Ex. 1 : *Find the inverse Laplace transforms of the following functions :*

$$(i) \quad \frac{3s+5}{(4s^2+12s+9)} \quad (ii) \ \frac{2s+5}{s^2+4s+13} \ (iii) \ \frac{s+7}{s^2+2s+2}$$

$$(iv) \quad \frac{5s-2}{3s^2+4s+8} \quad (v) \ \frac{s-1}{s^2-6s+25} \quad (vi) \ \frac{1}{\sqrt{7s+6}}$$

Sol. : (i) $L^{-1}\left[\dfrac{3s+5}{4s^2+12s+9}\right] = L^{-1}\left[\dfrac{3\,(s+3/2)-9/2+5}{4\,(s^2+3s+9/4)}\right]$

$$= \frac{1}{4}\,L^{-1}\left[\frac{3\,(s+3/2)+1/2}{(s+3/2)^2}\right]$$

$$= \frac{3}{4}\,L^{-1}\left[\frac{1}{(s+3/2)}\right] + \frac{1}{8}\,L^{-1}\left[\frac{1}{(s+3/2)^2}\right]$$

$$= \frac{3}{4}\,e^{-3t/2}\,L^{-1}\left[\frac{1}{s}\right] + \frac{1}{8}\,e^{-3t/2}\,L^{-1}\left[\frac{1}{s^2}\right]$$

[By the First Shifting Theorem]

$$= \frac{3}{4}\,e^{-3t/2}\,(1) + \frac{1}{8}\,e^{-3t/2}\,(t) = \frac{e^{-3t/2}}{4}\left(3+\frac{t}{2}\right)$$

(ii) $\quad L^{-1}\left[\dfrac{2s+5}{s^2+4s+13}\right] = L^{-1}\left[\dfrac{2\,(s+2)-4+5}{(s+2)^2+3^2}\right] = L^{-1}\left[\dfrac{2\,(s+2)+1}{(s+2)^2+3^2}\right]$

$$= 2\,L^{-1}\left[\frac{(s+2)}{(s+2)^2+3^2}\right] + L^{-1}\left[\frac{1}{(s+2)^2+3^2}\right]$$

$$= 2\,e^{-2t}\,L^{-1}\left[\frac{s}{s^2+3^2}\right] + e^{-2t}\,L^{-1}\left[\frac{1}{s^2+3^2}\right]$$

$$= 2\,e^{-2t}\,(\cos 3t) + e^{-2t}\left(\frac{\sin 3t}{3}\right)$$

$$= e^{-2t}\left(2\cos 3t + \frac{1}{3}\sin 3t\right)$$

(iii) $\quad L^{-1}\left[\dfrac{s+7}{s^2+2s+2}\right] = L^{-1}\left[\dfrac{(s+1)+6}{(s+1)^2+1}\right]$

$$= L^{-1}\left[\frac{s+1}{(s+1)^2+1}\right] + 6\,L^{-1}\left[\frac{1}{(s+1)^2+1}\right]$$

$$= e^{-t}\,L^{-1}\left[\frac{s}{s^2+1}\right] + 6e^{-t}\,L^{-1}\left[\frac{1}{s^2+1}\right]$$

$$= e^{-t}\,(\cos t) + 6\,e^{-t}\,(\sin t) = e^{-t}\,(\cos t + 6\sin t)$$

(iv)　$L^{-1}\left[\dfrac{5s-2}{3s^2+4s+8}\right] = L^{-1}\left[\dfrac{5s-2}{3\left(s^2+\dfrac{4}{3}s+\dfrac{8}{3}\right)}\right]$

$$= \dfrac{1}{3}\ L^{-1}\left[\dfrac{5\,(s+2/3)-10/3-2}{(s+2/3)^2+20/9}\right]$$

$$= \dfrac{5}{3}\ L^{-1}\left[\dfrac{(s+2/3)}{(s+2/3)^2+\left(2\sqrt{5}/3\right)^2}\right] - \dfrac{16}{9}\ L^{-1}\left[\dfrac{1}{(s+2/3)^2+\left(2\sqrt{5}/3\right)^2}\right]$$

$$= \dfrac{5}{3}\ e^{-2t/3}\ L^{-1}\left[\dfrac{s}{s^2+\left(2\sqrt{5}/3\right)^2}\right] - \dfrac{16}{9}\ e^{-2t/3}\ L^{-1}\left[\dfrac{1}{s^2+\left(2\sqrt{5}/3\right)^2}\right]$$

$$= \dfrac{5}{3}\ e^{-2t/3}\left(\cos\dfrac{2\sqrt{5}}{3}\ t\right) - \dfrac{16}{9}\ e^{-2t/3}\left(\dfrac{3}{2\sqrt{5}}\sin\dfrac{2\sqrt{5}}{3}\ t\right)$$

$$= e^{-2t/3}\left(\dfrac{5}{3}\cos\dfrac{2\sqrt{5}\,t}{3} - \dfrac{8}{3\sqrt{5}}\sin\dfrac{2\sqrt{5}\,t}{3}\right).$$

(v)　$L^{-1}\left[\dfrac{s-1}{s^2-6s+25}\right] = L^{-1}\left[\dfrac{(s-3)+3-1}{(s-3)^2+16}\right] = L^{-1}\left[\dfrac{(s-3)+2}{(s-3)^2+4^2}\right]$

$$= L^{-1}\left[\dfrac{(s-3)}{(s-3)^2+4^2}\right] + 2\,L^{-1}\left[\dfrac{1}{(s-3)^2+4^2}\right]$$

$$= e^{3t}\ L^{-1}\left[\dfrac{s}{s^2+4^2}\right] + 2\,e^{3t}\ L^{-1}\left[\dfrac{1}{s^2+4^2}\right]$$

$$= e^{3t}\,(\cos 4t) + 2e^{3t}\left(\dfrac{\sin 4t}{4}\right) = e^{3t}\left(\cos 4t + \dfrac{1}{2}\sin 4t\right)$$

(vi)　$L^{-1}\left[\dfrac{1}{\sqrt{7s+6}}\right] = \dfrac{1}{\sqrt{7}}\ L^{-1}\left[\dfrac{1}{\sqrt{s+6/7}}\right] = \dfrac{1}{\sqrt{7}}\ L^{-1}\left[\dfrac{1}{(s+6/7)^{1/2}}\right]$

$$= \dfrac{1}{\sqrt{7}}\ e^{-6t/7}\,L^{-1}\left[\dfrac{1}{s^{1/2}}\right] = \dfrac{1}{\sqrt{7}}\ e^{-6t/7}\dfrac{t^{1/2-1}}{\overline{|1/2}}$$

$$= \dfrac{e^{-6t/7}}{\sqrt{7\pi\,t}} \qquad \left\{\because\ L^{-1}\left[\dfrac{1}{s^n}\right]=\dfrac{t^{n-1}}{\overline{|n}}\ \text{and}\ \overline{|1/2}=\sqrt{\pi}\right\}$$

Ex. 2 : *Obtain the inverse Laplace transforms of the following functions :*

(i) $\dfrac{e^{-as}}{(s+b)^{5/2}}$　(ii) $\dfrac{e^{3-2s}}{(s+4)^{5/2}}$　(iii) $\dfrac{e^{-3s}}{s^2+8s+25}$　(iv) $\dfrac{e^{-2s}}{\sqrt{s+5}}$

Sol. : (i)　We have

$$L^{-1}\left[\dfrac{1}{(s+b)^{5/2}}\right] = e^{-bt}\ L^{-1}\left[\dfrac{1}{s^{5/2}}\right] = e^{-bt}\dfrac{t^{3/2}}{\overline{|5/2}} \qquad \text{(Dropping } e^{-as})$$

$$= \dfrac{4}{3\sqrt{\pi}}\ e^{-bt}\ t^{3/2}$$

Hence by the second shifting theorem, we get

$$L^{-1}\left[\frac{e^{-as}}{(s+b)^{5/2}}\right] = \begin{cases} \dfrac{4}{3\sqrt{\pi}}\, e^{b\,(t-a)}\,(t-a)^{3/2} & ,\quad t>a \\[2ex] 0 & ,\quad t<a \end{cases}$$

$$= \left\{\frac{4}{3\sqrt{\pi}}\, e^{b\,(t-a)}\,(t-a)^{3/2}\right\}\, U(t-a)$$

(ii) We can write $L^{-1}\left[\dfrac{e^{3-2s}}{(s+4)^{5/2}}\right] = e^3\, L^{-1}\left[\dfrac{e^{-2s}}{(s+4)^{5/2}}\right]$

Also we have $L^{-1}\left[\dfrac{1}{(s+4)^{5/2}}\right] = \dfrac{4\, e^{-4t}\, t^{3/2}}{3\sqrt{\pi}}$

Hence by the second shifting theorem, with a = 2, we get

$$L^{-1}\left[\frac{e^{3-2s}}{(s+4)^{5/2}}\right] = \begin{cases} e^3\left[\dfrac{4}{3\sqrt{\pi}}\, e^{-4\,(t-2)}\,(t-2)^{3/2}\right] & ,\quad t>2 \\[2ex] 0 & ,\quad t<2 \end{cases}$$

$$= e^3\left\{\frac{4}{3\sqrt{\pi}}\, e^{-4\,(t-2)}\,(t-2)^{3/2}\right\}\, U(t-2)$$

(iii) We have

$$L^{-1}\left[\frac{1}{s^2+8s+25}\right] = L^{-1}\left[\frac{1}{(s+4)^2+3^2}\right] = e^{-4t}\, L^{-1}\left[\frac{1}{s^2+3^2}\right]$$

$$= e^{-4t}\left(\frac{\sin 3t}{3}\right) = \frac{1}{3}\, e^{-4t}\sin 3t$$

Hence by the second shifting theorem, with a = 3, we get

$$L^{-1}\left[\frac{e^{-3s}}{s^2+8s+25}\right] = \begin{cases} \dfrac{1}{3}\, e^{-4\,(t-3)}\sin 3\,(t-3) & ,\quad t>3 \\[2ex] 0 & ,\quad t<3 \end{cases}$$

$$= \left\{\frac{1}{3}\, e^{-4\,(t-3)}\sin 3\,(t-3)\right\}\, U(t-3)$$

(iv) We have

$$L^{-1}\left[\frac{1}{\sqrt{s}+5}\right] = e^{-5t}\, L^{-1}\left[\frac{1}{\sqrt{s}}\right] = e^{-5t}\left(\frac{t^{-1/2}}{\lceil 1/2}\right)$$

$$= \frac{e^{-5t}}{\sqrt{\pi t}}$$

Hence by the second shifting theorem, with a = 2, we get

$$L^{-1}\left[\frac{e^{-2s}}{\sqrt{s+5}}\right] = \begin{cases} \dfrac{e^{-5(t-2)}}{\sqrt{\pi(t-2)}} & , \ t > 2 \\ 0 & , \ t < 2 \end{cases}$$

$$= \frac{e^{-5(t-2)}}{\sqrt{\pi(t-2)}}\, U(t-2)$$

Ex. 3 : If $L^{-1}\left[\dfrac{e^{-1/s}}{s^{1/2}}\right] = \dfrac{\cos 2\sqrt{t}}{\sqrt{\pi t}}$, find $L^{-1}\left[\dfrac{e^{-a/s}}{s^{1/2}}\right]$ where $a > 0$.

Sol. : Given that

$$L^{-1}\left[\frac{e^{-1/s}}{s^{1/2}}\right] = \frac{\cos 2\sqrt{t}}{\sqrt{\pi t}}$$

$$\therefore \quad L^{-1}\left[\frac{e^{-1/ks}}{(ks)^{1/2}}\right] = \frac{1}{k}\frac{\cos 2\sqrt{t/k}}{\sqrt{\pi(t/k)}} = \frac{1}{\sqrt{k}}\frac{\cos 2\sqrt{t/k}}{\sqrt{\pi t}} \qquad \text{[By the Change of Scale Theorem]}$$

$$\text{or} \qquad L^{-1}\left[\frac{e^{-1/ks}}{s^{1/2}}\right] = \frac{\cos 2\sqrt{t/k}}{\sqrt{\pi t}}$$

Putting $k = 1/a$, we get

$$L^{-1}\left[\frac{e^{-as}}{s^{1/2}}\right] = \frac{\cos 2\sqrt{at}}{\sqrt{\pi t}} \ .$$

Ex. 4 : *Find the inverse Laplace transforms of the following :*

(i) $\cot^{-1}\left(\dfrac{s-2}{3}\right)$ *(ii)* $\log\left(1+\dfrac{a^2}{s^2}\right)$

(iii) $\log\left(\dfrac{s^2+a^2}{s^2+b^2}\right)$ *(iv)* $\dfrac{s+1}{(s^2+2s+1)^2}$

Sol. : (i) Let $L^{-1}\left[\cot^{-1}\left(\dfrac{s-2}{3}\right)\right] = f(t)$

$$\therefore \qquad L^{-1}\left[\frac{d}{ds}\cot^{-1}\left(\frac{s-2}{3}\right)\right] = -t\,f(t) \qquad\qquad \text{[By result (30 a)]}$$

$$\therefore \qquad L^{-1}\left[\frac{-1/3}{1+(s-2)^2/3^2}\right] = -t\,f(t) \qquad \left\{ \because \ \cot^{-1}\left(\frac{s-2}{3}\right) = \frac{\pi}{2} - \tan^{-1}\left(\frac{s-2}{3}\right)\right.$$

$$\text{or} \qquad L^{-1}\left[\frac{-3}{(s-2)^2+9}\right] = -t\,f(t)$$

$$\therefore \qquad e^{2t}\, L^{-1}\left[\frac{3}{s^2+9}\right] = -t\,f(t) \qquad \text{[By the First Shifting Theorem]}$$

$$\therefore \qquad e^{2t}\,(\sin 3t) = t\,f(t)$$

Hence $\qquad L^{-1}\left[\cot^{-1}\left(\dfrac{s-2}{3}\right)\right] \;=\; f(t) \;=\; \dfrac{e^{2t}\sin 3t}{t}$

(ii) Let $\qquad L^{-1}\left[\log\left(1+\dfrac{a^2}{s^2}\right)\right] \;=\; f(t)$

$\therefore \qquad L^{-1}\left[\dfrac{d}{ds}\,\log\left(\dfrac{s^2+a^2}{s^2}\right)\right] \;=\; -t\,f(t)$

or $\;L^{-1}\left[\dfrac{d}{ds}\,\{\log(s^2+a^2)-\log s^2\}\right] \;=\; -t\,f(t)$

$\therefore \qquad L^{-1}\left[\dfrac{2s}{s^2+a^2}-\dfrac{2}{s}\right] \;=\; -t\,f(t)$

$\therefore \qquad 2\,(\cos at - 1) \;=\; -t\,f(t)$

or $\qquad \dfrac{2\,(1-\cos at)}{t} \;=\; f(t)$

Hence $\qquad L^{-1}\left[\log\left(1+\dfrac{a^2}{s^2}\right)\right] \;=\; \dfrac{2\,(1-\cos at)}{t}$

(iii) Let $\qquad L^{-1}\left[\log\left(\dfrac{s^2+a^2}{s^2+b^2}\right)\right] \;=\; f(t)$

$\therefore\; L^{-1}\left[\dfrac{d}{ds}\,\{\log(s^2+a^2)-\log(s^2+b^2)\}\right] \;=\; -t\,f(t)$

$\therefore \qquad L^{-1}\left[\dfrac{2s}{s^2+a^2}-\dfrac{2s}{s^2+b^2}\right] \;=\; -t\,f(t)$

$\therefore \qquad 2\,(\cos at - \cos bt) \;=\; -t\,f(t)$

or $\qquad \dfrac{2\,(\cos bt - \cos at)}{t} \;=\; f(t)$

Hence $\qquad L^{-1}\left[\log\left(\dfrac{s^2+a^2}{s^2+b^2}\right)\right] \;=\; \dfrac{2\,(\cos bt - \cos at)}{t}$

(iv) [**Note :** Since $\dfrac{d}{ds}\left(\dfrac{1}{s^2+2s+1}\right)=\dfrac{-2\,(s+1)}{(s^2+2s+1)^2}$ or $-\dfrac{1}{2}\dfrac{d}{ds}\left(\dfrac{1}{s^2+2s+1}\right)=\dfrac{s+1}{(s^2+2s+1)^2}$,

we use result (30a), to obtain required transform.]

We know that $\quad L^{-1}\left[\dfrac{1}{s^2+2s+1}\right] \;=\; L^{-1}\left[\dfrac{1}{(s+1)^2}\right] = e^{-t}L^{-1}\left[\dfrac{1}{s^2}\right] = e^{-t}t$

$\therefore \qquad L^{-1}\left[\dfrac{d}{ds}\left(\dfrac{1}{s^2+2s+1}\right)\right] \;=\; -t\,(e^{-t}t)$

$\therefore \qquad L^{-1}\left[\dfrac{-2\,(s+1)}{(s^2+2s+1)^2}\right] \;=\; -t\,(e^{-t}t)$

or $\qquad L^{-1}\left[\dfrac{s+1}{(s^2+2s+1)^2}\right] \;=\; \dfrac{1}{2}\,t^2\,e^{-t}$

Ex. 5 : *Find the inverse Laplace transforms of the following functions :*

(i) $\dfrac{s+2}{(s^2+4s+5)^2}$ (ii) $\dfrac{s+1}{(s^2+2s+2)^2}$ (iii) $\dfrac{s^2}{(s+a)^3}$

Sol. : (i) Let $\quad L^{-1}\left[\dfrac{s+2}{(s^2+4s+5)^2}\right] = f(t)$

$\therefore \quad L^{-1}\left[\displaystyle\int_s^\infty \dfrac{s+2}{(s^2+4s+5)^2}\,ds\right] = \dfrac{f(t)}{t}$ $\qquad$ [By result (31 a)]

$\therefore \quad L^{-1}\left[\left\{-\dfrac{1}{2(s^2+4s+5)}\right\}_s^\infty\right] = \dfrac{f(t)}{t}$

$\therefore \quad \dfrac{1}{2}\,L^{-1}\left[\dfrac{1}{s^2+4s+5}\right] = \dfrac{f(t)}{t}$

or $\quad \dfrac{1}{2}\,L^{-1}\left[\dfrac{1}{(s+2)^2+1}\right] = \dfrac{f(t)}{t}$

$\therefore \quad \dfrac{1}{2}\,e^{-2t}\,L^{-1}\left[\dfrac{1}{s^2+1}\right] = \dfrac{f(t)}{t}$ $\qquad$ [By the First Shifting Theorem]

$\therefore \quad \dfrac{1}{2}\,e^{-2t}\,(\sin t) = \dfrac{f(t)}{t}$

Hence $\quad L^{-1}\left[\dfrac{s+2}{(s^2+4s+5)^2}\right] = f(t) = \dfrac{1}{2}\,t\,e^{-2t}\sin t$

(ii) Let $\quad L^{-1}\left[\dfrac{s+1}{(s^2+2s+2)^2}\right] = f(t)$

$\therefore \quad L^{-1}\left[\displaystyle\int_s^\infty \dfrac{s+1}{(s^2+2s+2)^2}\,ds\right] = \dfrac{f(t)}{t}$

$\therefore \quad L^{-1}\left[\left\{-\dfrac{1}{2(s^2+2s+2)}\right\}_s^\infty\right] = \dfrac{f(t)}{t}$

$\therefore \quad L^{-1}\left[\dfrac{1}{2}\dfrac{1}{(s^2+2s+2)}\right] = \dfrac{f(t)}{t}$

$\therefore \quad \dfrac{1}{2}\,L^{-1}\left[\dfrac{1}{(s+1)^2+1}\right] = \dfrac{f(t)}{t}$

$\therefore \quad \dfrac{1}{2}\,e^{-t}\left[\dfrac{1}{s^2+1}\right] = \dfrac{f(t)}{t}$

$\therefore \quad \dfrac{1}{2}\,e^{-t}\sin t = \dfrac{f(t)}{t}$

Hence $\qquad L^{-1}\left[\dfrac{s+1}{(s^2+2s+2)^2}\right] = f(t) = \dfrac{1}{2}\, t\, e^{-t} \sin t$

(iii) We have

$$L^{-1}\left[\dfrac{1}{(s+a)^3}\right] = e^{-at} L^{-1}\left[\dfrac{1}{s^3}\right] = e^{-at}\,\dfrac{t^2}{2} \qquad \text{[By the First Shifting Theorem]}$$

$$\therefore \qquad L^{-1}\left[s\,\dfrac{1}{(s+a)^3}\right] = \dfrac{d}{dt}\left(\dfrac{1}{2}\,e^{-at}\,t^2\right) = \dfrac{1}{2}\,e^{-at}\,(2t - at^2) \qquad \text{[By result (32)]}$$

$$= \phi\,(t)\ (\text{say}), \qquad \text{where}\ \ \Phi(s) = \dfrac{s}{(s+a)^2}\ \text{and}\ \ \phi(0) = 0$$

$$\therefore \qquad L^{-1}\,[s\,\Phi(s)] = \dfrac{d}{dt}\,\phi(t) = \dfrac{d}{dt}\left\{\dfrac{1}{2}\,e^{-at}\,(2t - at^2)\right\}$$

$$= \dfrac{1}{2}\,e^{-at}\,(2 - 4\,at + a^2\,t^2)$$

Hence, $\qquad L^{-1}\left[\dfrac{s^2}{(s+a)^3}\right] = e^{-at}\left(1 - 2at + \dfrac{1}{2}\,a^2\,t^2\right)$

Ex. 6 : *Find the inverse of each of the following transforms :*

(i) $\dfrac{1}{s^2\,(s+1)}$ $\qquad$ (ii) $\dfrac{s^2+2}{s\,(s^2+4)}$ $\qquad$ (iii) $\dfrac{1}{s\,(s+1)^3}$

Sol. : (i) We have

$$L^{-1}\left[\dfrac{1}{s+1}\right] = e^{-t} \qquad\qquad \text{[Dropping the factor } 1/s^2]$$

$$\therefore \qquad L^{-1}\left[\dfrac{1}{s}\cdot\dfrac{1}{s+1}\right] = \int_0^t e^{-t}\,dt = [-e^{-t}]_0^t = 1 - e^{-t} \qquad \text{[By result (33)]}$$

$$= \phi(t)\ (\text{say}), \qquad \text{where}\ \Phi(s) = \dfrac{1}{s\,(s+1)}$$

$$\therefore \qquad L^{-1}\left[\dfrac{1}{s}\cdot\Phi(s)\right] = \int_0^t \phi(t)\,dt = \int_0^t (1 - e^{-t})\,dt \qquad \text{[By result (33)]}$$

Hence, $\qquad L^{-1}\left[\dfrac{1}{s^2\,(s+1)}\right] = [t + e^{-t}]_0^t = t + e^{-t} - 1$

(ii) $\qquad L^{-1}\left[\dfrac{s^2+2}{s\,(s^2+4)}\right] = L^{-1}\left[\dfrac{s^2+4-2}{s\,(s^2+4)}\right] = L^{-1}\left[\dfrac{1}{s} - \dfrac{2}{s\,(s^2+4)}\right]$

$$= L^{-1}\left[\dfrac{1}{s}\right] - L^{-1}\left[\dfrac{2}{s\,(s^2+4)}\right] = 1 - \int_0^t L^{-1}\left[\dfrac{2}{s^2+4}\right]\,dt$$

$$\text{[By result (33)]}$$

$$= 1 - \int_0^t \sin 2t \, dt = 1 - \left[-\frac{\cos 2t}{2}\right]_0^t$$

$$= 1 + \frac{\cos 2t}{2} - \frac{1}{2} = \frac{1 + \cos 2t}{2} = \cos^2 t$$

(iii) We have

$$L^{-1}\left[\frac{1}{(s+1)^3}\right] = e^{-t} L^{-1}\left[\frac{1}{s^3}\right] = e^{-t} \frac{t^2}{2}$$

$$\therefore \quad L^{-1}\left[\frac{1}{s} \cdot \frac{1}{(s+1)^3}\right] = \frac{1}{2} \int_0^t e^{-t} t^2 \, dt = \frac{1}{2}\left[t^2(-e^{-t}) - (2t)(e^{-t}) + (2)(-e^{-t})\right]_0^t$$

$$= \frac{1}{2}\left[(-t^2 e^{-t} - 2t \, e^{-t} - 2e^{-t}) - (-2)\right] = 1 - e^{-t}\left(\frac{t^2}{2} + t + 1\right)$$

Ex. 7 : *Find the inverse Laplace transforms of each of the following functions :*

(i) $\dfrac{s^2}{(s^2 + a^2)^2}$ (ii) $\dfrac{1}{(s^2 + a^2)^2}$ (iii) $\dfrac{1}{s} \, log\left(\dfrac{s+3}{s+2}\right)$ (iv) $\dfrac{1}{s} \, log\left(\dfrac{s^2 + a^2}{s^2 + b^2}\right)$.

Sol. : (i) We have

$$L^{-1}\left[\frac{1}{s^2 + a^2}\right] = \frac{\sin at}{a}$$

$$\therefore \quad L^{-1}\left[\frac{d}{ds}\frac{1}{s^2 + a^2}\right] = \frac{-t \sin at}{a} \qquad \text{[By result (30 a)]}$$

$$\therefore \quad L^{-1}\left[-\frac{2s}{(s^2 + a^2)^2}\right] = \frac{-t \sin at}{a}$$

or $$\quad L^{-1}\left[\frac{s}{(s^2 + a^2)^2}\right] = \frac{1}{2a} \, t \sin at$$

$$\therefore \quad L^{-1}\left[s \cdot \frac{s}{(s^2 + a^2)^2}\right] = \frac{1}{2a}\frac{d}{dt}(t \sin at)$$

$$\text{[By result (32) and } \because (t \sin at)_{t=0} = 0]$$

$$= \frac{1}{2a}(\sin at + at \cos at)$$

Hence $$\quad L^{-1}\left[\frac{s^2}{(s^2 + a^2)^2}\right] = \frac{1}{2a}(\sin at + at \cos at)$$

(ii) We have $$\quad L^{-1}\left[\frac{1}{s^2 + a^2}\right] = \frac{\sin at}{a}$$

$$\therefore \quad L^{-1}\left[\frac{d}{ds}\frac{1}{s^2 + a^2}\right] = \frac{-t \sin at}{a} \qquad \text{[By result (30 a)]}$$

$$\therefore \quad L^{-1}\left[\frac{s}{(s^2 + a^2)^2}\right] = \frac{1}{2a} \, t \sin at$$

$$\therefore \quad L^{-1}\left[\frac{1}{s} \cdot \frac{s}{(s^2 + a^2)^2}\right] = \frac{1}{2a} \int_0^t t \sin at \, dt \qquad \text{[By result (33)]}$$

$$= \frac{1}{2a}\left[t\left(-\frac{\cos at}{a}\right) - (1)\left(-\frac{\sin at}{a^2}\right)\right]_0^t$$

$$= \frac{1}{2a}\left(\frac{\sin at}{a^2} - \frac{t\cos at}{a}\right) = \frac{1}{2a^3}(\sin at - at \cos at)$$

Hence
$$L^{-1}\left[\frac{1}{(s^2 + a^2)^2}\right] = \frac{1}{2a^3}(\sin at - at \cos at)$$

(iii) Let
$$L^{-1}\left[\log\left(\frac{s+3}{s+2}\right)\right] = f(t)$$

$$\therefore \quad L^{-1}\left[\frac{d}{ds}\{\log(s+3) - \log(s+2)\}\right] = -t\,f(t) \qquad \text{[By result (30 a)]}$$

$$\therefore \quad L^{-1}\left[\frac{1}{s+3} - \frac{1}{s+2}\right] = -t\,f(t)$$

$$\therefore \quad (e^{-3t} - e^{-2t}) = -t\,f(t)$$

or
$$\frac{e^{-2t} - e^{-3t}}{t} = f(t)$$

Hence
$$L^{-1}\left[\frac{1}{s}\log\left(\frac{s+3}{s+2}\right)\right] = \int_0^t \frac{e^{-2t} - e^{-3t}}{t}\, dt \qquad \text{[By result (33)]}$$

(iv) Let
$$L^{-1}\left[\log\left(\frac{s^2 + a^2}{s^2 + b^2}\right)\right] = f(t)$$

$$\therefore \quad L^{-1}\left[\frac{d}{ds}\{\log(s^2 + a^2) - \log(s^2 + b^2)\}\right] = -t\,f(t) \qquad \text{[By result (30 a)]}$$

$$\therefore \quad L^{-1}\left[\frac{2s}{s^2 + a^2} - \frac{2s}{s^2 + b^2}\right] = -t\,f(t)$$

or
$$\frac{2(\cos bt - \cos at)}{t} = f(t)$$

Hence
$$L^{-1}\left[\frac{1}{s}\log\left(\frac{s^2 + a^2}{s^2 + b^2}\right)\right] = \int_0^t \frac{2(\cos bt - \cos at)}{t}\, dt \quad \text{[By result (33)]}$$

Ex. 8 : *Find the inverse Laplace transforms of the following functions :*

(i) $\dfrac{(s+2)^2}{(s^2 + 4s + 8)^2}$ *(ii)* $\dfrac{s^2 - a^2}{(s^2 + a^2)^2}$ *(iii)* $\dfrac{1}{(s-2)^4(s+3)}$

(iv) $\tan^{-1}\dfrac{2}{s^2}$

Sol. : (i) $L^{-1}\left[\dfrac{(s+2)^2}{(s^2+4s+8)^2}\right] = L^{-1}\left[\dfrac{(s+2)^2}{[(s+2)^2+4]^2}\right]$

$$= e^{-2t}\, L^{-1}\left[\dfrac{s^2}{(s^2+4)^2}\right]$$

Using the result of $L^{-1}\left[\dfrac{s^2}{(s^2+a^2)^2}\right]$ from Ex. 7 (i), we have

$$L^{-1}\left[\dfrac{(s+2)^2}{(s^2+4s+8)^2}\right] = e^{-2t}\left\{\dfrac{1}{4}\,(\sin 2t + 2t\cos 2t)\right\}$$

(ii) $\qquad L^{-1}\left[\dfrac{s^2-a^2}{(s^2+a^2)^2}\right] = L^{-1}\left[\dfrac{s^2}{(s^2+a^2)^2} - \dfrac{a^2}{(s^2+a^2)^2}\right]$

$$= L^{-1}\left[\dfrac{s^2}{(s^2+a^2)^2}\right] - a^2 L^{-1}\left[\dfrac{1}{(s^2+a^2)^2}\right]$$

Using results of Ex. 7 (i) and (ii), we get

$$L^{-1}\left[\dfrac{s^2-a^2}{(s^2+a^2)^2}\right] = \dfrac{1}{2a}\,(\sin at + at\cos at) - a^2\left\{\dfrac{1}{2a^3}\,(\sin at - at\cos at)\right\}$$

$$= \dfrac{1}{2a}\,(2at\cos at) = t\cos at$$

(iii) $\quad L^{-1}\left[\dfrac{1}{(s-2)^4(s+3)}\right] = L^{-1}\left[\dfrac{1}{(s+3-5)^4(s+3)}\right] = e^{-3t}\, L^{-1}\left[\dfrac{1}{s\,(s-5)^4}\right]$

$$= e^{-3t}\int_0^t L^{-1}\left[\dfrac{1}{(s-5)^4}\right]\,dt = e^{-3t}\int_0^t e^{5t}\,\dfrac{t^3}{3!}\,dt$$

$$= \dfrac{e^{-3t}}{6}\int_0^t t^3\,e^{5t}\,dt$$

$$= \dfrac{e^{-3t}}{6}\left[t^3\left(\dfrac{e^{5t}}{5}\right) - 3t^2\left(\dfrac{e^{5t}}{25}\right) + 6t\left(\dfrac{e^{5t}}{125}\right) - 6\left(\dfrac{e^{5t}}{625}\right)\right]_0^t$$

$$= \dfrac{e^{-3t}}{6}\left[e^{5t}\left(\dfrac{t^3}{5} - \dfrac{3t^2}{25} + \dfrac{6t}{125} - \dfrac{6}{625}\right) + \dfrac{6}{625}\right]$$

$$= e^{-3t}\left\{\dfrac{e^{5t}}{30}\left(t^3 - \dfrac{3t^2}{5} + \dfrac{6t}{25} - \dfrac{6}{125}\right) + \dfrac{1}{625}\right\}$$

$$= \dfrac{e^{2t}}{30}\left(t^3 - \dfrac{3t^2}{5} + \dfrac{6t}{25} - \dfrac{6}{125}\right) + \dfrac{e^{-3t}}{625}$$

(iv) Let $\qquad L^{-1}\left[\tan^{-1}\dfrac{2}{s^2}\right] = f(t)$

$\therefore \qquad L^{-1}\left[\dfrac{d}{ds}\tan^{-1}\dfrac{2}{s^2}\right] = -t\,f(t)$

$$\therefore \qquad L^{-1}\left[\frac{1}{1+4/s^4}\left(-\frac{4}{s^3}\right)\right] = -t\,f(t)$$

$$\text{or} \qquad L^{-1}\left[\frac{4s}{s^4+4}\right] = t\,f(t)$$

$$\text{or}\;\; L^{-1}\left[\frac{4s}{(s^2-2s+2)\,(s^2+2s+2)}\right] = t\,f(t)$$

$$\{\because\; s^4+4 = s^4+4s^2+4-4s^2 = (s^2+2)^2-(2s)^2\}$$

$$\text{or}\;\; L^{-1}\left[\frac{1}{s^2-2s+2}-\frac{1}{s^2+2s+2}\right] = t\,f(t)$$

$$\text{or}\;\; L^{-1}\left[\frac{1}{(s-1)^2+1}-\frac{1}{(s+1)^2+1}\right] = t\,f(t)$$

$$\therefore \qquad e^t\sin t - e^{-t}\sin t = t\,f(t)$$

$$\text{Hence} \qquad L^{-1}\left[\tan^{-1}\frac{2}{s^2}\right] = f(t) = \frac{2}{t}\sin t \sinh t$$

Ex. 9 : *Using the convolution theorem, find the inverse of each of the following transforms :*

(i) $\dfrac{s^2}{(s^2+a^2)^2}$ (ii) $\dfrac{1}{(s^2+a^2)^2}$ (iii) $\dfrac{s}{(s^2+a^2)^2}$ (iv) $\dfrac{1}{(s^2+1)^3}$

Sol. : (i) We can write $\dfrac{s^2}{(s^2+a^2)^2} = \dfrac{s}{s^2+a^2}\cdot\dfrac{s}{s^2+a^2}$

Let $\qquad\qquad F(s) = \dfrac{s}{s^2+a^2}$ and $G(s) = \dfrac{s}{s^2+a^2}$,

so that $\qquad\qquad f(t) = \cos at$ and $g(t) = \cos at$

Hence by convolution theorem, we have

$$L^{-1}\left[\frac{s^2}{(s^2+a^2)^2}\right] = \cos at * \cos at$$

$$= \int_0^t \cos au \cos a(t-u)\,du = \frac{1}{2}\int_0^t [\cos at + \cos a\,(2u-t)]\,du$$

$$[\because\; 2\cos A \cos B = \cos (A+B) + \cos (A-B)]$$

$$= \frac{1}{2}\left[\cos at\,(u) + \frac{\sin a\,(2u-t)}{2a}\right]_0^t$$

$$= \frac{1}{2}\left[\{(\cos at)\,(t)-0\} + \left\{\frac{\sin at}{2a}-\frac{\sin a\,(-t)}{2a}\right\}\right]$$

$$= \frac{1}{2}\left(t\cos at + \frac{\sin at}{2a}+\frac{\sin at}{2a}\right) = \frac{1}{2a}\,(\sin at + at \cos at)$$

(ii) We can write $\dfrac{1}{(s^2 + a^2)^2} = \dfrac{1}{s^2 + a^2} * \dfrac{1}{s^2 + a^2}$.

Let $\qquad F(s) = \dfrac{1}{s^2 + a^2}$ and $\qquad G(s) = \dfrac{1}{s^2 + a^2}$,

so that $\qquad f(t) = \dfrac{\sin at}{a}$ and $\qquad g(t) = \dfrac{\sin at}{a}$

Hence by the convolution theorem, we have

$$L^{-1}\left[\dfrac{1}{(s^2 + a^2)^2}\right] = \dfrac{\sin at}{a} * \dfrac{\sin at}{a}$$

$$= \int_0^t \dfrac{\sin au}{a} \cdot \dfrac{\sin a\,(t - u)}{a}\, du$$

$$= \dfrac{1}{2a^2} \int_0^t [\cos a\,(2u - t) - \cos at]\, du$$

$$[\because\ 2\sin A \sin B = \cos(A - B) - \cos(A + B)]$$

$$= \dfrac{1}{2a^2}\left[\dfrac{\sin a\,(2u - t)}{2a} - \cos at\,(u)\right]_0^t$$

$$= \dfrac{1}{2a^2}\left[\left\{\dfrac{\sin at}{2a} - \dfrac{\sin a\,(-t)}{2a}\right\} - \{(\cos at)\,(t) - 0\}\right]$$

$$= \dfrac{1}{2a^2}\left(\dfrac{\sin at}{a} - t\cos at\right) = \dfrac{1}{2a^3}(\sin at - at\cos at)$$

(iii) We can write $\dfrac{s}{(s^2 + a^2)^2} = \dfrac{s}{s^2 + a^2} \cdot \dfrac{1}{s^2 + a^2}$.

Let $\qquad F(s) = \dfrac{s}{s^2 + a^2}$ and $\quad G(s) = \dfrac{1}{s^2 + a^2}$,

so that $\qquad f(t) = \cos at$ and $\quad g(t) = \dfrac{\sin at}{a}$

Hence by the convolution theorem, we have

$$L^{-1}\left[\dfrac{s}{(s^2 + a^2)^2}\right] = \cos at * \dfrac{\sin at}{a}$$

$$= \int_0^t \cos au \cdot \dfrac{\sin a\,(t - u)}{a}\, du = \dfrac{1}{2a} \int_0^t [\sin at - \sin a\,(2u - t)]\, dt$$

$$[\because\ 2\cos A \sin B = \sin(A + B) - \sin(A - B)]$$

$$= \frac{1}{2a} \left[\sin at \, (u) + \frac{\cos a \, (2u - t)}{2a} \right]_0^t$$

$$= \frac{1}{2a} \left[\{(\sin at)\,(t) - 0\} + \left\{ \frac{\cos at}{2a} - \frac{\cos a \, (-t)}{2a} \right\} \right]$$

$$= \frac{1}{2a} \, (t \sin at)$$

(iv) We can write $\dfrac{1}{(s^2 + 1)^3} = \dfrac{1}{(s^2 + 1)^2} \cdot \dfrac{1}{(s^2 + 1)}$.

Let $\qquad\qquad F(s) = \dfrac{1}{(s^2 + 1)^2} \quad$ and $\quad G(s) = \dfrac{1}{(s^2 + 1)}$

so that $\qquad\qquad f(t) = L^{-1} \left[\dfrac{1}{(s^2 + 1)^2} \right]$ and $\quad g(t) = \sin t$

Hence by the convolution theorem, we have

$$L^{-1} \left[\frac{1}{(s^2 + 1)^3} \right] = f(t) * \sin t \qquad\qquad\qquad \dots \text{(i)}$$

Now $f(t) = L^{-1} \left[\dfrac{1}{(s^2 + 1)^2} \right] = L^{-1} \left[\dfrac{1}{s^2 + 1} \cdot \dfrac{1}{s^2 + 1} \right]$

$$= \sin t * \sin t$$

$$= \int_0^t \sin u \sin (t - u) \, du = \frac{1}{2} \int_0^t [\cos (2u - t) - \cos t] \, du$$

$$[\because 2 \sin A \sin B = \cos (A - B) - \cos (A + B)]$$

$$= \frac{1}{2} \left[\frac{\sin (2u - t)}{2} - \cos t \, (u) \right]_0^t$$

$$= \frac{1}{2} \left[\left\{ \frac{\sin t}{2} - \frac{\sin (-t)}{2} \right\} - \{(\cos t \, (t) - 0)\} \right]$$

$$= \frac{1}{2} \, (\sin t - t \cos t) \qquad\qquad\qquad \dots \text{(ii)}$$

Hence from (i),

$$L^{-1} \left[\frac{1}{(s^2 + 1)^3} \right] = \frac{1}{2} \, (\sin t - t \cos t) * \sin t$$

$$= \int_0^t \frac{1}{2} \, (\sin u - u \cos u) \cdot \sin (t - u) \, du$$

$$= \frac{1}{2}\left[\int_0^t \sin u \sin(t-u)\, du - \int_0^t u \cos u \sin(t-u)\, du\right]$$

$$= \frac{1}{2}\left[\frac{1}{2}(\sin t - t\cos t) - \frac{1}{2}\int_0^t u\,\{\sin t - \sin(2u-t)\}\, du\right] \qquad \text{[From result (ii)]}$$

$$= \frac{1}{4}\left[(\sin t - t\cos t) - \int_0^t u \sin t + \int_0^t u \sin(2u-t)\, du\right]$$

$$= \frac{1}{4}\left[(\sin t - t\cos t) - \left\{\sin t \left(\frac{u^2}{2}\right)\right\}_0^t + \left\{u\left(-\frac{\cos(2u-t)}{2}\right) - (1)\left(-\frac{\sin(2u-t)}{t}\right)\right\}_0^t\right]$$

$$= \frac{1}{4}\left[(\sin t - t\cos t) - (\sin t)\left(\frac{t^2}{2}\right) + \left\{\left(\frac{-t\cos t}{2} - 0\right) - \left(-\frac{\sin t}{4} - \frac{\sin t}{4}\right)\right\}\right]$$

$$= \frac{1}{4}\left(\sin t - t\cos t - \frac{t^2}{2}\sin t - \frac{t\cos t}{2} + \frac{\sin t}{2}\right) = \frac{1}{8}\left[(3-t^2)\sin t - 3t\cos t\right]$$

Ex. 10 : *Use the convolution theorem to find inverse Laplace transform of each of the following :*

(i) $\dfrac{1}{s^2(s+1)^2}$ (ii) $\dfrac{1}{(s-2)^4(s+3)}$ (iii) $\dfrac{s+2}{s^2(s-1)^2}$ (iv) $\dfrac{s+29}{(s+4)(s^2+9)}$

Sol. : (i) We can write $\dfrac{1}{s^2(s+1)^2} = \dfrac{1}{s^2}\cdot\dfrac{1}{(s+1)^2}$

Let $\qquad F(s) = \dfrac{1}{s^2}\qquad$ and $\qquad G(s) = \dfrac{1}{(s+1)^2}$,

so that $\qquad f(t) = t \qquad$ and $\qquad g(t) = t\,e^{-t}$

Hence by the convolution theorem, we have

$$L^{-1}\left[\frac{1}{s^2(s+1)^2}\right] = t * t\,e^{-t} = t\,e^{-t} * t$$

$$= \int_0^t (ue^{-u})(t-u)\, du = \int_0^t (ut-u^2)\,e^{-u}\, du$$

$$= \left[(ut-u^2)(-e^{-u}) - (t-2u)(e^{-u}) + (-2)(-e^{-u})\right]_0^t$$

$$= t\,e^{-t} + 2\,e^{-t} + t - 2$$

Check : $L[te^{-t} + 2e^{-t} + t - 2] = \dfrac{1}{(s+1)^2} + \dfrac{2}{s+1} + \dfrac{1}{s^2} - \dfrac{2}{s}$

$$= \frac{s^2 + 2s^2(s+1) + (s+1)^2 - 2s(s+1)^2}{s^2(s+1)^2} = \frac{1}{s^2(s+1)^2}$$

(ii) $L^{-1}\left[\dfrac{1}{(s-2)^4(s+3)}\right] = L^{-1}\left[\dfrac{1}{(s-2)^4(s-2+5)}\right]$ (Note the step)

$$= e^{2t}\, L^{-1}\left[\dfrac{1}{s^4(s+5)}\right] \qquad \dots \text{(i)}$$

Now to find $L^{-1}\left[\dfrac{1}{s^4(s+5)}\right]$, we use the convolution theorem.

Let $\qquad\qquad F(s) = \dfrac{1}{s^4} \qquad$ and $\qquad G(s) = \dfrac{1}{(s+5)}$

so that $\qquad\qquad f(t) = \dfrac{t^3}{6} \qquad$ and $\qquad g(t) = e^{-5t}$

$\therefore\qquad L^{-1}\left[\dfrac{1}{s^4(s+5)}\right] = \dfrac{t^3}{6} * e^{-5t}$

$$= \int_0^t \dfrac{u^3}{6}\, e^{-5(t-u)}\, du = \dfrac{e^{-5t}}{6}\int_0^t u^3 e^{5u}\, du$$

$$= \dfrac{e^{-5t}}{6}\left[u^3\left(\dfrac{e^{5u}}{5}\right) - 3u^2\left(\dfrac{e^{5u}}{25}\right) + 6u\left(\dfrac{e^{5u}}{125}\right) - 6\left(\dfrac{e^{5u}}{625}\right)\right]_0^t$$

$$= \dfrac{e^{-5t}}{6}\left[\left(t^3\dfrac{e^{5t}}{5} - 3t^2\dfrac{e^{5t}}{25} + 6t\dfrac{e^{5t}}{125} - \dfrac{6e^{5t}}{625}\right) + \dfrac{6}{625}\right]$$

$$= \dfrac{1}{30}\left(t^3 - \dfrac{3t^2}{5} + \dfrac{6t}{25} - \dfrac{6}{125}\right) + \dfrac{e^{-5t}}{625} \qquad \dots \text{(ii)}$$

Hence from (i) and (ii), we get

$$L^{-1}\left[\dfrac{1}{(s-2)^4(s+3)}\right] = e^{2t}\, L^{-1}\left[\dfrac{1}{s^4(s+5)}\right]$$

$$= \dfrac{e^{2t}}{30}\left(t^3 - \dfrac{3}{5}t^2 + \dfrac{6}{25}t - \dfrac{6}{125}\right) + \dfrac{e^{-3t}}{625}$$

(iii) $L^{-1}\left[\dfrac{s+2}{s^2(s-1)^2}\right] = L^{-1}\left[\dfrac{1}{s(s-1)^2}\right] + 2\,L^{-1}\left[\dfrac{1}{s^2(s-1)^2}\right]$ $\dots$ (i)

Now $L^{-1}\left[\dfrac{1}{s(s-1)^2}\right] = L^{-1}\left[\dfrac{1}{s}\cdot\dfrac{1}{(s-1)^2}\right] = 1 * t\, e^t$

$$= \int_0^t 1\cdot u\, e^u\, du = \left[u\, e^u - e^u\right]_0^t$$

$$= 1 + e^t(t-1) \qquad \dots \text{(ii)}$$

And $L^{-1}\left[\dfrac{1}{s^2(s-1)^2}\right] = L^{-1}\left[\dfrac{1}{s}\left\{\dfrac{1}{s(s-1)^2}\right\}\right] = \int_0^t [1 + e^t(t-1)]\, dt$ [Using (ii)]

$$= [t + \{(t-1)\,e^t - e^t\}]\Big]_0^t$$

$$= [(t + (t-1)\,e^t - e^t) - (0 - 1 - 1)]$$

$$= 2 + t + e^t\,(t-2) \qquad\qquad \dots \text{(iii)}$$

Using (i), (ii) and (iii), we get

$$L^{-1}\left[\frac{s+2}{s^2\,(s-1)^2}\right] = 1 + e^t\,(t-1) + 2\,[2 + t + e^t\,(t-2)]$$

$$= 5 + 2t + e^t\,(3t - 5)$$

(iv) We can write $\dfrac{s+29}{(s+4)\,(s^2+9)} = \dfrac{1}{s+4} \cdot \dfrac{s+29}{s^2+9}$.

Let $\qquad\qquad F(s) = \dfrac{1}{s+4} \qquad$ and $\qquad G(s) = \dfrac{s+29}{s^2+9}$

so that $\qquad\qquad f(t) = e^{-4t} \qquad$ and $\qquad g(t) = \cos 3t + \dfrac{29}{3}\,\sin 3t$

Hence by the convolution theorem, we have

$$L^{-1}\left[\frac{s+29}{(s+4)\,(s^2+9)}\right] = e^{-4t} * \left(\cos 3t + \frac{29}{3}\,\sin 3t\right)$$

$$= \int_0^t e^{-4\,(t-u)}\left(\cos 3u + \frac{29}{3}\,\sin 3u\right) du$$

$$= e^{-4t}\left[\int_0^t e^{4u}\cos 3u\,du + \frac{29}{3}\int_0^t e^{4u}\sin 3u\,du\right]$$

$$= e^{-4t}\left[\left\{\frac{e^{4u}}{16+9}\,(4\cos 3u + 3\sin 3u)\right\}_0^t + \frac{29}{3}\left\{\frac{e^{4u}}{16+9}\,(4\sin 3u - 3\cos 3u)\right\}_0^t\right]$$

$$= e^{-4t}\left[\left\{\frac{e^{4t}}{25}\,(4\cos 3t + 3\sin 3t) - \frac{4}{25}\right\} + \frac{29}{3}\left\{\frac{e^{4t}}{25}\,(4\sin 3t - 3\cos 3t) + \frac{3}{25}\right\}\right]$$

$$= e^{-4t}\left(\frac{-4+29}{25}\right) + \frac{1}{25}\,(4\cos 3t + 3\sin 3t + \frac{116}{3}\,\sin 3t - 29\cos 3t)\,]$$

$$= e^{-4t} + \frac{1}{25}\left(\frac{125}{3}\,\sin 3t - 25\cos 3t\right) = e^{-4t} + \frac{5}{3}\,\sin 3t - \cos 3t$$

Ex. 11 : *Show that* $\displaystyle\int_0^t\int_0^t\int_0^t f(t)\,dt^3 = \int_0^t \frac{(t-u)^2}{2!}\,f(u)\,du.$

Sol. : Consider inverse Laplace transform of $\dfrac{1}{s^3}\,F(s)$ as

$$L^{-1}\left[\frac{1}{s^3}\,F(s)\right] = \int_0^t\int_0^t\int_0^t f(t)\,dt^3 \qquad\qquad \dots \text{(i)}$$

and by the convolution theorem, we have

$$L^{-1}\left[\frac{1}{s^3} \cdot F(s)\right] = L^{-1}\left[\frac{1}{s^3}\right] * L^{-1}[F(s)] = \frac{t^2}{2!} * f(t)$$

$$= \int_0^t \frac{(t-u)^2}{2!}\, f(u)\, du \qquad\qquad \text{... (ii)}$$

Equating (i) and (ii), we get the required result.

Ex. 12 : *If* $L\,[J_0(t)] = \dfrac{1}{\sqrt{s^2+1}}$ *, then show that* $\displaystyle\int_0^t J_o(u)\, J_o(t-u)\, du = \sin t$

Sol. : Let $$h(t) = \int_0^t J_0(u)\, J_0(t-u)\, du$$

Then by the convolution theorem, we have

$$L[h(t)] = L\left[\int_0^t J_0(u)\, J_0(t-u)\, du\right] = L\,[J_0(t)]\, L\,[J_0(t)]$$

$$= \left(\frac{1}{\sqrt{s^2+1}}\right)\left(\frac{1}{\sqrt{s^2+1}}\right) = \frac{1}{s^2+1}$$

Hence $$h(t) = L^{-1}\left[\frac{1}{s^2+1}\right] = \sin t$$

or $$\int_0^t J_0(u)\, J_0(t-u)\, du = \sin t$$

[**Note :** This $J_0(t)$ is known as Bessel's function.]

Ex. 13 : Prove that $B(m, n) = \displaystyle\int_0^1 x^{m-1}(1-x)^{n-1}\, dx = \dfrac{\overline{|m}\ \overline{|n}}{\overline{|m+n}}$, where $m > 0$ and $n > 0$.

Sol. : Consider, $$h(t) = \int_0^t x^{m-1}(t-x)^{n-1}\, dx = t^{m-1} * t^{n-1}$$

Then by the convolution theorem, we have

$$L\,[h(t)] = L\left[\int_0^t x^{m-1}(t-x)^{n-1}\, dx\right] = L\,[t^{m-1}]\, L\,[t^{n-1}]$$

$$= \frac{\overline{|m}}{s^m} \cdot \frac{\overline{|n}}{s^n} = \frac{\overline{|m}\ \overline{|n}}{s^{m+n}}$$

Hence
$$h(t) = L^{-1}\left[\frac{\overline{m}\;\overline{n}}{s^{m+n}}\right] = \frac{\overline{m}\;\overline{n}}{\overline{m+n}}\; t^{m+n-1}$$

or
$$\int_0^t x^{m-1}(t-x)^{n-1}\,dx = \frac{\overline{m}\;\overline{n}}{\overline{m+n}}\; t^{m+n-1}$$

On putting $t = 1$, we get

$$B(m,n) = \int_0^1 x^{m-1}(1-x)^{n-1} = \frac{\overline{m}\;\overline{n}}{\overline{m+n}}$$

Ex. 14 : *Using partial fractions, find the inverse Laplace transform of :*

(i) $\dfrac{2s^2 - 6s + 5}{s^3 - 6s^2 + 11s - 6}$ (ii) $\dfrac{3s^3 + s^2 + 12s + 2}{(s-3)(s+1)^3}$

(iii) $\dfrac{1}{(s+2)(s^2 + 2s + 2)}$

(iv) $\dfrac{s^2 + 2s + 3}{(s^2 + 2s + 2)(s^2 + 2s + 5)}$ (v) $\dfrac{s^3}{s^4 - a^4}$ (vi) $\dfrac{s}{s^4 + s^2 + 1}$

(vii) $\dfrac{1}{s^3 + a^3}$ (viii) $\dfrac{s-2}{s(s+1)^3}$ (ix) $\dfrac{s^2 - 2s + 3}{(s-1)^2(s+1)}$

Sol. : (i) We have $\dfrac{2s^2 - 6s + 5}{s^3 - 6s^2 + 11s - 6} = \dfrac{2s^2 - 6s + 5}{(s-1)(s-2)(s-3)}$

Here denominator has non-repeated factors.

Let $\dfrac{2s^2 - 6s + 5}{(s-1)(s-2)(s-3)} = \dfrac{A}{(s-1)} + \dfrac{B}{(s-2)} + \dfrac{C}{(s-3)}$

Multiplying both sides by $(s-1)(s-2)(s-3)$, we get

$2s^2 - 6s + 5 = A(s-2)(s-3) + B(s-1)(s-3) + C(s-1)(s-2)$

Putting $s = 1$,   we get $A = 1/2$

Putting $s = 2$,   we get $B = -1$

Putting $s = 3$,   we get $C = 5/2$

$\therefore \quad L^{-1}\left[\dfrac{2s^2 - 6s + 5}{(s-1)(s-2)(s-3)}\right] = L^{-1}\left[\dfrac{1/2}{s-1} - \dfrac{1}{s-2} + \dfrac{5/2}{s-3}\right]$

$$= \frac{1}{2}\,e^t - e^{2t} + \frac{5}{2}\,e^{3t}$$

(ii) Let $\dfrac{3s^3 + s^2 + 12s + 2}{(s-3)(s+1)^3} = \dfrac{A}{s-3} + \dfrac{B}{s+1} + \dfrac{C}{(s+1)^2} + \dfrac{D}{(s+1)^3}$

Multiplying both sides by $(s-3)(s+1)^3$, we get

$3s^3 + s^2 + 12s + 2 = A(s+1)^3 + B(s-3)(s+1)^2 + C(s-3)(s+1) + D(s-3)$

Putting $s = 3$,   we get $A = 2$

Putting $s = -1$, we get $D = 3$

To determine B and C, equating coefficients of like powers of s^3 and s^2, we have

$$A + B = 3 \qquad \text{and} \qquad 3A - B + C = 1$$

$$\therefore \qquad B = 1 \qquad \text{and} \qquad C = -4$$

$$\therefore \quad L^{-1}\left[\frac{3s^3 + s^2 + 12s + 2}{(s-3)(s+1)^3}\right] = L^{-1}\left[\frac{2}{s-3} + \frac{1}{s+1} - \frac{4}{(s+1)^2} + \frac{3}{(s+1)^3}\right]$$

$$= 2e^{3t} + e^{-t} - 4e^{-t}(t) + 3e^{-t}\left(\frac{t^2}{2!}\right)$$

$$= 2e^{3t} + e^{-t} - 4t\,e^{-t} + \frac{3}{2}\,e^{-t}\,t^2$$

(iii) Here in denominator, quadratic factor can be written as product of linear factors with complex conjugate roots as

$$\frac{1}{(s+2)(s^2 + 2s + 2)} = \frac{1}{(s+2)(s+1+i)(s+1-i)}$$

Let $\dfrac{1}{(s+2)(s+1+i)(s+1-i)} = \dfrac{A}{s+2} + \dfrac{B}{s+1+i} + \dfrac{C}{s+1-i}$

Multiplying both sides by $(s+2)(s^2 + 2s + 2)$, we get

$$1 = A(s^2 + 2s + 2) + B(s+2)(s+1-i) + C(s+2)(s+1+i)$$

Putting $s = -2$, we get $\qquad A = \dfrac{1}{2}$

Putting $s = -1 - i$, we get $\qquad B = \dfrac{1}{(1-i)(-2i)} = -\dfrac{1}{4}(1-i)$

Putting $s = -1 + i$, we get $\qquad C = \dfrac{1}{(1+i)(2i)} = -\dfrac{1}{4}(1+i)$

$$\therefore \quad L^{-1}\left[\frac{1}{(s+2)(s^2 + 2s + 2)}\right] = L^{-1}\left[\frac{1/2}{s+2} + \left\{\frac{-\frac{1}{4}(1-i)(s+1-i) - \frac{1}{4}(1+i)(s+1+i)}{(s+1+i)(s+1-i)}\right\}\right]$$

$$= \frac{1}{2}L^{-1}\left[\frac{1}{s+2}\right] - \frac{1}{4}L^{-1}\left[\frac{2s}{s^2 + 2s + 2}\right]$$

$$= \frac{1}{2}e^{-2t} - \frac{1}{2}L^{-1}\left[\frac{(s+1) - 1}{(s+1)^2 + 1}\right]$$

$$= \frac{1}{2}e^{-2t} - \frac{1}{2}e^{-t}L^{-1}\left[\frac{s-1}{s^2 + 1}\right]$$

[By the First Shifting Theorem]

$$= \frac{1}{2}e^{-2t} - \frac{1}{2}e^{-t}(\cos t - \sin t)$$

Another method : We can write

$$\frac{1}{(s+2)(s^2 + 2s + 2)} = \frac{A}{s+2} + \frac{Bs + C}{s^2 + 2s + 2}$$

$$\therefore \qquad 1 = A(s^2 + 2s + 2) + (Bs + C)(s+2)$$

Equating coefficients of s^2, s and constant terms and after solving, we get A = 1/2, B = –1/2 and C = 0. Using these values we have the same result in above method.

(iv) Let $\dfrac{s^2 + 2s + 3}{(s^2 + 2s + 2)\,(s^2 + 2s + 5)} = \dfrac{p + 3}{(p + 2)\,(p + 5)}$ where $p = s^2 + 2s$

$$= \dfrac{1}{3\,(p + 2)} + \dfrac{2}{3}\,\dfrac{1}{(p + 5)}$$

$$= \dfrac{1}{3\,(s^2 + 2s + 2)} + \dfrac{2}{3}\,\dfrac{1}{(s^2 + 2s + 5)}$$

$$\therefore\ L^{-1}\left[\dfrac{s^2 + 2s + 3}{(s^2 + 2s + 2)\,(s^2 + 2s + 5)}\right] = \dfrac{1}{3}\,L^{-1}\left[\dfrac{1}{s^2 + 2s + 2}\right] + \dfrac{2}{3}\,L^{-1}\left[\dfrac{1}{s^2 + 2s + 5}\right]$$

$$= \dfrac{1}{3}\,L^{-1}\left[\dfrac{1}{(s + 1)^2 + 1}\right] + \dfrac{2}{3}\,L^{-1}\left[\dfrac{1}{(s + 1)^2 + 4}\right]$$

$$= \dfrac{1}{3}\,e^{-t}\,L^{-1}\left[\dfrac{1}{s^2 + 1}\right] + \dfrac{2}{3}\,e^{-t}\left[\dfrac{1}{s^2 + 4}\right]$$

$$= \dfrac{1}{3}\,e^{-t}\,(\sin t) + \dfrac{2}{3}\,e^{-t}\left(\dfrac{\sin 2t}{2}\right)$$

$$= \dfrac{1}{3}\,e^{-t}\,(\sin t + \sin 2t)$$

Note : We can also write

$$L^{-1}\left[\dfrac{s^2 + 2s + 3}{(s^2 + 2s + 2)\,(s^2 + 2s + 5)}\right] = L^{-1}\left[\dfrac{As + B}{s^2 + 2s + 2} + \dfrac{Cs + D}{s^2 + 2s + 5}\right]$$

Then determining A, B, C and D, we can obtain the same result in above method.

(v) We have $\dfrac{s^3}{s^4 - a^4} = s\left[\dfrac{s^2}{(s^2 - a^2)\times(s^2 + a^2)}\right] = \dfrac{s}{2}\left[\dfrac{1}{s^2 - a^2} + \dfrac{1}{s^2 + a^2}\right]$

$$= \dfrac{1}{2}\left[\dfrac{s}{s^2 - a^2} + \dfrac{s}{s^2 + a^2}\right]$$

$$\therefore\qquad L^{-1}\left[\dfrac{s^3}{s^4 - a^4}\right] = \dfrac{1}{2}\,L^{-1}\left[\dfrac{s}{s^2 - a^2}\right] + \dfrac{1}{2}\,L^{-1}\left[\dfrac{s}{s^2 + a^2}\right]$$

$$= \dfrac{1}{2}\,\cosh at + \dfrac{1}{2}\,\cos at = \dfrac{1}{2}\,(\cosh at + \cos at)$$

(vi) Since $\quad s^4 + s^2 + 1 = (s^2 + 1)^2 - s^2 = (s^2 + s + 1)\,(s^2 - s + 1)$

$$\therefore\qquad \dfrac{s}{s^4 + s^2 + 1} = \dfrac{s}{(s^2 + s + 1)\,(s^2 - s + 1)}$$

$$= \dfrac{As + B}{s^2 + s + 1} + \dfrac{Cs + D}{s^2 - s + 1}$$

$$= \dfrac{-1/2}{s^2 + s + 1} + \dfrac{1/2}{s^2 - s + 1}$$

Hence $\quad L^{-1}\left[\dfrac{s}{s^4 + s^2 + 1}\right] = \dfrac{1}{2}\left\{-L^{-1}\left[\dfrac{1}{s^2 + s + 1}\right] + L^{-1}\left[\dfrac{1}{s^2 - s + 1}\right]\right\}$

$$= \dfrac{1}{2}\left\{-L^{-1}\left[\dfrac{1}{(s + 1/2)^2 + (\sqrt{3}/2)^2}\right] + L^{-1}\left[\dfrac{1}{(s - 1/2)^2 + (\sqrt{3}/2)^2}\right]\right\}$$

$$= \frac{1}{2} \left\{ -e^{-t/2}\, L^{-1}\left[\frac{1}{s^2 + (\sqrt{3}/2)^2}\right] + e^{t/2}\, L^{-1}\left[\frac{1}{s^2 + (\sqrt{3}/2)^2}\right] \right\}$$

$$= \frac{1}{2} \left\{ -e^{-t/2}\left(\frac{\sin \sqrt{3}/2\, t}{\sqrt{3}/2}\right) + e^{t/2}\left(\frac{\sin \sqrt{3}/2\, t}{\sqrt{3}/2}\right) \right\}$$

$$= \frac{2}{\sqrt{3}}\, \sin\frac{\sqrt{3}}{2}\, t\, \left(\frac{e^{t/2} - e^{-t/2}}{2}\right)$$

$$= \frac{2}{\sqrt{3}}\, \sin\frac{\sqrt{3}}{2}\, t\, \sinh\frac{t}{2}$$

(vii) We have
$$\frac{1}{s^3 + a^3} = \frac{1}{(s + a)\,(s^2 - as + a^2)}$$

Let
$$\frac{1}{(s + a)\,(s^2 - as + a^2)} = \frac{A}{s + a} + \frac{Bs + C}{s^2 - as + a^2} \qquad \ldots (i)$$

Multiplying both sides by $(s + a)\,(s^2 - as + a^2)$, we get

$$1 = A\,(s^2 - as + a^2) + (Bs + C)\,(s + a) \qquad \ldots (ii)$$

Putting $s = -a$, we get $\quad A = \dfrac{1}{3a^2}$

To determine B and C, we equate the coefficients of like powers of s^2 and s, and we obtain

$$A + B = 0 \qquad\qquad \text{and} \quad -aA + aB + C = 0$$

$$\therefore \qquad B = -A = -\frac{1}{3a^2} \quad \text{and} \quad C = \frac{2}{3a}$$

$$\therefore \quad L^{-1}\left[\frac{1}{(s + a)\,(s^2 - as + a^2)}\right] = L^{-1}\left[\frac{1/3a^2}{(s + a)} + \frac{(-1/3a^2)\,s + 2/3a}{s^2 - as + a^2}\right]$$

$$= \frac{1}{3a^2}\, L^{-1}\left[\frac{1}{s + a}\right] - \frac{1}{3a^2}\, L^{-1}\left[\frac{s - 2a}{s^2 - as + a^2}\right]$$

$$= \frac{1}{3a^2}\, e^{-at} - \frac{1}{3a^2}\, L^{-1}\left[\frac{(s - a/2) - 3a/2}{(s - a/2)^2 + 3a^2/4}\right]$$

$$= \frac{1}{3a^2}\, e^{-at} - \frac{1}{3a^2}\, e^{at/2}\, L^{-1}\left[\frac{s - 3a/2}{s^2 + (\sqrt{3}\, a/2)^2}\right]$$

$$= \frac{1}{3a^2}\, e^{-at} - \frac{1}{3a^2}\, e^{at/2}\left(\cos\frac{\sqrt{3}\, a}{2}\, t - \sin\frac{\sqrt{3}\, a}{2}\, t\right)$$

(viii)
$$L^{-1}\left[\frac{s - 2}{s\,(s + 1)^3}\right] = L^{-1}\left[\frac{(s + 1) - 3}{(s + 1 - 1)\,(s + 1)^3}\right]$$

$$= e^{-t}\, L^{-1}\left[\frac{s - 3}{(s - 1)\,s^3}\right] \quad \text{[By the First Shifting Theorem]}$$

$$= e^{-t} L^{-1} \left[\frac{1}{s^3} \left(\frac{s-3}{s-1} \right) \right]$$

$$\text{(Dividing } -3 + s \text{ by } -1 + s) \text{ (Note this step)}$$

$$= e^{-t} L^{-1} \left[\frac{1}{s^3} (3 + 2s + 2s^2 - 2s^3) \right]$$

$$= e^{-t} L^{-1} \left[\frac{3}{s^3} + \frac{2}{s^2} + \frac{2}{s} - \frac{2}{s-1} \right]$$

$$= e^{-t} \left[3 \left(\frac{t^2}{2!} \right) + 2(t) + 2 - 2 e^t \right]$$

$$= e^{-t} \left(2 + 2t + \frac{3t^2}{2} \right) - 2$$

Note 1 : Before applying the method of partial fractions (to obtain inverse Laplace transform), it is advisable to find out whether the expression can be simplified by first shifting theorem.

Note 2 : It should be noted that the method given above is less tedious than writing the given expression as

$$\frac{s-2}{s(s+1)^3} = \frac{A}{s} + \frac{B}{s+1} + \frac{C}{(s+1)^2} + \frac{D}{(s+1)^3}$$

and then determining the coefficients A, B, C, D to obtain inverse Laplace transform.

(ix) $\qquad L^{-1} \left[\dfrac{s^2 - 2s + 3}{(s-1)^2 (s+1)} \right] = L^{-1} \left[\dfrac{(s-1)^2 + 2}{(s-1)^2 (s-1+2)} \right]$

$$= e^t L^{-1} \left[\frac{s^2 + 2}{s^2 (s+2)} \right]$$

$$= e^t L^{-1} \left[\frac{1}{s^2} \left(\frac{2 + s^2}{2 + s} \right) \right] \text{ [By the First Shifting Theorem]}$$

$$\text{(Dividing } 2 + s^2 \text{ by } 2 + s) \qquad\qquad \text{(Note this step)}$$

$$= e^t L^{-1} \left[\frac{1}{s^2} \left(1 - \frac{s}{2} + \frac{3s^2/2}{2+s} \right) \right]$$

$$= e^t L^{-1} \left[\frac{1}{s^2} - \frac{1}{2s} + \frac{3}{2} \frac{1}{s+2} \right]$$

$$= e^t \left(t - \frac{1}{2} + \frac{3}{2} e^{-2t} \right)$$

$$= \left(t - \frac{1}{2} \right) e^t + \frac{3}{2} e^{-t}$$

EXERCISE 4.4

1. Find the Inverse Laplace transform of each of the following functions :

(i) $\dfrac{s}{(s+a)^2}$ (ii) $\dfrac{1}{(s+4)^{3/2}}$ (iii) $\dfrac{s+7}{s^2+2s+2}$ (iv) $\dfrac{6s-4}{s^2-4s+20}$ (v) $\dfrac{8s+20}{s^2-12s+32}$

(vi) $\dfrac{2s+5}{s^2-2s-3}$ (vii) $\dfrac{1}{\sqrt{2s+3}}$ (viii) $\dfrac{1}{3\sqrt{8s-27}}$

Ans. (i) $e^{-at}(1-at)$ (ii) $2e^{-4t}\dfrac{\sqrt{t}}{\sqrt{\pi}}$ (iii) $e^{-t}(\cos t + 6\sin t)$

(iv) $2e^{2t}(3\cos 4t + \sin 4t)$

(v) $2e^{6t}(4\cosh 2t + 17\sinh 2t)$ or $(21\,e^{8t} - 13\,e^{4t})$

(vi) $e^{t}\left(2\cosh 2t + \dfrac{7}{2}\sinh 2t\right)$ or $\left(\dfrac{11}{4}\,e^{3t} - \dfrac{3\,e^{-t}}{4}\right)$

(vii) $\dfrac{e^{-3t/2}}{\sqrt{2\pi t}}$ (viii) $\dfrac{e^{27t/8}\,t^{-2/3}}{2\lceil 1/3}$.

2. Obtain the Inverse Laplace transforms of the following functions :

(i) $\dfrac{e^{-5s}}{(s-2)^4}$ (ii) $\dfrac{e^{4-3s}}{(s+4)^{5/2}}$ (iii) $\dfrac{e^{-3s}}{s^2-9}$ (iv) $\dfrac{e^{-s}}{\sqrt{s+1}}$ (v) $\dfrac{s\,e^{-s/2} + \pi e^{-s}}{s^2+\pi^2}$

(vi) $\dfrac{s\,e^{-\pi s}}{s^2-4s+29}$ (vii) $\dfrac{(s+1)\,e^{-\pi s}}{s^2+s+1}$ (viii) $\dfrac{e^{-s}+e^{-2s}}{s^2-3s+2}$ (ix) $\dfrac{(1-\sqrt{s})\,e^{-s}}{s^{3/2}}$

(x) $\dfrac{(1-\sqrt{s})^2\,e^{-s}}{s^3}$ (xi) $\dfrac{e^{-s}(1-e^{-s})}{s(s^2+1)}$

Ans. Notation used for displaced unit step function is $U(t-a) = \begin{cases} 0, & t < a \\ 1, & t \ge a \end{cases}$

(i) $\dfrac{1}{6}(t-5)^3\,e^{2(t-5)}\,U(t-5)$ (ii) $\dfrac{4(t-3)^{3/2}\,e^{-4(t-4)}}{3\sqrt{\pi}}\,U(t-3)$

(iii) $\dfrac{1}{3}\sinh 3(t-3)\,U(t-3)$ (iv) $\dfrac{e^{-(t-1)}}{\sqrt{\pi(t-1)}}\,U(t-1)$

(v) $\sin \pi t\,[U(t-1/2) - U(t-1)]$

(vi) $e^{2(t-\pi)}\left\{\cos 5(t-\pi) + \dfrac{2}{5}\sin 5(t-\pi)\right\}\,U(t-\pi)$

(vii) $\dfrac{e^{-(t-\pi)/2}}{\sqrt{3}}\left\{\sqrt{3}\cos\dfrac{\sqrt{3}}{2}(t-\pi) + \sin\dfrac{\sqrt{3}}{2}(t-\pi)\right\}\,U(t-\pi)$

(viii) $\{e^{2(t-1)} - e^{(t-1)}\}\,U(t-1) + \{e^{2(t-2)} - e^{(t-2)}\}\,U(t-2)$

(ix) $\left\{\dfrac{2\sqrt{t-1}}{\sqrt{\pi}} - 1\right\}\,U(t-1)$ (x) $\left\{\dfrac{(t-1)^2}{2} - \dfrac{8}{3}\dfrac{(t-1)^{3/2}}{\sqrt{\pi}} + (t-1)\right\}\,U(t-1)$

(xi) $\{1 - \cos(t-1)\}\,U(t-1) - \{1 - \cos(t-2)\}\,U(t-2)$.

3. Find the Inverse Laplace transforms of the following functions :

(i) $\tan^{-1}\dfrac{1}{s}$ (ii) $\tan^{-1}(s+1)$

(iii) $\log\left(\dfrac{s+2}{s+1}\right)$ (iv) $\dfrac{1}{2}\log\dfrac{s-1}{s+1}$ (v) $\log\left(\dfrac{1+s}{s}\right)$

(vi) $\log\left(\dfrac{s}{s-1}\right)$ (vii) $\dfrac{1}{2}\log\left(\dfrac{s^2-a^2}{s^2}\right)$ (viii) $\dfrac{1}{2}\log\dfrac{s^2+b^2}{(s-a)^2}$

(ix) $s\log\dfrac{s}{\sqrt{s^2+1}}+\cot^{-1}s$

Ans. (i) $\dfrac{\sin t}{t}$ (ii) $-e^{-t}\dfrac{\sin t}{t}$ (iii) $\dfrac{e^{-t}-e^{-2t}}{t}$ (iv) $\dfrac{\sinh t}{t}$ (v) $\dfrac{1-e^{-t}}{t}$ (vi) $\dfrac{e^t-1}{t}$

(vii) $\dfrac{1-\cosh at}{t}$ (viii) $\dfrac{e^{-at}-\cos bt}{t}$ (ix) $\dfrac{1-\cos t}{t^2}$

4. Use theorem on Inverse Laplace transform of derivative, to find

(i) $L^{-1}[1/(s-a)^3]$, given that $L^{-1}[1/(s-a)] = e^{at}$.

(ii) $L^{-1}[s/(s^2-a^2)^2]$, given that $L^{-1}[1/(s^2-a^2)] = \sinh at/a$.

5. Given that $L^{-1}\left[\dfrac{s}{(s^2+1)^2}\right] = \dfrac{1}{2}\,t\sin t$, find $L^{-1}\left[\dfrac{1}{(s^2+1)^2}\right]$.

[Hint : $L^{-1}\left[\dfrac{1}{(s^2+1)^2}\right] = L^{-1}\left[\dfrac{1}{s}\cdot\dfrac{s}{(s^2+1)^2}\right] = \displaystyle\int_0^t \dfrac{1}{2}\,u\sin u\,du = \dfrac{1}{2}\,(\sin t - t\cos t)\,]$

6. Find the Inverse of each of the following transforms :

(i) $\dfrac{1}{s^2+s}$ (ii) $\dfrac{1}{s^2(s^2+\omega^2)}$ (iii) $\dfrac{s+2}{s^2(s+3)}$ (iv) $\dfrac{1}{s^4-2s^3}$ (v) $\dfrac{1}{s}\left(\dfrac{s-a}{s+a}\right)$

(vi) $\dfrac{1}{s^2}\left(\dfrac{s-a}{s+a}\right)$ (vii) $\dfrac{1}{s^2}\left(\dfrac{s+1}{s^2+1}\right)$ (viii) $\dfrac{1}{s^3(s+1)}$

Ans.(i) $1-e^{-t}$ (ii) $\dfrac{1}{\omega^2}\left(t-\dfrac{\sin\omega t}{\omega}\right)$ (iii) $\dfrac{2}{3}\,t + \dfrac{1}{9} - \dfrac{1}{9}\,e^{-3t}$ (iv) $(e^{2t}-1-2t-2t^2)/8$

(v) $2e^{-at}-1$ (vi) $\dfrac{2}{a} - \dfrac{2}{a}\,e^{-at} - t$ (vii) $1+t-\cos t-\sin t$ (viii) $1-t+\dfrac{1}{2}\,t^2-e^{-t}$.

7. Find the Inverse Laplace transforms of the following functions :

(i) $\dfrac{s^2}{(s^2-a^2)^2}$ (ii) $\dfrac{1}{(s-1)^5(s+2)}$ (iii) $\dfrac{s}{(s-2)^5(s+1)^2}$ (iv) $\log\dfrac{s^2+1}{s^2+s}$

Ans. (i) $\dfrac{1}{2a}(\sinh at + at\cosh at)$ (ii) $\dfrac{e^t}{72}\left(t^4-\dfrac{4}{3}\,t^3+\dfrac{4}{3}\,t^2-\dfrac{8}{9}\,t+\dfrac{8}{27}\right) - \dfrac{e^{-2t}}{243}$

(iii) $e^{2t}\left(\dfrac{t^4}{36}+\dfrac{t^3}{54}-\dfrac{t^2}{54}+\dfrac{t}{81}-\dfrac{1}{243}\right) + \dfrac{e^{-t}}{243}$ (iv) $\dfrac{1}{t}\,(1+e^{-t}-2\cos t)$

8. Use the convolution theorem to find Inverse Laplace transforms of the following :

(i) $\dfrac{1}{(s-1)(s-2)}$ (ii) $\dfrac{1}{(s+3)(s-1)}$ (iii) $\dfrac{1}{s^2(s-a)}$ (iv) $\dfrac{1}{(s+2)^2(s-2)}$

(v) $\dfrac{s^2}{(s^2+4)^2}$ (vi) $\dfrac{1}{(s^2+9)^2}$ (vii) $\dfrac{s}{(s^2+4)^3}$ (viii) $\dfrac{1}{s^4-a^4}$

Ans. (i) $e^{2t}-e^t$ (ii) $\dfrac{1}{4}(e^t-e^{-3t})$ (iii) $\dfrac{1}{a^2}(e^{at}-at-1)$ (iv) $\dfrac{1}{16}(e^{2t}-e^{-2t}-4t\,e^{-2t})$

(v) $\dfrac{1}{2}\,t\cos 2t+\dfrac{1}{4}\sin 2t$ (vi) $\dfrac{1}{18}\left(\dfrac{\sin 3t}{3}-t\cos 3t\right)$ (vii) $\dfrac{1}{64}\,t(\sin 2t-2t\cos 2t)$

(viii) $\dfrac{1}{2a^3}\sinh at-\dfrac{1}{2a^4}\sin at.$

9. Show that $\displaystyle\int_0^t\int_0^t\ \ldots\ldots\ \int_0^t f(t)\,dt^n=\int_0^t\dfrac{(t-u)^{n-1}}{(n-1)!}\,f(u)\,du.$

[Hint : Consider Inverse Laplace transform of $\dfrac{1}{s^n}F(s)$ by division by $\dfrac{1}{s^n}$ and convolution theorem.**]**

10. Using partial fractions, find the inverse Laplace transforms of the following :

(i) $\dfrac{4s-5}{s^2-s-2}$ (ii) $\dfrac{s}{(s-1)(s-2)(s-3)}$ (iii) $\dfrac{2s^2-4}{(s+1)(s-2)(s-3)}$ (iv) $\dfrac{s^2+2s-3}{s(s-3)(s+2)}$

(v) $\dfrac{s+2}{(s+3)(s+1)^3}$ (vi) $\dfrac{2s+1}{(s+2)^2(s-1)^2}$ (vii) $\dfrac{s+2}{s^3(s-1)^2}$ (viii) $\dfrac{3s+1}{(s+1)^4}$

Ans. (i) $e^{2t}+3e^{-t}$ (ii) $\dfrac{1}{2}\,e^t-\dfrac{1}{2}\,e^{2t}+\dfrac{3}{2}\,e^{3t}$ (iii) $\dfrac{1}{6}\,e^{-t}-\dfrac{4}{3}\,e^{2t}+\dfrac{7}{2}\,e^{3t}$

(iv) $\dfrac{1}{2}\,t+\dfrac{4}{5}\,e^{3t}-\dfrac{3}{10}\,e^{-2t}$

(v) $\dfrac{1}{8}(2t^2+2t-1)\,e^{-t}+\dfrac{1}{8}\,e^{-3t}$ (vi) $\dfrac{1}{3}\,t(e^t-e^{-2t})$ (vii) $(3t-8)\,e^t+t^2+5t+8$

(viii) $e^{-t}\left(\dfrac{3}{2}\,t^2-\dfrac{1}{3}\,t^3\right)$

11. Using partial fractions, find the inverse Laplace transforms of the following :

(i) $\dfrac{5s+3}{(s-1)(s^2+2s+5)}$ (ii) $\dfrac{s^2-3}{(s+2)(s-3)(s^2+2s+5)}$

(iii) $\dfrac{27s-12s}{(s+4)(s^2+9)}$

(iv) $\dfrac{s^2+2s-4}{(s^2+2s+5)(s^2+2s+2)}$ (v) $\dfrac{s}{(s^2+1)(s^2+2)}$ (vi) $\dfrac{1}{(s^2+2s+5)^2}$

(vii) $\dfrac{s^3+3s^2-s-3}{(s^2+2s+5)^2}$ (viii) $\dfrac{s}{s^4+4}$ (ix) $\dfrac{a(s^2-2a^2)}{s^4+4a^4}$ (x) $\dfrac{1}{s^3-a^3}$ (xi) $\dfrac{s^3}{s^4+64}$

(xii) $\dfrac{s^3+16s-24}{s^4+20s^2+64}$

Ans. (i) $e^t - e^{-t} \cos 2t + \dfrac{3}{2}\, e^{-t} \sin 2t$ (ii) $\dfrac{3}{50}\, e^{3t} - \dfrac{1}{25}\, e^{-2t} - \dfrac{1}{50}\, e^{-t}(\cos 2t - 18 \sin 2t)$

(iii) $3\,(e^{-4t} - \cos 3t)$ (iv) $\dfrac{3}{2}\, e^{-t} \sin 2t - 2e^{-t} \sin t$ (v) $\dfrac{1}{2}\, \sin t - \dfrac{1}{2}\, t\, e^{-t}$

(vi) $\dfrac{1}{16}\, e^{-t}\,(\sin 2t - 2t \cos 2t)$ (vii) $e^{-t}(\cos 2t - 2t \sin 2t)$ (viii) $\dfrac{1}{2}\, \sinh t \sin t$

(ix) $\cos at \sinh at$ (x) $\dfrac{1}{3a^2}\left[e^{at} - e^{-at/2}\left\{ \cos \dfrac{\sqrt{3}}{2}\, at + \sqrt{3}\, \sin \dfrac{\sqrt{3}}{2}\, at \right\} \right]$

(xi) $\cosh 2t \cos 2t$ (xii) $\dfrac{1}{2}\, \sin 4t + \cos 2t - \sin 2t$

4.15 APPLICATIONS TO DIFFERENTIAL EQUATIONS

The Laplace transform is useful in solving differential equations and corresponding initial and boundary value problems. The solution of differential equations involving functions of an impulsive type can also be solved by the use of Laplace transform in a very efficient manner. The general process of solution consists of three main steps :

1. The given differential equation is transformed into an simple algebraic equation (called subsidiary equation).

2. The subsidiary equation is solved by pure algebraic manipulations.

3. The solution of the subsidiary equation is then transformed back to obtain the solution of the given differential equation.

In this way, the Laplace transform method reduces the problem of solving differential equation to an algebraic problem. Another advantage of this method over the classical method is that it solves initial value problem directly without first finding general solution (complete solution) and then evaluating the arbitrary constants. We shall now illustrate this method in the following applications.

Note :

(i) $L\left[\dfrac{dy}{dt}\right] = L\,[y'] = s\, Y(s) - y(0)$

(ii) $L\left[\dfrac{d^2 y}{dt^2}\right] = L\,[y''] = s^2\, Y(s) - s\, y(0) - y'(0)$

(iii) $L\left[\dfrac{d^3 y}{dt^3}\right] = L\,[y'''] = s^3\, Y(s) - s^2\, y(0) - s\, y'(0) - y''(0)$

(iv) $L\left[\dfrac{d^4 y}{dt^4}\right] = L\,[y^{iv}] = s^4\, Y(s) - s^3\, y(0) - s^2\, y'(0) - s\, y''(0) - y'''(0)$ etc.

4.16 SOLUTION OF ORDINARY DIFFERENTIAL EQUATIONS WITH CONSTANT COEFFICIENT

ILLUSTRATIONS

Ex. 1 : *Find the solution of each of the following differential equations which satisfy the given conditions :*

(i) $y'' - 3y' + 2y = 12\, e^{-2t}$, $y(0) = 2,$ $y'(0) = 6.$

(ii) $y'' + y = t$, $y(0) = 1,$ $y'(0) = -2.$

(iii) $y'' + 2y' + y = t\, e^{-t}$, $y(0) = 1,$ $y'(0) = -2.$

(iv) $y''' - 3y'' + 3y' - y = t^2 e^t$, $y(0) = 1,$ $y'(0) = 0,\ y''(0) = -2.$

(v) $y''' - y = e^t$, $y(0) = y'(0) = y''(0) = 0.$

Sol. : (i) Note : In the usual notation, given equation is

$$\frac{d^2 y}{dt^2} - 3\frac{dy}{dt} + 2y\,(t) = 12\, e^{-2t}$$

Taking the Laplace transform of both sides of the differential equation, we have

$$L\left[\frac{d^2 y}{dt^2}\right] - 3\,L\left[\frac{dy}{dt}\right] + 2\,L\,[y(t)] \;=\; 12\,L\,[e^{-2t}]$$

$$\therefore\ \{s^2\,Y(s) - s\,y(0) - y'(0)\} - 3\{s\,Y(s) - y(0)\} + 2Y(s) = \frac{12}{s+2}$$

Substituting the given conditions $y(0) = 2,\ y'(0) = 6$, we get

$$\{s^2\,Y(s) - s(2) - 6\} - 3\,\{s\,Y(s) - 2\} + 2\,Y(s) \;=\; \frac{12}{s+2}$$

or $$(s^2 - 3s + 2)\ Y(s) - 2s \;=\; \frac{12}{s+2}$$

$$\therefore\qquad (s^2 - 3s + 2)\,Y(s) \;=\; +2s + \frac{12}{s+2} \;=\; \frac{2s^2 + 4s + 12}{s+2}$$

$$\therefore\qquad Y(s) \;=\; \frac{2s^2 + 4s + 12}{(s^2 - 3s + 2)\,(s+2)} \;=\; \frac{2s^2 + 4s + 12}{(s-1)\,(s-2)\,(s+2)}$$

Using the method of partial fractions, we can express $Y(s)$ in the form

$$Y(s) \;=\; -\frac{6}{s-1} + \frac{7}{s-2} + \frac{1}{s+2}$$

Taking the inverse Laplace transform of both sides, we get

$$y(t) \;=\; -6\,e^t + 7\,e^{2t} + e^{-2t}$$

which is the required solution.

Check :

$$\because\ y = -6\,e^t + 7\,e^{2t} + e^{-2t}\ \therefore\ y' = -6\,e^t + 14\,e^{2t} - 2\,e^{-2t}\ \text{and}\ \ y'' = -6\,e^t + 28\,e^{2t} + 4\,e^{-2t}$$

Then $y'' - 3y'' + 2y = 12\,e^{-2t}$, $y(0) = 2$, $y'(0) = 6$ and the function $y(t)$ obtained is the required solution.

Note : Classical method will give the solution as

$$y = C_1 e^t + C_2 e^{2t} + e^{-2t}$$

where, C_1 and C_2 are to be evaluated from given conditions.

(ii) Taking the Laplace transform of both sides of the differential equation, we have

$$L[y''] + L[y(t)] = L[t]$$

$$\therefore \{s^2 Y(s) - s\,y(0) - y'(0)\} + Y(s) = \frac{1}{s^2}$$

Substituting the given conditions $y(0) = 1$, $y'(0) = -2$, we get

$$\{s^2 Y(s) - s(1) - (-2)\} + Y(s) = \frac{1}{s^2}$$

or $\qquad (s^2 + 1)\,Y(s) - s + 2 = \dfrac{1}{s^2}$

$$\therefore \qquad (s^2 + 1)\,Y(s) = s - 2 + \frac{1}{s^2}$$

$$\therefore \qquad Y(s) = \frac{s-2}{s^2+1} + \frac{1}{s^2(s^2+1)}$$

$$= \frac{s}{s^2+1} - \frac{2}{s^2+1} + \frac{1}{s^2} - \frac{1}{s^2+1} \quad [\text{By partial fractions}]$$

$$= \frac{1}{s^2} + \frac{s}{s^2+1} - \frac{3}{s^2+1}$$

Taking the Inverse Laplace transform of both sides, we get

$$y(t) = t + \cos t - 3 \sin t$$

which can be verified as the solution.

(iii) Taking Laplace transform of both sides, we have

$$L[y''] + 2[y'] + L[y(t)] = L[t\,e^{-t}]$$

$$\therefore \{s^2 Y(s) - s\,y(0) - y'(0)\} + 2\{s\,Y(s) - y(0)\} + Y(s) = \frac{1}{(s+1)^2}$$

Using the given conditions $y(0) = 1$, $y'(0) = -2$, it reduces to

$$\{s^2 Y(s) - s(1) - (-2)\} + 2\{s\,Y(s) - 1\} + Y(s) = \frac{1}{(s+1)^2}$$

or $\qquad (s^2 + 2s + 1)\,Y(s) - s = \dfrac{1}{(s+1)^2}$

$$\therefore \qquad (s^2 + 2s + 1)\,Y(s) = s + \frac{1}{(s+1)^2}$$

or $\qquad Y(s) = \dfrac{s}{(s+1)^2} + \dfrac{1}{(s+1)^4} = \dfrac{s+1-1}{(s+1)^2} + \dfrac{1}{(s+1)^4}$

$$= \frac{1}{(s+1)} - \frac{1}{(s+1)^2} + \frac{1}{(s+1)^4}$$

Taking the inverse Laplace transform of both sides, we get

$$y(t) = e^{-t} - t\,e^{-t} + \frac{t^3\,e^{-t}}{3!}$$

(iv) Taking the Laplace transform of both sides, we have

$$L\,[y'''] - 3\,L\,[y''] + 3\,L\,[y'] - L\,[y(t)] = L\,[t^2\,e^t]$$

$$\{s^3\,Y(s) - s^2\,y(0) - s\,y'(0) - y''(0)\} - 3\,\{s^2\,Y(s) - s\,y(0) - y'(0)\}$$

$$+\,3\,\{s\,Y(s) - y(0)\} - Y(s) = \frac{2}{(s-1)^3}$$

Using the given conditions $y(0) = 1$, $y'(0) = 0$, $y''(0) = -2$, we get

$$(s^3 - 3s^2 + 3s - 1)\,Y(s) - s^2 + 3s - 1 = \frac{2}{(s-1)^3}$$

$$\therefore \qquad Y(s) = \frac{s^2 - 3s + 1}{s^3 - 3s^2 + 3s - 1} + \frac{2}{(s^3 - 3s^2 + 3s - 1)\,(s-1)^3}$$

$$= \frac{s^2 - 3s + 1}{(s-1)^3} + \frac{2}{(s-1)^6}$$

$$= \frac{s^2 - 2s + 1 - s}{(s-1)^3} + \frac{2}{(s-1)^6}$$

$$= \frac{(s-1)^2 - (s-1) - 1}{(s-1)^3} + \frac{2}{(s-1)^6}$$

$$= \frac{1}{s-1} - \frac{1}{(s-1)^2} - \frac{1}{(s-1)^3} + \frac{2}{(s-1)^6}$$

and $\qquad y(t) = e^t - t\,e^t - \dfrac{t^2\,e^t}{2} + \dfrac{t^5\,e^t}{60},$ which is a particular solution.

Remark : If we assume $y(0) = A$, $y'(0) = B$, $y''(0) = C$, we find

$$Y(s) = \frac{As^2 + (B - 3A)\,s + 3A - 3B + C}{(s-1)^3} + \frac{2}{(s-1)^6}$$

Since A, B, C are arbitrary, so also is the polynomial in the numerator of the first term on the right. We can thus write

$$Y(s) = \frac{C_1}{(s-1)^3} + \frac{C_2}{(s-1)^2} + \frac{C_3}{s-1} + \frac{2}{(s-1)^6}$$

Taking inverse, we obtain general solution as

$$y(t) = \frac{C_1\,t^2\,e^t}{2} + C_2\,t\,e^t + C_3\,e^t + \frac{t^5\,e^t}{60}\,.$$

It should be noted that finding the general solution is easier than finding the particular solution. Since we avoid the necessity of determining the constants in the partial fraction expansion.

(v) Taking the Laplace transform of both sides, we have

$$L\,[y'''] - L\,[y(t)] = L\,[e^t]$$

$$\therefore \quad \{s^3\,Y(s) - s^2\,y(0) - s\,y'(0) - y''(0)\} - Y(s) = \frac{1}{s-1}$$

Using the given conditions $y(0) = y'(0) = y''(0) = 0$, we get

$$(s^3 - 1)\, Y(s) = \frac{1}{s-1}$$

$$\therefore \qquad Y(s) = \frac{1}{(s^3-1)\,(s-1)} = \frac{1}{(s-1)^2\,(s^2+s+1)}$$

Using the method of partial fractions, we can express $Y(s)$ in the form

$$Y(s) = \frac{-1/3}{s-1} + \frac{1/3}{(s-1)^2} + \frac{s/3 + 1/3}{s^2+s+1}$$

$$= -\frac{1}{3}\frac{1}{s-1} + \frac{1}{3}\frac{1}{(s-1)^2} + \frac{1}{3}\frac{(s+1/2)-1/2}{(s+1/2)^2+(\sqrt{3}/2)^2}$$

Taking inverse Laplace transform of both sides, we get

$$y(t) = -\frac{1}{3}\,e^t + \frac{1}{3}\,t\,e^t + \frac{1}{3}\,e^{-t/2}L^{-1}\left[\frac{s-1/2}{s^2+(\sqrt{3}/2)^2}\right]$$

$$= -\frac{1}{3}\,e^t + \frac{1}{3}\,t\,e^t + \frac{1}{3}\,e^{-t/2}\left\{\cos\frac{\sqrt{3}}{2}\,t + \frac{1}{\sqrt{3}}\,\sin\frac{\sqrt{3}}{2}\,t\right\}$$

Ex. 2 : *Solve each of the following by using Laplace transforms :*

(i) $\quad \dfrac{d^2x}{dt^2} + 9x\,(t) = 18\,t\,,\ x(0) = 0,\quad x\,(\pi/2) = 0.$

(ii) $\quad \dfrac{d^2y}{dt^2} + 2\,\dfrac{dy}{dt} + 5y = e^{-t}\sin t,\quad y(0) = 0,\ y'\,(0) = 1.$

(iii) $\quad y'' + 4y' + 13y = \dfrac{1}{3}\,e^{-2t}\sin 3t,\quad y(0) = 1,\ y'(0) = -2.$

(iv) $\quad (D^2 + n^2)\,x = a\sin(nt + \alpha),\qquad x(0) = x'(0) = 0.$

Sol. : (i) Taking Laplace transform of both sides, we get

$$L\left[\frac{d^2x}{dt^2}\right] + 9\,L\,[x(t)] = 18\,L\,[t]$$

$$\{s^2\,X(s) - s\,x(0) - x'(0)\} + 9\,X(s) = \frac{18}{s^2}$$

Since $x'(0)$ is not known, let $x'(0) = A$. Then

$$\{s^2\,X(s) - s(0) - A\} + 9\,X(s) = \frac{18}{s^2} \qquad\qquad \{\because\ x(0) = 0\}$$

or $\qquad\qquad (s^2 + 9)\,X(s) = A + \dfrac{18}{s^2}$

$$X(s) = \frac{A}{s^2+9} + \frac{18}{s^2\,(s^2+9)}$$

$$= \frac{A}{s^2+9} + \frac{18 + 2s^2 - 2s^2}{s^2\,(s^2+9)}$$

$$= \frac{A}{s^2 + 9} - \frac{2}{s^2 + 9} + \frac{2\,(s^2 + 9)}{s^2\,(s^2 + 9)}$$

$$= \frac{(A - 2)}{s^2 + 9} + \frac{2}{s^2}$$

Thus
$$x(t) = \left(\frac{A - 2}{3}\right) \sin 3t + 2t$$

To determine A, we put $t = \pi/2$ and obtain

$$x\left(\frac{\pi}{2}\right) = \left(\frac{A - 2}{3}\right) \sin 3\pi/2 + 2\pi/2$$

$$0 = \left(\frac{A - 2}{3}\right) (-1) + \pi \quad \text{or} \quad \left(\frac{A - 2}{3}\right) = \pi$$

$$\therefore \qquad x = \pi \sin 3t + 2t$$

(ii) Taking Laplace transform of both sides, we get

$$L\left[\frac{d^2y}{dt^2}\right] + 2\,L\left[\frac{dy}{dt}\right] + 5\,L\,[y(t)] = L\,[e^{-t} \sin t]$$

$$\therefore \ \{s^2\,Y(s) - s\,y(0) - y'(0)\} + 2\,\{s\,Y(s) - y(0)\} + 5\,Y(s) = \frac{1}{(s + 1)^2 + 1}$$

$$\therefore \quad \{s^2\,Y(s) - s(0) - 1\} + 2\,\{s\,Y(s) - 0\} + 5\,Y(s) = \frac{1}{s^2 + 2s + 2}$$

$$\left\{ \because \ y(0) = 0, \ y'(0) = 1 \right\}$$

$$\therefore \quad \{s^2\,Y(s) - s(0) - 1\} + 2\,\{s\,Y(s) - 0\} + 5\,Y(s) = \frac{1}{s^2 + 2s + 2}$$

$$\therefore \qquad (s^2 + 2s + 5)\,Y(s) - 1 = \frac{1}{s^2 + 2s + 2}$$

$$\therefore \qquad Y(s) = \frac{1}{(s^2 + 2s + 5)} + \frac{1}{(s^2 + 2s + 2)\,(s^2 + 2s + 5)}$$

$$= \frac{s^2 + 2s + 3}{(s^2 + 2s + 2)\,(s^2 + 2s + 5)}$$

$$\therefore \qquad y(t) = \frac{1}{3}\,e^{-t}\,(\sin t + \sin 2t) \ \text{[Refer solved example 14 (iv), sec. 5.9]}$$

(iii) Taking Laplace transform of each side, we have

$$L\,[y''] + 4\,L\,[y'] + 13\,L\,[y(t)] = \frac{1}{3}\,L\,[e^{-2t} \sin 3t]$$

$$\therefore \ \{s^2\,Y(s) - s\,y(0) - y'(0)\} + 4\,\{s\,Y(s) - y(0)\} + 13\,Y(s) = \frac{1}{3} \cdot \frac{3}{(s + 2)^2 + 9}$$

$\therefore\ \{s^2\,Y(s) - s(1) - (-2)\} + 4\,\{s\,Y(s) - 1\} + 13\,Y(s)\ =\ \dfrac{1}{(s+2)^2+9}$

$$\{\because\ y(0) = 1,\ y'(0) = -2\}$$

or $\qquad (s^2 + 4s + 13)\,Y(s) - s - 2\ =\ \dfrac{1}{(s+2)^2+9}$

or $\qquad Y(s)\ =\ \dfrac{s+2}{s^2+4s+13} + \dfrac{1}{(s^2+4s+13)\,[(s+2)^2+9]}$

$$=\ \dfrac{s+2}{(s+2)^2+9} + \dfrac{1}{[(s+2)^2+9]^2}$$

Taking inverse Laplace transform, we get

$$y(t)\ =\ L^{-1}\left[\dfrac{s+2}{(s+2)^2+9}\right] + L^{-1}\left[\dfrac{1}{\{(s+2)^2+9\}^2}\right]$$

$$=\ e^{-2t}\left[\dfrac{s}{s^2+9}\right] + e^{-2t}\,L^{-1}\left[\dfrac{1}{(s^2+9)^2}\right]$$

$$=\ e^{-2t}\cos 3t + e^{-2t}\,L^{-1}\left[\dfrac{1}{s^2+9}\cdot\dfrac{1}{s^2+9}\right]$$

$$=\ e^{-2t}\cos 3t + e^{-2t}\left\{\dfrac{\sin 3t}{3}\cdot\dfrac{\sin 3t}{3}\right\}\qquad \text{(By the convolution theorem)}$$

$$=\ e^{-2t}\cos 3t + \dfrac{e^{-2t}}{9}\int_0^t \sin 3u\,\sin 3\,(t-u)\,du$$

$$=\ e^{-2t}\cos 3t + \dfrac{e^{-2t}}{9}\int_0^t \dfrac{\cos (6u - 3t) - \cos 3t}{2}\,du$$

$$=\ e^{-2t}\cos 3t + \dfrac{e^{-2t}}{18}\left[\dfrac{\sin (6u - 3t)}{6} - u\cos 3t\right]_0^t$$

$$=\ e^{-2t}\cos 3t + \dfrac{e^{-2t}}{18}\left(\dfrac{\sin 3t}{3} - t\cos 3t\right)$$

$$=\ e^{-2t}\cos 3t + \dfrac{e^{-2t}}{54}\,(\sin 3t - 3t\cos 3t)\,.$$

(iv) Given equation is $x''(t) + n^2\,x(t) = a\sin nt\cos\alpha + a\cos nt\sin\alpha$.

Taking Laplace transform of the equation, we have

$$L\,[x''(t)] + n^2\,L\,[x(t)]\ =\ a\cos\alpha\;L\,[\sin nt] + a\sin\alpha\;L\,[\cos nt]$$

$$\{s^2 X(s) - s\, x(0) - x'(0)\} + n^2 X(s) = a \cos \alpha \left(\frac{n}{s^2 + n^2}\right) + a \sin \alpha \left(\frac{s}{s^2 + n^2}\right)$$

Using the given conditions $x(0) = x'(0) = 0$, we get

$$(s^2 + n^2)\, X(s) = a \cos \alpha \left(\frac{n}{s^2 + n^2}\right) + a \sin \alpha \left(\frac{s}{s^2 + n^2}\right)$$

$$\therefore \quad X(s) = a \cos \alpha \left[\frac{n}{(s^2 + n^2)^2}\right] + a \sin \alpha \left[\frac{s}{(s^2 + n^2)^2}\right]$$

Thus $\quad x(t) = (a \cos \alpha)\, L^{-1}\left[\frac{n}{(s^2 + n^2)^2}\right] + (a \sin \alpha)\, L^{-1}\left[\frac{s}{(s^2 + n^2)^2}\right]$

$$= (a \cos \alpha) \left\{\frac{n}{2n^3}(\sin nt - nt \cos nt)\right\} + (a \sin \alpha) \left\{\frac{t \sin nt}{2n}\right\}$$

$$= \frac{a \cos \alpha}{2n^2}(\sin nt - nt \cos nt) + \frac{a \sin \alpha}{2n}(t \sin nt)$$

$$\left[\textbf{Note : } \text{(i)} \quad L^{-1}\left[\frac{1}{s^2 + n^2}\right] = \frac{\sin nt}{n} \quad \therefore \; L^{-1}\left[-\frac{d}{ds}\frac{1}{s^2 + n^2}\right] = \frac{t \sin nt}{n}\right.$$

$$\therefore \qquad L^{-1}\left[\frac{2s}{(s^2 + n^2)^2}\right] = \frac{t \sin nt}{n} \quad \text{or} \quad L^{-1}\left[\frac{s}{(s^2 + n^2)^2}\right] = \frac{t \sin nt}{2n}$$

$$\text{(ii)} \qquad L^{-1}\left[\frac{1}{s}\cdot\frac{s}{(s^2 + n^2)^2}\right] = \int_0^t \frac{t \sin nt}{2n}\, dt = \frac{1}{2n^3}(\sin nt - nt \cos nt) \left.\vphantom{\int_0^t}\right]$$

Ex. 3 : *Solve the differential equation*

$$y'' + 4y = f(t), \quad y(0) = 0, \quad y'(0) = 1.$$

Sol. : Taking Laplace transform of both sides, we have

$$L\,[y''] + 4\,L\,[y(t)] = L\,[f(t)]$$

$$\{s^2 Y(s) - s\, y(0) - y'(0)\} + 4\,Y(s) = F(s)$$

Using the given conditions $y(0) = 0$, $y'(0) = 1$, we get

$$\{s^2 Y(s) - s(0) - 1\} + 4\,Y(s) = F(s)$$

or $$(s^2 + 4)\,Y(s) - 1 = F(s)$$

$$\therefore \qquad Y(s) = \frac{1}{s^2 + 4} + \frac{F(s)}{s^2 + 4} \qquad\qquad \dots \text{(i)}$$

Then using the convolution theorem, we have

$$y(t) = \sin t + f(t) * \frac{\sin 2t}{2} = \sin t + \frac{1}{2}\int_0^t f(u) \sin 2\,(t - u)\, du.$$

[Note that in this case, actual Laplace transform of f(t) does not enter into final solution.]

Ex. 4 : *Using the Laplace transform, solve the following differential equations :*

(i) $\dfrac{dy}{dt} + 3y\,(t) + 2 \displaystyle\int_0^t y(t)\,dt = t,\ \ given\ \ y(0) = 0$

(ii) $\dfrac{dy}{dt} + 2y\,(t) + \displaystyle\int_0^t y(t)\,dt = \sin t,\ given\ \ y(0) = 1.$ **(SUK Dec. 12)**

Sol. : (i) We have $L\left[\dfrac{dy}{dt}\right] + 3\,L\,[y(t)] + 2\,L\left[\displaystyle\int_0^t y(t)\,dt\right] = L\,[t]$

$\therefore\quad \{s\,Y(s) - y(0)\} + 3\,Y(s) + \dfrac{2}{s}\,Y(s) = \dfrac{1}{s^2}$

Using given condition $y(0) = 0$, it reduces to

$\left(s + 3 + \dfrac{2}{s}\right) Y(s) = \dfrac{1}{s^2}$

$\therefore\qquad\qquad Y(s) = \dfrac{s}{s^2\,(s^2 + 3s + 2)}$

$\qquad\qquad\qquad\quad = \dfrac{1}{s\,(s + 1)\,(s + 2)}$

$\qquad\qquad\qquad\quad = \dfrac{1/2}{s} - \dfrac{1}{s + 1} + \dfrac{1/2}{s + 2}$

$\therefore\qquad\qquad y(t) = \dfrac{1}{2} - e^{-t} + \dfrac{1}{2}\,e^{-2t}$

(ii) We have $L\left[\dfrac{dy}{dt}\right] + 2\,L\,[y(t)] + L\left[\displaystyle\int_0^t y(t)\,dt\right] = L\,[\sin t]$

$\therefore\quad \{s\,Y(s) - y(0)\} + 2\,Y(s) + \dfrac{1}{s}\,Y(s) = \dfrac{1}{s^2 + 1}$

Using given condition, it reduces to

$\left(s + 2 + \dfrac{1}{s}\right) Y(s) = 1 + \dfrac{1}{s^2 + 1}$

$\therefore\qquad\qquad Y(s) = \dfrac{s}{s^2 + 2s + 1} + \dfrac{s}{(s^2 + 2s + 1)\,(s^2 + 1)}$

$\qquad\qquad\qquad\quad = \dfrac{s}{(s + 1)^2} + \dfrac{s}{(s + 1)^2\,(s^2 + 1)}$

$$= \frac{1}{s+1} - \frac{1}{(s+1)^2} + \frac{-1/2}{(s+1)^2} + \frac{1/2}{s^2+1} \quad \text{(By partial fraction)}$$

$$= \frac{1}{s+1} - \frac{3/2}{(s+1)^2} + \frac{1/2}{s^2+1}$$

$$\therefore \quad y(t) = e^{-t} - \frac{3}{2} t\, e^{-t} + \frac{1}{2} \sin t$$

Note : Differential equations in Ex. 4 (i) and (ii) are called integrodifferential equations, since an integral as well as a derivative of the dependent variables appears in these equations.

Remark : The Laplace transform can also be used to solve some ordinary differential equations with variable coefficients. We can use the following result :

$$L\left[t^m y^{(n)}(t)\right] = (-1)^m \frac{d^m}{ds^m}\, L\left[y^{(n)}(t)\right]$$

EXERCISE 4.5

1. Find the solution of each of the following differential equations which satisfy the given conditions :

(i) $y'' + y = 0$, $y(0) = 1$, $y'(0) = 2$. **Ans.** $y(t) = \cos t + 2 \sin t$

(ii) $y'' - 3y' = 9$, $y(0) = y'(0) = 0$ **Ans.** $y(t) = e^{3t} - 3t - 1$

(iii) $y'' - 3y' + 2y = 4e^{2t}$, $y(0) = -3$, $y'(0) = 5$ **Ans.** $y(t) = -7e^t + 4e^{2t} + 4t\, e^{2t}$

(iv) $y'' + 4y' + 13y = 2e^{-t}$, $y(0) = y'(0) = 0$

Ans. $y(t) = \frac{1}{25} \left\{(13 - 2t)\, e^{-t} + 12\, e^{-4t}\right\}$

(v) $y'' + 4y + 8y = 1$, $y(0) = 0$, $y'(0) = 1$ **(SUK Dec. 11)**

Ans. $y(t) = \frac{1}{8} - \frac{1}{8}\, e^{-2t}(\cos 2t - 3 \sin 2t)$

(vi) $y'' - 2y' + y = e^{-2t}$, $y(0) = y'(0) = 0$ **Ans.** $y(t) = \frac{-1}{9}\, e^t + \frac{1}{3} t\, e^t + \frac{1}{9}\, e^{-2t}$

(vii) $y'' + 2y' + y = 6t\, e^{-t}$, $y(0) = 2$, $y'(0) = 5$

Ans. $y(t) = e^{-t}(t^3 + 7t + 2)$

(viii) $y'' - 7y' + 10y = e^{2t} + 10$, $y(0) = 0$, $y'(0) = \frac{-1}{3}$

Ans. $y(t) = 2 + \frac{4}{3}\, e^{5t} - \frac{10}{3}\, e^{2t} - \frac{t\, e^{2t}}{3}$

(ix) $y''' + y' = 2$, $y(0) = 3$, $y'(0) = 1$, $y''(0) = 2$

Ans. $y(t) = 5 + 2t - \sin t - 2 \cos t$

(x) $y'' + 4y' + 3y = 10 \sin t$, $y(0) = y'(0) = 0$

Ans. $y(t) = \dfrac{5}{2} e^{-t} - \dfrac{1}{2} e^{-3t} + \sin t - 2 \cos t$

(xi) $y'' + 9y = \cos 2t$, $y(0) = 1$, $y(\pi/2) = -1$

Ans. $y(t) = \dfrac{4}{5} \cos 3t + \dfrac{4}{5} \sin 3t + \dfrac{1}{5} \cos 2t$

(xii) $y'' + 2y' + 2y = 2 \cos 2t - 4 \sin 2t$, $y(0) = 0$, $y'(0) = 1$

Ans. $y(t) = \dfrac{3}{5} \cos 2t + \dfrac{4}{5} \sin 2t - \dfrac{3}{5} e^{-t} (\cos t + 2 \sin t)$

(xiii) $y'' + y' - 2y = 3 \cos 3t - 11 \sin 3t$, $y(0) = 0$, $y'(0) = 6$.

Ans. $y(t) = e^{t} - e^{-2t} + \sin 3t$

(xiv) $y'' + y' - 2y = 2 (1 + t - t^2)$, $y(0) = 0$, $y'(0) = 3$ **Ans.** $y(t) = t^2 - e^{-2t} + e^{t}$

(xv) $y'' + y = t \cos 2t$, $y(0) = y'(0) = 0$ **Ans.** $y(t) = \dfrac{4}{9} \sin 2t - \dfrac{5}{9} \sin t - \dfrac{1}{3} t \cos 2t$

(xvi) $y^{iv} + y'' - 2y = 0$, $y(0) = 0$, $y'(0) = -1$, $y''(0) = 0$, $y'''(0) = 1$.

Ans. $y(t) = -\dfrac{1}{3} \left(\sqrt{2} \sin \sqrt{2} \, t + \sinh t \right)$

(xvii) $y^{iv} + 2y'' + y = \sin t$, $y(0) = y'(0) = y''(0) = y'''(0) = 0$.

Ans. $y(t) = \dfrac{1}{8} \{ (3 - t^2) \sin t - 3t \cos t \}$

2. Solve each of the following by using Laplace transform :

(i) $\dfrac{d^2 y}{dt^2} + 3 \dfrac{dy}{dt} + 2y = f(t)$, $y(0) = y'(0) = 0$

where $f(t) = \begin{cases} 1 & , \quad 0 < t < 1 \\ 0 & , \quad \quad t > 1 \end{cases}$

Ans. $\dfrac{1}{2} - e^{-t} + \dfrac{1}{2} e^{-2t} - \left\{ \dfrac{1}{2} - e^{-(t-1)} + \dfrac{1}{2} e^{-2(t-1)} \right\} U(t-1)$

(ii) $\dfrac{d^2y}{dt^2} + n^2y = f(t), \quad y(0) = y'(0) = 0, \quad (n \ne 1)$

where $f(t) = \begin{cases} 0 & , \quad 0 < t < \pi \\ \sin t & , \quad \pi < t < 2\pi \\ 0 & , \quad t > 2\pi \end{cases}$

$$\textbf{Ans.}\ \frac{1}{n\,(n^2 - 1)}\ (1 + \cos n\pi)\ \sin nt,\ \pi < t < 2\pi$$

(iii) $y(t) + \displaystyle\int_0^t y(t)\, dt = 1 - e^{-t}.$ **Ans.** $y = t\, e^{-t}$

(iv) $\dfrac{dy}{dt} + 4y\,(t) + 5 \displaystyle\int_0^t y(t)\, dt = e^{-t},\ y(0) = 0$ **Ans.** $\dfrac{1}{2}\,(1 + e^{-2t} - 2e^{-t})$

(v) $\dfrac{dy}{dt} + y(t) - 2\displaystyle\int_0^t y(t)\, dt = \dfrac{t^2}{2},\ y(0) = 1,\ y(0) = -2.$

$$\textbf{Ans. } y(t) = \frac{1}{3}\,e^t + \frac{11}{12}\,e^{-2t} - \frac{t}{2} - \frac{1}{4}$$

3. A particle moves along a line so that its displacement x from a fixed point O at any time t is given by $\dfrac{d^2x}{dt^2} + 4\dfrac{dx}{dt} + 5x = 80 \sin 5t.$

If at t = 0, the particle is at rest at x = 0, find the displacement at any time t > 0.

$$\textbf{Ans. } x(t) = 2e^{-2t}\,(\cos t + 7 \sin t) - 2\,(\sin 5t + \cos 5t)$$

UNIT - V

FOURIER SERIES

5.1 INTRODUCTION

Fourier series and Fourier transform are main tools used in the analysis and design of many physical and engineering problems such as heat conduction, vibration, electrodynamics and linear time invariant systems. Fourier series is used in representation of periodic signals which involve the decomposition of signals in terms of sinusoidal components. Periodic functions encountered in practice are triangular waves, rectangular waves, square waves, sinusoidal waves etc. Fourier series is the basic mathematical representation of periodic functions. It is an infinite series of sines and cosines of multiples of x, satisfying certain conditions, known as Dirichlet's conditions. Fourier series are, in a certain sense, more universal than Taylor series, because many periodic functions of practical interest which are not infinitely differentiable or with finite number of discontinuities can conveniently be expanded in Fourier series, but do not have Taylor series representations. In the next sections, we discuss periodic functions and Fourier series.

5.2 PERIODIC FUNCTIONS

A function f(x) is said to be *periodic* if it is defined for all real x and if there is some positive number T such that

$$f(x + T) = f(x) \qquad \text{for all } x$$

The number T is then called period of f(x).

From the above definition it follows that, if n is any integer, then

$$f(x + nT) = f(x) \qquad \text{for all } x$$

Hence 2T, 3T, 4T, ... are also periods of f(x). We call T the fundamental period, or simply the period, it is the smallest period of f(x).

Example 1 : sin x, cos x, sec x and cosec x are periodic functions with fundamental period 2π while tan x and cot x are periodic functions with fundamental period π.

Example 2 : The constant function f(x) = c is also periodic function. Every positive number is a period of constant function.

Remark 1 : If f(x) is a periodic function of period T then f(ax), a $\neq$ 0 is a periodic function of fundamental period $\dfrac{T}{a}$.

For example, fundamental period of sin 2x is $\dfrac{2\pi}{2} = \pi$.

Remark 2 : The functions sin nx and cos nx are periodic functions with fundamental period $\dfrac{2\pi}{n}$ as $\sin n\left(x + \dfrac{2\pi}{n}\right) = \sin nx$ and $\cos n\left(x + \dfrac{2\pi}{n}\right) = \cos nx$.

For example, fundamental periods of sin x, sin 2x, sin 3x are 2π, π and $\dfrac{2\pi}{3}$ respectively.

Also, we know that, since any positive integral multiple of a period is also a period, it follows by multiplying $\dfrac{2\pi}{n}$ by n that 2π is also a period of sin nx and cos nx (Refer Fig. 5.1).

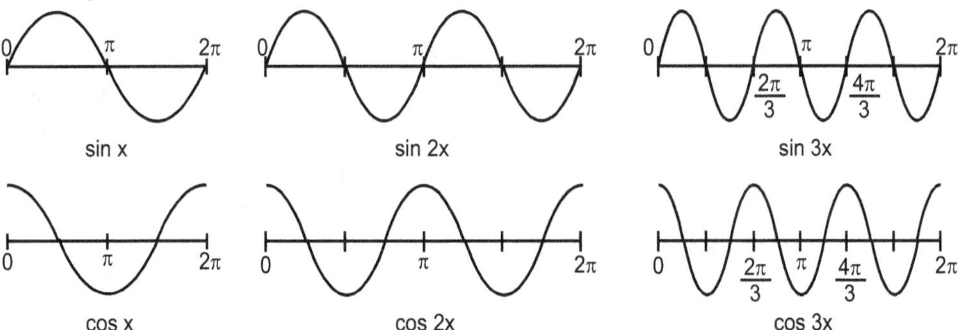

Fig. 5.1 : sine and cosine functions having a period 2π

Trigonometric Series : A series of the form

$$\frac{a_0}{2} + a_1 \cos x + b_1 \sin x + a_2 \cos 2x + b_2 \sin 2x + \ldots,$$

where $a_0, a_1, a_2, \ldots, b_1, b_2, \ldots$ are real constants, is called a trigonometric series and a_n, b_n are the coefficients of the series.

We see that each term of the series has the period 2π. Hence, if the series converges, its sum will be a function of period 2π.

5.3 FOURIER SERIES

If f(x) is a periodic function of period 2π, defined in the interval $c \le x \le c + 2\pi$ and satisfies the Dirichlet's conditions :

(i)   f(x) is finite and single valued and also its integral exists in the interval

(ii)   f(x) has at most finite number of finite discontinuities in the interval.

(iii)   f(x) has at most finite number of maxima and minima in the interval.

then f(x) can be represented by trigonometric series

$$f(x) = \frac{a_0}{2} + \sum_{n=1}^{\infty} (a_n \cos nx + b_n \sin nx)$$

This representation of f(x) is called *Fourier series* and its coefficients a_0, a_n, b_n are called the Fourier coefficients which are required to be determined from f(x) by the Euler's formulae, which we shall derive first.

Example 1 : $\sin^{-1} x$ cannot have a Fourier series expansion in any interval, since it is not a single-valued function.

Example 2 : tan x cannot have a Fourier series expansion in $(0, 2\pi)$, since it becomes infinite at $x = \dfrac{\pi}{2}$.

Example 3 : $f(x) = \dfrac{1}{x - 2}$ cannot have a Fourier series expansion, since it has infinite discontinuity at x = 2.

Example 4 : e^{ax} can be expanded as a Fourier series in any interval, since this function satisfies all Dirichlet's conditions.

5.4 NOTE (USEFUL RESULTS)

To determine the Fourier coefficients a_0, a_n and b_n, we shall read the following definite integrals which are valid for all values of c, provided m and n are integers, satisfying given restrictions.

(I) $\quad \displaystyle\int_{c}^{c+2\pi} \cos nx \, dx = \left[\dfrac{\sin nx}{n}\right]_{c}^{c+2\pi} = 0 \qquad\qquad (n \neq 0)$

(II) $\quad \displaystyle\int_{c}^{c+2\pi} \sin nx \, dx = \left[-\dfrac{\cos nx}{n}\right]_{c}^{c+2\pi} = 0 \qquad\qquad (n \neq 0)$

(III) $\quad \displaystyle\int_{c}^{c+2\pi} \sin mx \cos nx \, dx = \dfrac{1}{2} \displaystyle\int_{c}^{c+2\pi} [\sin (m + n) x + \sin (m - n) x] \, dx$

$$= \dfrac{1}{2}\left[-\dfrac{\cos (m + n) x}{(m + n)} - \dfrac{\cos (m - n) x}{(m - n)}\right]_{c}^{c+2\pi} = 0 \ (m \neq n)$$

If m = n,

$$\int_{c}^{c+2\pi} \sin mx \cos nx \, dx = \dfrac{1}{2} \int_{c}^{c+2\pi} \sin 2nx \, dx = 0 \qquad\qquad (m = n)$$

Hence, $\displaystyle\int_{c}^{c+2\pi} \sin mx \cos nx \, dx = 0$, for all m and n.

(IV) $\displaystyle\int_{c}^{c+2\pi} \cos mx \cos nx \, dx = \frac{1}{2} \int_{c}^{c+2\pi} [\cos (m + n) x + \cos (m - n) x] \, dx$

$$= \frac{1}{2} \left[\frac{\sin (m + n) x}{(m + n)} + \frac{\sin (m - n) x}{(m - n)} \right]_{c}^{c+2\pi} = 0 \qquad (m \neq n)$$

If m = n,

$$\int_{c}^{c+2\pi} \cos mx \cos nx = \int_{c}^{c+2\pi} \cos^2 nx \, dx = \frac{1}{2} \left[x + \frac{\sin 2nx}{2n} \right]_{c}^{c+2\pi} = \pi \qquad (m = n)$$

Hence, $\displaystyle\int_{c}^{c+2\pi} \cos mx \cos nx = \begin{cases} 0, & m \neq n \\ \pi, & m = n \end{cases}$

(V) $\displaystyle\int_{c}^{c+2\pi} \sin mx \sin nx \, dx = \frac{1}{2} \int_{c}^{c+2\pi} [\cos (m - n) x - \cos (m + n) x] \, dx$

$$= \frac{1}{2} \left[\frac{\sin (m - n) x}{(m - n)} - \frac{\sin (m + n) x}{(m + n)} \right]_{c}^{c+2\pi} = 0 \qquad (m \neq n)$$

If m = n,

$$\int_{c}^{c+2\pi} \sin mx \sin nx \, dx = \int_{c}^{c+2\pi} \sin^2 nx \, dx = \frac{1}{2} \left[x - \frac{\sin 2nx}{2n} \right]_{c}^{c+2\pi} = \pi \qquad (m = n)$$

Hence, $\displaystyle\int_{c}^{c+2\pi} \sin mx \sin nx \, dx = \begin{cases} 0, & m \neq n \\ \pi, & m = n \end{cases}$

5.5 DETERMINATION OF FOURIER COEFFICIENTS (EULER'S FORMULAE)

Let f(x) be a periodic function of period 2π which can be represented in the interval $c \leq x \leq c + 2\pi$, by

$$f(x) = \frac{a_0}{2} + \sum_{n=1}^{\infty} (a_n \cos nx + b_n \sin nx) \qquad \ldots (1)$$

To find a_0, a_n and b_n, we assume that the series (1) is uniformly convergent and it can be integrated term by term in the given interval.

We first determine a_0. Integrating both sides of (1) from c to c + 2π, we have

$$\int_{c}^{c+2\pi} f(x)\, dx = \int_{c}^{c+2\pi} \left[\frac{a_0}{2} + \sum_{n=1}^{\infty} (a_n \cos nx + b_n \sin nx) \right] dx$$

$$= \frac{a_0}{2} \int_{c}^{c+2\pi} dx + \sum_{n=1}^{\infty} \left[a_n \int_{c}^{c+2\pi} \cos nx\, dx + b_n \int_{c}^{c+2\pi} \sin nx\, dx \right]$$

$$= \frac{a_0}{2} (c + 2\pi - c) + 0 \qquad \text{[from results I, II]}$$

$$= a_0\, \pi$$

Thus, $$a_0 = \frac{1}{\pi} \int_{c}^{c+2\pi} f(x)\, dx \qquad \qquad \dots (2)$$

To determine a_n, multiply (1) by cos nx and then integrate from c to c + 2π, we have

$$\int_{c}^{c+2\pi} f(x) \cos nx\, dx = \int_{c}^{c+2\pi} \left[\frac{a_0}{2} + \sum_{n=1}^{\infty} (a_n \cos nx + b_n \sin nx) \right] \cos nx\, dx$$

$$= \frac{a_0}{2} \int_{c}^{c+2\pi} \cos nx\, dx + \int_{c}^{c+2\pi} \left(\sum_{n=1}^{\infty} a_n \cos nx \right) \cos nx\, dx$$

$$+ \int_{c}^{c+2\pi} \left(\sum_{n=1}^{\infty} b_n \sin nx \right) \cos nx\, dx$$

This is equivalent to integrate

$$= \frac{a_0}{2} \int_{c}^{c+2\pi} \cos nx\, dx + \int_{c}^{c+2\pi} a_m \cos mx \cos nx\, dx + \int_{c}^{c+2\pi} b_m \sin mx \cos nx\, dx$$

$$\text{where } m = 1, 2, \dots, n, \dots$$

$$= 0 + a_n\, \pi + 0 \qquad \text{(from results I, IV, III)}$$

$$= a_n\, \pi$$

Thus, $$a_n = \frac{1}{\pi} \int_{c}^{c+2\pi} f(x) \cos nx\, dx \qquad \qquad \dots (3)$$

To determine b_n, multiply (1) by $\sin nx$ and then integrate from c to $c + 2\pi$, we have

$$\int_{c}^{c+2\pi} f(x) \sin nx \, dx = \int_{c}^{c+2\pi} \left[\frac{a_0}{2} + \sum_{n=1}^{\infty} (a_n \cos nx + b_n \sin nx) \right] \sin nx \, dx$$

$$= \frac{a_0}{2} \int_{c}^{c+2\pi} \sin nx \, dx + \int_{c}^{c+2\pi} \left(\sum_{n=1}^{\infty} a_n \cos nx \right) \sin nx \, dx$$

$$+ \int_{c}^{c+2\pi} \left(\sum_{n=1}^{\infty} b_n \sin nx \right) \sin nx \, dx$$

This is equivalent to integrate

$$= \frac{a_0}{2} \int_{c}^{c+2\pi} \sin nx \, dx + \int_{c}^{c+2\pi} a_m \cos mx \sin nx \, dx + \int_{c}^{c+2\pi} b_m \sin mx \sin nx \, dx$$

$$\text{where } m = 1, 2, \ldots, n \ldots$$

$$= 0 + 0 + b_n \pi \qquad \text{(from results II, III, V)}$$

$$= b_n \pi$$

Thus, $\quad b_n = \dfrac{1}{\pi} \displaystyle\int_{c}^{c+2\pi} f(x) \sin nx \, dx \qquad\qquad \ldots (4)$

Thus, we have the following Euler's formulae

$$\boxed{\begin{aligned} a_0 &= \frac{1}{\pi} \int_{c}^{c+2\pi} f(x) \, dx \\[1em] a_n &= \frac{1}{\pi} \int_{c}^{c+2\pi} f(x) \cos nx \, dx \\[1em] b_n &= \frac{1}{\pi} \int_{c}^{c+2\pi} f(x) \sin nx \, dx \end{aligned}} \qquad \ldots (5)$$

In most applications, the interval over which the coefficients are computed is either $(0, 2\pi)$ or $(-\pi, \pi)$ and hence we have

Cor. 1 : If $c = 0$, the interval becomes $0 \leq x \leq 2\pi$ and the formulae given in (5) reduce to

$$
\begin{aligned}
a_0 &= \frac{1}{\pi} \int_0^{2\pi} f(x)\, dx \\[2ex]
a_n &= \frac{1}{\pi} \int_0^{2\pi} f(x) \cos nx\, dx \\[2ex]
b_n &= \frac{1}{\pi} \int_0^{2\pi} f(x) \sin nx\, dx
\end{aligned}
\qquad \ldots (6)
$$

Cor. 2 : If $c = -\pi$, the interval becomes $-\pi \leq x \leq \pi$ and the formulae given in (5) reduce to

$$
\begin{aligned}
a_0 &= \frac{1}{\pi} \int_{-\pi}^{\pi} f(x)\, dx \\[2ex]
a_n &= \frac{1}{\pi} \int_{-\pi}^{\pi} f(x) \cos nx\, dx \\[2ex]
b_n &= \frac{1}{\pi} \int_{-\pi}^{\pi} f(x) \sin nx\, dx
\end{aligned}
\qquad \ldots (7)
$$

Remark 1 : While determining Fourier coefficients it was assumed that $f(x)$ was continuous. If $f(x)$ has finite number of finite discontinuities, then the integral in (5) can be expressed as the sum of the component integral taken over the continuous portion of $f(x)$. Thus, if $f(x)$ is discontinuous at $x = x_0$, where $c \leq x_0 \leq c + 2\pi$, then coefficients of Fourier series can be expressed as

$$
a_n = \frac{1}{\pi} \left[\int_c^{x_0} f(x) \cos nx\, dx + \int_{x_0}^{c+2\pi} f(x) \cos nx\, dx \right]
$$

with similar expression for b_n.

Remark 2 : If the periodic function $f(x)$ with period 2π satisfies the Dirichlet conditions then Fourier series (1) with coefficients (5) converges to

(i) $f(x_0)$, if x_0 is a point of continuity (ii) $\dfrac{f(x_0 - 0) + f(x_0 + 0)}{2}$, if x_0 is a point of discontinuity.

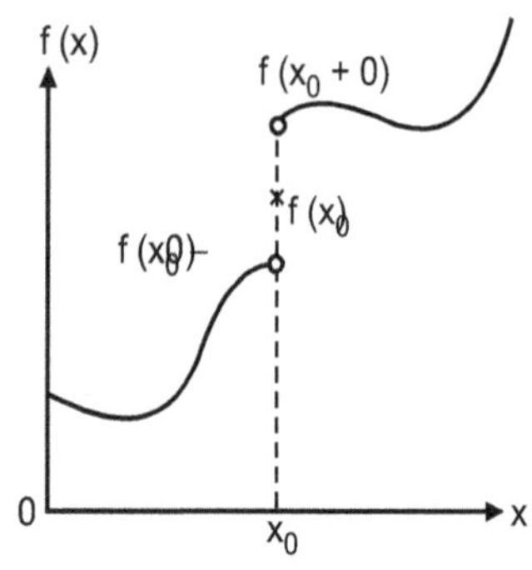

Here $f(x_0 - 0)$ and $f(x_0 + 0)$ are the left and right-hand limits of $f(x)$ at $x = x_0$, i.e.

$$\text{L. H. L.} = f(x_0 - 0) = \lim_{h \to 0} f(x_0 - h)$$

$$\text{R. H. L.} = f(x_0 + 0) = \lim_{h \to 0} f(x_0 + h)$$

Thus the value of $f(x)$ at the point of discontinuity $x = x_0$ is the arithmetic mean of these two limits as shown in Fig.5.2.

Fig. 5.2

5.6 EVEN AND ODD FUNCTIONS

When the function $f(x)$ possesses certain symmetrical properties the determination of Fourier coefficients in its Fourier expansion becomes quite simple. To consider the case of function to be even or odd, it must be defined in the interval where origin is the mid-point of the interval $-\pi \le x \le \pi$.

Even Function : A function $f(x)$ is said to be **even** if

$$f(-x) = f(x)$$

Thus x^2, $\cos x$, $x \sin x$, $e^x + e^{-x}$ are even functions. Geometrically, the graph of an even function is symmetrical about the vertical axis (y-axis) (Refer Figs. 5.3 and 5.4).

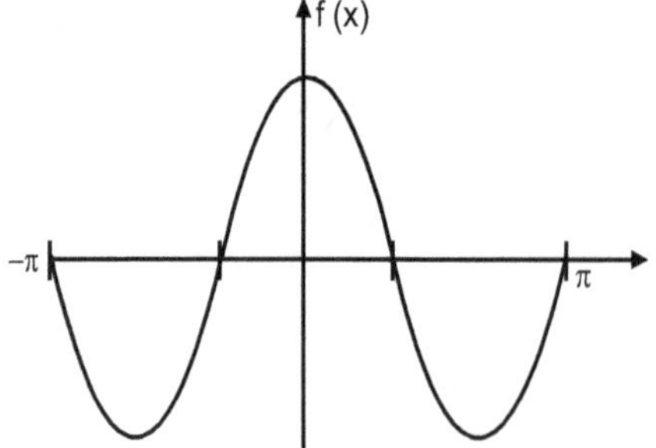

Fig. 5.3 : Even function

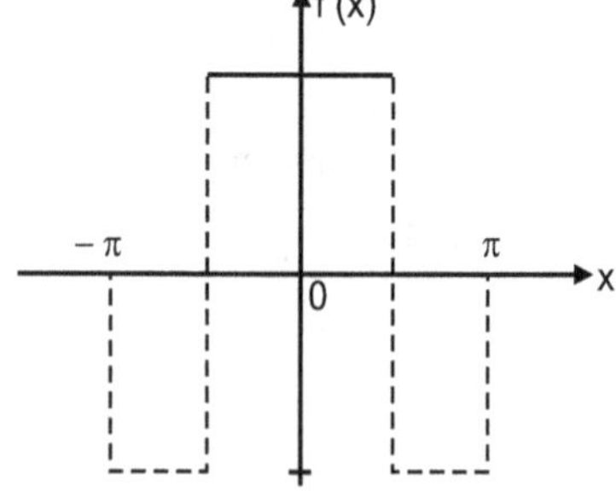

Fig. 5.4 : Even function

Odd function : A function $f(x)$ is said to be **odd** if

$$f(-x) = -f(x)$$

Thus x, sin x, x cos x, $e^x - e^{-x}$ are odd functions. Geometrically, the graph of an odd function is symmetrical through the origin (Refer Figs. 5.5 and 5.6).

Remark : The graph of an odd function for $-\pi \leq x \leq 0$ is the reflection across the vertical axis, and then across the horizontal axis.

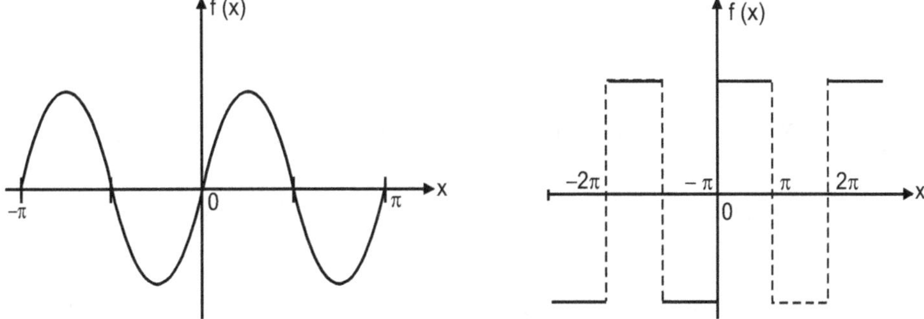

Fig. 5.5 : Odd function   **Fig. 5.6 : Odd function**

Following theorem is very useful in evaluation of integrals involving even and odd functions :

$$\int_{-a}^{a} f(x)\, dx = 2 \int_{0}^{a} f(x)\, dx \qquad \text{if } f(x) \text{ is even}$$

$$= 0 \qquad \text{if } f(x) \text{ is odd}$$

5.7 EXPANSIONS OF EVEN AND ODD PERIODIC FUNCTIONS

Case 1 : When f(x) is an even function : For even function f(x) defined in the interval $-\pi \leq x \leq \pi$, the Fourier coefficients a_0, a_n and b_n given by (5) are reduced as follows :

$$a_0 = \frac{1}{\pi} \int_{-\pi}^{\pi} f(x)\, dx = \frac{2}{\pi} \int_{0}^{\pi} f(x)\, dx \qquad [f(x) \text{ is even function}]$$

$$a_n = \frac{1}{\pi} \int_{-\pi}^{\pi} f(x) \cos nx\, dx = \frac{2}{\pi} \int_{0}^{\pi} f(x) \cos nx\, dx \quad [\text{Product } f(x) \cos nx \text{ is even}]$$

$$b_n = \frac{1}{\pi} \int_{-\pi}^{\pi} f(x) \sin nx\, dx = 0 \qquad [\text{Product } f(x) \sin nx \text{ is odd}]$$

Thus, for even function f(x) in $-\pi \leq x \leq \pi$, the Fourier coefficients are given by

$$a_0 = \frac{2}{\pi} \int_0^{\pi} f(x) \, dx$$

$$a_n = \frac{2}{\pi} \int_0^{\pi} f(x) \cos nx \, dx \qquad \cdots (8)$$

$$b_n = 0$$

Case 2 : When f(x) is an odd function : For odd function $f(x)$ defined in the interval

$-\pi \le x \le \pi$, the Fourier coefficients a_0, a_n and b_n are reduced as follows :

$$a_0 = \frac{1}{\pi} \int_{-\pi}^{\pi} f(x) \, dx = 0 \qquad \text{[f(x) is odd function]}$$

$$a_n = \frac{1}{\pi} \int_{-\pi}^{\pi} f(x) \cos nx \, dx = 0 \qquad \text{[Product f(x) cos nx is odd]}$$

$$b_n = \frac{1}{\pi} \int_{-\pi}^{\pi} f(x) \sin nx \, dx = \frac{2}{\pi} \int_0^{\pi} f(x) \sin nx \, dx \quad \text{[Product f(x) sin nx is even]}$$

Thus, for odd function $f(x)$ in $-\pi \le x \le \pi$, the Fourier coefficients are given by

$$a_0 = 0, \qquad a_n = 0$$

$$b_n = \frac{2}{\pi} \int_0^{\pi} f(x) \sin nx \, dx \qquad \cdots (9)$$

5.8 THE FOLLOWING RESULTS ARE QUITE USEFUL IN DETERMINING FOURIER COEFFICIENTS a_0, a_n AND b_n

1. The *generalised rule of integration by parts* is useful to evaluate interval for product of two functions, one of which is a power of x. If u, v are functions of x, then

$$\int uv \, dx = uv_1 - u'v_2 + u''v_3 - u'''v_4 + \dots$$

where dashes denote differentiation and suffixes denote integration.

For example,

$$\int (\pi^2 - x^2)\cos nx \, dx = (\pi^2 - x^2)\left(\frac{\sin nx}{n}\right) - (-2x)\left(-\frac{\cos nx}{n^2}\right) + (-2)\left(-\frac{\sin nx}{n^3}\right)$$

2. $$\int e^{ax} \sin bx \, dx = \frac{e^{ax}}{a^2 + b^2} (a \sin bx - b \cos bx)$$

$$\int e^{ax} \cos bx \, dx = \frac{e^{ax}}{a^2 + b^2} (a \cos bx + b \sin bx)$$

3. $2 \sin A \cos B = \sin (A + B) + \sin (A - B)$

           $2 \cos A \sin B = \sin (A + B) - \sin (A - B)$

           $2 \cos A \cos B = \cos (A + B) + \cos (A - B)$

           $2 \sin A \sin B = \cos (A - B) - \cos (A + B)$

4. $\sin A + \sin B = 2 \sin \dfrac{A + B}{2} \cos \dfrac{A - B}{2}$

           $\sin A - \sin B = 2 \cos \dfrac{A + B}{2} \sin \dfrac{A - B}{2}$

           $\cos A + \cos B = 2 \cos \dfrac{A + B}{2} \cos \dfrac{A - B}{2}$

           $\cos A - \cos B = 2 \sin \dfrac{A + B}{2} \sin \dfrac{B - A}{2}$

5. $\sin (A \pm B) = \sin A \cos B \pm \cos A \sin B$

           $\cos (A \pm B) = \cos A \cos B \mp \sin A \sin B$

6.   For any integer n, we note that

        $\sin n\pi = 0,$ $\sin 2n\pi = 0$

        $\cos n\pi = (- 1)^n,$ $\cos 2n\pi = 1$

7.   For any integer n, we note that

        $\sin (n \pm 1) \pi = 0,$ $\cos (n \pm 1) \pi = - \cos n\pi$

5.9 ILLUSTRATIONS ON EXPANSIONS OF PERIODIC FUNCTIONS

Type I : Functions having period $c \le x \le c + 2\pi$ or $-\pi \le x \le \pi$:

Ex. 1 : *Find the Fourier series of the function*

$$f(x) = e^{-x}, \; 0 \le x \le 2\pi \; \text{ and } \; f(x + 2\pi) = f(x)$$

Sol. : Let $\quad e^{-x} = \dfrac{a_0}{2} + \sum_{n=1}^{\infty} (a_n \cos nx + b_n \sin nx)$ ... (1)

where $\quad a_0 = \dfrac{1}{\pi} \displaystyle\int_{0}^{2\pi} f(x)\, dx = \dfrac{1}{\pi} \int_{0}^{2\pi} e^{-x}\, dx$

$$= \dfrac{1}{\pi} \left[\dfrac{e^{-x}}{-1} \right]_{0}^{2\pi} = \dfrac{1}{\pi} (-e^{-2\pi} + 1)$$

$$= \dfrac{1}{\pi} (1 - e^{-2\pi}) \qquad\qquad\qquad \text{... (2)}$$

$$a_n = \frac{1}{\pi} \int_0^{2\pi} f(x) \cos nx \, dx = \frac{1}{\pi} \int_0^{2\pi} e^{-x} \cos nx \, dx$$

$$= \frac{1}{\pi} \left[\frac{e^{-x}}{1^2 + n^2} (-\cos nx + n \sin nx) \right]_0^{2\pi}$$

$$= \frac{1}{\pi(1 + n^2)} \left[e^{-2\pi} (-\cos 2n\pi + n \sin 2n\pi) - e^{-0} (-\cos 0 + n \sin 0) \right]$$

$$= \frac{1}{\pi(1 + n^2)} \left[e^{-2\pi} (-1) - (-1) \right] \qquad \left(\because \cos 2n\pi = 1, \sin 2n\pi = 0 \right)$$

$$= \frac{(1 - e^{-2\pi})}{\pi(1 + n^2)} \qquad\qquad \ldots (3)$$

$$b_n = \frac{1}{\pi} \int_0^{2\pi} f(x) \sin nx \, dx = \frac{1}{\pi} \int_0^{2\pi} e^{-x} \sin nx \, dx$$

$$= \frac{1}{\pi} \left[\frac{e^{-x}}{1^2 + n^2} (-\sin nx - n \cos nx) \right]_0^{2\pi}$$

$$= \frac{1}{\pi(1 + n^2)} \left[e^{-2\pi} (-\sin 2n\pi - n \cos 2n\pi) - e^{-0} (-\sin 0 - n \cos 0) \right]$$

$$= \frac{1}{n(1 + n^2)} \left[e^{-2\pi} (-n) - (-n) \right]$$

$$= \frac{n(1 - e^{-2\pi})}{\pi(1 + n^2)} \qquad\qquad \ldots (4)$$

Substituting the values of a_0, a_n and b_n from (2), (3) and (4) in (1), we get

$$e^{-x} = \frac{(1 - e^{-2\pi})}{2\pi} + \sum_{n=1}^{\infty} \left[\frac{(1 - e^{-2\pi})}{\pi(1 + n^2)} \cos nx + \frac{n(1 - e^{-2\pi})}{\pi(1 + n^2)} \sin nx \right]$$

$$= \frac{(1 - e^{-2\pi})}{\pi} \left[\frac{1}{2} + \sum_{n=1}^{\infty} \frac{1}{(1 + n^2)} (\cos nx + n \sin nx) \right]$$

Ex. 2 : *Obtain Fourier series expansion for function $f(x) = \left(\dfrac{\pi - x}{2} \right)^2$ in the interval $0 \leq x \leq 2\pi$ and $f(x + 2\pi) = f(x)$.*

Deduce that,

(i) $\dfrac{1}{1^2} + \dfrac{1}{2^2} + \dfrac{1}{3^2} + \ldots = \dfrac{\pi^2}{6}$ *(ii)* $\dfrac{1}{1^2} - \dfrac{1}{2^2} + \dfrac{1}{3^2} - \dfrac{1}{4^2} + \ldots = \dfrac{\pi^2}{12}$

(iii) $\dfrac{1}{1^2} + \dfrac{1}{3^2} + \dfrac{1}{5^2} + \ldots = \dfrac{\pi^2}{8}$

Sol. : Let $f(x) = \dfrac{a_0}{2} + \sum\limits_{n=1}^{\infty} (a_n \cos nx + b_n \sin nx)$ ... (1)

where $a_0 = \dfrac{1}{\pi} \displaystyle\int_0^{2\pi} f(x)\, dx = \dfrac{1}{\pi} \displaystyle\int_0^{2\pi} \dfrac{(\pi - x)^2}{4}\, dx$

$\qquad = \dfrac{1}{4\pi} \left[\dfrac{(\pi - x)^3}{-3} \right]_0^{2\pi} = \dfrac{1}{12\pi} [\pi^3 + \pi^3]$

$\qquad = \dfrac{\pi^2}{6}$ ... (2)

$a_n = \dfrac{1}{\pi} \displaystyle\int_0^{2\pi} f(x) \cos nx\, dx = \dfrac{1}{\pi} \displaystyle\int_0^{2\pi} \dfrac{(\pi - x)^2}{4} \cos nx\, dx$

$\quad = \dfrac{1}{4\pi} \left[(\pi - x)^2 \left(\dfrac{\sin nx}{n} \right) - \{2\,(\pi - x)\,(-1)\} \left(-\dfrac{\cos nx}{n^2} \right) + 2(1) \left(-\dfrac{\sin nx}{n^3} \right) \right]_0^{2\pi}$

$\quad = \dfrac{1}{4\pi} \left[\left(0 + \dfrac{2\pi \cos 2n\pi}{n^2} - 0 \right) - \left(0 - \dfrac{2\pi \cos 0}{n^2} - 0 \right) \right]$

$\quad = \dfrac{1}{4\pi} \left[\dfrac{2\pi}{n^2} + \dfrac{2\pi}{n^2} \right]$ $\left(\because \cos 0 = \cos 2n\pi = 1 \right)$

$\quad = \dfrac{1}{n^2}$ ... (3)

$b_n = \dfrac{1}{\pi} \displaystyle\int_0^{2\pi} f(x) \sin nx\, dx = \dfrac{1}{\pi} \displaystyle\int_0^{2\pi} \dfrac{(\pi - x)^2}{4} \sin nx\, dx$

$\quad = \dfrac{1}{4\pi} \left[(\pi - x)^2 \left(\dfrac{-\cos nx}{n} \right) - \{2\,(\pi - x)\,(-1)\} \left(\dfrac{-\sin nx}{n^2} \right) + (2) \left(\dfrac{\cos nx}{n^3} \right) \right]_0^{2\pi}$

$\quad = \dfrac{1}{4\pi} \left[\left(-\dfrac{\pi^2 \cos 2n\pi}{n} + 0 + \dfrac{2 \cos 2n\pi}{n^3} \right) - \left(-\dfrac{\pi^2 \cos 0}{n} + 0 + \dfrac{2 \cos 0}{n^3} \right) \right]$

$\quad = \dfrac{1}{4\pi} \left[\dfrac{-\pi^2}{n} + \dfrac{\pi^2}{n} \right]$ $\left(\because \cos 0 = \cos 2n\pi = 1 \right)$

$\quad = 0$ ... (4)

Substituting the values of a_0, a_n and b_n from (2), (3) and (4) in (1), we get

$$\left(\dfrac{\pi - x}{2} \right)^2 = \dfrac{\pi^2}{12} + \sum\limits_{n=1}^{\infty} \dfrac{1}{n^2} \cos nx \qquad \text{... (5)}$$

We shall now deduce the given results from (5).

Putting $x = 0$ in (5), we have

$$\frac{\pi^2}{4} = \frac{\pi^2}{12} + \sum_{n=1}^{\infty} \frac{1}{n^2}$$

or $\qquad \displaystyle\sum_{n=1}^{\infty} \frac{1}{n^2} = \frac{\pi^2}{4} - \frac{\pi^2}{12} = \frac{\pi^2}{6}$

$\therefore \quad \dfrac{1}{1^2} + \dfrac{1}{2^2} + \dfrac{1}{3^2} + \ldots = \dfrac{\pi^2}{6}$ $\hspace{3cm}$ ... (6)

Again putting $x = \pi$ in (5), we have

$$0 = \frac{\pi^2}{12} + \sum_{n=1}^{\infty} \frac{1}{n^2} \cos n\pi$$

or $\qquad -\left[\displaystyle\sum_{n=1}^{\infty} \frac{1}{n^2} (-1)^n\right] = \dfrac{\pi^2}{12}$

$\therefore \dfrac{1}{1^2} - \dfrac{1}{2^2} + \dfrac{1}{3^2} + \dfrac{1}{4^2} - \ldots = \dfrac{\pi^2}{12}$ $\hspace{3cm}$ ... (7)

Adding (6) and (7), we get

$$2\left[\frac{1}{1^2} + \frac{1}{3^2} + \frac{1}{5^2} + \ldots\right] = \frac{\pi^2}{6} + \frac{\pi^2}{12} = \frac{\pi^2}{4}$$

$\therefore \qquad \dfrac{1}{1^2} + \dfrac{1}{3^2} + \dfrac{1}{5^2} + \ldots = \dfrac{\pi^2}{8}$ $\hspace{3cm}$ ... (8)

Hence (6), (7) and (8) are the required deductions.

Ex. 3 : *Expand f(x) = x sin x in the interval $0 \leq x \leq 2\pi$.*

Sol. : Let $x \sin x = \dfrac{a_0}{2} + \displaystyle\sum_{n=1}^{\infty} (a_n \cos nx + b_n \sin nx)$ $\hspace{2cm}$ ... (1)

where $\qquad a_0 = \dfrac{1}{\pi} \displaystyle\int_0^{2\pi} f(x)\, dx = \dfrac{1}{\pi} \int_0^{2\pi} x \sin x\, dx$

$$= \frac{1}{\pi} \left[x\,(-\cos x) - (1)\,(-\sin x)\right]_0^{2\pi}$$

$$= \frac{1}{\pi} \left[(-2\pi \cos 2\pi + 0) - (0 + 0)\right] = \frac{1}{\pi} \left[-2\pi\right]$$

$$= -2 \hspace{6cm} ... (2)$$

$$a_n = \frac{1}{\pi} \int_0^{2\pi} f(x) \cos nx \, dx = \frac{1}{\pi} \int_0^{2\pi} x \sin x \cos nx \, dx$$

$$= \frac{1}{2\pi} \int_0^{2\pi} x \, (2 \sin x \cos nx) \, dx = \frac{1}{2\pi} \int_0^{2\pi} x \, [\sin (n + 1) x - \sin (n - 1) x] \, dx$$

$$= \frac{1}{2\pi} \left[x \left\{ -\frac{\cos (n + 1) x}{(n + 1)} + \frac{\cos (n - 1) x}{(n - 1)} \right\} \right.$$

$$\left. - (1) \left\{ -\frac{\sin (n + 1) x}{(n + 1)^2} + \frac{\sin (n - 1) x}{(n - 1)^2} \right\} \right]_0^{2\pi} , \quad \text{for } n > 1$$

$$= \frac{1}{2\pi} \left[(2\pi) \left\{ -\frac{\cos 2 (n + 1) \pi}{(n + 1)} + \frac{\cos 2 (n - 1) \pi}{(n - 1)} \right\} - 0 \right] , \text{ for } n > 1$$

$$= -\frac{1}{(n + 1)} + \frac{1}{(n - 1)} , \text{ for } n > 1$$

$$= \frac{2}{n^2 - 1} , \text{ for } n > 1 \qquad\qquad \ldots (3)$$

When n = 1, we have

$$a_1 = \frac{1}{\pi} \int_0^{2\pi} x \sin x \cos x \, dx = \frac{1}{2\pi} \int_0^{2\pi} x \sin 2x \, dx$$

$$= \frac{1}{2\pi} \left[x \left(-\frac{\cos 2x}{2} \right) - (1) \left(-\frac{\sin 2x}{4} \right) \right]_0^{2\pi}$$

$$= \frac{1}{2\pi} \left[\left\{ -2\pi \left(\frac{\cos 4\pi}{2} \right) + \left(\frac{\sin 4\pi}{4} \right) \right\} - 0 \right] = \frac{1}{2\pi} [-\pi] = -\frac{1}{2}$$

$$b_n = \frac{1}{\pi} \int_0^{2\pi} f(x) \sin nx \, dx = \frac{1}{\pi} \int_0^{2\pi} x \sin x \sin nx \, dx$$

$$= \frac{1}{2\pi} \int_0^{2\pi} x \, (2 \sin x \sin nx) \, dx = \frac{1}{2\pi} \int_0^{2\pi} x \, [\cos (n - 1) x - \cos (n + 1) x] \, dx$$

$$= \frac{1}{2\pi} \left[x \left\{ \frac{\sin (n - 1) x}{(n - 1)} - \frac{\sin (n + 1) x}{(n + 1)} \right\} - (1) \left\{ -\frac{\cos (n - 1) x}{(n - 1)^2} + \frac{\cos (n + 1) x}{(n + 1)^2} \right\} \right]_0^{2\pi} , \text{for } n > 1$$

$$= \frac{1}{2\pi} \left[\left\{ 0 + \frac{\cos 2 (n - 1) \pi}{(n - 1)^2} - \frac{\cos 2 (n + 1) \pi}{(n + 1)^2} \right\} - \left\{ 0 + \frac{1}{(n - 1)^2} - \frac{1}{(n + 1)^2} \right\} \right] , \text{ for } n > 1$$

$$= \frac{1}{2\pi}\left[\frac{1}{(n-1)^2} - \frac{1}{(n+1)^2} - \frac{1}{(n-1)^2} + \frac{1}{(n+1)^2}\right]$$

$$= 0, \text{ for } n > 1 \qquad \qquad \dots (5)$$

When $n = 1$, we have

$$b_1 = \frac{1}{\pi}\int_0^{2\pi} x \sin x \sin x \, dx = \frac{1}{\pi}\int_0^{2\pi} x \sin^2 x \, dx$$

$$= \frac{1}{\pi}\int_0^{2\pi} x\left(\frac{1-\cos 2x}{2}\right) dx = \frac{1}{2\pi}\int_0^{2\pi} x\,(1-\cos 2x)\, dx$$

$$= \frac{1}{2\pi}\left[x\left(x - \frac{\sin 2x}{2}\right) - (1)\left(\frac{x^2}{2} + \frac{\cos 2x}{4}\right)\right]_0^{2\pi}$$

$$= \frac{1}{2\pi}\left[\left\{2\pi\,(2\pi) - \frac{4\pi^2}{2} - \frac{1}{4}\right\} - \left\{0 - \frac{1}{4}\right\}\right] = \frac{1}{2\pi}\,[2\pi^2]$$

$$= \pi \qquad \qquad \dots (6)$$

Hence using results (2), (3), (4), (5) and (6), we have

$$\therefore \quad x \sin x = \frac{a_0}{2} + a_1 \cos x + b_1 \sin x + \sum_{n=2}^{\infty} (a_n \cos nx + b_n \sin nx)$$

$$= -1 - \frac{1}{2}\cos x + \pi \sin x + \sum_{n=2}^{\infty} \frac{2}{n^2-1}\cos nx$$

Ex. 4 : *Determine the Fourier series for the function $f(x) = \sqrt{1 - \cos x}$ in the interval*

$0 \le x \le 2\pi$ and hence deduce that $\displaystyle\sum_{n=1}^{\infty}\frac{1}{4n^2 - 1} = \frac{1}{2}$.

Sol. : Given function $f(x) = \sqrt{1 - \cos x} = \sqrt{2\sin^2\frac{x}{2}} = \sqrt{2}\,\sin\frac{x}{2}$

$$\text{Let} \quad \sqrt{1 - \cos x} = \frac{a_0}{2} + \sum_{n=1}^{\infty}(a_n \cos nx + b_n \sin nx) \qquad \dots (1)$$

$$\text{where} \qquad a_0 = \frac{1}{\pi}\int_0^{2\pi} f(x)\, dx = \frac{1}{\pi}\int_0^{2\pi} \sqrt{2}\,\sin\frac{x}{2}\, dx$$

$$= \frac{\sqrt{2}}{\pi} \left[-2 \cos \frac{x}{2} \right]_0^{2\pi} = \frac{2\sqrt{2}}{\pi} \; [- \cos \pi + \cos 0]$$

$$= \frac{4\sqrt{2}}{\pi} \qquad \qquad \ldots (2)$$

$$a_n = \frac{1}{\pi} \int_0^{2\pi} f(x) \cos nx \, dx = \frac{1}{\pi} \int_0^{2\pi} \left(\sqrt{2} \; \sin \frac{x}{2} \right) \cos nx \, dx$$

$$= \frac{\sqrt{2}}{2\pi} \int_0^{2\pi} 2 \sin \frac{x}{2} \cos nx \, dx$$

$$= \frac{1}{\sqrt{2}\,\pi} \int_0^{2\pi} \left[\sin \left(n + \frac{1}{2} \right) x - \sin \left(n - \frac{1}{2} \right) x \right] dx$$

$$= \frac{1}{\sqrt{2}\,\pi} \left[- \frac{\cos \left(\frac{2n+1}{2} \right) x}{\left(\frac{2n+1}{2} \right)} + \frac{\cos \left(\frac{2n-1}{2} \right) x}{\left(\frac{2n-1}{2} \right)} \right]_0^{2\pi}$$

$$= \frac{2}{\sqrt{2}\,\pi} \left[\left\{ - \frac{\cos (2n+1)\,\pi}{(2n+1)} + \frac{\cos (2n-1)\,\pi}{(2n-1)} \right\} - \left\{ - \frac{1}{(2n+1)} + \frac{1}{(2n-1)} \right\} \right]$$

$$= \frac{\sqrt{2}}{\pi} \left[\frac{1}{2n+1} - \frac{1}{2n-1} + \frac{1}{2n+1} - \frac{1}{2n-1} \right] = \frac{\sqrt{2}}{\pi} \left[\frac{2}{2n+1} - \frac{2}{2n-1} \right]$$

$$= - \frac{4\sqrt{2}}{\pi \, (4n^2 - 1)} \qquad \qquad \ldots (3)$$

$$b_n = \frac{1}{\pi} \int_0^{2\pi} f(x) \sin nx \, dx = \frac{1}{\pi} \int_0^{2\pi} \sqrt{2} \sin \frac{x}{2} \sin nx \, dx$$

$$= \frac{\sqrt{2}}{2\pi} \int_0^{2\pi} \left(2 \sin \frac{x}{2} \sin nx \right) dx$$

$$= \frac{1}{\sqrt{2}\,\pi} \int_0^{2\pi} \left[\cos \left(n - \frac{1}{2} \right) x - \cos \left(n + \frac{1}{2} \right) x \right] dx$$

$$= \frac{1}{\sqrt{2}\,\pi} \left[\frac{\sin\left(\frac{2n-1}{2}\right)x}{\left(\frac{2n-1}{2}\right)} - \frac{\sin\left(\frac{2n+1}{2}\right)x}{\left(\frac{2n+1}{2}\right)} \right]_0^{2\pi}$$

$$= 0 \qquad \qquad \ldots (4)$$

$$\therefore \quad \sqrt{1-\cos x} = \frac{2\sqrt{2}}{\pi} - \frac{4\sqrt{2}}{\pi} \sum_{n=1}^{\infty} \frac{1}{(4n^2-1)} \cos nx \qquad \ldots (5)$$

Putting $x = 0$ in (5), we get

$$0 = \frac{2\sqrt{2}}{\pi} - \frac{4\sqrt{2}}{\pi} \sum_{n=1}^{\infty} \frac{1}{(4n^2-1)}$$

$$\therefore \quad \sum_{n=1}^{\infty} \frac{1}{4n^2-1} = \frac{1}{2}$$

Ex. 5 : *An alternating current i after passing through the rectifier has the form*

$$i = \begin{cases} I_o \sin x, & 0 \le x \le \pi \\ 0, & \pi < x < 2\pi \end{cases}$$

where I_o is the maximum current and the period is 2π. Express i as Fourier series. Also graph the function.

Sol. : Let $\quad i = \dfrac{a_0}{2} + \displaystyle\sum_{n=1}^{\infty} (a_n \cos nx + b_n \sin nx) \qquad \ldots (1)$

where $\quad a_0 = \dfrac{1}{\pi} \displaystyle\int_0^{2\pi} f(x)\,dx = \dfrac{1}{\pi} \left[\displaystyle\int_0^{\pi} I_o \sin x\,dx + \displaystyle\int_{\pi}^{2\pi} 0\,dx \right]$

$$= \frac{I_o}{\pi} \left[-\cos x\right]_0^{\pi} = \frac{I_o}{\pi} \left[-\cos \pi + \cos 0\right] = \frac{2I_o}{\pi} \qquad \ldots (2)$$

$$a_n = \frac{1}{\pi} \int_0^{2\pi} f(x) \cos nx\,dx = \frac{1}{\pi} \left[\int_0^{\pi} (I_o \sin x) \cos nx\,dx + \int_{\pi}^{2\pi} 0 \cos nx\,dx \right]$$

$$= \frac{I_o}{2\pi} \int_0^\pi 2 \sin x \cos nx \, dx = \frac{I_o}{\pi} \int_0^\pi [\sin (n + 1) x - \sin (n - 1) x] \, dx$$

$$= \frac{I_o}{2\pi} \left[-\frac{\cos (n + 1) x}{(n + 1)} + \frac{\cos (n - 1) x}{(n - 1)} \right]_0^\pi \quad \text{for } n > 1$$

$$= \frac{I_o}{2\pi} \left[\left\{ -\frac{\cos (n + 1) \pi}{(n + 1)} + \frac{\cos (n - 1) \pi}{(n - 1)} \right\} - \left\{ -\frac{1}{(n + 1)} + \frac{1}{(n - 1)} \right\} \right] \quad \text{for } n > 1$$

$$= \frac{I_o}{2\pi} \left[\left\{ \frac{\cos n\pi}{(n + 1)} - \frac{\cos n\pi}{(n - 1)} \right\} - \left\{ -\frac{1}{(n + 1)} + \frac{1}{(n - 1)} \right\} \right] \quad \text{for } n > 1$$

$$\left\{ \because \cos (n \pm 1) \pi = \cos n\pi \cos \pi \mp \sin n\pi \sin \pi = - \cos n\pi \right\}$$

$$= \frac{I_o}{2\pi} \left[\frac{1}{n + 1} - \frac{1}{n - 1} \right] (1 + \cos n\pi) = \frac{I_o}{2\pi} \cdot \frac{(-2)}{n^2 - 1} (1 + \cos n\pi)$$

$$= \begin{cases} 0 & \text{when } n \text{ is odd, except } n = 1 \\ -\dfrac{2 I_o}{\pi (n^2 - 1)} & \text{when } n \text{ is even} \end{cases}$$

Thus, $a_2 = -\dfrac{2I_o}{3\pi}, \quad a_4 = -\dfrac{2I_o}{15\pi}, \quad a_6 = -\dfrac{2I_o}{35\pi}, \ldots$ etc. $\ldots$ (3)

When n = 1, we have

$$a_1 = \frac{1}{\pi} \int_0^{2\pi} f(x) \cos x \, dx = \frac{1}{\pi} \left[\int_0^\pi I_o \sin x \cos x \, dx + \int_\pi^{2\pi} 0 \cos x \, dx \right]$$

$$= \frac{I_o}{2\pi} \left[\int_0^\pi \sin 2x \, dx \right] = 0 \qquad\qquad \ldots (4)$$

$$b_n = \frac{1}{\pi} \int_0^{2\pi} f(x) \sin nx \, dx = \frac{1}{\pi} \left[\int_0^\pi I_o \sin x \sin nx \, dx + \int_\pi^{2\pi} 0 \sin nx \, dx \right]$$

$$= \frac{I_o}{2\pi} \int_0^\pi 2 \sin x \sin nx \, dx = \frac{I_o}{2\pi} \int_0^\pi [\cos (n - 1) x - \cos (n + 1) x] \, dx$$

$$= \frac{I_o}{2\pi} \left[\frac{\sin (n - 1) x}{(n - 1)} - \frac{\sin (n + 1) x}{(n + 1)} \right]_0^\pi \quad \text{for } n > 1$$

$$= \frac{I_o}{2\pi} \left[\left\{ \frac{\sin(n-1)\pi}{(n-1)} - \frac{\sin(n+1)\pi}{(n+1)} \right\} - 0 \right]$$

$$= 0 \quad \text{for all n, except } n = 1 \qquad \ldots (5)$$

When $n = 1$, we have

$$b_1 = \frac{1}{\pi} \int_0^{2\pi} f(x) \sin x = \frac{1}{\pi} \left[\int_0^{\pi} I_o \sin x \sin x \, dx + \int_{\pi}^{2\pi} 0 \sin x \, dx \right]$$

$$= \frac{I_o}{\pi} \int_0^{\pi} \sin^2 x \, dx = \frac{I_o}{2\pi} \int_0^{\pi} (1 - \cos 2x) \, dx$$

$$= \frac{I_o}{2\pi} \left[x - \frac{\sin 2x}{2} \right]_0^{\pi} = \frac{I_o}{2} \qquad \ldots (6)$$

Hence using the results (2), (3), (4), (5) and (6), we have

$$i = \frac{a_0}{2} + (a_1 \cos x + a_2 \cos 2x + a_4 \cos 4x + a_6 \cos 6x + \ldots) + (b_1 \sin x)$$

$$= \frac{I_0}{\pi} + \left(0 - \frac{2I_o}{3\pi} \cos 2x - \frac{2I_o}{15\pi} \cos 4x - \frac{2I_o}{35\pi} \cos 6x + \ldots \right) + \left(\frac{I_o}{2} \sin x \right)$$

$$= \frac{I_o}{\pi} \left[1 - 2 \sum_{n=1}^{\infty} \frac{1}{(4n^2 - 1)} \cos 2nx + \frac{\pi}{2} \sin x \right]$$

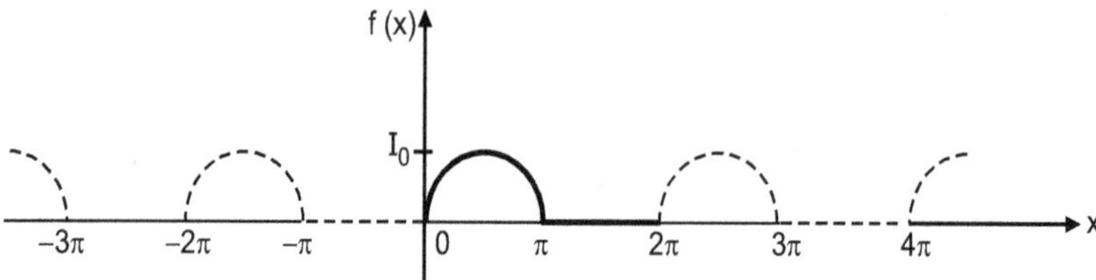

Fig. 5.7

Ex. 6 : *Obtain Fourier series expansion of $f(x) = \cos \alpha x$ in the interval $(0, 2\pi)$, where α is not an integer. Deduct that $\pi \cot 2\pi\alpha = \frac{1}{2\alpha} + \alpha \sum_{n=1}^{\infty} \frac{1}{\alpha^2 - n^2}$.*

Sol. : Let $\cos \alpha x = \frac{a_0}{2} + \sum_{n=1}^{\infty} (a_n \cos nx + b_n \sin nx)$ $\qquad \ldots (1)$

where $a_0 = \frac{1}{\pi} \int_0^{2\pi} f(x) \, dx = \frac{1}{\pi} \int_0^{2\pi} \cos \alpha x \, dx$

$$= \frac{1}{\pi} \left[\frac{\sin \alpha\, x}{\alpha} \right]_0^{2\pi} = \frac{1}{\pi} \left[\frac{\sin 2\pi\alpha}{\alpha} - 0 \right]$$

$$= \frac{\sin 2\pi\alpha}{\pi\alpha} \qquad\qquad \dots (2)$$

$$a_n = \frac{1}{\pi} \int_0^{2\pi} f(x) \cos nx \, dx = \frac{1}{\pi} \int_0^{2\pi} \cos \alpha\, x \cos nx \, dx$$

$$= \frac{1}{2\pi} \int_0^{2\pi} (2 \cos \alpha\, x \cos nx) \, dx$$

$$= \frac{1}{2\pi} \int_0^{2\pi} [\cos (\alpha + n)\, x + \cos (\alpha - n)\, x] \, dx$$

$$= \frac{1}{2\pi} \left[\frac{\sin (\alpha + n)\, x}{(\alpha + n)} + \frac{\sin (\alpha - n)\, x}{(\alpha - n)} \right]_0^{2\pi}$$

$$= \frac{1}{2\pi} \left[\left\{ \frac{\sin (2\pi\alpha + 2n\pi)}{(\alpha + n)} + \frac{\sin (2\pi\alpha - 2n\pi)}{(\alpha - n)} \right\} - 0 \right]$$

$$= \frac{1}{2\pi} \left[\frac{\sin 2\pi\alpha}{(\alpha + n)} + \frac{\sin 2\pi\alpha}{(\alpha - n)} \right] = \frac{1}{2\pi} \cdot \frac{2\alpha}{\alpha^2 - n^2} \sin 2\pi\alpha$$

$$= \frac{\alpha \sin 2\pi\, \alpha}{\pi\, (\alpha^2 - n^2)} \qquad\qquad \dots (3)$$

$$b_n = \frac{1}{\pi} \int_0^{2\pi} f(x) \sin nx \, dx = \frac{1}{\pi} \int_0^{2\pi} \cos \alpha\, x \sin nx \, dx$$

$$= \frac{1}{2\pi} \int_0^{2\pi} 2 (\cos \alpha\, x \sin nx) \, dx$$

$$= \frac{1}{2\pi} \int_0^{2\pi} [\sin (\alpha + n)\, x - \sin (\alpha - n)\, x] \, dx$$

$$= \frac{1}{2\pi} \left[-\frac{\cos (\alpha + n)\, x}{(\alpha + n)} + \frac{\cos (\alpha - n)\, x}{(\alpha - n)} \right]_0^{2\pi}$$

$$= \frac{1}{2\pi} \left[\left\{ -\frac{\cos (2\pi\alpha + 2n\pi)}{(\alpha + n)} + \frac{\cos (2\pi\alpha - 2n\pi)}{(\alpha - n)} \right\} - \left\{ \frac{-1}{(\alpha + n)} + \frac{1}{(\alpha - n)} \right\} \right]$$

$$= \frac{1}{2\pi}\left[\frac{(1-\cos 2\pi\alpha)}{(\alpha+n)} - \frac{(1-\cos 2\pi\alpha)}{(\alpha-n)}\right] = \frac{1}{2\pi}\cdot\frac{-2n}{(\alpha^2-n^2)}(1-\cos 2\pi\alpha)$$

$$= \frac{n(\cos 2\pi\alpha - 1)}{\pi(\alpha^2-n^2)} \qquad \qquad \dots (4)$$

Hence from (2), (3), (4), the required Fourier expansion is

$$\cos \alpha x = \frac{\sin 2\pi\alpha}{2\pi\alpha} + \frac{\alpha \sin 2\pi\alpha}{\pi} \sum_{n=1}^{\infty} \frac{1}{(\alpha^2-n^2)} \cos nx$$

$$+ \frac{(\cos 2\pi\alpha - 1)}{\pi} \sum_{n=1}^{\infty} \frac{n}{(\alpha^2-n^2)} \sin nx. \qquad \dots (5)$$

Now putting $x = 2\pi$ in (5), we get

$$\cos 2\pi\alpha = \frac{\sin 2\pi\alpha}{2\pi\alpha} + \frac{\alpha \sin 2\pi\alpha}{\pi} \sum_{n=1}^{\infty} \frac{1}{\alpha^2-n^2}$$

$$\therefore \qquad \pi \cot 2\pi\alpha = \frac{1}{2\alpha} + \alpha \sum_{n=1}^{\infty} \frac{1}{\alpha^2-n^2}$$

Ex. 7 : *What is the Fourier expansion of the periodic function whose definition in one period is*

$$f(x) = \begin{cases} -\pi, & 0 < x < \pi \\ x - \pi, & \pi < x < 2\pi \end{cases}$$

State the value of the series at $x = \pi$ and hence show that

$$\sum_{n=0}^{\infty} \frac{1}{(2n+1)^2} = \frac{\pi^2}{8}$$

Sol. : Let $f(x) = \dfrac{a_0}{2} + \sum_{n=1}^{\infty}(a_n \cos nx + b_n \sin nx)$ \qquad $\dots (1)$

where $a_0 = \dfrac{1}{\pi}\displaystyle\int_0^{2\pi} f(x)\, dx = \dfrac{1}{\pi}\left[\displaystyle\int_0^{\pi}(-\pi)\, dx + \displaystyle\int_{\pi}^{2\pi}(x-\pi)\, dx\right]$

$$= \frac{1}{\pi}\left[-\pi(x)_0^{\pi} + \left\{\frac{(x-\pi)^2}{2}\right\}_{\pi}^{2\pi}\right] = \frac{1}{\pi}\left[-\pi^2 + \left\{\frac{\pi^2}{2} - 0\right\}\right] = \frac{1}{\pi}\left[-\frac{\pi^2}{2}\right]$$

$$= -\frac{\pi}{2} \qquad \qquad \dots (2)$$

$$a_n = \frac{1}{\pi} \int_0^{2\pi} f(x) \cos nx \, dx$$

$$= \frac{1}{\pi} \left[\int_0^{\pi} (-\pi) \cos nx \, dx + \int_{\pi}^{2\pi} (x - \pi) \cos nx \, dx \right]$$

$$= \frac{1}{\pi} \left[(-\pi) \left\{ \frac{\sin nx}{n} \right\}_0^{\pi} + \left\{ (x - \pi) \left(\frac{\sin nx}{n} \right) - (1) \left(\frac{-\cos nx}{n^2} \right) \right\}_{\pi}^{2\pi} \right]$$

$$= \frac{1}{\pi} \left[0 + \left\{ \left(0 + \frac{1}{n^2} \right) - \left(0 + \frac{\cos n\pi}{n^2} \right) \right\} \right] = \frac{1}{\pi} \left[\frac{1 - \cos n\pi}{n^2} \right]$$

$$= \frac{1}{\pi n^2} \left[1 - (-1)^n \right] \qquad\qquad [\because \cos n\pi = (-1)^n]$$

$$= \begin{cases} 0, & \text{if n is even} \\ \dfrac{2}{\pi n^2}, & \text{if n is odd} \end{cases}$$

Thus $\quad a_1 = \dfrac{2}{\pi 1^2} \ , \ a_3 = \dfrac{2}{\pi 3^2} \ , \ a_5 = \dfrac{2}{\pi 5^2} \ , \dots$ etc. $\qquad\qquad \dots (3)$

$$b_n = \frac{1}{\pi} \int_0^{2\pi} f(x) \sin nx \, dx = \frac{1}{\pi} \left[\int_0^{\pi} (-\pi) \sin nx \, dx + \int_{\pi}^{2\pi} (x - \pi) \sin nx \, dx \right]$$

$$= \frac{1}{\pi} \left[(-\pi) \left\{ -\frac{\cos nx}{n} \right\}_0^{\pi} + \left\{ (x - \pi) \left(-\frac{\cos nx}{n} \right) - (1) \left(-\frac{\sin nx}{n^2} \right) \right\}_{\pi}^{2\pi} \right]$$

$$= \frac{1}{\pi} \left[\frac{\pi}{n} (\cos n\pi - 1) + \left\{ \frac{-\pi}{n} (\cos 2n\pi) + 0 \right\} \right]$$

$$= \frac{1}{n} \left[\cos n\pi - 2 \right] = -\frac{1}{n} \left[2 - (-1)^n \right]$$

Thus $\quad b_1 = -3, \qquad b_2 = -\dfrac{1}{2} \ , \qquad b_3 = -\dfrac{3}{3} = -1, \dots$ etc. $\qquad\qquad \dots (4)$

Hence the required Fourier series is

$$f(x) = -\frac{\pi}{4} + \frac{2}{\pi} \left[\frac{1}{1^2} \cos x + \frac{1}{3^2} \cos 3x + \frac{1}{5^2} \cos 5x + \dots \right]$$

$$+ \left[-3 \sin x - \frac{1}{2} \sin 2x - \sin 3x \dots \right]$$

$$= -\frac{\pi}{4} + \frac{2}{\pi} \sum_{n=0}^{\infty} \frac{\cos{(2n+1)}\,x}{(2n+1)^2} - \sum_{n=1}^{\infty} \frac{[2-(-1)^n]\sin nx}{n} \qquad \ldots (5)$$

Since f(x) is discontinuous at $x = \pi$, therefore, the value of f(x) at $x = \pi$, the point of discontinuity is calculated by rule

$$f(\pi) = \frac{f(\pi-0) + f(\pi+0)}{2} = \frac{\text{L. H. L.} + \text{R. H. L.}}{2}$$

where   L.H.L. $= f(\pi-0) = \lim_{h \to 0} f(\pi-h) = -\pi$

and   R.H.L. $= f(\pi+0) = \lim_{h \to 0} f(\pi+h) = \lim_{h \to 0} (\pi + h - \pi) = 0$

$\therefore \qquad f(\pi) = \dfrac{-\pi+0}{2} = -\dfrac{\pi}{2} \qquad\qquad \ldots (6)$

Thus from (5), on putting $x = \pi$, we have

$$-\frac{\pi}{2} = -\frac{\pi}{4} + \frac{2}{\pi} \sum_{n=0}^{\infty} \frac{\cos{(2n+1)}\,\pi}{(2n+1)^2}$$

$$\therefore \quad \sum_{n=0}^{\infty} \frac{1}{(2n+1)^2} = \frac{\pi^2}{8}$$

Ex. 8 : *Find the Fourier series expansion for periodic function f(x), if*

$$f(x) = \begin{cases} -\pi, & -\pi < x < 0 \\ x, & 0 < x < \pi \end{cases}$$

State the value of the series at x = 0 and hence deduce that $\displaystyle\sum_{n=1}^{\infty} \frac{1}{(2n-1)^2} = \frac{\pi^2}{8}.$

Sol. : Eventhough the origin is mid-point of the interval $-\pi < x < \pi$, f(x) is neither even nor odd. Thus, we use the formulae (7) of article 3.5.

Let $\displaystyle f(x) = \frac{a_0}{2} + \sum_{n=1}^{\infty} (a_n \cos nx + b_n \sin nx) \qquad\qquad \ldots (1)$

where $\displaystyle a_0 = \frac{1}{\pi}\int_{-\pi}^{\pi} f(x)\,dx = \frac{1}{\pi}\left[\int_{-\pi}^{0} (-\pi)\,dx + \int_{0}^{\pi} x\,dx\right]$

$$= \frac{1}{\pi}\left[-\pi\,(x)^0_{-\pi} + \left(\frac{x^2}{2}\right)^\pi_0\right] = \frac{1}{\pi}\left[-\pi^2 + \frac{\pi^2}{2}\right] = -\frac{\pi}{2} \qquad \dots (2)$$

$$a_n = \frac{1}{\pi}\int_{-\pi}^{\pi} f(x)\cos nx = \frac{1}{\pi}\left[\int_{-\pi}^{0}(-\pi)\cos nx\,dx + \int_{0}^{\pi} x\cos nx\,dx\right]$$

$$= \frac{1}{\pi}\left[-\pi\left(\frac{\sin nx}{n}\right)^0_{-\pi} + \left\{x\left(\frac{\sin nx}{n}\right) - (1)\left(-\frac{\cos nx}{n^2}\right)\right\}^\pi_0\right]$$

$$= \frac{1}{\pi}\left[\frac{\cos n\pi - 1}{n^2}\right] = \frac{1}{\pi}\left[\frac{(-1)^n - 1}{n^2}\right]$$

$$= \begin{cases} 0, & \text{if } n \text{ is even} \\ \dfrac{-2}{\pi n^2}, & \text{if } n \text{ is odd} \end{cases}$$

Thus $a_1 = \dfrac{-2}{\pi 1^2}, \quad a_3 = \dfrac{-2}{\pi 3^2}, \quad a_5 = \dfrac{-2}{\pi 5^2}, \dots$ etc. $\dots (3)$

$$b_n = \frac{1}{\pi}\int_{-\pi}^{\pi} f(x)\sin nx\,dx = \frac{1}{\pi}\left[\int_{-\pi}^{0}(-\pi)\sin nx\,dx + \int_{0}^{\pi} x\sin nx\,dx\right]$$

$$= \frac{1}{\pi}\left[(-\pi)\left\{-\frac{\cos nx}{n}\right\}^0_{-\pi} + \left\{x\left(-\frac{\cos nx}{n}\right) - (1)\left(-\frac{\sin nx}{n^2}\right)\right\}^\pi_0\right]$$

$$= \frac{1}{\pi}\left[\frac{\pi(1 - \cos n\pi)}{n} - \frac{\pi\cos n\pi}{n}\right] = \frac{1}{n}[1 - 2\cos n\pi]$$

$$= \frac{1}{n}\,[1 - 2\,(-1)^n]$$

Thus $b_1 = 3, \qquad b_2 = -\dfrac{1}{2}, \qquad b_3 = \dfrac{3}{3} = 1, \qquad b_4 = -\dfrac{1}{4}, \dots$ etc. $\dots (4)$

Substituting in (1), we get

$$f(x) = -\frac{\pi}{4} - \frac{2}{\pi}\left[\frac{1}{1^2}\cos x + \frac{1}{3^2}\cos 3x + \frac{1}{5^2}\cos 5x + \dots\right]$$

$$+ \left[3\sin x - \frac{1}{2}\sin 2x + \sin 3x - \frac{1}{4}\sin 4x + \dots\right] \quad \dots (5)$$

Since $f(x)$ is discontinuous at $x_o = 0$, therefore, the value of $f(x)$ at $x_o = 0$, the point of discontinuity is calculated by rule

$$f(0) = \frac{\text{L.H.L.} + \text{R.H.L}}{2} = \frac{f(0-0) + f(0+0)}{2}$$

where $\quad f(0-0) = \lim_{h \to 0} f(0-h) = -\pi$

and $\quad f(0+0) = \lim_{h \to 0} f(0+h) = \lim_{h \to 0} (0+h) = 0$

$\therefore \quad f(0) = \dfrac{-\pi + 0}{2} = -\dfrac{\pi}{2}$ $\hspace{3cm}$ ... (6)

Thus from (5), on putting $x = 0$, we have

$$-\frac{\pi}{2} = -\frac{\pi}{4} - \frac{2}{\pi}\left[\frac{1}{1^2} + \frac{1}{3^2} + \frac{1}{5^2} + \frac{1}{7^2} + \dots\right]$$

$$\therefore \quad \sum_{n=1}^{\infty} \frac{1}{(2n-1)^2} = \frac{\pi^2}{8}$$

Ex. 9 : *Find the Fourier series to represent e^{ax} in the interval $-\pi < x < \pi$.*

Sol. : Eventhough origin is the mid-point of the interval $-\pi < x < \pi$, $f(x)$ is neither even nor odd. Thus, we use the formulae (7) of article 5.5.

Let $\qquad e^{ax} = \dfrac{a_0}{2} + \sum_{n=1}^{\infty} (a_n \cos nx + b_n \sin nx)$ $\hspace{2cm}$ ... (1)

where $\qquad a_0 = \dfrac{1}{\pi} \int_{-\pi}^{\pi} f(x)\, dx = \dfrac{1}{\pi} \int_{-\pi}^{\pi} e^{ax}\, dx$

$$= \frac{1}{\pi}\left[\frac{e^{ax}}{a}\right]_{-\pi}^{\pi} = \frac{1}{\pi a}\left[e^{a\pi} - e^{-a\pi}\right]$$

$$= \frac{2 \sinh a\pi}{\pi a} \hspace{4cm} \text{... (2)}$$

$$a_n = \frac{1}{\pi} \int_{-\pi}^{\pi} f(x) \cos nx = \frac{1}{\pi} \int_{-\pi}^{\pi} e^{ax} \cos nx\, dx$$

$$= \frac{1}{\pi}\left[\frac{e^{ax}}{a^2 + n^2}(a \cos nx + n \sin nx)\right]_{-\pi}^{\pi}$$

$$= \frac{1}{\pi(a^2 + n^2)}\left[e^{a\pi}(a \cos n\pi) - e^{-a\pi}(a \cos n\pi)\right]$$

$$= \frac{a \cos n\pi \, (e^{a\pi} - e^{-a\pi})}{\pi(a^2 + n^2)} = \frac{2a \, (-1)^n \sinh a\pi}{\pi \, (a^2 + n^2)} \qquad \ldots (3)$$

$$b_n = \frac{1}{\pi} \int_{-\pi}^{\pi} f(x) \sin nx \, dx = \frac{1}{\pi} \int_{-\pi}^{\pi} e^{ax} \sin nx \, dx$$

$$= \frac{1}{\pi} \left[\frac{e^{ax}}{(a^2 + n^2)} \, (a \sin nx \, - n \cos nx) \right]_{-\pi}^{\pi}$$

$$= \frac{1}{\pi \, (a^2 + n^2)} \left[e^{a\pi} \, (- n \cos n\pi) - e^{-a\pi} \, (- n \cos n\pi) \right]$$

$$= - \frac{n \cos \, n\pi \, (e^{a\pi} - e^{-a\pi})}{\pi \, (a^2 + n^2)}$$

$$= - \frac{2n \, (- 1)^n \sinh a\pi}{\pi \, (a^2 + n^2)} \qquad \ldots (4)$$

Substituting the values of a_0, a_n, b_n in (1), we get

$$e^{ax} = \frac{\sinh a\pi}{\pi a} + \frac{2 \sinh a\pi}{\pi} \sum_{n=1}^{\infty} \frac{(-1)^n}{(a^2 + n^2)} \, (a \cos nx - n \sin nx)$$

Ex. 10 : *Determine the Fourier series for the following function*

$$f(x) = \begin{cases} \cos x, & -\pi < x < 0 \\ \sin x, & 0 < x < \pi \end{cases}$$

Sol. : Eventhough origin is the mid-point of the interval $-\pi < x < \pi$, $f(x)$ is neither even nor odd.

Let $f(x) = \dfrac{a_0}{2} + \displaystyle\sum_{n=1}^{\infty} (a_n \cos nx + b_n \sin nx)$ $\qquad \ldots (1)$

where $a_0 = \dfrac{1}{\pi} \displaystyle\int_{-\pi}^{\pi} f(x) \, dx = \dfrac{1}{\pi} \left[\displaystyle\int_{-\pi}^{0} \cos x \, dx + \int_{0}^{\pi} \sin x \, dx \right]$

$$= \frac{1}{\pi} \left[(\sin x)_{-\pi}^{0} + (- \cos x)_{0}^{\pi} \right] = \frac{1}{\pi} \, [1 + 1]$$

$$= \frac{2}{\pi} \qquad \ldots (2)$$

$$a_n = \frac{1}{\pi} \int_{-\pi}^{\pi} f(x) \cos nx \, dx = \frac{1}{\pi} \left[\int_{-\pi}^{0} \cos x \cos nx \, dx + \int_{0}^{\pi} \sin x \cos nx \, dx \right]$$

$$= \frac{1}{2\pi} \left[\int_{-\pi}^{0} \{\cos(1+n)x + \cos(1-n)x\} \, dx + \int_{0}^{\pi} \{\sin(1+n)x + \sin(1-n)x\} \, dx \right]$$

$$= \frac{1}{2\pi} \left[\left\{ \frac{\sin(1+n)x}{(1+n)} + \frac{\sin(1-n)x}{(1-n)} \right\}_{-\pi}^{0} + \left\{ -\frac{\cos(1+n)x}{(1+n)} - \frac{\cos(1-n)x}{(1-n)} \right\}_{0}^{\pi} \right]_{\text{for } n > 1}$$

$$= \frac{1}{2\pi} \left[0 + \left\{ -\frac{\cos(1+n)\pi}{(1+n)} - \frac{\cos(1-n)\pi}{(1-n)} + \frac{1}{1+n} + \frac{1}{1-n} \right\} \right]_{\text{for } n > 1}$$

$$= \begin{cases} 0, & \text{when } n \text{ is odd except } n = 1 \\[2mm] \dfrac{2}{\pi(1-n^2)}, & \text{when } n \text{ is even} \end{cases} \qquad \ldots (3)$$

When n = 1, we have

$$a_1 = \frac{1}{\pi} \int_{-\pi}^{\pi} f(x) \cos x \, dx = \frac{1}{\pi} \left[\int_{-\pi}^{0} \cos x \cos x \, dx + \int_{0}^{\pi} \sin x \cos x \, dx \right]$$

$$= \frac{1}{2\pi} \left[\int_{-\pi}^{0} (1 + \cos 2x) \, dx + \int_{0}^{\pi} \sin 2x \, dx \right] = \frac{1}{2\pi} \left[\left(x + \frac{\sin 2x}{2} \right)_{-\pi}^{0} + \left(-\frac{\cos 2x}{2} \right)_{0}^{\pi} \right]$$

$$= \frac{1}{2} \qquad \ldots (4)$$

$$b_n = \frac{1}{\pi} \int_{-\pi}^{\pi} f(x) \sin nx \, dx = \frac{1}{\pi} \left[\int_{-\pi}^{0} \cos x \sin nx \, dx + \int_{0}^{\pi} \sin x \sin nx \, dx \right]$$

$$= \frac{1}{2\pi} \left[\int_{-\pi}^{0} \{\sin(1+n)x - \sin(1-n)x\} \, dx + \int_{0}^{\pi} \{\cos(1-n)x - \cos(1+n)x\} \, dx \right]$$

$$= \frac{1}{2\pi} \left[\left\{ -\frac{\cos(1+n)x}{1+n} + \frac{\cos(1-n)x}{1-n} \right\}_{-\pi}^{0} + \left\{ \frac{\sin(1-n)x}{(1-n)} - \frac{\sin(1+n)x}{(1+n)} \right\}_{0}^{\pi} \right]_{\text{for } n > 1}$$

$$= \frac{1}{2\pi}\left[\left\{-\frac{1}{1+n}+\frac{1}{1-n}+\frac{\cos(1+n)\pi}{1+n}-\frac{\cos(1-n)\pi}{(1-n)}\right\}+0\right]_{\text{for } n>1}$$

$$= \frac{1}{2\pi}\left[-\frac{(1+\cos n\pi)}{(1+n)}+\frac{(1+\cos n\pi)}{(1-n)}\right] = \frac{1}{2\pi}\frac{2n}{(1-n)^2}(1+\cos n\pi)$$

$$= \begin{cases} 0, & \text{when n is odd except } n=1 \\[2mm] \dfrac{2}{\pi(1-n^2)}, & \text{when n is even} \end{cases} \qquad \dots(5)$$

When $n = 1$, we have

$$b_1 = \frac{1}{\pi}\int_{-\pi}^{\pi} f(x)\sin x\,dx = \frac{1}{\pi}\left[\int_{-\pi}^{0}\cos x\sin x + \int_{0}^{\pi}\sin^2 x\,dx\right]$$

$$= \frac{1}{2\pi}\left[\int_{-\pi}^{0}\sin 2x\,dx + \int_{0}^{\pi}(1-\cos 2x)\,dx\right] = \frac{1}{2\pi}\left[\left(-\frac{\cos 2x}{2}\right)_{-\pi}^{0}+\left(x-\frac{\sin 2x}{2}\right)_{0}^{\pi}\right]$$

$$= \frac{1}{2} \qquad \dots(6)$$

Thus from (1), (2), (3), (4), (5), and (6), the Fourier series is

$$f(x) = \frac{a_0}{2} + a_1\cos x + \left[a_2\cos 2x + a_4\cos 4x + a_6\cos 6x + \dots\right]$$

$$+ b_1\sin x + \left[b_2\sin 2x + b_4\sin 4x + b_6\sin 6x + \dots\right]$$

$$= \frac{1}{\pi} + \frac{1}{2}(\cos x + \sin x) + \frac{2}{\pi}\left[\sum_{r=1}^{\infty}\frac{1}{(1-4r^2)}\cos 2rx + \frac{2}{(1-4r^2)}\sin 2rx\right]$$

[Note n = 2r]

Type II : Even and Odd functions defined in the interval $(-\pi < x < \pi)$:

Ex. 11 : *Obtain Fourier expansion for function*

$$f(x) = \begin{cases} \pi + x, & \text{if } -\pi \le x \le 0 \\[2mm] \pi - x, & \text{if } 0 \le x \le \pi \end{cases} \qquad \text{and} \quad f(x+2\pi) = f(x)$$

Sol. : Here $\quad f(-x) = \begin{cases} \pi - x, & \text{if } -\pi \le -x \le 0 \\[2mm] \pi + x, & \text{if } 0 \le -x \le \pi \end{cases}$

$$= \begin{cases} \pi - x, & \text{if } 0 \le x \le \pi \\ \pi + x, & \text{if } -\pi \le x \le 0 \end{cases}$$

$$= f(x)$$

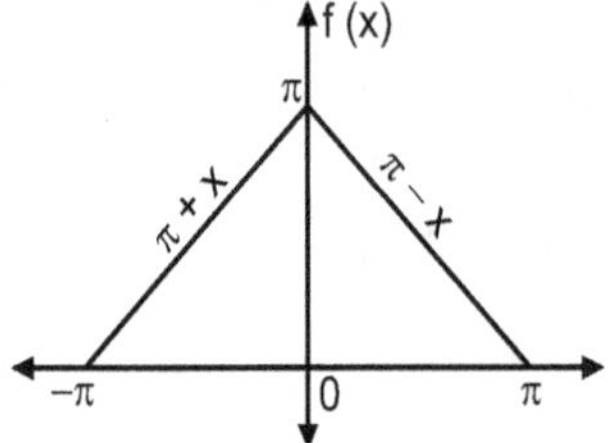

Fig. 5.8

Therefore, $f(x)$ is an even function of x in the interval $-\pi \le x \le \pi$. This is also clear from its graph (Refer Fig. 5.8) which is symmetrical about y-axis. Hence $b_n = 0$ and by result (8) of article 5.7, Fourier series is

$$f(x) \; = \; \frac{a_0}{2} + \sum_{n=1}^{\infty} a_n \cos nx \qquad \qquad \ldots (1)$$

where

$$a_0 \; = \; \frac{2}{\pi} \int_0^\pi f(x)\, dx = \frac{2}{\pi} \int_0^\pi (\pi - x)\, dx = \frac{2}{\pi} \left[\pi x - \frac{x^2}{2} \right]_0^\pi$$

$$= \; \frac{2}{\pi} \left[\pi^2 - \frac{\pi^2}{2} \right] = \frac{2}{\pi} \left[\frac{\pi^2}{2} \right]$$

$$= \; \pi \qquad \qquad \ldots (2)$$

$$a_n \; = \; \frac{2}{\pi} \int_0^\pi f(x) \cos nx\, dx = \frac{2}{\pi} \int_0^\pi (\pi - x)\, \cos nx\, dx$$

$$= \; \frac{2}{\pi} \left[(\pi - x) \left(\frac{\sin nx}{n} \right) - (-1) \left(-\frac{\cos nx}{n^2} \right) \right]_0^\pi$$

$$= \; \frac{2}{\pi} \left[\left\{ 0 - \frac{\cos n\pi}{n^2} \right\} - \left\{ 0 - \frac{1}{n^2} \right\} \right] = \frac{2}{\pi n^2} \left[1 - \cos n\pi \right]$$

$$= \; \begin{cases} 0, & \text{if n is even} \\ \dfrac{4}{\pi n^2}, & \text{if n is odd} \end{cases}$$

$$\therefore \qquad a_1 \; = \; \frac{4}{\pi 1^2}\, , \quad a_3 \; = \; \frac{4}{\pi 3^2}\, , \quad a_5 \; = \; \frac{4}{\pi 5^2}\, , \; \ldots \text{ etc.} \qquad \qquad \ldots (3)$$

From (1), (2) and (3) the required Fourier series is

$$f(x) = \frac{\pi}{2} + \frac{4}{\pi}\left[\frac{1}{1^2}\cos x + \frac{1}{3^2}\cos 3x + \frac{1}{5^2}\cos 5x + \ldots\right]$$

$$= \frac{\pi}{2} + \frac{4}{\pi}\sum_{n=0}^{\infty}\frac{1}{(2n+1)^2}\cos(2n+1)x.$$

Ex. 12 : *Obtain Fourier expansion for function*

$$f(x) = \begin{cases} \cos x, & -\pi < x < 0 \\[2mm] -\cos x, & 0 < x < \pi \end{cases} \quad \text{and} \quad f(x + 2\pi) = f(x).$$

Sol. : Here

$$f(-x) = \begin{cases} \cos(-x), & -\pi < -x < 0 \\[2mm] -\cos(-x), & 0 < -x < \pi \end{cases}$$

$$= \begin{cases} \cos x, & 0 < x < \pi \\[2mm] -\cos x, & -\pi < x < 0 \end{cases}$$

$$= -f(x)$$

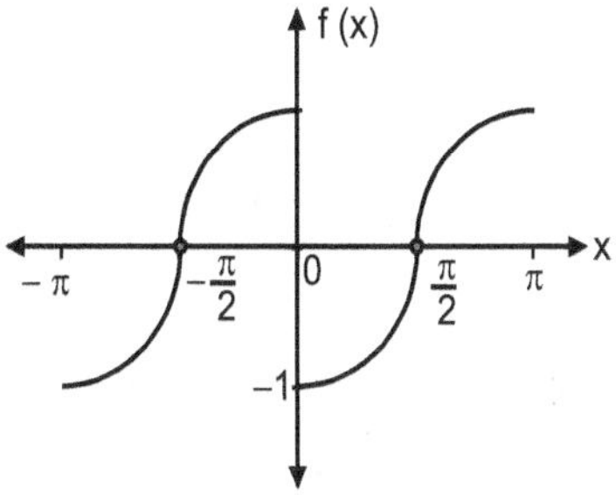

Fig. 5.9

Therefore f(x) is an odd function of x in the interval $-\pi < x < \pi$. This is also clear from its graph (Refer Fig.5.9) which is symmetrical in the origin. Hence $a_0 = 0$, $a_n = 0$ and by result (9) of article 5.7, Fourier series is

$$f(x) = \sum_{n=1}^{\infty} b_n \sin nx \qquad \ldots (1)$$

where

$$b_n = \frac{2}{\pi}\int_0^{\pi} f(x)\sin nx\, dx = \frac{2}{\pi}\int_0^{\pi}(-\cos x)\sin nx\, dx$$

$$= -\frac{1}{\pi}\int_0^{\pi}[\sin(1+n)x - \sin(1-n)x]\, dx$$

$$= -\frac{1}{\pi} \left[-\frac{\cos(1+n)x}{(1+n)} + \frac{\cos(1-n)x}{(1-n)} \right]_0^\pi \text{ for } n > 1$$

$$= -\frac{1}{\pi} \left[\left\{ -\frac{\cos(1+n)\pi}{(1+n)} + \frac{\cos(1-n)\pi}{(1-n)} \right\} - \left\{ -\frac{1}{(1+n)} + \frac{1}{(1-n)} \right\} \right]_{\text{for } n > 1}$$

$$= -\frac{1}{\pi} \left[\frac{(1+\cos n\pi)}{(1+n)} - \frac{(1+\cos n\pi)}{(1-n)} \right] = -\frac{1}{\pi} \cdot \frac{2n}{(n^2-1)}(1+\cos n\pi)$$

$$= \begin{cases} 0, & \text{if } n \text{ is odd except } n = 1 \\[2mm] -\dfrac{4n}{\pi(n^2-1)}, & \text{if } n \text{ is even} \end{cases}$$

$$\therefore \qquad b_2 = -\frac{4}{\pi}\frac{2}{(2^2-1)} \ , \ b_4 = -\frac{4}{\pi}\frac{4}{(4^2-1)} \ , \ b_6 = -\frac{4}{\pi}\frac{6}{(6^2-1)} \ , \ \dots \text{ etc. } \dots (2)$$

When $n = 1$, we have

$$b_1 = \frac{2}{\pi} \int_0^\pi f(x)\sin x \, dx = \frac{2}{\pi} \int_0^\pi (-\cos x)\sin x \, dx$$

$$= -\frac{1}{\pi} \int_0^\pi (\sin 2x) \, dx = 0 \qquad\qquad \dots (3)$$

From (1), (2) and (3), the required Fourier series is

$$f(x) = -\frac{4}{\pi} \left[\frac{2}{(2^2-1)}\sin 2x + \frac{4}{(4^2-1)}\sin 4x + \frac{6}{(6^2-1)}\sin 6x + \dots \right]$$

$$= -\frac{4}{\pi} \sum_{n=1}^{\infty} \frac{2n}{(2n)^2-1}\sin 2nx$$

Ex. 13 : *Obtain Fourier series for the function f(x) given by*

$$f(x) = \begin{cases} 1 + \dfrac{2x}{\pi}, & -\pi \le x \le 0 \\[3mm] 1 - \dfrac{2x}{\pi}, & 0 \le x \le \pi \end{cases}$$

Hence deduce that $\dfrac{1}{1^2} + \dfrac{1}{3^2} + \dfrac{1}{5^2} + \dots = \dfrac{\pi^2}{8}$

Sol. : Here

$$f(-x) = \begin{cases} 1 - \dfrac{2x}{\pi}, & -\pi \le -x \le 0 \\[2mm] 1 + \dfrac{2x}{\pi}, & 0 \le -x \le \pi \end{cases} = \begin{cases} 1 - \dfrac{2x}{\pi}, & 0 \le x \le \pi \\[2mm] 1 + \dfrac{2x}{\pi}, & -\pi \le x \le 0 \end{cases}$$

$$= f(x)$$

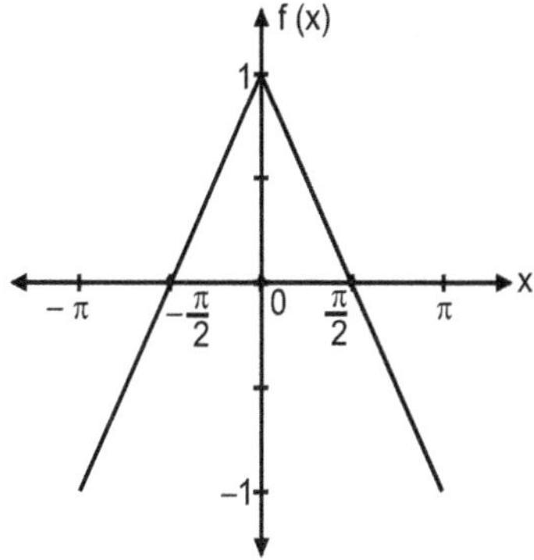

Fig. 5.10

Therefore f(x) is an even function of x in the interval $-\pi \le x \le \pi$. This is also clear from its graph (Refer Fig. 5.10) which is symmetrical about y-axis. Hence $b_n = 0$ and by result (8) of article 5.7, Fourier series is

$$f(x) = \frac{a_0}{2} + \sum_{n=1}^{\infty} a_n \cos nx \qquad \ldots (1)$$

where

$$a_0 = \frac{2}{\pi} \int_0^{\pi} f(x)\,dx = \frac{2}{\pi} \int_0^{\pi} \left(1 - \frac{2x}{\pi}\right) dx = \frac{2}{\pi} \left[x - \frac{x^2}{\pi}\right]_0^{\pi}$$

$$= 0 \qquad \ldots (2)$$

$$a_n = \frac{2}{\pi} \int_0^{\pi} f(x) \cos nx\,dx = \frac{2}{\pi} \int_0^{\pi} \left(1 - \frac{2x}{\pi}\right) \cos nx\,dx$$

$$= \frac{2}{\pi} \left[\left(1 - \frac{2x}{\pi}\right)\left(\frac{\sin nx}{n}\right) - \left(-\frac{2}{\pi}\right)\left(-\frac{\cos nx}{n^2}\right)\right]_0^{\pi}$$

$$= \frac{2}{\pi} \left[\left\{0 - \frac{2 \cos n\pi}{\pi n^2}\right\} - \left\{0 - \frac{2}{\pi n^2}\right\}\right] = \frac{4}{\pi^2 n^2}[1 - \cos n\pi]$$

$$= \begin{cases} 0, & \text{if n is even} \\[2mm] \dfrac{8}{\pi^2 n^2}, & \text{if n is odd} \end{cases}$$

$$\therefore \quad a_1 = \frac{8}{\pi^2}\frac{1}{1^2}, \qquad a_3 = \frac{8}{\pi^2}\frac{1}{3^2}, \qquad a_5 = \frac{8}{\pi^2}\frac{1}{5^2}, \ldots \text{etc.} \qquad \ldots (3)$$

From (1), (2) and (3), the required Fourier series is

$$f(x) = \frac{8}{\pi^2}\left[\frac{1}{1^2}\cos x + \frac{1}{3^2}\cos 3x + \frac{1}{5^2}\cos 5x + \ldots\right] \qquad \ldots (4)$$

at $x = 0$, $f(0) = 1$, on putting $x = 0$ in (4), we get

$$1 = \frac{8}{\pi^2}\left[\frac{1}{1^2} + \frac{1}{3^2} + \frac{1}{5^2} + \ldots\right]$$

$$\therefore \qquad \frac{1}{1^2} + \frac{1}{3^2} + \frac{1}{5^2} + \ldots = \frac{\pi^2}{8}\;.$$

Ex. 14 : *Prove that if* $-\pi < x < \pi,$

$$(i) \quad \cosh ax = \frac{2a}{\pi}\sinh a\pi\left[\frac{1}{2a^2} + \sum_{n=1}^{\infty}\frac{(-1)^n}{(n^2 + a^2)}\cos nx\right]$$

$$(ii) \quad \sinh ax = \frac{2}{\pi}\sinh a\pi\left[\sum_{n=1}^{\infty}\frac{(-1)^{n+1}\,n}{(n^2 + a^2)}\sin nx\right]$$

Sol. : (i) Let $f(x) = \cosh ax - \pi < x < \pi$

Here $f(-x) = \cosh(-ax) = \cosh ax = f(x)$

$\therefore$ $f(x)$ is an even function of x in $-\pi < x < \pi$.

Hence $b_n = 0$ and by result (8) of article 5.7, the Fourier series is

$$f(x) = \frac{a_0}{2} + \sum_{n=1}^{\infty}a_n\cos nx \qquad \ldots (1)$$

$$\text{where} \quad a_0 = \frac{2}{\pi}\int_0^{\pi}f(x)\,dx = \frac{2}{\pi}\int_0^{\pi}\cosh ax\,dx = \frac{2}{\pi}\left[\frac{\sinh ax}{a}\right]_0^{\pi}$$

$$= \frac{2\sinh a\pi}{a\pi} \qquad \ldots (2)$$

$$a_n = \frac{2}{\pi}\int_0^{\pi}f(x)\cos nx\,dx = \frac{2}{\pi}\int_0^{\pi}\cosh ax\cos nx\,dx$$

[Note : $\cos(n + ia)x = \cos nx\cosh ax - i\sin nx\sinh ax$**]** $\quad\begin{cases}\because \sin ix = i\sinh x \\ \text{and } \cos ix = \cosh x\end{cases}$

$$a_n = \frac{2}{\pi} \text{ R.P. of } \int_0^{\pi} \cos(n + ia)x \, dx = \frac{2}{\pi} \text{ R.P. of } \left[\frac{\sin(n + ia)x}{(n + ia)} \right]_0^{\pi}$$

$$= \frac{2}{\pi} \text{ R.P. of } \left[\frac{(n - ia)\sin(n\pi + ia\pi)}{(n^2 + a^2)} \right]$$

$$= \frac{2}{\pi} \text{ R.P. of } \left[\frac{(n - ia)(i \cos n\pi \sinh a\pi)}{(n^2 + a^2)} \right]$$

$$= \frac{(-1)^n \, 2a \sinh a\pi}{\pi (n^2 + a^2)} \qquad \qquad \dots (3)$$

From (1), (2) and (3), the required Fourier series is

$$\cosh ax = \frac{\sinh a\pi}{a\pi} + \frac{2a \sinh a\pi}{\pi} \sum_{n=1}^{\infty} \frac{(-1)^n}{(n^2 + a^2)} \cos nx$$

$$= \frac{2a}{\pi} \sinh a\pi \left[\frac{1}{2a^2} + \sum_{n=1}^{\infty} \frac{(-1)^n}{(n^2 + a^2)} \cos nx \right]$$

(ii) Let $\quad f(x) = \sinh ax, \, -\pi < x < \pi$

Here $\quad f(-x) = \sinh(-ax) = -\sinh ax = -f(x) \therefore f(x)$ is odd function of x in $-\pi < x < \pi$. Hence $a_0 = a_n = 0$ and by result (9) of article 5.6, the Fourier series is

$$f(x) = \sum_{n=1}^{\infty} b_n \sin nx \qquad \qquad \dots (1)$$

where $\quad b_n = \frac{2}{\pi} \int_0^{\pi} f(x) \sin nx \, dx = \frac{2}{\pi} \int_0^{\pi} \sinh ax \sin nx \, dx$

[**Note :** $\cos(n - ia)x = \cos nx \cosh ax + i \sin nx \sinh ax$]

$$b_n = \frac{2}{\pi} \text{ I.P. of } \int_0^{\pi} \cos(n - ia)x \, dx = \frac{2}{\pi} \text{ I.P. of } \left[\frac{\sin(n - ia)x}{(n - ia)} \right]_0^{\pi}$$

$$= \frac{2}{\pi} \text{ I.P. of } \left[\frac{(n + ia)\sin(n\pi - ia\pi)}{(n^2 + a^2)} \right]$$

$$= \frac{2}{\pi} \text{ I.P. of } \left[\frac{(n + ia)\,(-i \cos n\pi \sinh a\pi)}{(n^2 + a^2)} \right]$$

$$= \frac{(-1)^{n+1}\, 2n \sinh a\pi}{\pi\,(n^2 + a^2)} \qquad \ldots (2)$$

From (1) and (2), the required Fourier series is

$$\sinh ax = \frac{2}{\pi} \sinh a\pi \left[\sum_{n=1}^{\infty} \frac{(-1)^{n+1}\, n}{(n^2 + a^2)} \sin nx \right]$$

Ex. 15 : *Find Fourier series to represent the function $f(x) = \pi^2 - x^2$ in the interval $-\pi \le x \le \pi$ and $f(x + 2\pi) = f(x)$. Deduce that*

$$(i)\ \frac{1}{1^2} - \frac{1}{2^2} + \frac{1}{3^2} - \frac{1}{4^2} + \ldots = \frac{\pi^2}{12} \qquad (ii)\ \frac{1}{1^2} + \frac{1}{3^2} + \frac{1}{5^2} + \frac{1}{7^2} \ldots = \frac{\pi^2}{8}$$

Sol. : Here $f(-x) = \pi^2 - (-x)^2 = \pi^2 - x^2 = f(x)$. Therefore $f(x)$ is even function in $-\pi \le x \le \pi$. It is also clear from the graph (Fig. 5.11) that $f(x)$ is symmetrical about y-axis.

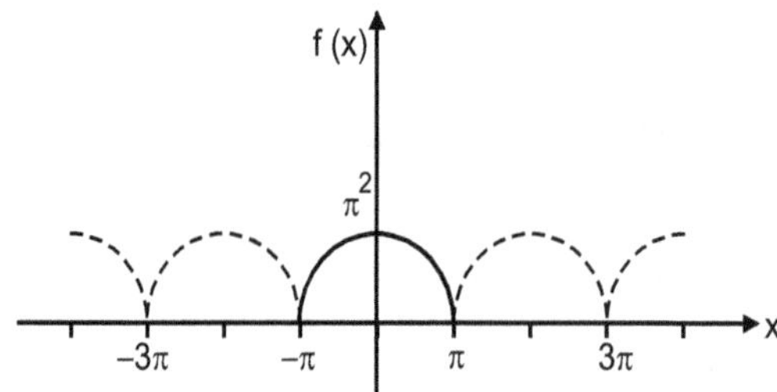

Fig. 5.11

Hence $b_n = 0$ and Fourier series for even function is

$$\pi^2 - x^2 = \frac{a_0}{2} + \sum_{n=1}^{\infty} a_n \cos nx \qquad \ldots (1)$$

where $a_0 = \dfrac{2}{\pi} \displaystyle\int_0^{\pi} f(x)\, dx = \dfrac{2}{\pi} \int_0^{\pi} (\pi^2 - x^2)\, dx = \dfrac{2}{\pi} \left[\pi^2 x - \dfrac{x^3}{3} \right]_0^{\pi}$

$$= \frac{4\pi^2}{3} \qquad \ldots (2)$$

$$a_n = \frac{2}{\pi} \int_0^{\pi} f(x) \cos nx\, dx = \frac{2}{\pi} \int_0^{\pi} (\pi^2 - x^2) \cos nx\, dx$$

$$= \frac{2}{\pi} \left[(\pi^2 - x^2)\left(\frac{\sin nx}{n} \right) - (-2x)\left(-\frac{\cos nx}{n^2} \right) + (-2)\left(-\frac{\sin nx}{n^3} \right) \right]_0^{\pi}$$

$$= \frac{2}{\pi}\left[\left\{0 - \frac{2\pi \cos n\pi}{n^2} + 0\right\} - 0\right] = \frac{4(-1)^{n+1}}{n^2} \qquad \ldots (3)$$

Substituting in (1) the values of a_0 and a_n from (2) and (3), we have

$$\pi^2 - x^2 = \frac{2\pi^2}{3} + 4 \sum_{n=1}^{\infty} \frac{(-1)^{n+1}}{n^2} \cos nx \qquad \ldots (4)$$

Now, putting $x = 0$ in (4), we get

$$\pi^2 = \frac{2\pi^2}{3} + 4 \sum_{n=1}^{\infty} \frac{(-1)^{n+1}}{n^2}$$

$$\therefore \qquad \frac{1}{1^2} - \frac{1}{2^2} + \frac{1}{3^2} - \frac{1}{4^2} + \ldots = \frac{\pi^2}{12} \qquad \ldots (5)$$

Again, putting $x = \pi$ in (4), we get

$$0 = \frac{2\pi^2}{3} + 4 \sum_{n=1}^{\infty} \frac{(-1)^{n+1}}{n^2} (-1)^n$$

$$\therefore \qquad \frac{1}{1^2} + \frac{1}{2^2} + \frac{1}{3^2} + \frac{1}{4^2} + \ldots = \frac{\pi^2}{6} \qquad \ldots (6)$$

Adding (5) and (6), we get

$$\frac{1}{1^2} + \frac{1}{3^2} + \frac{1}{5^2} + \frac{1}{7^2} + \ldots = \frac{\pi^2}{8} \qquad \ldots (7)$$

Hence (5) and (7) are required results.

Ex. 16 : *Find Fourier series to represent the function f(x) = x in the interval $-\pi < x < \pi$ and f(x + 2\pi) = f(x).*

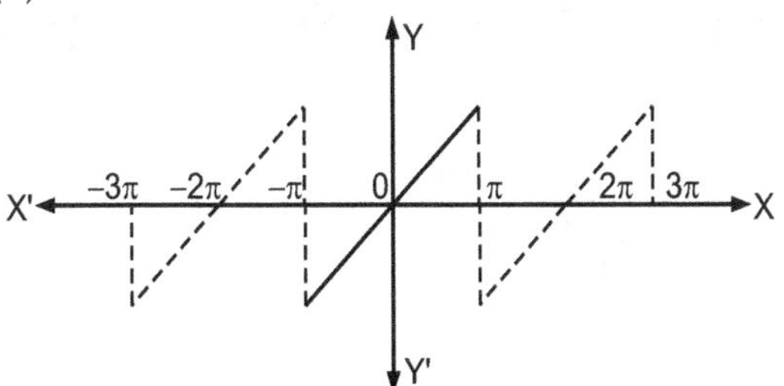

Fig. 5.12

Sol. : Here $f(-x) = -x = -f(x)$. Therefore $f(x)$ is an odd function of x in $-\pi < x < \pi$. This is also clear from the graph (Fig. 5.12) that $f(x)$ is symmetric through origin and represents the discontinuous function (saw-toothed waveform). Hence $a_0 = a_n = 0$ and Fourier series for odd function is

$$x = \sum_{n=1}^{\infty} b_n \sin nx \qquad \ldots (1)$$

where
$$b_n = \frac{2}{\pi} \int_0^\pi f(x) \sin nx \, dx = \frac{2}{\pi} \int_0^\pi x \sin x \, dx$$

$$= \frac{2}{\pi} \left[x \left(-\frac{\cos nx}{n} \right) - (1) \left(-\frac{\sin nx}{n^2} \right) \right]_0^\pi = -\frac{2 \cos n\pi}{n} \quad \ldots (2)$$

$$\therefore \qquad b_1 = \frac{2}{1}, \; b_2 = -\frac{2}{2}, \; b_3 = \frac{2}{3}, \; b_4 = -\frac{2}{4} \qquad \ldots (3)$$

Hence the required Fourier series is

$$x = 2 \left(\sin x - \frac{1}{2} \sin 2x + \frac{1}{3} \sin 3x - \frac{1}{4} \sin 4x + \ldots \right) \qquad \ldots (4)$$

Remark :

The graph of $y = (2 \sin x)$,

$$y = 2 \left(\sin x - \frac{1}{2} \sin 2x \right) \text{ and}$$

$$y = 2 \left(\sin x - \frac{1}{2} \sin 2x + \frac{1}{3} \sin 3x \right)$$

are as shown in Fig. 5.13 by the curves I (doted line), II (line) and (III) (bold line) respectively. From the adjacent figure we note that how successive approximations approach more and more closely to the $y = x$ for all values of x in $-\pi < x < \pi$, but not for $x = \pm \pi$

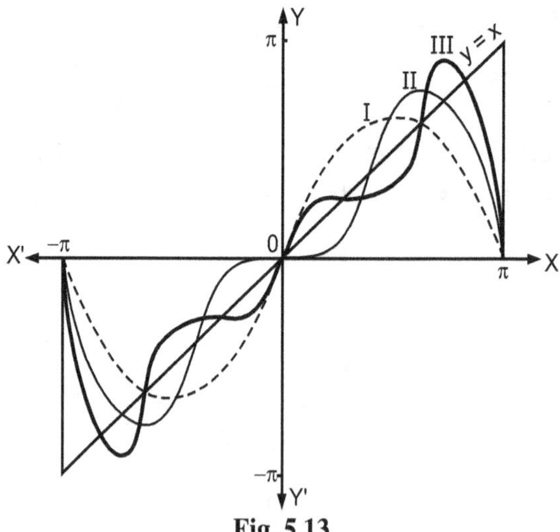

Fig. 5.13

Ex. 17 : *Find Fourier series of the function $f(x) = x + \dfrac{x^2}{4}$ when $-\pi < x < \pi$ and $f(x + 2\pi) = f(x)$, hence show that $\dfrac{1}{1^2} - \dfrac{1}{2^2} + \dfrac{1}{3^2} - \dfrac{1}{4^2} + \ldots = \dfrac{\pi^2}{12}$.*

Sol. : We use the following theorem on sum of functions :

Statement : The Fourier series of a sum $f_1 + f_2$ is the sum of corresponding Fourier series of f_1 and f_2.

Here $f(x)$ can be expressed as $f(x) = f_1(x) + f_2(x)$, where $f_1(x) = x$ is an odd function of x and $f_2(x) = \dfrac{x^2}{4}$ is an even function of x in the interval $-\pi < x < \pi$. Therefore, Fourier series of $f(x)$ is sum of the Fourier series of $f_1(x)$ and $f_2(x)$.

(i) Fourier series for odd function $f_1(x) = x$, $-\pi < x < \pi$:

$$\text{Let} \qquad f_1(x) = \sum_{n=1}^{\infty} b_n \sin nx \ dx \quad (a_0 = a_n = 0) \qquad \ldots (1)$$

$$\text{where} \qquad b_n = \frac{2}{\pi} \int_0^{\pi} f(x) \sin nx \ dx = \frac{2}{\pi} \int_0^{\pi} x \sin nx \ dx$$

$$= \frac{2}{\pi} \left[x \left(-\frac{\cos nx}{n} \right) - (1) \left(-\frac{\sin nx}{n^2} \right) \right]_0^{\pi}$$

$$= (-1)^{n+1} \frac{2}{n} \qquad \ldots (2)$$

$$\therefore \qquad f_1(x) = 2 \sum_{n=1}^{\infty} \frac{(-1)^{n+1}}{n} \sin nx \qquad \ldots (3)$$

(ii) Fourier series for even function $f_2(x) = \dfrac{x^2}{4}$, $-\pi < x < \pi$:

$$\text{Let} \qquad f_2(x) = \frac{a_0}{2} + \sum_{n=1}^{\infty} a_n \cos nx \qquad (b_n = 0) \qquad \ldots (4)$$

$$\text{where} \qquad a_0 = \frac{2}{\pi} \int_0^{\pi} f(x) \ dx = \frac{2}{\pi} \int_0^{\pi} \frac{x^2}{4} \ dx = \frac{1}{2\pi} \left[\frac{x^3}{3} \right]_0^{\pi}$$

$$= \frac{\pi^2}{6} \qquad \ldots (5)$$

$$a_n = \frac{2}{\pi} \int_0^{\pi} f(x) \cos nx \ dx = \frac{2}{\pi} \int_0^{\pi} \left(\frac{x^2}{4} \right) \cos nx \ dx$$

$$= \frac{1}{2\pi} \left[x^2 \left(\frac{\sin nx}{n} \right) - (2x) \left(-\frac{\cos nx}{n^2} \right) + (2) \left(-\frac{\sin nx}{n^3} \right) \right]_0^{\pi}$$

$$= \frac{1}{2\pi} \left[\left\{ 0 + \frac{2\pi \cos n\pi}{n^2} - 0 \right\} - 0 \right] = (-1)^n \frac{1}{n^2} \qquad \ldots (6)$$

$$\therefore \quad f_2(x) = \frac{\pi^2}{12} + \sum_{n=1}^{\infty} \frac{(-1)^n}{n^2} \cos nx \qquad \ldots (7)$$

Hence from (3) and (7), the Fourier series for f(x) is

$$x + \frac{x^2}{4} = \frac{\pi^2}{12} + \sum_{n=1}^{\infty} \frac{(-1)^n}{n^2} \cos nx + 2 \sum_{n=1}^{\infty} \frac{(-1)^{n+1}}{n} \sin nx \qquad \ldots (8)$$

Putting $x = 0$ in (8), we get

$$0 = \frac{\pi^2}{12} + \sum_{n=1}^{\infty} \frac{(-1)^n}{n^2} \quad \text{or} \quad - \sum_{n=1}^{\infty} \frac{(-1)^n}{n^2} = \frac{\pi^2}{12}$$

$$\therefore \quad \frac{1}{1^2} - \frac{1}{2^2} + \frac{1}{3^2} - \frac{1}{4^2} + \ldots = \frac{\pi^2}{12}$$

Ex. 18 : *Prove that, if $0 \leq x \leq 2\pi$, $\frac{1}{12} x\,(\pi - x)\,(2\pi - x) = \sum_{n=1}^{\infty} \frac{\sin nx}{n^3}$*

Sol. : Note : If f(x) is defined in the interval $0 \leq x \leq 2\pi$, then substitution $x = z + \pi$ transforms the function f(x) to a function F(z) in the interval $-\pi \leq z \leq \pi$. Now, if this transformed function is even or odd, then Fourier series for F(z) is obtained by determining the coefficients a_0, a_n and b_n from results (8) or (9). The Fourier series for f(x) is then obtained by replacing z by $x - \pi$. If F(z) is neither even nor odd, then we obtain Fourier series for f(x) by results (7).

Let
$$f(x) = \frac{1}{12} x\,(\pi - x)\,(2\pi - x), \text{ put } x = z + \pi$$

$$\therefore \quad F(z) = \frac{1}{12}(z + \pi)\,(-z)\,(\pi - z)$$

$$= \frac{1}{12} z\,(z^2 - \pi^2) \text{ in the interval } -\pi \leq z \leq \pi.$$

Also,
$$F(-z) = -\frac{1}{12} z\,(z^2 - \pi^2) = -F(z)$$

$\therefore$ F(z) is an odd function in $-\pi \leq z \leq \pi$ and Fourier series for F(z) is given by

$$F(z) = \sum_{n=1}^{\infty} b_n \sin nz \, dz \ (a_0 = a_n = 0) \qquad \ldots (1)$$

where
$$b_n = \frac{2}{\pi} \int_0^{\pi} F(z) \sin nz \, dz = \frac{2}{\pi} \int_0^{\pi} \frac{1}{12}(z^3 - \pi^2 z)\, \sin nz \, dz$$

$$= \frac{1}{6\pi} \left[(z^3 - \pi^2 z) \left(-\frac{\cos nz}{n} \right) - (3z^2 - \pi^2) \left(-\frac{\sin nz}{n^2} \right) \right.$$

$$\left. + (6z) \left(\frac{\cos nz}{n^3} \right) - (6) \left(\frac{\sin nz}{n^4} \right) \right]_0^\pi$$

$$= \frac{1}{6\pi} \left[\frac{6\pi \cos n\pi}{n^3} \right] = \frac{(-1)^n}{n^3} \qquad \qquad \dots (2)$$

From (1) and (2), the Fourier series for $F(z)$ is

$$F(z) = \sum_{n=1}^{\infty} \frac{(-1)^n}{n^3} \sin nz \qquad \qquad \dots (3)$$

Substituting $z = x - \pi$ in (3), the Fourier series for $f(x)$ is

$$f(x) = \frac{1}{12} x (\pi - x) (2\pi - x) = \sum_{n=1}^{\infty} \frac{(-1)^n}{n^3} \sin n (x - \pi)$$

$$= \sum_{n=1}^{\infty} \frac{(-1)^n}{n^3} \sin nx \cos n\pi$$

$$= \sum_{n=1}^{\infty} \frac{\sin nx}{n^3} \qquad \qquad [\because \ \cos n\pi = (-1)^n]$$

EXERCISE 5.1

1. Find the Fourier expansion for the following functions in the interval $0 \le x \le 2\pi$: (i) $f(x) = x$, (ii) $f(x) = x^2$, (iii) $f(x) = \frac{1}{2} (\pi - x)$, (iv) $f(x) = e^x$.

$$\textbf{Ans.:} \qquad \text{(i)} \quad x = \pi - \sum_{n=1}^{\infty} \frac{2}{n} \sin nx$$

$$\text{(ii)} \quad x^2 = \frac{4\pi^2}{3} + 4 \sum_{n=1}^{\infty} \frac{1}{n^2} \cos nx - 4\pi \sum_{n=1}^{\infty} \frac{1}{n} \sin nx$$

$$\text{(iii)} \quad \frac{1}{2} (\pi - x) = \sum_{n=1}^{\infty} \frac{1}{n} \sin nx$$

$$\text{(iv)} \quad e^x = \frac{e^{2\pi} - 1}{\pi} \left[\frac{1}{2} + \sum_{n=1}^{\infty} \frac{1}{(1 + n^2)} \cos nx - \frac{n}{(1 + n^2)} \sin nx \right]$$

2. Obtain the Fourier series for the periodic function f(x) defined in the interval $0 \le x \le 2\pi$ as

$$f(x) = \begin{cases} \sin x, & 0 \le x \le \pi \\ 0, & \pi \le x \le 2\pi \end{cases}$$

Deduce that $\dfrac{1}{1.3} + \dfrac{1}{3.5} + \dfrac{1}{5.7} + ... = \dfrac{1}{2}$.

Ans. : $f(x) = \dfrac{1}{\pi} - \dfrac{2}{\pi} \displaystyle\sum_{n=1}^{\infty} \dfrac{1}{4n^2 - 1} \cos 2nx + \dfrac{1}{2} \sin x.$

3. A function f(x) is defined within the range (0, 2π) by relations

$$f(x) = \begin{cases} x, & 0 \le x \le \pi \\ 2\pi - x, & \pi \le x \le 2\pi \end{cases} \quad \text{and } f(x + 2\pi) = f(x)$$

Express f(x) as a Fourier series in the range (0, 2π).

Ans. : $f(x) = \dfrac{\pi}{2} - \dfrac{4}{\pi} \displaystyle\sum_{n=0}^{\infty} \dfrac{1}{(2n+1)^2} \cos (2n+1) x.$

4. If $f(x) = \begin{cases} mx, & 0 < x < \pi \\ -mx + 2m\pi, & \pi < x < 2\pi \end{cases}$ and $f(x + 2\pi) = f(x)$.

Prove that $f(x) = \dfrac{m\pi}{2} - \dfrac{4m}{\pi} \left[\cos x + \dfrac{1}{3^2} \cos 3x + \dfrac{1}{5^2} \cos 5x + ... \right]$

5. Find the Fourier expansion of the function defined in one period by the relations

$$f(x) = \begin{cases} 1, & 0 < x < \pi \\ 2, & \pi < x < 2\pi \end{cases}$$

and deduce that $\dfrac{\pi}{4} = 1 - \dfrac{1}{3} + \dfrac{1}{5} - \dfrac{1}{7} + ...$

Ans. : $f(x) = \dfrac{3}{2} - \dfrac{2}{\pi} \left(\sin x + \dfrac{\sin 3x}{3} + \dfrac{\sin 5x}{5} + ... \right)$

6. Find the Fourier series for the function f(x) defined as

$$f(x) = \begin{cases} a, & 0 < x < \pi \\ -a, & \pi < x < 2\pi \end{cases} \quad \text{and } f(x + 2\pi) = f(x)$$

Hint : Substitution of x = π + z transforms function f(x) to F(z) as odd function in the interval (– π < z < π).

Ans. $f(x) = \dfrac{4a}{\pi} \displaystyle\sum_{n=0}^{\infty} \dfrac{1}{(2n+1)} \sin (2n+1) x$

7. Find the Fourier series for the following function f(x)

(i) $f(x) = \begin{cases} x, & -\dfrac{\pi}{2} < x < \dfrac{\pi}{2} \\ \\ \pi - x, & \dfrac{\pi}{2} < x < \dfrac{3\pi}{2} \end{cases}$ and $f(x + 2\pi) = f(x)$

(ii) $f(x) = \begin{cases} x, & -\dfrac{\pi}{2} < x < \dfrac{\pi}{2} \\ \\ 0, & \dfrac{\pi}{2} < x < \dfrac{3\pi}{2} \end{cases}$ and $f(x + 2\pi) = f(x)$

Ans. : (i) $f(x) = \dfrac{4}{\pi} \left(\sin x - \dfrac{1}{9} \sin 3x + \dfrac{1}{25} \sin 5x \; ... \right)$

(ii) $f(x) = \dfrac{2}{\pi} \sin x + \dfrac{1}{2} \sin 2x - \dfrac{2}{\pi 9} \sin 3x - \dfrac{1}{4} \sin 4x + \dfrac{2}{\pi 25} \sin 5x \; ...$

8. Find the Fourier series for the function f(x) defined as

$$f(x) = \begin{cases} 0, & -\pi \le x \le 0 \\ \\ x, & 0 \le x \le \pi \end{cases} \quad \text{and } f(x + 2\pi) = f(x)$$

Hint : Even though origin in the mid-point of the interval, f(x) is neither even nor odd.

Ans. : $f(x) = \dfrac{\pi}{4} - \dfrac{2}{\pi} \sum_{n=0}^{\infty} \dfrac{1}{(2n + 1)^2} \cos(2n + 1)x + \sum_{n=1}^{\infty} \dfrac{(-1)^{n-1}}{n} \sin nx$

9. The function f(x) is defined by

$$f(x) = \begin{cases} -\dfrac{x}{a}, & 0 < x < a \\ \\ \dfrac{\pi - x}{\pi - a}, & a < x < 2\pi - a \quad \text{and } f(x + 2\pi) = f(x) \\ \\ \dfrac{2\pi - x}{a}, & 2\pi - a < x < 2\pi \end{cases}$$

Show that for this function $a_n = 0$, $b_n = \dfrac{2 \sin na}{(\pi - a) n^2}$

10. If $f(x)$ is a periodic function defined over a period $(0, 2\pi)$ by

$$f(x) = \frac{(3x^2 - 6x\pi + 2\pi^2)}{12}$$

Prove that $f(x) = \sum_{n=1}^{\infty} \frac{\cos nx}{n^2}$ and hence show that $1 + \frac{1}{2^2} + \frac{1}{3^2} + \dots = \frac{\pi^2}{6}$.

11. Determine the Fourier expansion for the following periodic functions in the interval $-\pi \le x \le \pi$:

(i) $f(x) = |x|$ (ii) $f(x) = |\sin x|$ (iii) $f(x) = \begin{cases} -\dfrac{1}{2}, & -\pi < x < 0 \\ \dfrac{1}{2}, & 0 < x < \pi \end{cases}$

Ans. : (i) x | is an even function

$$\therefore \ |x| = \frac{\pi}{2} - \frac{4}{\pi}\left(\cos x + \frac{\cos 3x}{3^2} + \frac{\cos 5x}{5^2} + \dots\right)$$

(ii) $|\sin x|$ is an even function

$$\therefore \ |\sin x| = \frac{2}{\pi} - \frac{4}{\pi}\left(\frac{1}{3}\cos 2x + \frac{1}{15}\cos 4x + \frac{1}{35}\cos 6x + \dots\right)$$

(iii) $f(x)$ is an odd function $\therefore \ f(x) = \frac{2}{\pi}\left(\sin x + \frac{1}{3}\sin 3x + \frac{1}{5}\sin 5x + \dots\right)$

12. Prove that if $-\pi < x < \pi$ and a is not an integer,

(i) $\sin ax = \frac{\sin a\pi}{\pi}\left(\frac{\sin x}{1^2 - a^2} - \frac{2\sin 2x}{2^2 - a^2} + \frac{3\sin 3x}{3^2 - a^2} \dots\right)$

(ii) $\cos ax = \frac{2a \sin a\pi}{\pi}\left(\frac{1}{2a^2} + \sum_{n=1}^{\infty} \frac{(-1)^{n-1}}{n^2 - a^2}\cos nx\right)$

13. Obtain the Fourier series for the function $f(x) = x^2$, $-\pi < x < \pi$. Hence show that

(i) $\frac{1}{1^2} + \frac{1}{2^2} + \frac{1}{3^2} + \frac{1}{4^2} + \dots = \frac{\pi^2}{6}$

(ii) $\frac{1}{1^2} - \frac{1}{2^2} + \frac{1}{3^2} - \frac{1}{4^2} + \dots = \frac{\pi^2}{12}$

(iii) $\frac{1}{1^2} + \frac{1}{3^2} + \frac{1}{5^2} + \dots = \frac{\pi^2}{8}$ **Ans. :** $x^2 = \frac{\pi^2}{3} + 4\sum_{n=1}^{\infty} \frac{(-1)^n}{n^2}\cos nx$

14. Prove that in the interval $-\pi \leq x \leq \pi$,

(i) $\quad x \cos x = -\dfrac{1}{2} \sin x + 2 \displaystyle\sum_{n=2}^{\infty} \dfrac{(-1)^n}{(n^2-1)} \sin nx.$

(ii) $\quad x \sin x = 1 - \dfrac{1}{2} \cos x - 2 \displaystyle\sum_{n=2}^{\infty} \dfrac{(-1)^n}{(n^2-1)} \cos nx.$

Deduce that $\dfrac{1}{1.3} - \dfrac{1}{3.5} + \dfrac{1}{5.7} - \dfrac{1}{7.9} + \ldots = \dfrac{1}{4}(\pi - 2)$

15. Determine the Fourier series expansion for the function $f(x) = \sqrt{1 - \cos x},\ -\pi < x < \pi.$

$$\textbf{Ans. :}\ \sqrt{1 - \cos x} = \dfrac{2\sqrt{2}}{\pi} - \dfrac{4\sqrt{2}}{\pi} \sum_{n=1}^{\infty} \dfrac{1}{4n^2 - 1} \cos nx.$$

16. Find the Fourier series to represent $f(x) = x - x^2$ in the interval $-\pi \leq x \leq \pi.$

Deduce that $\dfrac{1}{1^2} - \dfrac{1}{2^2} + \dfrac{1}{3^2} - \dfrac{1}{4^2} + \ldots = \dfrac{\pi^2}{12}$

$$\textbf{Ans :}\ x - x^2 = -\dfrac{\pi^2}{3} - 4 \sum_{n=1}^{\infty} \dfrac{(-1)^n}{n^2} \cos nx - 2 \sum_{n=1}^{\infty} \dfrac{(-1)^n}{n} \sin nx.$$

17. Find the Fourier series to represent $f(x) = x + x^2$ in the interval $-\pi \leq x \leq \pi.$

Deduce that $\dfrac{1}{1^2} + \dfrac{1}{2^2} + \dfrac{1}{3^2} + \dfrac{1}{4^2} + \ldots = \dfrac{\pi^2}{6}.$

$$\textbf{Ans. :}\ f(x) = \dfrac{\pi^2}{3} + 4 \sum_{n=1}^{\infty} \dfrac{(-1)^n}{n^2 c} \cos nx - 2 \sum_{n=1}^{\infty} \dfrac{(-1)^n}{n} \sin nx.$$

18. Obtain the Fourier series in the interval $(-\pi, \pi)$ for the following functions :

(i) $f(x) = \begin{cases} 0, & -\pi \leq x \leq 0 \\ \sin x, & 0 \leq x \leq \pi \end{cases}$

(ii) $f(x) = \begin{cases} -x, & -\pi \leq x \leq 0 \\ x, & 0 \leq x \leq \pi \end{cases}$ and $f(x + 2\pi) = f(x)$

(iii) $f(x) = \begin{cases} \pi + x, & -\pi \leq x \leq -\dfrac{\pi}{2} \\[2mm] \dfrac{\pi}{2}, & -\dfrac{\pi}{2} \leq x \leq \dfrac{\pi}{2} \\[2mm] \pi - x, & \dfrac{\pi}{2} \leq x \leq \pi \end{cases}$

Ans. : (i) $a_n = -\dfrac{1 + \cos n\pi}{(n^2 - 1)\,\pi}$, $b_n = 0$, $a_1 = 0$, $b_1 = \dfrac{1}{2}$.

(ii) $f(x) = \dfrac{\pi}{2} - \dfrac{4}{\pi} \displaystyle\sum_{n=0}^{\infty} \dfrac{1}{(2n+1)^2} \cos(2n+1)x$

(iii) $f(x)$ is an even function $\therefore$ $f(x) = \dfrac{3\pi}{8} + \dfrac{4}{\pi} \displaystyle\sum_{n=1}^{\infty} \dfrac{\sin \dfrac{3n\pi}{4} \sin \dfrac{n\pi}{4}}{n^2} \cos nx.$

19. Obtain the Fourier series for the function $f(x) = \dfrac{\pi^2}{12} - \dfrac{x^2}{4}$ in the interval $-\pi \le x \le \pi$.

Ans. : $\dfrac{\pi^2}{12} - \dfrac{x^2}{4} = \cos x - \dfrac{1}{4}\cos 2x + \dfrac{1}{9}\cos 3x - \dfrac{1}{16}\cos 4x \ldots$

20. Prove that in the interval $-\pi < x < \pi$,

$$\dfrac{1}{2}(\pi - x)\sin x - \dfrac{1}{2} + \dfrac{1}{4}\cos x - \left(\dfrac{1}{1.3}\cos 2x + \dfrac{1}{2.4}\cos 3x + \ldots\right)$$

5.10 FUNCTIONS HAVING ARBITRARY PERIOD (CHANGE OF INTERVAL)

The functions considered so far had period 2π. In most of the engineering applications, the period of function to be expanded is not always 2π but some other arbitrary interval, say 2L. In such cases we transform, by simple change of variable, the interval of arbitrary length 2L into the interval of length 2π, and then determine the Fourier series.

Consider a periodic function $f(x)$ defined in the interval $c \le x \le c + 2L$. To change the problem to a period of 2π, we use substitution $z = \dfrac{\pi x}{L}$ or $x = \dfrac{Lz}{\pi}$

so that when $x = c$, $z = \dfrac{\pi c}{L} = d$, say

and when $x = c + 2L$, $z = \dfrac{\pi c}{L} + 2\pi = d + 2\pi$

Thus, the function $f(x)$ of period 2L in the interval $c \le x \le c + 2L$ is transformed into the function $f\left(\dfrac{Lz}{\pi}\right) = F(z)$, say, of period 2π in the interval $d \le z \le d + 2\pi$. Hence, if $F(z)$ has Fourier series, this series must be of the form

$$F(z) = \dfrac{a_0}{2} + \sum_{n=1}^{\infty} (a_n \cos nz + b_n \sin nz) \qquad \ldots (10)$$

$$\left.\begin{array}{l} a_0 = \dfrac{1}{\pi} \displaystyle\int\limits_{d}^{d+2\pi} F(z)\, dz \\[2em] a_n = \dfrac{1}{\pi} \displaystyle\int\limits_{d}^{d+2\pi} F(z)\cos nz\, dz \\[2em] b_n = \dfrac{1}{\pi} \displaystyle\int\limits_{d}^{d+2\pi} F(z)\sin nz\, dz \end{array}\right\} \qquad \dots (11)$$

where,

We can use these formulae directly, but change to variable x simplifies calculation.

Hence, making the inverse substitution $z = \dfrac{\pi x}{L}$, $dz = \dfrac{\pi}{L}\, dx$, so that

when $z = d,$ $x = c,$

and when $z = d + 2\pi,$ $x = c + 2L,$

In (10) and (11), the Fourier expansion of $f(x)$ in the interval $c \le x \le c + 2L$, is given by

$$f(x) = \frac{a_0}{2} + \sum_{n=1}^{\infty}\left(a_n \cos\frac{n\pi x}{L} + b_n \sin\frac{n\pi x}{L} \right) \qquad \dots (12)$$

where

$$\boxed{\begin{array}{l} a_0 = \dfrac{1}{L} \displaystyle\int\limits_{c}^{c+2L} f(x)\, dx \\[2em] a_n = \dfrac{1}{L} \displaystyle\int\limits_{c}^{c+2L} f(x)\cos\dfrac{n\pi x}{L}\, dx \\[2em] b_n = \dfrac{1}{L} \displaystyle\int\limits_{c}^{c+2L} f(x)\sin\dfrac{n\pi x}{L}\, dx \end{array}} \qquad \dots (13)$$

Cor. 1 : If $c = 0$, then result (13) gives

$$\boxed{\begin{array}{l} a_0 = \dfrac{1}{L} \displaystyle\int\limits_{0}^{2L} f(x)\, dx \\[2em] a_n = \dfrac{1}{L} \displaystyle\int\limits_{0}^{2L} f(x)\cos\dfrac{n\pi x}{L}\, dx \\[2em] b_n = \dfrac{1}{L} \displaystyle\int\limits_{0}^{2L} f(x)\sin\dfrac{n\pi x}{L}\, dx \end{array}} \qquad \dots (14)$$

Cor. 2 : If $c = -L$, then result (13) gives

$$
\boxed{
\begin{aligned}
a_0 &= \frac{1}{L}\int_{-L}^{L} f(x)\,dx \\[2ex]
a_n &= \frac{1}{L}\int_{-L}^{L} f(x)\cos\frac{n\pi x}{L}\,dx \\[2ex]
b_n &= \frac{1}{L}\int_{-L}^{L} f(x)\sin\frac{n\pi x}{L}\,dx
\end{aligned}
}
\qquad \ldots (15)
$$

5.11 EVEN AND ODD FUNCTIONS IN THE INTERVAL $-L \le x \le L$

Even Function : If $f(x)$ is an even function in $-L \le x \le L$, then the Fourier coefficients a_0, a_n and b_n given by (15) are reduced as follows :

$$
a_0 = \frac{1}{L}\int_{-L}^{L} f(x)\,dx = \frac{2}{L}\int_{0}^{L} f(x)\,dx \qquad\qquad [f(x)\text{ is even function}]
$$

$$
a_n = \frac{1}{L}\int_{-L}^{L} f(x)\cos\frac{n\pi x}{L}\,dx = \frac{2}{L}\int_{0}^{L} f(x)\cos\frac{n\pi x}{L}\,dx \quad \left[\text{Product } f(x)\cos\frac{n\pi x}{L}\text{ is even}\right]
$$

$$
b_n = \frac{1}{L}\int_{-L}^{L} f(x)\sin\frac{n\pi x}{L}\,dx = 0 \qquad\qquad \left[\text{Product } f(x)\sin\frac{n\pi x}{L}\text{ is odd}\right]
$$

Thus for even function $f(x)$ in $-L \le x \le L$, the Fourier coefficients are given by

$$
\boxed{
\begin{aligned}
a_0 &= \frac{2}{L}\int_{0}^{L} f(x)\,dx \\[2ex]
a_n &= \frac{2}{L}\int_{0}^{L} f(x)\cos\frac{n\pi x}{L}\,dx \\[2ex]
b_n &= 0
\end{aligned}
}
\qquad \ldots (16)
$$

Odd Function : If $f(x)$ is an odd function in $-L \leq x \leq L$, then the Fourier coefficients a_0, a_n and b_n given by (15) are reduced as follows :

$$a_0 = \frac{1}{L}\int_{-L}^{L} f(x)\,dx = 0 \qquad\qquad [f(x)\text{ is even function}]$$

$$a_n = \frac{1}{L}\int_{-L}^{L} f(x)\cos\frac{n\pi x}{L}\,dx = 0 \qquad\qquad \left[\text{Product } f(x)\cos\frac{n\pi x}{L} \text{ is odd}\right]$$

$$b_n = \frac{1}{L}\int_{-L}^{L} f(x)\sin\frac{n\pi x}{L}\,dx = \frac{2}{L}\int_{0}^{L} f(x)\sin\frac{n\pi x}{L}\,dx \qquad\qquad \left[\text{Product } f(x)\sin\frac{n\pi x}{L} \text{ is even}\right]$$

Thus for odd function $f(x)$ in $-L \leq x \leq L$, the Fourier coefficients are given by

$$\boxed{\begin{aligned} a_0 &= 0, \qquad a_n = 0 \\[2mm] b_n &= \frac{2}{L}\int_{0}^{L} f(x)\sin\frac{n\pi x}{L}\,dx \end{aligned}} \qquad \dots (17)$$

5.12 ILLUSTRATIONS ON EXPANSIONS OF PERIODIC FUNCTIONS HAVING ARBITRARY PERIODS

Type I : Functions having period $c \leq x \leq c + 2L$ or $-L \leq x \leq L$:

Ex. 1 : *Find the Fourier series expansion of the function*

$f(x) = 2x - x^2$, $0 \leq x \leq 3$ and period is 3.

Also graph the function.

Sol. : Here period $2L = 3$ $\qquad \therefore\ L = \dfrac{3}{2}$

$$\text{Let } 2x - x^2 = \frac{a_0}{2} + \sum_{n=1}^{\infty}\left(a_n\cos\frac{n\pi x}{L} + b_n\sin\frac{n\pi x}{L}\right) \qquad \dots (1)$$

$$\text{where} \quad a_0 = \frac{1}{L}\int_{0}^{2L} f(x)\,dx = \frac{2}{3}\int_{0}^{3}(2x - x^2)\,dx \qquad\qquad \left(\because L = \frac{3}{2}\right)$$

$$= \frac{2}{3}\left[x^2 - \frac{x^3}{3}\right]_{0}^{3} = \frac{2}{3}\left[9 - \frac{27}{3}\right]$$

$$= 0 \qquad\qquad\qquad \dots (2)$$

$$a_n = \frac{1}{L} \int_0^{2L} f(x) \cos \frac{n\pi x}{L} dx = \frac{2}{3} \int_0^3 (2x - x^2) \cos \frac{2n\pi x}{3} dx \quad \left(\because L = \frac{3}{2} \right)$$

$$= \frac{2}{3} \left[(2x - x^2) \left(\frac{3}{2n\pi} \sin \frac{2n\pi x}{3} \right) - (2 - 2x) \left(-\frac{9}{4n^2\pi^2} \cos \frac{2n\pi x}{3} \right) \right.$$

$$\left. + (-2) \left(-\frac{27}{8n^3\pi^3} \sin \frac{2n\pi x}{3} \right) \right]_0^3$$

$$= \frac{2}{3} \left[\left\{ 0 - \frac{9}{n^2\pi^2} \cos 2n\pi + 0 \right\} - \left\{ 0 + \frac{9}{2n^2\pi^2} + 0 \right\} \right]$$

$$\left(\because \ \cos 0 = \cos 2n\pi = 1 \right)$$

$$= \frac{2}{3} \cdot \frac{9}{n^2\pi^2} \left[-1 - \frac{1}{2} \right] = -\frac{9}{n^2\pi^2} \qquad \dots (3)$$

$$b_n = \frac{1}{L} \int_0^{2L} f(x) \sin \frac{n\pi x}{L} dx = \frac{2}{3} \int_0^3 (2x - x^2) \sin \frac{2n\pi x}{3} dx \quad \left(\because L = \frac{3}{2} \right)$$

$$= \frac{2}{3} \left[(2x - x^2) \left(-\frac{3}{2n\pi} \cos \frac{2n\pi x}{3} \right) - (2 - 2x) \left(-\frac{9}{4n^2\pi^2} \sin \frac{2n\pi x}{3} \right) \right.$$

$$\left. + (-2) \left(\frac{27}{8n^3\pi^3} \cos \frac{2n\pi x}{3} \right) \right]_0^3$$

$$= \frac{2}{3} \left[\left\{ \frac{9}{2n\pi} - 0 - \frac{27}{4n^3 \pi^3} \right\} - \left\{ 0 + 0 - \frac{27}{4n^3\pi^3} \right\} \right] = \frac{2}{3} \left(\frac{9}{2n\pi} \right)$$

$$= \frac{3}{n\pi} \qquad \dots (4)$$

Substituting the values of a_0, a_n and b_n from (2), (3) and (4) in (1), we get

$$2x - x^2 = 0 + \sum_{n=1}^{\infty} \left(-\frac{9}{n^2\pi^2} \cos \frac{2n\pi x}{3} + \frac{3}{n\pi} \sin \frac{2n\pi x}{3} \right)$$

$$= \frac{-9}{\pi^2} \sum_{n=1}^{\infty} \frac{1}{n^2} \cos \frac{2n\pi x}{3} + \frac{3}{\pi} \sum_{n=1}^{\infty} \frac{1}{n} \sin \frac{2n\pi x}{3}$$

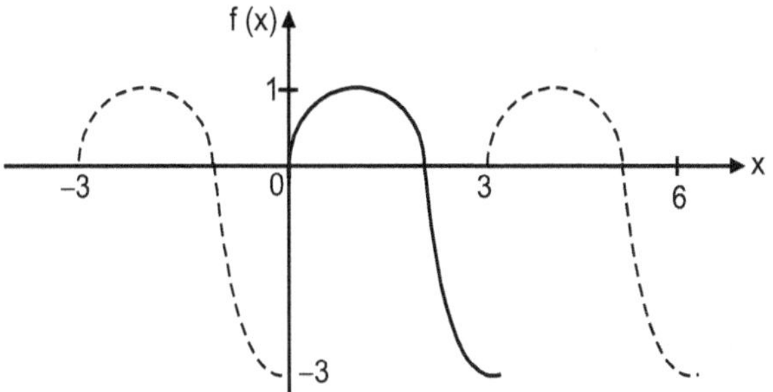

Fig. 5.14

Ex. 2 :　If $f(x) = \begin{cases} \pi x, & 0 \leq x \leq 1 \\ \pi(2-x), & 1 \leq x \leq 2 \end{cases}$　*period 2*

Show that in the interval $0 \leq x \leq 2$,

$$f(x) = \frac{\pi}{2} - \frac{4}{\pi} \sum_{n=0}^{\infty} \frac{1}{(2n+1)^2} \cos(2n+1)\pi x$$

Sol. : Here period $2L = 2$　　　$\therefore\ L = 1$

Let　$f(x) = \dfrac{a_0}{2} + \sum_{n=1}^{\infty}\left(a_n \cos \dfrac{n\pi x}{L} + b_n \sin \dfrac{n\pi x}{L}\right)$　　　... (1)

where　$a_0 = \dfrac{1}{L}\int_0^{2L} f(x)\,dx = \int_0^2 f(x)\,dx = \left[\int_0^1 \pi x\,dx + \int_1^2 \pi(2-x)\,dx\right]$　$(\because L = 1)$

$= \pi\left[\left(\dfrac{x^2}{2}\right)_0^1 + \left(2x - \dfrac{x^2}{2}\right)_1^2\right] = \pi\left[\dfrac{1}{2} + 4 - 2 - 2 + \dfrac{1}{2}\right]$

$= \pi$　　　... (2)

$a_n = \dfrac{1}{L}\int_0^{2L} f(x) \cos \dfrac{n\pi x}{L}\,dx = \int_0^2 f(x) \cos n\pi x\,dx$　　　$(\because L = 1)$

$= \int_0^1 \pi x \cos n\pi x\,dx + \int_1^2 \pi(2-x)\cos n\pi x\,dx$

$= \pi\left[\left\{x\left(\dfrac{\sin n\pi x}{n\pi}\right) - (1)\left(-\dfrac{\cos n\pi x}{n^2\pi^2}\right)\right\}_0^1 + \left\{(2-x)\left(\dfrac{\sin n\pi x}{n\pi}\right) - (-1)\left(-\dfrac{\cos n\pi x}{n^2\pi^2}\right)\right\}_1^2\right]$

$= \pi\left[\left\{\dfrac{\cos n\pi - 1}{n^2\pi^2}\right\} + \left\{\dfrac{-1 + \cos n\pi}{n^2\pi^2}\right\}\right] = \dfrac{2}{n^2\pi}(\cos n\pi - 1)$

$$= \begin{cases} 0, & \text{if n is even} \\[2mm] -\dfrac{4}{n^2\pi}, & \text{if n is odd} \end{cases}$$

i.e. $a_1 = -\dfrac{4}{\pi 1^2}$, $a_3 = -\dfrac{4}{\pi 3^2}$, $a_5 = -\dfrac{4}{\pi 5^2}$, ... etc.   ... (3)

$$b_n = \frac{1}{L} \int_0^{2L} f(x)\, \sin\frac{n\pi x}{L}\, dx = \int_0^{2} f(x)\, \sin n\pi x\, dx \qquad (\because\ L = 1)$$

$$= \int_0^{1} \pi x\, \sin n\pi x\, dx + \int_1^{2} \pi\,(2 - x)\, \sin n\pi x\, dx$$

$$= \pi\left[\left\{x\left(-\frac{\cos n\pi x}{n\pi}\right) - (1)\left(-\frac{\sin n\pi x}{n^2\pi^2}\right)\right\}_0^{1} + \left\{(2 - x)\left(-\frac{\cos n\pi x}{n\pi}\right) - (-1)\left(-\frac{\sin n\pi x}{n^2\pi^2}\right)\right\}_1^{2}\right]$$

$$= \pi\left[-\frac{\cos n\pi}{n\pi} + \frac{\cos n\pi}{n\pi}\right] = 0 \qquad ... (4)$$

From (1), (2), (3) and (4), the Fourier series is

$$f(x) = \frac{\pi}{2} - \frac{4}{\pi}\left[\frac{1}{1^2}\cos \pi x + \frac{1}{3^2}\cos 3\pi x + \frac{1}{5^2}\cos 5\pi x + ...\right]$$

$$= \frac{\pi}{2} - \frac{4}{\pi}\sum_{n=0}^{\infty} \frac{1}{(2n + 1)^2}\cos (2n + 1)\,\pi x.$$

Ex. 3 : *A sinusoidal voltage E sin ωt is passed through a half-wave rectifier which clips the negative portion of the wave as shown in Fig. 5.15. Find the Fourier series of the resulting periodic function.*

$$f(t) = \begin{cases} 0, & -\dfrac{T}{2} < t < 0 \\[4mm] E \sin \omega t, & 0 < t < \dfrac{T}{2} \end{cases} \qquad \text{where } T = \frac{2\pi}{\omega}$$

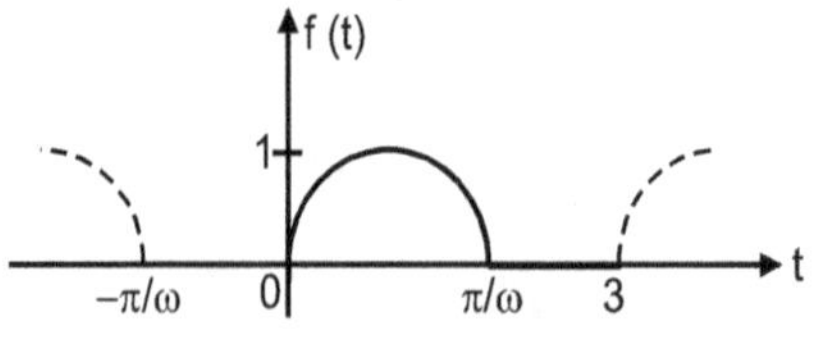

Fig. 5.15 : Half-wave rectifier

Sol. : Given function is

$$f(t) = \begin{cases} 0, & -\dfrac{\pi}{\omega} < t < 0 \\[3mm] E \sin \omega t, & 0 < t < \dfrac{\pi}{\omega} \end{cases}$$

Here period $2L = \dfrac{2\pi}{\omega}$ $\qquad \therefore \quad L = \dfrac{\pi}{\omega}$

Let $\qquad f(t) = \dfrac{a_0}{2} + \displaystyle\sum_{n=1}^{\infty} \left(a_n \cos \dfrac{n\pi t}{L} + b_n \sin \dfrac{n\pi t}{L} \right)$ $\qquad\qquad$ ... (1)

where $\qquad a_0 = \dfrac{1}{L} \displaystyle\int_{-L}^{L} f(t)\, dt = \dfrac{\omega}{\pi} \int_{-\pi/\omega}^{\pi/\omega} f(t)\, dt$ $\qquad \left(\because L = \dfrac{\pi}{\omega} \right)$

$$= \dfrac{\omega}{\pi} \left[\int_{-\pi/\omega}^{0} (0)\, dt + \int_{0}^{\pi/\omega} E \sin \omega t\, dt \right] = \dfrac{\omega}{\pi} \left[-\dfrac{E \cos \omega t}{\omega} \right]_{0}^{\pi/\omega}$$

$$= \dfrac{2E}{\pi} \qquad\qquad\qquad\qquad\qquad\qquad\qquad\qquad\qquad ... (2)$$

$$a_n = \dfrac{1}{L} \int_{-L}^{L} f(t) \cos \dfrac{n\pi t}{L}\, dt = \dfrac{\omega}{\pi} \int_{-\pi/\omega}^{\pi/\omega} f(t) \cos n\omega t\, dt \qquad \left(\because L = \dfrac{\pi}{\omega} \right)$$

$$= \dfrac{\omega E}{2\pi} \int_{0}^{\pi/\omega} 2 \sin \omega t \cos n\omega t\, dt = \dfrac{\omega E}{2\pi} \int_{0}^{\pi/\omega} [\sin (1 + n)\, \omega t + \sin (1 - n)\, \omega t]\, dt$$

$$= \dfrac{\omega E}{2\pi} \left[-\dfrac{\cos (1 + n)\, \omega t}{(1 + n)\, \omega} - \dfrac{\cos (1 - n)\, \omega t}{(1 - n)\, \omega} \right]_{0}^{\pi/\omega} \quad \text{for } n > 1$$

$$= \dfrac{E}{2\pi} \left[\left\{ -\dfrac{\cos (1 + n)\, \pi}{(1 + n)} - \dfrac{\cos (1 - n)\, \pi}{(1 - n)} \right\} - \left\{ -\dfrac{1}{(1 + n)} - \dfrac{1}{(1 - n)} \right\} \right]$$

$$= \dfrac{E}{2\pi} \left[\dfrac{\cos n\pi}{(1 + n)} + \dfrac{\cos n\pi}{1 - n} + \dfrac{1}{1 + n} + \dfrac{1}{1 - n} \right] \qquad \left[\because \cos (1 + n)\, \pi = -\cos n\pi \right]$$

$$= \dfrac{E}{2\pi} \left[\dfrac{1}{(1 + n)} + \dfrac{1}{(1 - n)} \right] (1 + \cos n\pi) = \dfrac{E}{2\pi} \dfrac{2}{(1 - n^2)} [1 + (-1)^n]$$

$$= \begin{cases} \dfrac{-2E}{\pi\,(n^2 - 1)}, & \text{if n is even} \\[4mm] 0, & \text{if n is odd, except } n = 1 \end{cases}$$

$$\therefore \quad a_2 = -\frac{2E}{\pi\,(2^2 - 1)}, \qquad a_4 = -\frac{2E}{\pi\,(4^2 - 1)}, \qquad a_6 = -\frac{2E}{\pi\,(6^2 - 1)}, \text{ etc.} \qquad \ldots (3)$$

When $n = 1$, we have

$$a_1 = \frac{1}{L} \int_{-L}^{L} f(x) \cos \frac{\pi t}{L}\, dt$$

$$= \frac{\omega}{\pi} \int_{0}^{\pi/\omega} E \sin \omega t \cos \omega t\, dt$$

$$= \frac{\omega E}{2\pi} \int_{0}^{\pi/\omega} \sin 2\omega t\, dt = \frac{\omega E}{2\pi} \left[-\frac{\cos 2\omega t}{2\omega} \right]_{0}^{\pi/\omega} = 0 \qquad \ldots (4)$$

$$b_n = \frac{1}{L} \int_{-L}^{L} f(t) \sin \frac{n\pi t}{L}\, dt = \frac{\omega}{\pi} \int_{-\pi/\omega}^{\pi/\omega} f(t) \sin n\omega t\, dt \qquad \left(\because L = \frac{\pi}{\omega} \right)$$

$$= \frac{\omega E}{2\pi} \int_{0}^{\pi/\omega} 2 \sin \omega t \, \sin \omega t\, dt = \frac{\omega E}{2\pi} \int_{0}^{\pi/\omega} [\cos (1 - n)\,\omega t - \cos (1 + n)\,\omega t]\, dt$$

$$= \frac{\omega E}{2\pi} \left[\frac{\sin (1 - n)\,\omega t}{(1 - n)\,\omega} - \frac{\sin (1 + n)\,\omega t}{(1 + n)\,\omega} \right]_{0 \text{ for } n > 1}^{\pi/\omega}$$

$$= 0 \quad \text{for all n except } n = 1 \qquad \ldots (5)$$

$$b_1 = \frac{1}{L} \int_{-L}^{L} f(x) \sin \frac{\omega t}{L}\, dt = \frac{\omega}{\pi} \int_{0}^{\pi/\omega} (E \sin \omega t) \sin \omega t\, dt$$

$$= \frac{E\omega}{\pi/\omega} \int_{0}^{\pi/\omega} \left(\frac{1 - \cos 2\omega t}{2} \right) dt = \frac{E\omega}{2\pi} \left[t - \frac{\sin 2\omega t}{2\omega} \right]_{0}^{\pi/\omega} = \frac{E\omega}{2\pi} \cdot \frac{\pi}{\omega}$$

$$= \frac{E}{2} \qquad \ldots (6)$$

Thus from (1), (2), (3), (4), (5) and (6), the Fourier series is

$$f(t) = \frac{E}{\pi} - \frac{2E}{\pi} \left[\frac{1}{(2^2 - 1)} \cos 2\omega t + \frac{1}{(4^2 - 1)} \cos 4\omega t + \frac{1}{(6^2 - 1)} \cos 6\omega t + \dots \right] + \frac{E}{2} \sin \omega t$$

$$f(t) = \frac{E}{\pi} - \frac{2E}{\pi} \sum_{n=1}^{\infty} \frac{1}{(4n^2 - 1)} \cos 2n\omega t + \frac{E}{2} \sin \omega t$$

Ex. 4 : *Find the Fourier expansion of the function $f(x) = 4 - x^2$ in the interval $0 < x < 2$. Graph the function and state the value of the series for $x = 0, 1, 2, 10, 11$.*

Sol. : Here period is $2L = 2$ $\therefore$ $L = 1$.

Let

$$4 - x^2 = \frac{a_0}{2} + \sum_{n=1}^{\infty} (a_n \cos n\pi x + b_n \sin n\pi x) \qquad \dots (1)$$

where

$$a_0 = \frac{1}{L} \int_0^{2L} f(x)\, dx = \int_0^2 (4 - x^2)\, dx \qquad \left(\because L = 1 \right)$$

$$= \left[4x - \frac{x^3}{3} \right]_0^2 = \frac{16}{3} \qquad \dots (2)$$

$$a_n = \frac{1}{L} \int_0^{2L} f(x) \cos \frac{n\pi x}{L}\, dx = \int_0^2 (4 - x^2)\cos n\pi x \, dx \qquad \left(\because L = 1 \right)$$

$$= \left[(4 - x^2)\left(\frac{\sin n\pi x}{n\pi} \right) - (-2x)\left(-\frac{\cos n\pi x}{n^2\pi^2} \right) + (-2)\left(-\frac{\sin n\pi x}{n^3\pi^3} \right) \right]_0^2$$

$$= \left[\left\{ 0 - \frac{4}{n^2\pi^2} + 0 \right\} - 0 \right] = -\frac{4}{n^2\pi^2} \qquad \dots (3)$$

$$b_n = \frac{1}{L} \int_0^{2L} f(x) \sin \frac{n\pi x}{L}\, dx = \int_0^2 (4 - x^2)\, \sin n\pi x \, dx \qquad \left(\because L = 1 \right)$$

$$= \left[(4 - x^2)\left(-\frac{\cos n\pi x}{n\pi} \right) - (-2x)\left(-\frac{\sin n\pi x}{n^2\pi^2} \right) + (-2)\left(\frac{\cos n\pi x}{n^3\pi^3} \right) \right]_0^2$$

$$= \left[\left\{ 0 - 0 - \frac{2}{n^3\pi^3} \right\} - \left\{ -\frac{4}{n\pi} - 0 - \frac{2}{n^3\pi^3} \right\} \right]$$

$$= \frac{4}{n\pi} \qquad \dots (4)$$

From (1), (2), (3) and (4), the required Fourier series is

$$4 - x^2 = \frac{8}{3} - \frac{4}{\pi^2} \sum_{n=1}^{\infty} \frac{1}{n^2} \cos n\pi x + \frac{4}{\pi} \sum_{n=1}^{\infty} \frac{1}{n} \sin n\pi x \qquad \ldots (5)$$

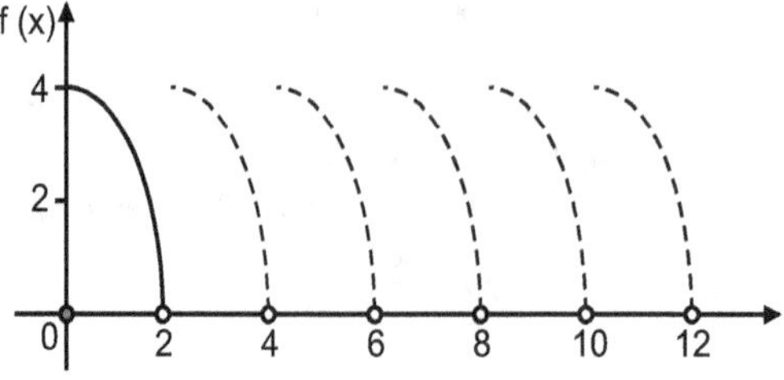

Fig. 5.16

Since function is discontinuous at points 0, 2, 4, 6, 8, 10 (Refer Fig. 5.16), we calculate the value of the series at $x = x_0$, the point of discontinuity, by the rule :

$$f(x_0) = \frac{\text{L. H. L.} + \text{R. H. L.}}{2} = \frac{f(x_0 - 0) + f(x_0 + 0)}{2}$$

$$\therefore \quad f(0) = \frac{f(0 - 0) + f(0 + 0)}{2} = \frac{\lim_{h \to 0} f(0 - h) + \lim_{h \to 0} f(0 + h)}{2} = \frac{0 + 4}{2} = 2$$

$$\text{and} \quad f(2) = \frac{f(2 - 0) + f(2 + 0)}{2} = \frac{\lim_{h \to 0} f(2 - h) + \lim_{h \to 0} f(2 + h)}{2} = \frac{0 + 4}{2} = 2$$

[**Note :** Since $f(x)$ is periodic function with period 2, its graph will repeat in the intervals (2, 4), (4, 6) and so on.]

Also $f(1) = 4 - 1 = 3$ [since function is continuous at $x = 1$].

Thus, the value of the series at $x = 0, 2, 4, 6, 8, 10$ and 11 is given by

$f(0) = 2, \quad f(1) = 3, \quad f(2) = 2, \ f(4) = 2, \quad f(6) = 2, \quad f(8) = 2, f(10) = 2$ and $f(11) = 3$

Ex. 5 : *Graph the following function and find its Fourier series :*

$$f(x) = \begin{cases} 0, & -5 < x < 0 \\ 3, & 0 < x < 5 \end{cases} \qquad \text{Period} = 10$$

How should $f(x)$ be defined at $x = -5, 0, 5$ in order that the Fourier series will converge to $f(x)$ for $-5 \le x \le 5$?

Sol. : [**Note :** Even though origin is mid-point of the interval, $f(x)$ is neither even nor odd.]

Here period is $2L = 10 \therefore L = 5$.

Choose the interval c to c + 2L as – 5 to 5, so that c = – 5.

$$\text{Let} \quad f(x) = \frac{a_0}{2} + \sum_{n=1}^{\infty} \left(a_n \cos \frac{n\pi x}{5} + b_n \sin \frac{n\pi x}{5} \right) \qquad \ldots (1)$$

$$\text{where} \quad a_0 = \frac{1}{L} \int_{-L}^{L} f(x)\, dx = \frac{1}{5} \int_{-5}^{5} f(x)\, dx \qquad \left(\because L = 5 \right)$$

$$= \frac{1}{5} \left[\int_{-5}^{0} (0)\, dx + \int_{0}^{5} (3)\, dx \right] = \frac{1}{5} \left[3x \right]_0^5 = 3 \qquad \ldots (2)$$

$$a_n = \frac{1}{L} \int_{-L}^{L} f(x) \cos \frac{n\pi x}{L}\, dx = \frac{1}{5} \int_{-5}^{5} f(x) \cos \frac{n\pi x}{5}\, dx \qquad \left(\because L = 5 \right)$$

$$= \frac{1}{5} \left[\int_{-5}^{0} (0) \cos \frac{n\pi x}{5}\, dx + \int_{0}^{5} 3 \cos \frac{n\pi x}{5}\, dx \right]$$

$$= \frac{3}{5} \left[\frac{5}{n\pi} \sin \frac{n\pi x}{5} \right]_0^5 = 0 \qquad \ldots (3)$$

$$b_n = \frac{1}{L} \int_{-L}^{L} f(x) \sin \frac{n\pi x}{L}\, dx = \frac{1}{5} \int_{-5}^{5} f(x) \sin \frac{n\pi x}{5}\, dx \qquad \left(\because L = 5 \right)$$

$$= \frac{1}{5} \left[\int_{-5}^{0} (0) \sin \frac{n\pi x}{5}\, dx + \int_{0}^{5} (3) \sin \frac{n\pi x}{5}\, dx \right]$$

$$= \frac{3}{5} \left[-\frac{5}{n\pi} \cos \frac{n\pi x}{5} \right]_0^5 = \frac{3\,(1 - \cos n\pi)}{\pi n} = \begin{cases} 0, & \text{if n is even} \\ \dfrac{6}{\pi n}, & \text{if n is odd} \end{cases}$$

$$\therefore \quad b_1 = \frac{6}{\pi.1}, \quad b_3 = \frac{6}{\pi.3}, \quad b_5 = \frac{6}{\pi.5}, \quad \ldots \text{etc.} \qquad \ldots (4)$$

From (1), (2), (3) and (4), corresponding Fourier series is

$$f(x) = \frac{3}{2} + \frac{6}{\pi} \left[\sin \frac{\pi x}{5} + \frac{1}{3} \sin \frac{3\pi x}{5} + \frac{1}{5} \sin \frac{5\pi x}{5} + \ldots \right] \qquad \ldots (5)$$

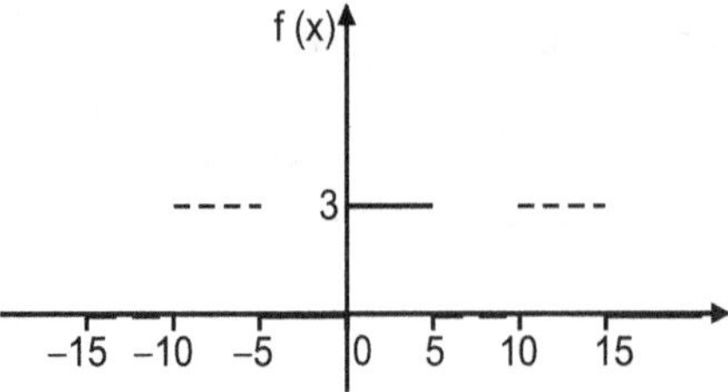

Fig. 5.17

Since f(x) satisfies the Dirichlet's conditions, we can say that the series converges to f(x) at all points of continuity and to $\dfrac{f(x_0 - 0) + f(x_0 + 0)}{2}$ at points of discontinuity.

At x = –5, 0 and 5, which are point of discontinuity, the series converges to $\dfrac{3+0}{2} = \dfrac{3}{2}$, as seen from the graph (Refer Fig. 5.15). The series will converge to f(x) for $-5 \leq x \leq 5$ if we redefine f(x) as follows :

$$f(x) = \begin{cases} 3/2, & x = -5 \\ 0, & -5 < x < 0 \\ 3/2, & x = 0 \\ 3, & 0 < x < 5 \\ 3/2, & x = 5 \end{cases} \qquad \text{Period} = 10$$

Type II : Even and Odd functions defined in the interval –L $\leq$ x $\leq$ L :

Ex. 6 : *Show that the Fourier series for the function f(x) = x² in the interval – l < x < l is given by*

$$f(x) = \frac{l^2}{3} + \frac{4l^2}{\pi^2} \sum_{n=1}^{\infty} \frac{(-1)^n}{n^2} \cos \frac{n\pi x}{l}$$

Sol. : Here f(x) = x² is even function of x in the interval $-l < x < l$. Hence, $b_n = 0$ and by result (16) of article 3.10, the Fourier series is

$$x^2 = \frac{a_0}{2} + \sum_{n=1}^{\infty} a_n \cos \frac{n\pi x}{l} \qquad\qquad (\because L = l) \quad \dots (1)$$

$$\text{where} \quad a_0 = \frac{2}{L} \int_0^L f(x)\, dx = \frac{2}{l} \int_0^l x^2\, dx = \frac{2}{l} \left[\frac{x^3}{3}\right]_0^l = \frac{2}{3} l^2 \qquad \dots(2)$$

$$a_n = \frac{2}{L} \int_0^L f(x) \cos\frac{n\pi x}{L}\, dx = \frac{2}{l} \int_0^l x^2 \cos\frac{n\pi x}{l}\, dx$$

$$= \frac{2}{l} \left[x^2 \left(\frac{l}{n\pi} \sin\frac{n\pi x}{l}\right) - (2x)\left(-\frac{l^2}{n^2\pi^2} \cos\frac{n\pi x}{l}\right) + (2)\left(-\frac{l^3}{n^3\pi^3} \sin\frac{n\pi x}{l}\right) \right]_0^l$$

$$= \frac{2}{l} \left[\left\{0 + \frac{2l^3}{n^2\pi^2} \cos n\pi - 0\right\} - 0 \right]$$

$$= \frac{4l^2\,(-1)^n}{n^2\pi^2} \qquad\qquad \ldots (3)$$

From (1), (2) and (3), the required Fourier series is

$$x^2 = \frac{l^2}{3} + \frac{4l^2}{\pi^2} \sum_{n=1}^{\infty} \frac{(-1)^n}{n^2} \cos\frac{n\pi x}{l} \qquad\qquad \ldots (4)$$

Note : Putting $x = 0$ in (4), we get

$$0 = \frac{l^2}{3} + \frac{4l^2}{\pi^2} \sum_{n=1}^{\infty} \frac{(-1)^n}{n^2}$$

$$\therefore \qquad \frac{\pi^2}{12} = \frac{1}{1^2} - \frac{1}{2^2} + \frac{1}{3^2} - \frac{1}{4^2} + \ldots$$

Ex. 7 : *Obtain Fourier expansion for sin ax in the interval $-l < x < l$, where a is not an integer.*

Sol. : Here $f(x) = \sin ax$, and $f(-x) = -\sin ax = -f(x)$ $\therefore$ $f(x)$ is an odd function of x. Hence, $a_0 = a_n = 0$, and by result (17) of article 5.10, the Fourier series is

$$\sin ax = \sum_{n=1}^{\infty} b_n \sin\frac{n\pi x}{l} \qquad\qquad \left(\because L = l\right) \quad \ldots (1)$$

where $\quad b_n = \dfrac{2}{L} \displaystyle\int_0^l f(x) \sin\frac{n\pi x}{L}\, dx = \dfrac{2}{l} \displaystyle\int_0^l \sin ax \sin\frac{n\pi x}{l}\, dx$

$$= \frac{1}{l} \int_0^l \left[\cos\left(\frac{n\pi}{l} - a\right) x - \cos\left(\frac{n\pi}{l} + a\right) x \right] dx$$

$$= \frac{1}{l} \left[\frac{l}{(n\pi - al)} \sin\left(\frac{n\pi - al}{l}\right) x - \frac{l}{(n\pi + al)} \sin\left(\frac{n\pi + al}{l}\right) x \right]_0^l$$

$$= \left[\frac{\sin(n\pi - al)}{(n\pi - al)} - \frac{\sin(n\pi + al)}{(n\pi + al)} \right] = \left[-\frac{\cos n\pi \sin al}{(n\pi - al)} - \frac{\cos n\pi \sin al}{(n\pi + al)} \right]$$

$$= -\frac{2n\pi}{(n^2\pi^2 - a^2 l^2)} \cos n\pi \sin al = \frac{(-1)^{n+1} \, 2n\pi \sin al}{(n^2\pi^2 - a^2 l^2)} \qquad \ldots (2)$$

Thus from (1), (2), we have

$$\sin ax = 2\pi \sin al \sum_{n=1}^{\infty} \frac{(-1)^{n+1} \, n}{(n^2\pi^2 - a^2 l^2)} \sin \frac{n\pi x}{l}$$

$$= 2\pi \sin al$$

$$\left[\frac{1}{(\pi^2 - a^2 l^2)} \sin \frac{\pi x}{l} - \frac{2}{(2^2\pi^2 - a^2 l^2)} \sin \frac{2\pi x}{l} + \frac{3}{3^2\pi^2 - a^2 l^2} \sin \frac{3\pi x}{l} - \ldots \right]$$

Ex. 8 : *Determine the Fourier expansion for*

$$f(x) = \begin{cases} 0, & -2 < x < -1 \\ 1 + x, & -1 < x < 0 \\ 1 - x, & 0 < x < 1 \\ 0, & 1 < x < 2 \end{cases} \qquad \text{Period } 4$$

Sol. :

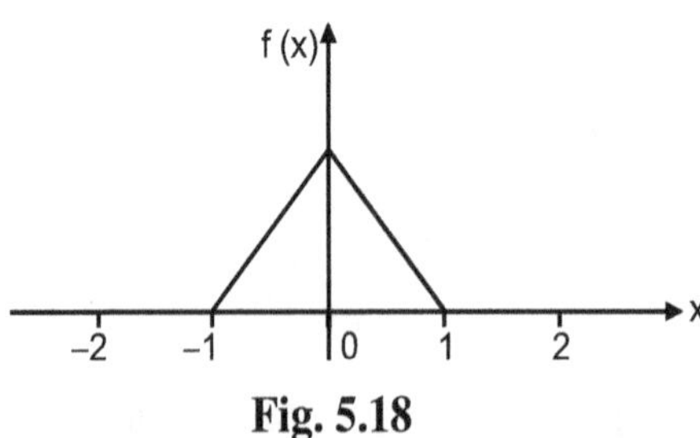

Fig. 5.18

Here we note that, in the range (0, 2), f(x) = 1 – x, 0 < x < 1 & f(–x) = 1 + x, –1 < x < 0. Thus, f(–x) = f(x) in the interval –2 < x < 2 (Refer Fig. 5.18). Therefore, f(x) is an even function of period 4 (= 2L). Hence $b_n = 0$ and the Fourier series is

$$f(x) = \frac{a_0}{2} + \sum_{n=1}^{\infty} a_n \cos \frac{n\pi x}{2} \qquad\qquad \left(\because L = 2\right) \;\dots (1)$$

where $\quad a_0 = \dfrac{2}{L} \displaystyle\int_0^L f(x)\, dx = \int_0^2 f(x)\, dx = \int_0^1 (1-x)\, dx + \int_1^2 (0)\, dx$

$$= \left[x - \frac{x^2}{2} \right]_0^1 = \frac{1}{2} \qquad\qquad \dots (2)$$

$$a_n = \frac{2}{L} \int_0^L f(x) \cos \frac{n\pi x}{L} = \int_0^2 f(x) \cos \frac{n\pi x}{2}\, dx$$

$$= \int_0^1 (1-x) \cos \frac{n\pi x}{2}\, dx + \int_1^2 (0) \cos \frac{n\pi x}{2}\, dx$$

$$= \left[(1-x)\left(\frac{2}{n\pi} \sin \frac{n\pi x}{2} \right) - (-1)\left(-\frac{4}{n^2\pi^2} \cos \frac{n\pi x}{2} \right) \right]_0^1$$

$$= \left[\left\{ 0 - \frac{4}{n^2\pi^2} \cos \frac{n\pi}{2} \right\} - \left\{ 0 - \frac{4}{n^2\pi^2} \right\} \right] = \frac{4}{n^2\pi^2} \left[1 - \cos \frac{n\pi}{2} \right] \qquad \dots (3)$$

From (1), (2) and (3), we have

$$f(x) = \frac{1}{4} + \frac{4}{\pi} \sum_{n=1}^{\infty} \frac{1}{n^2} \left(1 - \cos \frac{n\pi}{2} \right) \cos \frac{n\pi x}{2}$$

Ex. 9 : *Find Fourier series for the function $f(x) = x - x^2$ in the interval $-1 < x < 1$.*

Sol. : The given function can be expressed as $f(x) = f_1(x) - f_2(x)$, where $f_1(x) = x$ is an odd function and $f_2(x)$ is an even function in the interval $-1 < x < 1$. Thus, the Fourier series for the function $f(x)$ is the difference of the Fourier series of $f_1(x)$ and $f_2(x)$.

$f_1(x) = x$ is an odd function, $a_0 = a_n = 0$ and the Fourier series is

$$x = \sum_{n=1}^{\infty} b_n \sin \frac{n\pi x}{1} \qquad\qquad \left(\because L = 1\right) \;\dots (1)$$

where $\quad b_n = \dfrac{2}{L} \displaystyle\int_0^L f(x) \sin \frac{n\pi x}{L}\, dx = \frac{2}{1} \int_0^1 (x) \sin n\pi x\, dx$

$$= 2\left[x\left(-\frac{\cos n\pi x}{n\pi}\right) - (1)\left(-\frac{\sin n\pi x}{n^2\pi^2}\right)\right]_0^1$$

$$= -\frac{2\cos n\pi}{n\pi} = -\frac{2(-1)^n}{n\pi} \qquad \dots (2)$$

$f_2(x) = x^2$ is an even function, $b_n = 0$ and the Fourier series is

$$x^2 = \frac{a_0}{2} + \sum_{n=1}^{\infty} a_n \cos \frac{n\pi x}{1} \qquad \dots (3)$$

where $\quad a_0 = \frac{2}{L}\int_0^L f(x)\,dx = \frac{2}{1}\int_0^1 x^2\,dx = 2\left[\frac{x^3}{3}\right]_0^1 = \frac{2}{3} \qquad \dots (4)$

$$a_n = \frac{2}{L}\int_0^L f(x)\cos\frac{n\pi x}{L}\,dx = \frac{2}{1}\int_0^1 (x^2)\,\cos n\pi x\,dx$$

$$= 2\left[x^2\left(\frac{\sin n\pi x}{n\pi}\right) - (2x)\left(-\frac{\cos n\pi x}{n^2\pi^2}\right) + (2)\left(-\frac{\sin n\pi x}{n^3\pi^3}\right)\right]_0^1$$

$$= 2\left[\frac{2\cos n\pi}{n^2\pi^2}\right] = \frac{(-1)^n 4}{n^2\pi^2} \qquad \dots (5)$$

From (1), (2), (3), (4) and (5), the required Fourier series is

$$x - x^2 = \left[-\frac{2}{\pi}\sum_{n=1}^{\infty}\frac{(-1)^n}{n}\sin n\pi x\right] - \left[\frac{1}{3} + \frac{4}{\pi^2}\sum_{n=1}^{\infty}\frac{(-1)^n}{n^2}\cos n\pi x\right]$$

$$= -\frac{1}{3} - \frac{4}{\pi^2}\sum_{n=1}^{\infty}\frac{(-1)^n}{n^2}\cos n\pi x - \frac{2}{\pi}\sum_{n=1}^{\infty}\frac{(-1)^n}{n}\sin n\pi x.$$

EXERCISE 5.2

1. Graph the following functions and find their corresponding Fourier series :

(i)　$f(x) = \begin{cases} 0, & 0 \le x \le l \\ \\ a, & l \le x \le 2l \end{cases}$　　　Period $2l$

(ii)　$f(x) = \begin{cases} 8, & 0 < x < 2 \\ \\ -8, & 2 < x < 4 \end{cases}$　　　Period 4

(iii)　$f(x) = \begin{cases} l - x, & 0 < x \le l \\ \\ 0, & l \le x \le 2l \end{cases}$　　　Period $2l$

Ans. : (i) $f(x) = \dfrac{a}{2} - \dfrac{2a}{\pi}\left(\sin\dfrac{\pi x}{l} + \dfrac{1}{3}\sin\dfrac{3\pi x}{l} + \dfrac{1}{5}\sin\dfrac{5\pi x}{l} + \ldots\right)$

(ii) $f(x) = \dfrac{32}{\pi}\left(\dfrac{1}{1}\sin\dfrac{nx}{2} + \dfrac{1}{3}\sin\dfrac{3\pi x}{2} + \dfrac{1}{5}\sin\dfrac{5\pi x}{2} + \ldots\right)$

(iii) $f(x) = \dfrac{l}{4} + \dfrac{2l}{\pi^2}\left(\dfrac{1}{1^2}\cos\dfrac{\pi x}{l} + \dfrac{1}{3^2}\cos\dfrac{3\pi x}{l} + \dfrac{1}{5^2}\cos\dfrac{5\pi x}{l} + \ldots\right)$

$\qquad\qquad + \dfrac{l}{\pi}\left(\sin\dfrac{\pi x}{l} + \dfrac{1}{2}\sin\dfrac{2\pi x}{l} + \dfrac{1}{3}\sin\dfrac{3\pi x}{l} + \ldots\right)$

2. Determine the Fourier expansion for the following functions :

(i) $\quad f(x) = \begin{cases} \pi x, & 0 < x < 1 \\[2mm] 0, & 1 < x < 2 \end{cases}$ $\qquad$ Period 2

(ii) $\quad f(x) = \begin{cases} t, & 0 < t < 1 \\[2mm] 1 - t, & 1 < t < 2 \end{cases}$ $\qquad$ Period 2

(iii) $\quad f(x) = \begin{cases} 1 + x^2, & 0 \le x \le 1 \\[2mm] 3 - x, & 1 \le x \le 2 \end{cases}$ $\qquad$ Period 2

Ans. : (i) $f(x) = \dfrac{\pi}{4} - \dfrac{2}{\pi}\displaystyle\sum_{n=0}^{\infty}\dfrac{\cos(2n+1)\pi x}{(2n+1)^2} + \displaystyle\sum_{n=1}^{\infty}\dfrac{(-1)^{n+1}\sin n\pi x}{n}$

(ii) $f(x) = -\dfrac{4}{\pi^2}\displaystyle\sum_{n=0}^{\infty}\dfrac{\cos(2n+1)\pi t}{(2n+1)^2} + \dfrac{2}{\pi}\displaystyle\sum_{n=0}^{\infty}\dfrac{\sin(2n+1)\pi t}{(2n+1)}$

(iii) $f(x) = \dfrac{17}{2} + \left[-\dfrac{4}{\pi^2}\displaystyle\sum_{n=0}^{\infty}\dfrac{\cos(2n+1)\pi t}{(2n+1)^2} + \dfrac{1}{2\pi^2}\displaystyle\sum_{n=1}^{\infty}\dfrac{\cos 2n\pi t}{n^2}\right]$

$\qquad\qquad\qquad\qquad - \dfrac{4}{\pi^3}\displaystyle\sum_{n=0}^{\infty}\dfrac{\sin(2n+1)\pi t}{(2n+1)^3}$

3. Obtain the Fourier series expansion for the function $f(x) = 2 - \dfrac{x^2}{2}$ in the interval $0 \le x \le 2$.

$\qquad$ **Ans. :** $2 - \dfrac{x^2}{2} = \dfrac{4}{3} - \dfrac{2}{\pi^2}\displaystyle\sum_{n=1}^{\infty}\dfrac{1}{n^2}\cos n\pi x + \dfrac{2}{\pi}\displaystyle\sum_{n=1}^{\infty}\dfrac{1}{n}\sin n\pi x.$

4. Find the Fourier series for the function $f(x) = x^2$ in the interval $-a < x < a$.

$$\textbf{Ans. :}\ x^2 = \frac{a^3}{3} + \frac{a^2}{\pi^2} \sum_{n=1}^{\infty} \frac{1}{n^2} \cos \frac{2n\pi x}{a} - \frac{a^2}{\pi} \sum_{n=1}^{\infty} \frac{1}{n} \sin \frac{2n\pi x}{a}$$

5. If   (i) $f(x) = \dfrac{l}{2} - x,\ 0 < x < l$, prove that $\dfrac{l}{2} - x = \dfrac{l}{\pi} \sum_{n=1}^{\infty} \dfrac{1}{n} \sin \dfrac{2n\pi x}{l}$

(ii) $f(x) = x \cos\left(\dfrac{\pi x}{l}\right),\ -l \le x \le l,$ prove that

$$x \cos \frac{\pi x}{l} = -\frac{l}{2\pi} \sin \frac{\pi x}{l} + \frac{2l}{\pi} \sum_{n=2}^{\infty} \frac{(-1)^n\, n}{n^2 - 1} \sin \frac{n\pi x}{l}$$

6. Expand $f(x) = e^{-x}$ as a Fourier series in the interval $(-l,\, l)$.

$$\textbf{Ans. :}\ \sinh l \left[\frac{1}{l} + 2l \sum_{n=1}^{\infty} \frac{(-1)^n}{(l^2 + n^2\pi^2)} \cos \frac{n\pi x}{l} + 2\pi \sum_{n=1}^{\infty} \frac{n\,(-1)^n}{(l^2 + n^2\pi^2)} \sin \frac{n\pi x}{l} \right].$$

7. Show that the Fourier series for the function defined as

$$f(x) = \begin{cases} a, & -l < x < -\dfrac{l}{3} \\[2mm] b, & -\dfrac{l}{3} < x < \dfrac{l}{3} \qquad \text{Period } 2l \\[2mm] c, & \dfrac{l}{3} < x < l \end{cases}$$

is given by

$$f(x) = \frac{a+b+c}{3} + \frac{1}{\pi} \sum_{n=1}^{\infty} \frac{1}{n} \sin \frac{n\pi}{3} \times \left[(2b - a - c) \cos \frac{n\pi x}{l} + 2\,(c - a) \sin \frac{2n\pi}{3} \sin \frac{n\pi x}{l} \right]$$

8. Find the Fourier series of the following periodic functions :

(i) $f(x) = \begin{cases} x, & -1 < x \le 0 \\ x + 2, & 0 < x \le 1 \end{cases}$ Period 2

(ii) $f(x) = \begin{cases} 2x, & 0 \le x \le 3 \\ 0, & -3 < x < 0 \end{cases}$ Period 6

(iii) $f(x) = \begin{cases} 2, & -2 \le x \le 0 \\ x, & 0 < x < 2 \end{cases}$ Period 4

Ans. : (i) $f(x) = 1 + \dfrac{2}{\pi} \sum\limits_{n=1}^{\infty} \dfrac{1}{n} [1 - 2(-1)^n] \sin n\pi x$

(ii) $f(x) = \dfrac{3}{2} + \sum\limits_{n=1}^{\infty} \left[\dfrac{6(\cos n\pi - 1)}{n^2\pi^2} \cos \dfrac{n\pi x}{3} - \dfrac{\cos n\pi}{n\pi} \sin \dfrac{n\pi x}{3} \right]$

(iii) $f(x) = \dfrac{3}{2} + \sum\limits_{n=1}^{\infty} \left[\dfrac{2(\cos n\pi - 1)}{n^2\pi^2} \cos \dfrac{n\pi x}{2} - \dfrac{2}{n\pi} \sin \dfrac{n\pi x}{2} \right]$

9. Determine the Fourier coefficients of the function

$$f(x) = \begin{cases} 1, & -1 < x < 0 \\ \cos \pi x, & 0 < x < 1 \end{cases} \qquad \text{Period 2}$$

What is the sum of the series when $x = 1$?

Ans. : $a_0 = 1, \ a_n = 0, \ b_{2n} = \dfrac{4n}{\pi(4n^2 - 1)}, \ b_{2n+1} = -\dfrac{2}{\pi(2n + 1)}$

Value of the series when $x = 1$ is $\dfrac{1}{2} [f(1 - 0) + f(1 + 0)] = 0$.

10. Find the Fourier series of the following periodic functions :

(i) $f(x) = |x|, \quad -2 \le x \le 2 \quad$ Period 4

(ii) $f(x) = x^2 - 2, \ -2 \le x \le 2 \quad$ Period 4

(iii) $f(x) = \begin{cases} e^x, & -1 \le x \le 0 \\ e^{-x}, & 0 \le x \le 1 \end{cases} \qquad \text{Period 2}$

Hint : Given functions are even, $b_n = 0$

Ans. : (i) $|x| = 1 - \dfrac{8}{\pi^2} \left(\cos \dfrac{\pi x}{2} + \dfrac{1}{9} \cos \dfrac{3\pi x}{2} + \dfrac{1}{25} \cos \dfrac{5\pi x}{2} + \ldots \right)$

(ii) $x^2 - 2 = -\dfrac{2}{3} - \dfrac{16}{\pi^2} \left(\cos \dfrac{\pi x}{2} - \dfrac{1}{4} \cos \pi x + \dfrac{1}{9} \cos \dfrac{3\pi x}{2} - \ldots \right)$

(iii) $f(x) = \dfrac{e - 1}{e} + 2 \sum\limits_{n=0}^{\infty} \dfrac{e - (-1)^n}{e(n^2\pi^2 + 1)} \cos n\pi x$

11. Find the Fourier series of the following periodic functions :

(i) $f(x) = \begin{cases} -1, & -2 < x < 0 \\ 1, & 0 < x < 2 \end{cases}$ Period 4

(ii) $f(x) = \begin{cases} x + 1, & -1 < x < 0 \\ x - 1, & 0 < x < 1 \end{cases}$ Period 2

(iii) $f(x) = \begin{cases} -x, & -4 \le x \le 0 \\ x, & 0 \le x \le 4 \end{cases}$ Period 8

Hint : Given functions (i) and (ii) are odd, $a_0 = a_n = 0$ and

Function (iii) is even, $b_n = 0$.

Ans. : (i) $f(x) = \dfrac{4}{\pi} \sum_{n=1}^{\infty} \dfrac{\sin \dfrac{(2n + 1)\, \pi x}{2}}{(2n + 1)}$

(ii) $f(x) = -\dfrac{2}{\pi} \sum_{n=1}^{\infty} \dfrac{1}{n} \sin n\pi x$

(iii) $f(x) = 2 - \dfrac{8}{\pi^2} \sum_{n=1}^{\infty} \dfrac{(1 - \cos n\pi)}{n^2} \cos \dfrac{n\pi x}{4}$

12. Find the Fourier series for the function $f(x) = 1 - x^2$ in the interval $-1 \le x \le 1$.

Ans. : $1 - x^2 = \dfrac{2}{3} + \dfrac{4}{\pi^2} \left(\cos \pi x - \dfrac{1}{2^2} \cos 2\pi x + \dfrac{1}{3^2} \cos 3\pi x - \ldots \right)$

13. Find the Fourier expansion for the function $f(x) = x - x^3$ in the interval $-1 < x < 1$.

Ans. : $x - x^3 = \dfrac{12}{\pi^3} \left(\sin \pi x - \dfrac{1}{2^3} \sin 2\pi x + \dfrac{1}{3^3} \sin 3\pi x - \ldots \right)$

14. Obtain the Fourier series for the function defined as

$f(x) = \begin{cases} a\,(x - l), & -l < x < 0 \\ a\,(l + x), & 0 < x < l \end{cases}$

Deduce that $1 - \dfrac{1}{3} + \dfrac{1}{5} - \dfrac{1}{7} + \ldots = \dfrac{\pi}{4}$.

Hint : $f(x)$ is an odd function in $(-l, l)$, $a_0 = a_n = 0$

Ans. : $f(x) = \dfrac{2al}{\pi} \left[\dfrac{3}{1} \sin \dfrac{\pi x}{l} - \dfrac{1}{2} \sin \dfrac{2\pi x}{l} + \dfrac{3}{3} \sin \dfrac{3\pi x}{l} - \ldots \right]$

For deduction, put $x = \dfrac{l}{2}$, which lies between $0 < x < l$.

15. Determine the Fourier expansion for f(x) defined by

(i) $f(x) = \begin{cases} 0, & -3 < x < -1 \\ 1 + \cos \pi x, & -1 < x < 1 \\ 0, & 1 < x < 3 \end{cases}$ Period 6

(ii) $f(x) = \begin{cases} 0, & -2 < x < -1 \\ k, & -1 < x < 1 \\ 0, & 1 < x < 2 \end{cases}$ Period 4

Ans. : (i) $a_0 = \dfrac{1}{3}$, $a_n = \dfrac{-18}{\pi} \cdot \dfrac{1}{n\,(n^2 - 9)} \sin \dfrac{n\pi}{3}$ for all n except n = 3, $a_3 = \dfrac{1}{3}$

(ii) $f(x) = \dfrac{k}{2} + \dfrac{2k}{\pi} \left(\cos \dfrac{\pi x}{2} - \dfrac{1}{3} \cos \dfrac{3\pi x}{2} + \dfrac{1}{5} \cos \dfrac{5\pi x}{2} - \ldots \right)$

16. Obtain the Fourier series for $f(x) = e^{|x|},\ -2 < x < 2$.

Ans. : $e^{|x|} = \dfrac{e^2 - 1}{2} + \sum_{n=1}^{\infty} \dfrac{4\,[(-1)^n\, e^2 - 1]}{4 + n^2\, \pi^2} \cos \left(\dfrac{n\pi x}{2} \right)$

5.13 HALF-RANGE EXPANSIONS

In various engineering problems, it is required to obtain a Fourier expansion of function f(x) which is defined only in half period i.e. to expand a function f(x) in the range $0 \le x \le \pi$ in a Fourier series of period 2π or more generally in the range $0 \le x \le L$ in a Fourier series of period 2L.

Suppose that the conditions of a problem require us to consider the function f(x) in the interval $0 \le x \le L$, then it is immaterial what the function is outside the range. We are free to choose it arbitrarily in the interval $-L \le x \le 0$.

5.14 HALF-RANGE COSINE EXPANSION

If it is required to find cosine expansion of f(x) in $0 \le x \le L$, we extend the function f(x) from 0 to –L by reflecting it in the vertical axis (i.e. y-axis), so that $f(-x) = f(x)$, hence the original function together with its extension is even in the interval $-L \le x \le L$ (Refer Fig. 5.19 and Fig. 5.20) and also consider it is periodic with period 2L. Hence using result (16) of article 5.11; Fourier expansion will contain only cosine terms given by

$$f(x) = \frac{a_0}{2} + \sum_{n=1}^{\infty} a_n \cos \frac{n\pi x}{L} \qquad \ldots (18)$$

where

$$a_0 = \frac{2}{L} \int_0^L f(x)\, dx$$

$$a_n = \frac{2}{L} \int_0^L f(x) \cos \frac{n\pi x}{L}\, dx$$

$$\dots (19)$$

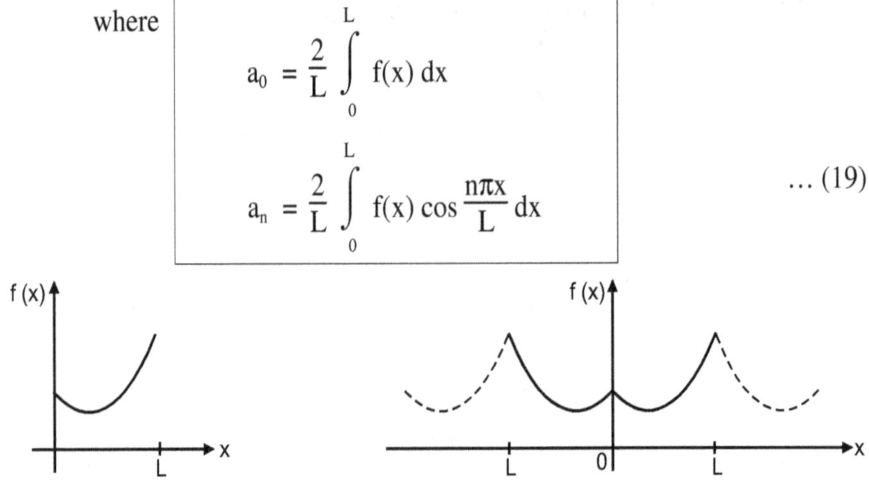

Fig. 5.19 : The given function f(x)   **Fig. 5.20 : Even extension**

Remark 1 : If $f(x)$ is defined in $0 \le x \le \pi$, then half-range cosine series is given by

$$f(x) = \frac{a_0}{2} + \sum_{n=1}^{\infty} a_n \cos nx \qquad \dots (20)$$

where

$$a_0 = \frac{2}{\pi} \int_0^\pi f(x)\, dx$$

$$a_n = \frac{2}{\pi} \int_0^\pi f(x) \cos nx\, dx$$

$$\dots (21)$$

Remark 2 : If $f(x)$ is defined in $0 \le x \le L$, then we can construct even function $F(x)$ by the equations :

$$F(x) = \begin{cases} f(x), & 0 \le x \le L \\ f(-x), & -L < x < 0 \end{cases} \quad \text{and} \quad F(x + 2L) = F(x)$$

Such a function $F(x)$ is known as the even periodic continuation (or extension) of $f(x)$.

5.15 HALF-RANGE SINE EXPANSION

If it is required to find sine expansion of $f(x)$ in $0 \le x \le L$, we extend the function $f(x)$ from 0 to $-L$ so that $f(-x) = -f(x)$, the extended function is odd in the interval $-L \le x \le L$ (Refer Fig. 5.21 and Fig. 5.22). Hence using result (17) of article 5.11; Fourier expansion will contain only sine terms given by

$$f(x) \;=\; \sum_{n=1}^{\infty} b_n \sin \frac{n\pi x}{L} \qquad \ldots (22)$$

where

$$\boxed{\; b_n \;=\; \frac{2}{L} \int_{0}^{L} f(x) \sin \frac{n\pi x}{L} \, dx \;} \qquad \ldots (23)$$

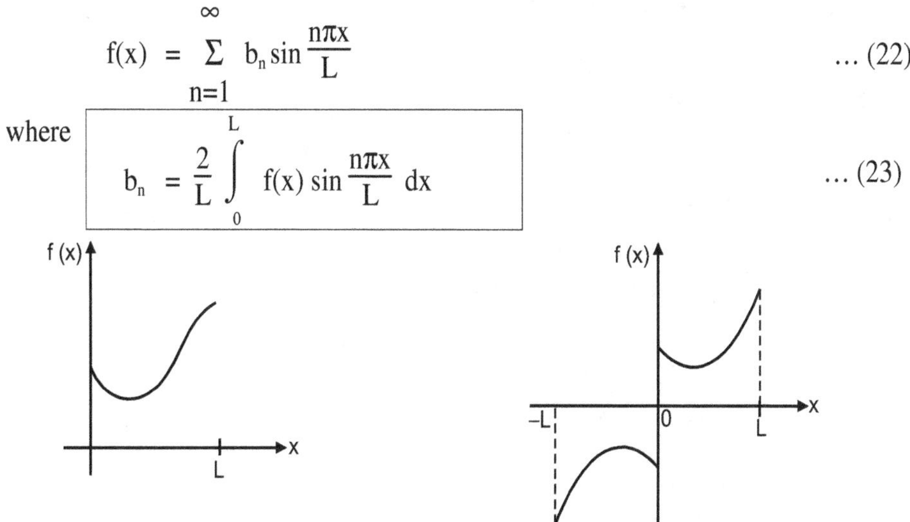

Fig. 5.21 : The given function f(x)   **Fig. 5.22 : Odd extension**

Remark 1 : If f(x) is defined in $0 \le x \le \pi$, then half-range sine series is given by

$$f(x) \;=\; \sum_{n=1}^{\infty} b_n \sin nx \qquad \ldots (24)$$

where

$$\boxed{\; b_n \;=\; \frac{2}{\pi} \int_{0}^{\pi} f(x) \sin nx \, dx \;} \qquad \ldots (25)$$

Remark 2 : If f(x) is defined in $0 \le x \le L$, then we can construct odd function F(x) by the equation

$$F(x) \;=\; \begin{cases} f(x), & 0 \le x \le L \\[2mm] -f(-x), & -L \le x \le 0 \end{cases} \quad \text{and} \quad F(x + 2L) = F(x)$$

Such a function F(x) is known as the odd periodic continuation (or extension) of f(x).

Remark 3 : The series expansion of f(x) given by (18) and (22) are valid for f(x) only in the interval (0, L) but not outside this interval.

5.16 ILLUSTRATIONS ON HALF-RANGE EXPANSIONS

Ex. 1 : *Find half-range (i) cosine series, (ii) sine series for the function*

$$f(x) \;=\; \begin{cases} x, & 0 < x < \dfrac{\pi}{2} \\[4mm] \pi - x, & \dfrac{\pi}{2} < x < \pi \end{cases}$$

Sol. : (i) Half-range cosine series :

Let
$$f(x) = \frac{a_0}{2} + \sum_{n=1}^{\infty} a_n \cos nx \qquad \dots (1)$$

Then from result (21), we have

$$a_0 = \frac{2}{\pi} \int_0^{\pi} f(x)\,dx = \frac{2}{\pi}\left[\int_0^{\pi/2} x\,dx + \int_{\pi/2}^{\pi} (\pi - x)\,dx\right]$$

$$= \frac{2}{\pi}\left[\left(\frac{x^2}{2}\right)_0^{\pi/2} + \left(\pi x - \frac{x^2}{2}\right)_{\pi/2}^{\pi}\right] = \frac{2}{\pi}\left[\frac{\pi^2}{8} + \left\{\left(\pi^2 - \frac{\pi^2}{2}\right) - \left(\frac{\pi^2}{2} - \frac{\pi^2}{8}\right)\right\}\right] \qquad \dots (2)$$

$$= \frac{2}{\pi}\left[\frac{\pi^2}{4}\right] = \frac{\pi}{2}$$

$$a_n = \frac{2}{\pi} \int_0^{\pi} f(x) \cos nx\,dx = \frac{2}{\pi}\left[\int_0^{\pi/2} (x) \cos nx\,dx + \int_{\pi/2}^{\pi} (\pi - x) \cos nx\,dx\right]$$

$$= \frac{2}{\pi}\left[\left\{x\left(\frac{\sin nx}{n}\right) - (1)\left(-\frac{\cos nx}{n^2}\right)\right\}_0^{\pi/2} + \left\{(\pi - x)\left(\frac{\sin nx}{n}\right) - (-1)\left(-\frac{\cos nx}{n^2}\right)\right\}_{\pi/2}^{\pi}\right]$$

$$= \frac{2}{\pi}\left[\left\{\frac{\pi}{2n}\sin\frac{n\pi}{2} + \frac{1}{n^2}\cos\frac{n\pi}{2} - \frac{1}{n^2}\right\} + \left\{-\frac{1}{n^2}\cos n\pi - \frac{\pi}{2n}\sin\frac{n\pi}{2} + \frac{1}{n^2}\cos\frac{n\pi}{2}\right\}\right]$$

$$= \frac{2}{\pi n^2}\left[2\cos\frac{n\pi}{2} - \cos n\pi - 1\right]$$

$$\therefore \quad a_1 = 0, \quad a_2 = \frac{2}{\pi 2^2}(2\cos\pi - \cos 2\pi - 1) = \frac{-8}{\pi 2^2}, \quad a_3 = 0, \quad a_4 = 0,$$

$$a_5 = 0, \quad a_6 = \frac{2}{\pi 6^2}(2\cos 3\pi - \cos 6\pi - 1) = \frac{-8}{\pi 6^2}, \quad a_7 = 0, \quad a_8 = 0,$$

$$a_9 = 0, \quad a_{10} = \frac{2}{\pi 10^2}(2\cos 5\pi - \cos 10\pi - 1) = \frac{-8}{\pi 10^2}, \dots \text{etc.} \qquad \dots (3)$$

Hence from (1), (2) and (3), required half-range cosine series is

$$f(x) = \frac{\pi}{4} - \frac{8}{\pi}\left[\frac{1}{2^2}\cos 2x + \frac{1}{6^2}\cos 6x + \frac{1}{10^2}\cos 10x + \dots\right]$$

Note : This series represents the even periodic extension of f(x) as shown in Fig. 5.23 below :

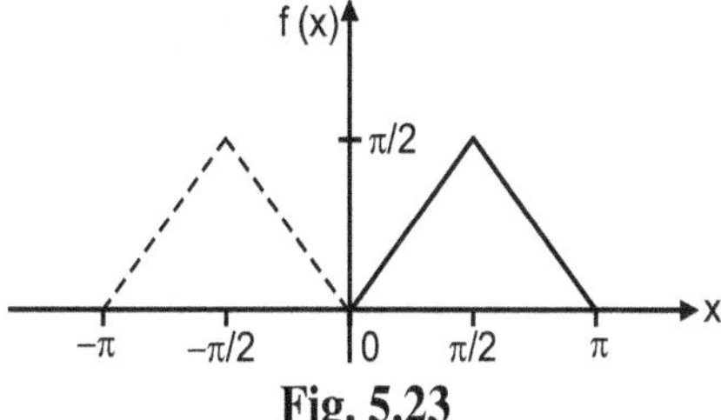

Fig. 5.23

(ii) Half-range sine series :

Let
$$f(x) \;=\; \sum_{n=1}^{\infty} b_n \sin nx \qquad\qquad \dots (1)$$

Then from result (25), we have

$$b_n \;=\; \frac{2}{\pi} \int_0^{\pi} f(x)\,\sin nx\,dx \;=\; \frac{2}{\pi}\left[\int_0^{\pi/2} (x)\,\sin nx\,dx \;+\; \int_{\pi/2}^{\pi} (\pi - x)\,\sin nx\,dx\right]$$

$$= \frac{2}{\pi}\left[\left\{x\left(-\frac{\cos nx}{n}\right) - (1)\left(-\frac{\sin nx}{n^2}\right)\right\}_0^{\pi/2} + \left\{(\pi - x)\left(-\frac{\cos nx}{n}\right) - (-1)\left(-\frac{\sin nx}{n^2}\right)\right\}_{\pi/2}^{\pi}\right]$$

$$= \frac{2}{\pi}\left[\left\{-\frac{\pi}{2n}\cos\frac{n\pi}{2} + \frac{1}{n^2}\sin\frac{n\pi}{2}\right\} + \left\{\frac{\pi}{2n}\cos\frac{n\pi}{2} + \frac{1}{n^2}\sin\frac{n\pi}{2}\right\}\right]$$

$$= \frac{4}{\pi n^2}\,\sin\frac{n\pi}{2}$$

$$\therefore \quad b_2 = b_4 = b_6 = \dots = 0$$

and $b_1 = \dfrac{4}{\pi 1^2}$, $b_3 = -\dfrac{4}{\pi 3^2}$, $b_5 = \dfrac{4}{\pi 5^2}$, ... etc. $\qquad\qquad \dots (2)$

Hence from (1) and (2), required half-range sine series is

$$f(x) \;=\; \frac{4}{\pi}\left[\frac{1}{1^2}\sin x - \frac{1}{3^2}\sin 3x + \frac{1}{5^2}\sin 5x \dots\right]$$

Note : This series represents odd periodic extension of f(x) as shown in Fig. 5.24 below :

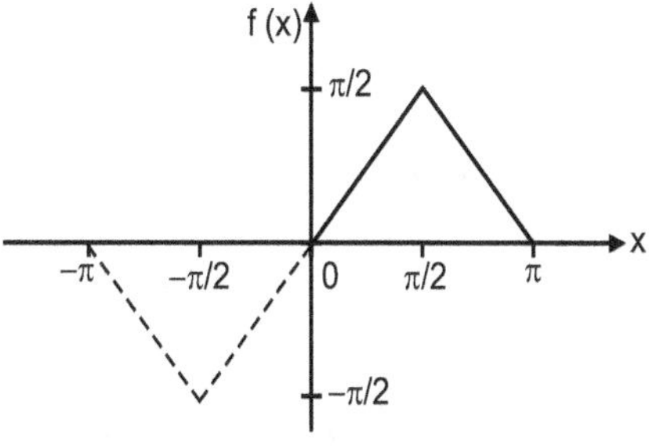

Fig. 5.24

Ex. 2 : *Find cosine series for sin x in the interval $0 < x < \pi$, hence deduce that*

$$1 - \frac{1}{3} + \frac{1}{5} - \frac{1}{7} + \dots = \frac{\pi}{4}$$

Sol. : Let $\qquad f(x) = \dfrac{a_0}{2} + \sum_{n=1}^{\infty} a_n \cos nx \qquad\qquad \dots (1)$

where $\quad a_0 = \dfrac{2}{\pi} \displaystyle\int_0^{\pi} f(x)\, dx = \dfrac{2}{\pi} \displaystyle\int_0^{\pi} \sin x\, dx = \dfrac{2}{\pi} \left[-\cos x\right]_0^{\pi}$

$$= \frac{4}{\pi} \qquad\qquad \dots (2)$$

$$a_n = \frac{2}{\pi} \int_0^{\pi} f(x) \cos nx\, dx = \frac{2}{\pi} \int_0^{\pi} \sin x \cos nx\, dx$$

$$= \frac{1}{\pi} \left[\sin (n+1)x - \sin (n-1)x\right] dx$$

$$= \frac{1}{\pi} \left[-\frac{\cos (n+1)x}{(n+1)} + \frac{\cos (n-1)x}{(n-1)}\right]_{0 \text{ for } n > 1}^{\pi}$$

$$= \frac{1}{\pi} \left[-\frac{\cos (n-1)\pi}{(n+1)} + \frac{\cos (n-1)\pi}{(n-1)} + \frac{1}{(n+1)} - \frac{1}{(n-1)}\right]$$

$$= \frac{1}{\pi} \left[\frac{\cos n\pi}{(n+1)} - \frac{\cos n\pi}{(n-1)} + \frac{1}{(n+1)} - \frac{1}{(n-1)}\right] \Big(\because \cos (n \pm 1)\pi = \cos n\pi \cos \pi\Big)$$

$$= \frac{1}{\pi} \left[\frac{1}{(n+1)} - \frac{1}{(n-1)}\right] (1 + \cos n\pi) = \frac{1}{\pi} \cdot \frac{-2}{(n^2 - 1)} \left[1 + (-1)^n\right]$$

$$= \begin{cases} -\dfrac{4}{\pi (n^2 - 1)}, & \text{if n is even} \\[2ex] 0, & \text{if n is odd, except } n = 1 \end{cases}$$

$$\therefore \quad a_2 = -\frac{4}{\pi(2^2 - 1)}, \quad a_4 = -\frac{4}{\pi(4^2 - 1)}, \quad a_6 = -\frac{4}{\pi(6^2 - 1)}, \dots \text{etc.} \qquad \dots (3)$$

When n = 1, we have

$$a_1 = \frac{2}{\pi} \int_0^{\pi} f(x) \cos x\, dx = \frac{2}{\pi} \int_0^{\pi} \sin x \cos x\, dx = \frac{1}{\pi} \int_0^{\pi} \sin 2x\, dx = 0 \qquad \dots (4)$$

From (1), (2), (3) and (4), required cosine series is

$$\sin x = \frac{2}{\pi} - \frac{4}{\pi}\left[\frac{1}{(2^2 - 1)}\cos 2x + \frac{1}{(4^2 - 1)}\cos 4x + \frac{1}{(6^2 - 1)}\cos 6x + \ldots\right]$$

$$= \frac{2}{\pi} - \frac{4}{\pi}\sum_{n=1}^{\infty}\frac{1}{(2n)^2 - 1}\cos 2nx \qquad \ldots (5)$$

Putting $x = \dfrac{\pi}{2}$ in (5), we get

$$1 = \frac{2}{\pi} - \frac{4}{\pi}\sum_{n=1}^{\infty}\frac{1}{(2n)^2 - 1}\cos n\pi$$

$$\frac{\pi}{2} = 1 - 2\sum_{n=1}^{\infty}\frac{1}{2}\left(\frac{1}{2n - 1} - \frac{1}{2n + 1}\right)(-1)^n$$

$$= 1 - \left[-\left(1 - \frac{1}{3}\right) + \left(\frac{1}{3} - \frac{1}{5}\right) - \left(\frac{1}{5} - \frac{1}{7}\right) + \ldots\right] = 1 - \left[-1 + \frac{2}{3} - \frac{2}{5} + \frac{2}{7} - \ldots\right]$$

$$= 2\left[1 - \frac{1}{3} + \frac{1}{5} - \frac{1}{7} + \ldots\right]$$

$$\therefore \quad \frac{\pi}{4} = 1 - \frac{1}{3} + \frac{1}{5} - \frac{1}{7} + \ldots$$

Ex. 3 : *Show that if* $0 < x < \pi$, $\cos x = \dfrac{8}{\pi}\displaystyle\sum_{m=1}^{\infty}\dfrac{m}{(4m^2 - 1)}\sin 2mx$

Sol. : Note : We have to find half-range sine series for cos x.

Let $\cos x = \displaystyle\sum_{n=1}^{\infty} b_n \sin nx \qquad \ldots (1)$

$$b_n = \frac{2}{\pi}\int_0^{\pi} f(x)\sin nx\, dx = \frac{2}{\pi}\int_0^{\pi}\cos x \sin nx\, dx$$

$$= \frac{1}{\pi}\int_0^{\pi}[\sin (n + 1) x + \sin (n - 1) x]\, dx$$

$$= \frac{1}{\pi}\left[-\frac{\cos (n + 1) x}{(n + 1)} - \frac{\cos (n - 1) x}{(n - 1)}\right]_0^{\pi} \text{ for } n > 1$$

$$= \frac{1}{\pi}\left[-\frac{\cos (n + 1) \pi}{(n + 1)} - \frac{\cos (n - 1) \pi}{(n - 1)} + \frac{1}{(n + 1)} + \frac{1}{(n - 1)}\right]$$

$$= \frac{1}{\pi} \left[\frac{\cos n\pi}{(n+1)} + \frac{\cos n\pi}{(n-1)} + \frac{1}{(n+1)} + \frac{1}{(n-1)} \right]$$

$$= \frac{1}{\pi} \left[\frac{1}{n+1} + \frac{1}{n-1} \right] (1 + \cos n\pi) = \frac{2n}{\pi(n^2-1)} [1 + (-1)^n]$$

$$= \begin{cases} 0, & \text{if n is odd} \\ \dfrac{4n}{\pi(n^2-1)}, & \text{if n is even} \end{cases} \quad \text{except } n = 1$$

$$\therefore \quad b_2 = \frac{8}{\pi(2^2-1)}, \ b_4 = \frac{16}{\pi(4^2-1)}, \ b_6 = \frac{24}{\pi(6^2-1)}, \ \dots \text{ etc.} \qquad \dots (2)$$

When n = 1, we have

$$b_1 = \frac{2}{\pi} \int_0^\pi f(x) \sin x \, dx = \frac{2}{\pi} \int_0^\pi \cos x \sin x \, dx = \frac{1}{\pi} \int_0^\pi \sin 2x \, dx = 0 \qquad \dots (3)$$

From (1), (2) and (3), we have

$$\cos x = \frac{8}{\pi} \left[\frac{1}{(2^2-1)} \sin 2x + \frac{2}{(4^2-1)} \sin 4x + \frac{3}{(6^2-1)} \sin 6x + \dots \right]$$

$$= \frac{8}{\pi} \sum_{m=1}^{\infty} \frac{m}{(4m^2-1)} \sin 2mx. \qquad \text{[Note n = 2m]}$$

Ex. 4 : *Prove that in the interval $0 < x < \pi$,*

$$\frac{e^{ax} - e^{-ax}}{e^{a\pi} - e^{-a\pi}} = \frac{2}{\pi} \left[\frac{\sin x}{a^2+1} - \frac{2 \sin 2x}{a^2+4} + \frac{3 \sin 3x}{a^2+9} - \dots \right]$$

Sol. : Here $\quad f(x) = e^{ax} - e^{-ax}, \ 0 < x < \pi$.

Note : We are required to express f(x) as half-range sine series.

Let $\quad f(x) = \sum_{n=1}^{\infty} b_n \sin nx \, dx \qquad \dots (1)$

where $\quad b_n = \frac{2}{\pi} \int_0^\pi f(x) \sin nx \, dx = \frac{2}{\pi} \int_0^\pi (e^{ax} - e^{-ax}) \sin nx \, dx$

$$= \frac{2}{\pi} \left[\frac{e^{ax}}{a^2+n^2} (a \sin nx - n \cos nx) - \frac{e^{-ax}}{a^2+n^2} (-a \sin nx - n \cos nx) \right]_0^\pi$$

$$= \frac{2}{\pi(a^2+n^2)} \left[\{ e^{a\pi}(-n \cos n\pi) - e^{-a\pi}(-n \cos n\pi) \} - \{ (-n) - (-n) \} \right]$$

$$= \frac{-2n \cos n\pi}{\pi(a^2+n^2)} (e^{a\pi} - e^{-a\pi})$$

$$\therefore \quad b_1 = \frac{2.1}{\pi(a^2+1)} (e^{a\pi} - e^{-a\pi}) \ , \ b_2 = -\frac{2.2}{\pi(a^2+4)} (e^{a\pi} - e^{-a\pi}) ,$$

$$b_3 = \frac{2.3}{\pi(a^2+9)} (e^{a\pi} - e^{-a\pi}) , \ \dots \text{ etc.} \qquad \dots (2)$$

From (1) and (2), we get

$$e^{ax} - e^{-ax} = (e^{a\pi} - e^{-a\pi}) \frac{2}{\pi} \left[\frac{\sin x}{a^2+1} - \frac{2 \sin 2x}{a^2+4} + \frac{3 \sin 3x}{a^2+9} \right]$$

$$\therefore \quad \frac{e^{ax} - e^{-ax}}{e^{a\pi} - e^{-a\pi}} = \frac{2}{\pi} \left[\frac{\sin x}{a^2+1} - \frac{2 \sin 2x}{a^2+4} + \frac{3 \sin 3x}{a^2+9} - \dots \right]$$

Ex. 5 : *Expand $f(x) = lx - x^2$, $0 < x < l$, in a half-range (i) cosine series, (ii) sine series.*
Deduce from sine series

$$\frac{1}{1^3} - \frac{1}{3^3} + \frac{1}{5^3} - \dots = \frac{\pi^3}{32}$$

Sol. : (i) Cosine series :

$$\text{Let} \qquad f(x) = \frac{a_0}{2} + \sum_{n=1}^{\infty} a_n \cos \frac{n\pi x}{l} \qquad\qquad (\because L = l) \qquad \dots (1)$$

$$\text{where} \qquad a_0 = \frac{2}{L} \int_0^L f(x)\, dx = \frac{2}{l} \int_0^l [lx - x^2]\, dx = \frac{2}{l} \left[\frac{lx^2}{2} - \frac{x^3}{3} \right]_0^l = \frac{l^2}{3} \qquad \dots (2)$$

$$a_n = \frac{2}{L} \int_0^L f(x) \cos \frac{n\pi x}{L}\, dx = \frac{2}{l} \int_0^l (lx - x^2) \cos \frac{n\pi x}{l}\, dx$$

$$= \frac{2}{l} \left[(lx - x^2) \left(\frac{l}{n\pi} \sin \frac{n\pi x}{l} \right) - (l - 2x) \left(-\frac{l^2}{n^2\pi^2} \cos \frac{n\pi x}{l} \right) + (-2) \left(-\frac{l^3}{n^3\pi^3} \sin \frac{n\pi x}{l} \right) \right]_0^l$$

$$= \frac{2}{l} \left[\left\{ 0 - \frac{l^3}{n^2\pi^2} \cos n\pi + 0 \right\} - \left\{ 0 + \frac{l^3}{n^2\pi^2} + 0 \right\} \right] = -\frac{2l^2}{n^2\pi^2} [1 + (-1)^n]$$

$$= \begin{cases} 0, & \text{if } n \text{ is odd} \\[2mm] -\dfrac{4l^2}{n^2\pi^2}, & \text{if } n \text{ is even} \end{cases}$$

$$\therefore a_2 = -\frac{4l^2}{2^2\pi^2} \ , \quad a_4 = -\frac{4l^2}{4^2\pi^2} \ , \quad a_6 = \frac{4l^2}{6^2\pi^2} \ , \ \dots \text{ etc.} \qquad \dots (3)$$

From (1), (2) and (3), we get

$$lx - x^2 = \frac{l^2}{6} - \frac{4l^2}{\pi^2}\left[\frac{1}{2^2}\cos\frac{2\pi x}{l} + \frac{1}{4^2}\cos\frac{4\pi x}{l} + \frac{1}{6^2}\cos\frac{6\pi x}{l} + \ldots\right]$$

$$= \frac{l^2}{6} - \frac{4l^2}{\pi^2}\sum_{n=1}^{\infty}\frac{1}{(2n)^2}\cos\frac{2n\pi x}{l}$$

(ii) Sine series :

Let
$$f(x) = \sum_{n=1}^{\infty} b_n \sin\frac{n\pi x}{l} \qquad\qquad \left(\because L = l\right) \ldots (1)$$

where

$$b_n = \frac{2}{L}\int_0^L f(x)\sin\frac{n\pi x}{L}\,dx = \frac{2}{l}\int_0^l (lx - x^2)\sin\frac{n\pi x}{l}\,dx$$

$$= \frac{2}{l}\left[(lx - x^2)\left(-\frac{l}{n\pi}\cos\frac{n\pi x}{l}\right) - (l - 2x)\left(-\frac{l^2}{n^2\pi^2}\sin\frac{n\pi x}{l}\right) + (-2)\left(\frac{l^3}{n^3\pi^3}\cos\frac{n\pi x}{l}\right)\right]_0^l$$

$$= \frac{2}{l}\left[\left\{0 - 0 - \frac{2l^3}{n^3\pi^3}\cos n\pi\right\} - \left\{-0 + 0 - \frac{2l^3}{n^3\pi^3}\right\}\right] = \frac{4l^2}{n^3\pi^3}\left[1 - (-1)^n\right]$$

$$= \begin{cases} 0, & \text{if } n \text{ is even} \\[2ex] \dfrac{8l^2}{\pi^3 n^3}, & \text{if } n \text{ is odd} \end{cases}$$

$$\therefore \quad b_1 = \frac{8l^2}{\pi^3 1^3}, \qquad b_3 = \frac{8l^2}{\pi^3 3^3}, \quad b_5 = \frac{8l^2}{\pi^3 5^3}, \quad \ldots \text{ etc.} \qquad\qquad \ldots (2)$$

From (1) and (2), we get

$$lx - x^2 = \frac{8l^2}{\pi^3}\left[\frac{1}{1^3}\sin\frac{\pi x}{l} + \frac{1}{3^3}\sin\frac{3\pi x}{l} + \frac{1}{5^3}\sin\frac{5\pi x}{l} + \ldots\right] \qquad\qquad \ldots (3)$$

$$= \frac{8l^2}{\pi^3}\sum_{n=0}^{\infty}\frac{1}{(2n + 1)^3}\sin\frac{(2n + 1)\,\pi x}{l} \qquad\qquad \ldots (4)$$

To obtain deduction, we put $x = \dfrac{l}{2}$ in result (3) above, then we have

$$l\left(\frac{l}{2}\right) - \left(\frac{l}{2}\right)^2 = \frac{8l^2}{\pi^3}\left[\frac{1}{1^3}(1) + \frac{1}{3^3}(-1) + \frac{1}{5^3}(1) \ldots\right]$$

$$\therefore \qquad \frac{\pi^3}{32} = \frac{1}{1^3} - \frac{1}{3^3} + \frac{1}{5^3} - \ldots$$

Ex. 6 : *Obtain a half-range sine series to represent*

$$f(x) = \begin{cases} \dfrac{2x}{3}, & 0 \le x \le \dfrac{\pi}{3} \\[3mm] \dfrac{\pi - x}{3}, & \dfrac{\pi}{3} \le x \le \pi \end{cases}$$

in the interval $0 \le x \le \pi$

Sol. : Let

$$f(x) = \sum_{n=1}^{\infty} b_n \sin nx \qquad \qquad \dots (1)$$

where

$$b_n = \frac{2}{\pi} \int_0^{\pi} f(x) \sin nx = \frac{2}{\pi} \left[\int_0^{\pi/3} \left(\frac{2x}{3}\right) \sin nx \, dx + \int_{\pi/3}^{\pi} \left(\frac{\pi - x}{3}\right) \sin nx \, dx \right]$$

$$= \frac{2}{3\pi} \left[\left\{ (2x) \left(-\frac{\cos nx}{n}\right) - (2) \left(-\frac{\sin nx}{n^2}\right) \right\}_0^{\pi/3} \right.$$

$$\left. + \left\{ (\pi - x)\left(-\frac{\cos nx}{n}\right) - (-1)\left(-\frac{\sin nx}{n^2}\right) \right\}_{\pi/3}^{\pi} \right]$$

$$= \frac{2}{3\pi} \left[\left\{ -\frac{2\pi}{3n} \cos \frac{n\pi}{3} + \frac{2}{n^2} \sin \frac{n\pi}{3} \right\} + \left\{ \frac{2\pi}{3n} \cos \frac{n\pi}{3} + \frac{1}{n^2} \sin \frac{n\pi}{3} \right\} \right]$$

$$= \frac{2}{3\pi} \left[\frac{3}{n^2} \sin \frac{n\pi}{3} \right] = \frac{2}{\pi n^2} \sin \frac{n\pi}{3}$$

$$\therefore \quad b_1 = \frac{2}{\pi.1^2} \frac{\sqrt{3}}{2}, \quad b_2 = \frac{2}{\pi.2^2} \frac{\sqrt{3}}{2}, \quad b_3 = 0, \quad b_4 = -\frac{2}{\pi.4^2} \frac{\sqrt{3}}{2}, \dots \text{ etc.} \dots (2)$$

Hence from (1) and (2), we get

$$f(x) = \frac{\sqrt{3}}{\pi} \left[\frac{\sin x}{1^2} + \frac{\sin 2x}{2^2} - \frac{\sin 4x}{4^2} - \frac{\sin 5x}{5^2} \cdots \right]$$

Ex. 7 : *Find the half-range sine series of the function*

$$f(x) = \begin{cases} \dfrac{2k}{l} x, & 0 \le x \le \dfrac{l}{2} \\[3mm] \dfrac{2k}{l}(l - x), & \dfrac{l}{2} \le x \le l \end{cases}$$

Sol. : Let

$$f(x) = \sum_{n=1}^{\infty} b_n \sin \frac{n\pi x}{l} \qquad \left(\because L = l \right) \dots (1)$$

where

$$b_n = \frac{2}{L} \int_0^{L} f(x) \sin \frac{n\pi x}{L} \, dx = \frac{2}{l} \left[\int_0^{l/2} \left(\frac{2k}{l} x\right) \sin \frac{n\pi x}{l} \, dx + \int_{l/2}^{l} \frac{2k}{l}(l - x) \sin \frac{n\pi x}{l} \, dx \right]$$

$$= \frac{4k}{l^2}\left[\left\{(x)\left(-\frac{l}{n\pi}\cos\frac{n\pi x}{l}\right) - (1)\left(-\frac{l^2}{n^2\pi^2}\sin\frac{n\pi x}{l}\right)\right\}_0^{l/2}\right.$$

$$\left. + \left\{(l-x)\left(-\frac{l}{n\pi}\cos\frac{n\pi x}{l}\right) - (-1)\left(-\frac{l^2}{n^2\pi^2}\sin\frac{n\pi x}{l}\right)\right\}_{l/2}^{l}\right]$$

$$= \frac{4k}{l^2}\left[\left\{-\frac{l^2}{2n\pi}\cos\frac{n\pi}{2} + \frac{l^2}{n^2\pi^2}\sin\frac{n\pi}{2}\right\} + \left\{\frac{l^2}{2n\pi}\cos\frac{n\pi}{2} + \frac{l^2}{n^2\pi^2}\sin\frac{n\pi}{2}\right\}\right]$$

$$= \frac{4k}{l^2}\left[\frac{2l^2}{n^2\pi^2}\sin\frac{n\pi}{2}\right] = \frac{8k}{n^2\pi^2}\sin\frac{n\pi}{2} \qquad \ldots (2)$$

From (1) and (2), we get

$$f(x) = \frac{8k}{\pi^2}\sum_{n=1}^{\infty}\left(\frac{1}{n^2}\sin\frac{n\pi}{2}\right)\sin\frac{n\pi x}{l}$$

Ex. 8 : *Find half-range sine series for f(x) given in the range (0, l) by the graph OAB in the diagram.*

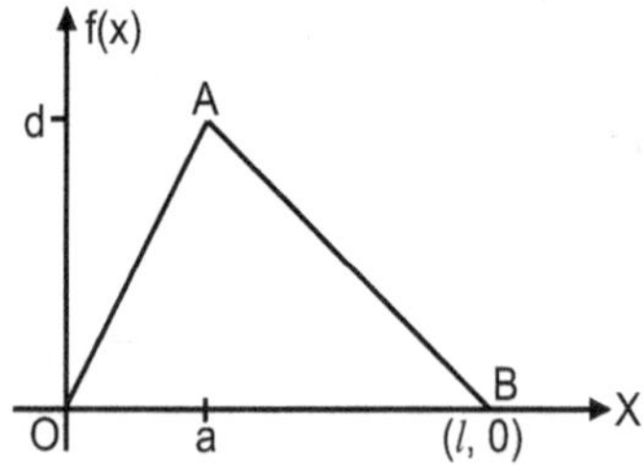

Fig. 5.25

Sol. : Here the equation of a line passing through points O(0, 0) and A(a, d) is

$$y = \frac{d}{a}x$$

$$\left[\text{Note} : \frac{y-y_1}{y_2-y_1} = \frac{x-x_1}{x_2-x_1}\right]$$

and the equation of a line passing through points A(a, d) and B(l, 0) is

$$y = -\frac{d}{l-a}(x-l)$$

∴   The function f(x) representing the graph OAB is defined by

$$f(x) = \begin{cases} \dfrac{d}{a}x, & 0 \le x \le a \\[3mm] -\dfrac{d}{l-a}(x-l), & a \le x \le l \end{cases}$$

Let half-range sine series of $f(x)$ be

$$f(x) = \sum_{n=1}^{\infty} b_n \sin\frac{n\pi x}{l} \qquad (\because L = l) \quad \dots (1)$$

where $b_n = \dfrac{2}{L}\int_0^L f(x)\sin\dfrac{n\pi x}{L}\,dx = \dfrac{2}{l}\left[\int_0^a \left(\dfrac{d}{a}x\right)\sin\dfrac{n\pi x}{l}\,dx + \int_a^l -\dfrac{d}{l-a}(x-l)\sin\dfrac{n\pi x}{l}\,dx\right]$

$= \dfrac{2d}{al}\left[(x)\left(-\dfrac{l}{n\pi}\cos\dfrac{n\pi x}{l}\right) - (1)\left(-\dfrac{l^2}{n^2\pi^2}\sin\dfrac{n\pi x}{l}\right)\right]_0^a$

$\qquad - \dfrac{2d}{l(l-a)}\left[(x-L)\left(-\dfrac{l}{n\pi}\cos\dfrac{n\pi x}{l}\right) - (1)\left(-\dfrac{l^2}{n^2\pi^2}\sin\dfrac{n\pi x}{l}\right)\right]_a^l$

$= \dfrac{2d}{al}\left[-\dfrac{al}{n\pi}\cos\dfrac{n\pi a}{l} + \dfrac{l^2}{n^2\pi^2}\dfrac{\sin n\pi a}{l}\right]$

$\qquad - \dfrac{2d}{l(l-a)}\left[-\dfrac{l(l-a)}{n\pi}\cos\dfrac{n\pi a}{l} - \dfrac{l^2}{n^2\pi^2}\sin\dfrac{n\pi a}{l}\right]$

$= \left[-\dfrac{2d}{n\pi}\cos\dfrac{n\pi a}{l} + \dfrac{2ld}{n^2\pi^2 a}\sin\dfrac{n\pi a}{l} + \dfrac{2d}{n\pi}\cos\dfrac{n\pi a}{l} + \dfrac{2ld}{n^2\pi^2(l-a)}\sin\dfrac{n\pi a}{l}\right]$

$= \dfrac{2ld}{n^2\pi^2}\left[\dfrac{1}{a} + \dfrac{1}{l-a}\right]\sin\dfrac{n\pi a}{l} = \dfrac{2l^2 d}{(l-a)\,a\pi^2 n^2}\sin\dfrac{n\pi a}{l} \qquad \dots (2)$

From (1) and (2), we get

$$f(x) = \dfrac{2l^2 d}{(l-a)\,a\pi^2}\sum_{n=1}^{\infty}\left(\dfrac{1}{n^2}\sin\dfrac{n\pi a}{l}\right)\sin\dfrac{n\pi x}{l}$$

Ex. 9 : *If $f(x) = x^2$, $0 < x < 2$ then find (i) Half-range cosine series, (ii) Half-range sine series, (iii) Fourier series.*

Sol. : (i) Half-range cosine series :

Let $\qquad x^2 = \dfrac{a_0}{2} + \sum_{n=1}^{\infty} a_n\cos\dfrac{n\pi x}{2} \qquad (\because L = 2) \quad \dots (1)$

where $\qquad a_0 = \dfrac{2}{L}\int_0^L f(x)\,dx = \dfrac{2}{2}\int_0^2 x^2\,dx = \left[\dfrac{x^3}{3}\right]_0^2 = \dfrac{8}{3} \qquad \dots (2)$

$\qquad\qquad a_n = \dfrac{2}{L}\int_0^L f(x)\cos\dfrac{n\pi x}{2}\,dx = \dfrac{2}{2}\int_0^2 x^2\cos\dfrac{n\pi x}{2}\,dx$

$$= \left[x^2 \left(\frac{2}{n\pi} \sin \frac{n\pi x}{2} \right) - (2x) \left(-\frac{4}{n^2\pi^2} \cos \frac{n\pi x}{2} \right) + (2) \left(-\frac{8}{n^3\pi^3} \sin \frac{n\pi x}{2} \right) \right]_0^2$$

$$= \frac{16}{n^2\pi^2} \cos n\pi \;\; = \frac{16(-1)^n}{n^2\pi^2} \qquad\qquad \ldots (3)$$

From (1), (2) and (3), we get

$$x^2 = \frac{4}{3} + \frac{16}{\pi^2} \sum_{n=1}^{\infty} \frac{(-1)^n}{n^2} \cos \frac{n\pi x}{2}$$

$$= \frac{4}{3} + \frac{16}{\pi^2} \left[-\frac{1}{1^2} \cos \frac{\pi x}{2} + \frac{1}{2^2} \cos \frac{2\pi x}{2} - \frac{1}{3^2} \cos \frac{3\pi x}{2} + \ldots \right] \qquad \ldots (4)$$

(ii) Half-range sine series :

Let
$$x^2 = \sum_{n=1}^{\infty} b_n \sin \frac{n\pi x}{2} \qquad\qquad \left(\because L = 2 \right) \ldots (5)$$

where
$$b_n = \frac{2}{L} \int_0^L f(x) \sin \frac{n\pi x}{2} \, dx = \frac{2}{2} \int_0^2 x^2 \sin \frac{n\pi x}{2} \, dx$$

$$= \left[x^2 \left(-\frac{2}{n\pi} \cos \frac{n\pi x}{2} \right) - (2x) \left(-\frac{4}{n^2\pi^2} \sin \frac{n\pi x}{2} \right) + (2) \left(\frac{8}{n^3\pi^3} \cos \frac{n\pi x}{2} \right) \right]_0^2$$

$$= \left[-\frac{8}{n\pi} \cos n\pi + \frac{8}{n^3\pi^3} \cos n\pi - \frac{16}{n^3\pi^3} \right]$$

$$= 8 \left[-\frac{1}{n\pi} \cos n\pi + \frac{1}{n^3\pi^3} (\cos n\pi - 2) \right]$$

$$\therefore \quad b_1 = 8 \left(\frac{1}{\pi} - \frac{3}{1^3\pi^3} \right), \; b_2 = -8 \left(\frac{1}{2\pi} + \frac{1}{2^3\,\pi^3} \right), \; b_3 = 8 \left(\frac{1}{3\pi} - \frac{3}{3^3\,\pi^3} \right) \ldots \text{etc.} \;\; \ldots (6)$$

From (5) and (6), we get

$$x^2 = 8 \left[\left(\frac{1}{\pi} - \frac{3}{1^3\pi^3} \right) \sin \frac{\pi x}{2} - \left(\frac{1}{2\pi} + \frac{1}{2^3\pi^3} \right) \sin \frac{2\pi x}{2} + \left(\frac{1}{3\pi} - \frac{3}{1^3\pi^3} \right) \sin \frac{3\pi x}{2} + \ldots \right] \ldots (7)$$

(iii) Fourier series :

Note : To obtain Fourier series, we note that

$$(0, 2) \equiv (0, 2L) \qquad\qquad \therefore \;\; 2L = 2 \text{ and } L = 1$$

Let
$$x^2 = \frac{a_0}{2} + \sum_{n=1}^{\infty} a_n \cos \frac{n\pi x}{1} + \sum_{n=1}^{\infty} b_n \sin \frac{n\pi x}{1} \qquad \ldots (8)$$

where
$$a_0 = \frac{1}{L} \int_0^{2L} f(x)\, dx$$

$$= \frac{1}{1} \int_0^{2} x^2\, dx = \left(\frac{x^3}{3}\right)_0^2 = \frac{8}{3} \qquad \ldots (9)$$

$$a_n = \frac{1}{L} \int_0^{2L} f(x) \cos \frac{n\pi x}{L}\, dx = \int_0^2 x^2 \cos n\pi x \; dx \qquad \left(\because L = 1\right)$$

$$= \left[x^2 \left(\frac{\sin n\pi x}{n\pi}\right) - (2x)\left(-\frac{\cos n\pi x}{n^2\pi^2}\right) + (2)\left(-\frac{\sin n\pi x}{n^3\pi^3}\right) \right]_0^2$$

$$= \frac{4}{n^2\pi^2} \qquad \ldots (10)$$

$$b_n = \frac{1}{L} \int_0^{2L} f(x) \sin \frac{n\pi x}{L}\, dx = \int_0^2 x^2 \sin n\pi x \; dx \qquad \left(\because L = 1\right)$$

$$= \left[x^2 \left(-\frac{\cos n\pi x}{n\pi}\right) - (2x)\left(-\frac{\sin n\pi x}{n^2\pi^2}\right) + (2)\left(\frac{\cos n\pi x}{n^3\pi^3}\right) \right]_0^2$$

$$= \left[-\frac{4}{n\pi} + \frac{2}{n^3\pi^3} - \frac{2}{n^3\pi^3} \right] = -\frac{4}{n\pi} \qquad \ldots (11)$$

From (8), (9), (10) and (11), the required Fourier series is

$$x^2 = \frac{4}{3} + \frac{4}{\pi} \sum_{n=1}^{\infty} \frac{1}{n^2} \cos n\pi x - \frac{4}{\pi} \sum_{n=1}^{\infty} \frac{1}{n} \sin n\pi x$$

Ex. 10 : *Expand $f(x) = \cos^2 x$ in a half-range sine series in the interval $0 < x < \pi$, and find first three non-zero terms in a series.*

Sol. : Let $\cos^2 x = \displaystyle\sum_{n=1}^{\infty} b_n \sin nx$ $\ldots (1)$

where,
$$b_n = \frac{2}{\pi} \int_0^{\pi} f(x) \sin nx \; dx = \frac{2}{\pi} \int_0^{\pi} \cos^2 x \sin nx \; dx$$

$$= \frac{2}{\pi} \int_0^\pi \left(\frac{1 + \cos 2x}{2} \right) \sin nx \, dx$$

$$= \frac{1}{\pi} \left[\int_0^\pi \sin nx \, dx + \frac{1}{2} \int_0^\pi 2 \sin nx \cos 2x \, dx \right]$$

$$= \frac{1}{\pi} \left[\int_0^\pi \sin nx \, dx + \frac{1}{2} \int_0^\pi \{ \sin (n + 2) x + \sin (n - 2) x \} \, dx \right]$$

$$= \frac{1}{\pi} \left[\left(-\frac{\cos nx}{n} \right)_0^\pi + \frac{1}{2} \left(-\frac{\cos (n + 2) x}{n + 2} - \frac{\cos (n - 2) x}{n - 2} \right)_0^\pi \right], \ n \neq 2$$

$$= \frac{1}{\pi} \left[\frac{1}{n} (1 - \cos n\pi) + \frac{1}{2} \left\{ \frac{1}{n + 2} [1 - \cos (n + 2) \pi] + \frac{1}{n - 2} [1 - \cos (n - 2) \pi] \right\} \right]$$

$$= \frac{1}{\pi} \left[\frac{1}{n} (1 - \cos n\pi) + \frac{1}{2} \left\{ \frac{1}{n + 2} (1 - \cos n\pi) + \frac{1}{n - 2} (1 - \cos n\pi) \right\} \right]$$

$$= \frac{1}{\pi} (1 - \cos n\pi) \left[\frac{1}{n} + \frac{1}{2} \left\{ \frac{1}{n + 2} + \frac{1}{n - 2} \right\} \right]$$

$$= \frac{1}{\pi} [1 - (-1)^n] \left[\frac{1}{n} + \frac{n}{n^2 - 4} \right], \quad n > 2$$

$$b_n = \begin{cases} 0, & \text{for all even } n > 2 \\ \dfrac{2}{\pi} \left[\dfrac{2n^2 - 4}{n(n^2 - 4)} \right], & \text{for all odd } n \end{cases} \qquad \ldots (2)$$

When n $= 2$, we have

$$b_2 = \frac{2}{\pi} \int_0^\pi \cos^2 x \sin 2x \, dx$$

$$= \frac{2}{\pi} \int_0^\pi \left(\frac{1 + \cos 2x}{2} \right) \sin 2x \, dx$$

$$= \frac{1}{\pi} \int_0^\pi (\sin 2x + \cos 2x \sin 2x) \, dx$$

$$= \frac{1}{\pi} \int_0^\pi \left(\sin 2x + \frac{1}{2} \sin 4x \right) dx = \frac{1}{\pi} \left[-\frac{\cos 2x}{2} - \frac{1}{2} \frac{\cos 4x}{4} \right]_0^\pi$$

$$= 0 \qquad \ldots (3)$$

Thus, $b_1 = \dfrac{4}{3\pi}, \quad b_2 = 0, \quad b_3 = \dfrac{28}{15\pi}, \quad b_4 = 0, \quad b_5 = \dfrac{92}{105\pi}, \quad \ldots\ldots(4)$

From (1), (2), (3) and (4), we have

$$\cos^2 x = \frac{1}{\pi}\left[\frac{4}{3}\sin x + \frac{28}{15}\sin 3x + \frac{92}{105}\sin 5x + \ldots\right]$$

EXERCISE 5.3

1. Expand the following functions $f(x)$ in a half-range (a) cosine series, (b) sine series and graph the corresponding periodic extension of $f(x)$:

(i) $f(x) = x,\ 0 \le x \le \pi$ (ii) $f(x) = x^2,\ 0 \le x \le \pi$ (iii) $f(x) = a\left(1 - \dfrac{x}{l}\right),\ 0 \le x \le l.$

Ans. :   (i) $x = \dfrac{\pi}{2} - \dfrac{4}{\pi}\left(\cos x + \dfrac{1}{3^2}\cos 3x + \dfrac{1}{5^2}\cos 5x + \ldots\right)$

$$x = 2\left(\sin x - \frac{1}{2}\sin 2x + \frac{1}{3}\sin 3x - \frac{1}{4}\sin 4x + \ldots\right)$$

$$\left(\textbf{Note :}\ \text{Put }\ x = 0;\quad \frac{\pi^2}{8} = \frac{1}{1^2} + \frac{1}{3^2} + \frac{1}{5^2} + \ldots\right)$$

(ii) $x^2 = \dfrac{\pi^2}{3} - 4\left(\cos x - \dfrac{1}{2}\cos 2x + \dfrac{1}{3^2}\cos 3x - \ldots\right)$

$$x^2 = \frac{2}{\pi}\left[\left(\frac{\pi^2}{1} - \frac{4}{1^3}\right)\sin x + \left(-\frac{\pi^2}{2}\right)\sin 2x + \left(\frac{\pi^2}{3} - \frac{4}{3^3}\right)\sin 3x + \ldots\right]$$

(iii) $a\left(1 - \dfrac{x}{l}\right) = \dfrac{a}{2} + \dfrac{4a}{\pi^2}\left(\dfrac{1}{1^2}\cos\dfrac{\pi x}{l} + \dfrac{1}{3^2}\cos\dfrac{3\pi x}{l} + \dfrac{1}{5^2}\cos\dfrac{5\pi x}{l} + \ldots\right)$

$$a\left(1 - \frac{x}{l}\right) = \frac{2a}{\pi}\left(\sin\frac{\pi x}{l} + \frac{1}{2}\sin\frac{2\pi x}{l} + \frac{1}{3}\sin\frac{3\pi x}{l} + \ldots\right)$$

2. Represent the following functions $f(x)$ by a half-range cosine series and graph the corresponding periodic extension of $f(x)$:

(i) $f(x) = e^x,\ 0 < x < l$

(ii) $f(x) = mx + c,\ \ 0 < x < p$

(iii) $f(x) = \cos \lambda x,\ 0 < x < \pi\ (\lambda$ is not an integer)

(iv) $\quad f(x) = \sin \dfrac{\pi x}{l}, \; 0 < x < l$

Ans. : (i) $\quad e^x = \dfrac{1}{l} (e^l - 1) + 2l \displaystyle\sum_{n=1}^{\infty} \dfrac{1}{l^2 + n^2 \pi^2} (e^l \cos n\pi - 1) \cos \dfrac{n\pi x}{l}$

(ii) $mx + c = c + \dfrac{mp}{2} - \dfrac{4mp}{\pi^2} \left[\dfrac{1}{1^2} \cos \dfrac{\pi x}{p} + \dfrac{1}{3^2} \cos \dfrac{3\pi x}{p} + \dfrac{1}{5^2} \cos \dfrac{5\pi x}{p} \cdots \right]$

$\left(\textbf{Note :} \text{ Put } x = 0; \text{ we get } \dfrac{\pi^2}{8} = \dfrac{1}{1^2} + \dfrac{1}{3^2} + \dfrac{1}{5^2} + \ldots \right)$

(iii) $\quad \cos \lambda x = \dfrac{\sin \lambda \pi}{\lambda \pi} + \dfrac{2\lambda \sin \lambda \pi}{\pi} \displaystyle\sum_{n=1}^{\infty} \dfrac{(-1)^n}{\lambda^2 - n^2} \cos nx$

(iv) $\quad \sin \dfrac{\pi x}{l} = \dfrac{2}{\pi} - \dfrac{4}{\pi} \left(\dfrac{1}{1.3} \cos \dfrac{2\pi x}{l} + \dfrac{1}{3.5} \cos \dfrac{4\pi x}{l} + \dfrac{1}{5.7} \cos \dfrac{6\pi x}{l} + \ldots \right)$

3. Obtain a half-range sine series for the following functions and graph the corresponding periodic extension.

(i) $f(x) = 2 - x, \; 0 < x < 2,$

(ii) $f(x) = x^2, \; 0 \le x \le c,$

(iii) $f(x) = \pi x - x^2, \; 0 < x < \pi,$

(iv) $f(x) = x^3, \; 0 < x < L.$

Ans. : (i) $2 - x = \dfrac{4}{\pi} \displaystyle\sum_{n=1}^{\infty} \dfrac{1}{n} \sin \dfrac{n\pi x}{2}$

(ii) $\quad x^2 = \dfrac{2c^2}{\pi^3} \displaystyle\sum_{n=1}^{\infty} \left(-\dfrac{\pi^2}{n} \cos n\pi + \dfrac{2}{n^3} \cos n\pi - \dfrac{2}{n^3} \right) \sin \dfrac{n\pi x}{c}$

(iii) $\quad \pi x - x^2 = \dfrac{8}{\pi} \left(\dfrac{1}{1^3} \sin x + \dfrac{1}{3^3} \sin 3x + \dfrac{1}{5^3} \sin 5x + \ldots \right)$

(iv) $\quad x^3 = \dfrac{L^3}{4} + \dfrac{6L^3}{\pi^2} \displaystyle\sum_{n=1}^{\infty} \dfrac{1}{n^2} \left[(-1)^n + \dfrac{2}{n^2 \pi^2} \{ 1 - (-1)^n \} \right] \cos \dfrac{n\pi x}{L}$

4. Find the half-range cosine series for the function f(x) defined by

(i) $f(x) = \begin{cases} kx, & 0 \le x \le \dfrac{l}{2} \\[2mm] k(l-x), & \dfrac{l}{2} \le x \le l \end{cases}$

(ii) $f(x) = \begin{cases} 2kx/l, & 0 < x < \dfrac{l}{2} \\[2mm] 2k(l-x)/l, & \dfrac{l}{2} < x < l \end{cases}$

Ans. : (i) $f(x) = \dfrac{kl}{4} - \dfrac{8kl}{\pi^2} \dfrac{1}{2^2} \cos \dfrac{2\pi x}{l} + \dfrac{1}{6^2} \cos \dfrac{6\pi x}{l} + \dfrac{1}{10^2} \cos \dfrac{10\pi x}{l} + \ldots$

(ii) $f(x) = \dfrac{k}{2} + \dfrac{4k}{\pi^2} \displaystyle\sum_{n=1}^{\infty} \left(\dfrac{2 \cos n\,\pi/2 - \cos n\pi - 1}{n^2} \right)$

5. Obtain (i) a half-range sine series and (ii) a half-range cosine series to represent $f(x) = x - x^2$ in the range $(0, 1)$.

Ans. : Sine series : $x - x^2 = \dfrac{8}{\pi^2} \displaystyle\sum_{n=0}^{\infty} \dfrac{1}{(2n+1)^3} \sin (2n+1)\,\pi x$

Cosine series : $x - x^2 = \dfrac{1}{6} - \dfrac{4}{\pi^2} \displaystyle\sum_{n=1}^{\infty} \dfrac{1}{(2n)^2} \cos 2n\pi x$

6. Expand $f(x) = \sin^2 x, \ 0 < x < \pi$, in a half-range (i) cosine series, (ii) sine series.

Ans. : Cosine series : $\sin x = \dfrac{1}{2} (1 - \cos 2x)$

Sine series : $\sin x = -\dfrac{8}{\pi} \displaystyle\sum_{n=1}^{\infty} \dfrac{1}{(2n-1)(2n+1)(2n+3)} \sin (2n-1) x$

7. Expand $f(x) = x, \ 0 < x < 2$, in a half-range (i) cosine series, (ii) sine series.

Ans. : Cosine series : $x = 1 - \dfrac{8}{\pi^2} \left(\dfrac{1}{1^2} \cos \dfrac{\pi x}{2} + \dfrac{1}{3^2} \cos \dfrac{3\pi x}{2} + \dfrac{1}{5^2} \cos \dfrac{5\pi x}{2} + \ldots \right)$

Sine series : $x = \dfrac{4}{\pi} \left(\sin \dfrac{\pi x}{2} - \dfrac{1}{2} \sin \dfrac{2\pi x}{2} + \dfrac{1}{3} \sin \dfrac{3\pi x}{2} - \ldots \right)$

8. Find a series of cosine of multiple of x which will represent x sin x in the interval $(0, \pi)$. Deduct that $1 + \dfrac{2}{1.3} - \dfrac{2}{3.5} + \dfrac{2}{5.7} - \ldots = \dfrac{\pi}{2}$.

Ans. : $x \sin x = 1 - \dfrac{1}{2} \cos x - 2 \left(\dfrac{\cos 2x}{1.3} - \dfrac{\cos 3x}{2.4} + \dfrac{\cos 4x}{3.5} + \ldots \right)$, put $x = \dfrac{\pi}{2}$.

9. Find the half-range cosine series for the function $f(x) = (x - 1)^2$ in the interval $0 < x < 1$. Hence show that

(i) $\dfrac{1}{1^2} + \dfrac{1}{2^2} + \dfrac{1}{3^2} + \ldots = \dfrac{\pi^2}{6}$ (ii) $\dfrac{1}{1^2} - \dfrac{1}{2^2} + \dfrac{1}{3^2} - \ldots = \dfrac{\pi^2}{12}$

(iii) $\dfrac{1}{1^2} + \dfrac{1}{3^2} + \dfrac{1}{5^2} + \ldots = \dfrac{\pi^2}{8}$

Ans. : $(x - 1)^2 = \dfrac{1}{3} + \dfrac{4}{\pi^2} \left(\cos \pi x + \dfrac{\cos 2\pi x}{2^2} + \dfrac{\cos 3\pi x}{3^2} + \ldots \right)$

10. Find the half-range sine series for

$$f(x) = \begin{cases} \dfrac{1}{4} - x, & 0 < x < \dfrac{1}{2} \\[2mm] x - \dfrac{3}{4}, & \dfrac{1}{2} < x < 1 \end{cases}$$

Ans. : $f(x) = \left(\dfrac{1}{\pi} - \dfrac{4}{\pi^2} \right) \sin \pi x + \left(\dfrac{1}{3\pi} + \dfrac{4}{3^2 \pi^2} \right) \sin 3\pi x + \left(\dfrac{1}{5\pi} - \dfrac{4}{5^2 \pi^2} \right) \sin 5\pi x + \ldots$

11. Expand $f(t) = \begin{cases} t, & 0 < t < \dfrac{\pi}{8} \\[2mm] \dfrac{\pi}{4} - t, & \dfrac{\pi}{8} < t < \dfrac{\pi}{4} \end{cases}$ in the range $\left(0, \dfrac{\pi}{4} \right)$ in a half-range sine series.

Ans. : $\dfrac{1}{\pi} \left(\sin 4t - \dfrac{1}{9} \sin 12t + \dfrac{1}{25} \sin 20t - \dfrac{1}{44} \sin 28t + \ldots \right)$

12. If $f(x) = \begin{cases} \dfrac{x}{a}, & 0 < x < a \\[2mm] \dfrac{l - x}{l - a}, & a < x < l \end{cases}$, prove that for all values of x in $(0, l)$,

$$f(x) = \dfrac{2l^2}{a(l - a) \pi^2} \sum_{n=1}^{\infty} \left(\dfrac{1}{n^2} \sin \dfrac{n\pi a}{l} \right) \sin \dfrac{n\pi x}{l}$$

13. Find the half-range cosine series for the following functions :

(i) $\quad f(x) = \begin{cases} c, & 0 < x < a \\ 0, & a < x < l \end{cases}$

(ii) $f(x) = \begin{cases} 1, & 0 \le x \le 1 \\ x, & 1 \le x \le 2 \end{cases}$

(iii) $\quad f(x) = \begin{cases} 1, & 0 < x < \dfrac{c}{2} \\ 1 - x, & \dfrac{c}{2} < x < c \end{cases}$

Ans. : (i) $\dfrac{ac}{l} + \dfrac{2c}{\pi}\left(\sin \dfrac{\pi a}{l} \cos \dfrac{\pi x}{l} + \dfrac{1}{2} \sin \dfrac{2\pi a}{l} \cos \dfrac{2\pi x}{l} + \dots \right)$

(ii) $\dfrac{5}{4} - \dfrac{4}{\pi^2}\left(\cos \dfrac{\pi x}{2} - \dfrac{1}{2} \cos \dfrac{2\pi x}{2} + \dfrac{1}{9} \cos \dfrac{3\pi x}{2} - \dots \right)$

(iii) $\left(1 - \dfrac{3c}{8} \right) +$

$\dfrac{2c}{\pi^2}\left[\left(\dfrac{\pi}{2} + 1 \right) \cos \dfrac{\pi x}{c} - \dfrac{1}{2} \cos \dfrac{2\pi x}{c} + \dfrac{1}{9}(1 - 3\pi) \cos \dfrac{3\pi x}{c} + \dots \right]$

14. Find the half-range sine series for the following functions :

(i) $\quad f(x) = \begin{cases} 0, & 0 < x < \dfrac{\pi}{4} \\ h, & \dfrac{\pi}{4} \le x < \dfrac{3\pi}{4} \\ 0, & \dfrac{3\pi}{4} \le x \le \pi \end{cases}$

(ii) $f(x) = \begin{cases} \dfrac{x}{2}, & 0 < x \le \alpha \\ \dfrac{\alpha}{2}, & \alpha \le x < \pi - \alpha \\ \dfrac{1}{2}(\pi - x), & \pi - \alpha \le x < \pi \end{cases}$

Ans. : (i) $f(x) = \dfrac{4h}{\pi} \displaystyle\sum_{n=0}^{\infty} \dfrac{(-1)^n}{(2n+1)} \sin \dfrac{(2n+1)\pi}{4} \sin (2n+1)x$

(ii) $f(x) = \dfrac{2}{\pi} \displaystyle\sum_{n=0}^{\infty} \dfrac{(-1)^n}{(2n+1)} \sin (2n+1)\alpha \sin (2n+1)x$

15. If
$$f(x) = \begin{cases} \dfrac{\pi}{3}, & 0 \le x < \dfrac{\pi}{3} \\[2mm] 0, & \dfrac{\pi}{3} \le x < \dfrac{2\pi}{3} \\[2mm] -\dfrac{\pi}{3}, & \dfrac{2\pi}{3} \le x \le \pi \end{cases}$$

then prove that
$$f(x) = \frac{2}{\sqrt{3}}\left(\cos x - \frac{1}{5}\cos 5x + \frac{1}{7}\cos 7x + \dots\right)$$

and also
$$f(x) = \sin 2x + \frac{1}{2}\sin 4x + \frac{1}{10}\sin 10x + \dots$$

16. If $f(x) = 1 - \dfrac{x}{L}$, $0 < x < L$ then find (i) half-range cosine series, (ii) half-range sine series of $f(x)$. Graph the corresponding periodic continuation of $f(x)$.

$$\textbf{Ans. : } a_0 = 1, \quad a_n = \begin{cases} \dfrac{4}{n^2\pi^2}, & n \text{ odd} \\[2mm] 0, & n \text{ even} \end{cases} \qquad b_n = \frac{2}{n\pi}$$

17. Represent $f(x) = \sin \dfrac{\pi x}{L}$, $0 < x < L$ by a half-range cosine series. Graph the periodic continuation of $f(x)$.

$$\textbf{Ans. : } a_0 = \frac{4}{\pi}, \quad a_1 = 0, \quad a_n = \begin{cases} -\dfrac{4}{\pi(n^2-1)}, & n \text{ even} \\[2mm] 0, & n \text{ odd} \end{cases}$$

18. In the following figure, OABC represents $f(\theta)$ in the range $(0, \pi)$. Find a half period sine series of the period 2π to represent $f(\theta)$ in the range $(0, \pi)$.

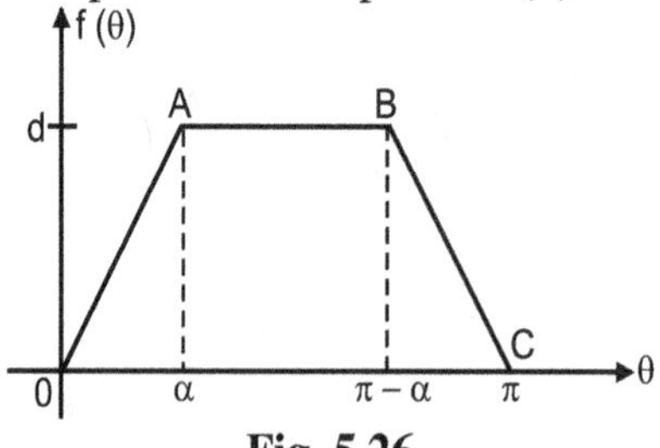

Fig. 5.26

$$\textbf{Ans. : } \quad f(\theta) = \frac{4d}{\pi\alpha} \sum_{n=0}^{\infty} \frac{\sin(2n+1)\alpha}{(2n+1)^2} \sin(2n+1)\theta$$

◈ ◈ ◈

UNIT- VI

APPLICATIONS OF PARTIAL DIFFERENTIAL EQUATIONS

6.1 INTRODUCTION

Partial differential equations arise in connection with various physical and geometrical problems when the functions involved depend on two or more independent variables. Most problems in fluid and solid mechanics (dynamics, elasticity), heat transfer, electromagnetic theory, quantum mechanics and other areas of physics lead to *partial differential equations.* The independent variables involved may be time and one or several co-ordinates in space. The present chapter is devoted to some of the most important partial differential equations occurring in engineering applications. We derive these equations as models of physical systems and consider methods for obtaining solutions of those equations corresponding to the given physical situations.

Since the general solution of a partial differential equation in a region R contains arbitrary constants or arbitrary functions, the unique solution of a partial differential equation corresponding to a physical problem will satisfy certain other conditions at the boundary of the region R. These are known as *boundary conditions.* When these conditions are specified for the time t = 0, they are known as *initial conditions.* A partial differential equation together with boundary conditions constitutes a *boundary value problem.*

In the applications of ordinary linear differential equations, we first find the general solution and then determine the arbitrary constants from the initial values. But the same method is not applicable to problems involving partial differential equations. Most of the boundary value problems involving linear partial differential equations can be solved by the method of separation of variables. In this method, right from the beginning, we try to find the particular solutions of the partial differential equation which satisfy all or some of the boundary conditions and then adjust them till the remaining conditions are also satisfied. A combination of these particular solutions gives the solution of the problem. Fourier series is a powerful aid in determining the arbitrary functions.

6.2 PRELIMINARIES

Differential equations in which partial derivatives are involved, are called *partial differential equations* (PDE). The order of the PDE is the highest order of partial derivatives present in it. It is obvious that the number of independent variables must be two or more than two.

Formation of Partial Differential Equations

A.   By eliminating arbitrary constants :

(i) $z = ax + by$

$\therefore \qquad \dfrac{\partial z}{\partial x} = a \qquad$ and $\qquad \dfrac{\partial z}{\partial y} = b$

$\therefore \qquad z = x\,\dfrac{\partial z}{\partial x} + y\,\dfrac{\partial z}{\partial y}$

i.e. a partial differential equation of order one obtained by eliminating two arbitrary constants a and b.

(ii) $(x-a)^2 + (y-b)^2 + (z-c)^2 = d^2,$ where z is a function of x and y.

Differentiating partially w.r.t. x and y respectively, we get

$$2\,(x-a) + 2\,(z-c)\,\frac{\partial z}{\partial x} = 0$$

and $2\,(y-b) + 2\,(z-c)\,\dfrac{\partial z}{\partial y} = 0$

Differentiating first equation partially w.r.t. x and second equation partially w.r.t. y, we get

$$1 + \left(\frac{\partial z}{\partial x}\right)^2 = -\,(z-c)\,\frac{\partial^2 z}{\partial x^2}$$

and $\qquad 1 + \left(\dfrac{\partial z}{\partial y}\right)^2 = -\,(z-c)\,\dfrac{\partial^2 z}{\partial y^2}$

$\therefore \qquad \dfrac{\partial^2 z}{\partial y^2}\left[1 + \left(\dfrac{\partial z}{\partial x}\right)^2\right] = \dfrac{\partial^2 z}{\partial x^2}\left[1 + \left(\dfrac{\partial z}{\partial y}\right)^2\right]$

i.e. a partial differential equation of order two obtained by eliminating four arbitrary constants a, b, c and d.

B.   By eliminating arbitrary functions :

(iii) $z = x\,f\left(\dfrac{y}{x}\right)$

$$\frac{\partial z}{\partial x} = f\left(\frac{y}{x}\right) + x\,f\,'\left(\frac{y}{x}\right)\left(-\frac{y}{x^2}\right)$$

and $\qquad \dfrac{\partial z}{\partial y} = x\,f\,'\left(\dfrac{y}{x}\right) \cdot \dfrac{1}{x}$

$\therefore \quad x\,\dfrac{\partial z}{\partial x} + y\,\dfrac{\partial z}{\partial y} = x\,f\left(\dfrac{y}{x}\right) = z$

i.e. a partial differential equation of order one obtained by eliminating one arbitrary function f. Note that it is same as obtained in (i).

(iv) $$z = f(y + ax) + \phi(y - ax)$$

$\therefore$ $$\frac{\partial z}{\partial x} = a\,f'(y + ax) - a\,\phi'(y - ax)$$

and $$\frac{\partial z}{\partial y} = f'(y + ax) + \phi'(y - ax)$$

$$\frac{\partial^2 z}{\partial x^2} = a^2\,f''(y + ax) + a^2\,\phi''(y - ax)$$

and $$\frac{\partial^2 z}{dy^2} = f''(y + ax) + \phi''(y - ax)$$

$\therefore$ $$\frac{\partial^2 z}{\partial x^2} = a^2\,\frac{\partial^2 z}{\partial y^2}$$

i.e. a partial differential equation of order two obtained by eliminating two arbitrary functions f and ϕ.

(v) $$z = ax + by + f\left(\frac{y}{x}\right)$$

$\therefore$ $$\frac{\partial z}{\partial x} = a + f'\left(\frac{y}{x}\right) \cdot \left(-\frac{y}{x^2}\right)$$

and $$\frac{\partial z}{\partial y} = b + f'\left(\frac{y}{x}\right) \cdot \frac{1}{x}$$

$\therefore$ $$x\frac{\partial z}{\partial x} + y\frac{\partial z}{\partial y} = ax + by$$

Differentiating partially w.r.t. x and y respectively, we get

$$x\frac{\partial^2 z}{\partial x^2} + \frac{\partial z}{\partial x} + y\frac{\partial^2 z}{\partial x\,\partial y} = a$$

and $$x\frac{\partial^2 z}{\partial y\,\partial x} + \frac{\partial z}{\partial y} + y\frac{\partial^2 z}{\partial y^2} = b$$

Multiplying first by x and second by y and adding, we get

$$x^2\frac{\partial^2 z}{\partial x^2} + xy\left(\frac{\partial^2 z}{\partial x\,\partial y} + \frac{\partial^2 z}{\partial y\,\partial x}\right) + y^2\frac{\partial^2 z}{\partial y^2} = 0$$

i.e. a PDE of order two obtained by eliminating two arbitrary constants a and b and arbitrary function f.

Note : We observe that there is some relationship between the order of PDE and the arbitrary constants or arbitrary functions involved in the most general solutions. The general solution must involve either arbitrary constants equal to twice the order of PDE or arbitrary functions equal to the order of PDE. In case both are involved then the sum of arbitrary constants divided by two and number of arbitrary functions must be equal to the order of PDE.

Some of the important partial differential equations involving two independent variables and one dependent variable which occur in the study of Engineering and Physical problems are :

I. The Wave Equation :

$$\frac{\partial^2 y}{\partial t^2} = c^2 \frac{\partial^2 y}{\partial x^2}$$

which occurs in the problems involving *vibrations of a stretched string*. It is also called as *one-dimensional wave equation.*

II. Diffusion Equation in One Dimension (One-dimensional heat flow equation) :

$$\frac{\partial u}{\partial t} = a^2 \frac{\partial^2 u}{\partial x^2}$$

which occurs in the conduction of heat flow along a bar.

III. Laplace's Equation in Two dimensions (Two-dimensional heat flow equation) :

(a)
$$\frac{\partial^2 u}{\partial x^2} + \frac{\partial^2 u}{\partial y^2} = 0 \quad \text{(Cartesian form)}$$

which occurs in the conduction of heat in a plate in steady state. The equation is also satisfied by electrostatic potential (ϕ).

(b)
$$r^2 \frac{\partial^2 u}{\partial r^2} + r \frac{\partial u}{\partial r} + \frac{\partial^2 u}{\partial \theta^2} = 0 \quad \text{(Polar form)}$$

There are various methods of solving PDEs. However, in what follows, we shall consider solution of linear PDE by the method of separation of variables. This method in general is used to reduce the PDE to the solutions of a set of ordinary differential equations each of which involves only one of the variables.

Note : We know that if an ordinary differential equation is linear and homogeneous then from known solutions, we can obtain further solutions by superposition. For a homogeneous linear partial differential equation, the situation is quite similar.

If y_1 and y_2 are any solutions of a linear homogeneous partial differential equation in some region R, then $\boxed{y = c_1 y_1 + c_2 y_2}$ where c_1 and c_2 are any constants, is also a solution of that equation in R.

6.3 MODELING OF VIBRATIONS OF A STRETCHED STRING (ONE-DIMENSIONAL WAVE EQUATION)

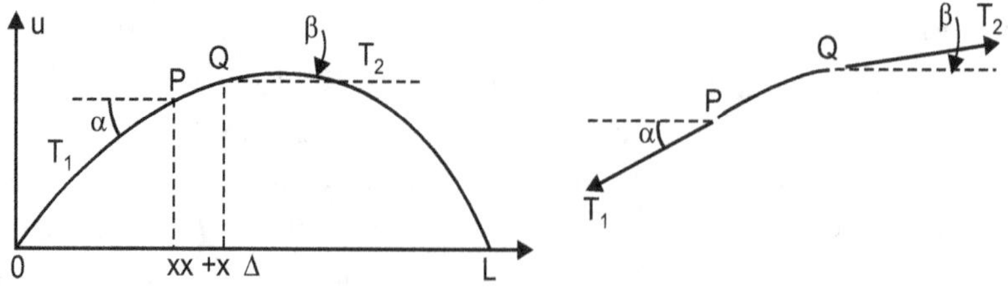

Fig. 6.1 : Deflected String at Fixed Time t

Let us derive the equation governing small transverse vibrations of an elastic string (such as a violin string). We stretch the string to length l and fix it at the ends. We then distort it and at some instant, say, $t = 0$, we release it and allow it to vibrate. The problem is to determine the vibrations of the string, that is, to find its deflection u (x, t) at any point x and at any time $t > 0$.

While deriving a differential equation corresponding to a given physical problem, we usually have to make simplifying assumptions to ensure that the resulting equation does not become too complicated.

We assume the following *physical assumptions* :
(a) The string is perfectly elastic and does not offer any resistance to bending.
(b) The mass of the string per unit length is constant.
(c) The tension caused by stretching the string before fixing it at the ends is so large that the action of the gravitational force on the string can be neglected.
(d) The string performs small transverse motions in a vertical plane; that is, every particle of the string moves strictly vertically and so that the deflection and the slope at every point of the string always remain small in absolute value.

Under these assumptions, we may expect that the solution u(x, t) of the differential equation to be obtained will reasonably well describe small vibrations of the physical non-idealized string of small homogeneous mass under large tension.

Consider the forces acting on a small portion of the string. Since the string does not offer resistance to bending, the tension is tangential to the curve of the string at each point. Let T_1 and T_2 be the tensions at the end points P and Q of that portion. Since there is no motion in horizontal direction, the horizontal components of the tension must be constant.

$\therefore$ $\qquad\qquad$ $T_1 \cos \alpha = T_2 \cos \beta = T = \text{constant}$ $\qquad\qquad\qquad$ ... (1)

In vertical direction, we have two forces, the vertical components $- T_1 \sin \alpha$ and $T_2 \sin \beta$ of T_1 and T_2 (minus sign appears because that component at P is directed downward.).

By Newton's second law, the resultant of these two forces is equal to the mass "m δx" of the portion times the acceleration $\dfrac{\partial^2 u}{\partial t^2}$, evaluated at some point between x and x $+ $ δx, where, m = mass of the undeflected string per unit length, δx $=$ the length of the portion of the undeflected string.

$\therefore$ $\qquad\qquad$ $T_2 \sin \beta - T_1 \sin \alpha = m\, \delta x \, . \, \dfrac{\partial^2 u}{\partial t^2}$

By using equation (1), we can divide this by $T_2 \cos \beta = T_1 \cos \alpha = T$,

$$\frac{T_2 \sin \beta}{T_2 \cos \beta} - \frac{T_1 \sin \alpha}{T_1 \cos \alpha} = \left(\frac{m\, \delta x}{T}\right) \frac{\partial^2 u}{\partial t^2}$$

$$\frac{T}{m} \frac{(\tan \beta - \tan \alpha)}{\delta x} = \frac{\partial^2 u}{\partial t^2}$$

Now $\tan \alpha$ and $\tan \beta$ are the slopes of the string at x and $x + \delta x$.

$$\therefore \quad \tan \alpha = \left(\frac{\partial u}{\partial x}\right)_x \quad \text{and} \quad \tan \beta = \left(\frac{\partial u}{\partial x}\right)_{x + \delta x}$$

Note : Here we write partial derivatives because u also depends on t.

$$\therefore \quad \frac{T}{m}\left[\frac{\left(\frac{\partial u}{\partial x}\right)_{x + \delta x} - \left(\frac{\partial u}{\partial x}\right)_x}{\delta x}\right] = \frac{\partial^2 u}{\partial t^2}$$

As $\delta x \to 0$,

$$\frac{T}{m} \cdot \frac{\partial^2 u}{\partial x^2} = \frac{\partial^2 u}{\partial t^2}$$

Let $\qquad c^2 = \dfrac{T}{m}$

$$\therefore \quad \boxed{\frac{\partial^2 u}{\partial t^2} = c^2 \frac{\partial^2 u}{\partial x^2}}$$

This is called one-dimensional wave equation. One-dimensional indicates that the equation involves only one space variable, x.

The notation c^2 (instead of c) for the physical constant $\dfrac{T}{m}$ has been chosen to indicate that this constant is positive.

Note : Vibration in membrane or drumhead, oscillations induced in a guitar or violin string is governed by wave equation.

6.4 SOLUTION OF WAVE EQUATION BY METHOD OF SEPARATION OF VARIABLES

The vibrations of an elastic string are governed by the one-dimensional wave equation :

$$\boxed{\frac{\partial^2 u}{\partial t^2} = c^2 \frac{\partial^2 u}{\partial x^2}} \qquad \qquad \dots (1)$$

where, u (x, t) is the deflection of the string.

To find out how the string moves, we determine a solution u (x, t) of (1) that also satisfies the conditions imposed by the physical system.

Since the string is fixed at the ends $x = 0$ and $x = l$, we have two **boundary conditions.**

$$\boxed{\textbf{B.C. : u (0, t) = 0, \quad u } (l \textbf{, t}) = \textbf{0} \quad \textbf{for all t}} \qquad \dots (2)$$

The form of the motion of the string will depend on the initial deflection, say f(x) (deflection at t = 0) and on the initial velocity, say g(x) (velocity at t = 0).

$\therefore$ We obtain the two **initial conditions.**

$$\boxed{\text{I.C. : } u(x, 0) \ = \ f(x) \ , \ \left(\frac{\partial u}{\partial t}\right)_{t = 0} = \ g(x)} \qquad \ldots (3)$$

Our problem is now to find a solution of (1) satisfying the conditions (2) and (3).

We take the following important steps :

Step 1 : By applying the so-called method of separation of variables (or product method), we shall obtain two ordinary differential equations.

Step 2 : We shall determine solutions of those two equations that satisfy the boundary conditions.

Step 3 : Using Fourier series, we shall compose those solutions, in order to get a solution of the wave equation (1) that also satisfies the given initial conditions.

Let us consider these steps one by one.

Step 1 : Two ordinary differential equations : In the method of separating variables (or product method), we determine solution of the wave equation (1) of the form :

$$\boxed{u \ (x, t) \ = F \ (x) \ . \ G \ (t)} \qquad \ldots (4)$$

where, F (x) is a function of x alone and G (t) is a function of t alone.

$$\frac{\partial u}{\partial t} \ = F \ (x) \frac{dG}{dt} \quad \therefore \quad \frac{\partial^2 u}{\partial t^2} \ = F \ (x) \cdot \frac{d^2 G}{dt^2}$$

$$\frac{\partial u}{\partial x} \ = \frac{dF}{dx} \ . \ G \ (t) \quad \therefore \quad \frac{\partial^2 u}{\partial x^2} \ = \frac{d^2 F}{dx^2} \cdot G \ (t)$$

But
$$\frac{\partial^2 u}{\partial t^2} \ = c^2 \ \frac{\partial^2 u}{\partial x^2}$$

$\therefore \qquad$
$$F \ (x) \ . \ \frac{d^2 G}{dt^2} \ = c^2 \ \frac{d^2 F}{dx^2} \cdot G \ (t)$$

Or
$$F \ G'' \ = c^2 \ F'' \ G$$

$$\frac{G''}{c^2 \ G} \ = \frac{F''}{F}$$

i.e.
$$\frac{F''}{F} \ = \frac{G''}{c^2 \ G}$$

Here L.H.S. is a function of x alone and R.H.S. is a function of t alone, hence above two expressions are independent of each other. Therefore we can equate to any constant, say k.

$\therefore \qquad$
$$\frac{F''}{F} \ = \frac{G''}{c^2 \ G} \ = k$$

This yields immediately two ordinary linear differential equations :

$$\frac{F''}{F} = k \;\Rightarrow\; F'' - kF = 0 \;\Rightarrow\; \frac{d^2F}{dx^2} - kF(x) = 0$$

Also,

$$\frac{G''}{c^2\,G} = k \;\Rightarrow\; G'' - c^2\,kG = 0 \;\Rightarrow\; \frac{d^2G}{dt^2} - c^2\,kG(t) = 0$$

Step 2 : Satisfying the boundary conditions : The boundary conditions are :

$$u(0, t) = 0\,,\; u(l, t) = 0 \quad \text{for all t.}$$

But

$$u(x, t) = F(x) \cdot G(t)$$

∴

$$u(0, t) = 0 \;\Rightarrow\; F(0) \cdot G(t) = 0$$

$$u(l, t) = 0 \;\Rightarrow\; F(l) \cdot G(t) = 0$$

If $G(t) = 0$ then $u = 0$ is a trivial solution. Thus $G(t) \ne 0$, and hence $F(0) = F(l) = 0$

Case (i) : Let $\quad k = 0$

∴

$$F'' = 0 \quad\Rightarrow\quad \frac{d^2F}{dx^2} = 0$$

whose solution is $\;F(x) = c_1 x + c_2.$

$$F(0) = 0 \Rightarrow c_2 = 0 \;;\; F(l) = 0 \Rightarrow c_1 = 0$$

∴ $\qquad\qquad F(x) = 0$ which is of no interest because then $u = 0.$

Hence we reject the case $k = 0$.

Case (ii) : Let $k > 0 \quad$ i.e. $\;k = m^2\;$ (say)

$$\frac{F''}{F} = \frac{G''}{c^2\,G} = m^2$$

$$\frac{F''}{F} = m^2 \;\Rightarrow\; F'' - m^2 F = 0$$

$$\frac{d^2F}{dx^2} - m^2 F = 0 \qquad \left(\text{let } D \equiv \frac{d}{dx}\right)$$

$$D^2 F - m^2 F = 0, \quad (D^2 - m^2)\,F = 0$$

$$\text{A.E.} \;:\; D^2 - m^2 = 0 \;\Rightarrow\; D = \pm m$$

∴

$$F(x) = c_1\,e^{mx} + c_2\,e^{-mx}$$

Now

$$F(0) = 0 \qquad\Rightarrow\qquad c_1 + c_2 = 0$$

$$F(l) = 0 \qquad\Rightarrow\qquad c_1\,e^{ml} + c_2\,e^{-ml} = 0$$

Solving we get $c_1 = 0,\; c_2 = 0 \quad\Rightarrow\quad f(x) = 0 \;\;\therefore\; u = 0$

Hence we reject the case $k > 0$ too.

Case (iii) (Important) : Let $k < 0$ i.e. $k = -m^2$ (say).

$$\frac{F''}{F} = \frac{G''}{c^2 G} = -m^2$$

$$\frac{F''}{F} = -m^2 \Rightarrow F'' + m^2 F = 0$$

$$\frac{d^2 F}{dx^2} + m^2 F = 0 \qquad\qquad \left(\text{let } D \equiv \frac{d}{dx}\right)$$

$$D^2 F + m^2 F = 0, \ (D^2 + m^2) \ F = 0$$

$$\text{A.E.} \ : \ D^2 + m^2 = 0 \ \Rightarrow \ D = \pm \ im$$

$\therefore \qquad\qquad F(x) = c_1 \cos mx + c_2 \sin mx.$

Now $\qquad\qquad F(0) = 0 \ \Rightarrow \ c_1 = 0$

$\therefore \qquad\qquad F(x) = c_2 \sin mx,$

and $\qquad\qquad F(l) = 0 \ \Rightarrow \ 0 = c_2 \sin ml.$

Now, $c_2 \neq 0$ since otherwise $F = 0$, and hence $u = 0$.

$\therefore \qquad\qquad \sin ml = 0 \ \Rightarrow \ ml = n\pi, \ n = 1, 2, 3, 4 \dots$ [Since $\sin n\pi = 0$ for all n]

$\therefore \qquad\qquad m = \dfrac{n\pi}{l}$

We thus obtain infinitely many solutions $F(x) = F_n(x)$, where

$$F_n(x) = c_2 \sin \frac{n\pi x}{l}, \ n = 1, 2, 3, \dots\dots$$

Also, $\qquad\qquad \dfrac{G''}{c^2 G} = -m^2 \qquad\qquad \left(\text{where } m = \dfrac{n\pi}{l}\right)$

$$G'' + c^2 m^2 G = 0 \qquad\qquad \Rightarrow \frac{d^2 G}{dt^2} + c^2 m^2 G = 0$$

Let $D \equiv \dfrac{d}{dt}$ $\therefore D^2 G + c^2 m^2 G = 0 \Rightarrow (D^2 + c^2 m^2) G = 0$

$$\text{A.E.} \ : \ D^2 + c^2 m^2 = 0 \ \Rightarrow \ D = \pm \ i \,(cm)$$

$\therefore \qquad\qquad G(t) = c_3 \cos cmt + c_4 \sin cmt$

Or $\qquad G(t) = G_n(t) = c_3 \cos \dfrac{n\pi ct}{l} + c_4 \sin \dfrac{n\pi ct}{l} \qquad \left(\because m = \dfrac{n\pi}{l}\right)$

Now, $\qquad\qquad u(x, t) = F(x) \cdot G(t) = F_n(x) \cdot G_n(t) = u_n(x, t) \ \dots$ (say)

$\therefore \qquad\qquad u_n(x, t) = \left(c_2 \sin \dfrac{n\pi x}{l}\right) \left[c_3 \cos \dfrac{n\pi ct}{l} + c_4 \sin \dfrac{n\pi ct}{l}\right]$

$$u_n(x, t) = \left[A_n \cos \frac{n\pi ct}{l} + B_n \sin \frac{n\pi ct}{l}\right] \sin \frac{n\pi x}{l}$$

where, $\qquad\qquad A_n = c_2 \, c_3, \ B_n = c_2 \, c_4, \ n = 1, 2, 3, \dots\dots\dots$

Step 3 : Solution of the entire problem : It is evident that no single solution of $u_n(x, t)$ can satisfy the initial conditions. However, the given P.D.E. is linear, principle of superimposition is valid meaning thereby that if, *we have several solutions then their sum is also a solution.*

Hence we take, $u(x, t) = \sum\limits_{n=1}^{\infty} u_n(x, t)$

$$\boxed{u(x, t) = \sum_{n=1}^{\infty} \left(A_n \cos \frac{n\pi ct}{l} + B_n \sin \frac{n\pi ct}{l} \right) \sin \frac{n\pi x}{l}} \qquad \dots (5)$$

as a *most general solution* which may yield a solution satisfying the initial conditions.

From (3) : $u(x, 0) = f(x)$, (5) becomes $u(x, 0) = f(x) = \sum\limits_{n=1}^{\infty} (A_n) \cdot \sin \frac{n\pi x}{l}$, $0 < x < l$.

We must choose A_n so that $u(x, 0)$ becomes the half range Fourier sine series of f(x).

$$\therefore \qquad \boxed{A_n = \frac{2}{l} \int_0^l f(x) \sin \frac{n\pi x}{l}\, dx}$$

To determine B_n, we have

$$\frac{\partial u}{\partial t} = \sum_{n=1}^{\infty} \left(-\frac{n\pi c}{l} A_n \sin \frac{n\pi ct}{l} + \frac{n\pi c}{l} B_n \cos \frac{n\pi ct}{l} \right) \sin \frac{n\pi x}{l}$$

From (3), $\left(\dfrac{\partial u}{\partial t} \right)_{t=0} = g(x)$.

$$g(x) = \sum_{n=1}^{\infty} \left(\frac{n\pi c}{l} B_n \right) \sin \frac{n\pi x}{l}$$

We must choose B_n so that $\left(\dfrac{\partial u}{\partial t} \right)_{t=0}$ becomes the half range Fourier sine series of g(x).

$$\therefore \qquad \frac{n\pi c}{l} B_n = \frac{2}{l} \int_0^l g(x) \cdot \sin \frac{n\pi x}{l}\, dx$$

$$\therefore \qquad \boxed{B_n = \frac{2}{n\pi c} \int_0^l g(x) \cdot \sin \frac{n\pi x}{l}\, dx}$$

Substituting values of A_n and B_n in (5), we get the required solution.

Result : Our discussion shows that u (x, t) given by (5) with coefficients A_n and B_n is a solution of (1) that satisfies all the conditions (2) and (3) of our problem, provided the series (5) converges.

Summary : To solve the one-dimensional wave equation,

$$\frac{\partial^2 u}{\partial t^2} = c^2 \frac{\partial^2 u}{\partial x^2} \quad \text{subject to the conditions}$$

1. $\qquad u (0, t) = 0$ $\left.\phantom{\begin{matrix}a\\b\end{matrix}}\right\}$ Boundary conditions

2. $\qquad u (l, t) = 0$

3. $\qquad u (x, 0) = f (x)$ $\left.\phantom{\begin{matrix}a\\b\end{matrix}}\right\}$ Initial conditions

4. $\qquad \left(\dfrac{\partial u}{\partial t}\right)_{t = 0} = g (x)$

The most general solution is given by

$$\boxed{u (x, t) = (c_1 \cos mx + c_2 \sin mx)\ (c_3 \cos cmt + c_4 \sin cmt)} \qquad \text{...(6)}$$

In obtaining solutions of the problems on vibration of tightly stretched string, we should directly assume the solution given in (6).

ILLUSTRATIONS

Ex. 1 : *If* $\dfrac{\partial^2 y}{\partial t^2} = c^2 \dfrac{\partial^2 y}{\partial x^2}$ *represents the vibrations of a string of length l fixed at both ends, find the solution with boundary conditions,*

(i) $y (0, t) = 0,$

(ii) $y (l, t) = 0$

and initial conditions,

(iii) $\left(\dfrac{\partial y}{\partial t}\right)_{t = 0} = 0$

(iv) $y (x, 0) = k (l x - x^2),\ 0 \leq x \leq l.$

Sol. : Given $\dfrac{\partial^2 y}{\partial t^2} = c^2 \dfrac{\partial^2 y}{\partial x^2}$. The most general solution is given by

$$y (x, t) = (c_1 \cos mx + c_2 \sin mx)\ (c_3 \cos cmt + c_4 \sin cmt)$$

Applying condition (i), $y (0, t) = 0,$

$$0 = [c_1 (1) + c_2 (0)]\ [c_3 \cos cmt + c_4 \sin cmt] \qquad \therefore \boxed{c_1 = 0}$$

$$\therefore \qquad y (x, t) = (c_2 \sin mx)\ [c_3 \cos cmt + c_4 \sin cmt]$$

To apply condition (iii), $\left(\dfrac{\partial y}{\partial t}\right)_{t=0} = 0$, we first obtain $\dfrac{\partial y}{\partial t}$.

$$\therefore \quad \frac{\partial y}{\partial t} = (c_2 \sin mx) \ [-cm \, c_3 \sin cmt + cm \, c_4 \cos cmt]$$

$$0 = (c_2 \sin mx) \ [0 + cm \, c_4]$$

Here, $\quad c_2 \neq 0, \quad \sin mx \neq 0 \quad \therefore \boxed{c_4 = 0}$

The most general solution will be

$$y(x, t) = (c_2 \sin mx) \ (c_3 \cos cmt)$$

$$y(x, t) = c_5 \sin mx \ \cos cmt \qquad \qquad \ldots (1)$$

Applying condition (ii), $y(l, t) = 0$

$$0 = c_5 \ \sin ml \cdot \cos cmt$$

Now, $\qquad c_5 \neq 0 \qquad$ (otherwise $y(x, t) = 0$ will become trivial solution.)

$$\cos cmt \neq 0$$

$\therefore \qquad \sin ml = 0 \Rightarrow ml = n\pi, \qquad \therefore \ m = \dfrac{n\pi}{l}, \ n = 1, 2, 3 \ldots\ldots\ldots$

$\therefore \quad$ Solution (1) becomes

$$y(x, t) = c_5 \ \sin \frac{n\pi x}{l} \ \cos \frac{n\pi ct}{l}, \ n = 1, 2, \ldots\ldots$$

Combining all these solutions, we get

$$\boxed{y(x, t) = \sum_{n=1}^{\infty} b_n \ \sin \frac{n\pi x}{l} \ \cos \frac{n\pi ct}{l}} \qquad \ldots (2)$$

Applying condition (iv),

$$y(x, 0) = k(lx - x^2), \ 0 \le x \le l$$

$$k(lx - x^2) = \sum_{n=1}^{\infty} b_n \ \sin \frac{n\pi x}{l}, \ 0 \le x \le l$$

This is Fourier's half range sine series for $f(x) = k(lx - x^2)$ in $0 \le x \le l$.

$$b_n = \frac{2}{l} \int_0^l f(x) \ \sin \frac{n\pi x}{l} \ dx = \frac{2}{l} \int_0^l k(lx - x^2) \ \sin \frac{n\pi x}{l} \ dx$$

$$= \frac{2k}{l} \left\{ (lx - x^2) \left(-\frac{l}{n\pi} \cos \frac{n\pi x}{l}\right) - (l - 2x) \left(-\frac{l^2}{n^2 \pi^2} \sin \frac{n\pi x}{l}\right) \right.$$

$$\left. + (-2) \left(\frac{l^3}{n^3 \pi^3} \cos \frac{n\pi x}{l}\right) \right\}_0^l$$

$$= \frac{2k}{l} \left(-\frac{2 \, l^3}{n^3 \pi^3}\right) \left[\cos \frac{n\pi x}{l}\right]_0^l$$

$$b_n = \frac{4\,k\,l^2}{\pi^3}\left(\frac{1-(-1)^n}{n^3}\right)$$

Substituting in (2), we get the required most general solution.

$$y\,(x,\,t) = \frac{4\,k\,l^2}{\pi^3}\sum_{n=1}^{\infty}\left(\frac{1-(-1)^n}{n^3}\right)\,\sin\frac{n\pi x}{l}\,\cos\frac{n\pi ct}{l} \qquad \textbf{... Ans.}$$

Note : $\qquad 1-(-1)^n = 2$; if n is odd

$$\qquad\qquad\qquad\quad = 0$; if n is even$$

$\therefore$ The above solution can be written as

$$y\,(x,\,t) = \frac{4\,k\,l^2}{\pi^3}\left\{\frac{2}{1^3}\,\sin\frac{\pi x}{l}\,\cos\frac{\pi ct}{l}+0+\frac{2}{3^3}\,\sin\frac{3\pi x}{l}\,\cos\frac{3\pi ct}{l}+0+\right.$$

$$\left.+\frac{2}{5^3}\,\sin\frac{5\pi x}{l}\,\cos\frac{5\pi ct}{l}+\,.........\right\}$$

$$y\,(x,\,t) = \frac{4\,k\,l^2}{\pi^3}\sum_{n=1}^{\infty}\frac{2}{(2n-1)^3}\,\sin\frac{(2n-1)\,\pi x}{l}\,\cos\frac{(2n-1)\,\pi ct}{l}$$

$$\boxed{\,y\,(x,\,t) = \frac{8\,k\,l^2}{\pi^3}\sum_{n=1}^{\infty}\frac{1}{(2n-1)^3}\,\sin\frac{(2n-1)\,\pi x}{l}\,\cos\frac{(2n-1)\,\pi ct}{l}\,}$$

Ex. 2 : *A string is stretched and fastened to two points l apart. Motion is started by displacing the string in the form $u = a\,\sin\dfrac{\pi x}{l}$ from which it is released at time $t = 0$. Find the displacement $u\,(x,\,t)$ from one end. $\left(Use\ wave\ equation\ \dfrac{\partial^2 u}{\partial t^2} = c^2\cdot\dfrac{\partial^2 u}{\partial x^2}\right).$*

Sol. : Given $\dfrac{\partial^2 u}{\partial t^2} = c^2\,\dfrac{\partial^2 u}{\partial x^2}$

Subject to the conditions

(i) $\quad u\,(0,\,t) = 0,\ \forall\,t$

(ii) $\quad u\,(l,\,t) = 0,\ \forall\,t$

(iii) $\left(\dfrac{\partial u}{\partial t}\right)_{t=0} = 0$

(iv) $\quad u\,(x,\,0) = a\,\sin\dfrac{\pi x}{l}$

The general solution is

$$u\,(x,\,t) = (c_1\cos mx + c_2\sin mx)\,(c_3\cos cmt + c_4\sin cmt)$$

Condition (i) $\Rightarrow c_1 = 0$

Condition (iii) $\Rightarrow c_4 = 0.$

$\therefore$ Solution becomes

$$u\,(x, t) = (c_2 \sin mx)\,(c_3 \cos cmt)$$

$$u\,(x, t) = c_5 \sin mx \cos cmt \qquad \qquad \qquad \text{... (1)}$$

Applying condition (ii), we get,

$$0 = c_5 \sin ml \cos cmt$$

$$c_5 \neq 0, \quad \cos cmt \neq 0 \qquad \therefore \ \sin ml = 0$$

$$ml = n\pi \qquad \qquad \therefore \ m = \frac{n\pi}{l},\ n = 1, 2, 3, ...$$

$\therefore$ Substituting in (1), we get

$$u\,(x, t) = c_5 \sin \frac{n\pi x}{l} \cos \frac{n\pi ct}{l},\ n = 1, 2, 3 ....$$

Combining these solutions, we get,

$$\boxed{u\,(x, t) = \sum_{n=1}^{\infty} b_n \sin \frac{n\pi x}{l} \cos \frac{n\pi ct}{l}} \qquad \qquad \text{... (2)}$$

Applying condition (iv), we get

$$u\,(x, 0) = a \sin \frac{\pi x}{l}$$

$$a \sin \frac{\pi x}{l} = \sum_{n=1}^{\infty} b_n \sin \frac{n\pi x}{l}$$

$$a \sin \frac{\pi x}{l} = b_1 \sin \frac{\pi x}{l} + b_2 \sin \frac{2\pi x}{l} + ...$$

$\therefore \ b_1 = a,\ b_2 = 0 = b_3 = ... = b_n = ...$

$\therefore$ (2) will become

$$u\,(x, t) = b_1 \sin \frac{\pi x}{l} \cos \frac{\pi ct}{l} + b_2 \sin \frac{2\pi x}{l} \cos \frac{2\pi ct}{l} + ...$$

$$\boxed{u\,(x, t) = a \sin \frac{\pi x}{l} \cos \frac{\pi ct}{l}}$$

which is the required general solution.

Ex. 3 : *A string is stretched tightly between $x = 0$, $x = l$ and both ends are given displacement $y = a \sin pt$ perpendicular to the string. If the string satisfies the differential equation $\dfrac{\partial^2 y}{\partial x^2} = \dfrac{1}{c^2} \dfrac{\partial^2 y}{\partial t^2}$, prove that the oscillations of the string are given by*

$$y = a\ \sec \frac{pl}{2c} \cos \left(\frac{px}{c} - \frac{pl}{2c} \right)\ \sin pt.$$

Sol. : We have the G.S.,

$$y = (c_1 \cos mx + c_2 \sin mx)(c_3 \cos cmt + c_4 \sin cmt) \qquad \ldots \text{(i)}$$

The condition $y = a \sin pt$ for $x = 0$ gives

$$a \sin pt = c_1(c_3 \cos cmt + c_4 \sin cmt)$$

This implies that $c_1 c_3 = 0$ $\qquad\qquad\qquad\qquad\qquad$ ... (ii)

$$c_1 c_4 = a \qquad\qquad\qquad\qquad \ldots \text{(iii)}$$

and $\quad cm = p$ $\qquad\qquad\qquad\qquad\qquad$ ... (iv)

From (ii), (iii), $c_3 = 0$ and from (iv), $m = \dfrac{p}{c}$

Substituting in (i), we get

$$y = \left(c_1 \cos \frac{px}{c} + c_2 \sin \frac{px}{c}\right) \cdot c_4 \, \sin pt$$

$$= \left(c_1 c_4 \cos \frac{px}{c} + c_2 c_4 \sin \frac{px}{c}\right) \sin pt$$

$$\Rightarrow \qquad y = \left(a \cos \frac{px}{c} + c_2 c_4 \sin \frac{px}{c}\right) \sin pt \qquad \ldots \text{(v)}$$

The condition $\qquad y = a \sin pt$ for $x = l$ gives

$$\boxed{a \sin pt = \left(a \cos \frac{pl}{c} + c_2 c_4 \sin \frac{pl}{c}\right) \sin pt}$$

$$\Rightarrow a\left(1 - \cos \frac{pl}{c}\right) = c_2 c_4 \sin \frac{pl}{c}$$

$$\Rightarrow \qquad c_2 c_4 = a \cdot \frac{2 \sin^2 \dfrac{pl}{2c}}{2 \sin \dfrac{pl}{2c} \cos \dfrac{pl}{2c}} = a \cdot \frac{\sin \dfrac{pl}{2c}}{\cos \dfrac{pl}{2c}}$$

Substituting in (v), we get

$$y = \left(a \cos \frac{px}{c} + a \, \frac{\sin \dfrac{pl}{2c}}{\cos \dfrac{pl}{2c}} \sin \frac{px}{c}\right) \sin pt$$

$$= a \cdot \frac{\cos \dfrac{px}{c} \cos \dfrac{pl}{2c} + \sin \dfrac{px}{c} \sin \dfrac{pl}{2c}}{\cos \dfrac{pl}{2c}} \sin pt$$

$$\Rightarrow \qquad \boxed{y = a \sec \frac{pl}{2c} \cos \left(\frac{px}{c} - \frac{pl}{2c}\right) \sin pt.}$$

Ex. 4 : *A tightly stretched string with fixed end points $x = 0$ and $x = l$ is initially in a position given by $y(x, 0) = y_o \sin^3\left(\dfrac{\pi x}{l}\right)$. If it is released from rest from this position, find the displacement y at any distance x from one end and at any time t.*

Sol. : The differential equation satisfied by y is $\dfrac{\partial^2 y}{\partial t^2} = c^2 \dfrac{\partial^2 y}{\partial x^2}$. The initial and boundary conditions are given by :

(i) $y(0, t) = 0$, (ii) $y(l, t) = 0$, (iii) $\left(\dfrac{\partial y}{\partial t}\right)_{t=0} = 0$,

(iv) $y(x, 0) = y_o \sin^3\left(\dfrac{\pi x}{l}\right)$

The most general solution is given by :

$$y(x, t) = (c_1 \cos mx + c_2 \sin mx)(c_3 \cos cmt + c_4 \sin cmt)$$

Condition (i) $\Rightarrow$ $c_1 = 0$

Condition (iii) $\Rightarrow$ $c_4 = 0$

$\therefore$ The most general solution will become

$$\boxed{y(x, t) = c_5 \sin mx \cdot \cos cmt} \qquad \text{... (I)}$$

Condition (ii) $\Rightarrow$ $0 = c_5 \sin ml \cdot \cos cmt$

$\therefore$ $\sin ml = 0$, $ml = n\pi$

$\therefore$ $m = \dfrac{n\pi}{l}$, $n = 1, 2, \ldots\ldots$

$\therefore$ Solution (I) becomes :

$$y(x, t) = c_5 \sin\frac{n\pi x}{l} \cos\frac{n\pi ct}{l}, \; n = 1, 2, \ldots\ldots$$

Combining all these solutions, we get

$$\boxed{y(x, t) = \sum_{n=1}^{\infty} b_n \sin\frac{n\pi x}{l} \cos\frac{n\pi ct}{l}} \qquad \text{... (II)}$$

Applying condition (iv),

$$y(x, 0) = y_o \sin^3\frac{\pi x}{l} = \frac{3y_o}{4}\sin\frac{\pi x}{l} - \frac{y_o}{4}\sin\frac{3\pi x}{l}$$

$$\left(\text{by using}\quad \sin^3\theta = \frac{3}{4}\sin\theta - \frac{1}{4}\sin 3\theta\right)$$

$\therefore$

$$y_o \sin^3\frac{\pi x}{l} = \sum_{n=1}^{\infty} b_n \sin\frac{n\pi x}{l}$$

$$\frac{3y_o}{4}\sin\frac{\pi x}{l} - \frac{y_o}{4}\sin\frac{3\pi x}{l}$$

$$= b_1 \sin\frac{\pi x}{l} + b_2 \sin\frac{2\pi x}{l} + b_3 \sin\frac{3\pi x}{l} + \ldots$$

Comparing we get, $b_1 = \dfrac{3\,y_o}{4}$; $b_2 = 0$; $b_3 = -\dfrac{y_o}{4}$; $b_4 = 0 = b_5 = b_6 = \ldots = b_n = \ldots$

Substituting in (II), we get,

$$y\,(x,\,t) \;=\; b_1 \sin\frac{\pi x}{l}\cos\frac{\pi ct}{l} + b_2 \sin\frac{2\pi x}{l}\cos\frac{2\pi ct}{l} + b_3 \sin\frac{3\pi x}{l}\cos\frac{3\pi ct}{l} + \ldots\ldots$$

$$\boxed{\,y\,(x,\,t) \;=\; \frac{3\,y_o}{4}\sin\frac{\pi x}{l}\cos\frac{\pi ct}{l} - \frac{y_o}{4}\sin\frac{3\pi x}{l}\cos\frac{3\pi ct}{l}\,}$$

Ex. 5 : *An elastic string is stretched between two fixed points at a distance l apart, one end is taken at the origin and at a distance $\dfrac{2l}{3}$ from this end the string is displaced a distance "a" transversely and is released from rest when in this position. Find y (x, t), if y satisfies the equation $\dfrac{\partial^2 y}{\partial t^2} = c^2\,\dfrac{\partial^2 y}{\partial x^2}$.*

Sol. :   Slope of OB $= \dfrac{a}{2\,l/3} = \dfrac{3a}{2l}$

Equation of OB is $y = \dfrac{3a}{2l}\,x$

Slope of BA $= \dfrac{a-0}{\dfrac{2l}{3} - l} = -\dfrac{3a}{l}$

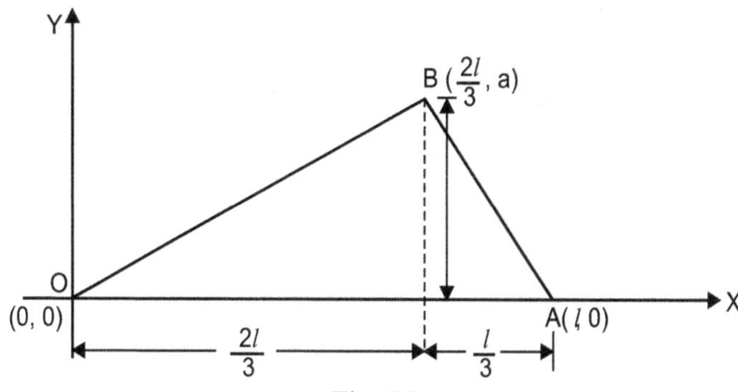

Fig. 6.2

Equation of BA is $y - 0 = -\dfrac{3a}{l}\,(x - l)$

$\therefore$ $y = \dfrac{3a}{l}\,(l - x)$

We have to solve $\dfrac{\partial^2 y}{\partial t^2} = c^2\,\dfrac{\partial^2 y}{\partial x^2}$

The boundary conditions are

(i) $y\,(0,\,t) = 0$

(ii) $y\,(l,\,t) = 0$

Initial conditions are

(iii) $\left(\dfrac{\partial y}{\partial t}\right)_{t=0} = 0$

(iv) $y(x, 0) = \dfrac{3a}{2l}\, x, \qquad 0 \le x \le \dfrac{2l}{3}$

$\qquad\qquad = \dfrac{3a}{l}\,(l - x), \qquad \dfrac{2l}{3} \le x \le l$

The most general solution is

$$y(x, t) = (c_1 \cos mx + c_2 \sin mx)\,(c_3 \cos cmt + c_4 \sin cmt)$$

Condition (i) $\quad\Rightarrow\quad c_1 = 0$

Condition (iii) $\quad\Rightarrow\quad c_4 = 0$

$\therefore$ $\qquad\boxed{y(x, t) = c_5 \sin mx \, \cos cmt}$ $\qquad\qquad$ ... (I)

Condition (ii) $\quad\Rightarrow\quad 0 = c_5 \sin ml \, \cos cmt$

$$\sin ml = 0, \ ml = n\pi \quad \therefore \quad m = \dfrac{n\pi}{l},\ n = 1, 2, \ldots\ldots$$

$$y(x, t) = c_5 \sin\dfrac{n\pi x}{l}\, \cos\dfrac{n\pi ct}{l},\ n = 1,\ 2,\ \ldots\ldots$$

Combining all these solutions, we get

$$\boxed{y(x, t) = \sum_{n=1}^{\infty} b_n \sin\dfrac{n\pi x}{l}\, \cos\dfrac{n\pi ct}{l}}$$ $\qquad$ ... (II)

Applying condition (iv), we have

$$y(x, 0) = \sum_{n=1}^{\infty} b_n \sin\dfrac{n\pi x}{l},\ \text{where}$$

$$f(x) = y(x, 0) = \dfrac{3a}{2l}\, x, \qquad 0 \le x \le \dfrac{2l}{3}$$

$$= \dfrac{3a}{l}\,(l - x), \qquad \dfrac{2l}{3} \le x \le l$$

$\therefore$ $\qquad b_n = \dfrac{2}{l} \displaystyle\int_0^l f(x) \sin\dfrac{n\pi x}{l}\, dx$

$$= \dfrac{2}{l}\left\{ \int_0^{\frac{2l}{3}} \dfrac{3ax}{2l} \sin\dfrac{n\pi x}{l}\, dx + \int_{\frac{2l}{3}}^{l} \dfrac{3a}{l}\,(l - x) \sin\dfrac{n\pi x}{l}\, dx \right\}$$

$$= \frac{6a}{l^2} \left\{ \left[\left(\frac{x}{2}\right)\left(-\frac{l}{n\pi}\cos\frac{n\pi x}{l}\right) - \left(\frac{1}{2}\right)\left(-\frac{l^2}{n^2\pi^2}\sin\frac{n\pi x}{l}\right) \right]_0^{\frac{2l}{3}} \right.$$

$$\left. + \left[(l-x)\left(-\frac{l}{n\pi}\cos\frac{n\pi x}{l}\right) - (-1)\left(-\frac{l^2}{n^2\pi^2}\sin\frac{n\pi x}{l}\right) \right]_{\frac{2l}{3}}^{l} \right\}$$

$$= \frac{6a}{l^2} \left\{ -\frac{l^2}{3n\pi}\cos\frac{2n\pi}{3} + \frac{l^2}{2n^2\pi^2}\sin\frac{2n\pi}{3} + \frac{l^2}{3n\pi}\cos\frac{2n\pi}{3} + \frac{l^2}{n^2\pi^2}\sin\frac{2n\pi}{3} \right\}$$

$$= \frac{6a}{l^2} \left(\frac{3}{2}\frac{l^2}{n^2\pi^2}\sin\frac{2n\pi}{3} \right) = \frac{9a}{\pi^2}\frac{1}{n^2}\sin\frac{2n\pi}{3}$$

$\therefore$ Substituting in (II), we get,

$$\boxed{y\,(x,\,t) \;=\; \frac{9a}{\pi^2}\sum_{n=1}^{\infty}\frac{1}{n^2}\sin\frac{2n\pi}{3}\sin\frac{n\pi x}{l}\cos\frac{n\pi ct}{l}}$$

EXERCISE 6.1

1. A taut string of a length $2l$ is fastened at both ends. The mid point of the string is taken to a height b and then released from rest in that position. Obtain the displacement.

Hint : B.C. : (i) $\left(\dfrac{\partial y}{\partial t}\right)_{t=0} = 0$, (ii) $y\,(2l,\,t) = 0$, Use $\dfrac{\partial^2 y}{\partial t^2} = c^2\dfrac{\partial^2 y}{\partial x^2}$

I.C. : (iii) $y\,(0,\,t) = 0$; (iv) $y\,(x,\,0) = \begin{cases} \dfrac{bx}{l},\; 0 \le x \le l \\[2mm] \dfrac{b}{l}(2x-x),\; l \le x \le 2l \end{cases}$

The most GS is $y(x,\,t) = (c_1\cos mx + c_2\sin mx)(c_3\cos cmt + c_4\sin cmt)$

and use formula for $b_n = \dfrac{2}{2l}\displaystyle\int_0^{2l} f(x)\sin\frac{n\pi x}{2l}\,dx = \dfrac{8b}{n^2\pi^2}\sin\frac{n\pi}{2}$.

$$\textbf{Ans. :}\;\; y\,(x,\,t) = \frac{8b}{\pi^2}\sum_{n=1}^{\infty}\frac{1}{n^2}\sin\frac{n\pi}{2}\sin\frac{n\pi x}{2l}\cos\left(\frac{n\pi ct}{2l}\right)$$

2. If a string of length l is initially at rest in its equilibrium position and each of its point is given a velocity $v\,(x)$ such that

$$v\,(x) = \begin{cases} cx, & 0 < x \le \dfrac{l}{2} \\[2mm] c\,(l-x), & \dfrac{l}{2} \le x \le l \end{cases}$$

Obtain the displacement $y\,(x,\,t)$ at any time t.

Hint : B.C. : (i) $y\,(0,\,t) = 0$, (ii) $y\,(l,\,t) = 0$, Use $\dfrac{\partial^2 y}{\partial t^2} = a^2\dfrac{\partial^2 y}{\partial x^2}$

(iii) I.C. : $\left(\dfrac{\partial y}{\partial t}\right)_{t=0} = \begin{cases} cx, & 0 \le x \le \dfrac{l}{2} \\[2mm] c\,(l-x), & \dfrac{l}{2} \le x \le l \end{cases}$,   (iv) $y(x, 0) = 0$

and use $b_n = \dfrac{2}{l} \displaystyle\int_0^l f(x) \sin \dfrac{n\pi x}{l}\, dx = \dfrac{4cl}{n^2\,\pi^2} \sin \dfrac{n\pi}{2}$.

Ans. : $y(x, t) = \dfrac{4\,c\,l^2}{a\,\pi^3} \displaystyle\sum_{n=1}^{\infty} \dfrac{1}{n^3} \sin \dfrac{n\pi}{2} \sin \dfrac{n\pi x}{l} \sin \dfrac{n\pi a t}{l}$

3. A tightly stretched string with fixed ends $x = 0$ and $x = l$ is initially at rest in its equilibrium position. If it is set vibrating giving each point a velocity $3x\,(l-x)$ for $0 < x < l$, find the displacement.

Hint : BC. : (i) $y(0, t) = 0$, (ii) $y(l, t) = 0$;

I.C. : (iii) $\left(\dfrac{\partial y}{\partial t}\right)_{t=0} = 3x\,(l-x)$, (iv) $y(x, 0) = 0$.

and use $b_n = \dfrac{2}{l} \displaystyle\int_0^l f(x) \sin \dfrac{n\pi x}{l}\, dx = \dfrac{12l^2}{n^3\,\pi^3}\,(1 - \cos n\pi)$

Ans. : $y(x, t) = \dfrac{24\,l^3}{\pi^4\,c} \displaystyle\sum_{n=1}^{\infty} \dfrac{1}{(2n-1)^4} \sin \dfrac{(2n-1)\,\pi x}{l} \sin \dfrac{(2n-1)\,\pi c t}{l}$

4. Work exercise 3, given that velocity is $v_o \sin^3 \dfrac{\pi x}{l}$, $0 \le x \le l$

Ans. : $y(x, t) = \dfrac{3v_o\, l}{4\pi c} \left[\sin \dfrac{\pi x}{l} \sin \dfrac{\pi c t}{l} - \dfrac{1}{9} \sin \dfrac{3\pi x}{l} \sin \dfrac{3\pi c t}{l} \right]$

5. A string is stretched and fastened to two points distance l apart is displaced into the form $y(x, 0) = 3\,(lx - x^2)$ from which it is released at $t = 0$. Find the displacement of the string at a distance x from one end.

Hint : B.C. : (i) $y(0, t) = 0$, (ii) $y(l, t) = 0$,

I.C. : (iii) $\left(\dfrac{\partial y}{\partial t}\right)_{t=0} = 0$, (iv) $y(x, 0) = 3\,(lx - x^2)$

and $b_n = \dfrac{2}{l} \displaystyle\int_0^l f(x) \sin \dfrac{n\pi x}{l}\, dx = \dfrac{18l^2}{n^3\,\pi^3}\,(1 - \cos n\pi)$

Ans. : $\dfrac{24l^2}{\pi^3} \displaystyle\sum_{n=1}^{\infty} \dfrac{1}{(2n-1)^3} \sin \dfrac{(2n-1)\,\pi x}{l} \cos \dfrac{(2n-1)\,\pi c t}{l}$

6. Work exercise 5, given that $l = 40$ and $y(x, 0) = 40x - x^2$, $0 \leq x \leq 40$.

$$\textbf{Ans.:} \quad y(x, t) = \frac{12800}{\pi^3} \sum_{n=1}^{\infty} \frac{1}{(2n-1)^3} \sin \frac{(2n-1)\pi x}{40} \cos \frac{(2n-1)\pi ct}{40}$$

7. An elastic string is stretched between two points at a distance l apart. One end is taken as origin and point $x = \dfrac{2l}{3}$ is displaced through distance "d" perpendicular to x-axis and released from rest from this position. Obtain the displacement.

Hint : B.C. : (i) $y(0, t) = 0$, (ii) $y(l, t) = 0$,

I.C. : (iii) $\left(\dfrac{\partial y}{\partial t}\right)_{t=0} = 0$,

(iv) $y(x, 0) = \begin{cases} \dfrac{3d}{2l}\, x, & 0 \leq x \leq \dfrac{2l}{3} \\[2mm] \dfrac{3d}{l}\,(l - x), & \dfrac{2l}{3} \leq x \leq l \end{cases}$

$$\textbf{Ans.:} \quad \frac{9d}{\pi^2} \sum_{n=1}^{\infty} \frac{1}{n^2} \sin \frac{2n\pi}{3} \sin \frac{n\pi x}{l} \cos \frac{n\pi ct}{l}$$

8. Work exercise 5, given that $y(x, 0) = y_0 \sin \dfrac{\pi x}{l}$

Hint : $b_1 = y_0$, $b_2 = b_3 = \ldots\ldots = 0$.

$$\textbf{Ans.:} \quad y(x, t) = y_0 \sin \frac{\pi x}{l} \cos \frac{\pi at}{l}$$

9. The points of trisection of a tightly stretched string of length l with fixed ends are pulled aside through a distance d on opposite sides of the position of equilibrium and the string is released from rest. Obtain the displacement of the string and show that mid-point always remains at rest.

$$\textbf{Ans.:} \quad y(x, t) = \frac{9d}{\pi^2} \sum_{n=1}^{\infty} \frac{1}{n^2} \sin \frac{2n\pi}{3} \sin \frac{2n\pi x}{l} \cos \frac{2n\pi at}{l}$$

$$\text{when } x = \frac{l}{2}, \ y\left(\frac{l}{2}, t\right) = 0 \text{ for all } t.$$

10. Work exercise 7, given that $x = \dfrac{3}{4}\, l$.

Hint : B.C. : (i) $y(0, t) = 0$, (ii) $y(l, t) = 0$,

I.C. : (iii) $\left(\dfrac{\partial y}{\partial t}\right)_{t=0} = 0$,

(iv) $y(x, 0) = \begin{cases} \dfrac{4d}{3l}\, x, & 0 \leq x \leq \dfrac{3l}{4} \\[2mm] \dfrac{4d}{l}\,(l - x), & \dfrac{3l}{4} \leq x \leq l \end{cases}$

$$\textbf{Ans.:} \quad y(x, t) = \frac{32\, d}{3\pi^2} \sum_{n=1}^{\infty} \frac{1}{n^2} \sin \frac{3n\pi}{4} \sin \frac{n\pi x}{l} \cos \frac{n\pi at}{l}$$

11. A uniform string stretched between the points $x = 0$ and $x = l$ is given the initial displacement $y(x, 0) = \sin\dfrac{\pi x}{l}$, $0 < x < l$ and initial velocity,

$$v(x) = \begin{cases} 0, & 0 < x < \dfrac{l}{4} \\[2mm] a, & \dfrac{l}{4} < x < \dfrac{3l}{4} \\[2mm] 0, & \dfrac{3l}{4} < x < l \end{cases}$$

Find subsequent displacement.

Ans. : $y(x, t) = \sin\dfrac{\pi x}{l} \cos\dfrac{\pi at}{l} + \dfrac{4l}{\pi^2} \sum_{n=1}^{\infty} \dfrac{1}{n^2} \sin\dfrac{n\pi}{2} \sin\dfrac{n\pi}{4} \sin\dfrac{n\pi x}{l} \sin\dfrac{n\pi at}{l}$

12. A string of length l fixed at its ends satisfies the wave equation $\dfrac{\partial^2 y}{\partial t^2} = c^2 \dfrac{\partial^2 y}{\partial x^2}$.

Find the solution if the string has initial triangular deflection given by :

$$y(x, 0) = \begin{cases} \dfrac{2k}{l} x, & 0 \le x \le \dfrac{l}{2} \\[3mm] \dfrac{2k}{l}(l - x), & \dfrac{l}{2} \le x \le l \end{cases}$$

and initial velocity zero.

Ans. : $y(x, t) = \dfrac{8k}{\pi^2} \sum_{1}^{\infty} \dfrac{(-1)^{n+1}}{(2n-1)^2} \sin\dfrac{(2n-1)\pi x}{l} \cos\dfrac{(2n-1)\pi ct}{l}$

13. Find the deflection $u(x, t)$ of a vibrating string $\left(\text{length } l = \pi, \text{ ends fixed and } c^2 = \dfrac{T}{\rho} = 1\right)$ corresponding to zero velocity and initial deflection $0.01(\pi - x)$.

Ans. : $u(x, t) = 0.02 \sum_{1}^{\infty} \dfrac{1}{n} \sin nx \cos nt$.

14. A flexible string of length π is tightly stretched between $x = 0$, $x = \pi$, on x-axis, its ends being fixed at these points. When set into small transverse vibration, the displacement $y(x, t)$ from x–axis of any point x at time t is given by

$$\dfrac{\partial^2 y}{\partial t^2} = 4 \dfrac{\partial^2 y}{\partial x^2}.$$

Find the solution of the equation which satisfies (i) $y(0, t) = 0$, (ii) $y(\pi, t) = 0$, (iii) $\left(\dfrac{\partial y}{\partial t}\right)_{t=0} = 0$ and (iv) $y(x, 0) = 0.1\ \sin x + 0.01 \sin 4x$ for $0 \le x \le \pi$.

Hint : $c^2 = 4$ $\therefore$ $c = 2$, $b_1 = 0.1$, $b_2 = 0$, $b_3 = 0$, $b_4 = 0.01$, $b_5 = b_6 = \dots = 0$.

Ans. : $y(x, t) = 0.1 \sin x \cos 2t + 0.01 \sin 4x \cos 8t$

6.5 MODELING OF ONE-DIMENSIONAL HEAT FLOW

Derivation of Equation :

We make use of following experimental facts or empirical laws :

(i)   Heat flows from higher temperature to lower temperature.

(ii) The rate of flow of heat through an area is proportional to the area and to the temperature gradient in degrees per unit distance $\left(\dfrac{\partial u}{\partial t}\right)$, where $u(x, t)$ is temperature distribution normal to the area. Constant of proportionality is called the *thermal conductivity* of the material and denoted generally by k.

(iii) The amount of heat required to change the temperature through a given range is proportional to the mass of the body and the change of temperature. The constant of proportionality is termed as specific heat and generally denoted by S.

Consider a homogeneous bar of uniform cross-section, sides coated with insulating material. It is assumed that the loss of heat from the sides by conduction or radiation is negligible. One end of the bar is treated as the origin and the direction of heat flow as positive X-axis. Let ρ be the density (gm/cm³), 'S' the specific heat (cal/gm deg) and 'k' the thermal conductivity (cal/cm-deg.sec). The temperature at any point of the bar depends on the distance x of the point from one end and time 't' and is denoted by $u(x, t)$ or u. Also the temperature distribution through a cross-section is same.

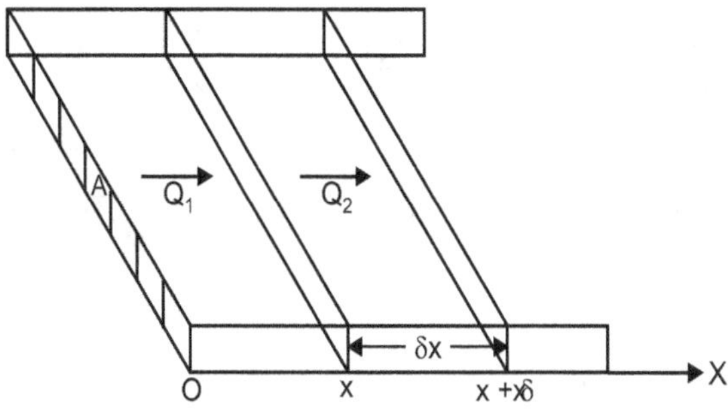

Fig. 6.3

Now, as the quantity of heat crossing any section of the bar is proportional to the area and the temperature gradient normal to the area, the quantity 'Q_1' flowing into the section at a distance x is,

$$Q_1 \;=\; -\,kA\left(\frac{\partial u}{\partial x}\right)_x$$

The quantity 'Q_2' flowing out of the section at a distance $x + \delta x$ is,

$$Q_2 \;=\; -\,kA\left(\frac{\partial u}{\partial x}\right)_{x + \delta x}$$

$\therefore$ Quantity of heat retained by the slab with thickness δx is,

$$Q_1 - Q_2 = kA \left[\left(\frac{\partial u}{\partial x} \right)_{x + \delta x} - \left(\frac{\partial u}{\partial x} \right)_{x} \right] \qquad \ldots (1)$$

But the rate of increase of heat in the slab

$$= S \rho A \delta x \frac{\partial u}{\partial t} \qquad \ldots (2)$$

$\therefore$ From equations (1) and (2),

$$S \rho A \delta x \frac{\partial u}{\partial t} = kA \left[\left(\frac{\partial u}{\partial x} \right)_{x + \delta x} - \left(\frac{\partial u}{\partial x} \right)_{x} \right]$$

$$\therefore \qquad S \rho \frac{\partial u}{\partial t} = k \left[\frac{\left(\frac{\partial u}{\partial x} \right)_{x + \delta x} - \left(\frac{\partial u}{\partial x} \right)_{x}}{\delta x} \right]$$

Taking limit as $\delta x \to 0$

$$S \rho \frac{\partial u}{\partial t} = k \lim_{\delta x \to 0} \left[\frac{\left(\frac{\partial u}{\partial x} \right)_{x + \delta x} - \left(\frac{\partial u}{\partial x} \right)_{x}}{\delta x} \right]$$

Or

$$\frac{\partial u}{\partial t} = \frac{k}{S \rho} \frac{\partial^2 u}{\partial x^2}$$

For $\dfrac{k}{S \rho} = c^2$, it reduces to $\dfrac{\partial u}{\partial t} = c^2 \dfrac{\partial^2 u}{\partial x^2}$ and is called *one-dimensional heat flow equation*. The constant $c^2 = \dfrac{k}{S \rho}$ is known as diffusivity of the material of the bar.

6.6 SOLUTION OF THE HEAT EQUATION BY METHOD OF SEPARATION OF VARIABLES

We have to obtain solution of the P.D.E.

$$\boxed{\frac{\partial u}{\partial t} = c^2 \frac{\partial^2 u}{\partial x^2}} \qquad \ldots (1)$$

Let $u(x, t) = F(x) \cdot G(t)$ be the solution. $\qquad \ldots (2)$

$$\therefore \qquad \frac{\partial u}{\partial t} = F(x) \cdot G'(t) \quad \text{and} \quad \frac{\partial^2 u}{\partial x^2} = F''(x) \cdot G(t)$$

Substituting in (1), we get

$$F(x) \cdot G'(t) = c^2 \, F''(x) \cdot G(t)$$

$$\frac{G'(t)}{c^2 \cdot G(t)} = \frac{F''(x)}{F(x)}$$

Since L.H.S. is a function of 't' alone and R.H.S. is a function of x alone, therefore both sides are independent of each other, hence can be equated to any arbitrary constant, say k.

$$\frac{G'(t)}{c^2 \cdot G(t)} = \frac{F''(x)}{F(x)} = k$$

Case (i) : Let $\quad k = 0 \Rightarrow G'(t) = 0 \quad \Rightarrow \quad G(t) = c_1$

and $\qquad F''(x) = 0 \Rightarrow F(x) = c_2 x + c_3$

$\therefore$ Complete solution is

$$u(x, t) = (c_2 x + c_3) \cdot c_1$$

Or $\qquad \boxed{u(x, t) = c_4 x + c_5}$ $\qquad$ ... (3)

Case (ii) : Let $\quad k > 0 \quad$ (say $k = m^2$)

$$\frac{F''(x)}{F(x)} = m^2 \quad \Rightarrow \quad F''(x) - m^2 F(x) = 0$$

$$\frac{d^2 F}{dx^2} - m^2 F = 0 \qquad \left(\text{Let } D \equiv \frac{d}{dx}\right)$$

$$(D^2 - m^2) F = 0 \Rightarrow F(x) = c_1 e^{mx} + c_2 e^{-mx}$$

Also, $\qquad \dfrac{G'(t)}{c^2 \cdot G(t)} = m^2$

$$\frac{G'(t)}{G(t)} = c^2 m^2 \quad \Rightarrow \quad \log G(t) = c^2 m^2 t + A$$

$\therefore \qquad\qquad G(t) = c_3 e^{c^2 m^2 t}$

Complete solution is

$$u(x, t) = \left(c_1 e^{mx} + c_2 e^{-mx}\right) c_3 \cdot e^{c^2 m^2 t}$$

Or $\qquad \boxed{u(x, t) = \left(c_4 e^{mx} + c_5 e^{-mx}\right) e^{c^2 m^2 t}}$ $\qquad$ ... (4)

Case (iii) : Let $\quad k < 0 \quad$ (say ($k = -m^2$)

$$\frac{F''(x)}{F(x)} = -m^2 \quad \Rightarrow \quad F''(x) + m^2 F(x) = 0$$

$$\frac{d^2 F}{dx^2} + m^2 F = 0 \qquad \left(\text{Let } D \equiv \frac{d}{dx}\right)$$

$$(D^2 + m^2) F = 0 \qquad \Rightarrow \quad F(x) = c_1 \cos mx + c_2 \sin mx$$

Also, $\dfrac{G'(t)}{c^2 \cdot G(t)} = -m^2 \implies \dfrac{G'(t)}{G(t)} = -c^2 m^2$

$\log G(t) = -c^2 m^2 t + A$

$G(t) = c_3 \ e^{-c^2 m^2 t}$

$\therefore$ Complete solution is

$$u(x, t) = \left(c_1 \cos mx + c_2 \sin mx\right) \ c_3 \ e^{-c^2 m^2 t}$$

Or $\boxed{u(x, t) = (c_4 \cos mx + c_5 \sin mx) \ e^{-c^2 m^2 t}}$ ... (5)

Again the question arises which solution we must adopt. In present case, we are concerned with conduction of heat from a source which has finite temperature. Naturally, the temperature u (x, t) cannot become unbounded as t increases. Naturally the solution given by (4) is therefore to be rejected and solution given by (5) is suitable in present case. Solution corresponding to k = 0 does not involve any t, hence it can be considered as steady-state solution i.e. solution when temperature no longer varies with time t.

Hence in obtaining solution of the problems of one-dimensional heat flow, we will always begin with solution given in (5) and consider solution (3) under steady-state conditions.

Note : Insulated boundary or end means no heat is flowing from it, meaning thereby $\dfrac{\partial u}{\partial x} = 0$ at that boundary or end.

ILLUSTRATIONS

Ex. 1 : *Solve* $\dfrac{\partial u}{\partial t} = \dfrac{\partial^2 u}{\partial x^2}$ *if (i) u is finite* $\forall t$, *(ii) u = 0 when x = 0, $\pi \forall t$, (iii) u = $\pi x - x^2$ when t = 0 and $0 \le x \le \pi$.*

Sol. : Given equation is $\dfrac{\partial u}{\partial t} = \dfrac{\partial^2 u}{\partial x^2}$. The boundary conditions are given as :

(i)   u (x, t) is bounded $\forall$ t

(ii)   u (0, t) = 0, $\forall$ t

(iii)   u (π, t) = 0, $\forall$ t

(iv)   u (x, 0) = $\pi x - x^2$, $0 \le x \le \pi$

The most general solution is

$\therefore$ $u(x, t) = (c_4 \cos mx + c_5 \sin mx) \ e^{-m^2 t}$ ... (1)

Applying the second condition :

$u(0, t) = 0 \implies c_4 = 0$

$\therefore$ $u(x, t) = c_5 \sin mx \ e^{-m^2 t}$

Applying the third condition u (π, t) = 0

$\implies$ $0 = c_5 \sin m\pi \ e^{-m^2 t}$

Now since $c_5 \neq 0$

　　and $e^{-m^2 t} \neq 0$ 　　$\therefore \sin m\pi = 0 \Rightarrow m\pi = n\pi$

$\therefore$ 　　$m = n$ for $n = 1, 2, 3, 4 \ldots\ldots$

$\therefore$ 　　Solution becomes $u(x, t) = c_5 \sin nx \, e^{-n^2 t}$ 　for $n = 1, 2, 3 \ldots\ldots$

Taking $n = 1, 2, 3 \ldots\ldots$ and varying the constant c_5 for each n, we see that the general solution is

$$u(x, t) = \sum_{n=1}^{\infty} b_n \sin nx \, e^{-n^2 t} \qquad\qquad \ldots (2)$$

Using aforesaid condition (iv) in (2), we get

$$\pi x - x^2 = u(x, 0) = \sum_{n=1}^{\infty} b_n \sin(nx); \quad 0 \le x \le \pi$$

In order to treat this as half range Fourier sine series of $(\pi x - x^2)$ in $0 \le x \le \pi$, b_n should be chosen as

$$b_n = \frac{2}{\pi} \int_0^{\pi} (\pi x - x^2) \sin nx \, dx$$

$$= \frac{2}{\pi} \left\{ (\pi x - x^2) \left(-\frac{\cos nx}{n} \right) - (\pi - 2x) \left(-\frac{\sin nx}{n^2} \right) + (-2) \left(\frac{\cos nx}{n^3} \right) \right\}_0^{\pi}$$

$$= \frac{4}{\pi n^3} (1 - \cos n\pi) = \begin{cases} 0, & \text{for } n \text{ even} \\ 8/\pi n^3, & \text{for } n \text{ odd} \end{cases}$$

$\therefore$ Solution (2) becomes

$$u(x, t) = \frac{4}{\pi} \sum_{n=1}^{\infty} \frac{1 - (-1)^n}{n^3} \sin(nx) \cdot e^{-n^2 t}$$

Or $u(x, t) = \dfrac{8}{\pi} \displaystyle\sum_{r=0}^{\infty} \dfrac{1}{(2r+1)^3} \sin[(2r+1)x] \cdot e^{-(2r+1)^2 t}$ which is the required

solution.

Ex. 2 : *Solve* $\dfrac{\partial V}{\partial t} = k \dfrac{\partial^2 V}{\partial x^2}$ *if*

(i) 　$V \neq \infty$ *as* $t \to \infty$ 　　　　　*(ii)* $\left(\dfrac{\partial V}{\partial x} \right)_{x=0} = 0, \ \forall t$

(iii) $V(l, t) = 0, \ \forall t$ 　　　　　*(iv)* $V(x, 0) = v_o, \ for \ 0 < x < l.$

Sol. : The most general solution is

$$V(x, t) = (c_4 \cos mx + c_5 \sin mx) \, e^{-m^2 k t}$$

$$\frac{\partial V}{\partial x} = (-m\,c_4\,\sin mx + m\,c_5\cos mx)\; e^{-m^2 k t}$$

Condition (ii) $\Rightarrow$ $c_5 = 0$

$\therefore$ $\qquad\qquad V(x, t) = c_4 \,.\, \cos mx \,.\, e^{-m^2 k t}$

Condition (iii) $\Rightarrow$ $0 = c_4 \cos ml\; e^{-m^2 k t}$

$\therefore$ $\qquad\qquad \cos ml = 0 \quad\Rightarrow\quad ml = \dfrac{n\pi}{2},\ (n\text{ is odd})$

or $\quad m = \dfrac{n\,\pi/2}{l},\ (n\text{ is odd})$ Or $m = \dfrac{(2n+1)\,\pi/2}{l},\ n = 0,\ 1,\ 2,\ \ldots\ldots$

$$V(x, t) = c_4 \cos\frac{[(2n+1)\,\pi/2]\,x}{l}\; e^{\dfrac{-[(2n+1)^2\,\pi^2/4]\,kt}{l^2}}\ ,\ n = 0, 1, 2, \ldots$$

Taking $n = 0, 1, 2, \ldots$ and combining all these solutions, we have the general solution

$$\text{as } V(x, t) = \sum_{n=0}^{\infty} a_{2n+1}\cos\frac{[(2n+1)\,\pi/2]\,x}{l}\; e^{-\dfrac{[(2n+1)^2\,\pi^2/4]\,kt}{l^2}}$$

Note : Notation a_{2n+1}, $n = 0, 1, 2, \ldots$ is used instead a_n because n is odd.

Applying condition (iv), we have

$$v_o = \sum_{n=0}^{\infty} a_{2n+1}\cos\frac{[(2n+1)\,\pi/2]\,x}{l}$$

which is nothing but half range Fourier cosine series for $f(x) = v_o$ in $(0, l)$ with $a_0 = 0$.

$$\therefore\quad a_{2n+1} = \frac{2}{l}\int_0^l v_o\cos\frac{[(2n+1)\,\pi/2]\,x}{l}\,dx = \frac{2\,v_o}{l}\left[\frac{2l}{(2n+1)\,\pi}\sin\frac{(2n+1)\,\pi x}{2l}\right]_0^l$$

$$a_{2n+1} = \frac{4\,v_o}{\pi}\,\frac{1}{(2n+1)}\sin(2n+1)\frac{\pi}{2} = \frac{4\,v_o}{\pi}\,\frac{(-1)^n}{2n+1}$$

$$\therefore\quad V(x, t) = \frac{4\,v_o}{\pi}\sum_{n=0}^{\infty}\frac{(-1)^n}{2n+1}\cos\frac{(2n+1)\,\pi x}{2l}\; e^{\dfrac{-(2n+1)^2\,\pi^2\,kt}{4l^2}}$$

Ex. 3 : *The equation for the conduction of heat along a bar of length l is* $\dfrac{\partial\theta}{\partial t} = k\,\dfrac{\partial^2\theta}{\partial x^2}$,
neglecting radiation. Find an expression for θ *if the ends of the bar are maintained at zero temperature and if initially the temperature is T at the centre of the bar and falls uniformly to zero at its ends.*

Sol. :

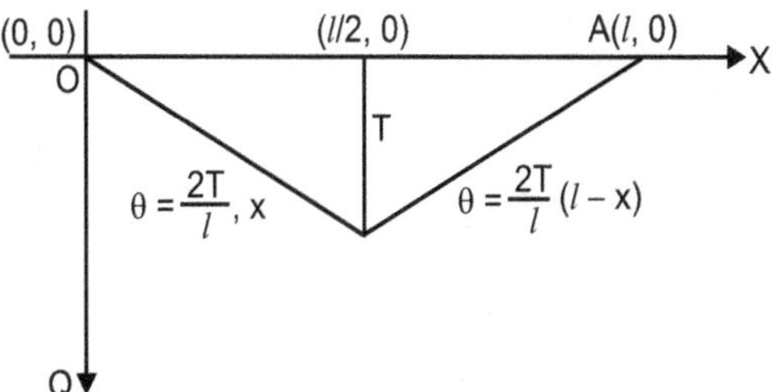

Fig. 6.4

Given equation is $\dfrac{\partial \theta}{\partial t} = k \dfrac{\partial^2 \theta}{\partial x^2}$ and the boundary condition is given as :

(i) $\theta(0, t) = 0$

(ii) $\theta(l, t) = 0$

(iii) $\theta(x, 0) = \dfrac{2T}{l} x$ for $0 \le x \le \dfrac{l}{2}$

$\qquad\qquad = \dfrac{2T}{l}(l - x)$ for $\dfrac{l}{2} \le x \le l$

The most general solution is

$$\theta(x, t) = (c_4 \cos mx + c_5 \sin mx)\, e^{-k m^2 t} \qquad \dots (1)$$

Applying condition (i), $\theta(0, t) = 0 \Rightarrow c_4 = 0$

$\therefore \qquad \theta(x, t) = c_5 \sin mx\, e^{-k m^2 t}$

Applying second condition, $\theta(l, t) = 0$

$\Rightarrow \qquad \sin ml = 0 \Rightarrow ml = n\pi$

i.e. $\qquad m = \dfrac{n\pi}{l}$ for $n = 1, 2, 3, \dots\dots\dots$

$\therefore$ Solution becomes

$$\theta(x, t) = c_5 \sin \dfrac{n\pi x}{l}\, e^{\frac{-k n^2 \pi^2 t}{l^2}}$$

Putting $n = 1, 2, 3 \dots\dots\dots$ and varying constant c_5 for each n, we have the general solution as

$$\theta(x, t) = \sum_{n=1}^{\infty} b_n \, \dfrac{n\pi x}{l}\, e^{\frac{-k n^2 \pi^2 t}{l^2}} \qquad \dots (2)$$

Applying the last condition, at $t = 0$

$$\theta = \sum_{n=1}^{\infty} b_n \sin \dfrac{n\pi x}{l}$$

where $b_n = \dfrac{2}{l} \displaystyle\int_0^l \theta \cdot \sin \dfrac{n\pi x}{l}\, dx$

$$= \dfrac{2}{l} \left[\int_0^{l/2} \dfrac{2T}{l}\, x\, \sin \dfrac{n\pi x}{l}\, dx + \int_{l/2}^{l} \dfrac{2T}{l}\, (l-x) \sin \dfrac{n\pi x}{l}\, dx \right]$$

$$= \dfrac{4T}{l^2} \left[\left\{ (x) \left(-\dfrac{l}{n\pi} \cos \dfrac{n\pi x}{l} \right) + \dfrac{l^2}{n^2\pi^2} \sin \dfrac{n\pi x}{l} \right\}_0^{l/2} \right.$$

$$\left. + \left\{ (l-x) \left(-\dfrac{l}{n\pi} \cos \dfrac{n\pi x}{l} \right) - \dfrac{l^2}{n^2\pi^2} \sin \dfrac{n\pi x}{l} \right\}_{l/2}^{l} \right]$$

$$\therefore \quad b_n = \dfrac{4T}{l^2} \left[-\dfrac{l^2}{2n\pi} \cos \dfrac{n\pi}{2} + \dfrac{l^2}{n^2\pi^2} \sin \dfrac{n\pi}{2} + \dfrac{l^2}{2n\pi} \cos \dfrac{n\pi}{2} + \dfrac{l^2}{n^2\pi^2} \sin \dfrac{n\pi}{2} \right]$$

$$= \dfrac{8T}{n^2\pi^2} \sin \dfrac{n\pi}{2}$$

Substituting in (2), we get

$$\theta(x, t) = \dfrac{8T}{\pi^2} \sum_{n=1}^{\infty} \dfrac{1}{n^2} \sin \dfrac{n\pi}{2} \cdot \sin \dfrac{n\pi x}{l}\, e^{\frac{-k\, n^2\, \pi^2\, t}{l^2}}$$

$$\theta(x, t) = \dfrac{8T}{\pi^2} \left[\sin \dfrac{\pi x}{l}\, e^{\frac{-k\, \pi^2\, t}{l^2}} - \dfrac{1}{3^2} \sin \dfrac{3\pi x}{l}\, e^{\frac{-9k\, \pi^2\, t}{l^2}} + \dots\dots \right]$$

Ex. 4 : *Solve* $\dfrac{\partial u}{\partial t} = k\, \dfrac{\partial^2 u}{\partial^2 x}$ *for the conduction of heat along a rod without radiation,* *subject to the following conditions :*

(i)   u is not infinite as $t \to \infty$

(ii) $\dfrac{\partial u}{\partial x} = 0$ for $x = 0,\ x = l$ (i.e. ends are insulated i.e. no heat flows through the ends) and (iii) $u = lx - x^2$ for $t = 0$ between $x = 0,\ x = l$.

Sol. : We have

$$u(x, t) = (c_4 \cos mx + c_5 \sin mx)\, e^{-k m^2 t} \qquad \dots (1)$$

Now applying the second condition,

$$\dfrac{\partial u}{\partial x} = 0 \quad \text{for } x = 0$$

$$\dfrac{\partial u}{\partial x} = (-m\, c_4 \sin mx + m\, c_5 \cos mx)\, e^{-k m^2 t}$$

$$\therefore \qquad \frac{\partial u}{\partial x} = 0, \ x = 0 \ \Rightarrow \ c_5 = 0$$

$\therefore$ Solution becomes

$$u = c_4 \cos mx \ e^{-k m^2 t}$$

Also,

$$\frac{\partial u}{\partial x} = - m\, c_4 \ \sin mx \ e^{-k m^2 t}$$

$$\frac{\partial u}{\partial x} = 0, \ x = l \ \Rightarrow \ 0 = - m\, c_4 \ \sin ml \ e^{-k m^2 t}$$

$$c_4 \neq 0 \qquad \therefore \ \sin ml = 0 \ \Rightarrow \ ml = n\pi$$

$$\therefore \qquad m = \frac{n\pi}{l}$$

$\therefore$ Solution is $u\,(x,\, t) = c_4 \ \cos \dfrac{n\pi x}{l} \ e^{\frac{-k\, n^2\, \pi^2\, t}{l^2}}$ for $n = 1, 2, 3, \ldots\ldots$

i.e.
$$u\,(x,\, t) = \sum_{n=1}^{\infty} a_n \ \cos \frac{n\pi x}{l} \ e^{\frac{-k\, n^2\, \pi^2\, t}{l^2}} \qquad \qquad \ldots (2)$$

Applying the third condition $u = lx - x^2$ for $t = 0$ between $x = 0$, $x = l$.

By putting $t = 0$,

$$\therefore \qquad u = \sum_{n=1}^{\infty} a_n \ \cos \frac{n\pi x}{l}$$

which is represented by Fourier half range cosine series for $lx - x^2$ in $(0,\, l)$ where

$$a_o = \frac{1}{l} \int_0^l (lx - x^2)\, dx = \frac{l^2}{6}$$

$$a_n = \frac{2}{l} \int_0^l (lx - x^2) \cos \frac{n\pi x}{l}\, dx$$

$$= \frac{2}{l} \left[(lx - x^2)\left(\frac{l}{n\pi} \sin \frac{n\pi x}{l}\right) - (l - 2x)\left(-\frac{l^2}{n^2 \pi^2} \cos \frac{n\pi x}{l}\right) + (-2)\left(-\frac{l^3}{n^3 \pi^3} \sin \frac{n\pi x}{l}\right) \right]_0^l$$

$$= \frac{2}{l} \left[-\frac{l^3}{n^2 \pi^2} \cos n\pi - \frac{l^3}{n^2 \pi^2} \right]$$

$$= -\frac{2l^2}{n^2 \pi^2} (1 + \cos n\pi) = \begin{cases} 0 & \text{for n odd} \\[2mm] -\dfrac{4l^2}{n^2 \pi^2} & \text{for n even} \end{cases}$$

Let $\qquad n = 2p$

$$a_{2p} = -\frac{4\, l^2}{4\, p^2\, \pi^2} = -\frac{l^2}{p^2\, \pi^2} \quad \text{for } p = 1, 2, 3, \ldots\ldots$$

Solution (2) becomes

$$u = a_0 + \sum_{p=1}^{\infty} a_{2p} \cos \frac{2p\pi x}{l} \, e^{\frac{-k4p^2\pi^2 t}{l^2}}$$

i.e.

$$u = \frac{l^2}{6} - \frac{l^2}{\pi^2} \sum_{p=1}^{\infty} \frac{1}{p^2} \cos \frac{2p\pi x}{l} \, e^{\frac{-4kp^2\pi^2 t}{l^2}}$$

which is the required solution.

Ex. 5 : *Solve* $\dfrac{\partial u}{\partial t} = k \dfrac{\partial^2 u}{\partial x^2}$ *if*

(i) $u(0, t) = 0$

(ii) $u_x(l, t) = 0$

(iii) $u(x, t)$ *is bounded and*

(iv) $u(x, 0) = \dfrac{u_o\, x}{l}$ *for* $0 \leq x \leq l.$

Sol. : The most general solution is

$$u(x, t) = (c_4 \cos mx + c_5 \sin mx)\, e^{-km^2 t}$$

Applying condition (i) $\Rightarrow$ $c_4 = 0$

$$u(x, t) = c_5 \sin mx \, e^{-km^2 t}$$

$$u_x(l, t) = 0 \quad \Rightarrow \quad \left(\frac{\partial u}{\partial x}\right)_{x=l} = 0$$

$$\frac{\partial u}{\partial x} = m \cdot c_5 \cos mx \, e^{-km^2 t}$$

$$0 = m \cdot c_5 \cdot \cos ml \, e^{-km^2 t}$$

$$\cos ml = 0, \quad ml = \frac{n\pi}{2} \ (n = \text{odd})$$

$$m = \frac{n\pi}{2l} \quad \text{or} \quad m = \frac{(2n+1)\pi}{2l}, \quad n = 0, 1, 2, \ldots\ldots$$

$$u(x, t) = c_5 \sin \frac{(2n+1)\pi x}{2l} \, e^{\frac{-k(2n+1)^2\pi^2 t}{4l^2}}$$

Or

$$u(x, t) = \sum_{n=0}^{\infty} b_n \sin \frac{(2n+1)\pi x}{2l} \cdot e^{\frac{-k(2n+1)^2\pi^2 t}{4l^2}}$$

Applying condition (iv), we get

$$\frac{u_o \cdot x}{l} = \sum_{n=0}^{\infty} b_n \sin \frac{(2n+1)\pi x}{2l}$$

$$\text{where} \qquad b_n = \frac{2}{l} \int_0^l \frac{u_0 \cdot x}{l} \sin \frac{(2n+1)\,\pi x}{2l} \, dx$$

$$b_n = \frac{2u_0}{l^2} \left\{ (x) \left(-\frac{2l}{(2n+1)\pi} \cos \frac{(2n+1)\,\pi x}{2l} \right) - (1) \left(-\frac{4\,l^2}{(2n+1)^2\,\pi^2} \sin \frac{(2n+1)\,\pi x}{2l} \right) \right\}_0^l$$

$$= \frac{8\,u_0}{\pi^2} \frac{1}{(2n+1)^2} \sin (2n+1) \frac{\pi}{2}$$

$$= \frac{8\,u_0}{\pi^2} \frac{1}{(2n+1)^2} \sin \left(n\pi + \frac{\pi}{2} \right)$$

$$b_n = \frac{8\,u_0}{\pi^2} \frac{1}{(2n+1)^2} \cdot (-1)^n$$

$\therefore$ The complete solution is

$$u(x, t) = \frac{8\,u_0}{\pi^2} \sum_{n=0}^{\infty} \frac{(-1)^n}{(2n+1)^2} \sin \frac{(2n+1)\,\pi x}{2\,l} \cdot e^{\frac{-(2n+1)^2\,\pi^2\,k\,t}{4\,l^2}}$$

Ex. 6 : *A homogeneous rod of conducting material of length 100 cm has its ends kept at zero temperature and the temperature initially is*

$$u(x, 0) = x \qquad , \qquad 0 \le x \le 50$$
$$= 100 - x , \qquad 50 \le x \le 100$$

Find the temperature u (x, t) at any time.

Sol. : We have to solve $\dfrac{\partial u}{\partial t} = c^2 \dfrac{\partial^2 u}{\partial x^2}$, subject to conditions

(i) $u(0, t) = 0$

(ii) $u(100, t) = 0$

(iii) $u(x, 0) = x \qquad , \ 0 \le x \le 50$

$\qquad \qquad = 100 - x, \ 50 \le x \le 100$

(iv) $u(x, t)$ is finite $\forall\, t$

The most general solution is

$$u(x, t) = (c_4 \cos mx + c_5 \sin mx)\, e^{-c^2 m^2 t}$$

Condition (i) $\Rightarrow \quad c_4 = 0$

$$u(x, t) = c_5 \sin mx \ e^{-c^2 m^2 t} \qquad\qquad \text{... (1)}$$

Condition (ii) $\Rightarrow \quad 0 = c_5 \sin 100\, m \ e^{-c^2 m^2 t}$

$$\sin (100\, m) = 0 \ \Rightarrow \ 100\, m = n\pi$$

$$m = \frac{n\pi}{100}, \quad n = 1, 2, 3, \ldots\ldots\ldots$$

Solution (1) becomes

$$u(x, t) = c_5 \ \sin\frac{n\pi x}{100} \ e^{-\frac{n^2\pi^2 c^2 t}{1000,00}}, \quad n = 1, 2, \ldots\ldots\ldots$$

Combining all these solutions

$$u(x, t) = \sum_{n=1}^{\infty} b_n \ \sin\frac{n\pi x}{100} \ e^{-\frac{n^2\pi^2 c^2 t}{100,00}} \qquad \ldots (2)$$

Applying condition (iii), we have

$$u(x, 0) = \sum_{n=1}^{\infty} b_n \ \sin\frac{n\pi x}{100}$$

and is half range sine series for $u(x, 0)$.

$$\therefore \quad b_n = \frac{2}{100} \int_0^{100} u(x, 0) \ \sin\frac{n\pi x}{100} \ dx$$

$$= \frac{1}{50} \left[\int_0^{50} u(x, 0) \ \sin\frac{n\pi x}{100} \ dx + \int_{50}^{100} u(x, 0) \ \sin\frac{n\pi x}{100} \ dx \right]$$

$$= \frac{1}{50} \left[\int_0^{50} x \ \sin\frac{n\pi x}{100} \ dx + \int_{50}^{100} (100 - x) \sin\frac{n\pi x}{100} \ dx \right]$$

$$= \frac{1}{50} \left[\left\{ (x) \times \left(\frac{-100}{n\pi} \cos\frac{n\pi x}{100}\right) - (1) \left(-\frac{100^2}{n^2\pi^2} \sin\frac{n\pi x}{100}\right) \right\}_0^{50} \right.$$

$$\left. + \left\{ (100 - x) \left(-\frac{100}{n\pi} \cos\frac{n\pi x}{100}\right) - (-1) \left(\frac{-100^2}{n^2\pi^2} \sin\frac{n\pi x}{100}\right) \right\}_{50}^{100} \right]$$

$$= \frac{1}{50} \left[-\frac{100}{n\pi}\left(50\cos\frac{n\pi}{2} - 0\right) + \frac{100^2}{n^2\pi^2}\left(\sin\frac{n\pi}{2} - \sin 0\right) - \frac{100}{n\pi}\left(0 - 50\cos\frac{n\pi}{2}\right) \right.$$

$$\left. - \frac{100^2}{n^2\pi^2}\left(\sin n\pi - \sin\frac{n\pi}{2}\right) \right]$$

$$\therefore \ b_n = \frac{1}{50}\left(\frac{100^2}{n^2\pi^2}\right) 2\sin\frac{n\pi}{2} = \frac{400}{n^2\pi^2} \ \sin\frac{n\pi}{2} = \begin{cases} 0, & \text{if n is even} \\ (-1)^n \dfrac{400}{n^2\pi^2}, & \text{if n is is odd} \end{cases}$$

Replace $n \to 2n + 1$

$$\therefore \qquad b_n = (-1)^n \cdot \frac{400}{(2n+1)^2\,\pi^2}$$

$\therefore$ Required solution is

$$u(x,t) = \sum_{n=0}^{\infty} \frac{(-1)^n \times 400}{(2n+1)^2\,\pi^2}\, \sin\frac{(2n+1)\,\pi x}{100} \cdot e^{\frac{-(2n+1)^2\,\pi^2\,c^2\,t}{100^2}}$$

Ex. 7 : *A bar with insulated sides is initially at temperature $0^\circ C$ throughout. The end $x = 0$ is kept at $0^\circ C$ for all time and the heat is suddenly applied so that $\dfrac{\partial u}{\partial x} = 10$ at $x = l$ for all time. Find the temperature function $u(x, t)$.*

Sol. : We have to solve the P.D.E.

$$\frac{\partial u}{\partial t} = a^2\,\frac{\partial^2 u}{\partial x^2}$$

Let

$$u(x,t) = F(x) \cdot G(t)$$

$$FG' = a^2\,F''G$$

$$\frac{F''}{F} = \frac{G'}{a^2\,G} = -m^2 \ \text{(say)}$$

then the solution is

$$u(x,t) = (c_1 \cos mx + c_2 \sin mx)\, e^{-a^2 m^2 t} \qquad \qquad \ldots (I)$$

Also,

$$\frac{F''}{F} = \frac{G'}{a^2\,G} = 0$$

then the solution is

$$u(x,t) = c_6 + c_7 \cdot x \qquad \qquad \ldots (II)$$

Conditions are

 (i) $u(x, 0) = 0$

 (ii) $u(0, t) = 0$

 (iii) $\left(\dfrac{\partial u}{\partial x}\right)_{x=l} = 10$, for all t.

Since the above conditions of the problem are such that any one of the above solutions (i.e. (I) and (II)) does not satisfy them. We use the combinations of the solutions to satisfy the given conditions i.e. sum of (I) and (II).

$$\therefore \qquad u(x,t) = c_6 + c_7 x + (c_1 \cos mx + c_2 \sin mx)\, e^{-m^2 a^2 t}$$

Now (ii) $\Rightarrow c_6 = 0, \quad c_1 = 0$

$$u(x,t) = c_7 x + c_2 \sin mx \cdot e^{-m^2 a^2 t}$$

Now (iii) $\Rightarrow \dfrac{\partial u}{\partial x} = c_7 + m\,c_2 \cos mx \ \ e^{-m^2 a^2 t}$

$$10 = c_7 + m\,c_2 \cos ml \ \ e^{-m^2 a^2 t}$$

$$\Rightarrow c_7 = 10$$

$$\cos ml = 0 \qquad ml = \frac{(2n + 1)\,\pi}{2}$$

$$u(x, t) = 10x + \sum_{n=0}^{\infty} c_{2n+1} \cdot \sin \frac{(2n+1)\,\pi x}{2l} \cdot e^{\frac{-a^2 (2n+1)^2 \pi^2 t}{4l^2}}$$

Now (i) $\Rightarrow$ $t = 0$, $u = 0$

$$-10x = \sum_{n=0}^{\infty} c_{2n+1} \sin \frac{(2n+1)\,\pi x}{2l}$$

$$c_{2n+1} = \frac{2}{l} \int_0^l (-10x) \sin \frac{(2n+1)\,\pi x}{2l} \cdot dx$$

$$= -\frac{20}{l} \left[(x)\left(-\frac{2l}{(2n+1)\,\pi} \cos \frac{(2n+1)\,\pi x}{2l}\right) + \frac{4l^2}{(2n+1)^2 \pi^2} \sin \frac{(2n+1)\,\pi x}{2l} \right]_0^l$$

$$c_{2n+1} = -\frac{80\,l}{(2n+1)^2 \pi^2} \sin \frac{(2n+1)\,\pi}{2}$$

$\therefore$ The complete solution is

$$u(x, t) = 10x - \frac{80\,l}{\pi^2} \sum_{n=0}^{\infty} \frac{1}{(2n+1)^2} \sin \frac{(2n+1)\,\pi}{2} \cdot \sin \frac{(2n+1)\,\pi x}{2l} \; e^{\frac{-a^2 (2n+1)^2 \pi^2 t}{4l^2}}$$

Ex. 8 : *A rod of length l has its ends A and B maintained at 20°C and 40°C respectively until steady-state conditions prevail. The temperature at A is suddenly raised to 50°C while that at B is lowered to 10°C and maintained thereafter. Find the subsequent temperature distribution of the rod.*

Sol. : Here initial conditions of temperature distribution are not explicitly given. We will first obtain the same. Initially steady-state conditions prevail, the temperature depends on x only, let it be $u_{s_1}(x) = Ax + B$.

$$x = 0, \ u_{s_1}(0) = 20°\,C, \ x = l, \ u_{s_1}(l) = 40°C, \ 20 = B, \ 40 = Al + 20, \ A = \frac{20}{l}$$

$$u_{s_1}(x) = \frac{20x}{l} + 20$$

Hence, we have to solve the P.D.E.

$$\frac{\partial u}{\partial t} = c^2 \frac{\partial^2 u}{\partial x^2}, \text{ subject to the boundary conditions}$$

(i) $u(0, t) = 50°\,C$

(ii) $u(l, t) = 10°\,C$ and initial condition

$$u(x, 0) = u_{s_1}(x) = \frac{20x}{l} + 20$$

Since the boundary conditions are not zero, we cannot proceed directly.

Note that after certain time, the temperature distribution of the rod has to reach steady state which implies that the solution has two parts :

(i)   Steady state part and

(ii)   Transient part which ultimately becomes zero.

We denote these as $u_s (x)$ and $u_t (x, t)$.

$$\therefore \qquad u (x, t) = u_s (x) + u_t (x, t)$$

where, $u_s (x)$ satisfies the P.D.E. under steady-state conditions i.e.

$$u_s (x) = cx + d$$

where, $\quad u_s (0) = 50°C \quad$ and $\quad u_s (l) = 10°C$

$$50 = 0 + d \qquad \therefore d = 50$$

$$10 = l\,c + 50 \quad \therefore \quad c = -\frac{40}{l}$$

$$\therefore \qquad u_s (x) = -\frac{40\,x}{l} + 50$$

$$\therefore \qquad u (x, t) = -\frac{40\,x}{l} + 50 + u_t (x, t).$$

Our problem reduces to obtain $u_t (x, t)$

where $\qquad u_t (x, t) = u (x, t) + \dfrac{40\,x}{l} - 50$

Substituting $u_t (x, t)$ in the P.D.E.

$$\frac{\partial u_t}{\partial t} = c^2\, \frac{\partial^2 u_t}{\partial x^2}$$

For obtaining boundary and initial conditions

$$u_t (0, t) = u (0, t) + 0 - 50$$

$$= 50 - 50 \qquad\qquad\qquad (\because\ u (0, t) = 50)$$

$$\boxed{u_t(0, t) = 0}$$

$$u_t (l, t) = u (l, t) + 40 - 50$$

$$= 10 + 40 - 50 \qquad\qquad\qquad (\because\ u (l, t) = 10)$$

$$\boxed{u_t (l, t) = 0}$$

$$u_t (x, 0) = u (x, 0) + \frac{40\,x}{l} - 50$$

$$= \frac{20\,x}{l} + 20 + \frac{40\,x}{l} - 50$$

$$\boxed{u_t (x, 0) = \frac{60\,x}{l} - 30}$$

Solution is $\quad u_t(x, t) = (c_1 \cos mx + c_2 \sin mx)\, e^{-c^2 m^2 t}$

$$u_t(0, t) = 0 \;\Rightarrow\; c_1 = 0$$

$$u_t(x, t) = c_2 \sin mx\; e^{-c^2 m^2 t}$$

$$u_t(l, t) = 0 \Rightarrow 0 = c_2 \sin ml\; e^{-c^2 m^2 t}$$

$$\sin ml = 0 \;\Rightarrow\; m = \frac{n\pi}{l},\; n = 1, 2, \ldots\ldots$$

$$u_t(x, t) = \sum_{n=1}^{\infty} b_n \sin \frac{n\pi x}{l}\, e^{-\frac{c^2 n^2 \pi^2 t}{l^2}}$$

$$u_t(x, 0) = \sum_{1}^{\infty} b_n \sin \frac{n\pi x}{l}$$

$$b_n = \frac{2}{l} \int_0^l \left(\frac{60\,x}{l} - 30\right) \sin \frac{n\pi x}{l}\, dx$$

$$= \frac{2}{l} \left\{\left(\frac{60\,x}{l} - 30\right)\left(-\frac{l}{n\pi}\cos\frac{n\pi x}{l}\right) - \left(\frac{60}{l}\right)\left(-\frac{l^2}{n^2\pi^2}\sin\frac{n\pi x}{l}\right)\right\}_0^l$$

$$= \frac{2}{l}\left\{-\frac{30\,l}{n\pi}(-1)^n - \frac{30\,l}{n\pi}\right\}$$

$$b_n = -\frac{60}{n\pi}\left[(-1)^n + 1\right]$$

$$u_t(x, t) = -\frac{60}{\pi}\sum_{1}^{\infty} \frac{(-1)^n + 1}{n} \sin \frac{n\pi x}{l}\, e^{-\frac{c^2 n^2 \pi^2 t}{l^2}}$$

$$u_t(x, t) = -\frac{60}{\pi} \times 2 \cdot \sum_{1}^{\infty} \frac{1}{2n} \sin \frac{2n\pi x}{l}\, e^{-\frac{4 c^2 n^2 \pi^2 t}{l^2}}$$

$$\therefore \quad \boxed{u(x, t) = 50 - \frac{40\,x}{l} - \frac{60}{\pi}\sum_{1}^{\infty}\frac{1}{n}\sin\frac{2n\pi x}{l}\, e^{-\frac{4 c^2 n^2 \pi^2 t}{l^2}}}$$

Ex. 9 : *Solve* $\dfrac{\partial u}{\partial t} = c^2 \dfrac{\partial^2 u}{\partial x^2}$ *if*

(i)   u is finite for all t

(ii) $u(0, t) = 0,\; \forall t$

(iii) $u(l, t) = 0,\; \forall t$

(iv) $u(x, 0) = u_0$ for $0 \le x \le l$, where l being the length of the bar.

Sol. : (i) The most general solution is

$$u(x, t) = (c_4 \cos mx + c_5 \sin mx)\ e^{-m^2 c^2 t}$$

(ii) $\Rightarrow$ $\quad c_4 = 0$

$$u(x, t) = c_5 \sin mx\ e^{-m^2 c^2 t}$$

(iii) $\Rightarrow$ $\quad 0 = c_5 \sin ml\ e^{-m^2 c^2 t}$

$$\sin(ml) = 0, \quad ml = n\pi$$

$$m = \frac{n\pi}{l}, \quad n = 1, 2, \ldots\ldots\ldots\ldots$$

$$u(x, t) = c_5 \sin\frac{n\pi x}{l}\ e^{-\frac{n^2 \pi^2 c^2 t}{l^2}}, \quad n = 1, 2, \ldots\ldots$$

Or

$$u(x, t) = \sum_{n=1}^{\infty} b_n \sin\frac{n\pi x}{l}\ e^{-\frac{n^2 \pi^2 c^2 t}{l^2}} \qquad \ldots (I)$$

Applying condition (iv),

$$u_0 = \sum_{n=1}^{\infty} b_n \sin\frac{n\pi x}{l}$$

$$b_n = \frac{2}{l} \int_0^l u_0 \sin\frac{n\pi x}{l}\ dx = \frac{2u_0}{l}\left(-\frac{l}{n\pi} \cos\frac{n\pi x}{l}\right)_0^l$$

$$b_n = \frac{2\,u_0}{\pi}\left(\frac{1 - (-1)^n}{n}\right)$$

$$u(x, t) = \frac{2\,u_0}{\pi} \sum_{n=1}^{\infty} \left(\frac{1 - (-1)^n}{n}\right) \sin\frac{n\pi x}{l}\ e^{-\frac{n^2 \pi^2 c^2 t}{l^2}}$$

Ex. 10 : *Solve the equation* $\dfrac{\partial u}{\partial t} = a^2 \dfrac{\partial^2 u}{\partial x^2}$ *where* $u(x, t)$ *satisfies the following conditions :*

(i) $u(0, t) = 0$

(ii) $u(l, t) = 0$ *for all t*

(iii) $u(x, 0) = x$ *in* $0 < x < l$

(iv) $u(x, \infty)$ *is finite.*

Sol. : The most general solution is

$$u(x, t) = (c_4 \cos mx + c_5 \sin mx)\ e^{-a^2 m^2 t}$$

(i) $\Rightarrow$ $\quad c_4 = 0$

$$u(x, t) = c_5 \sin mx\ e^{-a^2 m^2 t}$$

(ii) $\Rightarrow$ $0 = c_5 \sin ml \; e^{-a^2 m^2 t}$

$$\sin ml = 0, \quad ml = n\pi$$

$$m = \frac{n\pi}{l}, \; n = 1, 2, 3, \ldots\ldots$$

$$u(x, t) = c_5 \sin \frac{n\pi x}{l} \; e^{-\frac{a^2 n^2 \pi^2 t}{l^2}}, \; n = 1, 2, \ldots\ldots$$

Combining all these solutions, we get

$$u(x, t) = \sum_{n=1}^{\infty} b_n \sin \frac{n\pi x}{l} \; e^{-\frac{a^2 n^2 \pi^2 t}{l^2}}$$

(iii) $\Rightarrow$ $x = \sum_{n=1}^{\infty} b_n \sin \frac{n\pi x}{l}, \; 0 < x < l$

which is nothing but half range sine series for $f(x) = x$ in $(0, l)$.

$\therefore$ $$b_n = \frac{2}{l} \int_0^l x \sin \frac{n\pi x}{l} \, dx$$

$$= \frac{2}{l} \left\{ (x) \left(-\frac{l}{n\pi} \cos \frac{n\pi x}{l} \right) - (1) \left(-\frac{l^2}{n^2\pi^2} \sin \frac{n\pi x}{l} \right) \right\}_0^l$$

$$= \frac{2}{l} \left\{ -\frac{l^2}{n\pi} (-1)^n \right\} = -\frac{2l}{\pi} \left(\frac{(-1)^n}{n} \right)$$

$\therefore$ $$u(x, t) = \frac{2l}{\pi} \sum_{n=1}^{\infty} \frac{(-1)^{n+1}}{n} \sin \frac{n\pi x}{l} \; e^{-\frac{a^2 n^2 \pi^2 t}{l^2}}$$

Ex. 11 : *The temperature at any point of the insulated metal rod of one metre length is governed by the differential equation* $\dfrac{\partial u}{\partial t} = c^2 \dfrac{\partial^2 u}{\partial x^2}$. *Find u(x, t), subject to the following conditions :*

(i)   u (0, t) = 0 °C

(ii) u (l, t) = 0 °C

(iii) u (x, 0) = 50 °C and hence find the temperature in the middle of the rod at any subsequent time.

Sol. : The most general solution is

$$u(x, t) = (c_4 \cos mx + c_5 \sin mx) \; e^{-c^2 m^2 t}$$

(i) $\Rightarrow$ $c_4 = 0$

$$u(x, t) = c_5 \sin mx \; e^{-c^2 m^2 t}$$

(ii) $\Rightarrow$ $0 = c_5 \sin m \, e^{-c^2 m^2 t}$

$\sin m = 0$ $\therefore$ $m = n\pi, \quad n = 1, 2, \ldots\ldots\ldots$

$\therefore$ $u(x, t) = c_5 \sin n\pi x \, e^{-c^2 n^2 \pi^2 t}, \quad n = 1, 2, \ldots\ldots\ldots$

Combining all these solutions, we get

$$u(x, t) = \sum_{n=1}^{\infty} b_n \sin n\pi x \, e^{-c^2 n^2 \pi^2 t}$$

Applying condition (iii), we get

$$50 = \sum_{n=1}^{\infty} b_n \sin n\pi x, \quad 0 < x < 1$$

which is represented by half range Fourier sine series for $f(x) = 50$ in $(0, 1)$

$\therefore$ $b_n = 2 \int_0^1 50 \, \sin n\pi x \, dx$

$$= 100 \left[-\frac{\cos n\pi x}{n\pi} \right]_0^1 = \frac{100}{\pi} \left(\frac{1 - (-1)^n}{n} \right)$$

$\therefore$ $u(x, t) = \dfrac{100}{\pi} \sum\limits_{n=1}^{\infty} \dfrac{1 - (-1)^n}{n} \sin n\pi x \, e^{-c^2 n^2 \pi^2 t}$

Now the temperature in the middle of the rod at any subsequent time is

$$u\left(\frac{1}{2}, 0 \right) = \frac{100}{\pi} \sum_{n=1}^{\infty} \frac{1 - (-n)^n}{n} \sin \frac{n\pi}{2}$$

$$= 0, \quad \text{if } n \text{ is even}$$

$$= \frac{200}{\pi} \sum_{n=1}^{\infty} \frac{(-1)^n}{n}, \quad \text{if } n \text{ is odd.}$$

EXERCISE 6.2

Solve the one-dimensional heat flow equation $\dfrac{\partial u}{\partial t} = a^2 \dfrac{\partial^2 u}{\partial x^2}$ for function $u(x, t)$, subject to following conditions :

1. (i) $u(0, t) = 0$,   (ii) $u(l, t) = 0$, for all t

   (iii) $u(x, 0) = x, \quad 0 < x < l$ (iv) $u(x, \infty)$ is finite.

   Hint : $b_n = \dfrac{2l}{n\pi}(-1)^{n-1}$

   Ans. : $u(x, t) = \dfrac{2l}{\pi} \sum\limits_{n=1}^{\infty} \dfrac{(-1)^{n-1}}{n} \, e^{-\frac{n^2 a^2 \pi^2 t}{l^2}} \sin \dfrac{n\pi x}{l}$

2. (i) $u(0, t) = 0$,   (ii) $\dfrac{\partial}{\partial x} u(l, t) = 0$, for all t

(iii) $u(x, 0) = x$ (iv) $u(x, \infty)$ is finite

$$\textbf{Ans.:} \quad u(x, t) = \frac{8l}{\pi^2} \sum_{n=1}^{\infty} \frac{(-1)^n}{(2n+1)^2} \sin \frac{(2n+1)\pi x}{2l} \, e^{-\frac{a^2 (2n+1)^2 \pi^2 t}{4l^2}}$$

3. (i) $u(0, t) = 0$,   (ii) $u(\pi, t) = 0$, for all t

(iii) $u(x, 0) = \pi x - x^2$, $0 < x < \pi$ (iv) $u(x, \infty)$ is finite.

$$\textbf{Ans.:} \quad u(x, t) = \frac{8}{\pi} \sum_{n=1}^{\infty} \frac{\sin(2n-1)x}{(2n-1)^3} \, e^{-a^2(2n-1)^2 t}$$

4. (i) $\dfrac{\partial}{\partial x} u(0, t) = 0$, and   (ii) $\dfrac{\partial}{\partial x}(l, t) = 0$, for all t

(iii) $u(x, 0) = x^2$, $0 < x < l$ (iv) $u(x, \infty)$ is finite.

$$\textbf{Ans.:} \quad u(x, t) = \frac{l^2}{3} + \frac{4l^2}{\pi^2} \sum_{n=1}^{\infty} \frac{(-1)^n}{n^2} \cos \frac{n\pi x}{l} \, e^{-\frac{n^2 a^2 \pi^2 t}{l^2}}$$

5. Solve $\dfrac{\partial u}{\partial t} = \dfrac{\partial^2 u}{\partial x^2}$ if

(i) u is finite, $\forall$ t   (ii) $u(0, t) = 0$

(iii) $u(\pi, t) = 0$ (iv) $u(x, 0) = \pi x - x^2$, $0 \le x \le \pi$

$$\textbf{Ans.:} \quad u(x, t) = \frac{8}{\pi} \sum_{n=0}^{\infty} \frac{1}{(2n+1)^3} \sin(2n+1)x \, e^{-(2n+1)^2 t}$$

6. Solve $\dfrac{\partial u}{\partial t} = k \dfrac{\partial^2 u}{\partial x^2}$ if

(i) $u(x, t)$ is bounded   (ii) $u(0, t) = 0$

(iii) $u(l, t) = 0$ (iv) $u(x, 0) = \dfrac{u_o \, x}{l}$, $0 \le x \le l$

$$\textbf{Ans.:} \quad u(x, t) = \frac{2 u_o}{\pi} \sum_{n=1}^{\infty} \frac{(-1)^{n+1}}{n} \sin \frac{n\pi x}{l} \, e^{-\frac{k n^2 \pi^2 t}{l^2}}$$

7. The equation for the conduction of heat along a bar of length l is $\dfrac{\partial \theta}{\partial t} = k \dfrac{\partial^2 \theta}{\partial t^2}$,

neglecting radiation. Find an expression for θ if the ends of the bar are maintained at zero temperature and if initially the temperature is T at the centre of the bar and falls uniformly to zero at its ends.

Hint : (i) $\theta\,(0, t) = 0$, (ii) $\theta = (l, 0) = 0$, (iii) $\theta\,(x, 0) = \begin{cases} \dfrac{2T}{l}\,x, & 0 \le x \le l/2 \\[2mm] \dfrac{2T}{l}\,(-x), & l/2 \le x \le l \end{cases}$

$$\textbf{Ans. :}\ \theta\,(x, t) = \frac{8T}{\pi^2}\ \sum_{1}^{\infty}\ \frac{1}{n^2}\ \sin\frac{n\pi}{2}\ \sin\frac{n\pi x}{l}\ e^{-\frac{k\,n^2\pi^2 t}{l^2}}$$

8. Solve $\dfrac{\partial u}{\partial t} = c^2\,\dfrac{\partial^2 u}{\partial x^2}$, subject to the following boundary conditions :

(i) $u\,(0, t) = 0,$ (ii) $u\,(l, t) = 0,$ (iii) $u\,(x, 0) = \begin{cases} x, & 0 < x \le l/2 \\[2mm] l - x, & l/2 \le x < l \end{cases}$

$$\textbf{Ans. :}\ \ u\,(x, t) = \frac{4\,l}{\pi^2}\ \sum_{n=1}^{\infty}\ \frac{(-1)^n}{(2n-1)^2}\ \sin\frac{(2n-1)\,\pi x}{l}\ e^{-\frac{(2n-1)^2\pi^2 c^2 t}{l^2}}$$

9. The temperatures at the ends x = 0 and x = 50 cm in length of a rod are held at 0°C and 50°C respectively until steady-state conditions prevail. The two ends of the rod are suddenly insulated. Find the temperature distribution of the rod assuming that the surface of the rod is impervious to heat.

$$\textbf{Ans. :}\ \ u\,(x, t) = 25\ -\frac{200}{\pi^2}\ \sum_{n=1}^{\infty}\ \frac{1}{(2n-1)^2}\ \cos\frac{(2n-1)\,\pi x}{50}\ e^{\frac{-(2n-1)^2 a^2 \pi^2 t}{2500}}$$

10. A rod of length l is insulated along its length so that no heat is transformed from its sides, the uniform temperature of the rod is $50°\,C$. Suddenly the end x = 0 is cooled to $0°\,C$ and the end x = l heated to $100°\,C$ and these are maintained afterwards. Find the subsequent temperature distribution of the rod.

$$\textbf{Ans. :}\ u\,(x, t) = \frac{100\,x}{l} + \frac{100}{\pi}\ \sum_{n=1}^{\infty}\ \frac{1}{n}\ \sin\frac{2n\pi x}{l}\ e^{-\frac{4\,n^2 a^2 \pi^2 t}{l^2}}$$

11. A rod of length l has its ends A and B kept at $0°\,C$ and $75°\,C$, until steady-state conditions prevail. If the temperature of A is suddenly raised to $75°C$ and that of B to $175°C$ and maintained thereafter, find the subsequent temperature distribution of the rod.

$$\textbf{Ans. :}\ u(x, t) = 75 + \frac{100\,x}{l} - \frac{300}{\pi}\ \sum_{n=1}^{\infty}\ \frac{1}{(2n-1)}\ \sin\frac{(2n-1)\,\pi x}{l}\ e^{\frac{-(2n-1)^2 a^2 \pi^2 t}{l^2}}$$

12. A rod of length l has one end kept at $0°$ C and other end B at $100°$ C until steady-state conditions prevail. The temperature of A is suddenly raised to $50°$ C while the end B is insulated. These conditions are maintained thereafter, find the subsequent temperature distribution of the rod.

$$\text{Ans.}: u(x, t) = 50 + \sum_{n=1}^{\infty} \left[\frac{(-1)^{n-1}\,800}{(2n-1)^2\,\pi^2} - \frac{200}{(2n-1)\,\pi} \right] \sin\frac{(2n-1)\,\pi x}{2l}\; e^{\frac{-(2n-1)^2\,a^2\,\pi^2\,t}{4l^2}}$$

13. A rod of length l has its ends A and B maintained at 20°C and 40°C respectively until steady-state conditions prevail. The temperature at A is suddenly raised to 50°C while that at B is lowered to 10°C and maintained thereafter. Find the subsequent temperature distribution of the rod.

$$\text{Ans.}: u\,(x, y) = 50 - \frac{40}{l}\,x - \frac{60}{\pi} \sum_{n=1}^{\infty} \frac{1}{n} \sin\frac{2n\pi x}{l}\; e^{-\frac{4\,n^2\,a^2\,\pi^2\,t}{l^2}}$$

14. A uniform rod of length l whose surface is thermally insulated, is initially at temperature θ_0. At time $t = 0$, one end is suddenly cooled to temperature 0°C and subsequently maintained at this temperature and at the same time, the other end is thermally insulated. Find the temperature at end $x = l$ at any time t.

15. The ends A and B of a insulated rod of length l, have their temperatures at 20°C and 80°C respectively until steady-state conditions prevail. The temperatures at these ends are changed suddenly to 40°C and 60°C respectively. Find the temperature distribution of the rod at time t.

$$\text{Ans.}: u\,(x, t) = \frac{20\,x}{l} + 40 - \frac{40}{\pi} \sum_{1}^{\infty} \frac{1}{n} \sin\frac{2n\pi x}{l}\, e^{-\frac{4\,c^2\,n^2\,\pi^2\,t}{l^2}}\;.$$

6.7   MODELING OF TWO-DIMENSIONAL HEAT FLOW

Consider the flow of heat in a metal plate in XOY plane. If the temperature at a point does not depend upon z-coordinate and it depends only on x, y, and t, then the flow is called two-dimensional and the heat flow lies in XOY plane only and is zero along the normal to XOY plane.

Consider a rectangular element of the plate with sides δx and δy and thickness 'h'. As discussed in one-dimensional heat flow along a bar, the quantity of heat that enters the plate per second from the sides AB and AD is given by $-kh\,\delta x \left(\dfrac{\partial u}{\partial y}\right)_y$ and $-kh\,\delta y \left(\dfrac{\partial u}{\partial x}\right)_x$ respectively.

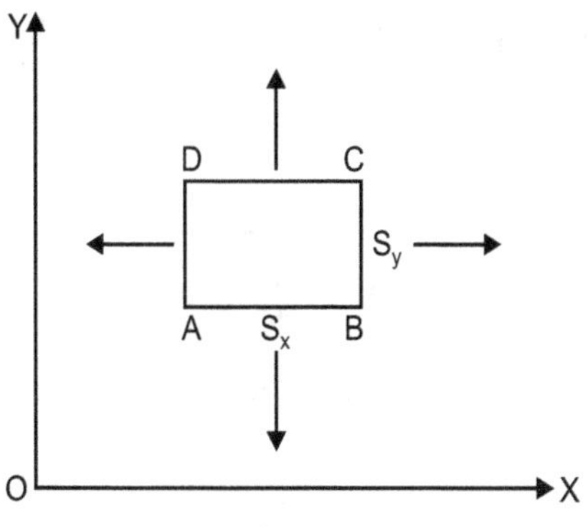

Fig. 6.5

Heat flowing out through sides CD and BC per second is $-kh\ \delta x\ \left(\dfrac{\partial u}{\partial y}\right)_{y\,+\,\delta y}$ and

$-kh\ \delta y\ \left(\dfrac{\partial u}{\partial x}\right)_{x\,+\,\delta x}$ respectively. Therefore, the total gain of heat by rectangular plate

ABCD per second

$$= -kh\ \delta x\ \left(\frac{\partial u}{\partial y}\right)_{y} \ \ kh\ \delta y\ \left(\frac{\partial u}{\partial x}\right)_{x} + kh\ \delta x\ \left(\frac{\partial u}{\partial y}\right)_{y\,+\,\delta y} + kh\ \delta y\ \left(\frac{\partial u}{\partial x}\right)_{x\,+\,\delta x}$$

$$= kh\ \delta x\ \delta y\ \left[\frac{\left(\dfrac{\partial u}{\partial x}\right)_{x\,+\,\delta x} - \left(\dfrac{\partial u}{\partial x}\right)_{x}}{\delta x} + \frac{\left(\dfrac{\partial u}{\partial y}\right)_{y\,+\,\delta y} - \left(\dfrac{\partial u}{\partial y}\right)_{y}}{\delta y}\right] \qquad \ldots (1)$$

The rate of gain of heat by the plate is also given by,

$$S\ \rho h\ \delta x\ \delta y\ \frac{\partial u}{\partial t} \qquad \ldots (2)$$

where, S = specific heat and ρ = density of the metal plate

$\therefore$ Equating equations (1) and (2), we get

$$kh\ \delta x\ \delta y\ .\ \left[\frac{\left(\dfrac{\partial u}{\partial x}\right)_{x\,+\,\delta x} - \left(\dfrac{\partial u}{\partial x}\right)_{x}}{\delta x} + \frac{\left(\dfrac{\partial u}{\partial y}\right)_{y\,+\,\delta y} - \left(\dfrac{\partial u}{\partial y}\right)_{y}}{\delta y}\right] = S\ \rho h\ \delta x\ \delta y\ \frac{\partial u}{\partial t}$$

Dividing by $h\ \delta x\ \delta y$ and taking limit as $\delta x \to 0,\ \delta y \to 0$, we get

$$k\left(\frac{\partial^2 u}{\partial x^2} + \frac{\partial^2 u}{\partial y^2}\right) = S\ \rho\ \frac{\partial u}{\partial t}$$

$$\therefore \qquad \frac{\partial u}{\partial t} = \frac{k}{S\rho}\left(\frac{\partial^2 u}{\partial x^2} + \frac{\partial^2 u}{\partial y^2}\right)$$

$$\text{Or} \qquad \frac{\partial u}{\partial t} = c^2\left(\frac{\partial^2 u}{\partial x^2} + \frac{\partial^2 u}{\partial y^2}\right) \qquad \ldots (3)$$

where $\quad \dfrac{k}{S\rho} = c^2$ is the diffusivity

Equation (3) represents temperature distribution of the plate in the transient state. For steady state when u is independent of t,

$$\frac{\partial u}{\partial t} = 0$$

∴ Equation (3) reduces to $\boxed{\dfrac{\partial^2 u}{\partial x^2} + \dfrac{\partial^2 u}{\partial y^2} = 0}$ ...(4)

and is called Laplace's equation in two-dimensions. Equations (3) and (4) can be extended to three-dimensional solids as,

$$\frac{\partial u}{\partial t} = c^2 \left(\frac{\partial^2 u}{\partial x^2} + \frac{\partial^2 u}{\partial y^2} + \frac{\partial^2 u}{\partial z^2} \right) \text{ and } \frac{\partial^2 u}{\partial x^2} + \frac{\partial^2 u}{\partial y^2} + \frac{\partial u^2}{\partial z^2} = 0$$

in a similar way and is called Laplace's equation in three-dimensions.

6.8 SOLUTION OF LAPLACE'S EQUATION IN TWO-DIMENSIONS BY THE METHOD OF SEPARATION OF VARIABLES

Laplace's equation in two-dimensions is $\dfrac{\partial^2 u}{\partial x^2} + \dfrac{\partial^2 u}{\partial y^2} = 0$ ... (1)

Let $u = XY$ ... (2)

where, X is a function of x alone and Y is a function of y alone, be a solution of equation (1).

Then, $\dfrac{\partial^2 u}{\partial x^2} = X'' Y \text{ and } \dfrac{\partial^2 u}{\partial y^2} = XY''$

Substituting these values in equation (1), we get

$$X''Y + XY'' = 0$$

∴ $\dfrac{X''}{X} = \dfrac{-Y''}{Y}$ ... (3)

As L.H.S. is being a function of 'x' alone and R.H.S. being a function of 'y' alone and x and y being independent variables, equation (3) will hold good only if both sides reduce to a constant, say 'k'.

∴ Equation (3) leads to,

$$\frac{X''}{X} = k \text{ and } \frac{-Y''}{Y} = k$$

Or $X'' - kX = 0$ and $Y'' + kY = 0$

∴ $(D^2 - k) X = 0$ and $(D^2 + k) Y = 0$ ... (4)

Case (i) : Let $k = 0$

$$D^2 X = 0 \implies X = c_1 x + c_2$$

$$D^2 Y = 0 \implies Y = c_3 y + c_4$$

∴ Complete solution is

$$\boxed{u(x, y) = (c_1 x + c_2)(c_3 y + c_4)}$$ ... (5)

Case (ii) : Let $k > 0$ i.e. $k = m^2$.

From equation (4),

$$(D^2 - m^2) X = 0 \implies X = c_1 e^{mx} + c_2 e^{-mx}$$

$$(D^2 + m^2) Y = 0 \implies Y = c_3 \cos my + c_4 \sin my$$

$\therefore$ Complete solution is

$$\boxed{u\,(x, y) = (c_1 e^{mx} + c_2 e^{-mx})\,(c_3 \cos my + c_4 \sin my)} \qquad \dots (6)$$

Case (iii) : Let $k < 0$, i.e. $k = -m^2$.

From equation (4),

$$(D^2 + m^2) X = 0 \implies X = c_1 \cos mx + c_2 \sin mx$$

$$(D^2 - m^2) Y = 0 \implies Y = c_3 e^{my} + c_4 e^{-my}$$

$\therefore$ Complete solution is

$$\boxed{u\,(x, y) = (c_1 \cos mx + c_2 \sin mx)\,(c_3 e^{my} + c_4 e^{-my})} \qquad \dots (7)$$

The most benefitting solution will be the one, consistent with the physical nature and the boundary conditions of the problem.

Note : To select the appropriate "most general solution", we will adopt the following procedure :

1. If in a physical problem, the plate subjected to steady temperature extends to infinity in the positive y-direction, we should take the constant $k = -m^2$ to represent each side of equation (3) i.e. if the condition given in a physical problem is $u = 0$ for $y = \infty$ for $\forall$ x between $(0, l)$ say or $u\,(x, \infty) = 0$, $\forall$ x in $(0, l)$, we always select the most suitable general solution of this nature as

$$\boxed{u\,(x, y) = (c_1 \cos mx + c_2 \sin mx)\,(c_3 e^{my} + c_4 e^{-my})}$$

2. If in a physical problem, the plate subjected to steady temperature extends to infinity in the positive x-direction, we should take the constant $k = m^2$ to represent each side of equation (3) i.e. if the condition given in a physical problem is $u = 0$ for $x = \infty$ for $\forall$ y between $(0, l)$ (say) or $u\,(\infty, y) = 0$, $\forall$ y in $(0, l)$, we always select the most suitable general solution of this nature as

$$\boxed{u\,(x, y) = (c_1 e^{mx} + c_2 e^{-mx})\,(c_3 \cos my + c_4 \sin my)}$$

3. The constant $k = 0$ is ruled out in physical applications.

4. When the constant $k = m^2$, the solution (6) can be written as

$$\boxed{u\,(x, y) = (c_1 \cosh mx + c_2 \sinh mx)\,(c_3 \cos my + c_4 \sin my)}$$

5. When the constant $k = -m^2$, the solution (7) can be written as

$$\boxed{u\,(x, y) = (c_1 \cos mx + c_2 \sin mx)\,(c_3 \cosh my + c_4 \sinh my)}$$

ILLUSTRATIONS

Ex. 1 : *Solve the equation* $\dfrac{\partial^2 V}{\partial x^2} + \dfrac{\partial^2 V}{\partial y^2} = 0$ *with conditions*

(i) $V = 0$ when $y \to +\infty$ for all x.

(ii) $V = 0$ when $x = 0$ for all values of y.

(iii) $V = 0$ when $x = 1$ for all values of y

(iv) $V = x\,(1-x)$ when $y = 0$ for $0 < x < 1$.

Sol. : Here in condition (i), $V = 0$ when $y \to \infty$, $\forall\, x$ is given, therefore we will select the most suitable solution as

$$V(x, y) = (c_1 \cos mx + c_2 \sin mx)\,(c_3\, e^{my} + c_4\, e^{-my})$$

Now condition (i) $\Rightarrow$ that $V(x, y)$ must remain finite as $y \to \infty$, this is possible only if $\boxed{c_3 = 0}$.

Also applying condition (ii), we must have $\boxed{c_1 = 0}$.

$\therefore$ The most general solution becomes

$$V(x, y) = c_5 \cdot \sin mx \cdot e^{-my}$$

Condition (iii) $\Rightarrow$ $0 = c_5 \sin m\; e^{-my}$, since $c_5 \neq 0$, otherwise $V(x, y) = 0$ will become the trivial solution and also, $e^{-my} \neq 0$.

$\therefore$ $\sin m = 0$, $m = n\pi$, $n = 1, 2, 3, \ldots\ldots$

and $V(x, y) = c_5\, \sin n\pi x\; e^{-n\pi y}, n = 1, 2, \ldots\ldots\ldots$

Combining all these solutions, we get

$$V(x, y) = \sum_{n=1}^{\infty} b_n \sin n\pi x\; e^{-n\pi y}$$

Applying condition (iv), we have

$$x(1-x) = \sum_{n=1}^{\infty} b_n \sin n\pi x, \quad 0 < x < 1$$

which is represented by half range Fourier sine series for $f(x) = x(1-x)$ in $(0, 1)$.

$$\therefore \qquad b_n = 2 \int_0^1 x(1-x) \sin n\pi x\; dx$$

$$= 2\left\{ (x - x^2)\left(-\frac{\cos n\pi x}{n\pi}\right) - (1 - 2x)\left(-\frac{\sin n\pi x}{n^2\,\pi^2}\right) + (-2)\left(\frac{\cos n\pi x}{n^3\,\pi^3}\right) \right\}_0^1$$

$$b_n = \frac{4}{\pi^3} \left(\frac{1 - (-1)^n}{n^3} \right)$$

$\therefore$ The complete solution is

$$\boxed{V(x, y) = \frac{4}{\pi^3} \sum_{n=1}^{\infty} \left(\frac{1 - (-1)^n}{n^3} \right) \sin n\pi x \cdot e^{-n\pi y}}$$

Ex. 2 : *An infinitely long uniform metal plate is enclosed between lines $y = 0$ and $y = l$ for $x > 0$. The temperature is zero along the edges $y = 0$, $y = l$ and at infinity. If the edge $x = 0$ is kept at a constant temperature u_o, find the temperature distribution $u(x, y)$.*

Sol. : We have to solve the P.D.E.

$$\frac{\partial^2 u}{\partial x^2} + \frac{\partial^2 u}{\partial y^2} = 0$$

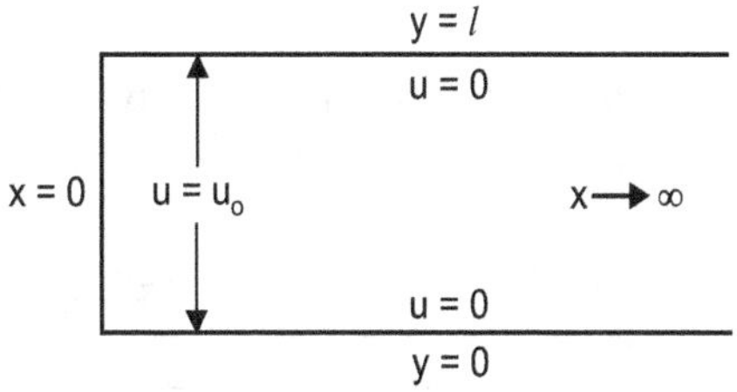

Fig. 6.6

Subject to the boundary conditions :

(i) $u(x, 0) = 0$,   (ii) $u(x, l) = 0$

(iii) $u(\infty, y) = 0$ (iv) $u(0, y) = u_o$

In condition (iii), $u = 0$ when $x \to \infty$ is given; therefore we will select the most general suitable solution as

$$u(x, y) = (c_1 e^{mx} + c_2 e^{-mx})(c_3 \cos my + c_4 \sin my)$$

Now condition (iii) $\Rightarrow$ $u(x, y)$ must remain finite as $x \to \infty$, this is possible only if $\boxed{c_1 = 0}$.

Condition (i) $\Rightarrow$ $\boxed{c_3 = 0}$

$\therefore$ $u(x, y) = c_5 \sin my \, e^{-mx}$

Condition (ii) $\Rightarrow$ $0 = c_5 \sin ml \, e^{-mx}$

$c_5 \neq 0$, $e^{-mx} \neq 0$, $\therefore$ $\sin ml = 0$

$$ml = n\pi \qquad \therefore m = \frac{n\pi}{l}, \ n = 1, 2, 3, \ldots\ldots\ldots$$

$$u(x, y) = c_5 \, \sin \frac{n\pi y}{l} e^{-\frac{n\pi x}{l}}, \ n = 1, 2, \ldots\ldots$$

Combining all these solutions, we have

$$u\,(x,\,y)\;=\;\sum_{n=1}^{\infty}\,b_n\,\sin\frac{n\pi y}{l}\,e^{-\frac{n\pi x}{l}}$$

Applying condition (iv), we have

$$u_o\;=\;\sum_{n=1}^{\infty}\,b_n\,\sin\frac{n\pi y}{l},\;\;0<y<l$$

which is represented by half range Fourier sine series for f (y) = u_o in (0, l).

$$\therefore\qquad b_n\;=\;\frac{2}{l}\int_0^{l}\,u_o\,\sin\frac{n\pi y}{l}\,dy\;=\;\frac{2\,u_o}{l}\left[-\frac{l}{n\pi}\cos\frac{n\pi y}{l}\right]_0^{l}$$

$$b_n\;=\;\frac{2\,u_o}{\pi}\left(\frac{1-(-1)^n}{n}\right)$$

$\therefore$ The complete solution is

$$u\,(x,\,y)\;=\;\frac{2\,u_o}{\pi}\sum_{n=1}^{\infty}\frac{1-(-1)^n}{n}\,\sin\frac{n\pi y}{l}\,e^{-\frac{n\pi x}{l}}$$

$$u\,(x,\,y)\;=\;\frac{4\,u_o}{\pi}\sum_{n=1}^{\infty}\left(\frac{1}{2n-1}\right)\,\sin\left(\frac{(2n-1)\,\pi y}{l}\right)\cdot e^{\frac{-(2n-1)\,\pi x}{l}}$$

Ex. 3 : *A rectangular plate is bounded by x = 0, x = a, y = 0, y = b. Its surfaces are insulated and temperature along three edges x = 0, x = a, y = 0 is maintained at 0°C while the fourth edge y = b is maintained at constant temperature u_o, until steady state is reached. Find u (x, y).*

Sol. : We have to solve the P.D.E. $\dfrac{\partial^2 u}{\partial x^2}+\dfrac{\partial^2 u}{\partial y^2}=0$, subject to the boundary conditions :

(i)   u (0, y) = 0

(ii) u (x, 0) = 0

(iii) u (a, y) = 0

(iv) u (x, b) = u_o

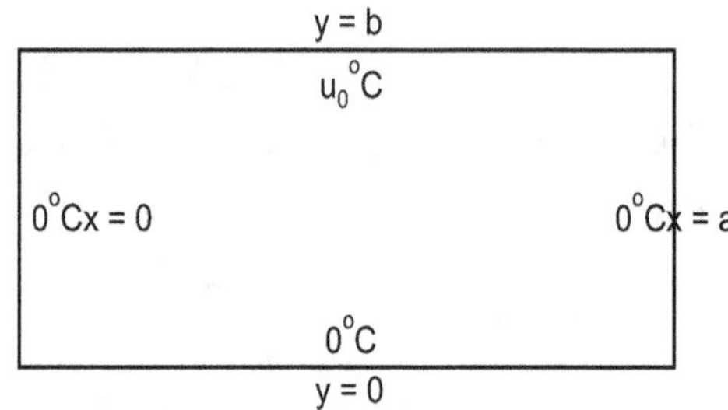

Fig. 6.7

If we consider u (x, y) = (c_1 cosh mx + c_2 sinh mx) (c_3 cos my + c_4 sin my) then by applying (i), c_1 = 0, but then u (a, y) cannot become zero because sinh am cannot be zero, for any non-zero value of m. Hence the possible solution may be given by

$$u\,(x,\,y)\;=\;(c_1\cos mx + c_2\sin mx)\,(c_3\cosh my + c_4\sinh my)$$

(i) $\Rightarrow$ c_1 = 0

(ii)　$\Rightarrow$　　　　$c_3 = 0$

$\therefore$　　　　　$u(x, y) = c_5 \sin mx \sinh my$

(iii)　$\Rightarrow$　　　　$0 = c_5 \sin ma \sinh my$

　　　　$c_5 \neq 0, \ \sinh my \neq 0 \quad \therefore \ \sin ma = 0$

$$ma = n\pi, \ m = \frac{n\pi}{a}, n = 1, 2, \ldots\ldots\ldots\ldots$$

$\therefore$　　　　$u(x, y) = c_5 \sin \frac{n\pi x}{a} \sinh \frac{n\pi y}{a}, \ n = 1, 2, \ldots\ldots\ldots$

Or　　　　$u(x, y) = \sum_{n=1}^{\infty} b_n \sin \frac{n\pi x}{a} \sinh \frac{n\pi y}{a}$

Applying condition (iv), we get

$$u_0 = \sum_{n=1}^{\infty} b_n \sin \frac{n\pi x}{a} \sinh \frac{n\pi b}{a}$$

$\therefore$　　　$b_n \sinh \frac{n\pi b}{a} = \frac{2}{a} \int_0^a u_0 \sin \frac{n\pi x}{a} \, dx$

$$= \frac{2 u_0}{a} \left[-\frac{a}{n\pi} \cos \frac{n\pi x}{a} \right]_0^a = \frac{2 u_0}{\pi} \left(\frac{1 - (-1)^n}{n} \right)$$

$$b_n = \frac{2 u_0}{\pi \sinh \frac{n\pi b}{a}} \left(\frac{1 - (-1)^n}{n} \right)$$

$\therefore$　　$u(x, y) = \frac{2 u_0}{\pi} \sum_{n=1}^{\infty} \frac{1 - (-1)^n}{n} \cdot \sin \frac{n\pi x}{a} \ \frac{\sinh \frac{n\pi y}{a}}{\sinh \frac{n\pi b}{a}}$

$$u(x, y) = \frac{4 u_0}{\pi} \sum_{n=1}^{\infty} \frac{1}{2n-1} \cdot \sin \frac{(2n-1)\pi x}{a} \cdot \frac{\sinh \frac{(2n-1)\pi y}{a}}{\sinh \frac{(2n-1)\pi b}{a}}$$

Ex. 4 : *A rectangular plate with insulated surfaces is 10 cm wide and so long compared to its width that it may be considered infinite in length without introducing an appreciable error. If the temperature along short edge y = 0 is given $u(x, 0) = 100 \sin\left(\frac{\pi x}{10}\right)$, $0 \leq x \leq 10$, while the two long edges x = 0 and x = 10 as well as the other short edge are kept at $0°C$. Find steady-state temperature u(x, y).*

Sol. : We have to solve the P.D.E. $\dfrac{\partial^2 u}{\partial x^2} + \dfrac{\partial^2 u}{\partial y^2} = 0$

Subject to the conditions :

(i) $u(x, \infty) = 0$

(ii) $u(0, y) = 0$

(iii) $u(10, y) = 0$

(iv) $u(x, 0) = 100 \sin\left(\dfrac{\pi x}{10}\right),$

$$0 \le x \le 10.$$

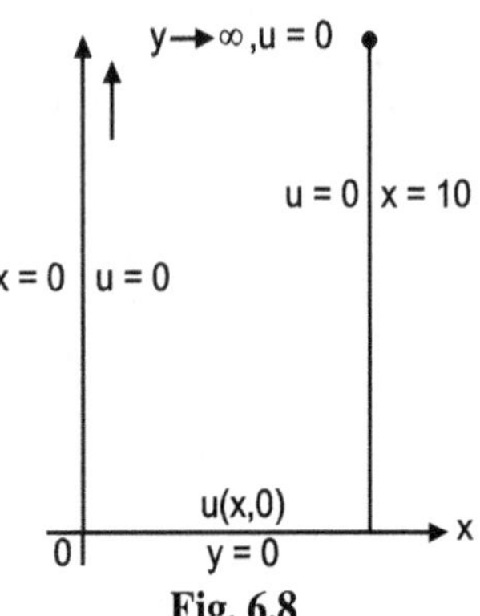

Fig. 6.8

The most general solution is

$$u(x, y) = (c_1 \cos mx + c_2 \sin mx)(c_3 e^{my} + c_4 e^{-my})$$

(i) $\Rightarrow$ $c_3 = 0$

(ii) $\Rightarrow$ $c_1 = 0$

$$u(x, y) = c_5 \sin mx \, e^{-my}$$

(iii) $\Rightarrow$ $0 = c_5 \sin 10 \, m \, e^{-my}$

$$\sin 10 \, m = 0, \quad 10 \, m = n\pi$$

$\therefore$ $m = \dfrac{n\pi}{10},$ $n = 1, 2, 3, \ldots\ldots$

$$u(x, y) = c_5 \sin \dfrac{n\pi x}{10} \, e^{-\frac{n\pi y}{10}}, \qquad\qquad n = 1, 2, \ldots\ldots$$

Or
$$\boxed{u(x, y) = \sum_{n=1}^{\infty} b_n \sin \dfrac{n\pi x}{10} \, e^{-\frac{n\pi y}{10}}}$$

Applying condition (iv), we have

$$100 \sin\left(\dfrac{\pi x}{10}\right) = \sum_{n=1}^{\infty} b_n \sin \dfrac{n\pi x}{10}$$

$$100 \sin\left(\dfrac{\pi x}{10}\right) = b_1 \sin \dfrac{\pi x}{10} + b_2 \sin \dfrac{2\pi x}{10} + \ldots\ldots$$

$$b_1 = 100, \quad b_2 = 0 = b_3 = b_4 = \ldots\ldots = b_n = \ldots\ldots$$

$\therefore$ The complete solution is

$$u(x, y) = b_1 \sin \dfrac{\pi x}{10} \, e^{-\frac{\pi y}{10}} + b_2 \sin \dfrac{2\pi x}{10} \, e^{-\frac{2\pi y}{10}} + \ldots\ldots$$

$$\boxed{u(x, y) = 100 \sin \dfrac{\pi x}{10} \, e^{-\frac{\pi y}{10}}}$$

Ex. 5 : *An infinitely long plane uniform plate is bounded by two parallel edges in the y-direction and an end at right angles to them. The breadth of the plate is π. This end is maintained at temperature u_o at all points and other edges at zero temperature. Find the steady-state temperature function u (x, y).*

Sol. : We have to solve the P.D.E. $\dfrac{\partial^2 u}{\partial x^2} + \dfrac{\partial^2 u}{\partial y^2} = 0$

Subject to the conditions :

(i) $u (0, y) = 0$

(ii) $u (\pi, y) = 0$

(iii) $u (x, \infty) = 0$ for $0 < x < \pi$

(iv) $u (x, 0) = u_o$ for $0 < x < \pi$.

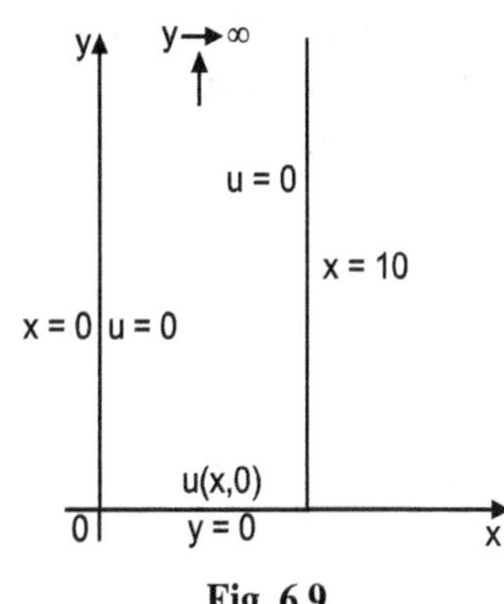

Fig. 6.9

The most general solution is

$$u(x, y) = (c_1 \cos mx + c_2 \sin mx)\ (c_3\ e^{my} + c_4\ e^{-my})$$

(iii) $\Rightarrow$ $\qquad\qquad c_3 = 0$

(i) $\Rightarrow$ $\qquad\qquad c_1 = 0$

$\therefore \qquad u (x, y) = c_5 \sin mx\ e^{-my}$

(ii) $\Rightarrow$ $\qquad\qquad 0 = c_5 \sin m\pi\ e^{-my}$

$\qquad c_5 \neq 0, \quad e^{-my} \neq 0, \quad \sin m\pi = 0$

$$m\pi = n\pi, \quad m = n, \quad n = 1, 2, \ldots\ldots$$

$\therefore \qquad u (x, y) = c_5\ \sin nx\ e^{-ny}, \quad n = 1, 2, \ldots\ldots$

Or

$$\boxed{u (x, y) = \sum_{n = 1}^{\infty} b_n\ \sin nx\ e^{-ny}}$$

Condition (iv) $\Rightarrow$

$$u_o = \sum_{1}^{\infty} b_n\ \sin nx, \qquad\qquad 0 < x < \pi$$

$$b_n = \frac{2}{\pi} \int_0^{\pi} u_o \sin nx\ dx = \frac{2\,u_o}{\pi} \left(\frac{-\cos nx}{n}\right)_0^{\pi} = \frac{2u_o}{\pi} \left(\frac{1 - (-1)^n}{n}\right)$$

$$\therefore \qquad u\,(x,\,y) \;=\; \frac{2\,u_0}{\pi}\,\sum_{n=1}^{\infty}\left(\frac{1-(-1)^n}{n}\right)\,\sin nx\ e^{-ny}$$

$$u\,(x,\,y) \;=\; \frac{4\,u_0}{\pi}\,\sum_{n=1}^{\infty}\,\frac{1}{2n-1}\ \sin\,(2n-1)\,x\ e^{-(2n-1)y}$$

Ex. 6 : *A rectangular plate with insulated surface is 10 cm wide and so long to its width that it may be considered infinite in length without introducing an appreciable error. If the temperature of the short edge y = 0 is given by,*

$$u \;=\; 20\,x \qquad\quad ;\ for\ 0\ \le x\ \le 5$$

$$=\; 20\,(10-x)\,;\ for\ 5\le x\le 10$$

and the two long edges x = 0, x = 10 as well as the other short edge are kept at $0^{\circ}C$, then prove that the temperature u at any point (x, y) is given by,

$$u \;=\; \frac{800}{\pi^2}\,\sum_{1}^{\infty}\,\frac{(-1)^{n+1}}{(2n-1)^2}\,\sin\,\frac{(2n-1)\,\pi x}{10}\,.\,e^{\frac{-(2n-1)\,\pi y}{10}}$$

Sol. : The temperature u(x, y) satisfies the equation :

$$\frac{\partial^2 u}{\partial x^2} \;+\; \frac{\partial^2 u}{\partial y^2} \;=\; 0$$

The boundary conditions being as follows,

(i) u (0, y) = 0   for all positive values of y including zero.

(ii) u (10, y) = 0   for all $y \ge 0$

(iii) u (x, ∞) = 0   for $0 \le x \le 10$ and

(iv) u (x, 0) = 20 x, $0 \le x \le 5$

$$= 20\,(10-x),\ 5 \le x \le 10$$

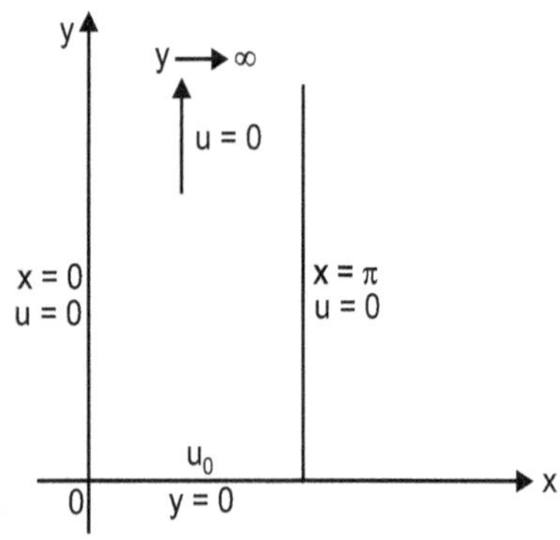

Fig. 6.10

The most suitable solution is

$$u\,(x,\,y) \;=\; (c_1 \cos mx + c_2 \sin mx)\,(c_3\,e^{my} + c_4\,e^{-my})$$

(iii) $\Rightarrow$ $\qquad\qquad c_3 = 0$

(i) $\quad\Rightarrow$ $\qquad\qquad c_1 = 0$

$$u\,(x,\,y) \;=\; c_5 \sin mx\ e^{-my}$$

(ii) $\quad\Rightarrow$ $\qquad\qquad 0 = c_5 \sin 10\,m\ e^{-my}$

$$c_5 \neq 0, \quad e^{-my} \neq 0, \quad \sin 10\,m = 0$$

$$10\,m = n\pi, \quad m = \frac{n\pi}{10}, \quad n = 1, 2, \ldots\ldots$$

$$u\,(x,\,y) = c_5 \sin \frac{n\pi x}{10}\, e^{\frac{-n\pi y}{10}}, \quad n = 1, 2, \ldots\ldots$$

Or
$$u\,(x,\,y) = \sum_{n=1}^{\infty} b_n \sin \frac{n\pi x}{10}\, e^{\frac{-n\pi y}{10}}$$

Applying condition (iv), we get

$$u\,(x,\,0) = \sum_{n=1}^{\infty} b_n \sin \frac{n\pi x}{10}$$

$$\therefore \qquad b_n = \frac{2}{10} \left\{ \int_0^5 20x \sin \frac{n\pi x}{10}\, dx + \int_5^{10} 20\,(10 - x)\, \sin \frac{n\pi x}{10} \cdot dx \right\}$$

$$= 4 \left\{ \left[(x) \left(-\frac{10}{n\pi} \cos \frac{n\pi x}{10} \right) - (1)\left(-\frac{100}{n^2\,\pi^2} \sin \frac{n\pi x}{10} \right) \right]_0^5 \right.$$

$$\left. + \left[(10 - x) \left(-\frac{10}{n\pi} \cos \frac{n\pi x}{10} \right) - (-1)\left(-\frac{100}{n^2\pi^2} \sin \frac{n\pi x}{10} \right) \right]_5^{10} \right\}$$

$$= 4 \left\{ -\frac{50}{n\pi} \cos \frac{n\pi}{2} + \frac{100}{n^2\pi^2} \sin \frac{n\pi}{2} + \frac{50}{n\pi} \cos \frac{n\pi}{2} + \frac{100}{n^2\pi^2} \sin \frac{n\pi}{2} \right\}$$

$$= \frac{800}{n^2\pi^2} \sin \frac{n\pi}{2}$$

The complete solution is

$$u\,(x,\,y) = \frac{800}{\pi^2} \sum_{n=1}^{\infty} \frac{\sin \dfrac{n\pi}{2}}{n^2} \sin \frac{n\pi x}{10}\, e^{-\frac{n\pi y}{10}}$$

Ex. 7 : *A square metal plate of side a has edges represented by lines x = 0, x = a, y = 0, y = a. The edges x = a and y = a are insulated. The edge x = 0 is kept at 0° C and y = 0 at $u_o\,^\circ$C where u_o is a constant. Obtain the temperature distribution u (x, y) under steady-state conditions.*

Sol. : We have to solve the P.D.E. $\dfrac{\partial^2 u}{\partial x^2} + \dfrac{\partial^2 u}{\partial y^2} = 0$

Subject to the boundary conditions :

(i) $u(0, y) = 0$

(ii) $\left(\dfrac{\partial u}{\partial y}\right)_{y = a} = 0$

(iii) $\left(\dfrac{\partial u}{\partial x}\right)_{x = a} = 0$

(iv) $u(x, 0) = u_0 \,°C$

If we take solution given by $k = m^2$

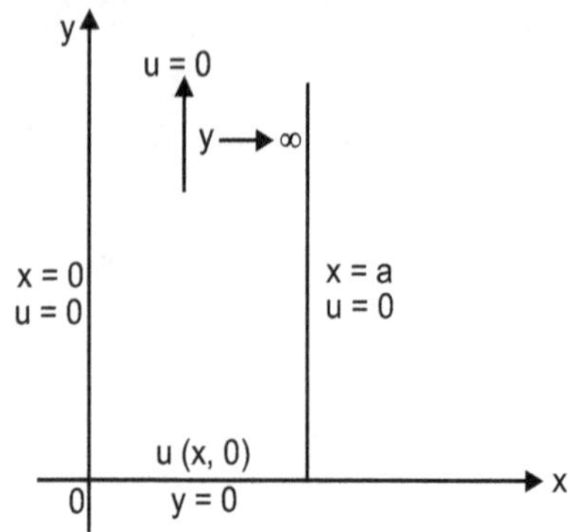

Fig. 6.11

i.e. $u(x, y) = (c_1 \cosh mx + c_2 \sinh mx)\,(c_3 \cos my + c_4 \sin my)$ then (i) is satisfied if $c_1 = 0$

but then $\dfrac{\partial u}{\partial x}\Big|_{x = a} = 0$ cannot be satisfied because cosh am can never be zero for any value of m.

Therefore, the most general solution is

$$u(x, y) = (c_1 \cos mx + c_2 \sin mx)\,(c_3 \cosh my + c_4 \sinh my)$$

(i) $\Rightarrow$ $c_1 = 0$

$\therefore$ $u(x, y) = \sin mx\,[c_3' \cosh my + c_4' \sinh my]$

$$\frac{\partial u}{\partial y} = (\sin mx)\,[m\,c_3' \sinh my + m\,c_4' \cosh my]$$

(ii) $\Rightarrow$ $0 = (\sin mx)\,[m\,c_3' \sinh ma + m\,c_4' \cosh ma]$

Here $m \neq 0$, $\sin mx \neq 0$ (otherwise we get trivial solution)

$$c_3' \sinh ma + c_4' \cosh ma = 0$$

$$c_4' = -\frac{c_3' \sinh ma}{\cosh ma}$$

$\therefore$ $u(x, y) = \sin mx\left[c_3' \cosh my - \dfrac{c_3' \sinh ma}{\cosh ma}\, \sinh my\right]$

$$= \frac{c_3' \sin mx}{\cosh ma}\,(\cosh my \cosh ma - \sinh ma \sinh my)$$

$$\frac{\partial u}{\partial x} = \frac{c_3'\, m \cos mx}{\cosh ma}\,\cosh (a - y)\, m$$

(iii) $\Rightarrow$ $0 = \dfrac{c_3' m \cos ma}{\cosh ma}\,\cosh (a - y)\, m$

$$\cos ma = 0, \qquad ma = \frac{(2n - 1)\,\pi}{2}$$

$$m = \frac{(2n-1)\,\pi}{2a}, \quad n = 1, 2, 3, \ldots\ldots\ldots$$

$$\therefore \quad u(x, y) = \frac{c_3'\, \sin\dfrac{(2n-1)\,\pi x}{2a}\, \cosh\left(\dfrac{(2n-1)\,\pi\,(a-y)}{2a}\right)}{\cosh\dfrac{(2n-1)\,\pi}{2}}$$

Or
$$u(x, y) = \sum_{n=1}^{\infty} \frac{b_n\, \sin\dfrac{(2n-1)\,\pi x}{2a}}{\cosh\dfrac{(2n-1)\,\pi}{2}}\, \cosh\left(\frac{(2n-1)\pi\,(a-y)}{2a}\right)$$

Applying condition (iv), we get

$$u_0 = \sum_{n=1}^{\infty} \frac{b_n\, \sin\dfrac{(2n-1)\,\pi x}{2a}}{\cosh\dfrac{(2n-1)\,\pi}{2}}\, \cosh\frac{(2n-1)\,\pi}{2}$$

$$u_0 = \sum_{n=1}^{\infty} b_n\, \sin\left(\frac{(2n-1)\,\pi x}{2a}\right)$$

$$\therefore \quad b_n = \frac{2}{a} \int_0^a u_0 \sin\frac{(2n-1)\,\pi x}{2a}\, dx$$

$$= \frac{2\,u_0}{a} \left[\frac{-2a}{(2n-1)\,\pi}\, \cos\frac{(2n-1)\,\pi x}{2a}\right]_0^a$$

$$= \frac{-4\,u_0}{\pi}\, \frac{1}{2n-1}\, [0-1] = \frac{4\,u_0}{\pi}\, \frac{1}{2n-1}$$

$$\therefore \quad u(x, y) = \frac{4\,u_0}{\pi} \sum_{n=1}^{\infty} \frac{\dfrac{1}{2n-1}\, \sin\dfrac{(2n-1)\,\pi x}{2a}}{\cosh(2n-1)\dfrac{\pi}{2}}\, .\, \cosh\left(\frac{(2n-1)\,\pi\,(a-y)}{2a}\right)$$

$$\therefore \quad u(x, y) = \frac{4\,u_0}{\pi} \sum_{n=1}^{\infty} \frac{\operatorname{sech}(2n-1)\dfrac{\pi}{2}\, \sin\dfrac{(2n-1)\,\pi x}{2a}\, \cosh\dfrac{(2n-1)\,\pi\,(a-y)}{2a}}{\cosh(2n-1)\dfrac{\pi}{2}}$$

EXERCISE 6.3

1. A thin sheet of metal bounded by the x-axis and the lines $x = 0$ and $x = 1$ and stretching to infinity in the y-direction has its upper and lower faces perfectly insulated and its vertical edges and edge at infinity are maintained at the constant temperature 0°C, while over the base temperature of 100°C is maintained. Find steady-state temperature $u(x, y)$.

$$\textbf{Ans.:}\ u(x, y) = \frac{400}{\pi} \sum_{n=1}^{\infty} \frac{\sin(2n-1)\,\pi x}{2n-1}\, e^{-(2n-1)\,\pi y}$$

2. Work example (1) if the temperature along short edge $y = 0$ is

$$u(x, 0) = (x - x^2) \text{ degrees}$$

$$\textbf{Ans.:} \ u(x, y) = \frac{4}{\pi^3} \sum_{n=1}^{\infty} \frac{\sin(2n-1)\,nx}{(2n-1)^3} \ e^{-(2n-1)\,\pi y}$$

3. Work example (1) if the temperature along short edge $y = 0$ is

$$u(x, 0) = \begin{cases} x & 0 < x \le 0.5 \\ \\ 1 - x & 0.5 \le x < 1 \end{cases}$$

$$\textbf{Ans.:} \ u(x, y) = \frac{4}{\pi^2} \sum_{n=1}^{\infty} \frac{(-1)^{n-1} \sin(2n-1)\,\pi x}{(2n-1)^2} \cdot e^{-(2n-1)\,\pi y}$$

4. The lower side $(y = 0)$ of a rectangular metal plate of length a and width b, with insulated upper and lower surfaces is kept at $100°C$ while upper side $y = b$ is insulated. If the other two sides are kept at $0°C$, find the steady-state temperature distribution of the plate.

$$\textbf{Ans.:} \ u(x, y) = \frac{200}{\pi} \sum_{n=1}^{\infty} \frac{1}{n} (1 - \cos n\pi) \sin \frac{n\pi x}{a} \left(\cosh \frac{n\pi y}{a} - \sinh \frac{n\pi y}{a} \tan \frac{n\pi b}{a} \right)$$

5. A square plate has its faces as well as edges $x = 0$ and $x = \pi$ $(0 < y < \pi)$ are insulated. Its edges $y = 0$ and $y = \pi$ are kept at temperature $0°C$ and $f(x)$ respectively. Show that

$$u(x, y) = \frac{a_0}{2} + \sum_{n=1}^{\infty} a_n \frac{\sinh ny}{\sinh nx} \cos nx$$

where, $\quad a_n = \dfrac{2}{\pi} \displaystyle\int_0^{\pi} f(x) \cos nx \, dx, \ n = 0, 1, 2, \ldots\ldots$

6. A rectangular plate bounded by lines $x = 0$, $x = a$, $y = 0$ and $y = b$, has its faces insulated while the edges $x = 0$, $x = a$ and $y = b$ are kept at zero degree and lower edge $(y = 0)$ is having temperature distribution. $5 \sin \dfrac{4\pi x}{a} + 3 \sin \dfrac{3\pi x}{a}$. Find the steady-state temperature distribution.

$$\textbf{Ans.:} \ u(x, y) = 3 \sin \frac{3\pi x}{a} \sinh \frac{3\pi (b-y)}{a} \operatorname{cosech} \frac{3\pi b}{a}$$

$$+ \ 5 \sin \frac{4\pi x}{a} \sinh \frac{4\pi (b-y)}{a} \operatorname{cosech} \frac{4\pi b}{a}.$$

7. A square plate has its faces insulated. The edges $x = 0$ and $x = \pi$ are also insulated while the edge $y = \pi$ is kept at $0°C$. The edge $y = 0$ has temperature distribution $u\,(x, 0) = x^2$. Find the steady-state temperature distribution.

$$\textbf{Ans. : } u\,(x, y) = \frac{\pi^2}{3} + 4 \sum_{n=1}^{\infty} \frac{(-1)^n \sinh n\,(\pi - y)\cos nx}{n^2 \sinh n\pi}$$

8. A rectangular metal plate is bounded by $x = 0$, $x = a$, $y = 0$, $y = b$. The edges $x = 0$, $x = a$, $y = b$ are insulated and the edge $y = 0$ is kept at temperature $u_o \cos \dfrac{\pi x}{a}$. Find the temperature distribution $u\,(x, y)$ in steady-state conditions.

$$\textbf{Ans. } u(x, y) = u \cos \frac{\pi x}{a} \cos \frac{\pi}{a} (b - y) \sec \frac{\pi b}{a}.$$

6.9 SOLUTION OF LAPLACE EQUATION BY THE GAUSS -SIEDEL ITERATIVE METHOD

The Laplace equation $\nabla^2 u = \dfrac{\partial^2 u}{\partial x^2} + \dfrac{\partial^2 u}{\partial y^2} = 0$ ...(A)

which occurs in the condition of heat in a plate in steady state.

Geometric representation of partial differential equation

Let (x,y) plane be partitioned into a network of rectangles of side $\Delta x = h$ $\Delta y = k$ by drawing the sets of lines.

The points of intersections of these families of lines are called mesh points, grid points ar lattice. Thus the points $(x, y), (x + h, y), (x + 2h, y)$, $(x - h, y)$, $(x - 2h, y),...$are the grid points as shown in figure below.

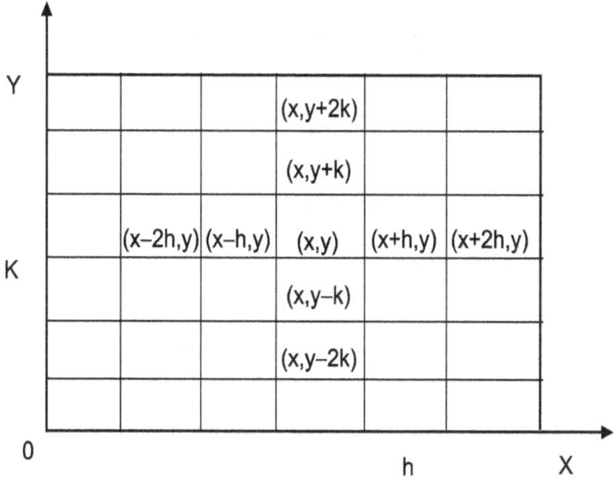

Fig. 6.12

Standard Five points formula and Diagonal five points formula

Consider the Laplace equation in two dimensions $\nabla^2 u = \dfrac{\partial^2 u}{\partial x^2} + \dfrac{\partial^2 u}{\partial y^2} = 0$

Its finite difference analog is $\dfrac{u_{i+1,\,j} - 2u_{i,j} + u_{i-1,\,j}}{h^2} + \dfrac{u_{i,\,j+1} - 2u_{i,\,j} + u_{i,\,j-1}}{k^2} = 0$

If we consider square mesh that is h = k, then above equation becomes

$$u_{i,j} = \frac{1}{4}\left[u_{i+1,\,j} + u_{i-1,\,j} + u_{i,\,j+1} + u_{i,\,j-1}\right] \qquad \ldots(B)$$

Above equation shows that the value of u at any point is the mean of its values at the four neighboring points as shown in figure below

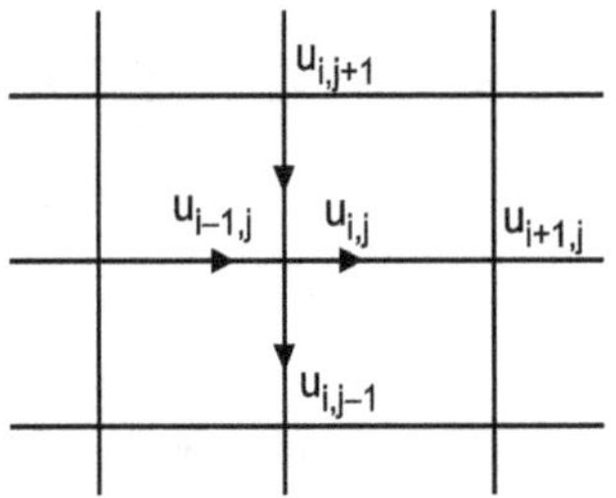

Fig. 6.13 : Standard five points formula

Equation (B) is called as standard five point formula.

If we rotate the coordinate axes through 45°, then the Laplace equation remains invariant. Therefore, we may use the function values at the diagonal points in place of the neighboring points. Then we may use the formula

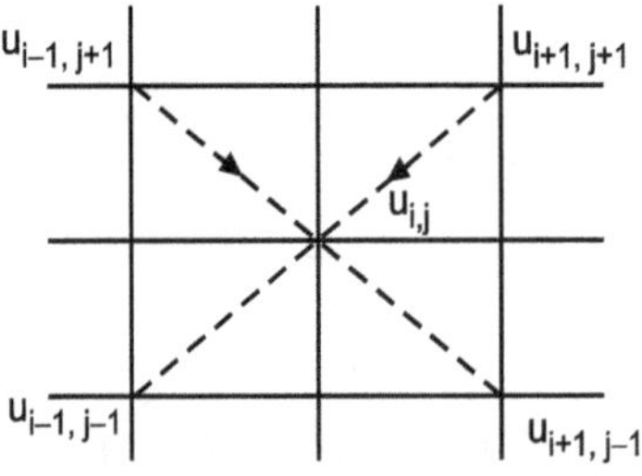

Fig. 6.14 : Diagonal five point formula

$$u_{i,j} = \frac{1}{4}\left[u_{i-1,\,j-1} + u_{i+1,\,j-1} + u_{i+1,\,j+1} + u_{i-1,\,j+1}\right] \qquad \ldots(C)$$

This formula is called as Diagonal five point formula.

Gauss- Seidel Method

This method uses the latest iterative values available and scans the mesh points systematically from left to right along successive rows. The formula is

$$u_{i,j}^{(n+1)} = \frac{1}{4}\left[u_{i-1,j}^{(n+1)} + u_{i,j+1}^{(n+1)} + u_{i,j-1}^{(n)}\right]$$

Note: We carry out the iteration till we get desired degree of accuracy.

ILLUSTRATIONS

Ex. 1 : *Solve Laplace equation* $\dfrac{\partial^2 u}{\partial x^2} + \dfrac{\partial^2 u}{\partial y^2} = 0$ *(or* $u_{xx} + u_{yy} = 0$*) for the square meshes with the boundary values shown in figure*

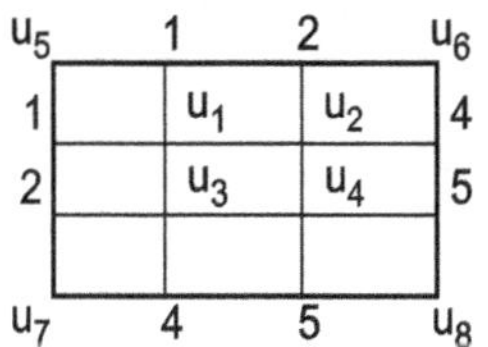

Fig. 6.15

Sol. : Using Diagonal five points formula, we have

$$u_1 = \frac{1}{4}[2 + 2 + u_4 + u_5] \qquad \ldots(1)$$

$$u_2 = \frac{1}{4}[1 + 5 + u_3 + u_6] \qquad \ldots(2)$$

$$u_3 = \frac{1}{4}[1 + 5 + u_2 + u_7] \qquad \ldots(3)$$

$$u_4 = \frac{1}{4}[4 + 4 + u_1 + u_8] \qquad \ldots(4)$$

If we use the standard five points formula, we have

$$u_1 = \frac{1}{4}[1 + u_2 + u_3 + 1] \qquad \ldots(5)$$

$$u_2 = \frac{1}{4}[4 + 2 + u_1 + u_4] \qquad \ldots(6)$$

$$u_3 = \frac{1}{4}[2 + + 4 + u_4 + u_1] \qquad \ldots(7)$$

$$u_4 = \frac{1}{4}[5 + 5 + u_2 + u_3] \qquad \ldots(8)$$

Equations (6) and (7) RHS is equal therefore $u_2 = u_3$

Thus the expressions (5),(6),(7) and (8) reduces to

$$u_1 = \frac{1}{4}[2 + 2u_2]$$

$$u_2 = \frac{1}{4}[6 + u_1 + u_4]$$

$$u_3 = \frac{1}{4}[6 + u_4 + u_1]$$

$$u_4 = \frac{1}{4}[10 + 2u_2]$$

If we start with the approximation $u_2 = 0$, then $u_2 = \frac{1}{2}$, $u_2 = 0$, $u_3 = 0$, $u_3 = \frac{5}{2}$

Then by Gauss-Seidel method, we have

$$u_1^{(1)} = \frac{1}{4}[1 + 0 + 1 + 0] = 0.5$$

$$u_2^{(1)} = \frac{1}{4}\left[\frac{1}{2} + \frac{5}{2} + 4 + 2\right] = \frac{9}{4} = 2.25$$

$$u_3^{(1)} = \frac{1}{4}\left[2 + 4 + \frac{5}{2} + \frac{1}{2}\right] = \frac{9}{4} = 2.25$$

$$u_4^{(1)} = \frac{1}{4}\left[5 + 5 + \frac{9}{4} + \frac{9}{4}\right] = \frac{5}{2} = 2.50$$

$$u_1^{(2)} = \frac{1}{4}[1 + 2.25 + 1 + 2.25] = 1.625$$

$$u_2^{(2)} = \frac{1}{4}[1.625 + 4 + 2.50 + 2] = 2.53125$$

$$u_3^{(2)} = \frac{1}{4}[2 + 4 + 1.625 + 2.50] = 2.53125$$

$$u_4^{(2)} = \frac{1}{4}[5 + 5 + 2.53125 + 2.53125] = 3.765625$$

$$u_1^{(3)} = \frac{1}{4}[1 + 1 + 2.53125 + 2.53125] = 1.765625$$

$$u_2^{(3)} = \frac{1}{4}[4 + 2 + 1.765625 + 3.765625] = 2.8828125$$

$$u_3^{(3)} = \frac{1}{4}[4 + 2 + 1.765625 + 3.765625] = 2.8828125$$

$$u_4^{(3)} = \frac{1}{4}[5 + 5 + 2.8828125 + 2.8828125] = 3.9414031$$

$$u_1^{(4)} = [1 + 1 + 2.8828125 + 2.8828125] = 1.94140625$$

$$u_2^{(4)} = \frac{1}{4}[2 + 4 + 1.94140625 + 3.9414031] = 2.970702338$$

$$u_3^{(4)} = \frac{1}{4}[2 + 4 + 1.94140625 + 3.9414031] = 2.970702338$$

$$u_4^{(4)} = \frac{1}{4}[5 + 5 + 2.970702338 + 2.970702338] = 3.985351169$$

$$u_1^{(5)} = \frac{1}{4}[1 + 1 + 2.970702338 + 2.970702338] = 1.985351169$$

$$u_2^{(5)} = \frac{1}{4}[2 + 4 + 1.985351169 + 3.985351169] = 2.992675585$$

$$u_3^{(5)} = \frac{1}{4}[2 + 4 + 1.985351169 + 3.985351169] = 2.992675585$$

$$u_4^{(5)} = \frac{1}{4}[5 + 4 + 2.992675585 + 2.992675585] = 3.996337793$$

$$u_1^{(6)} = \frac{1}{4}[1 + 1 + 2.992675585 + 2.992675585] = 1.996337793$$

$$u_2^{(6)} = \frac{1}{4}[2 + 4 + 1.996337793 + 1.996337793] = 2.998168897$$

$$u_3^{(6)} = \frac{1}{4}[2 + 4 + 1.996337793 + 1.996337793] = 2.998168897$$

$$u_4^{(6)} = \frac{1}{4}[5 + 5 + 2.998168897 + 2.998168897] = 3.999084449$$

$$u_1^{(7)} = \frac{1}{4}[1 + 1 + 2.998168897 + 2.998168897] = 1.999084449$$

$$u_2^{(7)} = \frac{1}{4}[2 + 4 + 1.99908449 + 3.99908449] = 2.999642224$$

$$u_3^{(7)} = \frac{1}{4}[2 + 4 + 1.999084449 + 3.999084449] = 2.999542224$$

$$u_4^{(7)} = \frac{1}{4}[5 + 5 + 2.999542224 + 2.999542224] = 3.999771112$$

As the values of 6th and 7th iterations agree up to two decimal places, hence

$$u_1 = 1.99908449, \quad u_2 = 2.999542224, \quad u_3 = 2.999542224, \quad u_4 = 3.999771112$$

Ex. 2 : *Solve Laplace equation $u_{xx} + u_{yy} = 0$ for the square meshes with the boundary values shown in figure*

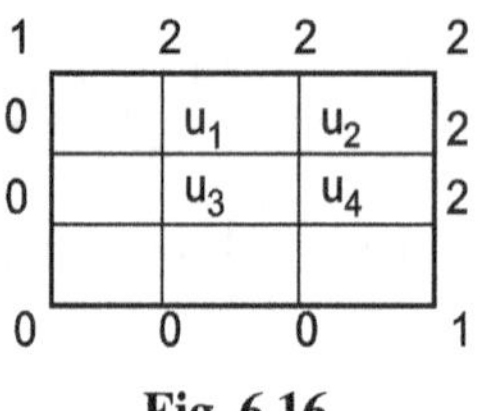

Fig. 6.16

Sol. : We assume that $u_4 = 0$

$$u_1 = \frac{1}{4}[1 + 2 + 0 + 0] = 0.75 \qquad \text{(Diagonal five point formula)}$$

$$u_2 = \frac{1}{4}[0.75 + 2 + 2 + 0] = 1.1875 \qquad \text{(Standard five point formula)}$$

$$u_3 = \frac{1}{4}[0 + 0 + 0.75 + 0] = 0.1875 \qquad \text{(Standard five point formula)}$$

$$u_4 = \frac{1}{4}[0.1875 + 2 + 0 + 1.1875] = 0.84375 \qquad \text{(Standard five point formula)}$$

Then by Gauss-Seidel method, we have

$$u_1^{(1)} = \frac{1}{4}[0 + 1.1875 + 0.1875 + 2] = 0.84375$$

$$u_2^{(1)} = \frac{1}{4}[0.84375 + 2 + 2 + 0.84375] = 1.421875$$

$$u_3^{(1)} = \frac{1}{4}[0 + 0.84375 + 0 + 0.84375] = 0.421875$$

$$u_4^{(1)} = \frac{1}{4}[0.421975 + 2 + 0 + 1.421875] = 0.9609375$$

$$u_1^{(2)} = \frac{1}{4}[0 + 2 + 1.421875 + 0.421875] = 0.9609375$$

$$u_2^{(2)} = \frac{1}{4}[0.96093975 + 2 + 2 + 0.9609375] = 1.48046875$$

$$u_3^{(2)} = \frac{1}{4}[0 + 0.9609375 + 0 + 0.9609375] = 0.48046875$$

$$u_4^{(2)} = \frac{1}{4}[0.48046875 + 2 + 0 + 1.48046875] = 0.990234375$$

$$u_1^{(3)} = \frac{1}{4}[0 + 1.48046875 + 0.48046875 + 2] = 0.990234375$$

$$u^{(3)}_2 = \frac{1}{4}\,[0.990234375 + 2 + 0.990234375 + 2] = 1.495117188$$

$$u^{(3)}_3 = \frac{1}{4}\,[0 + 0.990234375 + 0 + 0.990234375] = 0.495117188$$

$$u^{(3)}_4 = \frac{1}{4}\,[0.495117188 + 2 + 0 + 1.495117188] = 0.997558593$$

$$u^{(4)}_1 = \frac{1}{4}\,[0 + 1.495117188 + 2 + 0.495117188] = 0.997558594$$

$$u^{(4)}_2 = \frac{1}{4}\,[0.997558594 + 2 + 2 + 0.997558594] = 1.498779297$$

$$u^{(4)}_3 = \frac{1}{4}\,[0.0997558594 + 0 + 0.997558594] = 0.498779296$$

$$u^{(4)}_4 = \frac{1}{4}\,[0.498779296 + 2 + 0 + 1.498779297] = 0.999389648$$

Hence $u_1 = 0.99$, $u_2 = 1.49$, $u_3 = 0.49$, $u_4 = 0.99$

Ex. 3 : *Using the given boundary values, solve the Laplace equation $\nabla^2 u = 0$ at the nodal points of the square grid shown in figure*

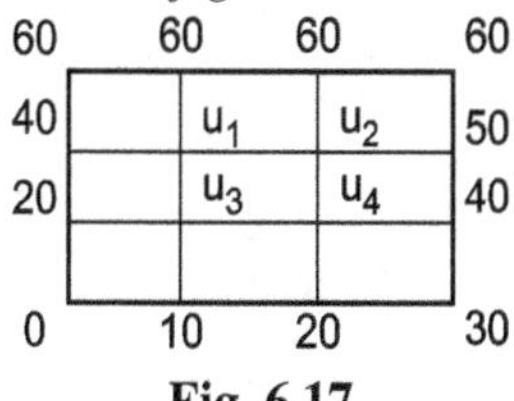

Fig. 6.17

Sol. : We assume that $u_4 = 0$

$$u_1 = \frac{1}{4}\,[20 + 60 + 60 + 0] = 35 \qquad \text{(Diagonal five point formula)}$$

$$u_2 = \frac{1}{4}\,[35 + 60 + 50 + 0] = 36.25 \quad \text{(Standard five point formula)}$$

Then by Gauss-Seidel method, we have

$$u^{(1)}_1 = \frac{1}{4}\,[60 + 40 + u_2 + u_3] = \frac{1}{4}\,[60 + 40 + 36.25 + 16.25] = 38.125$$

$$u^{(1)}_2 = \frac{1}{4}\,[60 + 50 + u^{(1)}_1 + u_4] = \frac{1}{4}\,[60 + 50 + 38.125 + 28.125] = 44.0625$$

$$u^{(1)}_3 = \frac{1}{4}\,[20 + 10 + u^{(1)}_1 + u_4] = \frac{1}{4}\,[20 + 10 + 38.125 + 28.125] = 24.0625$$

$$u^{(1)}_4 = \frac{1}{4}\,[40 + 20 + u^{(1)}_1 + u^{(1)}_3] = \frac{1}{4}\,[40 + 120 + 44.0625 + 24.0625] = 32.03125$$

Proceeding on the same manner we get,

$$u_1^{(2)} = 42.03125, \quad u_1^{(3)} = 43.0078125, \quad u_1^{(4)} = 43.25195311, \quad u_1^{(5)} = 43.31298827$$

$$u_2^{(2)} = 46.015625, \quad u_2^{(3)} = 46.50390625, \quad u_2^{(4)} = 46.62597655, \quad u_2^{(5)} = 46.65649412$$

$$u_3^{(2)} = 26.015625, \quad u_3^{(3)} = 26.50390625, \quad u_3^{(4)} = 26.625997656, \quad u_3^{(5)} = 26.65649414$$

$$u_4^{(2)} = 33.0078125, \quad u_4^{(3)} = 33.25195311, \quad u_4^{(4)} = 33.31298827, \quad u_4^{(5)} = 33.32824706$$

Hence $u_1 = 43.313$, $u_2 = 46.656$, $u_3 = 26.656$, $u_4 = 33.328$

Ex. 4 : *Solve Laplace equation* $\dfrac{\partial^2 u}{\partial x^2} + \dfrac{\partial^2 u}{\partial y^2} = 0$ *for the square meshes with the boundary values shown in figure*

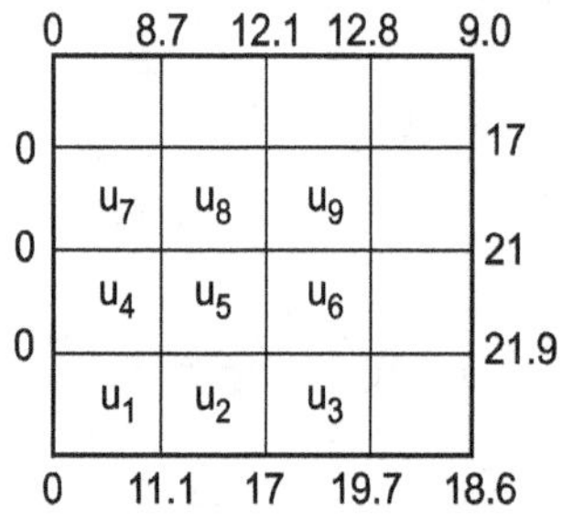

Fig. 6.18

Solution : For finding u_5, we use standard five point formula,

$$u_5 = \frac{1}{4}\,[0 + 21 + 12.1 + 17] = 12.52$$

By using diagonal five point formula we get the values of u_7, u_9, u_3, u_1

$$u_7 = \frac{1}{4}\,[0 + 12.52 + 12.1 + 0] = 6.15$$

$$u_9 = \frac{1}{4}\,[12.52 + 21 + 9 + 12.1] = 13.65$$

$$u_3 = \frac{1}{4}\,[17 + 18.6 + 21 + 12.52] = 17.28$$

$$u_1 = \frac{1}{4}\,[0 + 17 + 12.52 + 0] = 7.38$$

By using standard five point formula we get the values of u_8, u_6, u_2, u_4

$$u_8 = \frac{1}{4}\,[6.15 + 13.65 + 12.1 + 12.52] = 11.10$$

$$u_6 = \frac{1}{4}[12.52 + 21 + 13.65 + 17.28] = 16.11$$

$$u_2 = \frac{1}{4}[7.38 + 17.28 + 12.52 + 17] = 13.54$$

$$u_4 = \frac{1}{4}[0 + 12.52 + 6.15 + 7.38] = 6.51$$

Then by Gauss-Seidel method, we have

$$u_1^{(1)} = \frac{1}{4}[0 + 13.54 + 6.51 + 11.1] = 7.79$$

$$u_2^{(1)} = \frac{1}{4}[7.79 + 17.28 + 12.52 + 17] = 13.65$$

$$u_3^{(1)} = \frac{1}{4}[13.65 + 21.9 + 16.11 + 19.7] = 17.84$$

$$u_4^{(1)} = \frac{1}{4}[0 + 12.52 + 6.15 + 7.79] = 6.61$$

$$u_5^{(1)} = \frac{1}{4}[6.61 + 16.11 + 11.1 + 13.65] = 11.87$$

$$u_6^{(1)} = \frac{1}{4}[11.87 + 21 + 13.65 + 17.84] = 16.09$$

$$u_7^{(1)} = \frac{1}{4}[0 + 11.1 + 8.7 + 6.61] = 6.60$$

$$u_8^{(1)} = \frac{1}{4}[6.6 + 13.65 + 12.1 + 11.87] = 11.05$$

$$u_9^{(1)} = \frac{1}{4}[11.05 + 17 + 12.8 + 16.09] = 14.23$$

Proceeding on the same manner we get,

$u_1^{(2)} = 7.84$	$u_1^{(3)} = 7.83$	$u_1^{(4)} = 7.82$
$u_2^{(2)} = 13.64$	$u_2^{(3)} = 13.62$	$u_2^{(4)} = 13.64$
$u_3^{(2)} = 17.83$	$u_3^{(3)} = 17.86$	$u_3^{(4)} = 17.87$
$u_4^{(2)} = 6.58$	$u_4^{(3)} = 6.56$	$u_4^{(4)} = 6.58$
$u_5^{(2)} = 11.84$	$u_5^{(3)} = 11.90$	$u_5^{(4)} = 11.92$
$u_6^{(2)} = 16.22$	$u_6^{(3)} = 16.26$	$u_6^{(4)} = 16.27$
$u_7^{(2)} = 6.58$	$u_7^{(3)} = 6.62$	$u_7^{(4)} = 6.62$
$u_8^{(2)} = 11.19$	$u_8^{(3)} = 11.23$	$u_8^{(4)} = 11.24$
$u_9^{(2)} = 14.30$	$u_9^{(3)} = 14.32$	$u_9^{(4)} = 14.33$

Ex. 5 : *Solve Laplace equation* $\dfrac{\partial^2 u}{\partial x^2} + \dfrac{\partial^2 u}{\partial y^2} = 0$ *for the square meshes with the boundary values shown in Fig.*

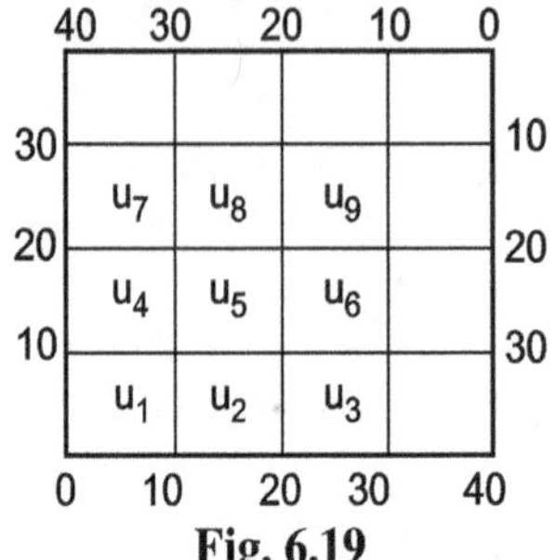

Fig. 6.19

Sol. : For finding u_5, we use standard five point formula.

$$u_5 = \frac{1}{4}\,[20 + 20 + 20 + 20] = 20$$

By using diagonal five point formula we get the values of u_7, u_9, u_3, u_1.

$$u_7 = \frac{1}{4}\,[\,20 + 20 + 20 + 40] = 25$$

$$u_9 = \frac{1}{4}\,[20 + 20 + 0 + 20] = 15$$

$$u_3 = \frac{1}{4}\,[20 + 40 + 20 + 20] = 25$$

$$u_1 = \frac{1}{4}\,[0 + 20 + 20 + 20] = 15$$

By using standard five point formula we get the values of u_8, u_6, u_2, u_4

$$u_8 = \frac{1}{4}\,[25 + 15 + 20 + 20] = 20$$

$$u_6 = \frac{1}{4}\,[20 + 20 + 15 + 25] = 20$$

$$u_2 = \frac{1}{4}\,[15 + 25 + 20 + 20] = 20$$

$$u_4 = \frac{1}{4}\,[20 + 20 + 25 + 15] = 20$$

Then by Gauss-Seidel method, we have

$$u_1^{(1)} = \frac{1}{4}\,[10 + 20 + 20 + 10] = 15$$

$$u_2^{(1)} = \frac{1}{4}\,[15 + 25 + 20 + 20] = 20$$

$$u_3^{(1)} = \frac{1}{4}\,[20 + 30 + 20 + 30] = 25$$

$$u_4^{(1)} = \frac{1}{4}\,[20 + 20 + 25 + 15] = 20$$

$$u_5^{(1)} = \frac{1}{4}\,[20 + 20 + 20 + 20] = 20$$

$$u_6^{(1)} = \frac{1}{4}\,[20 + 20 + 15 + 25] = 20$$

$$u_7^{(1)} = \frac{1}{4}\,[30 + 20 + 30 + 20] = 25$$

$$u_8^{(1)} = \frac{1}{4}\,[25 + 15 + 20 + 20] = 20$$

$$u_9^{(1)} = \frac{1}{4}\,[20 + 10 + 10 + 20] = 15$$

As the values of first iteration and first estimate is same, so no need to carry further iterations.

EXERCISE 6.4

1. Solve Laplace equation $\dfrac{\partial^2 u}{\partial x^2} + \dfrac{\partial^2 u}{\partial y^2} = 0$ for the square meshes with the boundary values shown in figure.

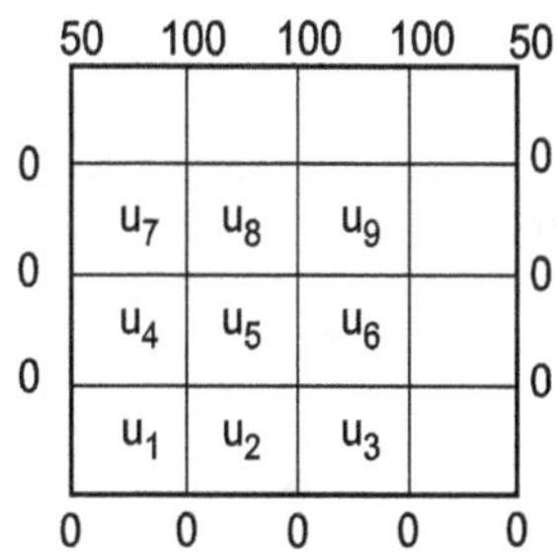

Fig. 6.20

2. Solve Laplace equation $\dfrac{\partial^2 u}{\partial x^2} + \dfrac{\partial^2 u}{\partial y^2} = 0$ for the square meshes with the boundary values shown in figure.

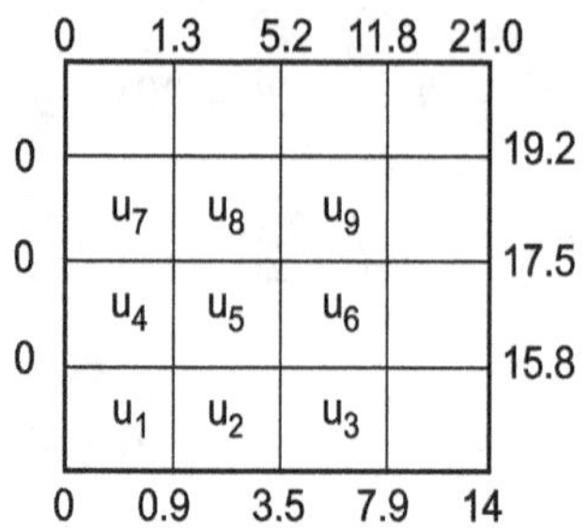

Fig. 6.21

3. Solve Laplace equation equation $\dfrac{\partial^2 u}{\partial x} + \dfrac{\partial^2 u}{\partial y^2} = 0$ for the square meshes with the

boundary values shown in figure.

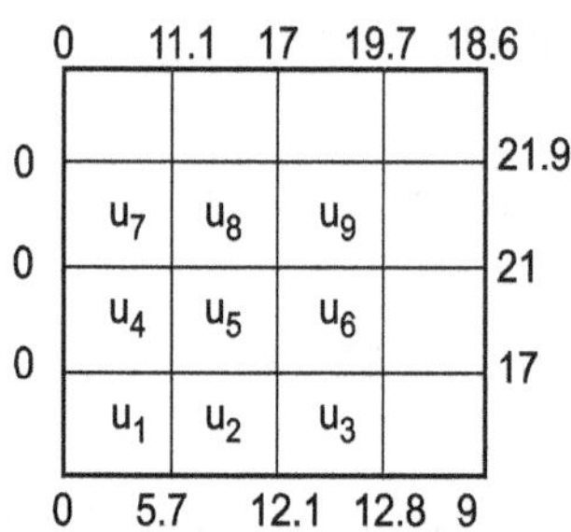

Fig. 6.22

4. Using the given boundary values, solve the Laplace equation $\nabla^2 u = 0$ at the nodal points of the square grid shown in figure.

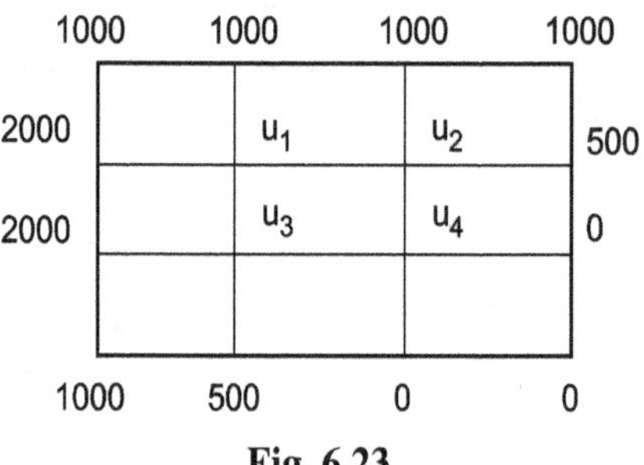

Fig. 6.23

❖ ❖ ❖